THE LAST WITCH

THE COMPLETE TRILOGY

KARPOV KINRADE
EVAN GAUSTAD

http://KarpovKinrade.com

~ ~ ~ ~ ~
Published by Daring Books
~ ~ ~ ~ ~
First Edition
ISBN: 978-1-939559-75-3

~ ~ ~ ~ ~

Aevelairith

Wiceraweil

KARPOV GAUSTAD

A
WEREWOLF
A VAMPIRE
AND A FAE
WALK INTO A BAR

http://KarpovKinrade.com

Copyright © 2020 Karpov Kinrade & Evan Gaustad
Cover Art Copyright © 2020 Karpov Kinrade

~~~~~

Published by Daring Books

~~~~~

First Edition
ISBN: 978-1-939559-67-8

~~~~~

CHAPTER ONE

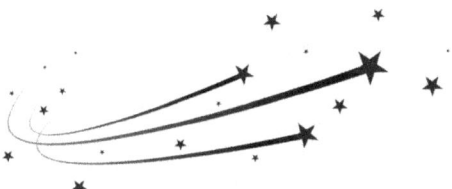

"So, a werewolf, a vampire and a fae walk into a bar..." Joe says, his lips pursed in exaggerated performance.

"What's a fae?" Frank asks from the end of the bar. He follows his question with a long drink of his Guinness, sloshing a bit out of his glass and onto the counter I just wiped down three seconds ago. Frank's a beefy type, with a thick body and a thick dark beard that covers his aging skin. He was a truck driver for 40 years and is now a professional barfly.

Joe shrugs, his eyes bloodshot and his beer belly hanging over his belt. "Like an elf. You know, like those movies." His alcohol habit has aged him by at least ten years. Well, that and grief. A broken heart will break your body just as fast. His 50 looks closer to 60, and his formerly brown hair is now streaked with gray.

"Nobody gives a shit about your stupid jokes, Joe," Phil says from his standard spot at a booth in the back. The youngest of them, Phil is tall and skinny, with a blond scruff of hair that dances wildly on his head, like it can hear music no one else can. He works construction, like most of the men around here, so he's always got filthy fingers wrapped around my otherwise clean pint glasses.

Joe's face falls, but he retains his optimism. "You care, don't ya, Bernie?"

I grin, rubbing a wet cotton rag over the spill Frank just made. "Sure I do, Joe. As long as you tip." I wink to take the sting out of my words, and he chuckles along with everyone else.

It's Tuesday, our slowest night of the week, and these guys are all regulars. They've been coming to Morgan's since before I was born, and will probably haunt the place long after I'm dead.

Joe takes a swig of his Smithwick's. "Okay fine. You're right. Vampires are dead. No one likes those bastards since they started to sparkle. Hold on, I've got another one. The past, present and future walked into a bar," he says, and before anyone can give him a hard time, he wraps the joke up. "It was tense."

That one actually makes me laugh out loud. What can I say? I'm a geek at heart. I just play the tough as nails Irish girl to keep the locals happy. I mean, it's not all an act. I *was* raised in a bar, my Irish heritage shines brightly in my pale skin and dark hair, and I'll absolutely punch a drunk who gets handsy. And if it weren't for these locals, I'd never have made it out of this town, even if I did end up right back where I started.

Fate is a bitch, and if she decides to walk into my bar, I'll show her ass out.

A twinge of pain flashes deep in my abdomen. I lean against the counter, exhaling quickly and holding onto my protruding belly. "Hey there, little one. What's going on? It's not time to meet yet."

Joe glances down at my stomach and is about to say something, a worry line creasing his forehead, when a loud crash sends him into full panic mode as the walls of Morgan's Irish Pub shake.

"What the hell was that?" he asks. "Is it aliens? Is this it? They've finally come for us!" He starts looking around the bar for... what? I'm not sure. A place to hide from the aliens maybe? A light saber?

I roll my eyes and make my clumsy way to the front door. "Relax, Joe. It's probably just a tree knocked down by the storm."

That's the other reason we're so slow tonight. A wicked blizzard that's going to make driving a bitch--if it hasn't already.

When I open the door, a gust of snow and wind nearly knock me to the floor. I hold tightly to the door frame and grab my coat from the rack, shrugging into it as I trudge out into the cold to check on the damage.

I shiver against the blistering winds, and suck in my breath at the scene before me. The roads are covered in inches of thick, fluffy snow, making it look like a winter wonderland. Winters are always harsh up here, but this is something else. In fact, this might be the worst we've had since I've been alive.

It will take out power for at least a few days, and I shudder to think what the homeless will do, but I can't help but marvel at the temporary beauty it's inspired.

I stand there so long my eyelashes begin to freeze shut. Blinking, I trudge through the inches of snow to the right, where the crashing sound came from.

I'm expecting a downed tree or power line, but I don't see anything unusual at first. Then I notice a hole in my wall the size of a grapefruit. I scoot closer, tugging my coat around my belly as best I can—I was too cheap to spring for a maternity coat and am really regretting that act of frugality right now—and peer into the hole looking for evidence of what caused it.

Something is stuck deep in the crumbling brick, but it's not a tree or a branch.

I reach in, my fingers numb from the cold, and feel around, hoping I'm not about to get bitten by a radioactive spider or feral chipmunk.

Nothing bites me, but I do feel the smooth edges of a rock. It's a little warm, but not hot enough to burn. Gripping the ridges, I nudge it out inch by inch as the brick crumbles around my hand into dust.

With one final tug, I pry the object free and hold it in my hand. Before I can get a good look, the light above flickers out. I turn to the road and watch the street lights do the same.

Awesome.

I take the rock with me, my thoughts bouncing between what category storm can toss around small boulders and how strong the generators at the maternity wing of the hospital are.

I hurry back to the warmth of the bar as fast as I can without slipping on the ice and falling on my ass. Heat blasts me as I step inside. Naturally, my alcoholic patrons have already started lighting candles so I won't kick them out. I love them, even with all their problems.

I take a moment to look at this rock. It's metallic gray with copper veins running through it. Veins that seem to glow, though I'm sure that's just a trick of the light. I shrug off my jacket and tuck the rock away on a shelf behind the bar.

"What you got there?" Joe asks, his voice slightly slurred because even I've lost track of how many Smithwick's he's had.

I look at it and shrug. "A rock, I guess. A bit unusual looking. You guys ever seen the wind throw stones before?"

I look around at Frank, Joe and Phil, the only patrons of our fine establishment tonight. Well, except Karl, but he's passed out in the back booth as always. There are stories that he has never moved, and he's actually a well-preserved corpse. I can neither confirm nor deny this. But his tab gets paid and he doesn't smell any worse than these other bastards. So we're good.

"It's bad out there, guys. One last round? Then I'm closing shop before you're stuck here all week."

There's a collective groan at being kicked out before nine (on a Tuesday, God forbid), but I shrug and top off drinks. They'll thank me in the morning when they wake up in their own beds rather than the floor of my bar. I'm just serving the last beer when the bell over the door dings, and I look up in surprise as a flurry of snow chases three men into my bar.

And by three men, I mean three absolute specimens. These are, hands down, the sexiest guys I've ever seen. It takes me all of two seconds to make that assessment.

I place a hand over my baby bump to remind myself what happens when I let a pretty face and a hot body talk me into bad decisions--and these guys look like a lot of bad decisions wrapped in a delicious bow.

Settle yourself, woman. You don't need more complications with a baby on the way.

"Close the door," Frank shouts. "You're letting in the storm and Bernie ain't mopping that shit in her condition."

A smile tugs at the corner of my lips. This town takes care of its own, that's for sure. And by the looks of these newcomers, they're definitely not from around here.

Though they came in together, I get the distinct impression they're not exactly friends as they glare at each other suspiciously.

What they're doing in my pub on a weeknight during a blizzard is beyond me.

They each choose separate tables near the back, though they don't take their eyes off each other. Strange. As I walk over to take their order, I also study them.

I may have sworn off men for the foreseeable future... like, until my kid is in college... but that doesn't mean I can't enjoy some eye candy when it walks into my bar.

"Hey guys, we just called last round, so I can get you something, but then we're closing up early on account of the storm."

"A whiskey on the rocks," Mr. Sexy #1 says, in an accent that sounds vaguely British. He is a tall drink of water and I am thirsty for it. I haven't had sex since the night this baby happened, but again, that's beside the point. His skin is pale, like moonlight, and his hair is as dark as midnight and matches the deep, dark depths of his eyes. He has a face chiseled from marble and full lips that are currently pinched in annoyance. He's dressed unusually--in fact, all three of them are. Like they've just come from a cosplay convention, though no cosplay convention would ever come to Rowley. This guy has a long black cloak and wears fitted leather pants and a black silk shirt underneath.

It takes all my will power to pry my eyes off of him and train them on Mr. Sexy #2. This boy is all wild energy--like an untamed forest, with eyes the color of deep green leaves, coppery brown hair that's tussled in that just-had-sex way, and a matching stubble that accentuates his rugged good looks. He's dressed in neutral colors and natural fabrics, and looks ready to lead a hike through the woods at night.

"What'll it be?" I ask, trying to sound like the hardened bar owner I should be and not the swoony undersexed pregnant lady I currently am. "And are these on the same tab?"

"An ale," he says, his voice deep and resonant, with a sexy lilt that's almost Irish. "And no."

"Alright, what about you?" I ask Mr. Sexy #3, whose eyes are the lightest blue I've ever seen. He has long, pale blond hair that only adds to his sex appeal, and wears a rich, velvet cloak pinned with a silver broach.

He looks unsure about his choices, so I size him up and suggest a Vesper Martini, even though it means more work for me.

"Very well," he says, and I can't place his accent, but it's definitely not American.

"What brings you boys to town?" I ask, keenly aware that everyone is watching this interaction.

The three Sexies silently glare at each other for a long moment before Sexy #2 finally answers. "A family errand," he says vaguely.

"Huh. Well, I hope you didn't drive. It's going to be a rough night on those roads."

When none of them reply, I turn and head back to the bar to get their drinks.

Joe wags his eyebrows as I work. "What's their deal?"

"I don't know. Never seen them before."

"You gonna bag one of 'em?" he asks with a dumb grin.

I roll my eyes. "You know I'm not interested in guys right now," I say, trying to hide the fact that I'm extremely interested in all three.

He sighs. "You deserve a nice guy to settle down with."

Before I can reply, another wave of pain grips me, and I lean against the bar to catch my breath.

Joe stands, clutching his beer as he does. "Bern, you okay?" He looks around, a panicked expression on his face. "Hey guys, Bernie's baby's coming. We got to get her help!"

"I'm fine. Relax. It's just Braxton Hicks. Totally normal."

Frank and Phil stand and drop some bills in front of them. "You sure you're okay?" Phil asks.

I nod, loading drinks on a tray to take to the newcomers.

"Alright then. Take care, Bernie. See you tomorrow," Phil says as he teeters out on slightly drunk legs.

Frank hesitates by the door, glancing at Joe then back at me. "You gonna be okay, kid?" he asks. I wince at the kid part, but he's been calling me that since I was born so it's hard to expect different.

"Yeah, it's fine. I'll be closing up soon anyways. Get home safe. Say hi to Alice and the kids."

He grimaces at the thought of his family. "Will do."

When the door opens, a flurry of snow and cold air blows in. Frank and Phil leave quickly, shivering as they step outside.

I hold the tray carefully and serve the new guys, studying them as I do. None of them speaks, but their simmering glares speak volumes.

"You three look like you're having fun," I say. "Bachelor party?"

Sexy #1 raises an eyebrow. "Are you Bernadette Morgan?" he asks.

It's my turn to raise an eyebrow in return. "Who's asking?"

"Hey Bern, one more drink, pretty please?" Joe asks, interrupting whatever Sexy #1 was about to say, if he was about to say anything at all. "I've only had... a couple? A few."

"Joe, you know that's not a good idea. You're drunk enough for a night like this."

I head back to the bar and start running through my closing check list when another pain grips my belly and I brace myself against the counter, taking quick breaths that sound a little too much like I'm in labor.

I'm not.

I can't be.

It's too soon and I'm snowed in. There would be no way to get to a hospital tonight.

I grab my phone to Google Braxton Hicks contractions. I mean, I've read all the damn books and I know what I'll find, but I need Dr. Google to make me feel better—or convince me I'm dying of a rare disease. Either way, as long as this baby doesn't make her debut today, I'm good.

I open my browser, but it lags. Shit. No service.

Joe is sweating profusely and cursing under his breath. "You okay there, buddy?" I ask through my own gritted teeth.

He looks up, his eyes widening. "Uh, yeah. It's just. You know. You look like shit."

I grimace. "Thanks. Every woman's dream compliment."

"Oh I didn't mean that, Bernie." He tugs at his overgrown facial hair nervously, his gray bushy eyebrows dancing atop his eyes like agitated caterpillars.

As the cramps in my belly ease, I take a relieved breath and smile. "There ya go. All better. I told you, false alarm."

He scoots himself back onto the barstool in front of me and grabs the remains of the drink Frank left, downing it in one long gulp that only seasoned alcoholics can manage with such aplomb.

I crack a wry grin, raising an eyebrow. "You good now?"

He swipes his forehead with the back of his hand. "Yeah. Sorry. I'm... not great in medical emergencies," he says shyly. "My wife always handled that shit... when... "

I pat his hand. " I know Joe, it's okay."

Outside the storm intensifies, the howling of the wind sending a shiver down my spine. "How long has it been now? Two years?"

He nods. "Last week marked two years since cancer stole my Betty." He sniffs, looking around for another drink.

"Did you drive here?" I ask.

"Nope. Walked."

I nod and pull out a clean tumbler. Normally on a night like tonight I'd pour two and share in the drink, but with this little one riding shotgun on my bladder, my drinking days are on pause. I pour two fingers of whiskey and scoot the glass to Joe, caving on my earlier resolution to cut him off.

"On the house," I say, pouring myself a club soda. I hold my glass up in toast. "To Betty."

Joe's eyes moisten as he raises his to clink against mine. "To Betty."

He throws back his whiskey, draining his glass before I've even brought mine to my lips. It's one of those nights, it seems, which, honestly, is a mood.

One I'm looking forward to giving into once I'm no longer an incubator to this little leech I already love more than is proper or right.

"Are you ready for motherhood?" Joe asks, leaning back as the whiskey relaxes him.

"Nope," I say, wiping down the already clean bar and throwing a glance at the Sexies to make sure they're still sexy. None of them have touched their drinks, but they are still sexy. I look back to Joe. "But is anyone ever really ready?"

He shrugs. "Betty was. She was born to it."

I don't bother telling him about the times she was in this very bar crying her heart out over a pint while bemoaning her mothering skills. I was a kid then, working the bar with my grandmother. We're a tight-knit community, so everyone turned a blind eye to my underage service. Even the cops who occasionally came by.

Betty is gone and he's all alone. Well, he's got a son, Alex, but he just reminds Joe of the life that got away so they don't really talk or see each other much. So I won't disabuse him of the notion that things were effortless for his wife. But dear god in heaven can we please stop acting like this shit isn't hard?

Cuz from what I've seen and heard—and growing up in a family-owned Irish pub, I've seen and heard a lot—this shit is the hardest.

"You know we just want you to be happy," he says, glancing at the three strangers nursing their drinks.

"I know... but guys are too much work, and I'm all full up with work at the moment." I glance at my protruding stomach and the bar that is now my full-time job since my grandfather died and my grandmother was put in a home.

Guys are the very last thing on my mind.

Especially since my grandfather ran this place into the red when my grandmother was no longer around to keep the books. Now I've got to salvage my family legacy if I have half a chance of supporting myself and my baby and keeping a roof over our heads.

Joe finishes up everyone's drinks that were left on the bar, and I check the time. 11:14 p.m.

"Okay, guys, wrap it up," I say as I wipe down all the tables, hobbling through the pub like that girl in Willy Wonka who eats the wrong candy and inflates into a ball. Most of the dishes are already washed, and I'm half tempted to leave the rest for the morning.

Joe stands and wobbles to the door, grabbing his coat from the rack. "I hate leaving ya like this, Bern. Want me to stay? I could sleep in one of the booths."

I yawn, suddenly feeling the weight of the day bear down on me. "Nah, I'm good. Get home before you can't."

"What about your Partner in Crime? Can she come?" he asks.

"Joe, I'm fine. AJ will be helping out with the bar and everything else nonstop once the baby arrives. I don't want to bother her till then. You know how things are there."

Joe shakes his head, and I know what he's thinking. AJ was my best friend growing up, but she never left town like I did. She married her high school boyfriend, a guy none of us like. But...we can't live her life for her. That's something she's got to figure out.

"Go on now. It's getting worse out there."

Finally, Joe nods, casting one last glance at the silent strangers, and leaves.

I want to go to bed, to get off my feet and zone out to Netflix, but I know if I leave the bar a mess, my future self won't be happy with me.

Begrudgingly, I grab a broom and start sweeping, but before I can get even half the job done, another contraction grips my belly, and for the first time tonight real fear worms its way into my heart.

It's easy to stay out of my head when I'm busy working, but in the silence of the night, I start to question all of my life choices.

Especially the one that landed me knocked up and single just as I was about to live my dream.

Tears burn my eyes as I take a seat on the piano bench, my hands cupping my belly, and I remind myself it wouldn't have mattered. Pregnant or not, my grandfather would still be dead, and I would still be the only Morgan left to carry on our family business.

There was no choice then, and there's no choice now. I can do this. I have to do this. It's no longer just my life on the line anymore.

I smile through my tears as my baby kicks out, already asserting her right to be here in my life.

Through gritted teeth and with steely determination, I stand and keep cleaning, though I have to stop regularly to let the contractions pass.

I'm still telling myself it's not the real deal when I feel a gush of liquid run down my legs.

Shit.

My water broke.

I'm having this baby. Right here. In the middle of the night. In the middle of a storm.

"Guys, um... I don't suppose any of you is a doctor?"

Instead of a hospital with an OBGYN, I'm stuck in my bar with three strangers, and I'm definitely going into labor.

I can no longer stand, so I slide to the floor, clutching my stomach, not sure what I'm going to do now. How can I have a baby alone? They don't teach this in the pregnancy books.

I can no longer keep my pain in, and as my muscles squeeze and my back spasms, I scream.

I fleetingly wonder if I can make it upstairs to my apartment. I could run a bath, get undressed, and give birth in the water. That wouldn't be too hard, would it?

Knowing I absolutely cannot do this on the floor of a bar, I attempt to pull myself up, but lose my grip and slide back down as my contractions quicken.

Shit.

Shit. Shit. Shit.

Terror latches onto me but I grit my teeth and wipe away the tears. I will do this. If not for me, for my child.

When the men all walk over to me, I suddenly feel terror of another sort. I have no idea who these guys are, and I'm completely vulnerable. I curse myself for kicking Joe out, but what would an old drunk do against these guys, who look made of pure muscles?

"In point of fact," Sexy #2 says. "I'm a healer. A doctor, if you like."

A doctor *if I like*. What the blazes does that mean?

"Have you ever delivered a baby?" I ask.

He nods. "Many."

"Good, cuz you're about to deliver mine."

CHAPTER TWO

I can't describe this kind of pain. Blinding comes to mind, but that might just be because my eyes are slammed shut while I wait for either the pain to pass or my life to end. In any case, the feeling of a baby wedging its way out of my uterus makes it hard to focus on anything else, even the outrageously sexy man propped between my legs barking orders at the other two.

"Get water boiling," he tells Sexy #1. "And you," he says to Sexy #3, "get me clean rags and the sharpest knife you can find."

"No," I say, trying to sit up. "Take me upstaAAAIIIIRRS... I need to LLLL-LIIIIIEEEEEE down."

Sexy #2 shakes his head. "No, you'll stay down here. You're in no condition to be moved right now." He locks eyes with me, and the pain ripping through me ceases momentarily as I get lost in his forest green gaze.

"Who are you?" I ask, panting through another contraction.

"My name is Zev, Bernadette. I'll make sure you deliver the child safely."

The brutal contractions fade again as my head spins. Zev? A doctor I've never met who knows my name and waltzed into my bar moments before I went into labor?

"No one calls me Bernadette unless they're trying to piiIIIIIIIIIIIIII-ISSSSSSS... me off. And I don't think you want to doOOOOOOOOOOOOOOOO... that."

"Anger won't help, but a charge of adrenaline can't hurt," Zev says, as he directs Sexy #1. "Get behind her and support her back."

I feel strong arms slip around my waist and I lean into his chest. I have no shits left to give. "What's your name, then?" I ask when I can speak again.

"Darius," he says, his lips brushing against my ear with his words.

"Zev and Darius," I repeat, mostly to make sure I heard right the first time. "And how about yoooOOUUUUUUUU?!" I say to Sexy #3 right as another contraction hits. This labor is progressing much more quickly than what the lady in my birthing class described.

Before the third mystery man can answer, Darius chimes in again. "Rune, take her other arm, even out the support." Okay, I guess Sexy #3 goes by Rune. It also seems as though these guys know each other, even if they like to sit at different tables when they go out.

The pain dulls enough for me to do some quick math. Outside, the storm's getting worse. Inside, I'm going into labor a week early. Most importantly, three oddly-named, unconscionably sexy men are helping deliver my baby with a calm very few men show in the labor ward. So... WTF?

"I'm surprised we all arrived at the same time," Rune says to the others. "I was sure I had a head start."

"We work off the same prophecy, old friend," Zev responds in his gruff baritone. "There's only one star to guide us."

"The only surprise," Darius says, "is that we never had a discussion as to what we'd do when it came time to take the child."

My head cranks toward Darius at these words. Is he talking about *my* child? I'd ask him directly but another contraction wracks my body and I scream, clutching Darius and Rune's hands with all my strength. Neither even flinches.

Meanwhile, with my eyes clamped shut, I feel a firm tugging at my pants. "You cannot deliver this child while wearing these," Zev says calmly.

Oh God, I hadn't thought about this part. Shit.

"Someone get me a blanket at least," I say through clenched teeth.

Darius and Zev look to Rune, who swiftly pops up and moves to the kitchen.

"He's good at finding things," Zev explains.

As advertised, Rune promptly returns with an armful of large towels

"Will this do?" he asks, suggesting he could go back into *my* kitchen and find more, somehow better towels.

"Those are fine."

He drapes the cover over my abdomen, as Zev gets me half naked.

"I will be watching you, dog," Darius says with an unfriendly bite to his voice. "Don't think for a second you're quick enough to catch the baby and escape."

Zev barks out a short laugh. "Oh, Darius, how I've missed your playful name calling. And don't expect me to run, I wouldn't want to deprive myself of tearing you apart."

"Now's not the time to revisit old wounds," Rune says in a condescending tone, like a bored professor explaining something simple to his students for the tenth time. "You can carry on with your bickering when the prophecy is fulfilled and the fae flourish once again."

"Cocky as ever," Darius mutters.

As fascinating as this exchange is, the language terrifies me. If I wasn't so actively birthing a child, I would absolutely sprint into a deadly storm to get away from these men.

"Who the hell are you people? How did you know my name? Why...aaa-AAAAAAHHHHHH!" I can't even finish the question, which is for the best because I didn't really know what to ask. Everything about this situation needs answers, but for now I'm just going to hope these men keep helping since I've got nowhere else to go.

"Hold my hands, Bernadette," Darius says from behind me. "Squeeze when you feel a contraction and focus on pushing."

"You three stop acting like psychopaths and I will." My face probably shows that I'm terrified, but I don't let on with my words. Growing up in a Massachusetts bar, I learned to talk tougher than I felt at a very early age.

Rune lowers himself to the floor, pressing gently against my knee, spreading my legs a little further and bringing back a shade of self-consciousness. He catches my eye and clearly sees a discomfort that goes beyond just the physical.

"When you feel a contraction, push your leg against my hand. That will activate the muscles you need to move the baby along."

I'm about to throw out another verbal lashing when I see Zev nod. "He's right. I'll keep my hand on the other knee."

I'm surrounded by men who might all be murderers, but without any other options I've landed on implicitly trusting Zev based on his word that he's a doctor...*if I like*. I hope it's the doctor claim that got Zev in my good graces and not the ruggedly handsome face, which has always been a weakness of mine.

Whatever the case, the new position helps. I scream and push between breaths, barely aware that Darius has put a wet washcloth over my forehead. I trust he grabbed a clean one and not the towel I'd been using to mop up Joe's beer.

Everything about this birth has gone wrong, and yet I find the situation strangely empowering. I'd planned on a very sterile, clinical, hospital bed delivery, none of that froufrou home or water birth stuff that the neighborhood midwives tried to sell me on. But now, sitting at an incline against a guy named Darius, two dudes named Zev and Rune side by side between my wide open legs, naked butt on the cold floor of an empty bar, I feel a small rush of pride over my natural birth. Who needs an epidural when you've got creepy intruders?

"The head is emerging," Zev says without a trace of happiness in his voice, casually explaining that my labor pains might soon come to an end. "Push harder with the next feeling of contraction."

"Oh, I'm sorry, have I not been pushing hard enough for you?"

Zev gives me a confused look, clearly not a sarcasm buff. This will make my feisty tone less effective.

As another wave of agony ripples through my torso, my legs start to close as my muscles flex. The pressure from Zev and Rune's hands gives me a little extra oomph in my push and suddenly the pain, while still incomprehensibly awful, takes on a new burn.

"She's out," Rune says, a look of awe on his face, just as the old clock behind the bar strikes midnight. I open my eyes, which have long been soaked with tears but now get a fresh coating. Just a few feet away, after growing inside me for the better part of a year, I see my baby. She's crying, bloody, and perfect. I'm a broken vessel, torn and sweaty and surrounded by demented intruders, but I don't care. I've never felt love like this.

"Rain…" I murmur, saying my baby's name out loud for the first time. She was always going to have that name, but I promised myself I wouldn't speak it until she arrived.

Rune holds the baby with great care, which at first puts me at ease before giving me a funny feeling. He stares at Rain with a kind of reverence that has my hackles up, and he's not making any move to hand her over my way.

"Give her to me," I say in a steady voice, my body absolutely giddy about being done with the throws of labor.

He hesitates. His eyes shift from me to Darius to Zev, and there's a palpable tension between the three. It pisses me off because… because give me my freaking baby.

He's still cradling my daughter when Zev stands, his impressive stature becoming apparent. Darius rises as well, also a taller-than-average man.

"Give the child to her mother," Zev says in a voice that's both calm and terrifying. "I know what you're doing, I know the impulse you feel, and neither Darius nor myself will let you move an inch from where you stand while you hold that baby."

Maybe it's that I'm still in agony and sitting in afterbirth, but these guys strike me as a special kind of crazy. Nevertheless, Rune seems to catch Zev's drift and he carefully leans over with Rain. I'm about to hold the baby I've been waiting so long to meet.

"Do you wrap the placenta around the child now or later?"

Rune's question feels like a mix of the right words in the wrong order. Wrap the baby in the placenta?

"Do I what now?"

"Or is that something the elders do while your body mends?"

It's late and I've labored, so I've got zero brain space for these weird questions. Fortunately, Zev steps in.

"She doesn't share your rituals. Here they eat the placenta. Just pass the child, Rune."

While I have no intention of eating the placenta, Zev's suggestion is less bonkers than the previous one. Rune does as he's told, with a mild look of disgust on his beautiful face.

As I take her into my arms, I feel my shirt being lifted. Darius, in the most forward and inappropriate move ever, is taking off my clothes while I'm incapacitated. My bar-owner instinct is to swing the baby at him like the bat I keep behind the counter to scare off the occasional drunk who has one too many. Fortunately, my maternal instinct steps in and stops me.

Darius manages to read the room and explains himself. "She needs to feel your skin." Of course I know about skin-to-skin time and how important it is, but this delivery and my new company has thrown me off my game. I drop a little of the tension and let Darius resume with the unprompted disrobing.

Finally, naked as a jaybird, I get to hold my baby. As soon as I press her up to my breast, she stops crying and my heart melts all over again. Her little lips inch along my skin, searching for a nipple, and it's absolutely the cutest thing that's ever happened in the world.

As she starts to nurse, a hand cups the underside of my breast to make the feeding angle easier. I honestly don't know which weirdo's weird hand it is, I'm too absorbed watching my sweet girl. While my eyes stay locked on Rain, I half-listen to more outlandish conversation from these men who should feel free to leave at any time.

"When did you notice the approach of the star?" Darius questions the other two, his calm voice floating over my head.

"We started watching the sky two weeks ago," Rune answers. "Violence in the realm had escalated, and the Readers announced the nearing of the date."

"I arrived last night," Zev adds. "Waited in the woods until the moment arrived. And you, Darius? Surely your kingdom knew of this day well in advance."

There's a tense moment between the two men, neither speaking, breathing or blinking.

Darius finally responds, "Of course. We've known for months."

While every inch of my being wants to scream, *what the hell is going on?!*, I resist. I'll learn more by listening, and I don't want to do anything that might startle Rain. She's lost the nipple and is making the softest little murmuring sounds.

"What now?" Rune asks, his voice quieter than before. "We've arrived at the moment we all expected but never spoke about. There's only one child, and I see only one way out."

Whatever Rune is saying makes Zev tense, as I feel his hand squeeze my thigh more tightly, and it sounds like he's... growling? Lack of sleep and an exhaustive labor have worn me out. I'm sure the growl was just in my head.

Darius puts his hands on my shoulders, sending a shiver down my spine that's both exhilarating and terrifying. "It may come to that, Rune, but you'll be up against Zev and myself if you make a false move. We all want the child, but she's of no use dead or unhealthy."

Now I've heard enough to pipe in. "I'm sorry, 'you want the child'? I don't know who you are or where-"

My voice stops. It's the craziest sensation, because I know what I wanted to say and now I'm silent, my brain's in a fog, and all I can do is stare into Darius' eyes, like I'm in a trance.

"Let her go," Zev says, though the words don't really register in my clouded head. "She needs her wits about her."

"Let's get her up to her bed," Rune says. "The baby is asleep so the mother should rest as well."

Maybe it's the mention of rest, but my mind suddenly becomes mine again and my voice returns. "Yes, please. And someone call a real doctor, I think I need actual help-"

"You'll be fine," Zev cuts me off. "Darius, carry her up. I'll clean the baby and then come up to tend to the mother's wounds."

"I'll tidy up down here," Rune says. "Needn't create a scene that garners unnecessary attention."

Zev gently pulls Rain away from me, which I allow because I'm not sure I have another option. As Darius lifts me from the ground and starts carrying me upstairs, my emotions overwhelm me. I'm scared shitless, utterly confused, and deeply in love with my newborn baby. And, while this situation makes me feel incredibly uneasy to say the least, it's not lost on me that I've currently got three dashing men waiting on me hand and foot. Unfortunately, from what I've gathered, they came to steal my baby, and the only way that'll happen is if they kill me and rip her from my cold, dead hands.

CHAPTER THREE

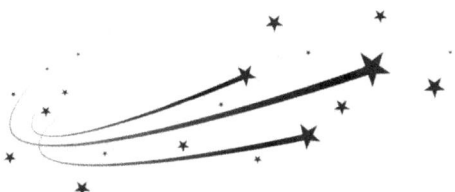

L ying in bed, Rain asleep in her crib in the corner, I slowly come to. I can't
have slept much, my body and brain ache for rest... but it's impossible to
ignore the conversation going on right outside my bedroom.

I still don't have a concrete idea of who - or what - Darius, Zev, and Rune are,
but I know they are different. Not just in the obvious ways, like being grossly
good-looking and able to help a first-time mother safely deliver a baby on the
floor of her bar, but in larger, more cataclysmic ways.

For starters, they're not from America. If I had enough to drink, I'd very
quickly tell you they aren't from Earth, but my brain still isn't ready to make that
leap. Nevertheless, they talk of places I've never heard of before and know things
they should have no way of knowing. And while those particulars could be
explained with a little con artistry, other things seem... magical.

It takes a lot of effort to get past my cynicism. On more than one occasion
I've made a magician cry by yelling "bullshit!" until he or she pulled back the
curtain to show me how the trick worked. Mysterious men, hot as they may be,
don't immediately have me believing in the paranormal.

And yet, things just seem... otherworldly. Everything from the timing of
their arrival to the ways they dress, talk, and move makes me feel like these men
can't be explained using traditional terms and ideas.

I nodded off a lot during birthing classes because I didn't think I was learning
anything, but I'm starting to wonder if I slept through the part where they tell
you that the pain of labor causes the most vivid hallucinations imaginable.
Though, if that were the case, wouldn't other women be talking about how they
thought their doctors and nurses morphed into exceedingly sexy strangers?

These thoughts are keeping me awake, as well as the conversation my possibly
hallucinated companions are having.

"Of course we can't arrange a deal, Darius," Zev says in a hushed tone. "We all want the child for the same reason. What are you prepared to offer that's equal in value to being eternally allied with the Fates and saving your people from extinction?"

"I haven't thought that far, friend," Darius responds. It's getting easier to distinguish their voices, and I'm still solidly pretending I'm asleep.

Growing up above a bar with very little privacy in our tiny two-room apartment, I learned the best way to get information the grown-ups didn't want you to have was to fake sleep. I'm a pro.

"There must be something in the prophecy to use as a guide," Rune says. "An impartial detail to determine who is the rightful courier."

"Don't be foolish." The condescension in his tone lets me know this is Darius. "The entire point of the prophecy is that this last step is undecided. We, in this room, are the final sentence of the scroll."

"Our version wasn't written, only spoken amongst elders and royals." Zev speaks with a tone that's calm, sophisticated, and gruff. His voice alone gives me goosebumps.

"You relied on an oral translation of the Fate's declaration?" Darius says snidely.

"Got me here at the same time as you, *friend.*"

I know I need sleep, but I can't stop listening, and I don't want them to stop talking. Also, for three beings who may or may not have superpowers, they are doing a crap job at noticing how loud they are and how nearby I am. Or maybe they just recognize that I'm vulnerable and powerless and they don't really care what I hear.

I shift slightly on account of the ever-present throbbing throughout my body, and the movement immediately shushes the conversation. This is as good a time as any to join in on the Sexies' little pow wow.

"What are you three talking about?"

There's a beat of silence, then the Sexies slowly shuffle into my doorway, looking like teens caught coming home after curfew. Look at me, only a few hours into motherhood and already commanding respect.

"You should keep resting, Bern-"

"Neeee," I jump in, knowing Zev is about to go with the full name. I've hated it since I was a kid and I'm not about to change my tune. Zev can deliver as many of my babies as he pleases, we're still not going full Bernadette.

"Yeah, I know I need rest. Thing is, there are three guys in my house that I don't remember asking to stay, and it's making it a little hard to sleep."

"We're only keeping an eye on you and the baby... Bern-E." I applaud Darius for the awkward attempt, even if his face looks ridiculous while he tries to make an E sound.

"Your health and safety is our chief concern," Rune picks up where Darius left off. "We can assure you of that."

Whether it's the constant chatter or it's actually feeding time, Rain starts to fuss. I'm sure she's hungry, but I'll use this as an opportunity to shame my trio of midwives.

"Well, you seem to be overlooking the importance of the baby sleeping, so maybe you can take the conversation to the living room while I feed her?"

I may have scored a small victory here, as the three turn to leave. Each moves differently, yet all possess the same silent grace that makes them so hard to look away from. A growing cry from my baby finally breaks my trance and I shuffle over to her.

Walking doesn't hurt the way I'd expect it to, and I take a moment to examine my nether regions. Jesus, Mary and Joseph... which one of them stitched me up? And when? Maybe that happened while I was first holding Rain, but you'd think I'd remember a hulking man running a needle and thread through my... you know. Again, I push thoughts of my visitors aside as my gaze lands on Rain.

She was perfect the first time I saw her and she's somehow even more incredible now, all swaddled up and clean. She's so beautiful in her little crib, more precious than I ever could have imagined.

"Come here, sweet little peanut. Momma's got you."

Her cries taper off as I pick her up and move her to my breast. I'm still scared of feeding, no real idea if I'm doing it right and no real advisor other than some of the wives of my drunken regulars. Still, she looks like she's eating, so I'll keep doing what I'm doing.

I ease into the rocker by the crib, going as slowly as possible because I'm still a little suspect of the stitch job downstairs. Just as I lean my back into the chair, three figures careen through the room, moving at a pace that makes them a literal blur.

In my state, I can't confidently describe what happens, but I'll swear on my mother's grave it didn't involve humans. Rune comes into the room first, but he doesn't enter, he *appears*. Like, out of thin air.

Before my brain processes that, a shadow travels along the ceiling, though nothing's there to cast it. The shadow is flying solo, and I know that's not how shadows work.

Just as this dark enigma is landing by my side, Zev explodes next to me. Explode doesn't sound right, but neither does the manner in which he arrives, because all I see out of the corner of my eye is a mix of fur and legs and face.

As fast as the dizzying movement starts, it ends, and now the guests I kicked out of my room thirty seconds ago are back.

"What in the flying f-"

"Move an inch and I'll rip your heart out through your back."

I'm *sure* Zev's not talking to me, but I still glance his way to see where his eyes are trained. He's clearly locked in on Darius, and he's got one of his enormous hands hovering centimeters from Rain's head. It scares the breath from my lungs, but that's as much as I dare to move.

"I'm standing between the fae and the baby, fool," Darius spits back. "He moved to come back in here the second he stepped into the living room."

"The wolf flinched first, not I," Rune hisses defensively.

"I smelled aggression on one of you, and clearly, I was right," Zev says, a low growl in his throat.

Wolf? Fae? The little corner of my brain that's been warning me we're no longer in Kansas finally has the microphone. This shit is *different*.

"Move your paw away from the baby, Zev." Rune speaks in a tone that seems less about commanding Zev and more about protecting Rain, which is finally something I can appreciate in this excruciating standoff.

The three men say nothing, each tense from teeth to toes as they wait to see if the other might move. I finally decide to speak, though I'm half expecting I'll startle Zev and get swallowed whole.

"Each of you," I start, talking as quietly and slowly as possible, "step to the center of the room and sit in front of me. Do it now, or I'll find a way to murder all of you, so help me God."

I feel their eyes on me as they consider my pitch. While I know they don't fear for their physical safety, it does seem they either respect me or need me for something, so my words carry a little weight. After a few more seconds of stillness, they do as directed, and the feeling of getting these three to follow instructions is borderline orgasmic.

As he moves to sit, I notice a small smirk on Rune's face. It might be the first emotion I've seen other than indifference and white-hot anger.

"Something funny, Runey Toons?" When in doubt, go schoolyard nicknames.

"Funny? I suppose, in its way. You say God. Singular. I always forget the simplicity of the earthly deities." His answer elicits a slight nod from Zev.

"Simplicity?" I respond, a little incredulous. "If religion here is simple, I'd hate to see the complex version. How do things work where you're from, pal?"

Rune stays silent. So do the others. It seems like my prying questions are going to get a little resistance, so I opt to go all in. It helps my confidence that they are sitting criss cross applesauce like children in front of me, all lined up in a row. I smirk at that and straighten my spine as I speak.

"You clearly need something from me, and none of you are happy with the others being here. So, if you want to get on my good side, one of you assholes better tell me what the bloody hell is going on."

I notice a feeling of safety creeping in, like my body trusts the people nearby and has released some tension. It's probably just the oxytocin from nursing flooding me with a happy hormone cocktail, but it's giving me the self-assurance to make demands, and hopefully that will help me keep a little control in a life that otherwise has gone way the hell off the rails in the last few hours.

Darius clears his throat, the first to man up and answer my damn question. Rune and Zev both look at him, apparently as eager to hear what he's got to say as I am.

"There's a prophecy, one you know not of, though it exists in your world."

"Great stopping point," I barge right in, needing clear answers in a hurry. "If this is my world, where are you from?"

"A different realm, I'm not sure you can understand it." His dark eyes flick away, like he's already bored with this conversation.

I narrow my eyes at his condescending tone. "Try me."

"We're in the same spheres of time, but a different world altogether," he says, and then adds under his breath, "One safe from the plague of humanity."

I'll unpack that plague of humanity bit in a minute. "Zev, Rune, this is true?" I ask for confirmation like I'm cross-checking the alibis of three kids who cut school. Talking like a principal is one of the few ways I can fake authority when I don't feel like I've really got it. The others nod and don't offer anything new, so I look back to Darius, prompting him to continue.

"The prophecy speaks of your child: when it would be born, the star that would guide its spirit, and the incomparable importance of its soul."

He lets those words hang as though they mean something, and clearly they do, but only to a person who's in league with these whackjobs.

"Okay," I shrug. "And?"

This time Zev butts in before Darius can continue. He seems to read the room a little better than his counterpart.

"Rain must leave this realm. Her soul is needed in another kingdom, for a purpose you're not ready to hear."

"Yeah, well, that's fine, because we're not going anywhere so it doesn't matter if I hear it or not." To punctuate my sentence, I quickly move my nursing child from one breast to the next, immediately regretting the decision as she nearly rips a nipple clean off.

When I get her settled and look back up, I'm met with three very serious, very stern sets of eyes.

"No, *you're* not going anywhere, that is true," Darius says. "Rain must come alone to the vampire's kingdom."

Zev snorts. "The vampires are at the root of these problems, dear Darius."

"Don't act as though the wolves are innocent, *dear Zev*," Rune interrupts. "Only the fae, with our connection to nature, can truly right this."

"Hold up, so Darius, you're a vampire?"

I'm waiting for someone to pop out of a corner and tell me I'm being pranked. But when no one does and Darius gives an imperceptible nod, I shift my gaze to Zev. "And you?"

"Werewolf, or wolf spirit, or wolf shifter, we have many names," he says, as if explaining his dad's half German.

"And I am fae," Rune says with a lofty pride the other two clearly don't care for.

I'm about three seconds from unleashing some serious mother bear energy on these three psychos, when a knock at the front door interrupts me.

All three guys turn their attention to the intrusion, and I stand with Rain clutched to my chest. Who could possibly be coming for the visit right now?

Darius looks unwilling to let me pass, but the pounding on the door gets louder.

"Bernie? You in there?" a voice calls from outside. "Joe called the station, said you might be in labor. I got here as soon as I could."

I glare at Darius, then share the glare with the others. "That would be the Chief of Police and a longtime family friend. If you don't let me answer that, you're going to have a much bigger problem to deal with very soon."

21

I mean what I say--if he thinks I'm in trouble, Chief Roland will try to give these guys hell without regard for his own safety. The question then becomes, what will these strangers do to him? And after that, what will they do to me?

CHAPTER FOUR

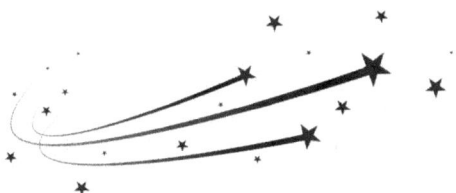

"Bernie?" The banging on the door becomes more aggressive and Rain hiccups and begins to cry. "I'm coming in one way or another, hon. Answer me, please?"

"What's it gonna be?" I ask the trio before me as I gently rock Rain, patting her back to soothe her.

This only seems to make her cry more loudly, and her screams echo through my small apartment.

"Bernadette!" Now the chief sounds panicked.

"He's using my full name. That's not a good sign," I say.

Darius steps aside. "Go. But watch what you say. We are not the ones who would be at risk were you to speak out of turn."

I narrow my eyes at the implied threat, but I hold my tongue when I see the unbridled violence simmering in his pitch black eyes. Turning away from his glare, I weave through the three guys towards my front door. When I yank it open, the chief--who was mid-knock--pulls his hand back, startled.

"My God, Bernie, you gave me a real scare." His gaze drops to the screaming bundle in my arms and his eyes widen. "So it's true. You had your baby."

"I certainly didn't steal this one from someone else," I joke.

He chuckles and runs a hand through his slightly balding hair. "You had us all worried," he says as he cranes his neck to scope out my apartment. "Who helped you?"

I glance back at the men crowding the entrance to my bedroom, wondering how much I should say. Could Chief Roland help me get rid of these guys? From what I've seen, I'm not sure, but it doesn't mean I'm not gonna try. "Why don't you come in and meet my knights in shining armor," I say with a saccharine smile.

The chief blinks, likely unused to me acting this way when I'm not on bar duty. "Uh, sure. Yeah, I'd like that."

He's dressed in street clothes, but he shifts his coat just enough to reveal the gun holstered at his hip. I nod in approval and lead him into my apartment, which--to be honest, has seen better days. The hardwood floor is pretty timeless--if scuffed in places, but the couch is threadbare and sagging; the recliner is a relic from a different epoch, and not in a cool antique kind of way; the kitchen is littered with dated dishes and appliances that scream 60s yard sale rejects; and the wallpaper is peeling. And this wallpaper...yeah, not the trend. Still, it's been home since my mom died and my grandparents took me in.

The chief looks a little misty-eyed as he studies the place. "I haven't been in here since...."

"Since my grandfather died," I say. "Well, you're always welcome. Grandpa would love to know his old friends were still coming by."

Rain has finally settled down and, though she doesn't fall back asleep, is enjoying snuggling against my chest. "Would you like to hold her?" I ask, though I'm reluctant to let go of my baby.

The chief's eyes widen. "Yes. I would."

He has four of his own kids and a handful of grandbabies, so he knows how to support her head, but as he takes her, the three men hiding out near my bedroom appear, their predatory instincts on high alert.

"Who might you be?" The chief asks, one hand dropping back to his gun as he clutches my child carefully with his other.

"These are the fine gentlemen who came to my rescue," I say, introducing them. "Zev here is a doctor *of sorts*, and he delivered little Rain with the help of his friends. They stayed to make sure I was okay. But your timing is perfect. They were looking for a place to stay in town. Maybe you could take them to Nancy's Bed and Breakfast and convince her to give them a room until the roads are clear enough for them to continue on their way?"

The chief frowns. "I'm sure Nancy could find you boys something."

Darius glares at me. "We are not in need of accommodations at this time."

"You're going to need somewhere to stay until the power comes back and the roads are safe for driving," I say sweetly.

The chief, sensing the tension, hands Rain back to me. "Why don't you boys come with me. We'll get you sorted. I'm sure Nancy will comp your stay for helping out our Bernie, here."

"Thanks, Chief," I say, nuzzling my baby. Why does she smell so good? How'd she get so perfect so fast?

When the guys don't move to follow him, the chief unsnaps his holster and pulls at his gun. "Do we have a problem here?"

Darius steps forward, his dark-as-sin eyes locked on the chief. "There is no problem here. You can leave. Bern--EE," he says, stumbling on my name, "is safe. We are friends here to help her. You will spread the word that we are staying with Bernie and everything is fine."

"Hey, hold up!" I say, turning to the chief, but his pupils are dilated and he nods.

"Of course. So glad you boys are here to take care of her. If you need anything, call." And then he walks out and closes the door behind him, leaving me speechless with the three Sexies--who might need a new nickname at this point. The three irritants perhaps. Or the three pains in my ass, maybe.

"What did you do to him?" I ask, poking Darius in his rock hard chest. I swear I nearly sprain my finger. But he doesn't even flinch.

"What had to be done. This child is too valuable to leave unprotected," he says.

"Um, excuse me? I'm the mother, in case you assholes forgot that tiny detail. I can protect my baby just fine. And I think it's past time the three of you left."

Darius sinks into my couch, frowning in discomfort. "I won't be going anywhere. Not without the child."

I look to Rune and Zev but they each shrug. "I'm afraid you're stuck with us," Zev says with a flirty grin and a wink. "You get free postpartum medical support, if that's any consolation."

I hesitate, because that is actually the best argument they've had so far given my shit insurance. I had no idea how I was going to cover the cost of giving birth to Rain, and yet here I am, in the clear. However, Zev fails to mention the part about them all wanting to steal my baby. "Yeah, that's great, right up until one of you tries to snatch my kid. Also, come on, you can't all expect to stay in my tiny apartment. Where will you sleep?"

They each glance at the second bedroom, the one my grandparents shared for fifty years. "All three of you will share a queen bed?" I ask, bemused.

Rune frowns. "I believe our sleeping needs are different."

"Is this seriously happening?" I ask, frustrated beyond measure and suddenly completely exhausted. I hobble to the recliner as Rain starts to fuss again and begin nursing her just as my stomach rumbles.

"When was the last time you ate?" Rune asks, casting a sideways glance at my sad kitchen.

I shrug. "It's been a while," I admit.

Rune heads to my kitchen and begins rummaging through cupboards. "When was the last time you acquired food?"

I shrug again. "Look, it's been a busy third trimester."

Rune looks to Darius and Mr. Tall, Dark and Sexy sighs in annoyance, then in a blink disappears through my window.

What the-- "Listen," I say, pulling my gaze from the window to the remaining two Sexies. "You guys need to start acting like normal human beings if you plan on staying here, or this isn't going to work."

Sadly, my point is undermined when I yawn, exhaustion overtaking me.

Zev saunters over, his gait like a wild animal, sleek and fluid. "Come. Get some rest. Your body is still healing."

Another yawn takes control of my face and I don't argue as he helps me up. I burp Rain while making my way to the bedroom. I have no energy left for arguing, and it's clear it won't do any good anyways. Maybe with some sleep I'll have a better idea how to get these guys out of my life for good.

Not wanting to let go of Rain, I take her to bed with me, and the moment my head hits the pillow, I pass out.

My dreams are feverish in nature, full of strange beasts and haunting images that blend my life in New York with other realms, and monsters chasing me. When I wake, I am covered in a sheen of sweat that makes my sheets stick to me.

I'm groggy as I try to figure out what woke me, and realize my breasts are painfully swollen and leaking milk all over my bed. Rain still sleeps, and my bladder feels ready to burst. Oh the joys of motherhood.

As I sit up and prepare to secure Rain with pillows while I head to the bathroom, I gasp.

This is my room, but it isn't. The wallpaper has been replaced with a pale blue paint and elaborate moulding. My bed is no longer the ancient mattress with springs that poke and prod, but instead seems to be made of clouds with a new four-poster rosewood canopy draped with shimmering silver silk. My sheets are luxuriously soft and match the walls, with a thick velvet white comforter embroidered with small flowers. New art hangs on my walls, and new furniture has replaced what I once had.

My urgent need to pee propels me forward despite my confusion, and I find the bathroom has also been redone with scented hand-carved soaps, new paint and light fixtures, and a thick carpet. Even the sink, toilet and bathtub have been replaced. What the actual hell?

Once I relieve myself, I head to the living room to find out what's going on. Am I hallucinating? Have I lost my damn mind?

Rune is in my kitchen plating food--a kitchen that now boasts new cabinets, new tile flooring, and state of the art appliances. Darius is sitting on an exquisite love seat, and Zev is stoking a fire in a fireplace I didn't have a few hours ago. My rickety upright out of tune piano has been replaced with a Steinway that easily cost $200,000. My fingers itch to play it, so much that my eyes burn with tears at the thought. It's been awhile since I've had one of those babies under my fingers.

"Could someone please explain to me how my entire apartment has changed while I slept?" I ask. "Wait, is this paranormal thing a bit, and you're actually part of an HGTV remodeling show?"

"H...G... what?" Leave it to Rune to be confused by everything and confirm that, no, I'm not on a reality show.

Darius looks up from a book he's reading. "The chosen one needed better accommodations," he says, simply, as if that explains everything.

Rune approaches with a plate--bone china, mind you--filled with chicken, a fresh salad and a side of grilled vegetables. "You must eat and replenish your strength."

"How'd you cook without power?" I ask, my stomach rumbling as I take a seat on the new couch and sigh at how comfortable it is.

"You now have a barbeque on your balcony," Rune says. "And you have a balcony."

I raise an eyebrow, and glance out the new door leading to said balcony. This isn't possible. "Where did all this stuff come from?" I ask, studying my surroundings.

"It wasn't easy," Zev says, "but we're resourceful."

"How did I not hear this? How did you add a balcony and change wallpaper and redo my floors in just a few hours while my baby and I slept through it all?"

"We have our ways," Rune says. "Ways that would not be comprehensible to your kind."

I shake my head, entirely bemused and befuddled, but also slightly ravenous.

The food is delicious and I make quick work of it. Rune is on hand to take my plate back to my entirely renovated kitchen. The apartment is still small, but it no longer feels that way. Everything is high quality and top of the line. I feel... pampered. It's a strange sensation and I don't know how to respond.

"What happened to my personal stuff?" I ask, looking around, my eyes landing on my family portrait with relief. I walk over, still careful with my stiff and fragile body, and study the four of us. "This was the last picture taken of us before my mom died," I say to the room, not really caring who's listening. "The day we had it done she and I had gotten into a huge fight. I don't even remember what about, just that I was still in a pissy mood when the photographer showed up."

I study my young face, all tween angst and drama. But my mom, she's glancing down at me with such fierce love. Sometimes this image is the only one I can clearly remember of her, the way the right side of her lip curls higher than the left when she smiles, and the tiny scar on her forehead that had a different story to it every time I asked her how she got it. She and I share the same bright blue eyes and dark hair, the same pale complexion. We both take after my grandmother, who is clutching my grandfather's hand in the portrait. "My grandparents raised me after my mom died," I say. I'll need to visit my grandmother soon. Introduce her to Rain. She may not remember us, but I want her to know her great-granddaughter nonetheless.

"Anything personal was kept," Zev says. "The rest was tossed."

Right. I really hope these guys know how to tell the difference between what's personal and what's not.

Now that I've eaten my fill, I can no longer resist the temptation of that piano, regardless of how they acquired all this shit in a black out snow storm.

"You didn't rob anyone, did you?" I ask, suddenly worried as I make my way to the piano bench.

Darius chuckles. "No. We have no need for that. Everyone was well compensated."

"Much of this was accomplished by magic," Rune says with a shrug, as if that explains it all.

As long as they didn't steal it, I'm satisfied enough to enjoy it for now. I let my fingers run over the ivory keys, closing my eyes as my memories drift back to my time in New York, to the life that could have been... if I hadn't gotten pregnant. If my grandfather hadn't died. If...if...if.

Too many ifs. I shove them away and begin to play. I start with something easy to warm up. I haven't had much time for this since I've been back. But as muscle memory kicks in, I move to more complicated pieces, finally landing on Ravel's *Gaspard de la Nuit,* one of the hardest piano pieces ever written. Everything disappears and I lose myself in the complex notes, reveling in the way my body feels, the way the music fills the apartment, the way I connect to the instrument like I am one with it.

When I finish, there is a profound silence in the room, and I turn to see all three guys staring at me in wonder.

Darius exhales a breath he seems to have been holding in. "I have never in my significantly long life heard anything so beautiful." His voice is soft, almost a breath against my mind, and his praise fills something in me that has been empty for far too long. I fall into the feeling, wishing I could have had the life that was once promised to me.

Before.

The mood is broken by the sound of someone knocking at the door.

Who's here now? I don't get this many visitors on a normal day, let alone in the middle of a freaking blizzard.

The guys exchange worried glances, and I sigh and go to answer.

My childhood bestie stands at the threshold, mascara running down her cheeks, long blond hair pulled into a messy bun, her clothing disheveled.

"AJ?" My gaze falls to the blood seeping through a bandage tied haphazardly around her arm. "What the hell?"

"Can I stay here for a few days?" she asks, sniffling. "John shot me."

CHAPTER FIVE

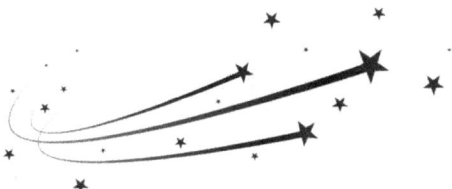

"Jesus Christ, AJ!" I guide her out of the cold, trembling with fear and rage. I disliked John when they started dating, loathed him a year into their marriage, and now I finally get to kill him.

We move toward the loveseat, and my sexy, irritating, home remodelers all gather round. I'm too focused on AJ's wound to consider the scene she finds herself walking into.

"Sweet Lord have mercy," AJ mutters under her breath, her head on a swivel as she looks between my gorgeous guests. "Shit, Bernie, did you win the lottery?"

AJ's the best. The bullet wound could be in her head and she'd still crack wise. I get her seated and, before I can make the request, Zev is there with a towel and some unmarked glass bottles. Those weren't here a day ago, so I guess he found an apothecary while he was piano shopping.

"Hi…" AJ manages to say as she falls into the wilderness that lives in Zev's green eyes.

"Good morning," Zev replies in his gruff but soothing voice. "I'm sorry, I didn't catch your name."

"I'm Anna Jane," she says softly, with an obvious subtext of "please ravage me."

Hearing AJ use her full name throws me. She *hates* her name, even more than I hate Bernadette. Clearly, she's overwhelmed by the magnitude of hotness in my apartment. Hell, she hasn't even noticed the million-dollar renovation yet--or my freaking baby!

Rune walks over with a glass of water for her. The manners on these intruders consistently surprise me. As he hands her the glass, he pours a single drop of something from another unmarked bottle.

"Here, this will help with the pain."

I stifle a laugh. Since walking in and laying eyes on Darius, Zev, and Rune, I don't think AJ's felt a thing.

"Thank you, I--oh my."

Her reaction to Zev ripping the sleeve off her undershirt is ridiculously muted. *Oh my?* This girl normally swears like a sailor, and now she's trying to pull off the demure act while my Sexies tend to her gunshot wound? I catch myself getting possessive and try to dial it back. *These uber-hot creeps are here to steal your baby, Bernie. Don't forget that.*

"It's a deep cut, but the instrument passed through surface tissue and didn't hit the bone," Zev explains, his words entirely lost on AJ as she studies his woodland god-like face.

"AJ," I say firmly, kneeling down and putting my hands on her knees. God, it feels good to kneel again. That's something you take for granted until you're eight months pregnant and trying to put on a shoe. "AJ, what happened? And where is that son of a bitch?"

She finally turns away from Zev and looks at me, a sadness settling in behind her big brown eyes.

"He was drunk and mad, because, you know, that's just his natural state of being," she starts, and I can see there's more anger than sadness in her look. It's a hard shift to notice, but after a few thousand heart-to-hearts with this girl, I pick up on her mood pretty fast.

"Then the power went out and he started getting drunker, and that made him madder. We yelled at each other a little last night and then he passed out, so I thought that was the end of it. But the bastard started drinking first thing this morning. I called him a deadbeat loser and may have said a thing or two about his mother, then I got shot."

She's a little too casual in her storytelling for my taste, but I know she's trying to keep her rage at bay. John started making life more difficult the day he and AJ met when he transferred to our high school senior year, but she always thought she could fix him. I wonder if this will be her breaking point.

"I'm so sorry. Of course you can stay--"

I'm interrupted by a cry from the bedroom, which serves as a great reminder that I have a baby. It also alerts AJ to a few of the changes.

"Holy shit! Bern! You're not pregnant!"

That was the obvious one. I'll give her time to catch up on the other tweaks as the day goes on.

She bursts to her feet and pulls me into a strong embrace, thwarting Zev's efforts to clean her wound.

"Where is she?" AJ asks, happy tears in her eyes. "I have to meet her."

"Stay right here, I'll bring her in," I say, giving AJ a gentle squeeze on her unshot arm as I go.

Just as I disappear into the bedroom, I hear my friend sounding a bit more like herself and not an overwhelmed schoolgirl as she addresses the unexpected guests.

"So, in the name of all that is good and holy, who the hell are you three?"

When I get to Rain, I can tell it's time for a diaper change and a feeding. I feel a little uncomfortable leaving AJ alone with the sexy stranger brigade, but she can stand up for herself as well as anyone, and I know they don't want any extra trouble.

I move Rain to her changing table and try to listen to the conversation in the front room in between the sobs. I can't hear much, just the occasional mention of countries as AJ tries to guess where everyone is from.

"Like, Paraguay? No, Portugal. Which one's in Europe? No, never mind, your hair's too light."

I love this girl so much. Her knowledge of the world outside of Massachusetts has, let's say, some gaps. That doesn't stop her from talking like she knows shit.

Their conversation makes me wonder--what *do* I tell AJ? Do I bring her into the loop? Will she believe me if I try? And what will these guys do, to me or her, if someone else knows what's going on? It might not be worth the risk.

I haven't quite decided on a plan of action as I head back out with Rain. AJ stands with the men in a circle around her, and I'm quite sure she orchestrated this positioning. Don't get me wrong, she's never been unfaithful, but she recognizes a thing--or three things--of beauty when she sees it. Plus, with John being the world's biggest piece of shit, I hope she takes all the time she wants to enjoy the view.

Still, she knows what's important and abandons the Sexies when she sees her goddaughter coming her way.

"She still needs to eat, so don't be offended if she screams the whole time you hold her," I say, like I'm a total expert on babies as I gently hand Rain to her.

"She can cry all she wants and I'll still love her forever," AJ says, and I know it's true. "My God, Bern, she's gorgeous. What's her name?"

"Rain," I answer, knowing full well--

"You and your weird hippie shit."

For being best friends since we were kids, AJ and I don't have a lot in common. It's why I left Rowley and she never did, nor did she ever plan to. Our differences have helped strengthen our bond over time, forcing us to appreciate and overlook traits we might not have had patience for if it weren't for the depth of our friendship.

I love seeing her hold Rain, and look forward to years of them spending time together, but she's still bleeding from a small hole on her upper arm.

"AJ, you need more time with my medics," I say, reaching for Rain. "You can play with the baby after you're stitched up."

She looks down at her arm, remembering the reason she came here.

"Right..." her voice trails off as she looks over her shoulder at the flawless men, quietly observing our every move. "Bernie, what's happening? When was she born? Who are these guys? Why... I don't know, why everything?"

Before I can start to respond, Zev comes over and gently guides AJ back to the loveseat. The moment he touches her, she's lost again in a sexy fog.

"I'm going to numb your arm then suture the wound," Zev explains as he sits AJ down, her eyes never leaving his face. "My thread will help you to heal."

AJ offers a slight nod to Zev, then looks at me questioningly.

"Wait, Bernie, for real, who are these guys? I appreciate the medical attention and all, but this is too weird to ignore."

Well. Shit. Now I've got half a second to decide how to play this. I don't know what to do, what's going to happen, or how much danger any of us are in, but my gut tells me to keep up the ruse. If nothing else, that might give me more time to figure something out.

"Um, where do I start? This is Zev, Rune, and Darius." All male eyes are glued to me, also interested in how my introduction will go. "They showed up at my bar last night, on their way to... Montreal. Got stuck here when the power went out, and that's pretty much why Rain and I are alive."

AJ's eyes go wide. "Are you serious?"

I nod, and it dawns on me that I mostly told the truth. A little fib about where they're headed, but I don't know what would have happened if these men didn't have some insane prophecy guiding them to my doorstep. As for that final part, I'll fill AJ in after I figure out how we're going to survive.

"I mean... that's insane," AJ very astutely observes. "And you're all doctors?"

There's a momentary silence as the men figure out who will field questions addressing the group. Darius takes the lead.

"We all have medical training, if not the actual title of doctor."

"And what's in Montreal?" AJ's always been a talker, especially around cute guys. With so many years lost to a loveless marriage, I imagine it's only going to be worse now. "Are you all going to a medical conference or something?"

Another beat. So handsome, smart, and strong, but the quick wit is severely lacking. They look between one another, hoping someone will speak. Naturally, AJ fills the dead air.

"What's up, fellas? No one remembers why they're going to Montreal?"

"Yes," Rune blurts out, clearly an unskilled liar. "A medical conference or something."

Zev and Darius nod, trying to show how they're all on the same page. AJ just stares--then starts to laugh.

"Okay, whatever. You guys are lying through your teeth, but you're fixing my arm so I'll let it slide." Her ability to brush things off has always astounded me. It's probably made her a little complacent at times, but right now it's really bene-fiting us all.

"So, um, Bernie," AJ says, changing the subject. "When did you get all this amazing shit?"

Goddammit. And I thought explaining the hottest men in the universe being in my house would be the biggest challenge. This is definitely going to be harder.

"Oh, yeah, I forgot you hadn't seen the place yet," I gesture around, trying to buy myself some thinking time. Won the lottery? Took out a loan? Lie and say nothing's changed? None of those will fly. Gotta go random.

"I... inherited everything," I start, having no trouble sounding surprised because I'm not entirely sure what'll come out of my mouth next. "An older cousin on my mom's side left a bunch of stuff to my mom. I guess he's got no next of kin and somehow didn't know my mom was dead. Honestly, I keep waiting for someone to come back and reclaim it all. A truck showed up a few days ago and now I'm wicked fancy."

AJ stares at me, her right eyebrow cocked in a very disbelieving fashion. The Sexies all stare at me as well, none of them with a clue as to what I said.

"Clearly," AJ says, and I'm half-sure she's about to call out my bullshit. But then she goes on, "this is the universe trying to get you to live in Rowley forever. And I appreciate it, powers that be," she says, looking up and doing a kind of cross thing over her chest that I'm pretty sure is made up, "but I won't allow it. Bernie's too good for this dumb town, so she's back to playing concert halls and shit as soon as Baby Rain's old enough to stay with her auntie."

If she's moved on to taking shots at our hometown, she's good with my story. AJ will kill a bitch who bad mouths Rowley if they're not from here, but when it comes to me and pursuing my dreams, she thinks this town can "get bent." I'd never felt like AJ was truly mad at me about anything until I moved back. That's something we're still working out.

"Finished," Zev cuts in, having swiftly tended to AJ's arm while we talked it out.

"Oh. Whoa." AJ looks at her wound and isn't sure how to react. It's so tightly stitched the gash is only barely noticeable. And yet, from a few feet away, I can hardly see the thread.

"What kind of invisible synthetic shit is this?" AJ asks.

"It's... not a material you would know about," Zev offers, and I'm curious to hear how he handles a barrage of follow-up questions. Before he can continue, Darius' voice interrupts. But the words don't come from his mouth, instead they go straight into my freaking head.

The thread is made of his own hair, Bernadette.

I make eye contact with Darius, and I know he's talking directly with me, but doing it so AJ can't hear him. It gives me the funniest feeling, like I'm having a casual conversation against my will. He's overpowering my mind and, frankly, I wish I didn't like it so much.

It's what he used to stitch the tearing after Rain was born. You have werewolf hair sewn throughout your va--

"Get out!" I scream to make Darius leave my mind, but unlike his words, mine resound loudly throughout the room. Everyone looks up, worried. Sticking with the theme of the day, I improvise.

"Get out... of here with those medical stories, Zev! We don't have time to learn the history of medicine from wherever you're from. I've got a baby to tend to, AJ needs to decide how many charges she wants to press against her husband, and you three need to learn how to tend bar."

I pulled that last one out of my ass, and couldn't be happier with myself.

"Oh yeah, I forgot to mention," I say to AJ, though my words are mostly meant for the men I'm going to try like hell to turn into my sexy slaves. "Since I'm on mom duty, these guys are going to handle the business downstairs for a day or two while they're stranded. Win win, am I right?"

AJ smiles, because I am right. The three men frown, because they don't necessarily agree.

KARPOV KINRADE & EVAN GAUSTAD

"If you don't mind, maybe you can teach them some tricks of the trade? Start by showing Rune where the kegs are and how to change a tap?"

"Of course I don't mind," AJ answers, giving my arm a squeeze and Rain's head a tiny kiss. "Rune is... blondie, right? Follow me."

I watch them head out the door, and I'm thrilled to death that AJ is here, even if it does complicate my living arrangements even more than they already were. My immediate future is still incredibly vague, but she brings a burst of hope and happiness into my life that I'm grateful for, especially now.

After they leave, I turn to Darius and Zev.

"First off, don't pull that shit again, Darius. Stay out of my head."

He offers a curt nod, but I'm not sure he's going to follow my order. Then I turn to Zev.

"And you--did you really stitch me up downstairs with your own hair?"

"Downstairs? No, you were up in your bedroom-"

"You know what I mean. The wounds *below my waist.*"

"Ah," Zev says, finally catching on. "Yes. You'll find no thread as strong or as sterile as the hair of a wolf. Not an Earth wolf, of course, but from-"

"Got it, thank you," I cut him off, my brain not needing any more information to process. I head for the hallway, taking Rain to the comfort of our own bedroom.

"You two can join Rune, down in the walk-in fridge," I say as I reach the door. "This is a small town, where everyone knows me and everyone talks. If people don't think you should be here, they'll make their feelings clear."

I look at Rain and her beautiful little face. We just met, but I'd die for her in an instant.

"You might have powers we don't," I say with renewed passion, "but a town of angry Massholes looking out for their own isn't something you want to reckon with."

"Be that as it may," Darius says, stepping forward, his dark eyes mesmerizing me into temporary silence, "we cannot leave the child unprotected." He glances at Zev then back at me. "While you slept, we agreed that at least two of us would stay near her at all times."

I glare at the man before me. "First, she's not unprotected. She's with me, and I will not let anything happen to her. Second, you three don't get to make decisions about my baby. You don't get to make any decisions about--"

But before I can finish, the sound of a gunshot coming from outside my door interrupts me.

Rain screams bloody murder in my arms, my breasts pulse in pain from the pressure of the milk, and Zev growls like a wild animal.

My front door crashes in and slams to the floor, a hulk of man on the other side, his dirty blond hair a greasy mess, his wife-beater shirt stained with dirt and beer, his brown eyes wild with fury, and a double-barreled shotgun cocked in his hands.

It's John, AJ's good for nothing husband.

"I know she's here you dumb bitch. Give me back my wife or you and that brat of yours are gonna get shot."

CHAPTER SIX

It's not an exaggeration to say that having a gun pointed at you and your newborn child is one of the most terrifying things that can happen to a person.

But my terror is short lived.

As short lived as that asshole's life in my apartment.

Several things happen at once, and I only have time to step back and tighten my arms around my irate child as a scene straight out of a horror movie unfolds before me.

First, Zev's body shifts from man to wolf in one astounding moment. It's like a controlled burst of energy--he takes in a breath, then his features and limbs transform in a smooth, exotic motion, his bones reshaping as white fur grows over skin. He lands gracefully on all fours, majestic and intimidating. I've seen a couple wolves in my life, and Zev's at least twice as big as any of them.

Before I can even unpack that transition, Darius moves with lightning speed, disarming John just as the gun goes off, blowing a hole in my ceiling and traumatizing my eardrums.

Next, Zev leaps into the fray, his claws digging into John's chest and tearing through flesh, muscle and bone like the bastard is made of butter.

And finally, Darius's teeth sharpen into knives, and he twists John's neck to the side, sinking his fangs into John's pulsing vein.

I don't know what kills him. The wolf mauling or the vampire draining, but within seconds, his lifeless form is dropped to my floor like a bag of flour.

The thunk he makes is slightly wet, like a splat, and I swallow back vomit and shield Rain's eyes from the gore, even though I know she technically can't see that far yet.

"What the f--" I can't even finish my thoughts before Rune appears, his body blocking what remains of the door frame as his sharp blue eyes take in the scene.

Darius glances at him. "There was a situation," he says before looking down at the body and then back to Rune. "It's been resolved."

I nearly choke on his casual tone.

Rune nods. "Good. AJ is in the bar. You might need to..."

Darius nods. "Understood." He disappears downstairs, while Zev remains a wolf, sitting by the door like a guard dog.

"And the child?" Rune locks his gaze with mine, and in four long strides is by my side, assessing both Rain and me. "You are shaking. It's shock. Come."

He guides me out of the living room and into my bedroom, then sits me on the bed and gently removes the screaming child from my arms. "She is hungry but safe." He looks at me with more compassion than I've ever seen from any of them. "If you cannot feed her, I can make her a formula that will satisfy."

My mind is having trouble translating sound to words, but it clicks into place when he starts to leave with her.

"No. Give her to me. I can do it."

He nods and hands Rain back, and without regard for modesty--as that ship has long since sailed--I pull out a breast and let my baby latch on.

Rune watches, his eyes mostly locked on Rain, I'm sure to confirm she's okay after everything that transpired. Still, his eyes spend a little more time on me than they have in the past. His gaze trails over my naked breast, then along my neck and up to my eyes. A hint of modesty creeps back into my psyche, as I realize how disheveled and generally disgusting I must look. I know I certainly feel beyond gross after a day of work, childbirth, intermittent sleep and no bathing.

I break eye contact before he does, checking on Rain to make sure she's drinking all right. She's chugging away, blissfully unaware of everything. I wonder how old she'll be when I can finally tell her the story of her birth. Right now, it seems like it would be too traumatic at any age. I smile to myself as I think of getting a picture of the three Sexies holding Rain, each looking deathly serious, to put in her baby book. Then I laugh out loud when I imagine Darius not showing up in the picture--if that adage about vampires is true.

"What? What's wrong?" Rune asks.

Is laughter a sign of distress where he's from?

"Do vampires show up in mirrors or pictures?" I ask.

Rune frowns. "Is there a reason they wouldn't?"

I shrug. "Just trying to figure out how much of what I think I know is real."

He sniffs. "Well, I wouldn't put a lot of stock in what most humans imagine any of us to be like. Honestly, I have no idea where they come up with some of it."

"Right. Well. You'll have to fill me in on what's real and what's not." I switch Rain to my other breast. "In the meantime, I'm going to finish feeding and change her, you should go see--"

"What the actual mother-loving hell is this?"

It would appear AJ has seen the body of her now-dead husband.

I hear one of the guys saying something to her, but she comes busting into my room, her eyes wide, blood drained from her skin. "Oh my Lord, woman, you scared the shit out of me. I thought that bastard..."

She rushes me and the baby, evading Rune who tries to stop her as she sits next to me on the bed and wraps her arms awkwardly around me as Rain continues to feed.

"Are you okay? Is my god-baby okay?" she asks, tears now streaming down her face.

I lean my head against her forehead, the way we used to do, like cats head-butting each other. "We're safe. But...I'm sorry? About... you know." It's a pretty weak apology for, I don't know, being an accessory to murder? Not really sure what my role was so I can't figure out the appropriate response. Hallmark doesn't make cards for 'sorry the three supernatural beings who came here to kidnap my kid killed your abusive asshole husband in the most violent way possible.' I'm guessing the demand isn't high for that sort of thing. Very niche market.

But AJ just shakes her head. "Girl, there's a lot you need to explain, but right now I'm just relieved you and cutie-pie here are okay. That asswipe can burn in hell for all I care."

"You're not mad?" I ask. I mean, I'm not mad he's dead. I'm mad there's blood all over my newly refurbished apartment, but John can rot, as she said. Still, AJ has had a complicated relationship with him since high school. I know this can't be easy, even if he was an animated piece of evil dog shit.

She shakes her head, letting blond curls spill in front of her eyes. "Listen, this marriage has been dead for a long time. It was just...living in a small town, with nowhere else to go, it always felt too hard to get out." AJ wipes her eyes, then smiles. "Now the marriage is literally dead, and I didn't have to do the murder-ing, so I guess--"

Rain interrupts our heart to heart by pulling off my nipple, satisfied with a full tummy. Before I can burp her, Rune--who I nearly forgot was there, that boy is stealth--holds his hands out for her. "I'd like to check her ears, if that's okay?"

When I frown, confused, he adds. "From the gunshot? And I can burp her and get her back to sleep."

Shit. What kind of mother am I that I didn't even consider the effect a gunshot so close to her head would have? I nod and hand her to Rune.

Zev, who is still a giant white wolf, appears at the door and hovers near Rune as they leave my room. The wolf glances at me briefly, then walks away.

I gracelessly shove my breast back into my shirt and sigh as AJ narrows her eyes. "You gonna tell me what the hell is going on now? For real? Who are these guys?"

I inwardly wince, not wanting to lie, but knowing I must. For reasons. "I already told you, they were on their way to a medical convention when--"

"Shut your lying mouth, B. Look, I know I've never been as smart as you. I still hear the same dumb blond jokes from the idiots and assholes who were saying that shit in high school, so I'm not delusional about how clever I am. But, of all people, you know I'm not as stupid as I look." Her eyes narrow and I see the lifetime of pain and disappointment hidden in them. A lifetime of living up to the very low expectations everyone had for her.

I want to argue, to tell her none of that is true, but I won't insult her intelli-gence. I was a musical prodigy in a tiny town with no competition. It set me up to be some kind of weird local mascot. I could do no wrong. I was pretty, sure, but I wasn't AJ's level of pretty. Instead, I was the smart one with all the talent. She was the blond bombshell who filled out early. Her nickname in middle school was jailbait. Her family life was shit, so she had no support. I became her family, with my grandparents doing what they could for her. But nothing we did could shake this town from their prejudices.

It's no wonder she never left John. She had nowhere else to go. I'm the only person in Rowley who's ever loved her back, and I was gone for half a decade.

So, I make a decision I hope I won't regret.

And I tell her everything.

She is completely silent through it all, the only sign that she's still listening is the occasional widening of her eyes.

When I'm done, we sit in silence for a long minute, both of us absorbing the absurdity of my tale. Saying it all out loud does nothing to make this situation sound saner. If anything, I feel like I'm in an alternate reality.

"So, Zev is the werewolf, Rune is the fae, and Darius is the vampire?" she asks, finally.

I blink. "Yes."

She nods. "Makes sense. I vibe with that."

I blink again. "You... *vibe with that?*"

"I mean, at first, I wasn't sure if Rune or Darius was the vampire. They both have a bit of that energy, but I for sure knew Zev was a werewolf the moment I met him."

"What the hell are you going on about?" I ask. "When you *met him?*"

AJ sighs, like she's trying to explain something basic to a child. "I don't know how you *didn't* know what they were the moment they walked into the bar, B. It was super obvious. You think I bought any part of that story about them going to a medical convention together?" She rolls her eyes. "I have read enough books and seen enough TV shows to know the real deal when I meet it. First of all, no normal men are that incredibly hot unless their last names are Hemsworth. Second, I could smell it on them."

Now my eyes are surely bugging out of my freaking skull. "You could *smell it on them.* AJ, what does that even mean?"

My best friend shrugs, all casual-like. "I dunno. They didn't smell human."

She glances at me sharply, her perfect little nose scrunching in disgust. "Speaking of, momma, when did *you* last bathe." It's not even a question, just a clear testament to my current hygiene. And she's not wrong, so I don't argue when she drags me to the bathroom and begins running the tub.

"Strip down. It ain't nothing I haven't already seen. We need to clean you up before we go deal with the mess my dead husband left."

She's so matter-of-fact about it all, I feel equally relieved and confused. Am I the only one surprised by the presence of the supernatural in our world? And what will the Sexies say when they find out AJ knows? I worry Darius will try his mind tricks with her, and no one is messing with my girl's brain if I can help it.

AJ hums as she works, adding bath salts and bubbles, and when I finally sink into the hot water, I moan in pleasure. My body truly feels like it's been put through a military boot camp. Everything hurts, and I don't even care if baths are recommended after birth or not. It feels too good to be bad for me. Plus, my new bath came with jets, which work perfectly to massage out some of my aches and pains as I soak.

AJ washes my hair for me, bless her, and once I'm done and dressed in fresh clothes, I feel like a whole new person. Ready to face whatever awaits me on the other side of my bedroom door, more or less.

Also, I need my baby back. Being apart from her is strange, after carrying her in me for so long. My body doesn't feel complete without her. I glance at the clock and see it's already afternoon. The day is slipping away, soon we'll have to light candles because it doesn't seem like the power is coming back by tonight. Thank God for the gas water heater.

I can hear the three Sexies bickering as we walk into the living room together, though the scene that awaits us is not what I'm expecting.

"This has nothing to do with her," Rune says. He's sitting in a rocking chair holding Rain so tenderly, my heart nearly melts.

Darius and Zev are playing chess in the corner, which is strange because I thought they hated each other and I'm very certain I don't own a chessboard. It's also strange that Zev can transform from wolf to human and immediately become lust worthy again.

"It certainly has something to do with her," Darius says, not bothering to look at the fae as he studies his next move on the chess board. "She died trying to sort out this prophecy, and now the three of us are here, just as she foresaw."

Darius looks over at Rune now. "You think that's a coincidence?"

Zev clears his throat. "I think we should discuss this later."

"Discuss what later?" I ask, when it's clear they won't keep talking like I'm not in the room.

"Nothing important," Zev says with a grimace. "Just digging up old bones that should stay buried."

"Speaking of bones and being buried, what did you do with..." I was about to say, the body, but I glance at AJ to see how she's doing first.

"The body," she finishes for me. "Where's that asshole's body?"

Turns out my girl is holding her shit together better than I could have imagined.

It also turns out John's body is gone. It's like it never happened. The floors are spotless, the ceiling is repaired, even the smell of burnt gunpowder is gone. The room now smells like cinnamon and apples, from something boiling in a cast iron pot over the fire.

Darius, who was just sitting across from Zev, is now standing before us in a blink.

"Stop doing that," I say. "Walk like a normal person unless it's absolutely necessary."

He narrows his dark eyes, but nods. "We have handled the situation." Then he glances at AJ. "All that remains is taking care of her."

I grip AJ's hand harder. "I've told her everything. There's nothing to take care of. She's in the know and it's gonna stay that way."

Zev growls under his throat and Rune looks up from the baby, but doesn't make a move to intervene.

Darius frowns. "That won't be possible. The more people who know, the more dangerous this situation becomes for the child and you."

Before I can argue with him, his eyes begin to glow a faint silver and he speaks to AJ in a hypnotic voice. "You saw nothing and heard nothing. Your last memory is being downstairs at the bar. There was no gun shot, and you don't know what happened to your husband."

AJ blinks, then begins to laugh. "Oh, this must be some vampire mind voodoo shit, right? I knew that was real. Yeah, sorry, buddy. Doesn't work on me."

Darius' face hardens and Rune chuckles under his breath.

Darius tries again. "You will forget everything that happened."

AJ shakes her head. "Sorry not sorry, dude. But A for effort."

"Looks like you've lost your touch," Rune says, amused.

Zev stalks over, his muscles flexing like he's on the prowl. He sniffs at AJ, who doesn't seem to find this weird at all. Zev's green eyes widen in surprise. "Hmmm. Seems like this one isn't human."

CHAPTER SEVEN

I'm shocked, confused, and conflicted. On the one hand, it's a relief to know AJ's mind isn't open for vampire business. On the other, my best friend for as long as I can remember, the godmother to my only child, the one person in this world I can trust--isn't human? What am I supposed to do with that information?

"What?" I ask Zev, ready to throw a massive fit if he doesn't elaborate.

"Yeah, what?" AJ echoes.

My head snaps to her, every sense I can control focused on studying her thoughts, expressions, and movements. I've always been able to read AJ's tells, knowing when she lied about where she spent the night, what was going on with her dad, which boy she was making out with. Throughout all of that, at no point did I think, *hang on, I wonder if she's lying about being the same species as me.*

Even as I look her over, getting close enough to take a discreet sniff and see if I can smell whatever Zev smelled--I definitely cannot--AJ keeps her eyes on the werewolf.

"What do you mean I'm not human? Bernie, what's he saying?"

AJ finally looks at me and sees how freaked out I am.

"Are you… Bernie, are you freaking serious? Do you not think I'm a person?" The look of disbelief on her face makes me wonder if I am being a little crazy about this. "We've been having sleepovers since we were like five. We've gone skinny dipping a thousand times."

She's not lying, but I'm not sure if anatomy is the defining human factor. After all, I've spent a fair amount of time thinking about the anatomy of my visiting Sexies, and I don't want those fantasies to be dashed right now.

"Why didn't you fall under the spell, A? I'll believe whatever you say, but I need you to help me understand."

She looks at me, then at Zev, then back at Darius, who's still pretty steamed about having his mental advances rebuffed.

"I mean… I don't know. All he did was tell me to forget shit and it's like, why? So you're a gorgeous vampire, I don't have to hand you the damn keys to my mind."

The logic doesn't win me over, but analytics have never meant much in our relationship. Still, I need a second opinion.

"Zev?" I ask, still wanting an explanation from the doctor with K-9 smelling powers.

"Humans have a bitter smell," he explains, eyes wandering over AJ. "The toxins from your body, the harmful chemicals your brains produce, the scent is almost overwhelming."

He walks back to AJ, very much invading her personal space as he places his nose at the base of her neck and inhales deeply. She doesn't fight it at all, instead placing her hands on his hips to steady herself as she tilts her head to the side and gives Zev better access. From the way they're standing, you wouldn't know AJ's husband died twenty minutes ago and Zev's the one who killed him. As Zev takes in whatever otherworldly pheromone my friend's producing, he keeps his eyes locked with mine. For the briefest second I imagine standing where AJ is, Zev's face next to mine, his breath on my neck. A warm shiver runs through me and I shake my head to snap out of it.

Zev steps back, his gaze returning to the woman he just inhaled. "She has no such smell. You may have human blood, but there's more to you than that."

I need a break from this new reality, so I cross the room to take my baby back from Rune. She might be less than a day old, but she feels like the one constant I've got in life, now that I know AJ is an alien or a bird or a pile of crabs wearing a human suit.

Darius comes in hot, wanting answers like the rest of us, but also with a personal bone to pick since AJ beat him in a game of mentalist. "Where are you from?"

"I'm from Rowley, idiot."

Her immediate snark is so common for people in this area, it makes me think either Zev can't handle the smell of New Englanders or I've grown up amongst nonhumans. Frankly, both options sound plausible.

Rune's been quiet to this point, observing with a blank face. When he stands and strides over to AJ, Zev and Darius clear the way, almost deferentially.

"I sense nymph."

He speaks with a quiet authority. It's a side of Rune I hadn't seen until this point. He stares into AJ's eyes while describing her to us.

"She attracts, clearly. There's fluidity, grace… and fire. That must be the human side."

Zev and Darius join the fae, the three of them all standing inches from AJ, whose body is tense but unmoving. My mind drifts again to a quick body swap, placing myself in the middle of that Sexy circle, but I push the thought out for fear of fainting.

"It's on the father's side," Darius speaks barely above a whisper.

"How do you know?" asks Zev. It's the first time I've seen the werewolf seek knowledge from another, and it adds another layer to his intelligent charm.

"Because if the trait came from her mother," Darius says, turning away from AJ to show his inspection has concluded.

"...she'd know." Rune picks up the sentence where Darius left off. "She had no example of who she was. No role model."

"Hey, blondie, maybe stop talking shit about my mom." AJ's heart is in the right place, even if she misses the point.

I've still got no fewer than a million questions, but the Sexies seem pretty content with this reasoning. AJ's a nymph, not on her mom's side, case closed, I guess?

"Hang on," I finally chime in, not ready for this conversation to move to the next point. "How many nymphs and wolf people and, friggin', I don't know, orcs are living around me? Or is AJ, and AJ's dad, are they the only ones?"

"Certainly not the only ones," Zev answers, reclaiming his role as the smartest man in the room. "But there are very few."

The werewolf walks into the attached kitchen, taking a glass and filling it with water from the sink.

"A small number of Earthlings aren't human," he continues, "many concentrated in this area."

"What, in Rowley?" AJ asks. I can hear from the tenor of her voice that she's not into the idea of other non-humans living in her town. She doesn't want anyone cheapening her Nymphness.

"Your world has a long history with paranormals," Rune explains. "Centuries ago, when witches sought refuge in this region--"

"Quiet, Rune," Darius says with a roll of his eyes. "You sound like a tired professor."

"Someone had to pay attention during seminars, Prince Darius," Rune fires back.

"Hang on," I say, not wanting the seminar detail to slip through the cracks. "You two went to school together?"

"All three of us," Zev says, walking over with his glass and joining the conversation. "We have a backstory that predates your country, Bernie."

"That's right," Darius says, a menacing look in his eyes. "Our friendship started lifetimes ago. Or at least *one* lifetime."

"We don't need to have this conversation now," Rune says, his anger starting to boil over.

"Then when?" Darius asks. "Generations have passed. When will you feel comfortable talking about Cara's death? Or are you happy to silently blame me until the kingdoms collapse?"

A hush takes over the room, each man staring daggers at the others. It would appear that the Sexies not only have history, but some heavy history.

"Later," Zev says. "You deserve the conversation, Darius, but not right now."

And with that, the werewolf turns to AJ and shocks us all by throwing the water from his glass at her face.

"What the... you son of a bitch!" As mad as AJ looks, she's too startled to act on her anger, staying put while staring daggers at Zev.

Darius moves over to look at AJ. Rune also looks from her face to the floor around her, giving the scene of the crime a thorough inspection.

"Interesting," Darius says.

"Quite," Rune agrees.

"Water nymph," Zev announces.

"More like beat-your-ass-with-a-tire-iron nymph, you piece of--"

"A." I cut her off in part so she won't start a fight with three superpowered beings, but also because of the sight before me.

She might be livid, but AJ is completely dry. In front of her, there's a perfect ring of water. Like she had a forcefield that repelled it and, save a few drops on her clothes, kept her from getting wet.

I point to the floor and she follows my finger, noticing the water and then putting her hands to her face.

"Why... why'd you miss?" she asks Zev, who smiles in response.

"Because you're a water nymph," he responds in an oddly reassuring tone. "You control the water around your body, just like you can control men."

At that, both AJ and I burst into laughter. Attract, seduce, allure, maybe. But control? If AJ could actually *control* men, her life would have been way different.

"I'll give you the water gag," she says, looking from Zev to me and then back to her assailant. "But I've got no power over men. If anything, it's the other way around."

"Do you live near the water?" Darius asks, a hint of annoyance in his voice at having to teach someone about why they could dodge his mind tricks.

"Yeah, dumbass, the ocean's like five miles from here."

"Can you see it from your home?" If Darius sounded annoyed earlier, he's now fully vexed.

AJ thinks, though she knows the answer. "No, not... no. But why does that matter? Also, plenty of people have thrown beer in my face and it hasn't, like, bounced off me."

"You don't have power over fluids, and just a minimal control over the water near your body," Zev clarifies. "I also imagine you relinquished your power over men."

"What? When? Why?" Her string of questions showcases how little either of us understand what's being said.

"If you don't believe in your own strength," Darius cuts in, "you turn what should be a power into a weakness."

It's a very backhanded compliment, and I think AJ takes it as such. She might've let guys walk all over her up to this point in her life, but if she actually starts to believe in herself, she could put a stop to it now.

"But," Darius continues, "a nymph in the house only complicates things further." He steps toward her, mouth open, teeth sharpening with each step. "I'd like to know what everyone proposes we do."

"How about this," I say, putting my foot down before this conversation gets further out of hand. "This is my house and you three are the entire complication. So why don't you go down to the bar, clean a little, talk things over, sit on the stools and try to look normal. With the power out and nothing to do at home, people will start showing up soon, and I'd love it if you refrained from killing anyone else today."

I look at AJ, still weirded out by her not being human, but nevertheless taking a lot of comfort in her presence. I need a shot of Jameson and a cry on a shoulder, and I know she'll help with both.

"AJ and I are going to have a quick talk and then we'll join you," I finish, trying not to leave room for any follow-up questions.

The Sexies seem content, or are at least eager to discuss the new situation. They move out of the apartment, with Darius being the last to go, his eyes lingering on AJ.

As soon as he closes the door, she turns to me with a twinkle in her eye I don't think I've ever seen before. "Can you believe this shit? I'm not human!"

I don't know why this makes her so ecstatic, but I guess it's better than her being devastated.

"Are you sure, though?" I'm not ready to buy into all this, especially because we don't know what any of it means. Can she breathe underwater? Talk to fish? Or just stay dry without an umbrella?

"I mean, not really," AJ says, and I take solace in her at least being a little apprehensive. "But that water trick was something, and I'm riding a wave of dead-husband endorphins."

Right. That's still a thing. At some point, when we know what's going on and, well, what she is, we'll need to address the issue of the murdered and now officially missing John.

"What I do know," AJ continues, "is that a sexy vampire tried to get in my head, and then a wicked hot werewolf sniffed my neck and told me I'm not human. Who am I to argue with those facts?"

I stroll into my bedroom while considering her words. It's time for Rain to have a proper sleep in her crib before I have to feed her again. My breasts are already starting to feel heavy again. AJ follows me in, her face going soft at the sight of my daughter.

"So," I say as I lay Rain down. "What now? What do we do?"

There's a quiver in my voice as I speak, and I know a monsoon of tears are on the way. I'm overwhelmed by everything and need to cry out some stress before I can use my brain or body again.

AJ recognizes all of this, of course, and brings me in for a hug just as the weeping begins. I bury my head into her shoulder to stifle my sobs and she leads me out of the bedroom away from Rain.

"First off, let's get downstairs and drink some whiskey." As expected, AJ's comfort game is unassailable.

"Second, let's remember who has the dead husband and yet is for some reason doing all the consoling."

It's a fair point, and one that forces me to break from crying long enough to let out a laugh.

"You're right," I say as I dry my eyes with my sleeves. "I've got a beautiful baby and run a halfway house for hotties from other realms. And that includes you, apparently."

"It's a pretty good setup," she says. "Even so, I'll kick your ass if you stay in Rowley longer than is absolutely necessary."

"AJ, I have to run--"

"Nope," she cuts me off before I can launch into my speech about being responsible for the family business. "No buts. You have a gift, it got you out of this place, and as soon as we deal with...whatever it is we're dealing with, you gotta go, girl."

We share a brief moment, speaking no words, just smiling gratefully at each other. Thank God for true friends.

"Okay," I say, feeling a bit of a second wind coming on. "I've got to figure out how to run this bar and... well, I've got to figure out everything."

"*You*," AJ starts, looking at me like I'm nuts, "don't have to do anything. I was going to step in for you after the baby came, and that doesn't change just because she's here early."

I knew AJ would help when Rain arrived, but I was always hesitant to put this on her plate. She's got--well, had--enough to deal with in her personal life, and I can't really afford to pay her beyond what the customers tip. Morgan's is a small bar in a small town, meaning we'll always have enough customers to stay open and never quite make enough money to pay all our bills. The fact that my family has kept this place going for multiple generations is nothing short of a miracle.

"I mean, I'm not going to turn down your help, but I completely understand if you need to go off and think or cry or just fire a gun into the sky for a while."

"Nope, I'm good," AJ says with a shrug. "I don't want to leave you, don't mind being around them, and I'll happily stuff some tips in my bra." She flashes a sexy smile. "I'm going to control the shit out of these human men."

She undoes a button on her shirt to show a little more cleavage. What a strange new version of the same old AJ.

"Great," I say as I turn back to my room. "I'm going to watch my baby sleep for a while, then we'll come meet you downstairs, Nympho."

AJ bounds off to the bar, not at all bothered by the new moniker. I step into my room and catch a glimpse of myself in the mirror over my dresser; looks like the bath did me good. Face is still a little puffy and I'm not even going to think about my midsection, but I'm not the monster I felt like earlier this morning.

A cold breeze ripples over my skin, alerting me to an open window on the other side of my bed. What kind of horrible mother leaves a window open in the dead of winter next to a newborn? Even if she's only alone for like five minutes, she could still...

I stop dead in my tracks, standing between the window and the crib.

The empty crib.

My baby's gone.

CHAPTER EIGHT

I look out the window, my heart pounding so hard in my chest I fear my ribs will break. Panic crowds my mind, filling it, not so much with words, but horrifying images of all the things that could be happening to my baby.

Outside I see only sheets of snow blurring the town I know so well, covering it all in a blanket of white that earlier looked ethereal and beautiful, but now has a sinister undertone.

Rain is hungry. Cold. She needs me.

And someone has taken her.

Fear jolts me into action, turning to rage in a blink, and I raise my voice as I race downstairs as fast as my still-healing body can go.

"Which one of you assholes took my goddamned child?" I scream, storming into the bar so hard the door hinge comes undone. The building seems to shake, startling me for a moment. The storm outside must be worse than I thought, which only makes me more angry and scared for Rain.

The three Sexies and AJ all turn to look at me, and none of them are holding my baby.

Darius is the first to blink over to me, and I don't even reprimand him for using his superspeed this time. "What has happened?" he asks, his eyes burning into my soul with their dark intensity.

"She's gone," I say, tears springing up as a wave of emotion threatens to drown me. "Rain is gone."

And then, Darius is gone. Presumably upstairs to investigate. I don't even know. My stupid human eyes can't track his movements.

I cover my face, sobs shaking me, and feel strong arms wrap around me. "We will find her. Trust us on this," Rune says, and his words hold power that seem to calm me despite myself.

With a howl, Zev, already back in wolf form, leaps across the bar and crashes out a window. Dude is really going to have to learn to use doors, but that's a lesson for less urgent times.

"Aren't you going to help search?" AJ asks Rune, who is still holding me close, like I might fall apart if he wasn't there to keep me together, and maybe that's not far from the truth.

"I must stay to protect Bernie. We do not know what we're dealing with yet, though I have my suspicions."

"If you're staying with B, then I'll go."

I push against Rune's chest just enough to create a bit of space between us. I need to clear my head, and whether it's his magic or natural magnetism, I can't do that when he's holding me. "I'm going too," I say.

"Not a chance, B," AJ says with a frown. "It's freezing out there. You just gave birth. You'll be no use to Rain if you get sick or dead."

AJ glances at Rune, who nods. But though her words make sense on some level, it feels wrong for me to stay behind doing nothing while my child is in danger.

As if reading my mind, AJ reaches for my hand. "I know this goes against everything inside you. You're a badass, no question, but you. Just. Had. A. Baby. Most women are still in the hospital recovering and getting fed sad, alcohol-free jello shots. You shouldn't be dealing with any of this. Let me help."

"Werewolves and vampires are the best trackers you can find," Rune says. "And however else I might feel about Darius and Zev, they are powerful, even amongst their kind. They will find your child."

"And I've never been sick a day in my life," AJ says, and with a start I realize that's true. I never thought about it before, how odd that was. "Turns out, the cold never bothered me anyway." She shrugs with an impish smile. "Snow is just water in a different form, and apparently that's my jam. So, I'm gonna go out there and see what I can do."

She kisses my cheek. "I'll be back soon."

Then she glances at Rune. "Get her a shot, make her rest. And protect her with your life or I will carve out your liver and feed it to that wolf out there."

"Duly noted," Rune says with a glint in his silver-blue eyes.

I watch helplessly as my best friend heads outside, into the blizzard, and hiccup softly as a new wave of emotion overwhelms me.

My breasts feel about ready to burst, and when I look down I notice I'm leaking. Fantastic. As if I needed one more problem right now.

Rune takes my hand and guides me to the bar, indicating I should sit.

My legs are wobbly, my head is spinning, and now that the adrenaline is wearing off, the ache in my body from my recent birthing experience is returning, so I take the seat normally reserved for Joe and marvel at how odd it feels to be on this side of things.

Rune moves around like he belongs back there, pulling out two glasses and the finest whiskey we have. He pours a generous amount into each tumbler, then takes something from a hidden pocket and sprinkles it into mine. It makes the liquor sparkle, like liquid gold.

I take the glass, staring at the mesmerizing drink. "What did you do to it?

And honestly, I shouldn't be drinking this while nursing. A tiny bit once a week is fine, according to Doctor Internet, but more than that could be harmful for... for Rain."

Saying her name brings up a surge of terror once again, and Rune comes around the bar to sit next to me. He takes my free hand, and at the touch of his skin that calmness I felt before flows over me. "That powder will change how your body perceives the alcohol. It will excrete it more slowly, breaking it down and keeping it from passing through your milk. I've also added something that will help you recover more quickly from the birth. It's quite safe, I assure you."

My eyes widen. "We could make a lot of money selling your magical drinks here," I say, sipping at the concoction. It dances on my tongue and burns going down in the kind of smooth, rich way only the best whiskey can offer.

Instantly I feel my body melt a bit. Every nerve is still on fire, worried for my child. Wondering what's happening. What the three of them are out there doing.

But the drink and Rune's presence take the edge off--which part of me resents. I have a right, a responsibility, even, to be hysterical and in full-on rage mode right now. At the same time, AJ is right. I'm no use to Rain if I'm sick, and I don't want to--I don't know--feed her angry milk. Is that a thing? I don't even know anymore, but I don't want to risk it.

So I continue sipping the magic whiskey as my gaze locks with Rune's pale blue eyes. "You don't look like a fae," I say at last. "At least not how I imagined."

His lips twitch in a smile. "I appear how I must in this realm to not stand out too much. Would you like to see my true form?"

I suck in a breath and nod.

With a flick of his wrist, his appearance shifts. It's subtle, but I take in each detail. The irises of his eyes are larger, more luminescent. His face is more defined, his skin so perfect it doesn't look real. His hair glows silver, like moonlight. But the most striking difference is his ears. They are longer, with pointed tips.

"You're beautiful," I say with a shaky breath, temporarily overwhelmed by the vision of him.

He lifts a hand to caress my cheek, his gaze consuming me. "Would that you could see yourself through my eyes, to truly know real beauty."

His words send a shiver down my spine, but the temporary distraction is short-lived as my mind crashes back to why we're sitting here.

When a new tear slides down my cheek, Rune uses the pad of his finger to wipe it away. "They will be back soon. With Rain."

"How can you be so sure?"

"I just am," he says, as if that explains everything. "The cost of failure is too high."

"Tell me what's really going on here," I demand. Since these guys walked into my bar, it's been madness. The irony that this is the first pause we've had to actually talk is not lost on me.

"Your child is at the crux of a prophecy that will have a profound impact on all of us. Human, vampire, werewolf, fae, and all others. It is said she is the Last

Witch that will be born, the last one of your kind who can save us all from extinction."

"My kind?" I ask, sure the magical alcohol is now playing with my hearing.

"Yes," Rune says softly. "You're more special than you know, Bernie. In time, this will all make sense, and you'll understand the true importance of your beautiful girl."

"Is that why she's been kidnapped? Because of this stupid prophecy?" I ask, my hand clutching the tumbler so hard it might crack as my anger returns more powerful than before.

Once again, the bar shakes, like a mini-earthquake, though we don't get earthquakes here. My baby is out in a storm so powerful it's shaking buildings. I'm beyond angry. I'm ready to tear into whoever did this the same way Darius and Zev tore into John.

"We are not the only ones who seek her," Rune says.

"Fantastic," I say, downing the last of my whiskey. "As if having three supernatural alphas showing up demanding my child wasn't bad enough."

Rune frowns. "I'm truly sorry our presence has been so disruptive to you. I will admit, I never quite thought about your role in the prophecy. For thousands of years, this edict has been passed down in my family, that we would be ready to retrieve the one who could save us. It has made us all a bit...myopic in our approach."

Ugh. I can't be like, sure it's totally fine you want to steal my kid, but also, I don't know what I would have done if they hadn't been around to help deliver so, shit. "Right now I just want her back in my arms. The rest can wait. But know this, none of you are taking her away from me. She's mine." I pause, fighting a sudden urge to overshare, then give in when I realize it would be nice to have someone to talk to about the things weighing on my heart. I hold up my glass, and Rune reaches for the whiskey, pouring me another and sprinkling in his magic glitter once again.

"I didn't want her at first," I confess finally, after taking another drink. "She wasn't planned... obviously. And I gave serious consideration to..." I pause, drinking again. It's so hard to think about. To talk about. To have her or not have her was the most difficult choice I've ever made. "I was in a master's program at Julliard--"

When Rune looks at me confused, I explain. "It's a music school in New York. Very prestigious, hard to get into it."

His eyes soften. "I'm not surprised you attained that level of acclaim. Your music is truly magical."

His words send a thrill through me, which I attempt to ignore. "I had opportunities coming out my ass," I say. "But I guess the prospect of success made me stupid. I had an affair with one of my teachers... and ended up pregnant. He wanted me to have an abortion, and I was ready to. Having a baby would derail my career, my life. Everything I'd worked so hard for. But on the day of the appointment, I couldn't go through with it. I stayed at school as long as I could while pregnant, but then my grandfather died and I knew it was all coming to an end. My life, my dreams. Everything."

I swallow my tears along with more whiskey. "And then she was born and I looked into her perfect elfin face and I knew I'd made the right choice. I would give up everything for her. Everything."

I glare at Rune fiercely. "She is mine to protect. She is mine to raise. And that is non-negotiable. But I don't expect you to understand."

I turn away, overcome by my own emotions, hating myself for talking tough about my parenting moments after my baby was stolen from her room.

Rune reaches for my hand. "Bernie, I would like to show you something, with your permission."

"Show me what?" I ask, returning my gaze to his.

"Close your eyes," he says, as he places his hands on both sides of my face and leans in until our foreheads are touching. The gesture feels deeply intimate, and I inhale his scent of wildflowers and cinnamon. "I understand more than you know."

His fingers heat up against my skin and my inner mind glows silver, then everything changes.

I am standing in a forest at night, a gentle breeze tickling the hair on my neck and swaying the branches around me. Dozens of small glowing bugs buzz in the air, casting silver light against the iridescent flowers spread over a vast valley that starts at the edge of the trees.

The sound of insect life scurrying under layers of leaves and mulch fills my ears, and when I inhale, I smell a faint sweetness from the flowers and the musky scent of the rich green foliage surrounding me.

Everything feels so damn real, it's like being in the most advanced, futuristic virtual reality game.

"Come this way," Rune says, startling me with his presence. He reaches for my hand and a spark of energy dances on my skin when our palms touch.

He looks down at me, a look of surprise and something else... on his face before he schools his expression to neutral.

Our fingers link and I let him lead me through the trees towards the sound of running water. Of waterfalls and rushing rivers.

A man stands at the edge of the water, placing flowers into a narrow boat.

I gasp, tightening my grip on Rune's hand when I realize the man we are watching... is him.

He leans to whisper into my ear. "This is the night my wife and child died. I am saying goodbye." His voice is choked with emotion. "She was the last of our kind to get pregnant and give birth. We hoped it was a sign that the plague on our people was ending. That the prophecy we feared wasn't coming to pass. That perhaps our combined royal lineage could break this curse. But alas, the child came early, and was stillborn. The birth took her life in the process, and there was nothing I could do with any of my magic to save either of them."

We watch silently, our grip on each other's hands tightening, as the Rune of the past pushes the boat into the water. Once it's moving down the river, he raises an arrow and lights it with a blue fire, then draws his bow and releases. His aim is true, and the boat alights in glowing flames that fill the night sky. He falls to his knees as his wife and child sink, his cries of anguish raw and visceral.

The Rune by my side looks down at me again, his silver eyes glistening with emotion. "I know your fear. Your pain. Your worry. It is mine as well. It is what brought us all here."

He holds up a hand before I can say anything. "I'm not trying to justify taking your child from you. I just wanted you to understand why."

There's an argument to be had, but I see the point Rune's making. It's just... not a conversation I know how to have right now, after what I just bore witness to. So, I change the subject.

"I know so little about you three. Can you take me back further? To your time with Darius and Zev?"

A fleeting smile passes over the fae's face, quickly replaced by a look of longing.

"I'm sorry," he says, his eyes glistening with unshed tears as he stares into a past I cannot enter. "I'm afraid my heart cannot bear revisiting the memory of another loved one lost to me."

There are times to question and times to be silent, and I know this is the latter. As much as I want to know more, and even as much as I feel I have the right to know more, sometimes we must choose to be kind over being right. I give him what little solace a squeeze of my hand can provide.

I'm pulled out of the trance by the sound of the bar door slamming open, my heart heavy and my mind thick.

Rune is now sitting next to me, just as he was. But his eyes are still full of the pain I just witnessed. As powerful as our moment was, my mind switches gears immediately when I see AJ race in, a small bundle in her arms.

Darius follows, dragging a man with a hood over his head and his hands tied behind his back, a large white wolf nipping at his heels.

"Rain's okay," says AJ, handing my child to me. I grip Rain so tight, probably squeezing air out of her tiny lungs, but I can't help myself. Now that she's back, I finally let myself consider the thought I pushed back against so hard--I might have never seen her again.

"I'm so sorry, baby," I say to her. "Mama won't ever let you go again."

"And this," AJ says, reminding me there's more to this story, "is the bastard who took her."

I glare as she pulls off his hood... and then I gasp.

"Karl?"

The deadbeat who's always passed out in my bar? The man who's known my family for years? That's the person who kidnapped my baby?

What the hell alternate reality have I stumbled into?

CHAPTER NINE

I stare into Karl's familiar face, snow sticking to his ever-present stubble. His large hazel eyes are full of fear and confusion. The fear I understand because he should know he's about to die; the confusion doesn't make sense, because there should be no question as to why he's about to die.

"Karl..." I let the word hang, carrying all the weight of a full sentence.

"Bernie..." Karl responds in kind, and I listen closely to his tone, hoping it will explain his inexplicable behavior.

It doesn't.

Darius, lacking the patience to read the man's facial expression, slams him against the bar, holding his face down on the copper surface.

"Who are you?" Darius snarls, his sharp teeth centimeters from Karl's pulsing jugular vein. "Who sent you for the child?"

Karl keeps his eyes trained on me, ignoring the vampire's questions.

"Bernie, you know me."

"I thought I did," I snap back. It seems like he's got some point to make, something to say in his defense, but he's not getting there fast enough.

"These guys, they aren't what they seem." If Karl thought that generic under-statement was going to win any points, he's sorely mistaken.

"Neither are you!" My yell startles Rain and makes her cry, but AJ is at my side immediately with a blanket. In a surprisingly swift motion, I wrap the baby, pop out a boob, begin to feed and then return my fiery stare to Karl. I strut toward the bar, feeling incredibly emboldened with these three powerful men backing me up.

"Have you been plotting this? Pretending to be passed out in my bar so you'd know when the baby came?"

Of course, the answer will be no. Karl's too much of a deadbeat drunk to formulate a plan and then carry it--

"Yes."

The word doesn't come from Karl's mouth, but rather from Rune's. The two look at each other, reading one another's faces and movements, before Karl looks back at me. His silence confirms the fae's assessment.

"You don't understand, Bernie."

Another cliche one-liner, but he's not wrong. In a day where every single thing has been strange and stupefying, this is somehow the most unexpected event so far. A regular at the family bar for years, a guy who could never manage to drive himself home at the end of the night, a person everyone in town knows, stole my baby. From my window, on the second floor, in the dark, in a blizzard.

"I'm trying to help you," Karl says earnestly. "We're trying to save your baby."

"Who," Darius asks, stepping menacingly close to Karl's face, "is we?"

Zev circles around the captive man, sniffing. Rune grabs Karl by the wrist, inspecting his hand. I'm not sure what answers they're looking for, but they're looking intently.

Suddenly, Zev growls. At first I think something about Karl has angered him, but then I see his wolf eyes have moved to the front door. I follow his look and seconds later, the doorknob starts to turn. Jesus, who's here to steal my baby now?

The door opens about an inch, then slams shut and locks itself. As my frazzled brain tries to remember if the bar door has always made its own decisions, I see the vampire's hand extended in that direction and realize he did the closing and locking. It'll take a while for me to get used to all the magic.

AJ moves quietly to a window at the front of the bar and peeks out. "It's Joe and Frank," she says, then adds with a smile, "they brought flashlights so you can't make them leave when the candles burn out."

"Don't let them in," Darius says. "There are too many bodies in here as it is."

He makes a good point, but sending these guys home almost guarantees they'll come back fifteen minutes later with Frank's wife to check up on me. And if she shows up and starts talking, I doubt the most powerful magic in the universe could get her to stop.

"They won't go without a fight," I explain.

"Bernie?!" A voice comes from outside, right on cue. "You okay in there? It's Joe and Frank, we brought some baby toys, pacifiers and shit."

Sweet, stupid, drunk old men.

When I look back to Darius, he's gone. As is Karl. And yet I still hear his voice as if he's inches away.

"Where can I take this intruder?" the invisible Darius asks.

"Wait," I interrupt, too confused to let this go. "Where are you?"

"He's right where you last saw him."

Rune places his hand gently on my shoulder as he speaks, washing that wave of calm over me. God, I need him touching me always.

"I've created an illusion along the back of the bar. Darius, gag him now while we let these people in." Rune looks at me with a sweetness in his eyes, and I'm truly starting to feel he's on my side. "We'll run business as usual, if that's what you think is best. Though, may I suggest closing early so you can get some rest?"

"I'll be back in a moment," the invisible Darius says. "I'm going to stitch this cretin to the ceiling upstairs."

I don't really know what that means, but I'm also sure he isn't lying.

"Bern?!" Joe calls again from outside. It would never cross his mind that the bar might be closed, especially because my grandparents had the place open every day except Christmas.

Rune takes a seat at the bar, assuming the role of a customer, I guess. AJ comes over and takes the now-sleeping Rain, who fell asleep while feeding because she's just so goddamn cute. I walk over to the door, a little jealous I can't just unlock it from thirty feet away like Darius.

I open up and present Joe and Frank with a big, fake smile, even as a gust of cold nearly knocks me on my ass.

"Hey, guys! Sorry, the wind blew the door open earlier so I locked it. Come on in!"

I turn away to lead them inside, but don't hear footsteps behind me. When I look back, they're still frozen in place, staring at the far end of the bar. I follow their eye line and quickly realize the hesitation.

"Oh yeah, that. Ummm... I got a dog."

I wish I'd had a conversation with Zev about how to explain his presence, but it's too late for that. Now I'm a dog owner. When people come to my bar, I have a husky the size of a small horse. What a great way to drum up business.

"Where... where'd you get it?" asks Frank, looking legitimately afraid to step foot in the bar. "Cuz that ain't no dog. That's a wolf."

"Maybe it has some mix in it, but he's totally tame," I say, as Zev looks up at me and growls under his breath. I want to kick him as a reminder to watch his manners, but that would definitely look bad. "As to where I got him, it's a long story, Frank. Now, get your ass inside so I can close the door, and I'll tell you once you've had a beer and loosened up."

They do as they're told, giving me a few seconds to start thinking of a husky-the-size-of-a-huge-wolf buying story that can't be verified. Fortunately, by the time they reach the bar, they see AJ and what she's holding. Joe spins back toward me.

"Whoa! Bern! Holy shit! Your baby!"

Holy shit indeed. It's like every time someone notices Rain, I remember that I'm a brand new mother who should be asleep constantly.

"Yeah, that's baby Rain," I say, walking back behind the bar to get her from AJ. "She arrived last night with the help of this guy. Rune."

Rune has been sitting at the bar, doing his best to be ignored, but I figure it's less suspicious to open up the introductions now than it is to wait for the guys to ask questions.

Joe and Frank size him up. Normally they'd make fun of a clean man with a handsome face, but Rune's obvious size and strength keep the jokes at bay. Plus, they take kindly to anyone who helped me out.

"Oh yeah, you were here last night," Joe says. "Are you a, uh, you know, you a..."

My tired brain is about to answer, "a fae," but fortunately AJ steps in to save me from myself.

"He's a doctor. He and another doctor friend are passing through town, thinking of opening up a practice somewhere in Mass. Couldn't have timed their visit to Morgan's any better."

Solid work, AJ. She's clearly better than me at lying on the spot, which makes it even more important to have her around.

"Where's the other doctor friend?" Frank asks. "And wait, weren't there three guys here last night?"

I look down at Zev the wolf, wondering how to answer this question. He returns my gaze, and I get a very strange feeling sharing a look with a wolf who I know is not just a wolf.

"No, just the two guys that I remember," I answer, unwittingly locking Zev into wolf form whenever the bar is open.

"The other guy, Darius, he is…" I launch into this sentence before I have any idea of where it's headed, but the bar door swings open and finishes my story for me.

"He is here!"

Darius enters casually, giving me a slight nod and taking a seat by Rune. I watch the two lock eyes briefly and I'm positive they just linked brains, filling each other in on everything missed. When they finish their mind gossip, Darius turns to Joe and Frank, offering a forced smile.

"Do you gentlemen know Karl? I was speaking with him last night. He said he… had some lodging recommendations."

Joe and Frank start laughing immediately as I put my hand over my eyes. I've never seen someone so bad at lying to small town folk.

"Talking to Karl?" Joe says with a chuckle. "He must have been sleep talking, drunken fool."

"Of course we know Karl," Frank adds. "Grew up with his dad, our grandpas went to war together. Known his family for generations."

Joe nods, not going into his family history, even though I'm sure it's similar.

Rune and Darius share a knowing look and probably a little mental dialogue that I wish I could hear, despite my earlier insistence that they stay out of my head.

With Rain asleep in my arms and my own eyelids feeling like they're made of lead, I decide this is as good a chance as any to duck away for sleep. AJ's quick enough on her feet to answer questions, Rune can create an illusion if necessary, and as long as Darius doesn't lose his cool and rip someone's throat out, we should be fine.

I bid my goodnights and grab a candle as I head for the backdoor. Before I can leave, I sense the familiar feeling of another's words penetrating my mind.

I'm sorry to enter your thoughts and break my promise, Bernie, Darius says, *but I want you to know the intruder is bound to the kitchen ceiling with unbreakable ropes. You'll be safe upstairs, but perhaps avoid that room. Zev will join you.*

It's a fair warning, as I for sure would have shit myself if I walked into the kitchen and saw Karl magically roped to the ceiling.

I look back at Darius, who now has his eyes trained on the wolf. After a few seconds, Zev rises and clambers up the stairs. I turn back to Darius.

Thanks, I think, guessing at how telepathic communication works.

You're welcome, I hear in response.

I pat Joe on the shoulder, kiss AJ on the cheek, and head upstairs, baffled and amused at the state of my life.

MY DREAMS ARE full of Rune. We're standing in the snow, but everything feels warm. His hands touch every inch of my skin, starting at my shoulders, stroking down my arms, then moving to my torso, rubbing my back at first, then turning me away from him so he can caress my stomach and breasts. I feel him pressed against me, and it's clear we both enjoy the feel of each other's skin.

"You're beautiful," he whispers in my ear, over and over. I'm in the state of sleep where I know this is a dream, and yet it's as vivid as any I've ever had. His breath tickles my ear, sending shivers down my spine and raising goosebumps on my sensitive flesh.

When I turn back to face him, he's naked, his body chiseled and smooth. As I reach down for him, he puts a hand on my shoulder, stopping me.

"Bernie," he says.

"Yes?" I reply, moving my face to his, eager to taste his lips.

"Bernie," he repeats, this time a little more forcefully.

"Bernie," he says a third time, and now the snow drifts away, the white glow morphing into a dim flicker, and I'm suddenly in my bedroom.

I bolt up, an immediate sense of panic overtaking me. Where's Rain? Who's dead? What now?

Rune sits in front of me, his presence providing an immediate calm.

"Shhh, you're all right. Rain's all right." It's as though he can read my thoughts, which, duh, he probably can. Yikes. How much of that dream was he privy to?

"What time is it?" I ask. "How long did I sleep? Where's everyone else?"

"It's morning," Rune says. "You finally got some quality rest. Unfortunately-
-"

The rest of his sentence is cut off when we hear AJ bounding up the stairs, two at a time like she's done since junior high.

When she enters the room, I see worry etched on her face.

"I don't see him out front. No sign of a car, either. He must have gone out the back."

"What? Who?" I'm still groggy and there are too many "he's" that she could be referring to.

A lot of my grogginess dissolves when Darius does his appearing act right next to AJ, nearly causing her to fall in surprise.

"Zev is trying to catch his scent in the woods," he says to Rune. "We saw no prints in the snow."

I'm still completely lost, but I think I've got a good guess.

"Karl?"

Darius says nothing, though the angry clench of his jaw speaks volumes. AJ just wrings her hands, confused and alarmed. Rune looks back to me, giving a slight nod.

"He disappeared."

"What do you mean, *disappeared*? He just escaped? I thought Darius had--"

"I had," the vampire cuts me off forcefully, a little defensive. "And he disappeared. The ropes are all in place, unmoved, unbroken. A human can't escape those bonds."

In an instant, Zev the wolf appears at the top of the stairs, and in just as little time Zev in human form stands beside Darius. It happens far too quickly, and by the time I notice he's completely naked, he's already started slipping into a pair of pants. But not before I see everything.

"No scent, no tracks, no sounds," the half-naked werewolf says, his voice pulling my eyes up from his waistline to his mouth.

"Darius, what do you mean?" AJ asks. "He did escape those bonds, so what are you saying?"

"I can't be sure," Darius starts, choosing his words carefully. "But it appears that Karl spends his time in the company of witches."

CHAPTER TEN

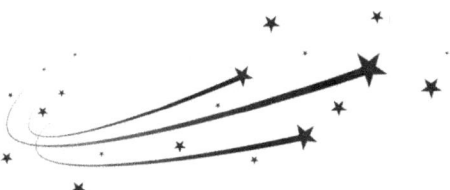

"Awesome, let's bring some witches into the mix," I say sarcastically. My nerves are frayed and I'm definitely using snark to hide that. AJ sees right through me though, and reaches for my hand, offering what comfort she can.

"I anticipated push back from those who wish to thwart us," Darius says, "but I'm surprised the witches are getting involved."

"I'm not," Rune says calmly. "This directly affects all magical races, particularly the witches. If your kind hadn't hunted them out of our world, we might not be in this mess in the first place."

Darius bares his teeth, and fangs protrude, his eyes darkening even further. "Push me too far, fae, and I'll develop a taste for *your* blood."

Zev studies them both and shakes his head. "My kind has the reputation for being hotheads, but I think you're both stealing that title."

"Please," Darius says. "We've seen you at your angriest, Zev, and it's not something either of us can compete with."

The werewolf walks over and gets in the vampire's face, forcing me to take a few steps back just in case a fight breaks out.

"And if your cold, dead heart could make room for emotions, you would have been angry as well."

They're back at it again with whatever beef developed during their years at, I don't know, magic school. It's like siblings who can't let something go, and as an only child, I'm annoyed enough to put an end to it.

"Jesus Christ, what are you talking about? Get it out in the open so we don't have to pause every hour for this redundant shit fit."

Neither Darius nor Zev looks at me, still locked on each other and fuming. Rune steps forward to speak, putting a hand on Zev as he does so and hopefully delivering some calm to the furious wolf.

"We learned of this prophecy at the same time, centuries back," the fae says.

"As it affected each kingdom, the three of us were part of an ancient council that aimed to work with some sense of a common goal."

"Four of us," Darius says, still not turning away from Zev.

"Yes, there was a fourth," Rune continues. "A witch named Cara. A dear friend to us all."

"Not dear enough," Zev says, leaving no question as to who he's addressing.

I look at Darius, a new level of rage on his face. It seems like he needs a chance to speak about this through a mediator, so I ask him the next question.

"Darius," I say in as gentle a voice as I can muster, "what happened?"

The vampire finally takes his attention off Zev and looks at me. The room immediately feels a shade less hostile.

"We all worked together to translate and understand the prophecy," Darius says, gazing at the wall like his memories are projected there. "Cara wanted to work on a spell that might illuminate the meaning of the language. We initially told her not to, that there was too much magic in play, but she insisted. And I was the first to take her side."

Zev opens his mouth to speak, but Rune tightens his grip on the wolf's shoulder and silences him.

"So… your friend died?" Their silence seems like a pretty solid affirmation. "And you were all there when she did whatever she did, and Darius maybe didn't push back as hard as you two would have liked. And instead of talking it out, you've been mad for, what, a millennium?"

More confirming silence.

"Okay," I say, coming to the end of my usefulness as a paranormal counselor when they continue staring in silence. "I'm glad that got explained. It's… a lot."

The tension breaks a little when Rain begins crying, and I feel bad at how happy I am to hear my child fussing. "We'll get back to that, because right now we need to find Karl," I say, my mind spinning with a plan. "Or whoever he's working with, since I'm pretty sure he's not a witch."

"He's not," Zev says. "Witches are exclusively women. Always have been."

Huh. That's interesting and slightly unexpected. "Okay, so as I said, we need to find him and figure out who he's working with and why they also want my baby. How many magical species will we be fighting to keep her safe?" I clutch her more closely, fear and a fierce maternal protectiveness clouding my thinking.

"If he has magic, he might not be easy to track," Zev says gruffly. "As for how many others might be after her, that's hard to say. There are many races, but the witches, werewolves, fae, and vampires are the primary. All others are derived from us over the course of thousands of years."

"So nymphs are, like, some kind of blend? A magical mutt?" AJ asks, disappointment clear in her voice. She definitely wanted to be higher on the pyramid.

"In a manner of speaking," Zev says. "But this all happened ages ago. Right now, we need to formulate a better plan for protecting Rain and Bernie."

"Agreed," Rune says.

Darius nods but says nothing.

"And who will protect us from you three?" I ask, my words thrown like daggers at each of them. Rain finishes feeding and I cover myself and burp her as

I stare the three men down. "You came here to take her, just like Karl. How are you any different? The only reason you're still here is because you're all keeping each other in check."

The Sexies look at each other with some level of discomfort. "It is... complicated," Rune says.

I know it's complicated, especially after getting insight from Rune, but that doesn't warm me to the idea of someone stealing my child. "You all have your reasons for what you're trying to do. So does Karl. And I appreciate that you're staying and helping. But at the end of the day, why should I trust any of you? You all want the same thing. My baby. And you all see her as a savior to your people without regard for me, or her as a person."

Tears sting my eyes and the whole situation crashes into me like a tsunami I can't contain. I turn away so they don't see me cry. "I'd like to be alone, please. Can you all leave my room?"

Before anyone argues it's not safe, I turn back to glare at them. "I'll protect Rain, and you can all wait in the other room, but I need a freaking minute with my child and myself, is that too much to ask after all this?"

I raise my voice for emphasis, and Rune especially flinches like I just slapped him, but I can't muster enough energy to care. I feel beaten and bruised after nearly losing my child, knowing it could happen again. AJ leads the men out, Rune leaving last and closing the door behind him with a sharp click.

I lock it, knowing damn well it won't make any difference to men with magical powers and super strength, but it gives me some small semblance of control over an entirely uncontrollable situation. I shuffle over to my bed and crawl into it, pulling the blankets over both myself and my child until it is just the two of us in my mini make-shift fort. She's already fallen back to sleep, content and safe in my arms, and I stare at her for some time, wondering what it is that makes her so special. I know what makes her special to *me*. But why is everyone else in all the worlds after her, and how can I possibly keep her safe against such threats?

Eventually, those guys will figure out how to best each other. One of them will take her from me, and I will have no recourse. No way of fighting back. I would die for her, of course I would, and it just might come to that, but I fear my blood is not powerful enough or valuable enough to matter in this battle. This is far beyond the skills of a barmaid turned pianist turned barmaid again.

The tears come hard and fast, and I'm solidly wallowing in my own pain when I hear the whir of the electricity coming back to life. Through the thick comforter, a flicker of light confirms our power has returned.

It looks like we'll be back to business as usual, and I'll need to muster my own courage to get my business up and running before I lose that too.

I crawl out of bed and use a Baby Bjorn to strap Rain to my chest, then I freshen up in the bathroom before returning to the guys in the living room.

"We've got a lot of prep work to do now that the power's back on. Are you going to help?"

Everyone nods and follows me silently downstairs.

I spend the next several hours giving instructions and teaching everyone what to do. AJ insists she can handle everything, but I need something to keep my body and my mind occupied. The alternative is more wallowing, and I'm not a fan.

We clean, prep and have everything ready when our first customers arrive. Tonight it's all regulars. The power's back and the snow stopped, but tall snow banks and black ice keep people from venturing far from home, and we've never been good at pulling in tourists anyways.

That suits my mood just fine. I don't really want to deal with strangers right now.

Everyone who comes in oohs and ahhs over the baby, but I refuse any requests to hold her, and keep her strapped to my chest all night except when I sneak away to feed or change her.

AJ and my new sexy staff do their part. Rune and Darius wash glasses and buss tables while Zev just chills in his wolf body--and by just chills I mean he glues himself to my heels. I swear I nearly trip on him at least three times.

When we finally close up shop that night, I'm dead on my feet, though the guys look as refreshed as always. Damn them.

Rune approaches me with hesitancy as I straighten my back, cracking it in at least five painful places.

"Let me take her and put her to bed, Bernie. You need a break."

When I don't answer, and instead clutch Rain closer to my chest, Rune lays a hand on me, and a rush of warmth and calm flows over me.

I jerk away. "Stop. Don't manipulate my emotions right now. I get to be pissed and scared and... and pissed."

He nods. "You do. I apologize. I just hate to see you so unhappy. I come from a long line of healers. It is in my blood to want to soothe and help. Forgive me for overstepping."

Well now I feel like part ass, part justified mama bear and 100% exhausted. Rune has been nothing but kind to me and Rain. Tender even. And as I look up the staircase, I wonder if I can even make it with her on my chest. I worked too hard and didn't accept the help that was offered. It's classic Bernie and I usually push through, but my body isn't used to recovering from childbirth.

With a sigh and some nervousness, I unclasp the straps and hand the bundle--baby included--to Rune's outstretched arms. His silver-blue gaze drops to Rain, and his expression is so gentle, so loving, so full of awe and hurt for what he's lost, that the wall I built around my heart cracks just a little. "Go. Before I change my mind."

He nods and with fluid speed, hastens upstairs.

I pause a moment, trying to will my broken body forward, when I feel strong arms lift me up.

Zev flashes a cheeky smile. "You don't look capable of making it up those stairs, love. Let me help."

I'm about to argue, but he's probably right. Everything in my body hurts so much I feel tears coming, though I refuse to let them fall. I will not show weakness, but dear heaven I could use a bath.

Using that magically heightened intuition, Zev carries me to the bathroom and gently places me on the toilet as he runs the hot water. Rune appears with a vial of herbs and dumps it into the bath. "It will help with your pain," he says, softly.

I can see more words unspoken in the depths of his eyes, but he turns to leave before I can ask. Zev raises an eyebrow but leaves as well, allowing me to undress in private.

As I slink off my clothes and sink into the tub, I groan in pleasure. Worry for Rain still filters through the relaxation, but the scent of lavender and rose and the feel of my muscles unknotting does a lot to calm my mind.

My mind is drifting when a knock at my door pulls me back. "Uh, yeah?"

Zev walks in holding a small jar of oil as I try to strategically place bubbles to allow for some level of modesty. Though, the werewolf doesn't seem concerned about such things, and maybe it's just my prudish puritan culture getting in the way of things.

"Your back was bothering you. I thought I might offer my massage services to alleviate a bit of that discomfort," he says, his gaze taking in the parts of my body that are still exposed, and lingering on the parts that aren't.

His words send a promise directly to my body, which responds before my mind even gets a chance to talk me out of it. I pull my knees to my chest and lean forward, exposing as much of my back as I can.

Zev shrugs out of his shirt, revealing his perfectly sculpted abs of steel before taking a seat on the edge of the tub. I raise an eyebrow at that and he shrugs. "Wouldn't want to get it wet."

"Sure," I say, shaking my head. "I think you're just allergic to clothing."

He lays his large hands on my shoulders, the heat from his skin seeping into my perpetually chilled body, and I moan at the simple pleasure of it.

Zev leans in, his lips coming dangerously close to my ear, his chest pressing up against my naked back. "Not allergic," he whispers. "But clothes do get in the way of some of life's most delicious moments, don't you think?"

"They can be cumbersome at times," I agree, trying to keep my voice steady as he begins to massage the tension out of my muscles.

As he works his way down my spine, I'm lost to his touch. He knows every tender muscle and how to coax the pain out of my body. I try not to sound like I'm having an orgasm over this massage, but it's damn hard, and I can tell my attempt at silence isn't fooling the werewolf.

"I can smell your arousal," he says, once again bringing his mouth to my ear.

In a bold move that feels more like AJ than myself, I reach back with my hand and graze it over his pants. "And I can feel yours."

Even just the hint of my touch inspires a deep growl low in his chest. The timbre of it resonates through my body and ignites a fresh wave of desire that I do my best to fight.

So I ask a question that could definitely kill the mood, and most likely will.

"Do you have someone? Back home?"

I let my hair fall over my face as I turn from him. Whatever his answer, I don't want to wear my heart on my sleeve right now.

He clears his throat and pulls back, his hands lingering at my side, lightly grazing the sides of my breasts. "No, no mate at home."

"Never?" I ask.

His fingers dig into my flesh and he moves against me, his mouth hovering over my shoulder. "Wolves mate for life, love," he says, his voice cracking with emotion. "And you don't know how dangerous these questions are for you." His lips brush against my shoulder, then his teeth nip my flesh, followed by a soft kiss.

And then he stands and leaves, pulling the door closed behind him firmly.

My skin is on fire from his touch, from his bite and his kiss. I rub at the faint teeth marks left in my skin and lean back, closing my eyes as I try to process what just happened. I can't sort out of my emotions. All I know is my skin is buzzing and my heart is racing.

By the time I'm done with the bath and dried off, I feel like a whole new woman--and am mostly recovered from my time with Zev. Though I still feel a small bruising pain in my shoulder from his bite, and it brings to mind all manner of places I'd like to feel his mouth next. Shoving aside any sexy thoughts of the Sexies, I check on Rain, who's sleeping soundly in her crib. Ah, to be so sheltered from the reality of the world. I tuck a blanket around her and then head to the living room where the guys are all there.

"Where's AJ?" I ask.

"She said she had some errands to run and will be back in a 'hot second'," Darius says somewhat awkwardly.

"Okay... why do you all look so weird right now?" I ask, searching their faces. They're sitting around the kitchen table facing each other and seem to be in the middle of a very tense discussion.

"We have given thought to the situation," Rune says after a moment. "And we have all come to realize there is more going on than we initially...considered. Regarding the prophecy, your child, and... you."

Zev clears his throat, his gaze landing on my shoulder before moving to my face. "This is more complicated than my realm understood. I'm sure if my mother..."

"Your mother?" I ask, ignoring the way his forest green eyes make me weak in the knees. "Who's your mother and what's she got to do with any of this?"

Zev looks to the other two, who remain silent, so he continues, reluctantly. "My mother is the queen of our realm. All three of us are princes. It was--is--our duty to fulfill the prophecy in order to save our people. That's why we were schooled together, along with Cara, the princess sent by the witches."

Princes? Like actual freaking princes. Shit. No wonder they wanted to give my apartment a huge makeover. And here I've been putting them to work tending bar and cleaning floors. The thought makes me smirk just a smidgen.

"As I was saying," Zev continues, his eyes narrowing on my mouth, "we do not believe our families understood the whole picture. So we have decided to send messages back to our realms explaining plans have changed."

"Plans?" That snaps me out of any sexy thoughts. "The plans to kidnap my kid? So you're not going to try to take Rain?" I ask, hope rising in me despite my best attempt to quash it.

Darius grunts with a mixture of annoyance and impatience. "What *Prince* Zev is trying to say is that while the prophecy still holds, and the need is still dire, we want to try to find another way."

"So you're all leaving?" I ask, and my heart sinks at that thought despite being entirely pissed off at all of them five minutes ago. In a game of Kiss, Marry, Kill, all three Sexies would qualify for each column. These postpartum hormones are a bitch.

"No." Rune's voice is firm. More alpha than I've ever heard it. "You and Rain still need protection. We will not abandon you. But while we wait for word from our respective families, we have decided to take a pledge that will give you--and us--reassurance of each of our intentions."

Darius and Zev both shift uncomfortably as Rune speaks. Whatever he's talking about, it's meaningful. But... a pledge? Like... of allegiance? To the flag? That's the only pledge I can think of and it sounds pretty useless.

"So, what, this is like a glorified pinky swear? How is this supposed to reassure me?"

"This pledge will bind us to you--for the time being," he adds when Darius glares at him. "We will not be able to take your child without your consent."

"Pft. Then you might as well throw in the towel. I'll never consent."

Rune nods. "I know that is how you feel now. It is our hope you will reconsider, given the consequences."

Before I can interrupt to tell him where he can shove his pledge, and his hope, he holds up his hand. "Regardless, this pledge cannot be broken by any of us. It will run its course at the spring solstice, at which point we can all reassess. In the meantime, it will mean we no longer have to watch each other so closely. One of us can be with you while the others are tending to the bar or helping in whatever way you need."

Rune pauses, then locks his gaze with mine and says softly, "We will be here at your whim, to serve, care for, and assist you. And, most importantly, to ensure the safety of your child."

Oh my. Heat flushes my cheeks and my knees feel a bit wobbly suddenly. I want to fan my face but that seems a tad extra, so I hold myself in check. *Play it cool, Bernie. Play it cool.*

"Right. Okay. That sounds... fine. So when will you do this?" My emotions are tumbling around inside me. Relief, fear, gratitude, lust, all of it making me an emotional mess.

"We need the right ingredients," Rune says, still leading the conversation. "The proper herbs, a dusting of fresh snow..."

"Sure. That sounds... reasonable, I guess."

"And..." Rune hesitates, and Darius grunts again.

"Unicorn blood," Darius says, finally. "We need unicorn blood."

CHAPTER ELEVEN

"Cool story, bro."

It's the answer I would have given, but it actually comes from AJ, standing in the

doorway, having returned from whatever errand took her away in the dead of night.

"Unicorn blood?" She chuckles. "Yeah, sure, I'll just swing by my uncle's ranch and grab a vile."

Darius studies AJ seriously, as is his way. It's hard to tell if he's annoyed by her sarcasm or wondering--

"Who is your uncle? What's his family line?"

Yep. Wondering if her uncle really has a freaking unicorn.

AJ walks into the kitchen, laughing to herself, and pulls a beer from the fridge. Apparently grandpa didn't finish all his Budweiser before he passed. Jesus, have I not cleaned out the fridge since I moved home?

"My uncle doesn't have a unicorn, numbnuts," she responds, leaning against the counter and popping the bottle cap off with a lighter.

Darius bolts to his feet, fast enough to startle even his magical buddies.

"Watch yourself, nymph," he hisses, teeth bared. "Your powers are few and the stakes are higher than you can fathom. Cross me any further and you'll see--"

Rune grabs Darius by the elbow, and it looks like those fae calming powers have at least some effect on vampires. Darius takes a deep breath and then slowly moves back into his seat, like a predator biding his time.

AJ looks between the two for a second, then laughs. She smells a little boozy. I'm starting to think her errand was a stupid one.

"So, what's the plan?" I ask, trying to get the conversation back on track. "One of you goes to your world and comes back with some blood?"

"We can't return until the message has been received," Zev says, shaking his head. "For any of us to show up without the child and no prior notification would send the kingdom into a panic."

"Really?" I ask. "Even if you told people, er, your kind, that you were coming right back to protect the baby?"

Now all three of them shake their heads, solemn looks on their faces. I'll never be able to empathize with the severity of their situations, since I'm the mom of the baby they want to steal, but a small part of my brain recognizes the gravity of what they're dealing with.

"Okay, three things need to happen," I say as I turn toward the fridge, lost in thought and also immediately ravenous. I've been working too hard, sleeping too little, and acting as a full-time milk generator for a hungry newborn. I need to eat my bodyweight in carbs.

The minute I open the fridge door, AJ sprints past me, through the living room and out the door, yelling, "Don't eat!" on her way out. The guys watch her go suspiciously, then turn back to me.

"She moves, and thinks, erratically," Rune observes.

I nod. That's as good a way as any to describe AJ.

I hear her feet scampering back up the outdoor steps, and she enters seconds later with a giant smile on her face and a massive pizza box in her hands.

"House of Pizza... " I trail off, hoping I'll still be able to chew while crying tears of joy. AJ and I spent half our high school years inhaling pizzas from this place. She opens the box, displaying a steaming, extra-large pie covered in sausage and mushrooms. It's the best gift I've ever received.

"I thought you might want something other than Rune's salad bar," AJ says. "Also, while I was there I had a couple beers and practiced nymphing, so the pizza was free."

"That's... not a thing," Darius says, perplexed.

AJ just grins. "It is now, bitches."

Oh Lord. Nymph AJ is going to be a lot to handle. But also a lot of fun.

I walk over to her and take the box, mouthing "I love you" as I do. Then I turn back to the guys. Not wanting the Sexies to see what I'm about to do to this pizza, I compose myself and finish my thought from earlier.

"All right, four things need to happen. First, I'm gonna eat every slice of this thing. Second, I want to know what's actually in this goddamn prophecy you keep talking about. Third, you figure out where you're going to get unicorn blood and then let me know if I can help. But, like, that better not involve killing a unicorn, okay? I've seen all the Harry Potter movies and read the books. I know how that shit ends. And fourth," I conclude, moving toward my bedroom, "I'm going to sleep, waking only to feed my baby, and I don't want to see anyone until morning."

I hear no protest as I walk off, excited beyond measure for the face stuffing I'm about to do. But then, an unexpected blast of nostalgia, one unrelated to AJ, punches me in the gut and stops me in my tracks. The smell of the pizza takes me back a couple decades, to a summer day when I was a child.

I spin around, facing my housemates.

"Sorry, there's a fifth thing. I need to go see my grandma."

. . .

RAIN ONLY WAKES me twice during the night to feed, otherwise sleeping like a little angel because that's what she is. When I get out of bed in the morning, I quickly eat one of the four remaining pizza slices and then sneak into the bathroom to brush my teeth before heading to the front room.

I'm not expecting to literally run into a naked werewolf.

I smack Zev with the bathroom door, and he gracefully dodges the brunt of the impact--though it would do little to harm him regardless.

He grins and steps in my direction, not bothering to hide his nudity or the evidence that he's happy to see me.

I pry my gaze away from his huge--

"Can I be of service?" he asks, and dear heaven help me I just want to throw myself at this man.

"Um. Sorry. I didn't know anyone was in here."

He takes another step closer, until our bodies are almost touching. "I don't mind sharing."

I don't even know what we're talking about anymore. All I can think is 1: why aren't we both naked? 2: how can I brush my teeth before this goes any further? And 3: who cares what my third thought is. Let's go back to one.

Why aren't we both naked?

I feel lost in the woods when I look into his eyes, and as his arm slides around my waist, pulling me against the hard length of his body, I go weightless.

He brushes his lips against my neck. "You feel it too."

I don't know what 'it' means, but yes, I certainly feel something.

He flicks his tongue against the spot he bit in the bath, and heat pools in my abdomen as my body aches in need of him.

"Careful, woman. You're playing with fire."

When he pulls away from me, I feel like a balloon that's been deflated. And as he walks out, closing the door behind him, I lean against the bathroom counter and take a deep breath.

Damn him.

Once I can stand without shaking, I groom and dress for the day, then head to the living room.

The Sexies are still gathered around the table, and I wonder if they just stayed up all night staring at each other like weirdos--with the exception of Zev, of course, who at least had a brief break to torture me in the bathroom.

They explain that they did not, with Rune and Zev sleeping in shifts, while Darius of course remained awake since he's a creature of the night.

While I slept, a few plans were hatched. I'm not allowed to travel without a guard, and I can't be alone with just one prince until the pledge takes effect. Therefore, Rune and Zev will accompany me on my journey to see my grandma. Journey is their word, not mine--we're driving like fifteen minutes down to Ipswich.

In the meantime, Darius will stay here to get his two hours of sleep and ask AJ questions about potential places to find a unicorn. AJ's still asleep and it makes me really, really sad to know I won't be in the house to see her face when Darius starts inquiring about the local mythical creature scene.

After feeding, changing, and bundling Rain, I get myself ready to step into the world for the first time since I became a mother. It's an odd sensation, thinking of who I might see and what they might say, and it's all made odder by the fact that I'll have to explain the gorgeous, mysterious company I'm keeping.

As I buckle Rain down in the carseat in the back of my 2004 Subaru Forester--affectionately named The Boobaru by AJ--I'm surprised by how excited I am. I'm outside! I get to go for a drive! I'm like a happy retriever.

I try to hide my giddiness as Rune gets into the passenger seat next to me. His presence is a strange mix of calming and electric, accelerating my heart rate while wrapping me in a warm sense of security. Two days postpartum and I'm developing a schoolgirl crush on at least two hunks from another realm. Hard to tell if I'm lucky or cursed.

The roads from Rowley to Ipswich are shit, which makes the drive longer but gives Zev and Rune more time to break down the prophecy that's upended my life and the lives of many others. From the way they talk, three realms are in the throes of chaos and on the verge of collapse because of this... situation.

"The issue for so many," Rune explains, "is that you have to look back to the beginning of time, the origin story of each race, to understand the problems underlying our societies today. Most of the brightest fae, werewolves and vampires are not capable of that scope of thought."

"Certainly not vampires," Zev growls from the back.

"Well, let's see how a human can handle it," I say. "Start from the beginning."

Rune nods, and it seems like both an affirmation to my request and like he's queuing up a really long story in his head. I ease off the gas a little; no need to hurry when I've got the history of an entire world coming my way.

"The story starts with the Fates, who originally spawned the--"

"What's a Fate?" I ask, crashing Rune's story before it even has a chance to begin.

"They were the original witches--sisters, who had great power," Zev offers from the back. He leans forward and grips my seat, his fingers brushing against my arm, not that I'm paying attention to that. "In addition to their own kind, they created all races of magical beings."

"The first witch created vampires from her blood," Rune says, continuing as if Zev hadn't interrupted. "The second turned a rib into the first of the wolves, and the third gave life to the fae with the air from her lungs."

"Okay," I say, skeptically. "So far it sounds like the parts of the Bible I find hardest to believe."

"I've read your Bible and I don't disagree," Zev says with a gruff chuckle that sends shivers up my spine. "But the fae have documented history from the second generation of existence."

"And vampires being what they are, many direct descendants of the Fate's creation still live today," Rune adds. "Darius is only three generations removed."

Well, shit. Looks like the paranormals brought receipts.

"Fine, you're all made from witch parts," I concede as snarkily as possible. "What was the prophecy written on? One of the Fate's arm fat?"

"The different races dictated the Fate's words in their own way," Rune says, dismissing my attitude. "Werewolves maintained the story orally, speaking it to pups."

"Singing," Zev corrects. "We pass on our history through song."

I make a mental note to start a karaoke night at Morgan's and force Zev to sing this prophecy in wolf form.

"Very well," Rune says, "*sung* by the wolves. Fae, as Zev mentioned, wrote fastidious notes, and the vampires tasked a group of immortals to preserve the story. Aside from a slight discrepancy here or there, each of the three races maintains a similar version of the Fates' original decree."

"So, wait..." I'm now invested in the story and want to parse out some details. "What about witches? We've got three races invented by witches. Did the Fates forget to, you know, have babies or something?"

Rune shifts in his seat, brow furrowed as he thinks of the best way to answer me. Zev laughs again, and I swear he does this in the sexiest way possible, like he's rehearsed sexy laughs in the mirror so much that it now seems totally natural. But there's nothing natural about his level of sexiness. Nothing.

"The Fates did indeed spawn more witches," Zev says. "For many ages they were the most powerful race, then they stood on an equal plane for centuries as the other races grew and eventually began to outnumber the witches. Then..."

He drifts off, his gaze shifting toward the increasingly uncomfortable Rune.

"Until what?" I ask, my eyes spending way too much time on Zev in the rearview mirror and not enough time on the road.

Rune takes his cue from Zev and picks up the story, though it clearly pains him to do so.

"A feud began between the fae and the witches, over the rights to some of nature's gifts."

"The fae began killing witches for their land and the magical materials they cultivated," Zev says, clearly annoyed at Rune's milder retelling.

"Which led to the vampires taking advantage of a weakened race," Rune says, "and enjoying the powerful blood of witches fleeing the war. And, unless I'm mistaken, many a wolf helped the vampires with their tracking during that era."

Now it's Zev who's looking out the window, unhappy with the truth that's just been leveled at him. I feel like they're both too close to the story and need a third party's summation.

"So... you shit-birds killed all the witches?"

"Not all," Rune quickly explains. "Once the vampires began to attack, a great many witches came to Earth, taking human form as we have done, and beginning new lives amongst your kind. They came to this very continent, around the same time as the Europeans, hoping to find a new world of their own."

When the story transitions from a magical realm I can't quite fathom to the land where pilgrims and puritans settled--where I grew up and studied the local history--a circuit breaker trips in my brain.

"Hang on... that witch shit from the 1600s was... that was real?"

Rune slowly shakes his head, giving Zev the opportunity to jump in.

"Yes and no," the werewolf says. "Witches were here, living alongside and even marrying humans. However, it was almost exclusively human women burned in your horrific trials."

"Easy there," I fire back, not wanting to be lumped in with the old white men who burned women at the stake because they were afraid of getting boners. "Those weren't *my* trials. But please, continue."

"Vampires tracked the witches to this world," Zev says, "now constantly thirsting for their blood. Once the rumor of witches spread, it was the vampires who took human form and pointed fingers at ordinary women, even controlling minds during the trials to create the needed spectacle."

I've known witches were real for a few hours, and I'm already ready to kick Darius square in the balls for what his kind did.

"Okay," I say, trying to put things back on track as I notice our exit is approaching. "That's super fascinating and I want to hear more, but how does this tie in to present day? Why are the races fighting, and what in God's name does it have to do with my baby?"

"If you'll remember back to the beginning of the story," Rune says with a professorial nod, happy to connect the dots for me, "the Fates created us all. They are inextricably tied to each race... and we to them. As they died out, hardships engulfed each kingdom, and the elders who had been crying about the prophecy for generations were finally heard."

"Each version of the prophecy," Zev explains slowly, giving my human brain a little breathing room as it processes the wildest shit I've ever heard, "acknowledges that if the witches die, so will all the beings they created."

I look from Zev to Rune, and they both return sullen stares, waiting for me to speak.

"I take it a lot of the witches have died?"

They both nod, then Zev speaks in a softer voice than I've heard him use previously.

"There are no more in our world, and very few here. Few enough... " he pauses, giving his words extra weight. "That we've come to the final part of the prophecy."

I can tell Zev is just going to stare at me until I guess again, so I turn to Rune in hopes he'll just spill the goddamn beans. The sweet and sexy fae doesn't disappoint.

"When the Last Witch is born," he says, as though reciting the thesis for his doctorate, "the kingdom that harnesses her life will survive while the others perish."

His words filter slowly through my ears and into my brain, with only one phrase having a lasting impact: *The Last Witch?*

I nearly miss my turn as I try to process the information, slamming on the brakes and skidding along the icy road, then fishtailing into a parking lot. Having driven in the snow since I was a teen, the move doesn't scare me that much. For once, the nerves of the fae and werewolf are more frazzled than mine. But that might be because I'm in a state of complete shock.

I autopilot into a spot right in front of Nanny's assisted living home in Ipswich and exit the car, still fighting with the words floating inside my brain. *The Last Witch?*

Zev and Rune get out and fall in line behind me as I walk toward the entrance. Thankfully Zev grabs Rain out of her car seat, as I'm in such a haze I walk away from the car without even getting my baby. I would have remembered within seconds, but it's still a moment I know I'll beat myself up for until I die.

We pass people as I walk through the door, only half noticing the looks given to my companions. My weary brain is pretty used to the way they look and dress, but ten seconds in public reminds me how much they stick out in these small New England towns.

The Last Witch? At this point I'm not just thinking the phrase, I'm mouthing it as well. We've arrived at the front desk and I'm about to sign in when Zev hands me my child and the obvious connection finally clicks.

"Holy SHIT. *She's* the last witch?!?"

Zev and Rune don't respond, probably because they're contemplating using magic to disappear. I look around the room, feeling no fewer than eighteen sets of eyes on me. The harshest glare comes from the young nurse working the reception desk.

"Hi," I say, trying to compose and cover for my outburst. "They're catching me up on a TV show and just gave away a huge spoiler." I playfully punch Zev in the arm for effect, forgetting again that his body is made of muscle armor.

I give a half-hearted smile, sign in at the front desk, and lead the way toward Nanny Tilly's room. There are more questions I want to scream, but this clearly isn't the place for it.

When we get to Nanny's door, I stop, the trailing Sexies halting behind me. I face them, giving as serious a look as I can muster, even while Rune's eyes melt me and Zev's eyes consume me.

"I need you two to wait out here," I say. "There's a window in the door so you can keep an eye on me, but my grandma's been in a… let's say, disturbed mental state since my mom died when I was 11. She's been worse since she started living here a few years ago, and I never know what kind of mood she'll be in. I don't want any extra bodies in the room that might stress her out. Also, be prepared for no fewer than a billion questions when I get back."

Neither of them likes the idea of me going in alone, but they both give a subtle nod of agreement. I put my hand on the cold brass handle, overwhelmed by this revelation but still excited about introducing Rain to her only living relative.

I have such fond memories of life with my grandparents, Matilda and Edwin, or Tilly and Ed. They'd always take me to get pizza, even when my mom told them I couldn't eat more junk food. We'd spend long days on the beach, take camping trips into the mountains, sail to the Cape and drive to Boston to go see movies my mom said I was too young to watch.

Everything changed in an instant when my mom died. Nanny was reclusive for weeks, and then I became very sick and she just went insane. Couldn't speak in full sentences, would wail and point at things that weren't there. I recovered

72

from my mysterious illness, but she never did. Gramps could keep her calm most times, though she was in and out of institutions until I went away to school. Once I was out on my own I became focused on my life and didn't check in with my grandparents as much as I should have, and suddenly Nanny was moving into a home. I came back for a week to help Gramps make the transition, getting her room set up and personal items in order. She and I took a walk in the woods before I helped her settle into her new apartment that day, and it was the most peaceful I'd seen her in years.

I've visited with her a handful of times since moving back, but I can't tell if she recognizes me. I don't know if she's aware her husband died. I struggle to come see her because it makes me sad; I regret not spending more time with her, and I miss the moments we had before everything changed.

I take a breath to steady myself and then walk into her room.

She's lying in her bed, staring out the window. She's still beautiful in her old age, long silver hair hanging just below her shoulders, deep lines on a face that was once so youthful. When she's still, it's easy to see the old Tilly, and it warms my heart.

"Hi, Nanny."

She slowly turns away from the window until her eyes meet mine. We hold each other's gaze for a second, and she gives me a soft smile.

But then her eyes drift down to Rain, locked into her harness, blissfully unaware of the world around her.

Tilly stares at the baby, her smile fades.

And then she screams.

CHAPTER TWELVE

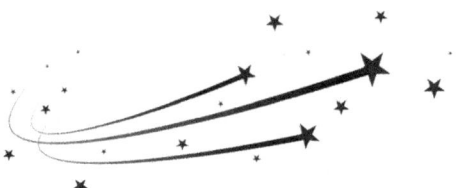

anny's screams wake the sleeping child in my arms, whose own wails join the cacophony of crazy. Within seconds, Zev and Rune burst into the room, Zev already partially shifting into a wolf, both of their gazes trained on my grandmother like they're going to attack.

"Stop!" I shout, startling everyone except Rain, whose lungs seem to have grown exponentially since we got here, if her volume is any indication. "Do not hurt her," I tell the guys. "And get back into full human before someone sees you," I hiss at Zev, whose arms are already paws. Looks like I stopped him in time before he ripped through yet another outfit.

He's barely shifted back when a nurse hurries into the room. "What happened?" she asks, breathless from running down the hall. She immediately checks on Nanny, who stopped screaming but is moaning and clearly agitated as she shifts around in the bed like she's fighting her blankets.

I hand Rain to Rune, whose gifts of calm wash over the child until she's back asleep in his exceptionally chiseled arms. Prying my gaze from his guns, I move quickly to Nanny's side and try to calm her. "You're okay, Nanny. It's me, Bernie. Shh..."

The nurse checks her blood pressure and temperature and tsks at me like she's scolding a child. "Tilly doesn't need this kind of stimulation. It isn't good for her health."

"I'm aware of that," I say, trying to hold back my irritation. "We didn't do anything. She just started screaming the moment I walked in. What's wrong with her? Has she had more episodes? I normally get notified if it seems like she's taking a turn for the worse."

"She's been just fine until today, just now," the nurse says with more than a little accusation in her tone. "I think it's best if you go. Her blood pressure is much higher than I'd like it to be."

74

"I just need a few minutes with her," I say. "And my cousin, he always knows how to calm her down, don't you, Rune?"

Zev smirks. "That's right, *cousin.*"

Rune frowns at the werewolf but hands him the baby as he joins my side. "Of course. He smiles at Tilly. "Hello, great-aunt." He places a hand on hers, and her thrashing slows as she responds to Rune's calming powers.

The nurse narrows her eyes at us, then shrugs. "Fine. Five minutes. Then you must let her rest."

Once the nurse is gone, I focus my attention back on Nanny. Rune stays by her side, holding her hand. "If I leave, she will become agitated again," he says sadly.

I nod, blinking away unwanted tears.

Zev joins us, and kneels next to me while holding Rain so Tilly can see her.

"This is your great-granddaughter," I say, fighting the emotion making my words crack. "And Rain, this is your great-grandmother. She raised me through my terrible tweens and teens. She made sure I always had a tutor for my piano, even when they could barely afford to keep the bar open. She made me a dress for prom so I wouldn't feel left out when we couldn't afford to buy one." I can no longer fight the tears that stream down my face. "She's the best. You're a lucky little girl," I tell my child, then I turn to the woman who's been everything to me for so long. "Oh Nanny, I wish you were here. Really here. I don't know how to do this without you. You always had the answers, and now I feel so lost."

It's more than I wanted to say in front of the Sexies, but the words pour out of me before I can sensor them.

"Come back to me, okay? To us."

Zev slides his free arm around my waist and helps me stand, my legs already cramping.

Rune nods and pulls his hand away. He and Zev take Rain out while I say a final goodbye. I feel a sickening sadness as I smooth her brow one more time before leaving. "I'll come visit you as soon as I can, Nanny," I whisper.

When I pull my hand away, she reaches for me, grabbing my wrist with an iron grip that surprises me. Her voice is monotone and her eyes glazed over as she speaks. "Beware the stars, beware the moon, beware the language that ends with doom." Her nails dig into me and she hisses. "I am you. She is here. You are she."

I pry my wrist out of her grip, a bruise already forming. "Nanny, what do you mean?" Tears stream down my face and I watch helplessly as Nanny's face scrunches up and her body starts to seize.

The nurse returns with a needle. Without preamble, she injects Nanny with it, and my grandmother instantly calms, her eyelids fluttering shut.

I don't want to go, but the nurse stands by the bed watching me, her expression clearly annoyed.

I leave with a heavy heart, pulling the door closed behind me. Rune and Zev are waiting for me in the hall, and when Zev sees the tears in my eyes, he pulls me into a hug.

I want to resist, to push him away as I think about my Nanny instead of this witch business. Instead I melt into his arms, grateful for his strength, for his comfort, even for his presence. If I can set aside why he's here, the fact that I'm not alone is a relief.

Zev rubs my back as I cry into his shoulder. He smells like the woods and feels so solid, so grounded, that my heart slows and my mind calms just by being this close to him. "You okay, love?" he asks softly, his lips brushing against the top of my head, creating a whole other sensation in my body.

I nod against his chest. Then, when I feel strong enough, I step back to look into his forest green eyes. "I've never seen her like that before. She's had breakdowns in the past, but nothing like that."

"I heard what she said," Zev says, which seems impossible considering he was on the other side of a closed door, but then I remember he has dog abilities and is probably listening to everyone in Rowley all the time. "Did her words mean anything to you?"

I think for a second then shake my head. "Not really. Something about the language of doom? But she's always spouted strange things, ever since her mind started to go. I just don't understand why seeing Rain freaked her out so much."

We head back to the car, and I feel distant and drained as Rune locks the baby into the carseat and stays in the back with her while Zev sits up front with me. "I guess it's time to find some unicorn blood?" I say with all the enthusiasm of someone about to go to the dentist.

"That can wait," Zev says gruffly. "You're shaking."

I look down at my hands and realize he's right. And I can't stop. I feel panic rising in me, unlike anything I've ever felt before.

Zev takes one of my hands in both of his and the warmth from them infuses my skin, spreading over my body.

"Crazy shit has been happening to me, ever since the three of you walked into my bar," I say, turning to glare at each of them. "And then you spring on me that you think my daughter is a witch. Oh, and by the way, she's not just a witch, she's the last witch. What does that even mean?"

Zev turns my hand over and brushes the pad of his thumb over my palm in rhythmic strokes, like he's trying to calm a wild animal--which maybe isn't far from the truth. "That night we followed the signs of the prophecy. At this point I don't know much more than you, I'm afraid. We followed the fallen star and it led us to you both."

"The rock." I haven't thought about it since that night, but the rock I pulled out of the wall; it didn't look like a regular stone because it most definitely is not.

"So Rain's a witch? How? This isn't like AJ's situation. Rain's dad isn't magical. I'm sure of it."

"This wouldn't be passed down through her father's lineage," Rune says softly.

The implication of his words takes a moment to settle into my frazzled mind. "So you're saying she got it from me?" I choke out a laugh. "I'm definitely not a witch."

Zev frowns. "Stranger things have happened... but you almost certainly are."

My eyes widen. "So, you're saying my mother was a witch? And--"

"--And your grandmother," Rune, finishes my thought. "I could feel her power. It was confused. Untamed. But very strong. Overwhelming, perhaps. I've never felt more clarity regarding the prophecy."

"Tilly is a witch?" I feel like I'm in an episode of The Twilight Zone.

"Undeniably," Rune says.

I look to Zev who's nodding, clearly no question in his mind either.

The next ten minutes pass in silence, as Zev and Rune respect my need to process. I can't just accept this witch business the way I did with AJ being a nymph (especially since with everything they've said about nymphs that one makes *perfect* sense).

They're saying I'm a witch. My daughter, who can't yet see an inch in front of her face, is a witch. Before my mother died, I was apparently being raised by a witch. And after she went, when I spent my days and nights with Nanny and Gramps, I was still under a witch's guidance.

What is a witch? I don't know what this means on the most basic level. And yet, the more I reflect, the more I have to consider the possibility. Tilly was always a little off, but in that quiet, grandmother kind of way. She fully departed reality when my mother died, but even then she went mad in her own, interesting way. A lot of nights spent at the cliffside where my mom killed herself, and a lot of lucid conversations with Gramps about why they needed to go look for Lauren (my mom). I remember overhearing those talks from my room, knowing Nanny was losing it but still wishing she was right.

As we get closer to Morgan's, I decide to break the silence with a question. "If my mom was a witch with powers and shit, why'd she kill herself?"

Zev looks over his shoulder at Rune, the two sharing a thoughtful stare before replying. Is Zev trying to figure out what the answer is, or are the two conspiring about how much I'm allowed to know. Rune finally speaks up.

"As you know from my story, magical abilities don't keep one safe from anguish."

It's a good answer. Doesn't help me at all, but I can't blame Rune for that.

WE PARK the car and I get Rain out of her carseat. She's going to wake up screaming for food any minute, but I'm hoping she'll put that off just a bit longer to give my mind time to settle.

It's only a little after 1 pm, a much earlier return time than I expected thanks to Nanny's episode and the nurse with no manners. I figure Darius is still sleeping or hanging out in one of his darkened rooms and AJ is either on a unicorn scavenger hunt or taking a nap in preparation for another long night of bartending.

As I walk into the living room, those expectations get dashed in a hurry. AJ's sitting on the kitchen counter, drinking a beer and looking very proud of herself. Darius sits in the corner, furthest from the blacked out windows and safe from errant rays of sunlight.

And in the middle of the room, tied to a chair and looking woefully confused, is Michael Lawrence. My high school boyfriend.

"Mike?"

"Bernie?"

We speak at the same time, matching exasperated tones.

"What are you doing here?" I ask before my brain can catch up to my mouth. *He's tied to a chair, Bernie. He's not the one you should be asking.*

I whip my head toward AJ, who's stifling a laugh. "AJ, with God and three creatures from other realms as my witness, I will beat you to death with a ham hock if you don't tell me what's so funny right now."

My burst of anger only makes her laugh harder, and she coughs up some of her beer in the process.

"Bernie," Darius starts, "There's no need to worry. We've brought this man--"

"No, no," AJ cuts him off, "I need to tell her. You don't understand comedy, Darius, your timing will suck and the joke won't land."

"I don't believe there's anything to joke about in this situation, Anna."

There's a real sibling vibe developing between Darius and AJ, one that I'm sure she likes and he can't stand. I think for a second about what AJ would have been like in high school if she had an older brother who was a vampire. That's not a thought I want to revisit.

"Okay, Jesus, just tell me!"

"Yeah, and tell me!" Michael looks terrified, and it's clear he's been told nothing.

"Okay!" AJ snaps back. "God, it's not like anyone's late for anything. All right, hold on, I have to set this up right."

She takes another sip of beer, but neither Michael nor I say anything this time because we know another interruption will just set her off and she'll take longer. Silence from Darius shows he's learned the same lesson.

"Bernie, this is Michael, you may remember him from high school when you two dated and he took your V card... "

I did not expect this part of my past to come up, and my face immediately turns fire engine red. When I turn away so Michael doesn't see me blush, I point my face at Zev and Rune, who look entirely confused.

"Anyway," AJ wisely gets back to her story before they can derail this ludicrous conversation with more questions, which is the first good thing that's happened to me all day. "Turns out that while you and Michael were getting your hump on, Michael was also busy making little girls' dreams come true."

I couldn't possibly be more confused, and I'm about to say as much when AJ finally spits out what she's been dying to say this whole time.

"Because your high school beau was a freaking unicorn."

CHAPTER THIRTEEN

"AJ, what the damn hell is wrong with you?" I shout, waking Rain who begins to howl at the top of her lungs. I sigh, pull her from her car seat and pop out a breast to stick into her greedy mouth.

Michael's eyebrows raise, and he clears his throat. "Um, can someone let me out of these restraints and explain to me what's going on?" He speaks in a very formal and polite tone for a kidnapee.

AJ hops down from the counter and saunters over to him. "You know what's going on, Mikey Mike. Why don't you tell Bernie here what you really are?"

He glances at me, then back at AJ, then his shoulders sag. "How did you find out?" he asks.

I nearly choke on my own tongue. "Wait, it's true? You're a... you're a unicorn?"

He nods, not able to maintain eye contact with me.

I switch Rain to my other breast and begin pacing the room while she feeds. "What the hell is going on? Does Rowley have any humans here? Is Joe an ogre and Frank, what is he? A leprechaun?"

No one answers as I vent. I think back to high school, to the giddy days of new lust that felt like love. Michael was unquestionably the best looking guy in the school, with his golden hair and matching eyes, his perfectly tanned skin and sleek muscles. He was on the track team, and won more medals than I can remember. We used to make out under the bleachers when he snuck away from practice. He seemed magical at the time, but a unicorn? That's beyond the scope of what I can handle right now. Though maybe it helps to explain him being such a fast runner.

"Let him go," I command everyone--anyone--in the room.

AJ sighs and goes to release his bonds, but not before glaring at him. "One wrong move and my vamp boy will eat you, got it?"

Michael's eyes widen and he nods his head nervously. I throw a look at AJ, a little annoyed that she's talking tough to the majestic creature she brought here against his will.

I haven't seen Michael since graduation. Last I heard he moved out of town and didn't keep in touch with anyone here. It's the goal for most people growing up in Rowley, and he's one of the few who accomplished it. I bet he's really loving this homecoming party.

"So now we're kidnapping people?" I ask. Rain finishes feeding and I hand her to the closest person--Darius. The vampire looks at Rain in confusion, then walks over to the changing table while I try to figure out what to do next.

"It wasn't kidnapping," AJ says, barely containing her laughter. "More like... horsenapping." Now she's literally doubled over in laughter, and as much as I want to be mad, I start to laugh too, because this is just too absurd.

"I'm so... sorry, Michael," I say, as my hysterical laughter escalates. Now I can't control the fits and AJ and I are both doubled over as the guys all watch us warily.

Well, everyone but Darius, who seems to be having some trouble at the changing station. "Is this normal? I think the young human is ill."

I dash over there, worry replacing all other emotions, then my laughter returns when I realize what he's going on about. "Nope, that's just normal newborn poop. Fun, right?

He wrinkles his nose. "It's smelly. And oddly colored and formed."

AJ hoots and slaps her leg. "I can't with these guys. It's too much."

"Listen," Michael says, sidestepping us. "I'm just gonna get going if that's all right."

Darius stands and in a blink has handed the baby off to Rune and is blocking Michael's path to the door. "You may not leave."

Michael looks around nervously as Zev growls under his throat and Rune, who's skillfully getting Rain diapered up and ready for a snooze, watches casually--in the way a cat is casual until it strikes.

"What do you want with me?" Michael asks, giving up and sinking into my new, luxurious couch. "No one knows what I am. I live a quiet life. I don't want to cause trouble."

"We need your blood," Darius says with his whole 'I'm gonna eat you and you'll like it' vibe.

"How much of it?" Michael asks, in an exasperated tone that makes it clear someone--or something--has asked for his blood before.

But Darius, who clearly doesn't like being questioned, hisses, flashing extra pointy teeth. "Who are you to question us? Do you know who we are?"

Oh Lord. "Chill your tits, vamp boy." I step forward and grab Darius by the arm. "You need some serious schooling in how to win friends and influence people."

His ink-dark gaze locks with mine. "I am fully capable of influencing people," he says.

"I mean without voodoo powers," I say. "You catch more flies with honey than vinegar."

His brows crease in confusion.

"Nevermind. Look, just let me handle this. You and AJ have done quite enough." I focus my attention on Michael, and as I look closely at him for the first time, I realize how ageless he is. Like a model stepping off the cover of a magazine, sculpted from clay and photoshopped to perfection. He's obviously matured since his teenage years, but he hasn't been ravaged by time in the way one would expect. Now I can see it. The supernatural beauty at work in him. "We just need a vial or so," I say. "I'm sorry they brought you in like this. I had no idea they were going to do that. And, to state the obvious, I had no idea you were a unicorn."

He stares at me for some time, the room quiet. "It's good to see you again, Bernie," he says, surprising me. "It's been too long."

"It has," I say, cocking my head.

"I meant to come by... when I heard." He pauses. "I'm sorry. For your loss. But. I didn't know if you'd want to see me after--"

"After you dumped her like the piece of shit you are," AJ says, getting in his face. "You broke her heart, you bastard. She was a wreck for weeks over your pathetic ass."

"For crying out loud, AJ, shut the hell up! That was like ten years ago."

She glances at me, nonplussed, but steps back a fraction. She still looks ready to cut a bitch though.

Michael shrugs sheepishly. "Yeah, I'm sorry about that. I was worried. We were getting so close and if you found out what I was... I was scared."

"It was a long time ago," I say, and I know I'll be sitting with this later, worrying over every memory of Michael, reframing the end of my first serious relationship in light of all I've learned. But I'm a big girl now and have too much on my plate to stress about my high school broken heart. "I would be grateful if you could spare some blood though. I know it sounds weird and all but--"

"It's fine," he says as he pulls up his sleeve and holds out his arm. "Take what you need."

"We can't take it from your human form," Rune says, inserting himself into the awkward conversation.

"Right," Michael says. "Um. You'll need to stand back. I don't want to hurt anyone."

I move towards the kitchen to give him room, the realization washing over me that I'm about to watch the first guy I ever slept with turn into a horse.

A unicorn, not a horse.

I glance at Darius, who smirks.

Out of my head, vampire. And excuse me, a unicorn.

But I soon see that the distinction is an important one. Before my very eyes, Michael begins to glow an ethereal white. He doesn't contort and bend out of shape like Zev. Instead, I'm blinded by the light he emanates, and in a flash, he's transitioned from man to a gleaming white unicorn standing in my freaking living room.

"Michael?" I step forward tentatively and hold out my hand to him. He leans his head down and I touch the softness of his mane and let my hand slide over his golden horn. A tingling pulses up my arm, like magic infusing me, and a euphoric kind of happiness overwhelms me. I smile, soaking up the feeling like it's water and I'm dying of thirst.

Darius clears his throat, rudely interrupting the exchange. "I will extract his blood now."

Rune shakes his head. "I don't think so. You'll contaminate it with centuries-old bacteria. Allow me." Rune produces from some pocket or another a small silver blade and a crystal vial covered in etchings.

I cringe as he slices into Michael's back leg and golden blood drips into the vial.

Once it's full, Rune waves his hand over the wound and mutters a few words in, I don't know, Elvin or some shit, and when he removes his hand, Michael's unicorn flesh is once again unblemished.

"This should be enough," Rune says, studying the glowing golden contents.

Michael nods and, in another blast of light, turns from unicorn to man once more. Unlike Zev, he still has his clothes on, and I try to convince myself I'm not the least bit disappointed by that. But I am curious. "You keep your clothes when you shift?" I ask, totally nonchalantly.

AJ blows my cover by snorting.

Michael grins like he knows what I'm thinking. "Sorry to disappoint. But yes, unlike shifters, my powers are pure magic. My body isn't changing form, my essence is returning to its true nature."

"Right. Sure. Makes perfect sense."

Michael looks around and frowns. "If there's nothing else, I assume I'm free to go?"

The Sexies don't object, and I sigh, assuming that means it's fine. "Let me buy you a drink first. It's the least I can do." I glance at Rune. "Keep an eye on Rain?"

He nods, and the other two narrow their eyes like they're jealous, though that can't possibly be true.

Michael and I walk downstairs to the bar, and I pour us both a shot of whiskey. "Cheers," I say.

He downs his drink and I refill, then move to the other side to sit with him.

"I see your apartment's gotten an upgrade," he says.

"Uh, yeah. Those guys, they're kind of a big deal and decided they wanted to live in style while here."

Michael frowns. "They're dangerous, Bernie. I don't really know what's going on, but I've got a bad sense. Be careful with them."

"I know," I say. "It's... complicated."

He chuckles. "It always is with you."

"What does that mean?" I ask.

"Just that life was never easy for you." He pauses. "I hated ending things the way we did, but after your grandmother talked to me, I--"

"Nanny talked to you?" I ask, shocked. "About what? Why?"

"She didn't tell you?"

"Tell me what?"

He sighs and sets his tumbler down. "After prom, she came to my house. Said she knew what I was and that I needed to leave you alone. That being with you would ruin your life. She was--convincing. I didn't want to hurt you, but really didn't feel like I had a choice. It was the hardest thing I've ever done."

I lean back against my barstool, a wave of conflicting emotion flooding me. "She didn't say anything to me, for obvious reasons, I suppose. All of this magic shit was kept secret from me up until Rain was born."

"Congratulations, by the way. On your baby. She's beautiful, just like her mother."

His compliment makes me flush. "What about you? I heard you left town. Just north of Boston, right? What do you do? Do you have kids? A wife?"

"Yeah, we're in Saugus." He pauses. "And I write fantasy novels for a living."

I can't help but smile at that. "They say write what you know. I guess that works out for you."

He laughs. "Yeah, something like that. And, I have a daughter. Ellie. He reaches for his phone and pulls up a picture of a blond girl with big blue eyes who looks about kindergarten age.

"She's lovely," I say. "I'm glad you found happiness. Is her mother still in the picture?"

"Actually, my husband and I are her parents. We used a surrogate."

"Husband?" I'm not sure if I'm more shocked my old flame is a unicorn or gay. Both are unexpected.

"Yeah. I didn't know, or didn't want to acknowledge it fully when we were together. It wasn't until college that I finally came out. That's when I met Robert. We've been together ever since." He looks at me cautiously, waiting for my response.

I smile and take his hand. "I'm so happy for you, Michael. How, um, did your parents take it?" I ask with a sheepish look, already knowing the answer. Michael came from the type of family that wouldn't be too keen on a gay son.

He returns my look and shakes his head, but then relief fills his eyes as he swipes the picture on his phone to one of him and his husband. "This is Robert."

"You two make a gorgeous couple," I say honestly. "Does he know about... "

"That I'm a unicorn?" he asks with a chuckle. "Yes, it was kinda hard to hide. We used his DNA for our daughter to avoid any... complications with her down the road. And he'd never betray my secret. Just like I won't betray yours."

I raise an eyebrow. "Yeah, about all this. I can't apologize enough. I've been thrown into the deep end of this supernatural shit, and it's been a hard ride. You shouldn't have been pulled into this."

"It's okay. I'm glad I could help." He takes one last swig from his glass. "But next time, just ask?"

I laugh as we both stand. "I will."

We hug and he pulls away to look at me. "It was good seeing you again, Bernie. Even under the circumstances."

"You too, Michael. Don't be a stranger. And bring your family by sometime."

I let him out the front door and lock it behind him, then walk back up to my apartment, my mind lost in the past to what was and what could have been. What did my grandmother know about this new world I now find myself thrust into? And why didn't she tell me the truth back then?

Rune is in the kitchen cooking something in a pot when I return. Darius and Zev are playing chess, and AJ is sitting at the piano picking at keys. She looks up when I walk in. "Wild, isn't it?" she says with a cheeky grin.

"That's one word for it," I say grimly. "How on earth did you know he was a unicorn?"

"Well, Darius pieced it all together," she explains. "He asked about the families that have been in Rowley the longest, and I said the Lawrences since I've never heard of a Lawrence leaving town, until Michael, and even he didn't get too far. Then he asked some weird questions about who was whose son and suddenly I'm off to kidnap Michael while Darius waits in his bat cave." She gives me a ho-hum shrug and glances at the clock on the wall. "Time to open the bar. Ready boys?"

"I cannot leave the potion until it is complete," Rune says.

"How long will that be?" AJ asks.

"You cannot rush magic."

"Are you cooking Michael's blood in my kitchen?" I ask, marching over to look into the pot. It has a golden hue and sparkles, just like something that would come out of a unicorn.

"Once it is done, we can complete our pledge and you will feel safe," Rune says softly, and I realize in that moment he's not just doing this to keep the three of them honest, but so that I will trust them. It softens me just a little.

"Thank you," I say. "For trying to make me feel better about all this."

Rune stops stirring for a moment to turn to me, his eyes looking a deeper blue than before, like the ocean pulling me into its depths. He takes my hands in his, stepping forward so our bodies are mere inches apart. "I cannot say that I know how hard this has been for you, but I can feel your pain, your worry, your fear. I know it's hard to trust us, but I hope you can at least believe that I want to make this easier for you while we work out what must be done."

He drops one of my hands and brushes his knuckles lightly against my cheek. "I did not expect to feel the way I do about you and the child. It has complicated things. But I would not change that for anything."

I suck a breath in, my body humming with pent up desires I can't act on. His eyes drop to my lips, and I want more than anything for him to come closer, but then AJ tugs at my sweater, breaking the spell between us. "Let's go, before our regulars show up."

"Right," I say, reluctantly pulling my hand--and my gaze--from his. I turn away as Rune resumes stirring his pot. "AJ and I will go open up while you finish brewing up your potion," I say, trying to clear my head. "Bring Rain down when you're done. I don't want her left alone while those nutcases are out there."

The three of them nod and AJ and I head to the bar. Even before they finish their pledge, I'm already comfortable with them being around Rain. A lot has changed in a couple days. Everything, really.

We wipe down counters and prep the bar for whoever might wander in tonight. AJ peppers me with questions about Michael, from what we talked about to whether he was 'hung like a horse' in high school.

"You're terrible, you know that?" I say, spraying her with the water hose at the sink.

She shrieks, but before it hits her, she holds up her hands and the water turns to steam and dissipates into the air.

I shake my head. "I need some powers of my own." I wipe up the mess I made and walk to the door to unlock it. "Speaking of, I found out some news about me and Rain today. Apparently we come from a long line of witches."

She stares at me for a second, mouth agape, then rushes over and pulls me into a hug. "I always knew you were special. More special than me for sure."

I lean back to lock eyes with her. "AJ, that's not true. I don't even have powers, not that I know of. You're special. You've always been more special than you know."

"Pft," she says, walking back to the bar. "You're just saying that because you're a very friendly, accommodating witch."

"No, it's because you're my best friend and it's true," I counter, grabbing a rag left on one of the tables. "You just turned water into steam with your mind and you can make dudes do whatever you want. You're, like, the most special. And maybe Rain has some hidden powers, but I'm just as ordinary as I was yesterday."

She flicks me with the rag in her hand. "Stop it. I see how those three sexy men upstairs look at you. Rune is ready to lay down his damn life for you. Zev looks like he's about to hump your leg. And Darius wants to eat you, in the best possible way." She wags her eyebrows, and I can't help but laugh. "They didn't hunt a unicorn and make a vow for nothing. They want in your pants, bad. So don't give me any bullshit about being ordinary. There's never been anything ordinary about you."

Our conversation is cut short when the bell at the door rings. I expect to see Joe and Frank, but am surprised when it's Chief Roland.

I stand and smile. "Hey! Can I get you a drink?" I ask. "Scotch on the rocks, right?"

He smiles grimly. "Good memory, but no, I'm not here to drink. Unfortunately, I'm on official business."

"About what?" I ask, my heart suddenly pounding nervously in my chest. "Did something happen to Tilly?"

He shakes his head. "No nothing like that. It's about John Marsden." He looks over at AJ. "A few neighbors said he was driving this way the morning he disappeared."

AJ freezes and I hold my breath, waiting to see how she responds. "And? You can drive this way without coming to this bar," she says, and I can almost feel the blast of her powers being thrown at the chief.

His eyes widen and his mouth drops open as he struggles to find his words. "We found... we found some blood, and the lab results finally came back."

"What do you mean?" I ask, repeating AJs words like an idiot.

"It was John's blood. And we found it in front of Morgan's. I'm going to need to talk to both of you, and definitely to those strange men that have been hanging around. This has officially become a murder investigation."

CHAPTER FOURTEEN

"How can I help you, Officer?"

AJ and I both turn to see Darius walking into the bar from the back entrance. He's inexplicably wearing a designer suit and tie, rather than his usual cos-play dress up, and his dark eyes are locked onto the Chief, who startles at the unexpected arrival.

"Uh, yes, I have a few questions for all of you about the night of John Marsden's disappearance. But I'll need to speak with your... the other men as well?"

Darius crosses the room quickly--normal human quickly not vampire quickly--and stands in front of the chief, towering over the stout man by at least two feet. "There were only two of us, and my colleague is in the middle of an important meeting. I can answer any questions you may have."

What kind of brain damage is the good chief going to suffer after being blasted by both AJ's nymphness and the vampire's mind melts, I wonder. Poor guy. I feel bad for him, but not bad enough to intervene, cuz I sure as shit do not want to get caught up in John's well-deserved murder.

"Right, well, this is... as I said, a murder investigation," Chief Roland mutters, looking around like he needs that drink after all.

I reach for his arm to guide him to a table. "Why don't you have a seat, and I'll get you something to wet your whistle while you talk to Darius and AJ, hm?"

He nods vaguely and sits as I direct him. I give AJ and Darius pointed looks that I hope communicate something along the lines of 'do not mess him up too badly but also get us out of this stat' and start pouring a scotch on the rocks, which I serve with a napkin and a smile as Nanny always taught me.

I take the fourth seat at the table and wait for the chief to begin.

Relying on familiar habits, he pulls a small notebook out of his breast pocket and puts his reading glasses on, then takes a swig of the drink before clearing his throat. "Where were you the day of Mr. Marsden's disappearance?"

"We were all here," I say. "I had just had my baby, which Darius and Rune helped deliver by a miracle from heaven. AJ came over as planned to help take care of me, the baby, and the bar while I recovered, and we were dealing with the power outage and the storm."

The chief nods, pushing his glasses up onto his nose before it slides off. "Right. Right. Can anyone else corroborate this?"

"Other than all four of us?" AJ asks with way too much snark. I kick her under the table and she flips me off when the chief isn't looking.

Darius rolls his eyes like an exacerbated teacher and leans in. "We know nothing of this man's disappearance. We were here throughout the power outage with no visitors. You will stop looking into this and determine John left town of his own volition. He was abusive, angry, and erratic. He walked around town looking for his wife, cut himself on a broken bottle of beer, grew frustrated, and left."

I sit silently, waiting to see if his Jedi mind tricks work.

The chief takes notes, then nods. "Right. Right. Yes, just had to dot all my i's and cross all my t's. You know how it is."

"Sure," AJ says, sitting forward in her chair, her face a mask. She doesn't have the same benevolent relationship with the chief that I do. To her, he's the dick-head who never stood up for her when she called in John's abuse. The jackass who always berated her for her youthful indiscretions. It's taken me too long, but I'm finally seeing the truth. AJ and I did not have the same childhood, despite growing up the exact same way.

My heart hurting, I reach for her hand and squeeze it, as the chief and Darius stand.

"How do you know Bernie, again?" The chief asks as they walk to the door.

Darius glances back at me. "Oh, I'm an old friend of her grandmother, Tilly's. We go way back."

His cheeky answer grates my nerves, but I hold in my ire until the chief is in his car and driving away. Then I walk up to Darius and punch him in the arm.

The act of defiance predictably hurts my fist more than it hurts his steel arm, but I don't care. "Don't you dare bring my grandmother into this again, you hear me?"

He stares at me long and hard, making me think the punch was a bad idea.

"First of all," he says, "it was a good cover. Second, it was a warning shot."

I raise an eyebrow, now more confused than angry. "A warning… what, to warn the police chief not to do his job?"

"You think we would have left any trace of the man we murdered?" Darius says, his voice utterly patronizing. "He's here on behalf of the same people who sent Karl. The nymph's dead husband is just his excuse to get us all talking."

AJ and I share a look, both a little miffed by the vampire's assessment. Does this mean the whole police department's in on this? That seems excessive.

In any event, I can't think about that right now. I've got to save my baby from literally everyone and try to run a bar while I'm at it.

"Let's just get this pledge over and done with," I say, preparing to follow him upstairs, but he stops me.

"You cannot be present. It must be done with only those taking the pledge in attendance for it to work."

Sounds like a lot of bullshit to me, but honestly, I don't even care anymore. "Fine. Whatever. Go."

I wave dismissively, sending Darius off to join the others for their little pledge, then turn to AJ. She's chewing her nails and staring at the wall. With as much as I've been through, it's easy to forget the tumultuous times that befell my friend these last couple days: getting shot, losing her dickhead husband, finding out she's not human, becoming a full-time bartender.

"Hey," I whisper as I put a hand on her back. "How are you?"

She turns to me quickly, the distant look gone from her face and replaced by a sweet smile.

"I… I think I'm fine."

She sounds earnest, but it's still a little hard to believe. How could either of us be fine right now? She sees my doubt and works to convince me.

"I'm almost ashamed about it, but I've only felt relief since John… you know. And I might go home and look at a picture or find an old birthday card and get hit with some grief, but right now I'm only worried about you. It sounds a little messed up, but the last two days are the best I've had in a long, long time."

"That does sound messed up, A," I agree. "I wish we could have turned this page a long time ago."

She smiles again and puts a reassuring hand on my shoulder, turning the tables on who's doing the comforting.

"No use thinking about what could have been. I'm a godmother to an angel and a freaking nymph now. Let's open this damn bar!"

A FEW HOURS LATER, Morgan's is in full swing. And by full swing, I mean nine people are quietly drinking beers. We get a little rowdy on St. Patrick's Day, but otherwise we're just a place for locals to escape into a pint and bide their time before they have to go back to lives they've mostly grown tired of.

AJ's pouring drinks and I'm letting Joe tickle Rain's toes while she's wrapped in her little holster. As much as I'd love to let him hold her, I'm still too afraid. Joe's as trustworthy as they come, but no one in my life is what they seem anymore. I remind myself of that everytime I look at Karl's normal spot in the back.

Finally, the three Sexies arrive. Each looks a little off. Darius lacks his normal aggressive intensity, Rune has slight bags under his eyes, and Zev, in wolf form, is panting a bit. I guess the hangover from a pledge potion is legit.

The fae and the vampire sit at the bar next to a younger guy named Max who's been coming to Morgan's since his 21st birthday. He's a couple years older than me and pops in a few times a week then goes home and lies to his wife about how much he drank. Max looks at Darius questioningly.

"You're not from around here, are you?"

"No," Darius mutters back.

"Where you from?" Max says, unaware of how poorly this small talk will go.

89

"Elsewhere."

Max looks at me, eyebrows raised. "Got a real chatterbox over here, Bern."

"I know, Max. He's an old... *family* friend," I say, my inflection dripping with distaste. "Can't get rid of him, despite how much we want to."

"I hear that," Max says with a smile. "My wife's two sisters are staying with us. It's like the three of them can't talk without screaming. Don't matter if they're happy or mad, just constantly yelling."

Jennifer's sisters are in town, huh? The beginnings of a plan start to percolate.

I look from Darius to Rune, then down to Zev. All three are here for the long haul, whatever that haul may be. They also just chased down a unicorn and chugged some serious moonshine in order to earn my trust. I'm not shutting down the bar because I need money and a home for my daughter, so I think I ought to make the best of this hand I've been dealt.

"Max, call Jen and tell her to bring her sisters here."

"What?" Max says, terror in his eyes. "Not on your goddamn life-"

"Max, call your wife and tell her to come to Morgan's," I say, "and I'll tell her you've had two beers instead of six. And your kids can play out back with my husky."

There's a moment of silence, then Max reaches for his phone. I knew this would be an easy win.

I look down at Zev, his head cocked to the side, undoubtedly thinking angry thoughts. I scratch him behind the ears and coo at him like a dog. Darius almost laughs at that, his permanent frown twitching into a near-smile.

While Max begrudgingly texts, I move over to the stool where Rune is sitting. He's sipping what looks like a rum and coke, but I'm pretty sure it's just water with some rum-colored magic.

"How are you doing?" I ask softly, feeling an almost uncontrollable urge to care for the man who's done so much for me recently.

"Rather ill," he answers. He doesn't look up from his drink, but he does place his hand gently on my waist. It's intimate and exhilarating. In response, I put my hand on his leg, my fingers falling over the inside of his thigh.

"Well, if you're feeling up to it," I say, fighting the urge to let my hand creep higher, "I have a favor to ask."

"Anything."

His response comes immediately, his eyes penetrating mine, and suddenly I want to ask an entirely different favor that would require a trip to the bedroom.

"They'll be here in ten, Bern."

Max's voice reminds me of what I really wanted to ask, and possibly keeps me from passing Rain to the nearest person with hands and leading Rune upstairs.

"Thanks, Max," I say quickly before turning back to my Elvin crush. "There are some ladies on their way. Think you can make a cool looking drink that's the most delicious thing they've ever tasted and it gets them good and drunk but with no hangover in the morning?"

My request is utter BS and I'm about to laugh, but Rune answers with a curt nod.

"Of course. Should it be fizzy? Perhaps an alluring shade of pink? I'll provide a few options."

With that, he's up and behind the bar, looking through my liquor selection and pulling small vials from the inside of his coat. AJ, now a little territorial as my head bartender, gives Rune an angry look.

"A, you're on break," I say. "Come hold the baby while I play piano."

She smiles widely, jumping at the chance to hold Rain. It feels like weeks since I had my baby, but it's only been days, and the opportunities for AJ to snuggle her goddaughter have been few and far between.

I may not trust many people right now, but I trust AJ with my life. Always will.

As she gently embraces my sleeping angel, I glide toward the piano, wondering what I'll play. I'm instantly overcome with emotion, thinking back to my youth when I'd play for bar patrons all the time. Gramps used to tell me the bar would go out of business if people didn't come to hear me.

I sit on the bench and uncover the keys. So many memories are tied to this instrument and this bar. My mom bought the piano when I was five, then a couple years later Tilly moved it into this bar, right where it still sits today. This is where I grew up, and now I feel like I'm trying to grow up all over again.

"Play, Bernie."

Joe's voice is soft and sweet, tied in with all those memories. It's the perfect motivation to get my fingers moving.

I decide on Chopin's Nocturne Op. 9, No. 2 in E-Flat Major, which was always Tilly's favorite. Even after her mind went, this song would make her smile and give her a moment of respite from whatever was ailing her. It's not the most complicated piece, which made it one I mastered early, and as my fingers glide over the keys, pulling from strings and ivory a hypnotic melody that carries its own kind of magic, that same relief washes over me. The music takes me out of myself and away from all the fear and uncertainty that have plagued me since Rain arrived.

I can't wait to teach my baby to play piano.

I don't realize how quiet the bar has grown until I finish, the pads of my fingers resting on the last notes. After a breath of silence, there's a smattering of applause that seems much louder than our few patrons should justify. I turn towards the bar and notice AJ has tears in her eyes, the kind of crying you do when you're incredibly proud of your friend. Rune has stopped mixing drinks, his enchanting face looking extra enchanted by my music. Darius looks calm and content, which is a big mood change for him. Even Zev seems affected and is now curled up by my barstool watching me.

"Girl's night!! WOOOOOOO!!!"

No voice shatters a mood quite like Jennifer's.

She and her sisters waltz through the door, looking like three women who refuse to let spring break end. They're all attractive enough, even if each of them is wearing a dress that's one size too small.

"Bernie, I'd kiss your baby but Miles has been wiping snot all over the house for three days and I don't want you to have to deal with that shit. Holy Christ, who the hell are you?"

God, I love Jennifer. She's finally spotted Rune behind the bar, where he's got his sleeves rolled up as he firmly muddles some mint leaves.

"Good evening," he says before throwing a quick wink at me. Rune is totally in on my plan. "We've got a special drink tonight if you ladies would like to try it."

Jennifer and her sisters, who I think are named Rebecca and Amy, belly up to the bar, none of them even taking the time to acknowledge Max. He almost has to raise his hand to get his wife's attention.

"Babe, where are the kids?" Good question, Max.

"At your parents' place, playing video games with headphones on," Jennifer answers, eyes still on Rune. "I told your mom to call you if they get too annoying."

Max studies his wife and her sisters for a moment, then polishes off his beer and waves to me. It's a clear signal that he wants another, and I'm to remember not to tell Jennifer how many he's already had.

"A," I half-whisper, loud enough to get her attention. "Time to get back behind the bar and do some beer pouring and nymphing. I'm going to make Jennifer's night and really piss off a vampire."

AJ nods her understanding and hands me Rain, who somehow slept through Jennifer's booming entrance. I walk over to the girls, all three of them so entranced by Rune that they don't even notice my approach.

"Thanks for coming in, ladies," I say with a semi-forced smile. Older men have always been the lifeblood of this bar, and I'm not entirely sure how to feel about three women here for "ladies night." Still, I've got bills to pay and sexy men to exploit.

"This is Rune, he's visiting from Europe and he'll be making some fancy, foreign drinks. And this… " I say, putting a hand on Darius' shoulder and feeling him tense as I do so, "is Darius."

The vampire stares at me, looking unamused as he waits to see what kind of description he gets. I can read in his eyes that he fears what I'll say next.

"He's an exotic dancer."

Time practically stands still. The girls turn their heads in slow motion, pulling away from Rune and focusing on a new object of desire. Darius stares into my eyes and I feel the familiar, uncomfortable sensation of a voice entering my mind.

You'll pay for this, Bernie.

It's not an empty threat, but he doesn't scare me like he used to. I send a thought back his way.

Maybe I just want to see you naked, Darius. And this is the best way I can think of to make my dreams come true.

A little of the anger leaves his face, replaced by a slight trace of intrigue. I turn away, proud of myself for the sly reply, and also wondering how much truth there is to it.

I join AJ behind the bar, surveying the scene I've created: a few girls swarmed around Darius, all of them sipping magical cocktails whipped up by Rune, Joe scratching a man-turned-wolf behind the ears. Also, we've got five guys lined up at the bar staring at AJ, ready to order a tenth beer if it means she'll give even the slightest smile. Not a bad night at Morgan's, I'd say.

"I'm sneaking upstairs to feed and change Rain," I tell AJ. "You keep everyone happy and drinking."

"Try this before you go." AJ hands me a cocktail that fizzes with magic. "It's called a Sexy Runedezvous," she says, unable to hold in her giggling. "Get it? *Rune*dezvous, like rendezvous but--"

"I get it," I say with a laugh, 100% sure Rune did not name or approve of the name for his concoction. That's all AJ. I sip on the drink and the flavors burst on my tongue, then the magic and alcohol mix in my body to create a nice mellow buzz. "Damn. No wonder this is such a hit."

I hand the drink back to AJ and duck over to the back exit, hoping to make a discreet getaway since I know the Sexies get nervous if I'm out of sight. Once I get up the stairs and into my bedroom, I quickly change Rain and then start to feed her. When she's got a good latch and a steady gulp going, I head into the living room--

--And run smack into Darius.

"Jesus!" I yell, causing Rain's eyes to flare open before going back to a contented half-mast. "What the hell are you doing up here?"

He stands very close to me, closer than he's ever been, aside from the times he was showing his teeth and hissing some kind of threat.

"We don't want you and the child alone, Bernie. Under no circumstances, no matter how quickly you think you'll be back."

He's serious but sweet, a tone I've never heard in his voice. Then he does something even more unexpected.

"I was very upset I had to follow you. I was about to start dancing."

Oh my God. Darius made a joke. I'm too surprised to laugh. His lips twitch into something close to a smile, and that's about as much of a reaction to humor as I can expect from him.

"Right, sorry," I say. "I thought maybe the pledge would have mellowed that protectiveness."

Darius shakes his head. "We aren't worried about each other. We worry about whoever else might be out there."

Again he smiles, this time it even reaches the edges of his lips, and I'm getting exposed to a whole new Darius. He steps even closer, our faces now inches apart. With all the antagonizing, I'd forgotten how perfect his features are, how easy it is to get lost in his dramatic gaze. As he starts to speak into my mind, it nearly causes my knees to buckle.

I must say, Bernie, the thought of you dreaming about me in the nude was... stirring.

Oh shit. I awoke a lusting vampire.

Minutes ago I was ready to take a fae right there on the bar, not long ago I was sharing bathroom space with a naked werewolf, and now my body's begging to be wrapped in a vampire's arms. This kind of sexual energy can't be normal for

93

a new mother. The werewolf hair stitching must be having an effect. That feels like a safe thing to blame all this on.

Before I can think of how to respond to this advance, Darius stiffens. My gaze had been locked on his lips but now I glance up and realize his eyes have gone completely white. His body trembles and he stares blindly into the empty space above my head.

"Darius? Darius, what's wrong?"

I don't want to raise my voice, but I'm seconds away from running down the stairs and screaming for help. Just as my nerves are about to break, he comes to, his body relaxing and his eyes returning to their normal piecing darkness.

He stays still, thoughts clearly whirring around in his mind.

"What? What happened?" I ask, afraid of the answer.

"I've communed with my father, the King. He received word of our predicament… and passed on some news."

All news is bad news at this stage of my life, so I don't have any question that I'm about to hear something terrifying.

"Apparently… " Darius continues, "The Order of the Star has returned."

And, once again, the bad news makes zero sense to me.

"Okay. And I care because…?"

"Because that's the group after your child," he says. "It's a collection of witches with bad intentions, but the members disbanded over a decade ago. It appears they've reconvened."

Of course. More magical enemies to deal with. "If they're witches, do I know any of them?"

Darius thinks for a moment. "I don't know." He looks at the floor, then back into my eyes to deliver the real bombshell.

"But it was amongst the Order that I first met your grandmother."

CHAPTER FIFTEEN

"W hat the--" I lean away from Darius, so far that he has to reach out and catch me before both Rain and I fall ass over tea kettle. I have so many questions, I don't even know where to begin. "What does Nanny have to do with this Order of the Star? And what do you mean that's when you met her?"

He looks deep into my eyes. There's a pain in his gaze, and I can't tell if it stems from a past hurt of his own, or if he fears hurting me with his words. Either way, he's showing a vulnerability I never expected to see.

Just as he opens his mouth to speak, I hear footsteps pounding up the stairs. They're coming up two at a time, so I know it's AJ.

"Hey, what are you dorks doing up here?" She seems a little out of breath, and I can tell it's not just from her trip up to the apartment.

"The bar is, like, packed. Jennifer called a hoard of horny moms when you said there was an exotic dancer."

I peek back at Darius who's already staring my way. I no longer notice that sweet vulnerability from two seconds earlier.

AJ is oblivious to the non-verbal conversation happening as she talks. "They brought cash and they're like, I dunno, tigers at feeding time. If someone doesn't start dancing soon, I think they're gonna burn the place down."

Stubborn as he is, I've got no idea if Darius will actually help us out. As much as I want to see him dancing while the ladies of Rowley stuff dollar bills into his thong, it's a little hard to imagine. On top of all that, we still have to deal with the bombshell he just dropped on me.

To my surprise, Darius simply nods at AJ. "Mustn't disappoint the ladies," he says. He winks at me and then follows her quickly down the stairs.

Not one to let someone else have the last word, I mentally shout at him. *This conversation isn't over, vamp boy.*

He doesn't reply, but I do hear him laughing in my mind.

He's such a damn pain in the ass.

I strap Rain into her carrier and follow them down. The moment I open the door to the bar I stop short, staring in wonder at a sight I've never seen in my life.

Like AJ said, the place is packed. Mostly with women, which is definitely a first for Morgan's. The few men I see are regulars, all looking fairly uncomfortable. I'll have to remember to comp their drinks tonight as an apology. Or maybe AJ can nymph them all into high spirits. That might be a better plan. I also spot Michael and his husband in the corner drinking a few of Rune's magical elixirs. When Michael sees me, he grins and raises a glass.

I smile and nod, then follow his gaze to a makeshift stage one of the guys must have rigged while I was upstairs. Rune, no longer behind the bar, is playing a harp--where the hell did we get a harp?--in a way I've never heard one played before. It's majestic, both the song he's playing and the way that he plays. I could watch him all night, but it appears the crowd is getting antsy for something else.

"Where's the strippah?!" A female voice yells from the middle of the room, inspiring a cheer of assent from the ladies around her. I scan the room for Darius but don't see him. Did he bail? Is dancing the one thing in life that scares him, and he's fled back to his realm?

I get my answer almost immediately, as a shadowy figure drops from the ceiling and lands in a crouch on the stage. I don't know if he climbed to the ceiling earlier or just tricked the crowd with some vampire shit, but either way they all lose their freaking minds.

Darius is still fully dressed and he doesn't move anything except his eyes as he surveys the audience before him. The crowd falls into a hush, waiting for what will come next. I see Darius give a quick look at Zev, then he turns to Rune who begins to play something different.

This new harp song is nothing like the first. It's fast and intense, and it has me imagining a bunch of serious-faced fae at a rave.

As the music ramps up, the Dance of Darius begins. It's rhythmic and fast, almost violent, but controlled and intoxicating. It's like he's breakdancing and gyrating and booty shaking all at the same time, and he hasn't even taken his clothes off. That's going to have to change if he wants to keep all the ladies interested.

As if on cue, Zev lunges at Darius, his teeth sinking into the vampire's black silk shirt, pulling it off dramatically. The crowd screams with fear and excitement. A wolf just attacked the dancer, but now the dancer is shirtless with his six... no wait, eight-pack on full display. Good grief vamp boy is ripped.

If there was any question as to whether or not Darius would enjoy dancing for a crowd, that doubt has disappeared. I dare say he's in his element. As he moves into a handstand and does an aerial split, I wonder if he worked as a dancer to pay his way through vampire college. Then, when Zev approaches again to bite off Darius' pants, I wonder if the two of them had a traveling stripshow act.

I move behind the bar to try and get a better view, since the place is packed with patrons. Before I can find the perfect vantage point, AJ taps me on the shoulder.

When I turn to her, I'm met with an enormous smile. Her eyes are wide as saucers as she opens the register to show me piles of cash within. "Rune's drinks are a hit. And the guys are tipping me like money's going out of style. Plus, two kegs are tapped and we're running out of all the well liquors. As long as these guys are around, you might have to start running this place like it's a successful bar."

The thought is equal parts exciting and sobering. What happens to the bar, to us--to me--when the Sexies leave? Surely this can't be the status quo forever.

My sad musings are put on hold when Zev growls and pounces from across the floor, pinning Darius to the wall, who's now only wearing a pair of red silk boxers that do little to hide his significant... size.

AJ snorts as my gaze locks on the sexy vampire. His muscles glisten like he's been rubbed in oil, and as he continues his dance-fight with the wolf, I'm mesmerized by his fluid grace and his flexing muscles.

"Looks like someone's falling for vamp boy," AJ whispers with a mischievous smile.

I tear my eyes off of the stage to glare at her. "I can admire the view without wanting to pay the price to live there," I say.

"Suuuure," she says as she saunters off to fill a drink order.

To avoid falling into a lust-filled daydream about Darius, I focus instead on Rune, whose long, graceful fingers strum the strings of the harp with such mastery, I can't help but feel a kindred connection to him. To his music. To his craft and skill.

As if he knows I'm thinking of him, he glances over to me, his silver eyes gleaming in the dim light of the bar, and he winks. My cheeks heat with the attention and I turn away, flustered by all of them.

"Bernie, where did you find these guys?" Jennifer asks, her eyes glazed from too much drink. Or too much man meat. It's hard to tell.

"It's a long story," I say, shrugging. I'm super tired of the doctor lie, and I don't think this particular crowd will buy that one anyways. It makes me a little nervous; we may be digging ourselves into too many lies and sooner or later the walls will cave in. But that's a problem for future Bernie. Today's Bernie has enough to deal with.

When Darius and Zev finish up their weird--and perhaps rehearsed?--routine, the crowd screams and shouts, begging for more, but it seems the boys are done.

Darius locks his dark gaze with mine and smirks. *Was that sufficient?*

I swallow, still a little weak-kneed as he stands there mostly naked. *It'll do.*

He raises an eyebrow, then disappears with his clothes to the bathroom, where he emerges a few moments later completely dressed, to the utter disappointment of everyone.

For the rest of the night, Rune's drinks flow, Darius and AJ charm everyone with their powers, and Zev sticks close to me and Rain, nearly tripping me several times.

When Rain demands to be fed again, I sneak upstairs to take a break and rest.

AJ, Rune and Darius are handling things well enough, and I'm exhausted. When I think of how little time has passed since I gave birth, I'm amazed. I should still be in the hospital. Or at the very least resting a lot while kind neighbors bring me casseroles.

I read *What to Expect When You're Expecting* at least three times. There for sure wasn't a single chapter on what to expect when a werewolf, a vampire and a fae walk into your bar and try to steal your baby, then proceed to protect you, then you find out your best friend is a nymph and your ex-boyfriend is a gay unicorn, and your grandmother is a witch who might have been part of a secret society. Someone should publish a new edition that takes all these issues into account, if you ask me.

Once in my apartment, I sink into the couch, my feet aching, my back about to break, and my head pounding.

I close my eyes as I pull my breast out to nurse Rain and am startled when my front door opens and a large white wolf walks in. "Jesus, Zev, you scared the living daylights out of--" I lose track of my thoughts when he transforms from beast to man and stands before me naked. I've already seen the goods, but I'm sitting and he's standing and he's on full display at eye level. Forgive me, but it's really hard to not stare. Holy hell, do all paranormals come packing, or just my three?

"Not all of us, no," Zev says in a deep voice, his green eyes twinkling flirtatiously. I blush three shades of red when I realize I spoke out loud. I must be more exhausted than I thought. "But if it bothers you, I'll clothe myself."

"It's not that..." I start to say, but then I stop. Of course he needs to put clothes on. I can't just hang out with him naked. Pull yourself together, Bernie.

"What's that?" Zev asks, turning toward me as he walks to the guest bedroom, his ass cheeks like perfectly sculpted boulders that I have to resist the urge to stand up and touch.

"Get dressed," I finally say when my brain starts to work again.

He chuckles as he disappears into the room, as if he knows what I'm thinking. Undoubtedly I'm not hard to read at the moment.

When he returns, he's only wearing jeans. Which I guess helps a bit. But those chiseled abs are just as distracting as everything else. "Did you lose all your shirts?" I ask, bundling Rain into a burrito and walking over to the living room crib to let her sleep.

Zev grins. "I'm not a big fan of excess clothing."

"Right." My throat feels suddenly dry, so I head to the kitchen for a glass of water, then go back to the couch to sit down.

Zev joins me and without asking permission, pulls my legs over his lap, forcing me to recline against the sofa. "What are you doing?"

"Giving you what you need," he says, which brings to mind all manner of tempting ideas, none of which involve my feet.

"Is that part of the pledge potion?" I ask. I have no idea how this thing works, so while my question is a bit cheeky it might also be spot on.

"In a way," he answers. "We're committed to respecting your wishes, as a mother and a woman. But, pledge or no pledge, I understand what you've been through and the care you need. And deserve."

He begins massaging my legs. As he works his way up my calf and toward my thigh I give in completely, moaning as his strong hands relieve the tension in my body.

"You've pushed yourself too hard too soon," he reprimands, his voice as much of a caress as his hands. "Rune's potions will help, but you still need your rest."

"I didn't exactly schedule this craziness to come into my life right now." I lose my words for a moment when his fingers dig into a particularly painful spot on my foot.

"By the way," I say, switching gears to a much more pressing topic. "Do you know anything about the Order of the Star?"

I haven't had a chance to ask Darius about his involvement, and since the Sexies have a mysterious shared past, I figure Zev might be able to answer some of my questions.

He frowns, his lips tightening. "Why do you want to know?"

"Okay, sounds like you do know something. Explain.""

"Others will have more information than I do. The Order has a torrid history amongst my race. It was an organization of witches who used their magic to attack my kind, targeting our pups and killing our mates in order to weaken our packs."

"Tell her the whole story," a new voice demands. Darius has appeared out of practically nowhere, and now stands before us, glowering. "The witches organized in order to protect themselves from persecution. From being hunted."

Zev stops rubbing my feet, much to my great sadness, and stands to face Darius, bristling at the interruption. "We weren't the only ones, nor the first, to hunt the witches," he growls.

Rain--disturbed by the men raising their voices--wakes up from her nap screaming, and I scowl at the two of them. "You've already had this fight, and now you've woken the baby. Shame on you both."

I sound like an old school marm, but I don't care. A sleeping infant is not to be messed with.

Zev's demeanor changes in an instant, turning from combative to repentant. He shuffles over, tail between his legs, to change Rain's diaper and try to get her back to sleep. I use the moment to confront Darius.

"Now's the time you explain how, when, and why you met my grandmother," I say, patting the cushion next to me and inviting Darius to sit.

The vampire casts a glance at Zev, who pretends like he's not paying attention, but I know he totally is. Darius takes a seat beside me, close enough for our legs to touch and the recent memories of his gleaming body to flood my brain. His words snap me back to the reality at hand.

"I had business with the Order, before you or your mother were born. That is when I met Tilly. She was a powerful witch--their leader, and we were at war."

"So you were some kind of emissary?" I ask.

He gives a shrug that could mean anything.

"And what did you learn?"

"That they were waiting for the Last Witch to be born as well. The one who would spell the end to all other kinds and return power to the witches."

"Oh good, another power grab," I say dryly. "So their motives are about as pure as all of yours."

Zev grunts, proving he has in fact been listening, and Darius just scowls. "At least we now know who Karl is working with and what they want."

"But we don't know who's leading the Order now," I say. "It's clearly not Tilly."

Darius looks out the window and Zev tilts his head back, staring up in thought. They don't know.

"No, we don't," the vampire says as he lays a hand on my leg.

The touch makes me shiver, and not just from his unnaturally cold skin. Why are all three of these men so good at gentle touches that make me want to be ravaged when there are so many other things I need to be thinking about?

"But if the leader is not from your bloodline," Darius continues, "that's something of concern."

"Why's that?" I ask just as Rune and AJ enter the apartment, finally done closing the bar just after one in the morning. On our best night pre-Sexies, the place would be empty by 10:15.

"Not all witches have the best intentions," the vampire says, a knowing look in his eye. "Outside of your lineage, we can't really know what the Order intends to do with the child."

FOR THE NEXT FEW WEEKS, things fall into a bit of a routine--certainly more routine than the first few chaotic days of Rain's life. AJ moves back to her own house to escape the cramped quarters at my apartment but continues to bartend and incorporate more of Rune's drinks into our regular menu. Darius--much to his eternal consternation--becomes a favorite amongst the locals, and even folks from out of town. He and Zev perform their act nightly now, bringing in tourists from Salem, Boston, and all over to witness their ever-changing show. Rune plays the harp and has talked me into playing piano with him, and I have to admit, the effect is pretty damn magical. Several patrons record us and put us up on instagram, which delights Rune beyond measure for some reason.

And I can't deny, having these hunky paranormals around has made my bar a whole new type of intoxicating.

I thought Rain's arrival would kill Morgan's financially, and the antics that ensued made me sure the business would collapse, but things have turned around drastically. In addition to all of our new female patrons, now that AJ has a grasp of her seductive powers, men who would stop in for a beer after work are now staying for three or four drinks.

Meanwhile, I get to be a mother. I tend to my baby without constantly looking over my shoulder, and I wrap her in a Bjorn and stroll through the bar when I feel like it. I've set up a swing next to the piano and Rune and I play her to sleep while the patrons watch and listen. For fleeting moments, I feel a happiness I haven't experienced in years.

But it's a momentary sensation, clouded by the uncertainty of what isn't happening. Despite our best attempts, we've learned nothing new about the Order of the Star or what Karl was involved in. We don't know who else might be part of this. I'm half expecting sweet old Joe will turn out to be the Devil himself, maybe with plans to burn me alive? At this point, nothing will surprise me.

So when we have yet another week of no new leads, I make a decision. One that won't be popular with anyone.

"I need to see my grandmother again," I announce one afternoon, looking at Darius specifically. "And I want you to come with me."

"Why me?" the vampire asks, setting down the leather bound book he was reading.

"Because you knew Tilly back in the day, and you've got those voodoo mind powers. Maybe you can get through to her. We'll leave Rain at home with Rune and Zev so she'll be safe. And hopefully we can avoid triggering my grandmother into another panic attack."

Darius frowns. "I cannot go out during the day, and there are no visiting hours at night," he reminds me. Like what, did he study the damn brochure?

I smile. "I know. That's why we're going to break in."

CHAPTER SIXTEEN

I'd love to leave right after sunset, but AJ tells me I should wait until after the bar closes so Zev doesn't have to be in wolf form and she's not too busy creating a "lust tornado of nymphiness." Her words, not mine.

So Darius and I plot behind the bar between his dances, deciding how exactly we'll get inside.

"I should go in first," I say, trying to take charge of our strategy. "If anyone's inside, at least I'm a family member and I can make up some story about being worried."

Darius smiles condescendingly, and I realize immediately that my plan is unrealistic. "You understand that we're breaking in, yes? Trying to enter unnoticed."

He makes a very good point. Planning for an encounter with a nurse or a custodian sort of handicaps the whole operation.

"Fine," I say, reluctantly relinquishing my authority. "How do we get in undetected? Without tripping the alarms?"

"Well," Darius says with a casual shrug, "the alarms sense either motion or heat, and since my blood runs cold and I move too quickly, I'll just go inside and disable the system."

Right. The fact that I thought I should take the lead on a heist with a vampire shows my mom brain still isn't firing on all cylinders.

We agree on the strategy and that we'll leave as soon as the bar doors lock, and I decide I'll catch a quick nap before we go. As I start for the stairs, Darius stops me.

"Remember, we've pledged not to take your child without your permission."

"Right. That's why I can leave her while we go." I feel like I've got this, but Darius gives me a look that suggests I'm missing something.

"That's correct," he says, "as long as you don't give permission."

"So, what, I need to just leave her on the floor and walk away?" Either I don't understand what the word permission means, or these paranormal pledge rules are a little vague.

"No," Darius responds, doing a better job than normal at staying patient. "You can hand the child to any of us, as you've been doing. You can say 'play with Rain,' or 'hold my baby.' The only phrase you cannot say, without breaking the pledge, is 'take the child.'"

Take the child. This is good to know, and the type of thing someone might have told me earlier, but maybe each of them was hoping for a slip. So strange to think that these men, now my companions, maybe even friends, definitely objects of many affections, could still turn on me. But it's nice to know they can't do it unless I give them the go-ahead.

"Can I say, 'take the *baby*,'?" My question's half in jest, and yet these semantics seem to have cosmic importance.

Darius nods. "Only the phrase *take the child* will break the bond."

With that, he struts toward the dance floor and I head upstairs, happy to know I have powers--and terrified I might slip up.

AT FIVE PAST MIDNIGHT, Rune carries the last drunk out the door and AJ locks up. I pass her the baby, ensuring I won't misspeak and destroy my life, and head to the car with Darius.

As we buckle in, I realize I'm alone with him for the first time. Yes, we've had moments in one room while everyone else was in another, but now we're in a car, driving away. A few weeks ago I would have accepted this as a death sentence, now I can't help but feel a thrill run through my body. Ever since our shared moment in my room, the chemistry between me and Darius has changed. Less antagonism, lots of sexual tension. It certainly doesn't help that he strips down to almost nothing in the bar night after night.

Darius stares out the window as we drive to Ipswich, taking in the scenery, which I'm sure he can see just fine even though it's dark.

"Does anything look familiar?" I ask, wondering how much time he's actually spent in this area. He's been alive forever, so maybe he's summered in Eastern Mass for eons. Who the hell knows? I realize with a sudden sobriety no matter how much we talk, or how long I end up living with the Sexies, they will always remain mysteries. They have lived longer than I can even imagine. This is nuts.

"Only vaguely," Darius answers, pulling me out of my thoughts. There's a hint of sorrow in his voice that he covers quickly. "A lot has changed since I last visited. Both here and in my world."

He seems a little melancholic, so I leave it at that. Plus, I've got to start steeling my nerves for the crimes I'm about to commit.

There are three other cars in the lot when we arrive, which doesn't seem like a lot. Maybe two nurses and a security guard? Thin staff to care for a building full of invalids. I'm worried for Nanny, but also relieved that our scheme might be easier to pull off than expected.

We pull around to the back and Darius does a quick survey of the building.

"Are you sure about this?" I ask. "They might have a more complex system than you're used to."

He looks at me, the condescension roaring back into his striking eyes. "I've broken into kingdoms protected by magic spells and guarded by dragons."

"Dragons? You're just going to throw that out there willy nilly? Dragons?" But he doesn't respond. He's already out of the car and moving swiftly toward a ladder that leads to a ventilation duct near the roof, leaving me to stew about dragons and unicorns and whatever else might exist that I always thought was fairytale. It's probably safest to assume everything is real, but that might make my brain explode.

I shove my existential crisis to the side as I get out of the car and glance around, not really sure what to do next. Darius has taken full control of the plan, and I'm just along for the ride, which isn't a position I enjoy being in.

It only takes a few seconds before the back emergency exit pops open and he waves me toward him. I jog over, noticing how good my legs feel. I've recovered very quickly from this birth, and if anyone asks me how I did it I'll just say some bullshit like kale smoothies and yoga. Namaste, bitches. Who would believe the truth anyways? I can barely wrap my mind around my current situation, and I'm living it.

As soon as I get inside, I see Darius hasn't gone totally unnoticed--a security guard lies unconscious on the ground by the door.

"I assume this was necessary?" I say in an aggressive whisper.

Darius looks down at the guard and shrugs. "Sometimes an elbow to the temple works more effectively than mind control. Let's go to Tilly."

Before I can show him the way, Darius starts striding down the hall toward her room.

"How do you know where you're going?"

"Magic," is all he responds. At first it seems like he's brushing me off, but then I think about it a little more.

"Your magic? Or hers?"

Darius throws a quick glance over his shoulder, "the latter."

When we get to her door, I'm about to ask how we'll get it unlocked, but my brain catches up fast enough for me to keep my mouth shut. With a flick of his wrist, I hear a soft click and the door pops open. I'm excited to someday learn the extent of his powers, because right now the man feels like a walking cheat code.

With a final look behind us, we tiptoe into Nanny's room. Well, I tiptoe. He just walks in his normal stealth mode.

Enough moonlight spills through the window that we're able to see her bed. Nanny's asleep, but tossing a bit like she's having a bad dream. As I move toward her, Darius stands back by the door.

"Stop," he quietly commands. I do as I'm told, though I can't imagine what his concern is with me getting closer to my grandmother. "She's not well."

I roll my eyes at the obvious statement; *that's why she's in a home, bro.* I realize immediately that my thoughts have been heard, because Darius takes slow steps toward Nanny while explaining the dilemma.

"She's powerfully afflicted. The episodes you've talked about have nothing to do with you or her surroundings, and everything to do with what's going on in her mind."

He arrives at her bedside and kneels, every step taken in silence. Ever so slowly, he reaches up and grasps her hand. The move is done gently, but Darius seems to tense as the two connect, like a shock has gone up his arm.

Seconds later, Nanny's eyes start to flutter open. She looks at the ceiling, then slowly turns to me. After my last visit, I'm terrified at how she might react. Screaming would be bad for our cover, of course, but I assume the vampire could fix those problems. I'm more worried about the emotional damage another episode might cause her and me both.

However, instead of becoming agitated or distressed, my sweet Nanny smiles. It's a smile I haven't seen in years, not since I was a little girl and my mother was alive.

Then she lets her head fall to the other side, facing Darius, and something even more unexpected happens.

"It's you," she says softly, the smile still on her face.

"Hello, Matilda," Darius responds, his voice so full of kindness that unexpected tears spring to my eyes.

It's beyond beautiful, seeing Tilly recognize a face and speak coherent words. At the same time, I just want to scream until everything makes sense. After all these years and so much mental unrest, she recognizes the effing vampire?

"Where am I?" she asks Darius, who's still holding her hand. His jaw is clenched tightly and his muscles are tense, like he's the one in distress.

"In a room that keeps you safe from the outside," Darius answers, "but not safe from yourself."

"Can you take me away?"

The vampire shakes his head, a look of pity etched on his brow. "I can't take you anywhere you'd be better off. Matilda, do you recognize your granddaughter?"

She turns toward me, the warm smile still there, and nods her head.

"Bernie. I'm so sorry."

"What for, Nanny?" I can't imagine what she feels the need to apologize for. The tears I've been holding back begin to spill as I rush to her side, kneeling next to Darius, and only slightly resenting that it's his hand she's holding instead of mine.

"I couldn't save you," Nanny says. "I couldn't save my Lauren, and after I tried, I couldn't save you."

"Save me from what?" When she doesn't respond immediately, I turn to Darius. "Save me from what? What's she talking about?"

He throws me a quick look, and with it a mental warning. *If you want me to learn anything, you'll stay calm.*

I nod, his point well taken, and he gives his attention back to Tilly.

"You've more power than I remember," Darius says, a slight quiver in his voice. "Do you know what changed? What happened to your mind?"

Nanny keeps her eyes on the ceiling, and I see a tear fall down her weathered cheek.

"I thought I could end the line," she says matter-of-factly, her voice clear and strong. "I thought, perhaps, I could be the last one."

I don't understand what's going on, and I can't quite tell if Darius does either. His face looks pained, like he's having this conversation while squatting a thousand pounds.

"Why didn't you know better?" the vampire asks. The question isn't so much scornful, as one filled with regret. A sadness born from whatever my grandmother did.

She turns to him again, the smile coming back, though this time with a mischievous curl in her lip. "Why don't any of us know better, my sweet?"

My *sweet*? That better be some endearing grandmother shit, because I'm not prepared to hear that Nanny and my vamp boy had a thing before I was born.

"Matilda," Darius says, the strain in his voice more pronounced. "The Order is back. Or perhaps never left. We know they want the baby, but we don't know their intention. Without your guidance, I fear they're being misled."

Tilly's smile fades, replaced by a look of concern.

"I know nothing. Leadership came through my bloodline, protection spells from our family books. It... it must be a new--"

Before she can finish her sentence, the door to her room crashes open, shattering the fragile silence.

"Get away from the bed!" screams a male voice.

I look over to see a man dressed in black, his face covered by a hood just like Karl's, only it's not Karl's voice. It's obviously not medical staff, unless they've really changed their methods since last I was here.

"You! Get up. Let go of the woman's hand!" he shouts, holding up a gun and pointing it at Darius.

The vampire raises his left hand, the one not locked with Tilly's, to show he's defenseless. Then he leans in and whispers to my grandma, just loud enough for me to hear.

"This will hurt, and I'm sorry. But you're strong."

With that, he releases her hand and she immediately starts to convulse violently. It's worse than I've ever seen before, and I'm sure her neck is going to snap.

"What did you do?" the man at the door shouts, stealing my question. He makes a move toward Tilly's bed, but as soon as he lifts his leg, Darius waves an arm and sends the man flying through the doorway, crashing against the wall on the opposite side of the hall.

"More will be here soon," Darius says, his voice raspy and his eyes bloodshot. "Follow me through the window."

"I can't leave Nanny. What if they hurt her?"

"They won't," he says as he unlocks and opens the window frame. "If the Order of the Star wanted her dead, she'd be dead."

"That's not as comforting as you might think," I hiss, but I know he's right. We have to get out of here, and we can't take Tilly. I glance once more at my Nanny, my heart breaking that I have to leave her like this. "I'm sorry, Nanny," I whisper, but before I do as Darius says, I dart into the hall, needing whatever answers I can find.

The man he threw against the wall is barely conscious, definitely concussed. As he moans, I lift the ski mask that was covering his face.

It's Alex.

Joe's son.

What the hell?

The sound of footsteps running down the hall forces my hand, and I sprint back through Nanny's room and Darius hoists me through the window. We run around the building, the sound of sirens in the distance and getting closer by the second, and finally reach the car.

There's only one driveway leading away from the facility, and that road's about to be filled with cop cars or Order members. The other option is to drive through the fence in front of me and down a hill. So that's what I do.

I start the engine, leave the lights off, and slam on the gas. We crash through the chainlink and roll into the darkness, just as the lights from the squad cars blink in my rearview mirror.

As my Subaru rolls downhill, I realize I just drove us off a snow-covered slope in the dark. I pump the brakes to no avail, the car still rolling and picking up steam.

"Um, Darius? Think you could…?"

I don't bother finishing the question, assuming his best solution will be better than whatever I could think up.

When he doesn't answer I give a quick sideways glance, and don't love what I see. He's breathing hard and still looking haggard. The one time I decide to rely on his magic, and he's got the flu or something.

"Darius! I know you can't die, but I've still got bones and organs and shit that will not survive when we hit a tree. So WAKE. UP!"

As I yell the last part, I dig my nails into his leg and feel a jolt of electricity shoot through me. It's strong enough to knock me against the car door, my head bumping hard against the window.

I try to shake it off, but my vision is blurred and it's pitch black anyway. Instead of last-minute ideas for how to save us, I've just got pictures of Rain dancing in my head. Her tiny toes, her sweet little nose. Who's going to take care of my baby?

And then my body lurches forward, my sternum slamming painfully against the steering wheel. My eyes are shut and I'm positive we just collided with a huge maple tree. The only reason I'm not feeling intense pain is because I'm already dead.

For a moment, there's nothing but silence. Finally I pry open my eyes, for no other reason than to see what heaven looks like. Or hell, I guess. No point in being presumptuous.

Instead, I see the inside of my car. I look to the side and see Darius, his hands pressed against the dashboard in front of him. He looks at me, his face less pained than before, the beginning of a smile at the corners of his mouth.

When I turn my head again, I can see faintly out the windshield. No more than ten feet in front of us is a crumbling stone wall, one of those old property lines people made with huge boulders in the 1700s. If we had stopped a second later, I'd be dead.

I look back at Darius. "Why'd you wait?!" I yell, the emotion from the near-death experience boiling over. "We... I, almost died!"

He puts his hand on my knee, trying to calm me as he speaks.

"When I clasped hands with your grandmother, I took on the burden of her powers. She has a tremendous amount of magic inside her, that's the reason she's been... the way she's been."

He takes a moment, clearly still recovering from whatever he's trying to describe.

"The longer I held her hand, the stronger it became. Had we stayed in contact a moment longer I might have been knocked unconscious. It took everything I had to disable that man. I barely made it to the car."

"And then...?"

"And then you grabbed me. I'm not sure what you felt, but I felt whatever power that had been constricting me release."

I raise my hand to my head, feeling the knot forming where I bounced off the window.

"I felt something, all right. Guess Nanny's powers almost took us both out."

I smile at Darius, glad he's okay, even more glad I'm alive.

"So I timed it out perfectly, then," I say with a slightly unhinged chuckle. "I screamed and pinched your leg just in time for you to stop the car."

Darius returns the smile, though he also shakes his head--there's still something I'm missing.

"No, Bernie. I didn't stop the car." He looks out at the line of rocks that would have instantly killed me, then returns his focus to my eyes, a new and exciting energy brewing there.

"You did."

CHAPTER SEVENTEEN

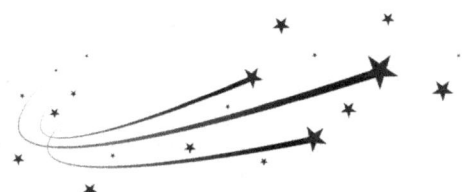

"I'm sorry, I must have hit my head harder than I thought, because it sounded like you said *I* magically stopped our car from killing me and--I don't know--wrinkling your outfit?" My voice carries in it all the disbelief I feel, mixed with an unhealthy dose of adrenaline and raw nerves.

"That is correct," he says, tugging on his jacket. "My clothing is not wrinkled."

I raise an eyebrow. "*That's* your takeaway from this?"

"My takeaway is that a small thread of your grandmother's powers traveled through me and into you, though I do not know how such a thing would be possible." He tightens his lips in annoyance.

"Oh, is that hard for you?" I say, laying the sarcasm on real thick. "Something's out of the ordinary and confusing? Poor little vampire."

He ignores my comment, so I ignore him, and instead I look down at my hands like I just grew them from scratch and they might start spitting out lightning or magic balls any moment. When nothing extraordinary happens, I sigh, a little disappointed. I've never understood in books and movies why the heroine or hero resists when they find out they're special or have magic. Music was what made me special, and I was--and am--grateful for it. Otherwise, I would have been just another small-town girl who ended up married to her high school sweetheart and popping out kids while stealing away every week for a night at the pub.

I close my eyes, letting the painful truth wash over me. If it weren't for the Sexies showing up, that's exactly where my life was headed even with this musical gift I've been cultivating for years. Well, maybe except the part about being married to my high school sweetheart.

How did I end up here? I was on the right path, the path that led out of

Rowley and into the great wide world where all my dreams lived, when I self-sabotaged and ended up right back where I started.

I wouldn't trade Rain for anything, but I wish I could have had her under...smarter circumstances. But then again, aren't these the circumstances that brought these men into my life? Things might be difficult and complicated, but I'm not particularly eager to see them leave, if I'm being honest with myself. Even though that's what will ultimately happen, with or without my baby.

Okay, enough self-loathing. Jesus, a fleeting moment of thinking I was magical and now I want to throw a huge pity party. *Buck up, Bernie.*

I look back at Darius, who's watching me carefully.

"What? Did I grow horns or something?"

He shakes his head. "But you are exhibiting signs of a serious concussion."

"Pft. I'm fine." But even as I say it, I realize I've been slurring my words this whole time, and everything is a bit fuzzy around the edges. The fact that I didn't even notice scares me more than the actual symptoms. "Let's just get back to the bar."

But as I try to start the car, it sputters and dies. "Shit."

"You are in no position to drive. Nor is your vehicle, it would appear."

"Ha, very funny mister. What do you recommend?"

"First, we must heal you. Then, I will carry you home."

My head begins to pound, like the pain was on a temporary leave of absence and is back in full form. I slump against my seat and close my eyes. Just for a moment.

I start awake at the sound of Darius calling my name.

"Shhh... " I hiss, not opening my eyes. "You're making it worse."

"Bernie, you need to look at me."

I really want vamp boy to back the hell off and let me sleep, but then I remember where we are and what just happened and my heart starts thumping aggressively against my rib cage, jolting me back to reality. "Shit. Okay, I'm here. You mentioned healing? Yes, let's do that before I lose it again. Do you have something like Rune's magic elixirs?"

Darius smirks. "Something like that. But it's more... direct from the source."

"Right, well, lay it on me. I'm ready to go home."

I expect the vampire to pull a vial of some glowing shit out of his pocket, like a normal magical dude. Instead, his eye teeth elongate and he brings his wrist up to his mouth and... bites!

"What are you doing?"

He offers me his blood, pulsing out of his vein, like it's a delicacy.

"What am I supposed to do with that?" I ask, my stomach roiling in displeasure.

"Drink. It will heal you."

"Um, no thanks, I'm good. Plan B."

"There is no Plan B, Bernie. This is the plan. The only plan. We need to get you home, but not in your current condition." He stares at me, his dark eyes wide and pleading. "Now, drink."

I feel the compulsion and I smack him without thinking. "Don't you dare mind control me," I hiss. "That is against the rules."

"What rules?" he asks with all the arrogance of an eternal being of beauty and power who's used to getting whatever he wants.

"The rules I put in place. I'm the queen of this castle, and what I say goes."

He narrows his eyes at me. "Fine, then drink before you pass out, you foolish, stubborn woman. Or do you want to leave Rain without her milk source and mother?"

"That's a low blow," I say, but I can't argue with him. Not about that. I would do anything for that little girl. Including, it would seem, sucking on some vampire blood.

Just as I lean in, I pause. "Wait, this won't make me a vampire will it?"

"No. Our transformation ceremony is much more complicated."

"Good," I say. "I'm rather fond of the sun."

Bracing myself for the grossest shit ever, I move my mouth apprehensively toward his bleeding arm, nervous about how his blood will taste, what it will make me feel… and how I'll react to having my lips on his skin.

My mouth reaches the wound and I feel a drop of blood on my tongue. There's not a strong taste to it, maybe a little bitter, but it's thin like water and doesn't have me gagging.

As soon as I swallow, I feel a surge ripple through my body. It's like the feeling of getting goosebumps, but the bumps are in my veins. The rush flows to every part of my body, and as it reaches my head I feel the ache start to fade. Add this to the list of things to sell at the bar: Tylenol capsules filled with vampire blood.

"Do you feel better?" Darius asks, but the tone of his voice shows that he already knows the answer. I realize I must be sucking pretty hard on his wrist, but I can't make myself stop. Every drop makes me feel better and gives me more energy.

Finally, the sexy vampire takes his arm away from my hungry mouth. "Enough," he says with a playful smile. "I need to keep at least a little in my veins."

He starts to pull his sleeve back down, but I notice a drop of blood trickling down his wrist. Before I can stop myself, I lunge at his arm, my tongue flicking out for that last drop of powerful blood.

Our faces are now inches apart. I hold his gaze as I lick my lips, savoring every molecule of his lifeforce. What started as an unappealing proposal has turned into an arousing endeavor, and I'm quite sure Darius feels the same way. Perhaps this was his plan from the beginning.

I'm already so close. I already tasted him.

What's the harm in a little kiss?

No harm at all, he whispers into my mind, and before I can think another thought, our lips are touching, our tongues swirling around each other's. It seems Darius has regained all of his strength since being overwhelmed by witch power, as he reaches around me and pulls our bodies tighter together.

His kisses are forceful but soft, firm but sweet. I run my hands through his pitch-black hair and over his neck, his smooth skin so intoxicating that I just want to touch him everywhere. I bite his earlobe as he moves a hand slowly down my side and then slips it under the waist of the back of my jeans. The feeling of his touch on my bare skin makes me nibble his ear almost too hard, so I move my mouth back to his.

He continues to rub and caress in all the right ways, and I find my hands undoing his pants and dancing my fingers along the top of his silk boxers. I break the kiss so I can look into his eyes as my hand starts to move under the waistband. He returns my stare with a fiery passion, and I know exactly where this "little kiss" is headed. If we weren't in a car, our clothes would be scattered about the room and we'd already be under the sheets.

But we are in my car. My car that won't start. Miles and miles from my home… and my baby.

As much as my body is screaming for this, it's not right. My mind is elsewhere, and that's where my body should be, too. Even if it means I have to stop touching the beautiful man in my arms.

Darius senses my hesitation, and it seems he understands the timing is all wrong. He also probably snuck in and listened to my thoughts.

"You're right," he says, his lips still brushing against mine, my fingertips still inches from their prize. "When we finish this--and make no mistake, we *will* finish this," he says, his voice deep and hypnotic against my ear, "it will not be under such limiting circumstances. I will take my time memorizing every inch of you, playing your body like you play that piano, making you sing for my touch until you are begging uncontrollably."

His words, the thrill of them, the feel of him still pressed against me, does nothing to deescalate the growing need in my body.

And then, as if he knows just how aroused he's made me, he pulls away with a smirk. "In the meantime, I will carry you back."

He starts to retreat, but no way am I letting him get the last word. I pull him back for one last kiss, and as I claim his mouth with mine, I grab his hand and slide it up to my breast until he is arching against me, as full of desire as I am. Then I force myself away and try to put myself back together.

"*Now* your clothes are wrinkled," I say with a wink.

When I emerge from my car, everything feels different. Not only are all my injuries healed, but it's like I've gained extra senses. I can hear a night owl in the distance, its wings ruffling as it hunts its dinner. The sound of snow falling. The breathing of a small critter hiding in a log fifty feet away. It's all overwhelming and I don't know where to focus.

I look to Darius, wide-eyed. "Is this your blood or more of my grandmother's power?"

"My blood," he says, his gaze taking in my disheveled clothing.

Despite the cold, my cheeks heat as I think about how close we got to… everything. How close we will get again if either of us have our way.

Traditionally, it would be a bit too soon to explore these urges after giving birth. But I'm pretty sure the fae magic, vampire blood and… I cringe at the thought, but werewolf hair... have all done their part in getting my body to a better place than it was even before I got pregnant.

"You might notice... other side effects as well," he says, and before I can reply or ask what he means, he literally sweeps me off my feet and into his arms.

There is no chance to talk as Darius begins to run. I would have expected it to be uncomfortable, bouncing around in his arms, but he's so fluid, so graceful, it's like we're flying. The wind blows through my hair, snow collecting in it, but I don't even notice the cold. My body is still hot from within, and with my face tucked in his shoulders and his arms gripping me firmly, it's so very easy to get lost in the fantasies of what we almost did.

By the time we arrive home--which should have taken hours or days, I'm almost disappointed the trip happened so fast. It's just after 2 AM when we walk into the apartment, where Rune, Zev and AJ are waiting in the front room.

One look from AJ and it's clear she knows I had some sexy times with vamp boy. She arches her eyebrow and looks between us in a not-so-subtle way.

Since that wasn't the point of the trip, I ignore her and head straight to Rain, who's happily snuggled in the arms of a werewolf. As I quietly approach my sweet, sleeping girl, Darius fills everyone in on what we discovered.

"Tilly possesses more power than I've ever seen in one witch, and tonight we were confronted by another member of the Order of the Star."

Rain is sleeping, and she looks so peaceful with Zev that I don't want to disturb her; instead I slide onto the couch next to him. He glances at me with a warm smile as Rune brings me a cup of coffee sprinkled with magic--like coffee needs anything extra to make it wonderful. It is the drink of the gods, after all.

"Did they hurt Tilly?" AJ asks, hopping from her chair like she's ready to cut a bitch.

I shrug, my eyes stinging again at the memory of leaving her so vulnerable. "Darius doesn't think they will. But, A, you should have seen her, when Darius held her hand, I got her back. Just for a few moments, but I got Nanny back."

Zev uses his free arm to wrap around my shoulder and pull me into a warm hug, dispelling any remnants of chill from the trip through the snow, and offering me unspoken comfort as I grapple with my emotion.

"And that's not all," I say, before Darius can continue. "You're never going to believe who it was this time." This is obviously directed at AJ, since no one else in the room would specifically care.

"Who?" AJ asks, her eyes widening.

"Joe's son!"

My best friend's jaw drops. "Alex? That's... that's impossible," she sputters.

"I know!" I say, as flabbergasted as she is.

The guys just stare at us, waiting for one of us to make sense.

AJ explains. "Alex was in an accident on prom night years ago. He was in a car crash and flew through the windshield. His brain... it never worked right after that. He's been in a home ever since."

I shake my head. "I don't get it. He seemed... normal, given the circum-stances. But it was definitely him. I checked myself."

AJ begins to pace the room while I snuggle more into the nook of Zev's arms.

He looks down at me, concern in his eyes. "You've had vampire blood. What happened?"

"Oh yeah, that's the other thing. I wrecked the car. Hit my head. Darius healed me."

A growl forms deep in Zev's chest. "I'm sure he did."

Darius scowls at the werewolf. "It was that or let her pass out and suffer worse injury. What would you have me do?"

"Not bind her to you," he says gruffly.

Rune comes over and lays a finger on my wrist, while staring into my eyes, then nods. "Darius did the right thing. It could have been much worse if he hadn't acted quickly."

This shuts Zev up, but I can feel the tension in his body. The werewolf is definitely pissed, and now I have a lot of questions about this binding shit.

But Rain has clearly not enjoyed the change in Zev, and she wakes up screaming and ready for her midnight snack. The werewolf's demeanor changes instantly, cooing and loving on her as he passes her to me. It's really incredible to see how each of the Sexies are with my baby. All their bad boy bravado shuts down when my little one is around. She's got them wrapped around her tiny, adorable, little finger.

I take her into my bedroom and close the door, wanting some privacy for myself and knowing Rain could use less stimulation right now. You could cut the tension in the living room with a knife.

I ease into my bed and cuddle my child as she feeds, my mind worrying over all the different threads in my life that seem to be unraveling. I want to get Darius back in to see Nanny, but that seems risky after the ruckus we've made. Even if Darius doesn't come with, I need to check in on Nanny to make sure she's okay. I also need to get my car back. And...I'm going to need to talk to Joe and find out what the hell is going on with his son.

Determined to do just that, I fall asleep with Rain in my arms and am ready the next day to confront a man I've known literally my entire life.

Only catch is, he doesn't show up to Morgan's that night.

Or the next.

Or the next.

I ask Frank about it, but Frank is as perplexed as me, saying he hasn't heard from Joe in days.

By the end of the week, I've called to make sure Nanny is safe: she is. Though the staff gives me very few details about 'an incident' that disrupted her. I also know something is definitely off with Joe. At the close of the night, I pull the Sexies aside and voice my concern. "I think something happened to Joe. We need to go check on him and find out what's going on."

Leaving the baby with AJ and Rune, Zev, Darius and I head to Joe's. One of the Sexies managed to bring back my car, but Darius determined it was a waste of metal and somehow acquired me a brand new Jaguar.

"You realize you've painted a big red target on me with this, right?"

Darius sniffs. "You can just tell people it is mine, if you must."

Zev snorts in the back. "Darius has always been a bit pompous. He can't help it."

"You know, when AJ and I were little and would get into fights, Nanny would lock us in the bathroom together until we resolved our differences," I say, turning onto Joe's street. I park in front of his house and twist to face both of them. "We would 'pretend' to make up, and we thought we were so clever, but of course in the process of negotiating our fake peace, we actually made up in the end. I'm thinking you three need some quality time in the bathroom together. Seems like you were close once upon a time, and I think you could be again. You have a lot in common." I wink and get out of the car, with the boys following.

We approach the house cautiously, but we don't get far before both Darius and Zev stop and look at each other, their faces unreadable.

"What?" I ask, walking to stand between them.

Zev glances at me. "I'm so sorry, Bernie."

The werewolf just stops there, leaving Darius to finish his thought.

"Joe's dead."

CHAPTER EIGHTEEN

I stand in stunned silence staring at the house AJ and I had visited many times as teenagers, back when AJ and Alex dated. Before John came along and before Alex's accident. It wasn't something I ever talked about with Joe or my grandparents, what happened that night. Michael and I went to the prom with AJ and Alex, but Alex got too drunk and none of us were willing to drive with him, so he left alone. And then he crashed.

It's a night that weighed heavy on all of us. I always thought it was part of the reason Michael broke up with me. Now I know better, but still.

Emotion clogs my throat and my eyes pool with unshed tears as Darius and Zev each take one of my hands. They don't speak, and they don't demand anything from me. They just stand by my side, holding my pain in the silence.

After several minutes, a tear finally escapes and falls down my cheek. Darius turns to face me, using his free hand to catch the tear with the pad of his thumb.

It takes me a moment before I can speak. "H--how?"

"We'll find out," Darius swears.

I nod and release their hands, missing the contact instantly--the cold touch of the vampire and the heat of the werewolf, but I know they can't get me answers if they're tied to my side.

Crossing my arms over my chest to ward off a chill, I watch as Zev sheds his clothes and shifts into wolf form, then sniffs around the perimeter of the house. Darius dashes toward the side door with his impossible speed and is inside before I can blink.

Nothing makes sense in my world anymore, so logically I know Joe could've been evil or mixed up in some dark magic, but my gut says otherwise. Maybe Alex did recover from permanent brain damage, and maybe my ex is a unicorn and my best friend's a nymph and I'm from a line of witches. But it'll take a lot more than that to convince me Joe is anything but good. He was always so sweet, looking out for Tilly while she still lived at home, then taking care of Ed once he was alone. And then he took care of me.

Even if Darius and Zev come back and tell me he was part of this ridiculous Order and he got killed for not stealing my baby when he was supposed to, I'm not ready to believe them. Some people are still good. Not everyone is tricking me with magic and lying about their past. Joe's on the right side of this, I'm certain.

Zev returns first, shifting back into human form and standing naked on Joe's front lawn. Darius arrives a moment later as Zev is getting back into his pants and shirt. I'm just hoping none of Joe's neighbors are watching us. If so, they just got an eyeful.

Now clothed, Zev steps over to me. "I'm so sorry, Bernie," he says as he pulls me into a hug.

"What happened?" I ask, hoping they'll say it was natural causes, but knowing they won't. Nothing is natural in my world anymore.

Darius answers first. "I can't say. He's seated at the dining room table, a glass of water by his hand. No blood, no sign of struggle."

Zev nods, stepping away from me but keeping his hands on my shoulders. "The smell works with our timeline. He's been dead for four days, five at the most. I will say..." He pauses mid-sentence, taking a long, full breath, then slowly breathing out. "Bernie, do you know Joe's wife?"

I shake my head. "I *knew* her, past tense. She died a couple years back."

Darius and Zev share a look.

"What do you smell?" the vampire asks.

"I don't know," Zev answers. "But it's not a scent that should be here. Not if Joe's wife really died two years ago. Not if he's been living alone."

"How... how the hell do you smell that?" I probably sound angrier than I am, but I take so many impossible outcomes as fact these days that I just need a little piece of logic to hold onto.

The werewolf frowns, bringing me in for another hug and whispering the answer in my ear. "The same way I smell your fear and your sorrow. And the many other things you feel."

His answer doesn't really have a science behind it, but it'll have to do for now. It also makes me a little bashful, knowing that not only can the vampire hear my thoughts but the wolf can smell my feelings. Not a lot of privacy around a group of men who make me think and feel the types of things I'd rather keep secret.

I pull out of Zev's arms and take a deep breath, trying to steady myself and think clearly. "What do we do? About Joe?"

The question brings a steady flow of tears, as the reality of his death starts to sink in. Darius steps forward, putting a hand on my shoulder and softly running it down to my elbow.

"Anything we do will only bring attention to us, and there's already too many watching."

"But we can't just leave him there. I'll call the police, or an ambulance..."

I start to pull my phone from my pocket, but Darius stops me. "Make that call, but not while we're here. We need to be back with Rain. I'm more convinced of that now than ever."

My phone is in my hand, and I have half a mind to ignore Darius even though he's probably right. Joe just deserves so much better. He's a stone's throw away, lying dead at his table, and I'm just going to leave?

I nod, acquiescing to the vampire's point. As I look down, I notice I have a new text message.

It's from AJ. Two minutes ago.

And it just says, *Help.*

THE INSTANT I show the message to Darius, I'm in his arms and we're bounding through the woods of Rowley. Joe lives just a few blocks from Morgan's, and clearly this vampire thinks it will be quicker to leap over fences and barrel through snow banks than take my fancy new ride. Zev follows close behind, once again in wolf form, sprinting on all fours.

Darius comes to a stop when we get close to Morgan's, waiting two seconds for Zev to catch up. I watch the two of them make eye contact, surely discussing an unspoken plan, and then Zev darts off into the shadows. Before I can ask where he's going, which, like an idiot, I was about to do, Darius whispers into my mind.

We mustn't speak. Zev's going to check the perimeter to make sure we're not being lured into a trap. Then we'll follow him inside.

I think some sort of affirmation, probably just the phrase "uh-huh," and then hold my breath while I wait for Zev to lead us in. My baby's in there, and while I take the slightest bit of comfort in knowing Rune's nearby, I'm starting to think that there's a limit to the powers my Sexies possess.

There, Darius mind-speaks, and I follow his gaze to the roof where the wolf now stands. *Hold tightly to my neck.*

I wrap my arms around him as firmly as I can and a rush of wind hits my face as Darius takes three huge steps and then leaps into the sky. I guess he's jumping, but I feel like springing from the ground to the top of a two-story building is more like flying. And just as impressive as him going airborne is the silence with which he lands. Dude is high level stealth mode.

Zev gestures us forward, leading us toward the roof above the bathroom. As he nears the edge, he shifts back from a wolf to a naked human. The cold doesn't seem to bother him. It also doesn't affect him in the ways it might affect other men, I can't help but notice.

"The baby is in the bedroom," Zev says in a whisper, not nearly as aware as I am of his nudity. "I'm guessing she's being concealed by Rune. There are at least four bodies in the front room, though I can't hear all their movements because… well, because AJ won't stop talking. She seems very angry."

I bet she is. But whatever rage she's dishing out now, it's going to look like a soft rap on the knuckles compared to the fury I'll unleash.

"Darius, go in first," Zev continues. "Careful of any energies you feel--I'm not sure what's Rune's magic and what's not."

"I'll know," Darius says in a deathly serious tone, then he quickly vanishes over the edge of the roof.

I shiver, glad I'm not on the receiving end of him when he's angry.

Zev turns to me. "We need to get inside, but I want you to stay in the bathroom."

"Not a chance," I hiss with as much quiet rage as I can. "I need to find my baby."

"You won't be able to see her," Zev says. "I'm sure Rune took every precaution, and now you need to do the same. You're too important, Bernie. Please do as I ask." His forest green eyes, practically aglow in the moonlight, plead with me.

I give the slightest nod, knowing he's right, but not trusting myself to heed his advice. I've said before that I'll die for my child, and I don't think anyone can talk me out of that.

Zev takes me under an arm, then uses his free hand to lower us down to the window that Darius left open. I can't imagine the strength it would take to hold two adult bodies with one arm, but I suppose his strength is as magical as all the other magical shit that's taken over my life.

Once in the bathroom, he returns to wolf form and creeps to the door, listening to whatever sounds are coming from the bedroom. He's probably trying to hear movements and smell feelings or some shit, because the dialogue is plenty audible from where I'm standing even with my bullshit human hearing. Mostly because of AJ.

"I don't care, Alex!" my friend yells. "There's nothing you could say that would make me give two shits about our past, because what you're doing is wrong. Now get this goddamn blindfold off of me!"

"How can you trust these guys and not me, AJ?" Alex sounds serious.

"How can I... you pretended to have brain damage for ten years!" AJ makes a really good point.

"I wasn't pretending, I was... look, you don't understand, and you're not--"

"Alex, stop." Another voice enters the conversation, this one a woman's. She sounds familiar, but I can't place her.

"We don't have time to debate these issues," the woman continues. "I've come for the child, and I'm not going to waste time trying to convince you."

"You sound familiar," AJ says, mirroring my own thoughts. The voice has a nostalgic quality. Like a high school teacher or someone I once knew long ago. Chances are pretty strong that's who it is. AJ and I definitely called Ms. Day a witch all the time; maybe the reason she got so mad is because we were right.

The voice ignores AJ entirely and speaks directly to Rune. "Fae, you're running out of options. I've got plenty of spells left to try, and sooner or later you'll lose consciousness and any mystique you've created will vanish."

Jesus. I can't tell what's going on, but it appears Rune doesn't have the upper hand. Whatever he did to help hide Rain seems to have put him in a bind. Zev's hackles are up, and his left paw is raised, like a hunting dog ready to strike. But where the hell is Darius?

I hear Rune clear his throat before speaking. "Like you said, Witch, we're not debating anything. Please, continue with your spells." His voice is extremely strained, even if he's still putting up a verbal fight. I can only imagine what's been done to make such a strong man suffer so much. I wish I could do something to help him, but I know I'm way out of my depth.

"Very well," the voice says with a trace of disappointment. God, she sounds more familiar with every word. *Who is she?*

I hear the clinking of some glass, maybe a spoon hitting the edges of a cup as it stirs. "Would you like to drink this one on your own, Fae? Or shall I pour it in your eye like the last?"

Before Rune can respond--or not respond, depending on how he prefers his torturing--Alex speaks up.

"Hey, we might have a problem."

"What?" the mystery woman asks sharply.

"I, um… I just looked at AJ's phone." Alex fumbles his words, sounding pretty nervous, just like the guy I remember from high school. "She… she sent a text to Bernie before I took it away, I guess."

After a second of silence, I hear a loud slap.

"Ow! Goddammit, that hurt!" Alex screams, obviously on the receiving end of a smack across the face.

"Did it?" the woman asks. "Because if that hurts, you're not going to enjoy being ripped apart by a werewolf at all."

"You certainly won't."

Darius has joined the mix, probably appearing out of nowhere in his annoying way, which I swear I will never reprimand him for again if he can get us out of this mess.

His arrival seems to put a temporary halt on conversation as fighting ensues.

I hear crash after crash and loud growls from Zev, who sped out of the bath-room without me even noticing.

"Hold on, Rune!" Darius says. I don't know what he's asking the fae to hold on to, but the fear in the vampire's voice is tangible and makes my own fear that much stronger.

Snapping myself out of panic mode, I scan the bathroom, searching for any sign of Rain or a weapon I can use, anything to make myself useful. Maybe this is my chance to sneak into the bedroom and try to find my baby.

I feel the urge to help, to do something more proactive than just sit on my ass like a damsel in distress. I want to help Rune, or distract the attackers so Zev can maul them or Darius snap their spines. But more than that, I want to find my baby.

I creep toward the door, trying to be wary of the fight that's going on while staying under the radar. Peering down the hallway, I see a whirlwind of activity. Chairs crash against the wall, flashes of light scorch my plants, and AJ lies slumped against the floor, a blindfold tied around her eyes. I'm about to throw caution to the wind and rush to help when I see her push herself up.

"Rune!" Darius sounds more anxious this time, causing my anxiety levels to spike as well. How dire is the situation out there? Is Rune going to die? Where the hell is he?

But before I can worry about the guys, I need to find Rain. I take a deep breath and slink down the hallway toward the bedroom, hoping I can turn the corner into my room before someone grabs me.

I make it through and close the door quietly behind me, leaning against it while I reach behind my back to turn the lock. I search the room, starting with the crib and moving over to my bed, hoping a mother's intuition will help me find a baby that's shrouded in a magical illusion.

As I fumble around checking the most obvious and oddball places for a baby, I hear a soft cry. It doesn't sound like she's in distress, but it still makes me that much more panicked about finding her. I move more slowly, listening as hard as I can, inching closer to the source of the whimpers...

And then the world goes dark.

I can't see anything, and sounds are muffled.

My first guess is that the lights went out. My second is that I've been knocked out. My third is that a bag's been put over my head.

When I try to lift my hands up to my face, someone with an iron grip grabs my wrists and thrusts them behind my back, binding them with something warm. It ties too fast for a normal rope but doesn't hurt like a zip tie. Before I can guess what's holding me in place, I'm hoisted over someone's shoulder and carried toward the back wall. I'm helpless with no hands or vision, and I can only scream as I feel myself falling out the window and through the cold night air.

I DON'T HAVE a clue where I am when I come to. It's still dark, my hands are still tied behind my back, and I'm shivering from cold.

At first I panic, trying to fight out of my tethers and shake off whatever's covering my head. All that does is fill my hood with noise and make me less aware of my surroundings, so I stop. I take a few deep breaths, then try my best to be still and listen.

There's the sound of a fire crackling nearby. Not close enough for me to feel its warmth, but not too far away. There are also voices--soft and distant, but loud enough to make it through whatever fabric covers my ears.

Another sound cuts through it all. The same sound that rose above the chaos in my apartment. Rain is crying.

As I listen, her tiny voice gets closer, as do the voices of others, along with the sound of footsteps crunching in the snow. My heart races as I prepare for the people, witches, or monsters that are coming my way. To kill me? Maybe. To kill my baby? That's the only thing that worries me.

I feel a body come close, stopping right beside me. Suddenly, the hood over my head gets ripped off, and cold air hits my face. The distant fire provides the only light, and I blink my blindness away, allowing my eyes to focus. The first thing I see is trees everywhere, branches heavy with the recent snowfall, the ground covered by a fresh layer. I can't hear or see any signs of city life. We must be deep in the woods.

Whoever lifted my hood steps behind me and unties my wrists. Moments later another captor passes me Rain. I cry through a painfully dry throat and pull her close, trying to give her every ounce of warmth in my body, doing whatever I can to protect her and make her feel safe. My touch seems to settle her a little, which in turn calms my nerves the slightest bit.

"Beautiful."

I hear that same voice, the familiar woman from my apartment, though now she sounds soft and nurturing. I look up to find the source of the sound, and see a cloaked figure a few paces away. She's outlined by the fire in the background, so I can't see anything except her profile.

"She's absolutely beautiful," the woman says again.

Who the hell is this? Who kidnaps a mother and child, only to tell the bound-up mom how pretty her baby is?

The figure steps closer until she's right next to me, and as the moonlight illuminates her face, I finally get to see her.

"I'm so proud of you," she says as she kneels down and touches my cheek.

It takes another moment before I can place her, because it's been almost twenty years... but that smile. Those eyes. That voice. The small scar on her forehead that I used to run my finger over.

I'm staring into the face of my dead mother.

CHAPTER NINETEEN

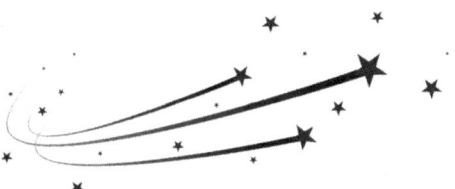

"...Mom?" My voice catches on the word. Is this a trick? Some kind of magical illusion making me see things that couldn't possibly be here? My mom is dead, and therefore this can't be real.

An icy numbness burrows into my heart, steeling me against unwanted emotions. My entire adult life has been defined by the day I lost my mother. A part of me died with her, as I shut myself off from feeling the type of love that could lead to that type of loss. More than one therapist tied her death to me seeking companionship with unavailable or inappropriate men, like my music professor. Her death crushed me in a way nothing else ever would or could.

But now she's here. And I don't know what to feel.

"Hi, Sunshine," she whispers, tears rolling down her cheeks and coming to rest on her smiling lips.

Sunshine. She always called me Sunshine, and I haven't heard that nickname since. I wonder how much that word, stuck deep in the recesses of my psyche, led me to name my daughter Rain. Like somehow the opposite word would lead to the opposite outcome. I squeeze my baby a little tighter, needing her for emotional support right now far more than she needs me.

My mom looks from me to the baby, a grandmother's love radiating off her face. She doesn't move to touch Rain, probably because she knows my guard is still way up. If she was hoping for a joyful mother-daughter reunion, she picked the wrong way to go about it.

"How?" I ask, choosing the only question I can give voice to right now. A deep hurt in my chest is threatening to crash over me, and I have to keep it at bay if I want to get through this.

"Come, join me by the fire," she says, extending a hand to help me up. "I'll tell you everything, but I also need to prepare you for what's to come. You're still in danger."

Yeah, no shit. I'm surrounded by the people who have been trying to steal my baby.

Seeing no other choice if I want answers, I stand and follow, my gaze taking in everything I can as I try to figure out where I am and who I'm with. About a dozen figures cloaked in dark robes form a circle around us, pretty much exactly what you'd expect a creepy cult to do. Their faces are cast in shadows from their hoods, and none of them move. They could be statues for how still they are, but I wouldn't bet on it. My guess is they are armed, with magic and weapons. Whatever they're packing, they're no doubt ready to intervene if I go off-script. I clutch Rain harder to my chest, then ease off when I realize I'm about to wake her. My skin thrums with the power in this place, and I suddenly feel desperately alone.

I try to quiet the sound of my heart pounding in my head and reach for that small strand that still connects me to Darius. Will he feel where I am? Will he know I'm in danger? Try as I might, I can no longer sense him tethered to me, and this breaks me almost more than anything else has. That sense of loneliness is now completely consuming.

With hesitant steps, I join my mother by the fire. My uneasiness is at war with another, deeper part of myself--the child in me who recognizes with longing the way my mother walks as if her feet barely touch the ground; the way she flicks her wrists like a ballerina, so graceful and lithe. She had been a dancer once upon a time, and though she mostly abandoned her studio sessions when I came along, my fondest memories are of us dancing together in the kitchen while baking banana bread.

I study the woman before me now, and I see that same grace, that same easy fluidity, and I know that part of my mother couldn't possibly be faked. Which makes all of this so much harder. While I'm desperately clinging to my fear to keep me alive, I'm also trying hard not to fall into that safety net she always provided. It's a dichotomy I don't know how to justify within myself, and I'm torn apart by it. Once I'm close enough to the flames to feel their warmth penetrating the cold that has sunk into my bones, I look for a place to sit. My legs feel unstable, whether from exhaustion or from the recent revelations I'm not sure. As I search for a stump or a log, I hear my mother speak in a slightly affected tone.

"*Lángol.*"

I look her way just as she finishes waving a wand--like, an actual witch's wand, and suddenly two flames leap from the fire, turning a radiant blue as they split from their source, one landing behind each of us. I jump a little, afraid of getting burned--since that's what fire does. Meanwhile, my mother sits back into the blue flames beneath her, and the fire expands around her body like a really bizarre bean bag chair.

"Go ahead, Bernie," she says in her soothing tone. "It's safe."

Safe is debatable, but I'm curious despite myself. I inch closer to the blaze, noticing that it's warm but not painfully hot. I ease my body down and feel a resistance come up to meet me. It molds around my body like a cushion, and just like that, I'm relaxing in a fire chair. Well, relaxing may be too strong a word, but tensely sitting for sure.

I have plenty of questions about the seat she just conjured, and my mom must notice because she starts to explain.

"Fire is one of the greatest tools for a witch," she says. "It's part of the reason we've been able to survive despite--"

"Why are you after my baby?" I ask, cutting her off.

As much as I want--and need--to know what she is and where she's been all these years if not dead, my most immediate concern is keeping Rain safe.

My mom just shakes her head, a pained look in her eyes and a quiver in her lip. "To save you, sweetheart. We've been trying to save you."

She seems entirely earnest, but things haven't been as they seem for quite some time. Recent events have primed me to stay skeptical of everyone, and that definitely includes my dead mother.

"I don't understand." I really don't. I don't know what to ask, because I'm too overwhelmed. Too many questions are crowding my thoughts to pick just one.

"I know, Sunshine. There's no way you could. Even after I explain, there will still be parts that don't make sense, but I'll do my best to ease your mind." My mom takes a moment to compose herself, wiping away some tears and dabbing a handkerchief under her nose. In the most extreme, unnatural circumstances, she's still kind of normal. Like a regular mom, sitting in a chair made of fire after pulling off a supernatural kidnapping. Someone sign us up for our reality TV show, stat.

"You might never trust me," she says. "I accept that, and part of me expects it. But I won't stop trying to save you, and hopefully, you'll come to under-stand..." she pauses again, her voice cracking with emotion. "You'll come to understand that everything I've done is because I love you. More than anything."

I want to believe her, almost as much as she wants to be believed. She sounds so sincere. Her tears, the emotion straining her voice, the look of love she gives me that's so reminiscent of my memories of her. It's almost too perfect. Too much like a movie scene. Either I've become jaded, or I'm missing something here. Still, the child in me wants more than anything to trust what she says, because the alternative might just break me.

She leans forward, her gaze locked on mine, her words earnest as she contin-ues. "I found out I was a witch on my twelfth birthday, which is the year most girls' powers manifest. I fought it for a long time, not wanting to believe I was different. You know how it is at that age. You just want to fit in. Then I went through a rebellious phase, discovering all the worst uses for my powers and--"

"And what does this have to do with me?" I ask sharply, leaning forward with Rain held firmly in my arms. "With what's happening now? Kidnapping me and my child?" I really do want to hear my mother's life's story, but there's a time and a place. This is neither.

"Everything changed when you were born, Bernie," she says quickly. "I'm not trying to ramble on about my past, but I think you understand how becoming a mother upends your world. And you're starting to understand how much crazier it is when you know magic exists, for better and for worse."

Her words give me pause as I realize my estranged mother and I have something very much in common. *Well-played, mom.*

"Nanny filled me in on the prophecy after you were born, and I briefly lost my shit on her for waiting until I'd had a child to drop that bombshell." It's nice to hear mom sounding a little like me. "But once I cooled down, I knew what I had to do. I went all in. I wanted to master my powers, to harness my capabilities, all so I could protect you. And then…"

My breath catches, knowing she's about to talk about the day she died. Or, rather, didn't die.

"I still didn't really understand my magic, but I knew that I was part of this prophecy, and so were you, and it was too much to bear. I didn't want you to suffer the way I and your nanny had."

"So to ease my suffering you faked your own death?" I ask bitterly, on the verge of losing the battle to control my sorrow and anger.

She shakes her head. "I tried to cast a spell, just before you turned twelve. I wanted to protect you. I just… I wanted you to be safe forever."

"What happened?"

"I almost killed you," she says, wiping away more tears wetting her cheeks. "I put my baby girl in a coma. Nanny had to pull out some deep, dark magic to bring you back."

"Wait, when I was eleven? I don't remember any of this." Even if I didn't remember the coma, wouldn't I have at least remembered all the magic spell stuff leading up to it? Wouldn't I have any memory of missing school? Wouldn't AJ remember something this big?

"Tilly took care of your memories," she says.

"What about school? Friends? AJ?" I ask, shaken to the core that my kind old Nanny messed with my brain.

"It was summertime, and Nanny handled the rest."

The rest being AJ. Jesus, what kind of family do I belong to?

My mom continues, seemingly oblivious to my own horror at learning all this. "She tried to tell me it was okay, that you would be okay and I should forgive myself, but I couldn't. I couldn't look at you after what I'd done. So…" she forms a fist with her hand like she's trying to hold in all the pain as she speaks. "I decided you would be safer without me. I chose to end my life."

I exhale, letting out a breath I didn't know I was holding. "Except you didn't," I point out.

"I tried," my mom says, sounding even more remorseful than before. "I threw myself off a cliff into the ocean."

I shiver as the memories I keep carefully suppressed come rushing back. Finding her suicide note. Searching the shoreline for her body. Friends with fishing boats patrolling the coastline day and night. Her body was never found. She was presumed dead. After all, how could anyone live through that fall?

"How did you survive?" I ask. "And where have you been all these years?"

She sighs and looks away, her gaze lost in the darkness of the surrounding trees. "I woke up here, in this very forest, staring into my mother's face."

That's actually something I can imagine quite readily, though her circumstances were a bit different. "So what, this is like some weird recreation reunion for you?"

"No. But I wanted you to understand why I did what I did. Why Nanny did what she did."

My heart skips a beat. "What did Nanny do?"

My mother stands and approaches me, then kneels down and takes one of my hands into hers. "She stole your magic to bring me back from the dead."

My throat goes dry and a cold sweat covers my skin as I yank my hand from hers. "What do you mean, stole my magic?"

"I didn't want her to. I never meant for any of this to happen. I didn't consider what it would do to a mother to lose her child. She snapped, even before she absorbed too much power. The grief turned her into someone else." My mother rocks back on her heels, her eyes, the same deep blue as my own, locked on mine. "She used dark magic, blood magic, to pull your power from you and then harnessed it to find my body and bring me back. When I woke up in this forest, I was yanked from the afterlife. The use of that much power made her crazy."

"That's why she lost her mind? Why she's in the hospital now?"

My mother nods. "It is. Magic. Power. It isn't natural. It's always been a curse, causing more problems than it solves. And those monsters who are living with you, they are born of the oldest magic, and they are using you, and your daughter, to empower their own races."

"I already know what they want," I say, impatiently. "I know why they came. But it's more complicated than that."

I think back to all the shared moments, the private conversations, the memories I've already made with each of them. Complicated definitely describes my current relationship status.

My mother smiles sadly, then stands and waves her wand over the fire. The golden-red flames turn blue, like our magic chairs, and begin to dance against the night sky, forming shapes that tell a story.

"They told you what they wanted you to know. They used their powers of mental manipulation and seduction on you."

As I watch, I see scenes played out from my life with Darius, Rune and Zev. Private moments none other were privy to.

"Did they tell you what they will do with the child, once they have her?" she asks, the form of a baby appearing in the flames.

"They need her to save their people," I say softly, feeling sick to my stomach.

"That much is true," my mom says. "But there's much more to it than that." With another flick of her wand, the flames change shapes once more. "Each race believes they understand the prophecy of the Last Witch. And each believes they know what must be done to save the magic flowing in their veins, giving life to their race."

A wolf appears in the flames, several wolves, in fact, surrounding the baby laying on the ground. The wolves then descend upon the child, ripping it apart. I turn my head from the gruesome scene, but cannot erase it from my mind.

"The wolves would eat her, consuming her flesh and bones in order to take in her magic and save themselves."

I glance back at the flames as they shift again, this time to the fae, who lay the baby in a hole dug in the ground. "The fae would put her to earth, burying her alive so that her blood, bones, and final breath can become part of the nature they worship, so that she will become one with the Great Tree and give them their lives and magic back."

I clutch Rain tighter to my chest. "Stop this," I whisper, anger and fear and disgust boiling in me.

"You must see the truth, my daughter. You must know, otherwise, I cannot save you."

The flames dance again, this time bringing forth the vampires. The baby in the fire is strapped to an altar, her blood drained as the vampires feed on her. My mother doesn't need to explain this one. It's all too clear.

She circles her wand a final time and the flames die down, turning back to their normal color. "You see? They've been using you. They don't care about you or the child, only their own immortal selves. They were never meant to exist. Not in the world of humans. Not anywhere. They are aberrations and they must never get their hands on the Last Witch. We must keep Rain safe, for her sake and for the sake of all of humanity."

"So you've been trying to kidnap her to keep her safe?" I ask.

My mom smiles, relief in her eyes. "Yes. Exactly!"

"And what about Joe? Why did you kill him?"

She flinches. "That was out of my control. Joe found out about Alex, and he…"

She drifts off but I press on, needing info faster than she seems prepared to give it.

"And Nanny? Why send Order members to her room?"

"To keep her safe," she says. "The Order has been watching over Nanny since her mind went, trying to keep other creatures away from the powers stored in that frail body. Like that vampire who nearly killed her before Alex arrived."

Except… that's not what happened. Nanny had been relieved to see him. Happy. Or was that just what Darius wanted me to see?

I rub my temples, a massive headache forming. I don't know what's real and what's not. Who to trust and who to fight.

"Then why not come to me yourself earlier? Why all the theatrics? You put me and Rain at risk."

My mother sinks back into her fire chair, looking slightly defeated. "I wanted to. Sunshine, I've wanted to come see you every day since I disappeared. Being so close and yet so far has made life almost unbearable. But how could I explain myself? How could I tell you anything and still keep you safe? I wish I got to you before those monsters did, and now I'm trying to fix this, I swear it."

I close my eyes, squeezing through tears as I try to find the truth in my heart, when a voice invades my mind.

Bernie, do not trust her. It's not what it seems. I'm coming to save you both.

My breath hitches. *Darius.*

CHAPTER TWENTY

D*on't move.*
   Darius' final command makes me hold my breath and my eyes go wide. The reaction is not lost on my mother.

"What is it, Bernie?" She leans in, inspecting me, clearly on high alert. I don't know if she senses something, or if she's just constantly on edge because she lives in a secret society in the woods.

"I'm... I'm afraid, mom." I decide not to mention the voice in my head, because I still don't know who to trust. The only thing I can think to do is keep this conversation going and hope the truth appears in big, flashing, neon lights.

"I'm afraid of everyone. Including you."

Probably not what a mom wants to hear from her daughter, but she takes it in stride.

"Of course you are. I lied to you and broke your trust, and I don't expect to fix that just by showing my face. I only hope you take it better than Joe did when he saw Betty."

And the hits just keep on coming.

"Betty? His wife who died from cancer, whose funeral I went to?" I mean, has anyone ever actually died? And like... stayed dead?

Mom nods. "She's here. She's a witch."

As shocking as that is, I'm more heartbroken for Joe.

"And Joe found out?"

"About her, and about Alex," my mom says. "Betty worked for years on a spell that would bring her son's mind back, and it was finally a success. But the deception and the loss--and the knowledge that his wife was a witch, it was too much for Joe."

Of course it was. Sweet old man stopped caring about anything except beer these last two years, and to then find out he didn't have to go through that agony? That his wife chose to leave him? No matter what her reasoning, that's a pill not a lot of people could swallow without choking.

"Why?" I ask. "Why'd she have to leave, or pretend to die?"

My mother looks into the distance, searching for the words that might make me understand. Open-minded as I'm trying to be, I doubt she'll find them.

"It's too much to explain in one conversation, Sunshine. That might sound like a cop-out, but there's a long history of witches that makes everything--"

"Yeah, I know the history," I interrupt.

"Well," she says, doubt heavy in her voice, "you know the history as told by the races that have been killing us for generations."

It's a fair point, though it's not like Darius, Zev and Rune minced words. None of them painted the treatment of witches in a flattering light. God, how is it that it feels like everyone on both sides of this argument is telling the truth and lying to me at the same time?

I want to ask more questions, about Betty, Alex, Mom--shit, I haven't even thought to ask about the father I never met, who was almost undoubtedly a minotaur or talking fish. However, all questions will have to wait, as a deep red glow ignites in the sky above us, accompanied by a low, bone-rattling hum.

Every member of The Order is on guard, and my mom is out of her chair the moment it happens.

"Where's the breach?" she yells to no one in particular. "Are they inside the field?"

A younger woman who I don't recognize runs over, her fiery red hair flying behind as her hood falls to her back. She speaks with some sort of accent, one I can't place except to say the girl ain't from Mass.

"Someone crossed the river basin," she explains, her words rushed and breath short. "Non human. Three."

My hopes rise as I realize all three Sexies are coming for me, but they fall just as quickly. Are they coming for me *and* my baby, or just my baby?

"Arm yourselves and take your posts!" my mother yells, transitioning from chill witch mom to intimidating general in an instant. "There's a vampire in the woods, so don't show any hesitation."

She turns on me, suspicion clouding her eyes. "Bernie, what's your relationship with these men?"

"What? You know more about them than I do, you've been--"

"No," she cuts me off, searching for specifics. "I know they've stolen your trust, but have they taken your heart? Have you slept with them?"

This feels way too much like I'm a teenager coming home from the drive-in movies, and I don't really know what to make of it.

"No," I answer defensively but truthfully.

"Any acts of passion? Any connection that's more than skin deep?"

Her insistence seems strange, but the pointed questioning does make me think more clearly.

"I... there was a car crash, with Dar--with the vampire, and to keep me conscious, to help me recover..."

I don't finish the sentence because it's clear my mom has already heard enough.

"Oh, Sunshine," she says, with a mix of pity and scorn. "He gave you his blood. And now he owns you."

Before I can respond, she sprints off into the night, leaving me and Rain alone by the fire.

The Order is preparing for battle with the Sexies. The Sexies have come for me and Rain and will probably kill any member of the Order that gets in their way. Including my mother.

I'm caught in the middle and don't know which way to turn.

A howl in the distance lets me know that Zev is near. It'll be an interesting twist if he can convince the wolves of New England to join the fight.

I stay by the fire, as it's my only source of light in these unfamiliar surroundings. I know both sides of this skirmish say they want to keep me safe, but I still feel the need to duck and take cover. That need only gets stronger when the sky lights up again in a bright crimson, and a shrill siren wakes Rain. I cover her ears, trying to protect her. She probably wants to feed, but the poor thing will have to wait a bit longer.

"They're on the last ridge!" a man calls from the darkness.

"Ready yourselves!" my mother responds. "Stun, confuse, or kill, whatever you need to do to stay alive and protect the child!"

Moments later, clusters of light burst out of the trees and into the clearing. I can't tell where the Order's assault is targeted, but I know it's unending. I fear for the men who have come to save me, though I still wonder how much it's them I should be fearing.

Suddenly, I see the shadow of a tree uproot, and the sound of branches cracking echoes through the woods.

"To the East!" a voice screams. "Target the fae!"

More fire and lighting bolts erupt from the witches stationed in the trees, now all directed nearer to where Rain and I sit. If this fight moves any closer to us, we're liable to get barbecued by an errant blast of fire.

Another tree tears from the ground, and I hear the sound of a man screaming as he falls from his perch in the branches, then a sickening thud as his body hits the snow. Seconds later, a beam of white light scorches the ground beneath the tree, and I hear Rune cry out in agony.

I'm compelled to move towards him, to see if I can help, to offer some sort of protection, but I know that's a fool's errand. I have my baby. I can't walk blindly into a firefight. Instead, I take the only action I can think of.

"STOP!"

I scream at the top of my lungs, clutching Rain to my chest, trying to top the sound of the magical powers clashing around me. I don't expect my cry to be heard, but it's all I've got.

A few more shots are fired, but then the chaos seems to settle. A trace of quiet enters the night. Either everyone died, or my plea worked. Neither seems likely, so I keep Rain hugged against me, waiting for another outburst.

Instead of fire, the next thing I see flying through the air is my pet wolf. Zev lands at my feet, then quickly begins circling me, staring and sniffing in every direction.

Around us, I hear the sound of bodies scurrying down trees, swinging from branch to branch as they head towards the ground. Footsteps come from every direction as the Order surrounds us. Zev looks more like a frightened animal than I've ever seen him, moving around me in a low crouch, a constant growl humming in his throat.

The Order members begin closing in on us, but there's still no sign of Rune or Darius. I don't understand what could have happened to them. They're both too strong, too powerful, too cunning. What are we up against? And of course, I'm once again torn by the lingering question in my mind… which of them is truly my enemy?

Darius, are you here? I think, hoping for an answer but afraid of what he'll say. Silence is the only answer I get.

"Get away from the baby, Wolf," my mother orders. Zev makes no move to obey.

"You're outnumbered and up against a magic your teeth can't cut through," she says savagely. "Move away and die quickly, or stay put and I'll make the pain linger much longer."

Zev only growls and continues his guard of me and Rain. I don't like where this is headed, and I'm terrified of how it might end.

"Mom," I say, fighting past the lump in my throat so I can speak clearly. "Please don't."

"I'm sorry, this isn't your conversation." Her response is quick and firm, putting me in my place like I'm a child and, in the process, pissing me the hell off.

"Of course it's my conversation!"

"Sunshine--"

"Don't 'Sunshine' me, Lauren." Her name escapes my lips before I even know what I'm saying.

"I'm late to the party, but I'm also the one holding the Last Witch," I say, glancing down at my baby. "If I'm going to bear this cross, I get a seat at the table."

My mom--Lauren--takes a few steps closer, seeming to accept that she won't win this argument with her I'm-in-charge attitude.

"Sweetheart, you're at the table. I won't keep anything from you…" she pauses, looking from my face down to the wolf. "…As soon as you're safe."

No sooner have the words left her lips than her wand is in the air, pointed at Zev, a golden light bursting from it. He's quick enough to move his head out of the way, but the blast catches him in the shoulder, sending him flailing away into the snow. The yelp he lets out as he crashes and falls still breaks my heart.

"No!" I shout, whirling back to face my mother.

"Baby," she starts, ready to dish out another lie, or tell me the truth. I get the feeling I may not know who I should actually trust until it's too late.

She takes another step toward me, but before her foot can settle, a blur of darkness streaks through my vision, toppling my mother and sending other members of the Order scrambling. Before my eyes can follow the movement, the shadow appears behind a hooded member and knocks them unconscious with a blow to the head before they can even turn around.

The vampire has arrived.

Fire starts to fly again and I duck down, hunching over my shrieking baby to keep her out of harm's way. I look behind me to see if I can spot Zev. I can only make out what might be the outline of a rock, or perhaps a motionless wolf.

Suddenly, I feel a body at my side.

"We need to flee, Bernie."

Order members are scattered about, some heading our way but ceasing the onslaught for fear of hitting Rain. This is as good a time as any to escape, but…

"Not without Zev and Rune."

"Bernie, they may not survive--"

"It's a three-way pledge, Darius," I say firmly. "We're not leaving if they're still alive."

Darius stands his ground, his face conflicted. He's trying to respect my wishes, but it's clear his chief concern is keeping me alive. I can't imagine a world in which this man would hurt me, no matter what consequences he may face. If I had to choose between my mom and the vampire this instant…

"Bernie, you need to trust me!"

My mother's voice comes from the ground near the fire. She's slowly getting to her feet, obviously hurt from the blow she took.

"No matter how charmed you are, or protected you feel, each of these men is trying to save his own race! The stakes are too high to be blinded by their powers--or your feelings! Don't you think they would snap your neck in an instant if it meant saving everything and everyone they care about? Do you really think you and your child matter to them more than their entire realm? More than their own lives?"

She limps toward me, looking hurt and afraid, and speaking words that ring true. It would be foolish to think about how each man has treated me without remembering why they came in the first place.

"Matilda's daughter, I presume," Darius says calmly.

"Don't say her name like you know her," my mom says.

Interesting. It looks like I know something my mother doesn't. What to do with this information, I'm not sure.

"You don't know of what you speak, woman," the vampire spits back, sounding much more like the Darius I was first introduced to. "None of you know the first thing about this child, its powers, or the prophecy."

While Darius gives my mother a verbal lashing, the other members of the Order fall in behind her. It's me, my baby, and a vampire against a much larger, seemingly more powerful group. My baby might have magic one day, but that day is not today, and I already know I don't have any--thanks to Nanny. So really, it's Darius against the Order, which doesn't seem like great odds, even for a super powerful vampire.

I look back toward the clearing, vaguely making out the movements of a body slumped against a tree. I know in my heart it's Rune. He's alive at least, though it's hard to say for how long.

"Is that why you've killed so many of us, you monster?" my mom fires back. "Just racing to get to the last one so you could feast on the innocent for eternity?"

I throw another glance back toward Zev, and see that he's starting to rise. I may not know who to trust, but I know I'm not ready to see any of these strange, beautiful men die.

When I turn back, I see my mom slowly raising her wand.

"Mother," I say in my most admonishing voice. "Do not."

I expect her to ignore me, but instead she looks at the ground and starts to cry.

"Oh, Sunshine,' she whispers between sobs. "Why won't you let me save you?"

Her words strike a chord, and I see how painful this is for her. She knows she hasn't earned my trust, and yet I think she truly believes that I'll die without her help. But then, her expression shifts, a new malice in her eyes and a harsher tone in her voice.

"Don't you see what this magic becomes?" she wails, gesturing to the fire and devastation all around us. "There's no end to this, Sunshine. Everyone will always want to achieve the greatest power, to live forever, to rule over the others. There's only one way to end this."

She lowers her wand and reaches out to me with her other hand. "Give me the baby, Bernadette. She is the sacrifice that will save us all. Her death will end the wars forever."

A collective gasp comes from the Order members behind my mother. A figure steps forward and removes her hood--it's Joe's wife, Betty. She hovers over my mother's shoulder and speaks while keeping her eyes on me and the vampire.

"What are you talking about?" Betty asks. "The objective was always to save the child, Lauren."

"No," my mom says firmly. "It was always to save our families, our husbands and brothers, our sisters and mothers... our daughters."

She turns her attention back to me. "I'm asking you to do something impossible, Sunshine. No mother could ever willingly harm her child."

Except you, I think to myself. *By trying to take my baby from me.*

"But this goes beyond your pain, or mine, or my mother's. You have a chance to end so much suffering. If we don't do the right thing, these cursed magic creatures will haunt the world for another million years."

This whole time, my mom has been trying to convince me of the evil forces conspiring against me. I know she believes what she says, but she's lost sight of who the real monster is.

I look down at Rain--cold, hungry, and crying. I need to get her away from here. Away from the witches who are supposed to be her family.

I turn to Darius, whose eyes have been locked on my mother this whole time, every muscle in his body ready to spring into action and save the baby he pledged to protect.

That's it. The pledge.

He takes his eyes off my mother to look at me, a hesitant expression on his face. I know he heard my thoughts. "Bernie..."

"Darius," I say, not giving him a chance to stop me. "Take the child."

"What are you doing?" my mother yells, her wand hand raised again.

"I'm taking your advice, mother," I say, with every ounce of sass I can muster. "I'm doing the right thing."

I hold Rain out toward the vampire. He's the only one who can keep her safe right now, and that's all I care about. "Take the child."

He looks at the baby so tenderly, a sort of compassion on his face I never thought could have existed. And then he raises his gaze to me.

"No."

I don't understand. Neither does my mother or any member of the Order, who all seem dumbstruck at the scene unfolding before them.

"Darius, I've broken the pledge," I say. "All I want is for her to be safe, away from all this, and you're the only one I trust to make that happen. Please, Darius, take my baby."

He pushes Rain back into the nook of my arm, then reaches up and touches my cheek.

"She's safest with you. Your love for her is as strong as any magic, and has already kept her alive against all odds. I refuse to take her from her mother, no matter what."

When I open my mouth to object, he inches closer, wrapping an arm around me while keeping his other hand on Rain.

"I can't allow any harm to come to the child," he says softly, his dark eyes penetrating all the defenses I had built up around my heart. "But I can't allow any harm to come to you either. I followed the star that night expecting to find a savior for my people. Instead, I found a savior for my own soul, and I will not let her go now."

For the briefest moment, all the fear drifts out of me as I lose myself in Darius' eyes, feeling secure in the midst of this madness.

"All right," I say, knowing I can't change his mind and realizing how much I need him by my side. I linger on his eyes for a second longer, finding strength in them that I know I'll need for the fight ahead.

And then, before I can turn away, Darius and I are hit with a blast of magic that sends me flying back several feet and crashing into the snow. My grip on Rain tightens as I hold her close to my chest and pray she isn't hurt. The wind is knocked out of me and my head spins from the impact.

I look around frantically for Darius and scream when I see him.

He is on fire. Blue flames licking at his flesh, burning him from the inside out. I try to crawl to him, but every part of my body flares with pain and I fall back when I realize my right leg is broken. Darius crashes to the ground flailing wildly as flames engulf his entire body. His cries are excruciating and echo through the forest as the trees themselves seem to absorb his pain.

"What have you done?" I scream as my mother stands over him, wand pointed down, smoke still curling from the tip. Then she turns, her face a mask void of any emotion, as she locks her gaze with mine and takes a step toward Rain and me.

CHAPTER TWENTY-ONE

"Y ou stupid girl." My mother's voice is cold, harsh, absent any warmth it once held. She moves toward me slowly, wand still raised. I push my heels into the earth below, trying to put as much distance as possible between us and this murderous lunatic who is my mother. My heart is hammering in my chest, cold sweat slicking my skin, tears burning my eyes as I glance over to Darius, his body now still and smoldering in the snow.

"After all the horrors you've been through in the last few days," my mother says, taking another step forward. "After watching your grandmother lose her mind and live the rest of her life in agony, destroying her husband's life in the process. After growing up without a mother, you still can't see where all the trouble stems from."

I stop scooting along the ground, knowing I won't get away. Hopefully, I'll have better luck hurling words.

"You're blaming all those things on *my child*? Every problem for the last fifty generations can be pinned on this tiny, defenseless girl?"

"It's what she represents, Bernie," my mother says, a little exasperated with my defiance. Not sure what else she expected.

"You won't understand now, you'll probably hate me until I'm dead and gone, but this is the only choice." My mom softens her voice, toning it down so she sounds more like the woman who almost won me over just moments ago. "Please, Sunshine. Hand her over. Don't make me hurt you as well."

It's a sweet attempt at saying the most hateful thing ever, and I'm not buying it.

"Oh, mom." I'm overrun with emotions, but my voice is calm and clear. "All these years wishing I had one more minute with you, could see you one last time. And now I just wish you really were dead."

Her face twists with anger, then she stands tall, composes herself, and aims her wand at me. "Me too, Sunshine. *Szünet.*"

There's a flash, and then I feel nothing. No pain, but also no cold, no touch. I know Rain is pressed against me, but I can't even feel her. My thoughts still tumble around in my mind, my eyes still see, but it's like my head has no body. Every effort to move a leg or an arm fails. As my mother reaches down and extracts my baby from my arms, all I can do is watch through blurry, tear-filled eyes.

"Please don't," I mouth, my lips barely moving while the sound stays trapped in my throat.

She lifts Rain and tucks her under her chin, gently cooing as she walks away from me, toward the fire. "What a sweet girl you are. What a sweet, beautiful girl."

What a goddamn psychopath.

I fight to move again, but it's all for naught. Whatever connection there used to be between my brain and body has gone offline. I've still got control over my eyes, and I look as far as I can in every direction.

I can barely make out Zev in my periphery, and I've got no clue if he's breathing or not. Rune's too far away, hidden amongst the trees, at least that's where I hope he is.

Darius is much easier to spot. Not twenty feet away, I see smoke rising off his motionless body. Fear hits me in the gut at the sight. I know vampires are hard to kill, but a witch's fireball seems like it would be deadly to just about anyone.

I shift my eyes back towards my mother, helpless to do anything but watch as she waves her wand and summons a platform of blue fire under her feet. It lifts her into the air, hovering above the open flame. Along with my baby.

"Gather round," she announces to her followers. The forest has fallen silent, save for the sound of footsteps shuffling across the snow-covered earth. Rain doesn't even cry. She seems to be in some kind of trance. The eerie quiet is much worse than the cacophony of battle from earlier. Paralyzed from the neck down, my baby dangling above a sprawling fire, and all I hear is pounding, merciless silence.

"I know you've fought to save the Last Witch," my mother says as the Order members circle around the fire. "But as you've seen here tonight, it's an impossible task. It took everything we had, every spell we could muster, to fend off just three attackers, and more will come." She gestures to the woods, as if enemies lurk there even now. "The vampires, the werewolves and the fae will have armies at their backs. Kingdoms to come against us, if we do not end this now. Who amongst us wants to die at the hands, teeth, or claws of these abominations?"

There are murmurs from the circle, voices offering both agreement and protest.

"Remember that this was never about a single child," my wretched mother continues. "This was about all of our futures, and the future of humanity. This is about righting centuries of wrongs that our ancestors had to endure at the mercy of those monsters!"

She's talking about my princes, men who risked so much for me and for Rain. How could this be my reality? The three sent to steal my child, once the most frightening of foes, now lay around me dying, because they chose to defend me and my baby from the mother I thought to be long dead. So many twists of fate, and all so cruel.

I hear muffled whines coming from Rain, still under my mom's control. I choke on my sobs, wishing more than anything that it was my body hanging above that fire. If only Tilly had sacrificed me after I was born, shattering my mother and putting an end to these magical tragedies. So many lives could have been saved, and I'd have never experienced the greatest loss of all.

But Nanny would have never done that. She broke herself trying to bring her daughter back. I feel that connection to her now, stronger than ever before. I recognize the love she felt, and the sacrifices she made because her heart told her to. God, I wish Nanny was here. To comfort me, and to talk some sense into her craven daughter.

My chest burns, and I feel like it's the actual sensation of my heart giving out. Rain is about to die and I have nothing left to live for, so why should my heart keep beating?

"The Order should vote," a woman yells, interrupting my mother's tirade. "It's how we've always addressed issues in the past. We've thwarted the attack and we're safely convened at the coven fire. Let us vote, Lauren."

"There isn't time for a vote!" my mother shouts back. "You think the attack is over? That we're safe? Each and every one of us will die if we don't act swiftly."

The threat of death seems to quiet her dissenters, yielding control back to my mother.

"We stand before the First Fire, ignited by the Fates, the sacred flames that have burned even as our numbers dwindled. We now have the chance to restore the order they once sought to create, by letting the flames consume the Last Witch, bringing an end to the powers that have long been a source of death and destruction among ours and all races. This child's sacrifice will quench these eternal flames, allowing the great magic to consume itself, and thus end these powers forever."

As she lifts my baby into the air, the burning in my soul becomes almost unbearable. I want to move so badly, to break free of this pain, but my body won't allow it.

I want to scream, to rage against what is happening. And then, just as I think I'm about to succumb to the heat building in my chest, a soft amber glow shines in the sky. Perhaps my heart did burst, and this is my journey to the other side. Or maybe Rain has been fed to the fire, and the world is twinkling with the magical brightness that existed in that beautiful, perfect baby.

Bernie, my dear.

I hear the voice in the same way I hear Darius when he speaks to my mind, but it is not the vampire who speaks to me now.

It's Tilly.

Nanny?

A shimmering form appears before me, clarifying within the amber glow, a silver wisp that takes on the form of my grandmother. She steps forward, her translucent arms outstretched, her body an effervescent figure pulled straight from a dream, hovering just about the snow. The glow from her being washes the whole forest in a warm, golden light.

My eyes snap from her back to the fire, to the scene I'd looked away from because I thought it might kill me to watch. My mother is frozen, holding Rain above the fire. Everyone is frozen.

Everyone but Nanny and me.

What did you do? I ask the figure before me.

I have slowed time, but only for a moment. I've come to give you back what I took from you so long ago. Nanny approaches me, kneeling to touch my cheek with her ghostly finger. Warmth infuses my skin, and I feel tears slide down my cheeks as sensation in my body slowly returns.

I have to go now, Nanny says, stroking my cheek like she did when I was scared as a child.

Where? I ask, still feeling stuck in something between a dream and a nightmare.

No one knows. She smiles gently. *That is the great adventure, to discover what life looks like on the other side of the door we call death. Thank you for bringing me. For releasing me.*

What's she talking about? What did I do? *Nanny, what do you mean?*

You called out to me, your voice a source of pure love. When I heard you, I knew it was okay to let go, she says, her tone so calm and sweet as she delivers this crushing news.

No! I feel my heart crack open, emotions too big to bottle up spilling out of it even as my body refuses to feel it all. *I need you. Rain needs you. Don't leave us.*

Oh child, I'm not leaving you. I'm leaving an old body in a hospital bed. I'll always be in here. She removes her hand from my cheek and places it over my heart, and I watch in awe as a blinding light flashes in her soul and pushes through her hand and into me, filling the cracks that have formed at my core. As I fill with that light, that magic, my body comes to life again, pulsing with every sensation. My broken leg mends itself and my very skin begins to glow with the kind of power I have never felt or even imagined in my life.

Nanny's eyes are full of light even as the rest of her begins to fade. *I committed a great act of evil that was inspired by the greatest love when I stole your magic to bring your mother back. It is not for witches to interfere with the destinies of others. My beautiful granddaughter, I am giving you back your destiny. I will be here, watching over you. Watching over Rain.*

My body burns, but this time it is a welcome fire that sparks my soul to life, a part of me I didn't even know was dead until now.

But at what cost? My Nanny has almost entirely disappeared. The outlines of her body are fading like smoke dissipating on the wind. Only her face remains clear. Her eyes, still full of so much love.

But girl, know this, she says, her voice becoming faint even in my mind. *It was always you.*

And then, she is gone. I feel it the moment her soul departs this world, as all the power she released slams into me.

I scream.

The sound of my voice rings through the forest, waking up all the creatures who live here, driving magic into each leaf, each blade of grass, each stray rock.

Time--which was at a standstill--now snaps into motion, my mother moving to sacrifice my child over the fire. The whole interlude with Nanny happened in the blink of an eye, so my mom never saw Tilly. She doesn't see what has changed in me.

With instinct born of desperation and fear, I push it all out of me, every drop of magic I feel swelling within. I can't tell if I'm reigning power in from the natural world or if it's all emanating from my own being. I'm acting without thinking, and the result is a tsunami of electricity.

Light crashes over the Order, my mother, everyone near me.

While the world bends and shakes around me, I set my intention to one thing only.

Save Rain.

I must save Rain.

My eyes stay focused squarely on my baby as wave after wave of brilliant light crashes through the others. They scatter and fall to the ground, stunned or unconscious. If a fallen witch tries to stand back up, she's immediately struck down again. Meanwhile, Rain floats gently on a soft, glowing cloud, safely above the fire.

My gaze never leaves her as I walk to the fire's edge. She's hovering just above the flames, the same ones that were meant to consume her life, and yet I feel no fear. She'll wait for me. She is safe.

I pull her from the floating stasis and move away from the blaze, squeezing her in my arms. "Oh sweetheart, are you okay?" I check her little body for any injury, the light from my fingertips soaking into her soft skin. She coos, grasping at the glowing streaks my magic leaves.

I stand amidst the chaos my power has created, but my feet do not sink into the snow. Instead, I find myself floating above the earth, moving toward my mother, who was blasted to the ground and now struggles to right herself.

She stares at me, slack jawed. While the other Order members lay motionless, my mother is still alert. Whether that's because she's the stronger witch or my subconscious intention was to leave her standing I cannot say.

"How did… where did you get such power?" she asks, fear in her eyes for the first time tonight.

"It is mine by blood," I say. "And you are done here."

My mother's lips curl like a rabid dog and she reaches for her wand and pulls at the blue fire still burning between us.

"I didn't want it to be this way," she says. "I wanted to spare you. But you've made that impossible."

With a flick of her wrist, she casts the fire at Rain and me, intent on completing what she started, even if it means I die with my daughter.

Without thought, without knowing what I'm doing, I call my magic to me on instinct. My intent is enough. A golden shield forms around my child and myself, and when the blue fire comes for us, it is repelled backward by the vibrant light.

141

My mother's eyes widen. Before she can manage a scream, the fire wraps around her body, her own flames consuming her.

As relieved as I am to be alive, I can't help but feel the pain of losing her all over again.

I hold Rain so she can't see her grandmother die, but I watch. I bear witness to the consequences of messing with dark magic. Of bringing back the dead. And trying to kill the innocent.

When her screams die to nothing, the fire flashes. I blink, and when I open my eyes again, my mother is gone. Nothing remains of her body but a dim blue light fading out into the night.

Around the eternal witch's fire lay the remains of the Order, all unconscious but alive.

But they are not my concern.

I look around, seeking out the three men who have turned my life--and my heart--upside down in such a short time.

I find Zev first, in wolf form. Laying a hand on him, I press my magic into his fur and close my eyes, willing him to heal, to live.

His body twitches, then jerks and he shifts to human under my hand, his green eyes opening. I exhale in relief as he pulls me into a hug, careful not to crush the baby between us.

My tears fall on his shoulder, and he pulls away to wipe them. "I guess it's not so bad," he says with a smirk.

"What's not so bad?" I ask.

"Being mated to a witch. It could be worse."

If his words are a shock, the kiss that comes next nearly undoes me. My body is already raw, exposed from the inside out, so when he takes my lips with his, cupping the back of my head with one hand as the other wraps around my waist, I feel everything. Every sensation, every emotion, every shift in his body against mine. I feel him under my skin, in my heart, in some primal part of me I've been denying my whole life, and if I were a wolf, I would howl right now. But, alas, I am human.

Or rather, I am witch. And so I kiss him back, deeply, passionately, with nips at his bottom lip as my fingers dig into his back.

I pull away, painful as it is to do so, but I can't go on knowing there are two of our pack still missing. "We will talk more later," I say. "About this mate business."

His eyes are filled with need, but he nods, nuzzling my neck once more before pulling away. "I'll go to Rune. I can hear him in the clearing. He is alive. You find Darius. He will need your blood."

I hand him Rain. "Take her," I say. "If I have to feed Darius my blood, it's best if she's somewhere else."

He nods, accepting the child, his face softening as it always does when he looks at her.

Before I can leave, Zev cups my face with his palm. "It was always you," he says softly.

The very same words Tilly spoke to me before she died.

I kiss him once more, then turn to find Darius. Around me, the night fills with the scents and sounds of the forest. With a heightened sense, I experience every shift of the trees groaning deep in their roots, every tiny movement of each animal and insect, every shimmering moonbeam lighting my way. It's heady, intoxicating and dizzying. I have to stop and lean over to catch my bearings again. The world around me is too bright, too noisy, too filled with wonder. I feel as if my head will explode.

But Darius. I need to find him. He could be almost dead, meaning I have no seconds to spare.

I push through the discombobulation, but I can't remain upright. Instead, I crawl through the snow, my ability to hover now gone as I struggle to settle my mind and stabilize this new power surge I'm having. If not for Darius' blood flowing in my veins, increasing our connection, sending me a guiding ribbon of light to follow, I'm not sure I would have been able to find him through the snow now falling once more. It's as if nature is trying to reclaim the forest we have defiled with fighting and death.

I choke back emotion as my mind wanders to Tilly and my mom. To everything that has happened here.

I blink against tears, and against the memory of Darius bursting into flames.

Feeling through the snow with hands that are becoming numb from cold, I hit on what I know is the vampire's body. Relief surges through me as I sense the smallest speck of life still present in him.

I pull myself up to where he lays, my head swimming as I study his too perfect face, which is now covered in charred burn marks. Rage swells up again at my mother and the suffering she caused, but I push it back. I can't afford anger right now.

I need healing. Love. Peace. I need to bring this man back to me.

I search his cloak for the knife I know he keeps there, and hold it to my wrist. Praying it's sharp enough but not too sharp, I swipe at my vein, releasing a crimson ribbon across my arm that glows with the same golden light as my skin. I squeeze my eyes against the pain that follows the swell of blood, then I hold it over my vampire's mouth.

I hope the magic in my bloodstream will be an extra healing elixir for Darius.

It takes a moment, but as my blood drips into his mouth, his body comes back to life, the burn marks on his face healing first to pink puckered scars, and then to smooth, clear skin.

When his eyes open, revealing the dark orbs that always pull me in, my heart skips a beat in relief.

When he pulls me into him, replacing my wrist with my neck as he continues to feed, my heart skips a beat in desperate desire. The pain of his teeth sinking into my flesh is turned to pleasure as his lips caress my neck, as his hands grip my body laying on top of his. As his strength returns to all parts of him.

And when he continues to feed, to consume my blood, and my reality dips and spins and closes into darkness, my heart skips several beats. And then is silent.

CHAPTER TWENTY-TWO

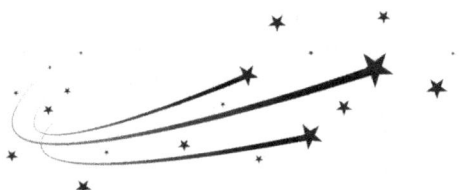

"Bernie?" A voice calls my name, but he sounds so far away. Like a dream through mist and clouds.

"I think she's coming to," another voice says.

It isn't until I hear a heart-rending cry that I find my way out of the fog I feel I've been lost in for ages.

When I open my eyes, three beautiful faces stare down at me. Silver eyes that glow with an inner light. Forest green eyes that take me into the wilds of the woods. And eyes so black I am lost in their eternal darkness.

"Welcome back," Rune says, his voice filled with worry. "You've given us quite a scare."

"Rune used every potion and herb on you," Zev says. "I've never seen his magic so useless."

Rune glares at the werewolf who just shrugs.

"Even my blood did nothing to revive you," Darius says, his voice choking on more emotion than I've ever heard from him. "I nearly killed you. You should never have offered yourself that way to me. I had no control."

Zev, much to my surprise, puts a comforting hand on the distraught vampire. "But you did stop. You stopped in time. Because you love her and would never hurt her."

It's the first time I've truly seen a glimpse of who they might have been had they not turned on one other so many eons ago, and it makes me hopeful for what might yet be. But also... *love?* That's a big word. One I'll have to unpack later.

I try to lift myself, to get a sense of where I am, of what happened, but the room is spinning.

Strong hands support my back. "Easy there. You've been out a long while."

"Rain?" I whisper, my throat dry as sandpaper.

Someone hands me a glass of water. "Drink," Zev says.

I do. And someone else hands me a bundle that squirms in my arms. "Rain." Tears fall as I hold her close to me. As my vision clears, I realize I'm in my bedroom. The Sexies are all here. I've got my baby. And AJ is sitting in the chair in the corner, her head lolled to the side in sleep.

"Is she okay?"

Rune nods. "She hasn't left your side. We didn't want to wake her."

"What happened?" I ask, instinctively pulling out a breast to feed my daughter.

Before they can answer, I notice my skin and pull Rain away, handing her to whichever Prince is closest. "What's wrong with me?"

It takes me a moment for memories to return. The power I inherited from my grandmother. The surge of energy I felt when my mother died. The glowing skin and glowing blood.

I stand, pushing away the hands that try to stop me, and stumble to the full-length mirror on my closet door. I can't believe what I'm seeing.

"I'm still glowing. How... why?" From head to toe. My skin shines like diamond dust, my eyes shimmering like living sapphire and even my hair is streaked with gold and silver glitter. I didn't expect it to last past that night. It'll be real hard to live a normal life if I... sparkle. Oh Jesus, I can already imagine the jokes at the bar.

"The power you possess is too much for a single body," Darius says, the worry clear in his tone. "When your grandmother returned your magic, she also gave you what was left of her own. And then, when your mother died by her own flame, the magic in her blood flowed into yours."

"So, what are you saying?" I ask. "I'm three witches in one?"

Darius nods. "Essentially." The vampire comes up behind me and slips his arms around my waist. "You have more magic than your body knows what to do with, which is why you can't control the glow of your skin."

I cling to him and lean my head against his chest, feeling suddenly unstable, nearly blinded by my own reflection. My head is spinning and I twist away to vomit, but there's nothing in my stomach, so it's a painfully dry heave.

"You're being poisoned by the magic in you," the vampire whispers, laying a cool hand over my fevered forehead.

I turn to face him, gripping his biceps. "What does that mean? What do I do to stop it?"

"I can bleed some off of you by drinking your blood," he says. "That seemed to help. But it's only a temporary solution."

Rune approaches. "Darius is correct. That won't keep you alive long term. We need a more permanent solution, and soon."

"The Council has reconvened," Zev says, approaching us. "All of our kind have united in one purpose."

My stomach tightens and my pulse races. "What purpose is that?"

"Rain," he says simply. "They all want your child. They've decided they will share her, to try and save everyone."

"Share her," I say, my brain coming to life slowly. "You mean kill her?"

They each nod solemnly.

"And you're going to help them?" I ask, pulling away, my voice full of hurt and accusation. As I do a blast of light rips out of me and slams into Darius, pushing him across the room and into my wall, where he makes a man-sized cut out.

"What the hell?" I run over to him. "Are you okay? I'm so sorry."

Darius steps out of my wall and dusts himself off. "I will be fine. Your blood still flows in my veins, and it's very powerful. It's you we need to worry about right now."

I'm shaking as I look again at my hands, which seem to have a mind of their own. I pull away from all of them, retreating into a corner of the room like a scared animal. "What if I hurt one of you?" I ask, then my gaze lands on the bundle in Rune's arms. "What if I hurt my child?"

"You'd never," AJ says, sitting up and stretching. "That's bullshit and you know it."

"But how can we be sure," I ask. "Maybe my mother was right about one thing. This power is dangerous. Unnatural." I've never feared myself, what I'm capable of, and it's not a good feeling.

Darius clears his throat. "I have an idea. Wait just a moment."

With vampire speed he disappears from the room and reappears a moment later holding something I'd entirely forgotten about.

It's the star that brought these men to me. The rock I pulled from the wall just before Rain arrived. I inch forward to look at it, wondering if my magic is causing my eyes to play tricks on me. "It's glowing the same color as my skin."

Darius nods. "It's been glowing since you got your powers back. Maybe it can help you control them until we think of something more permanent."

He offers the rock to me and I reach out nervously to take it. I don't know what to expect, but the moment I wrap my hand around it, I feel a shift inside myself, a settling. Light from my skin pours into the star until my body stops glowing and I return to normal.

"How do you feel?" Rune asks, passing Rain to Zev to come kneel before me. He peers into my eyes, studies my palm, takes my pulse.

"A bit better," I say with relief. "Not so dizzy or out of control."

"Try setting the star aside," Rune suggests.

My eyes widen. "What if I hurt you?"

"I'll be alright and Zev won't let anything happen to Rain. But we need to see what we're dealing with."

I nod and carefully set the star on the ground and then release my hand from it. The moment I do, power rushes back into me like a tidal wave. My hands blaze with lightning and the dresser near me explodes in shards of wood.

Quickly, I grab the star and hold it to my chest, my breathing rapid, my body practically buzzing.

Once again the star absorbs the excess power and I feel myself stabilize.

Rune reaches for my hand to help me stand.

With one hand clutching the star, I give my other to him and let him pull me up.

"It would appear she needs to be in physical contact--"

"With the star to control her magic, yeah," AJ cuts Rune off, not needing the play by play. "We were literally all here watching, Elfie."

Before the two can get into one of their sibling spats, I interrupt. "Okay, so I'm a magical bomb about to explode and all of your kingdoms are coming for my kid. What about you three?" I ask, looking at each of them. "The pledge you made is broken. I broke it." I glance at Darius who holds my gaze with his. "Will you go home? Take your rightful places and help them?"

"We are not working with our kingdoms," Zev says.

Rune nods. "We have taken a new pledge."

"What kind of pledge?" I ask.

Darius takes my hand in his, speaking directly into my mind. *We are yours, Bernie. Yours and Rain's. We will each lay down our lives for you if we must. Forever.*

I suck in a breath, unsure what to believe. But then he pulls up his sleeve and shows me a tattoo he didn't have before. A triangle with a star in the middle. Rune and Zev have the same marking on their arms. And then I notice my own arm--it has a matching symbol.

"We are bound to you," Rune says. "And we will do whatever we must to protect you."

So many emotions flood me. After nearly losing my child, watching my grandmother die, watching my mother die, worrying the men I've come to care for would betray me, and now being filled with so much magic I can't control, I don't know what to do or think, but I know what I feel.

For the first time in a long time. I feel hope.

Darius caresses my cheek. "We will find a way to keep both you and Rain safe. You have my oath."

I STARE into the glowing full moon that casts its silver light over the water, breaking through the surrounding fog and giving a soft glow to the night sky. It's peaceful. A peace I don't think I've ever felt before.

"Shall we?" Rune says, extending his hand to guide me.

I turn and look at the handsome fae, his expression genuine and understanding. Zev and Darius stand behind him, both wearing tailored black suits, as is Rune. Dashing as ever, but now in a more formal, earthly way.

Darius' mind brushes mine lightly, and I feel his emotions. A steady calm mingled with great tenderness. This is a new thing between us that started after he fed on me. I can't say that I mind. Now, it's as if we can touch each other even when we aren't together. It's a comfort I never imagined I would find so valuable.

Darius stays with me as I extend my hand and give it to Rune. Under the light of the moon, my skin is glowing, and not in the way people said it glowed while I was pregnant, which I still think was bullshit since I was red and sweaty through most of it. No, my skin very literally glows these days, a soft amber hue flowing through my pores, even when I'm holding the star. Darius will need to feed on me again soon, or I'll never be able to leave the house.

And just as intimately, I feel the wave of a wild, primal connection when I look at Zev. We still haven't talked about what he meant when he called me his mate, though I have ideas. And the thought of it, while slightly terrifying, also heals something in my heart I didn't know was broken.

I look forward to exploring these complex emotions with each of the men in my life, once things get back to normal.

Or whatever normal now looks like for me.

I finally take Rune's hand and we join the others, then move as a group to the cliff's edge. Below us waves crash against the rocky coast, spraying sea mist into the air and creating a steady rhythm with the intervals of the break.

It's been a little over a week since I saved Rain from my mother. Since I became overwhelmed with magical powers that cause my skin to glow and silver streaks to run through my hair. Since I brought Darius back to life with my blood. Since my Nanny died. We've kept the bar closed in mourning, just as we did after my grandfather passed. But patrons have taken to slipping envelopes of cash under our door, with notes and cards. I've also found a casserole or dessert on the porch leading to my apartment nearly every day. My community has come together to take care of me and Morgan's Pub while I process my Nanny's death.

Now we stand at the cliff my mother leapt from, back when she was still good, before dark magic warped her perception of right and wrong. A tear rolls down my cheek as I think of how much her heart must have hurt, how broken she must have been to decide that the best thing for her child would be for her to take her own life.

But we're here for Tilly. As much as I hated losing my mother twice, saying goodbye to my Nanny is just as hard. I plant a kiss on the top of Rain's head, her cute little body strapped tightly against mine in her carrier. She won't have any memories of her great grandmother, but I'll see Nanny in everything my baby girl does, and Rain will have no question about where she inherited her greatness.

We stand a few feet back from the precipice, wind whipping through our hair, a steady stream of light coming from the moon. Hard to call this a funeral, but I feel it's the right service to honor Tilly and everything she meant to me.

Darius and Zev flank me and Rune stands just behind, his hands resting on my waist. Supported on all sides. It's so strange to stand with these princes and have an aura of calm about us. The Order members who posed a threat not that long ago are now just grateful the baby is alive and that I'm protected. Betty came to see me after I regained consciousness and made clear the misguided intentions were my mother's alone. After my final moments with Tilly and the magical stand off with my mom, I know she's telling the truth.

So now I have a moment to reflect and feel safe. And yet there's still an anxious knot in my stomach. I can't place the cause, but the feeling won't go away.

"I'm here! I got it!"

Our little ceremony has been waiting on one last guest, and we all turn to watch AJ bounding through the grass.

"I had to look through like six boxes before I found it," she says, handing me the final item we needed before this ceremony could get underway.

"That's fine, thank you so much for going back," I say. "I can't believe I forgot it."

"Yeah, it's not like you've got anything else on your mind," AJ jokes. "Vampire wound, killed your mom, skin freaking glows all the time."

I stifle a laugh. The "killed your mom" thing is almost off color, but that's how AJ rolls. Also, when you break it down, I did kill my mother, and I'd do it again if I had to.

I look down at the keepsake she brought, and my lip immediately starts to quiver and tears bubble up.

Nanny's old Red Sox hat.

Before she lost her mind, we'd watch baseball together all the time, going down to Boston to watch the Red Sox and even driving up to Portland for minor league games. Nanny was a fanatic, though she wouldn't shout or cheer at the games; she'd just watch, her eyes wide, a constant smile on her face. It was like a kind of magic she couldn't understand, these men batting around and chasing after this tiny orb.

After the incident, which I now see in a *very* different light, baseball was the one thing that could pull her through an episode. I always thought it was the boring commentary from the announcers, but it was something deeper. It was a peace she found in the skill and strategy, and watching the little ball take flight.

I don't have many other trinkets of Nanny's, and I don't really feel a connection to her possessions. I truly do feel her inside my heart, a piece of her soul living inside mine, flowing through the magic she returned to my veins. So I'm going to throw this hat off the cliff and into the waters below, saying goodbye to the hardships Tilly endured while in her physical form, and turning the page on this chapter of her magical existence.

The princes each bring their own element to this goodbye ritual. I said they didn't need to make any grand gestures, but they clearly feel a sense of gratitude for Tilly, as they should. Darius squeezes a drop of blood into the hat, Zev adds a tuft of hair, and Rune places a single leaf, one from a tree in his homeland, he says.

AJ pours in a shot of Powers Irish Whiskey, which was the first thing she got drunk on, stolen from our bar during a sleepover when she was 14. Tilly helped her through the hangover and never told her parents, something AJ has never forgotten.

When everyone finishes their moment with the hat, I take it back and add one more thing. Her ashes. Finally, she will be free.

I walk it to the cliff's edge and conjure an image of my grandmother, of times I spent with her growing up. Of her smile. Of the love in her eyes. "Thanks for saving me, Nanny. Me and Rain."

I feel a slight ripple in my stomach, like the sensation when you're on a rollercoaster. It's just a little tickle from my Nanny and it makes me smile.

I throw the hat off the edge and watch as her ashes begin to glow as they are carried to sea by the wind. In the distance, I could swear I hear Nanny's laughter, like she's on a great adventure and enjoying every minute of it.

After a long moment of silence, I turn back to this utterly bizarre and beautiful little family I now have.

"Okay," I say, forcefully wiping tears away from my eyes. "Now we have to head back to the bar so the community can say their goodbyes to Tilly and Joe the Irish way."

"Here, here," AJ says, taking a swig from the bottle of Powers.

I pass Zev the baby and walk over to Darius, who's still standing at the cliff's edge, his gaze lost in the horizon.

I slip a hand into his and he squeezes it. "She was an incredible woman," he says, referring to Nanny.

"Yes, she was."

He looks down at me. "She was so proud of you."

That means more than he'll ever know, or maybe he does know, I realize, as I feel a swell of love for him.

"It's time to go," I say softly. "But I can't show up to the bar glowing."

His nostrils flare and eyes dilate as I tilt my neck.

As his teeth sink into my flesh, I close my eyes and wrap my arms around him.

He holds me up as my legs wobble, and he takes just enough to ease the magic building up in me. The pleasure and pain spiral in me and I wish we were alone, because there's so much more I want to do with this man.

But that will have to wait.

We have time now.

We have my whole life, it would seem.

THERE's a line outside Morgan's when we return. I keep the star tucked in my pocket, with a small hole so it can stay in contact with my skin. It's not an elegant solution, but it works well enough for now.

Zev shifts into wolf form before we enter, since that's how he's known here. Though he complains about it, I think he secretly enjoys not having to talk to anyone.

We go in through the back so I can unlock the front door from the inside.

Rune and AJ get in place behind the bar. Zev stays at my side wherever I am-- a gesture that now carries added weight given our relationship, and Darius takes the baby so I have free hands to hug and greet people.

I unlock the door and folks I've known my whole life pour in. That night, everyone shares stories about my grandmother, from her younger days to more recent years. She touched so many lives. There are many toasts and many tears, but also so much laughter. And Joe's spot at the bar is kept empty, with his favorite beer in front of it. We toast to him, to the man who would wake in the middle of the night to help a friend, no questions asked.

Rain is passed around as everyone greets her. Zev sniffs each person who touches her and makes sure they know if they hurt her they will regret that choice.

For one night, I forget about the looming war with three powerful kingdoms and just focus on this moment, being surrounded by friends and family, celebrating two lives that were well-lived and will be well-remembered.

My eyes are red-rimmed and my face hurts from laughing as we close up and let the last patron out.

When I finally lock the door I'm ready to pass out for a few days straight, but Darius halts that plan as he approaches with a box.

"What's all this?" I ask.

"Some personal effects of your grandparents we found when we upgraded your living environment. I thought you might like to look through them. Maybe they can bring you some comfort."

I walk over to him and peek into the box. I've seen it before. There are pictures, letters, newspaper clippings and cards spanning almost half a century. Nanny and I spent many nights pouring over the contents.

Darius sets it on one of the tables, and I sit and begin removing items one by one to show them to the others. The Sexies all sit with me, while AJ, who has seen the box before, goes upstairs to put Rain to bed.

I smile at the picture on the top of the pile. "This was their wedding day," I say. They were just teenagers with a lifetime ahead of them. I wonder if they could have imagined what their lives became. Can anyone ever truly know what path they will ultimately end up traveling?

There are newspaper clippings from weddings, funerals and births in the family. And love letters my grandparents sent back and forth during the war. One of these days I will curl up with a glass of wine in front of the fire and read these. Nanny always said I should.

My hand drifts over another letter, and I freeze.

This one is new.

My name is scrawled across the envelope.

The handwriting is familiar.

"My grandfather must have written this... but I never received it," I say, opening the envelope and pulling out the letter within. The paper looks fairly new, and the writing seems to be scribbled hastily in black ink. My throat tightens as I read the letter, my hands shaking.

MY SWEET BERNIE. *If you are reading this, then I am dead. More than that, my life was taken by forces more powerful than you can imagine, all so that you will return to Rowley. Bernie, you need to leave. Forget about Morgan's. Save yourself and my grandchild. I wish I could have been there for her birth. I know Nanny does as well.*

Please heed my warning. You are not safe. Go to Budapest. There you will find a man named Timothy Trendle. Tell him I sent you. Tell him... tell him you are his daughter. He will help you.

I DROP THE LETTER, and it floats to the floor as tears begin to sting my eyes.

"What's wrong?" asks Darius, as Rune takes my hand, and Zev meets my gaze.

"My grandfather says he was murdered, and that my father…" I say, my voice cracking. "My father is alive."

KEEP READING FOR MORE!

KARPOV GAUSTAD

A
WEREWOLF
A VAMPIRE
AND A FAE
GO TO BUDAPEST

http://KarpovKinrade.com

Copyright © 2020 Karpov Kinrade & Evan Gaustad
Cover Art Copyright © 2020 Karpov Kinrade

~~~~~
Published by Daring Books
~~~~~
First Edition
ISBN: 978-1-939559-69-2

~~~~~

CHAPTER ONE

The candles are lit and we are all sitting around the ouija board.

Me and the three Sexies, of course. Plus AJ and Michael.

My ex-unicorn was a last-minute decision--one motivated by his particular brand of magic. He was just glad we didn't need his blood again.

My palms are sweating and I wipe them on my jeans as I wait for Rune to tell us how to start.

I glance over at Rain, who's in the corner in her travel crib, worry gripping me whenever I'm not holding her, but she's still sleeping peacefully.

While her mother sits in a pentagram trying not to look nervous.

It's not working. I look very nervous.

This is the first time I've ever tried talking to the dead--on purpose at least-- and there's a lot at stake.

Rune insisted on carving the ouija board himself after AJ suggested we 'ring up Nanny or Gramps on the ol' ouija' to find out what the letter means, what we should do about my glow-in-the-dark powers, and what they know about my dad.

Kind of a lot to ask from someone trying to enjoy the afterlife.

Much discussion has been had about the mysterious letter I found from my grandfather, predicting his own death as a murder and directing me to Budapest to find my father who I thought was dead. None of us, not even my all-knowing Sexies, has a clue what to make of it. How much, if any, can be believed?

So when AJ suggested we use her old ouija board from high school, everyone agreed it could work, but not with that 'crude mimicry of true magic.' Rune's words, not mine.

And now here we are. In the basement of the pub, surrounded by cobwebs and boxes of storage, with dust coating everything, we are having a seance.

AJ squirms, then leans in to look at the board. Again. "It's just wicked crazy," she says for the zillionth time. "I see something different in the wood depending on how I look at it."

Rune smiles, pleased by the compliment to his craftsmanship.

AJ glances up, squinting. "It's like those trippy paintings. The ones that have a shape when you squint."

"What is the matter with your eyes?" Rune asks. "Are you experiencing discomfort?"

AJ bursts out laughing and punches the fae in the shoulder. "You elves have no sense of humor."

Rune just blinks.

I clear my throat. "Okay, let's get going. How do we start?"

Darius pulls out a dagger. "We each need to give a drop of our blood to the board."

Michael groans. "You said you didn't need my blood this time."

"I said we weren't inviting you for your blood," Darius replies. "And that is still true. But as you accepted the invitation, we now need your blood--as well as everyone else's--to proceed. If you object, you may wait upstairs."

With that dismissal, Darius cuts into his palm and holds it over the board, letting a drop hit the surface.

The blood sizzles and then is absorbed by the wood. I can almost hear a contented sigh coming from the board once the vampire blood is no longer visible.

Darius and Zev are flanking me, so the vampire hands me the knife next. My first thought is how unsanitary this is. "Shouldn't we, I don't know, sterilize this between each use?"

Darius rolls his eyes. "It is a blade forged with magic and dipped in the running waters of Valiace. Your methods are rudimentary in comparison."

"Right." I sigh and accept the dagger. With an intake of breath, I slice, flinching at the sharp shock of pain. I watch in fascination as my blood hits the board, sizzles like frying bacon, then is absorbed. Again I hear--or rather sense--that same sigh. This time it's louder.

I pass the blade to Zev, who conducts his part of the ritual, then hands it to Rune. AJ's next, and when it gets to Michael, we all wait to see if he will do it or leave.

I think Michael himself is the only one surprised by his choice to slice open his flesh, releasing the silvery magic that is his blood. This time, there's an audible sigh followed by a burp, then a giggle, as Michael's blood is taken in by the board.

I glance at Rune, who shrugs. "This board has been given life so that it may become a portal between worlds. It is the only way to get truly accurate results."

"Are you telling me we just used our blood to make a new life form? One that can open doors to the dead?" I ask, thinking about every Buffy the Vampire Slayer episode I've ever watched. Which is all of them. More than once.

Rune cocks his head, his expression confused. "Did you not want to open the veil so that you could communicate with your ancestors?"

"I mean, just my grandparents, but sure, I guess. I just didn't want to, you know, make a whole new life for it." I glance down at the board suspiciously. "It's creepy."

"Well, it's done," says AJ. "So let's call them!"

AJ is way too excited about all of this.

I just feel slightly nauseous.

But that could just be the bitter green wild salad Rune made me eat earlier.

Darius nods to me and I clear my throat. "Everyone, take hands."

I close my eyes and focus my energy, trying to carefully recall the words Darius told me I must use. "By the powers of earth, air, fire, water, and spirit, I do call thee, oh ancestors of my blood. By the sacred and most holy. By the sun and the moon. By the light and the darkness, I call thee. Come to me now in my time of need. Nanny and Gramps, come to me."

I release a breath and open my eyes, and we all lean in to place a hand on the planchette--the name for which I learned from Rune and refers to the little heart-shaped thingamabob that the spirits allegedly move to spell shit. I can't stop thinking about how close the earth-made ouija boards are to this deftly made object created by an actual magical being.

"Are there any spirits with us tonight?" I ask, and though I'm not trying to modulate my voice into a spooky seer, it happens anyways, much to my embarrassment when AJ snickers.

Nothing happens immediately following my question, and just as I'm about to ask it again, the planchette jerks across the board and stops over the word YES.

I look around the circle, eyes wide, slightly out of breath. "Did one of you do that?"

They all shake their heads.

And I believe them. I mean, why would they try to prank me on ghosts? I already know everything is real. I'm a glowing witch, sitting in a room with a werewolf, a vampire, a fae, a sea nymph and a unicorn.

A ghost is nothing.

Still, I haven't done this since I was a silly kid with AJ and we were trying to freak each other out. It was never this dramatic back then.

"Is this Ed--Gramps?"

It jerks to the NO.

I swallow, beads of sweat forming on my forehead.

"Tilly?" I ask, a painful swelling of hope causing my voice to shake.

The planchette circles around the NO, then lands back on it.

Shit.

"Can you reach Tilly or Ed? I need to speak to them."

Again, NO.

I lock eyes with Darius, and his voice floats into my mind like a caress. *Ask if it intends harm.*

I nod. "Do you intend anyone in this room harm?"

This time it lands in the middle of NO and YES.

"What does *that* mean?" I ask, frustrated.

It was rhetorical, mostly, but the spirit begins to answer, moving the planchette over the board with such force and speed that we all have to let go or get dragged around.

And now it's moving on its own from letter to letter.

N-E-U-T-R-A-L

"So you have no intention one way or another?" I ask.

It moves to YES.

Darius frowns. *See if it can tell you about your father.*

"My grandfather left me a letter before he died telling me to go to my father. Do you know anything about that?"

YES.

My heart flutters in my chest as I struggle to think of questions that can be answered with YES or NO or a simple word.

"Is my father still alive?"

It moves to the spot between YES and NO again.

"Maybe?"

Again it circles itself and settles back on the middle spot.

"How clarifying," I mumble.

"Should I go to Budapest to find my father?"

YES.

Ask if you will be safe, Darius insists.

"Will we be safe?"

Nothing moves for a long moment, then it begins to spell a word.

D-E-A-T-H F-O-L-L-O-W-S Y-O-U

"Death follows you," I say. "Like, follows me to Budapest?"

Though there are no windows down here, a gust of wind blows through the room, extinguishing the magically lit candles. The floor begins to shake, and everything in the room rattles. The planchette moves around the board wildly, settling on nothing particular, then Michael stiffens, his eyes widening and going white.

"I told him," he says, but it's not his voice coming through his mouth.

"Nanny?" I ask, reaching across the board.

Michael/Nanny takes my hand, and I swear I feel her paper-thin skin against mine. "It is, my dear. I only have a moment. They are... pulling me back."

"Tell me quickly," I say. "What's going on? Who's my father? Who killed Gramps? What's in Budapest."

"I told him," she says again. "I told him they'd come for him. But he didn't listen. He was a part of them once. Then they came for him. But they were all too late, weren't they?"

"Nanny, what are you talking about? I don't understand."

"Find your father," she says, eyes refocusing on me. "Find him and then you will know the truth."

Michael slumps forward, his eyes returning to normal. The wind around us calms, and even the candles re-light.

"Are you okay?" I ask Michael.

He nods. "That was... wild."

"Unicorns are particularly receptive to visitors from the other side," Rune says in his lecture voice that's starting to grow on me.

"Do you think the other spirit is still here?" I ask. When no one answers, I look to the board. "Are there any spirits present?"

When nothing happens, I ask one more time.

Still nothing.

"I guess that's all we get," I say, disappointment coloring my voice. I had hoped to answer this latest riddle with something other than just more riddles.

AJ yawns. "At least we can all go to bed now. I'm exhausted."

"This doesn't help us," I say as I stand, my joints creaking with the movement. Lord, when did I turn into a 95-year-old woman? "What she said doesn't clarify anything. Maybe she told my grandfather something that made him believe someone was trying to kill him. Maybe she mentioned my dad. But what does any of that mean? Why didn't someone save Ed?"

"And who was the rando party crasher?" AJ asks as she dusts off her jeans. Before anyone can answer the question, her mind shifts gears at a pace I can barely keep up with. "You know, this space is huge. You should really fix it up. You could do a lot with it."

"Ha. Right. With what money?" I ask as I pick up Rain.

Zev grabs her crib, collapsing it in one fluid movement like a damn pro. It feels weird that he's the sexiest when he's doing mundane tasks, but I can't help it. Any one of them could melt my panties off by doing the dishes, burping Rain, or sweeping. It's ridiculous.

AJ huffs and heads towards the stairs leading to the bar. "That's very limiting thinking that will not help you manifest a higher path."

"Oh Lord, AJ, are you reading self-help books again?"

She shrugs. "I figure if I want to tap into all my sexy-ass power, I should do some research. Find my center. Become one with the universe. All that jazz."

I nod. "If you learn anything that could help me stop glowing, pass it on. I'm so over being a perpetual night light."

She chuckles. "It's pretty. But yeah, I will."

We all head upstairs, Rain staying asleep in my arms the whole time, which I count as a small blessing in a very strange night.

Once at the bar, Zev sets up the crib again and I lay Rain into it as Rune makes us all drinks.

We sit around a table and clink our glasses together as I say my favorite Irish toast. "May the best of our past be the worst of our future."

It always makes me think of my ancestors, and the stories Nanny used to tell that were passed down to her from her great great grandmother. Those stories seemed like fables at the time, legends of the old world, of fairies and magic and fanciful imaginings. But given what I know now, I wonder how many of those stories were closer to the truth than I realized.

"So I guess we're all going to Budapest," I say, my mind returning to our current reality. "Well, you don't have to go, Michael. Obviously."

He shrugs, his golden blond hair glinting under the dim pub lighting, his blue eyes twinkling with mischief. "My husband and daughter might not like me leaving, but if you get into a bind, you know you can call me, Bernie."

"Thanks, Michael. I appreciate it." Nothing like having a unicorn on call in case of emergencies.

"I won't be going either," AJ says, setting her glass down firmly and locking eyes with me.

"What do you mean? Of course you will."

"B, someone has to keep the bar open while you're gone. I won't let you lose this place. I know how to run it, so I'll stay and handle shit while you go figure out your destiny."

I've given thought to what would happen to the bar, but I figured we could close temporarily in hopes that Budapest wouldn't take too long.

As if reading my thoughts, she shakes her head. "You know you can't afford it. Let me do this." She leans over the table to grasp my hands, her expression earnest. "I won't let you down. Let me prove myself."

Tears sting my eyes. "Oh hon, you have nothing to prove. Of course I trust you with the bar. I'm just gonna really miss you."

She smiles through her own teary eyes. "We'll see each other soon enough."

Michael stands. "I think this is my cue to head home. But just so you know, I'm happy to help out in any way I can while you're gone. I just finished writing a book so I'm taking a break to research my next novel."

"What kind of research does a unicorn need to do to write fantasy?" AJ asks with a snicker.

I kick her under the table. "Be nice. He's offering to help."

She nods. "Sorry. Yeah. Thanks. I can see some serious uses for those abs of yours."

Michael turns a darker shade of pink as AJ laughs, then stands to join him. "I've got to get going too."

She links arms with Michael. "Care to give me a ride home?"

He nods and as they walk to the door, I stand. "Thank you. Both of you."

Once they are gone, Darius flashes over there to lock up, then flashes back before I can blink.

I think I'm actually getting used to it. Which freaks me out a little. It's astonishing how quickly we can adjust to the insane. But I guess it's how we've survived over the centuries.

I sink back into my chair and take another drink, studying the three Sexies sharing the table with me.

Darius keeps his face impassive, but his emotions are bubbly. At least that's the best word I have for it. *Why do you feel weird?* I ask through our mental connection.

He raises an eyebrow, his dark eyes boring into me. *Weird? Whatever do you mean?* He shrugs and fusses with his pitch black hair, though it is as perfectly coiffed as always.

"You two care to share what you're discussing?" Zev asks, and his unique accent combined with the huskiness of his voice makes even such benign words sound seductive, sending a shiver up my spine. "Darius is bubbly," I say.

Zev nearly spits out his drink when he laughs. "Bubbly?"

Darius narrows his eyes. "I am not *bubbly*. Nor have I ever been *bubbly*." His clipped British accent is even more striking when his feathers are ruffled, I notice.

"Fine, edgy," I say, choosing another adjective.

"I am concerned by the seance this evening. It did not go as planned."

Rune finishes the last of his drink and stands to collect everyone's glasses. "Spirits are always temperamental," he says. "The fae are very careful about contacting them. Once a soul passes into the next life, they are meant to move on. When we seek their spirits, we are tethering them to this reality."

I sigh. "Damnit Rune, why didn't you tell me that part before we did this? Now I have a sentient ouija board and an upset ghost to deal with and I still didn't get any answers."

Rune shrugs as he walks to the bar to begin cleaning up. "I assumed you knew."

Zev chuckles. "Rune always thinks everyone knows everything he does. It's his most annoying trait."

"At least I assume the best of others," the fae says from behind the bar as he washes the glasses. "You, on the other hand, think everyone is an idiot until proven otherwise."

Rune looks smug, his long silver-blond hair pulled back in a leather strap, his sky blue eyes twinkling with humor.

"And you both have the tedious tendency to pontificate on your own genius-es," Darius says with an exaggerated yawn. "It's exhausting."

"You're like squabbling siblings," I say with a chuckle.

Darius glances at the werewolf, whose forest green eyes look shadowed by thoughts of the past. Zev's jaw clenches, and he brushes a lock of brown hair from his eyes as he nods at the vampire. "We were once just as siblings, were we not?" he says softly.

Darius breaks eye contact, and stares into the distance. "We were. But that was many years ago."

"Not so long for those with no expiration date," I say, pulling my grandfa-ther's letter out of my pocket and studying the words I've already memorized. My eyes get watery as I think of the time I lost with him while I was in New York. Time I'll never get back now. "You have more opportunities than most to make things right with those you love," I remind them.

Darius flinches and Zev looks away. Rune is the only one who holds eye contact with me, but freezes as a glass slips from his hands, shattering onto the floor. The fae straightens, staring at his empty hand. "Something is here," he whispers.

Just as he utters the words, a cold wind blows through the bar and the lights flicker on and off, then all the glasses begin flying off the shelves.

"Curses," Darius says as Zev growls and shifts into wolf form.

"What is it?" I ask, the hairs on my arms rising, magic crashing through me and lighting up my skin.

Just as I look down at my glowing fingers, I see the letter in my hand burst into flames. I scream and drop it to the table, then scream again when I realize my fingers are on fire. Pain flares in me, burning not my skin but my insides as my powers take control of me.

Before I can ask for help, more glass shards explode around us as chairs flip on end. "Looks like one of our ghost friends has decided to stay," Darius says grimly.

CHAPTER TWO

"Make it stop!"

I'm not sure if I'm talking about the flying dishes or the fire raging from my fingers, but as I say the words, my hands sizzle out, returning to their normal color and temperature. There's a small pile of ashes on the singed table-- what's left of the letter to my grandfather, but no flames.

I shake from the surge of power I couldn't control. Time seems to stop as I look at the remains of the letter; the only evidence of my father, of what happened to Gramps, destroyed..

But when another glass shatters to the left of me, I'm brought back to the present. A ghost is haunting me. And ruining my bottom line. I'm honestly more concerned with replacing pint glasses than I am the haunting part. As scary as a specter flinging dishes would have been a week ago, my perception has changed drastically and now I find myself more annoyed by paranormal problems than frightened.

Glasses keep flying and crashing, followed by a few bottles of whiskey. Rune stands behind the bar, closest to the pesky spirit and tries to trace its movements. He stays deathly still, biding his time, while I watch my restocking fees soar.

I want to intervene, to do something, but fear paralyzes me. Fear that my fingers will light fire again and I won't be able to control it. So I wait, watching as Rune handles the ghost.

With his usual deftness, the fae unleashes a handful of dark orange powder into the air above the bar. It settles around a form, creating a vibrant outline of a man. It looks like a 3D graphic from a video game or something, but it's there, in real life, hovering above the countertop.

As soon as the dust touches the figure, it freezes. I can't tell if that's an effect of whatever Rune threw or if this ghost is just embarrassed he got caught throwing all my shit around.

"Be still, specter," Rune says, slowly advancing toward the ghost.

"Ask him who he is!" I yell, eager to finally get some answers. "Where did you come from? Why the hell are you breaking my things?"

"Easy, Bernie," Zev says in his bassy, calming voice. "Unless I'm wrong, and I'm sure professor Rune will correct me if I am, a deceased spirit cannot communicate without the proper medium."

Rune nods. "That's true. We can only hope to send him--"

"I can hear you."

The voice emanates from the spirit, which causes Darius to instinctively grab my arm while Zev growls and Rune prepares to throw another ghost-thwarting powder.

"And you can hear me," the ghost continues.

"How?" Rune asks, barely above a whisper.

"You brought me into your realm," the spirit answers calmly. "You created a door, and now I walk between here and the afterlife."

Perfect. We've got an angry ghost that now lives at Morgan's Pub, breaking my shit and free to come and go as he pleases.

"What do you want?" I ask, exasperation clear in my voice. I don't have time for this.

"I want you to leave," the ghost responds, being a complete dick about everything.

"Yeah, well this is my freaking bar and I--"

"Because if you don't leave," he cuts me short, the volume and echo in his voice intensifying. "You, your baby, and all of your friends will die."

The spirit's words could be interpreted as threatening, but that's not the vibe I'm getting from him. More like he's trying to help.

Due to either the eerie tone of the ghost's voice or all the shattered glass, Rain wakens, crying softly for me. I rush to her, picking her up and tucking her against my chest, doing my best to protect her from... my life.

"Who's coming?" Darius asks, sharing my belief that the ghost isn't planning to do any killing.

We all wait with bated breath, standing in silence and hoping for an answer. Instead, the sparkling flakes thrown by Rune start to fall, dissolving the form of the ghost. The figure isn't moving to another spot in the room, just disappearing before our eyes.

As the last bits of colorful dust fall to the bar, we hear a final whisper from the invisible visitor.

"They all are."

And then he's gone, leaving a layer of powder on the copper bar.

I exhale a breath I've been holding in too long and my shoulders slump as I realize we're alone. For now.

Rain begins to cry again, and I think at first it's because I'm holding her too hard in my efforts to protect her. But when I look down, I see her blanket is singed, her tiny little arms have glowing red fingerprints on them... and my fingers are burning.

Darius is at my side in an instant, taking Rain from me before I drop her on the floor of the bar. And without a word I race outside, swallowing the sob that's rising in me.

I hurt my child. I burned her soft, perfect skin.

A light rain starts, and as the water hits my flesh, it sizzles.

I slump down against the wall and bury my head in my hands, sobbing.

It isn't long before I feel a wet nose pushing into my hands.

I flinch back, worried I'll burn him, but Zev shifts from wolf form to take my hands in his.

"You can't hurt me," he says softly. "I burn like you, hot and fierce." He puts a hand on my heart and takes mine to place on his naked chest.

His skin is hot to the touch, just like mine. And his heart is pounding in beat to my own, too fast, too loud.

"I hurt my baby," I say, the tears turning to steam on my cheeks.

"Rain is fine. Rune cooled her skin and says there's no injury to speak of."

"It could have been so much worse," I say with a sinking heart. "I can't hold her." The words ache as I say them, but I know this is how it must be for now. To protect her. "Not until I get my powers under control. I can't risk her."

Zev's eyes are sad but he nods. "We will make sure she has her every need met. And you will master this. I know it." His gaze bores into my soul as he speaks. "I know you."

I nod. "You're right. I will. I have no choice."

He kisses my lips lightly, then stands, lifting me up as he does. "Let's go deal with the ghost, shall we?"

THE SEXIES TRIED to talk me out of calling AJ, but they lost that fight before it even started. Either my friend is coming with us to Budapest, or she's moving to another state, but she's sure as shit not bartending at my haunted establishment. Morgan's can close, for all I care. There must be a "brought back a creep from the dead who won't leave and can't be killed" clause in my insurance policy, right?

Turns out there isn't. Also turns out AJ is exactly as stubborn as I could have guessed she would be.

"Not on your life, B," she says, staring up at me while sitting on my bed. "The ghost we brought out of retirement gave you a warning and now I can't help you? Bullshit, the bar stays open."

"AJ, he was throwing glasses--"

"Do you know how many of your pint glasses *I've* thrown?" she asks, knowing damn well I'm still mad about the number of times I got in trouble as a teen after a hammered AJ broke a bunch of glasses.

It's a standoff. My worry for AJ against her worry for me and Rain. Even if I tell her not to, she'll come back and open up the bar. Aside from caring about my future, she loves flirting and knowing she's in control. She's the happiest she's been... probably ever. Who am I to take that away from her?

"Fine," I say. "Stubborn bitch."

"Takes one to know one."

I'm proud of us for maturing so well as we've aged.

"Alright, since you're here and you've already shot down one request, can I ask you to help me pack?"

Her face falls and I move toward my closet, needing to get my bags filled while Rain's with the Sexies in the other room. If she didn't like being told not to tend bar, she really won't like hearing that we've decided to leave in the morning.

"Look, I think you're right," I say as I look for the duffle that hasn't been used since I moved back from New York. "The ghost came to warn us, not to haunt us. All signs point toward us leaving ASAP."

"But…" AJ trails off, knowing there's nothing she can say or do. Her eyes drift over to Rain's empty crib, and I realize that I might still be AJ's fave, but my baby is a close second.

"We're coming back, A."

This isn't the type of goodbye you can prepare for. I have every intention of returning home after I find out who or what my dad is, and figure out a way to control these ridiculous powers, and fend off a council of magical beings trying to steal my kid. But AJ and I both know I'm not making any promises.

I start throwing shit into my duffle, tossing every type of clothing for every type of season because I know nothing about Budapest. AJ just stands a few feet away watching me, not helping or speaking. If someone was just observing our body language through the window, they'd think this was an awkward breakup.

"I know you're coming back, but…"

AJ can't quite finish her thought before turning away to hide her tears. My girl's not much of a crier--didn't shed a single tear in front of me when I moved to New York, even though she later confessed to sobbing her way through two full pints of mint chocolate chip later that night. I'm not surprised she's trying to keep up that tough exterior, but we're both scared shitless right now and this conversation is pretty emotionally overpowering.

"Look," I say, picking up where she left off. "I'm traveling with the most powerful dudes in the universe. And dudes who have pledged to protect *me*, not just my baby."

AJ nods, then gives me a questioning stare. "For the record, I'm not keeping this bar open so you have a job when you get home. I'm planning to take Morgan's over when you move away to be famous at piano or whatever. Because that's still what's going to happen."

I laugh, despite knowing she's totally serious.

"Fair enough," I say. "But that's all the more reason for me to go now. No concert hall's going to book a piano player who glows and needs a vampire to drain her neck every few hours. Speaking of…" I look down at my hands which are starting to crackle with electricity. Panic grips me for a moment, but I take a few breaths and try to center myself the way Rune taught me. I don't think I'm in danger of losing control, as long as this power is drained from me soon.

Oh, Darius?

I've taken to calling my vampire footman with my thoughts whenever I need a reduction in magical powers. Whether it's practice or a strengthened bond from Darius constantly sucking my blood, I've become far more adept at conversing with my mind.

Within seconds, he's standing in the doorway, mixed emotions on his face. He doesn't like being told what to do, but I know he loves my blood and he certainly doesn't seem to mind pressing his body against mine as he feeds from me.

You sparkle, he says, the teasing lilt of his voice clear even through mind speak.

Yes, ha ha. It's very funny. I raise an eyebrow. *Now come do something about it, please. It freaks me out.*

Though the vampire succeeded in lightening my mood, he can still sense the fear in me. He dashes across the room and is behind me in a flash. He runs his thumb over the pulsing vein in my neck as he presses his chest against my back.

I shiver in anticipation of what he's about to do.

"I'd tell you two to get a room," AJ says with a disgusted sigh as she heads to the door, "but I know this *is* your room, so I'll be on my way."

The moment she reaches the hallway, Darius flicks his wrist, closing the door firmly behind her, and with a small twist of his fingers, the door clicks locked.

He still has a hand on my neck, the coolness of his skin sending waves of heat through me in a striking juxtaposition of sensations. Our bodies are so close I can feel the hard flexing of his abs as he shifts, dropping his hand from my neck to my arm, letting his finger trail my sensitive flesh. I suck in a breath as my legs become less stable than I would like and the butterflies in my stomach begin to swarm.

He slides his other arm around my waist, pulling me closer to him. I feel his breath on my neck as his mouth hovers above my flesh.

My skin pulses--from pleasure or power it's hard to say--but I feel alive with a kind of energy I can't describe. And the electricity of his every touch feels heightened to an extreme that is becoming harder and harder to endure while keeping my clothes on.

You smell delicious, he says to my mind, his mental voice husky and layered with need.

I'm sure I'll taste even better, I say, trying to keep my voice cool and unaffected and failing miserably.

I feel the proof of his arousal against my back, and I lean into him, teasing his hardness with the friction.

It's his turn to suck in a breath, but before I can gloat about my small victory, his arm tightens around my waist and he plunges his teeth into my neck.

The pain is a dark thrill running down my spine and pooling at my feet, and I moan and drop my arm over his, intertwining my fingers with his as he drinks deeply from me.

My head spins, my knees buckle, but he doesn't let me fall. His grip is firm without being bruising, just enough support so that I can lose myself in him without fear.

He asked me once if I worried he would take too much. I told him no, and it's true. Each time he feeds from me the silver threads that dance between us grow stronger, forming a deeper bond than I knew was possible. It's impossible to feel fear of him hurting me, when we've already saved each other's lives.

I can feel the moment he approaches that invisible line by taking too much, like my soul is dancing on the edge of life and death, and once again he pulls back just before going too far.

When his lips pull away, when air hits the tiny bite marks on my neck, the distance between us feels immeasurable. I fight back tears once again at the absence of him and wonder if this is a normal vampire effect. It's a good predatory move, making the prey crave the hunter as much as the hunter craves the prey.

His tongue flicks at the small wounds, instantly healing them.

I look down at my hands and note they are no longer glowing or sparking like fireworks. Turning in the vampire's arms so I can face him, I'm about to offer my thanks for once again saving me--and distracting me--when he cuts off my words with his mouth on mine, crushing us together in an almost painful embrace.

His tongue brushes against mine as he deepens our kiss, exploring my mouth with his as his hands rub down my back and over my ass.

I arch into him, my breasts aching as they press into his hard chest, my fingers digging into his back, clutching at his clothes.

I want you. His mental voice is full of need and urgency.

His hands move to cup my ass as he lifts me up. I wrap my legs around his waist and he carries me to the bed. At this angle, I feel the hardness of his arousal pressing against my own desperately aching body, the clothing between us a hardship I can no longer bear.

He lowers me to the bed and with supernatural ease he pulls off my pants and underwear.

I feel suddenly self-conscious about my postpartum body, and I try to move in a way that will maximize my sexiness and hide the mommy bits, but Darius places himself between my knees, spreading them as he runs his hands up my thighs.

"I don't need to read your thoughts to know what you're thinking," he whispers, his fingers lightly brushing up against the sensitive flesh between my legs.

My body quivers with pleasure and a growing need and impatience. "You're too dressed," I tell him, even as my mind is a bit in shock that this is really happening.

Am I actually about to have sexy time with a vampire prince? My life is wild.

"Very well," he says, and moves apart from me just enough to pull off his shirt and remove his pants. He does this much more slowly than I know he can... which means he wants me to enjoy the show.

So I do.

He moves with such fluid grace it's mesmerizing, pulling me into a trance-like state that I have no desire to fight. Once he is naked, he stands before me, every line of his hardened body a testament to nature's artistry, and I nearly choke on my own tongue as I finally get a really good look at all that awaits me.

Holy heaven help me.

He grins, clearly reading me like a splayed open and ready-to-be-devoured book. "Now it is you who wears too much," he says, crawling onto the bed and over me. He makes quick work of the rest of my clothing, reverting back to his vampire speed and impatience, which suits me just fine.

With nothing between us but flesh, he presses into me, our bodies conforming to each other's as he slides a hand under my head and gazes deeply into my eyes. The dark depths of his undo me, like a black star he uses gravity against me as I fall into him.

"I don't know if my kind have a soul," he says, as one hand caresses my head while the other dips between us to tease my body into greater need. "But if I do, you are its mate."

His words, the movement of his fingers, the feel of his mouth on mine again, claiming my lips… all of it brings my body to the very edge of a cliff. But before I can tip over that cliff and enjoy the explosive freedom of that bodily flight, he tenses and then disappears, the weight of him replaced by an awful emptiness and a chill in the air. I blink and he's fully dressed, hand on doorknob.

His face is a cold mask. "Get dressed and run!"

And then he is gone.

It takes me a moment to realize he's not coming back, and the throbbing of my body for his will be left unmet, even as I struggle to understand what the hell could have torn him from my bed and that moment with such haste.

I'm afraid of learning the answer to that question.

I follow his instructions, getting dressed quickly as I strain to sense anything amiss.

I nearly trip over my Budapest bag on the way out, and I kick it to the side. It has everything I need for international travel, but I keep unpacking and packing it, nervous in a way I can't explain.

I step out of the bedroom, my nerves on edge as I look around for Darius.

When I walk into the living room, I'm surprised to see no one. Darius only walked out of the room seconds before, so he should be here, and I can't imagine where the others would have gone. And AJ? Where's she?

I stand alone in silence, and that's when I notice it's not actually that silent. There are sounds coming from the bar.

And a smell.

Smoke.

I run out the back door and down the stairs, the crackling of fire getting louder with every step. I can also hear people struggling, and a baby crying.

I glance down at my hands, an irrational fear that I started this fire overtaking me, but no, that's not possible. This wasn't me. But if not me, then who?

Before I reach the back entrance, the door flings open and Rune sprints out, his beautiful silver hair singed by the flame. Right behind him is Zev, in wolf form, carrying--with his enormous, intimidating jaws--the knotted end of a blanket bundle that squirms and lets out little cooing sounds.

"Rain?"

"Run, Bernie," Rune says, taking me by the arm and turning me away. "You must run!"

The urgency of his voice makes me want to obey, but I can't blindly follow. "Darius?" I ask, resisting Rune's pull.

"We'll meet Darius in the woods," Rune says, giving me another tug. "If he survives."

CHAPTER THREE

I don't have time to react or respond before Zev the wolf ducks his head between my legs and hoists me onto his back. I clutch his fur, holding on for dear life as we bound into the woods.

"What about AJ?" I cry out, remembering that she was here before Darius and I had our alone time.

"She left before they arrived," Rune answers, annoyingly light on the details as we charge further and further from the bar. I can see smoke billowing out of the windows, but no visible flame.

"Who are *they*?" It's frustrating to have to ask this question, but I get that neither Rune nor Zev feels like talking right now.

"They're fae," Rune answers through pursed lips, clearly not happy with the acts of his kin.

As we near the woods' edge, I roll off of Zev, my fall broken by a patch of leaves and snow. The werewolf and the fae have to stop and turn back to me.

"Bernie, we must hurry," Rune pleads with me. "We're outnumbered and can't allow them near you or the child."

"And I can't survive more than half a day without Darius sucking my blood," I fire back. "So we're not going to just watch one of our own die before this stupid quest even starts."

It's weird saying one of our own, especially referring to this group that doesn't have two members of the same species. But here we are, bound by incomprehensible trials and near-death experiences, and about to go through a few more. If Darius isn't one of our own, who is?

Rune doesn't move right away, weighing my words. Zev, however, morphs from wolf to human, transitioning Rain from his jaws to his arms as he rises. It shouldn't be sexy, but so help me Jesus it is.

171

"She's right," Zev says, a few burn marks on his naked body. "We're out and we've regrouped. On top of that, we've got a secret weapon."

He looks me dead in the eye, and I understand what he's asking. The trouble is, I have no idea how to do it.

"What should I do? I don't have any control, I don't know--"

He raises a hand to my lips, stopping my panic from escalating any further.

"I've seen what magic can do when your heart's behind it," Zev says. "Darius needs you. Let's go."

He puts an arm around me and we turn back toward Morgan's, a knot forming in my stomach as I consider the task before me. I'm not ready for this. I can't face off against a magical being, let alone match any power that's too great for my three princes. This is too much. I'm about to turn back to Zev and Rune and tell them I need help, that I need Darius...

But that's just it.

I need Darius.

And if I'm being honest with myself, I don't just need him. I want him. I crave him. He may not know if he has a soul, but I know he does, and ours are inextricably bound. I will not leave him.

Darius.

The knot in my stomach doubles in size, but now it feels like a raging fire and not a fit of nerves.

An intense tingling spreads through my body, igniting every inch of my flesh and blood as it works toward my fingers. I have the same sensations I did the night I killed my mother--nothing makes sense, I know not what I do, but I'm acting on impulses that can't be denied.

I feel Zev fall away from me as trails of white-hot light shoot out of my fingertips. An ear-piercing cry erupts from my lungs and through my mouth, a sound so loud and shrill I can't believe it came from a human.

The light blasts into the bar, shaking the foundation and making me worry for a moment I've done more harm than good. I hold the scream and the magic outpouring as long as I can, until my head grows faint and my knees buckle beneath me. I hit the ground in a heap, spent from my unbridled outburst.

Zev and Rune are immediately beside me, each with a hand under my arms and helping me stand.

"Are you alright?" Rune asks.

I nod slowly, trying to control my breathing and settle my heart rate.

While the fae and the werewolf have their focus on me, my eyes catch some movement at the back door of the bar.

Through the smoke and ash, I see a sexy, disheveled, smoldering vampire walking my way.

Darius... I speak in my mind.

Thank you, he whispers back.

Zev catches my gaze and looks up. You'd have to be paying close attention to notice, but the slightest hint of a smile crosses his face.

"Look who's still immortal," the werewolf says.

Rune speaks a little less playfully. "The others?"

"Dead," Darius responds. "They can swap bar stories with the ghost now."

Rune breathes a sigh of relief. Whatever his feelings about Darius and his fellow fae, it's clear he has no trouble choosing a side in this fight.

I look past the vampire and see that, somehow, my bar is still standing. Smoke drifts out of the windows, but it's not billowing like before. Darius reads my face and addresses my obvious concern.

"Morgan's is fine," he says. "Your spell put out the fire... or rather, sent it after the fae. Once we clean out the bodies and replace a few floorboards, it will look just as it did."

It feels silly to care so much about a building when death seems to be nipping at our heels, but Morgan's is like a family member. It *is* a family member.

"Is it safe to stay here tonight?" I ask.

Darius shakes his head. "We need to leave immediately. There will be more attacks, and we've nowhere to hide in Rowley." He looks at me lovingly with his dark eyes. "It's not fair to ask you to save my life a third time."

Compliments from such a powerful man carry a little extra weight, and I want to bask in this one for as long as I can.

Unfortunately, he's right. We need to leave yesterday.

"Are we safe to go back inside?" I ask the group, thinking about all the baby gear I don't currently have with me.

"Every second is precious," Zev says, sniffing the passing breeze for signs of assassins. "But we can gather things before we set off."

Without so much as a glance at any of us, Rune starts walking toward the bar. "I'll clear the fallen," he says, his voice ice cold. We all watch him go; Darius might have been closest to death, but these events have been just as traumatic for Rune.

"Okay," I say, turning back to Zev, who's holding Rain. I inch closer, peering at her small face, making sure she's unharmed. Making sure not to touch her. "I need to grab my phone to text AJ and throw some stuff for Rain in her diaper bag, then we'll head to the airport."

WE HEAD out about 10 PM and the roads between Rowley and Boston are mostly empty. We're in the airport parking lot in less than half an hour, giving us just enough time in the car for everyone to agree that the fae went after Darius first, and he'd be dead if not for my newfound powers.

After texting AJ a long, final plea to stay the hell away from Morgan's, I get a chance to reflect on what happened. These magical bursts are still new to me; I've only focused on how to keep my powers from consuming me, not about what they can actually do. Tonight, for the first time, someone told me to use my magic... and I did.

It's thrilling. And a little scary. Given I nearly ignited my daughter with those same powers.

As I get out of the car and grab the diaper bag, I look up and catch Darius' eye. There's a hard look to his gaze that softens when it lands on me, and I shiver with delight at the effect I have on the vampire, and the effect he has on me. It's intoxicating.

"Bernie," Rune says, breaking me out of my trance as he carries Rain in her car seat. "You'll have to take the lead on this. I have no experience with your aero ports."

Rune's pronunciation of airports reminds me that while these guys might pass for normal humans, they actually hail from entirely different worlds. I'll need to remember that as we embrace the exciting adventure of international travel together.

"Right. It's easy, you just follow me and... " I stop explaining when it dawns on me I haven't thought any of this through. "Who here has money?"

Rune pulls a small bag of coins from his cloak. Zev just shrugs. Darius takes a long gold chain from his pocket, something I keep expecting to have a watch on the other end, but it doesn't.

"Okay, put your non-money away," I say, confident we won't be able to pay for tickets in pure gold. "I'm going to use credit cards, probably five or six of them, so just don't try to help."

We cross the bridge from the parking structure to the terminals and walk through the sliding glass doors.

Heading toward the ticketing counter, I realize how little Earth stuff I've done with these three. I smile to myself, thinking there's no place like an airport--or should I say *aero port*-- to show some paranormals a good time.

"Hi there, where are we going today?" a friendly young clerk asks as we approach.

"Um, Budapest. One way." I almost laugh when I say the words, the absurdity of everything hitting me hard now that I'm out of my magical bar and in the real world. Just buying four one-way tickets to Budapest on a whim. No biggie.

"Alright," the attendant says as he starts typing away. I steal a glance behind me, enjoying the sight of the Sexies trying to act normal and failing miserably. No one can look this good and hope to blend in.

"We've actually got seats on a flight leaving in just under an hour," the clerk says. "Will that work or do you need more ti--"

"We'll leave now," Darius cuts in, unable to control his take-charge instincts.

No talking from you, I scold him in my thoughts.

"The soonest flight would be wonderful," I say to the clerk with a smile.

Why is this taking so long? Darius asks my mind.

It's been ten seconds, I think back.

Exactly.

God give me the patience to endure a twelve-hour flight with these men.

With our boarding passes in hand, we head from the ticketing area to the security checkpoint, and I'm overrun with fear about the photo ID situation. Do fae have driver's licenses? I'm pretty sure werewolves don't. Is Darius going to show a centuries-old birth certificate? Why the hell did I think we'd be able to board a flight?

Naturally, my worries subside as soon as we get to the front of the line and I hear Darius speak to the TSA agent.

"We are allowed to pass without showing you documentation. It's of no concern to you and you'll go about your business."

With a blank look on her face, the middle-aged woman at her tiny kiosk just waves us through. TSA Pre-Check has nothing on vampire mind control.

Passing through security takes a little more finesse. I have to tell the Sexies to take their shoes off four times before they acquiesce, and Rune gets some very suspicious looks when he loudly asks how he could possibly hide a bomb in the sole of his boot. I'm seriously regretting not discussing airport etiquette on the drive over.

"What's a belt?" I hear Zev ask the young female agent ushering travelers past the bag scanner.

"The hell you mean, 'what's a belt'?" she rightly fires back. "Put it through the loops, hold your damn pants up."

Zev looks confused, maybe even a little angry. Like the woman is toying with him. "Then how does it come off?"

"He's not from… here," I interrupt from the next row, hoping I can end this conversation before the woman gets growled at. "Zev, you don't have a belt, just walk through the thing!"

He might know a lot about earthly designs and have no trouble ripping through clothes, but now it's clear that werewolves can't handle belts.

"Just put it in the bin, sir."

Another TSA agent sounding more perturbed than usual alerts me to Darius refusing to put down his coat. It looks like she got as far as making him take it off, but parting with it makes Darius a little too uncomfortable.

Darius, I say in my mind. *How many knives are in your coat?*

Why?

The response has me thinking the number is somewhere between four and ten.

Tell Rune to create an illusion, you can't take those on the plane. My spoken thoughts are hasty, and I wonder if he can still hear them clearly.

Why can't I take them on the--

"Just do it!" I say out loud, then immediately hold my phone up to my ear so it looks like I was yelling at someone on the phone. Sort of.

I look over in time to see Rune nod at Darius and then casually wave towards the conveyor belt. Once Darius' jacket passes through without any alarms sounding, I go back to my shoes.

With the biggest hurdles cleared, I do take a modest amount of pleasure in watching each prince walk through the metal detector and then stand still while a tired old man with no patience for bullshit runs his wand over their pockets. Rune has to go through the X-ray thingy three times before finally getting his pockets completely empty. One of the agents is about to confiscate some of his small containers when Darius steps in and forcefully changes the man's mind.

Shoes on and bags scanned, we head toward the boarding area.

"People live here?" Rune asks as we pass a couple of young travelers sleeping with their heads on their bags.

"No, probably just a long layover, waiting to board their next flight," I say.

"Why did they fly to the wrong destination?" Zev asks, but we thankfully arrive at our gate before I'm forced to answer.

I have my three handsome companions go ahead of me, and I feel like a mother escorting her children onto a plane for the first time. I snicker at the thought of putting them all on little child leashes. What a sight that would be. All the adrenaline from blasting magic out of my fingertips an hour ago has been replaced by a dull sense of responsibility.

When we finally get to the jetway and head for the airplane doors, I breathe a sigh of relief. I'll be able to sit back and rest for at least a few hours.

Naturally, no sooner has that thought passed through my head than Rain starts to cry. Poor little girl. She should be asleep in her crib and instead I'm hauling her across the globe on a mission I don't even understand.

The flight's about three-quarters full, which is nice for us late arrivals. We can get our bags into overhead compartments and find our seats without stepping over too many people. We get a mix of looks from the other passengers; some are annoyed to see a baby joining them for a red eye, others can't take their eyes off the strapping men moving down the aisle.

When we get to our seats, I sit between Rune and Darius, and Zev takes the row behind us, keeping Rain with him as he preps her bottle.

Let me know when you need a release, Darius whispers into my head. Instantly I'm imagining my last *near release* in all its glorious detail, despite knowing the vampire is talking about taking some of my magic blood.

But he looks at me and smirks. *Of either kind*, he adds, clearly picking up on my thoughts.

Heat pools in my belly at the thought of what that might be like and, despite the circumstances, I feel a burning need filling me. One glance at Darius' lap proves he feels it too. I smile. *I will, thank you. Ever thought about joining the mile-high club?*

The what?

Nevermind.

I turn my attention back to my baby, happily sucking down her bottle while a werewolf cuddles her. I hate that I can't hold her, that the thought of cradling her in my arms fills me with fear. I try to push those feelings aside, finding a tiny bit of comfort in knowing how well my co-travelers will care for her while I try to fix my broken, magical self.

Without a baby to occupy my energy, my thoughts return to Darius, and how fun it would be to have a stealthy fling while we're in the air. The plane is dark, passengers are mostly sleeping. We could slip into the lavatory and then he could slip into…

The direction of my thoughts become too distracting, and when Darius takes my hand, gripping it firmly, his eyes dilating with need, I realize I've gotten him all hot and bothered too. To redirect both of our minds, I turn to Rune, wanting to ask a question I didn't get a chance to earlier.

"Why do you think the fae came after us first? I thought it was a council from all three realms."

Rune doesn't look at me right away, and it's clear these thoughts were already swirling inside his head. Finally, he speaks, though he still does not look me in the eye.

"It suggests, to me, that there was never any intention to discuss or negotiate a safe passage for you and the child."

"What do you mean?"

"A group of fae might be seen as a diplomatic envoy," he explains, "as we're largely viewed as the more trustworthy of the races. But those who attacked us went directly after Darius, not so much as speaking a word before blasting everyone with fire."

There's anger in his voice. Perhaps a sense of betrayal. It's funny, because these princes who have bound themselves in the common interest of my protection, they are surely viewed as traitors by their kinfolk. And yet that seems to be exactly how Rune feels about the fae sent after us this evening.

"Why would they go after him and not all three of you?" I ask. "Or just come directly for the baby? Or me?"

"It's a coordinated attack," he answers matter-of-factly. "They intend to weaken us systematically until no one can protect Rain. Which is why…"

Rune looks worried, which makes me insanely nervous. He kept me calm when someone stole my baby in the middle of a storm, when things, at least to me, seemed much more dire than they are right now. Now he's struggling to finish a sentence.

"Which is why, once you are settled, and protected, and in control of your powers… Zev, Darius and I must return to our realms."

A tiny, shrinking sliver of myself has always known the day would come. Even as our bonds grew stronger and our love grew deeper, I knew my princes wouldn't just keep tending bar in a small town in Massachusetts. Still, the fae's words worm into the deepest part of my heart and plant a dark seed full of pain.

"But… I don't know if I can do this, if I can do anything without you three," I say, sounding exactly as needy as I feel.

Rune takes and gently kisses the top of my hand. "I don't think any of us are prepared to go on with a life that doesn't have you in it. Sadly, that's the exact reason we need to return. To put an end to this madness and stop the senseless onslaught."

"How would you do that? How could any of you get your kingdoms to stand down?"

He gives a thoughtful shrug. "We can't say with any certainty. Zev might have the easiest route, with the way wolf kingdoms establish hierarchy. Darius would need to convince a council of ancients who have never changed their mind about anything. I'd have to prove to my mother that the child is nothing without her bond to you." He looks at me, tenderness is his bright eyes. "None of it would be easy. Any success would be worth it."

I glance at Darius, whose mental presence caresses my worried mind. *Do not fear. We are oath-bound to protect you always. And if we have to bring down our kingdoms from within to do so, we will. But we will find our way back to you. I will find you always.*

Tears burn my eyes and clog my throat, but I refuse to let them fall. Instead, I twist in my seat to face Zev, who has remained quiet during this. His path may be the simplest, but Rune hinted at something that sounded much harder.

With the werewolf, I say nothing. I just dive into his forest green eyes, getting lost in them until the bittersweet bliss of his presence eases my heart. And I know there will be an unquenchable hurt inside me every day that I am apart from these men.

He leans forward so that we are forehead to forehead. "This war must end. For everyone's sake." With his free hand he cups my face, pulling away to make eye contact with me. "But we won't leave until you are safe."

That actually brings me a perverse kind of comfort. Since I seem to never be safe anymore, the chances of them being allowed to leave are slim.

Still, I know they're right. Eventually, they will have to face their families. I only wish I could protect them from the pain that will come.

As the plane starts to accelerate down the runway, I reach my hand into my pocket, gripping the fallen star tightly and sending some of my anxieties into its magical form. My nerves have nothing to do with flying and everything to do with where I'm flying to. *What* I'm flying to. And what I might lose when I finally gain what I'm so desperately seeking. Control.

I'm a witch.

I say that to myself probably twenty times each day, and every time it feels a little more real. Tonight it's stronger than ever before. I'm ready to take these powers, and then I'm ready to take on whatever comes my way. But first, I really have to pee.

I wait for the plane to get some altitude and then stand. I feel Darius' eyes on me as I scoot into the aisle, and I may or may not take a little extra time stepping over and straddling him as I go. It's possible I push my breasts against his face briefly as well, but that's only because the seating is so cramped.

In the row behind us, Zev has his eyes closed and is gripping the armrests fiercely, Rain strapped into her car seat next to him. I hope this is the last airplane experience we force on the poor wolf.

The bathrooms are empty since I'm technically still supposed to be seated, but that stuff is just a suggestion. I've been holding in a pee for the last five hours and don't give a shit about turbulence right now.

I'm just finishing up my business when there's a knock at the door. It's pretty ridiculous, because I know there's an empty bathroom a few feet away.

"Yeah, I'm in here," I say.

Instead of a response, I see the small lock on the door start to slide from *occupied* to *vacant*. Not exactly what a girl wants to see when she's plunked down on the toilet.

"Hey, I said I'm in--"

I know you are.

I stop talking and my fear turns to excitement as Darius speaks into my mind. I scoot my feet back to make room for the door to fold in, and he quietly and quickly steps inside the cramped stall.

My eyes trail down to see that his pants are already unbuttoned and he's wasting no time pushing them down.

I stand, stepping out of my panties instead of pulling them back up, and bring his face to mine while his hand slides between my thighs.

I'd like to finish what we started, he says.

So would I, I answer.

Jesus Lord God, so would I.

CHAPTER FOUR

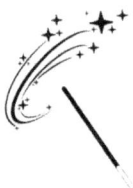

My body hums with energy as he presses himself against me, his hands sliding over my ass, and I don't waste any time. I pull his head down lower so I can reach his lips and kiss him with everything in me. Passionately, bruisingly, with such urgent need that I'm breathless from it.

I feel him in my mind. In my blood. In my soul.

And when he slips one of his hands between my legs, I feel him inside me.

I moan into his lips and he hardens against me.

I would question if this is prudent or safe, but my body is healed and prudent can go to hell.

I need this man.

Desperately.

When he turns me around to bend me over the toilet, I miss the heat of his lips but crave what's about to happen.

Are you ready? He asks in my mind, as his fingers dig into my hips and he positions himself against me.

More than ready, I reply.

"Excuse me," someone says, knocking on the bathroom door and totally ruining the mood. "Please return to your seats. The fasten seatbelt sign is on."

"I'm feeling sick," I say. "It'll be a minute."

Hurry.

I can practically hear the smirk in his mental voice. *As you wish.*

I doubt that he means to call to mind my favorite movie when he says that, but the effect is the same and somehow that's even more of a turn on.

Just as he's about to fulfill his promise to me and my horny body, the plane lurches, hitting an air pocket or a flock of flying bison, something with enough force to make everything in the bathroom shake violently.

I lose my footing and knock my head against the cabinet. As Darius tries to

180

catch me, his... well let's just say his most-protruding body part has an unfortunate run-in with the sink.

He curses in my mind, loudly and creatively.

I feel a trickle of something on my head and realize I'm bleeding.

When I move to grab a paper towel to catch the blood now dripping into my eyes I trip over the underwear wrapped around my ankles and crash into the vampire, pushing us both into the door, which collapses outward under our combined weight, spilling us into the cramped hall where we land on the floor with our pants down.

Then three things happen in such quick succession it might as well be simultaneous.

Darius uses his super speed to set us on our feet.

He somehow gets both of our pants pulled up quickly.

And he speeds over to the flight attendant who witnessed all of this and uses his mind voodoo on her so she won't remember seeing what she saw.

The lights are out in the cabin and most everyone else on the flight seems to be asleep, so we've avoided the worst of the humiliation. We do, however, get a few knowing smirks from the nosier passengers as we walk back up the aisle.

By the time we make it to our seats, I'm dizzy and bleeding from my head. If it wasn't for the pain, I'd probably feel more embarrassed than at any other point in my life.

On top of all that, I'm still horny—a condition that feels like it's going to be permanent.

I do not like your aero planes.

Darius sounds like a sulky teenager in my mind and I can't help but laugh.

My smile fades when I see Rune's expression.

"What happened to you?" He asks as I take the seat next to him.

"Um. Turbulence."

Immediately he sets to work examining my head and dressing my wound with a smelly poultice that he snuck through security.

It stings but then a pleasant numbness sets in and I lean back in my chair.

I don't realize how tense Darius is until I take his hand, and the ripples of his hunger burn through my mind.

When I look at him, his jaw is clenched and he's facing forward, staring at the back of the chair in front of him.

You okay?

I'm. Fine.

Yeah, you sound fine. Do you need to feed on me?

No. It's too soon and you're too weak.

Well you can't stay like this the whole damn flight to Budapest.

I can.

You're a stubborn ass.

He has no reply to that. I smirk and make sure he can hear it in my thoughts.

When he glances my way, I tilt my head. *Do it.*

Darius narrows his eyes at me, then abruptly stands.

When Zev also stands and moves out of his seat I realize the two are communicating.

Are you serious? You'd rather change seats than feed?

You are too tempting and I will not risk your safety.

I expect Zev to sit next to me, but instead they approach the nearest flight attendant and within two minutes I'm being escorted to first class.

You did not tell me we had better options for our travel.

We didn't, I say. *I would have needed five more credit cards to pay for these seats.*

When we get to the other side of the curtain, the difference is night and day.

Zev takes a seat next to me and Darius and Rune sit together to the right of us, Rune now cradling my sleeping baby. The chairs are much larger and they recline into a nearly horizontal position. I'm informed by the flight attendant we will be served a gourmet breakfast in a few hours but if I need anything just ask.

I don't know why Darius thinks I can't handle giving him more blood. I'm touched by his concern but definitely feel he's making more of an issue of this than he needs to. It isn't until Rune's meds start to wear off and my headache returns that I reluctantly admit I hit my head pretty damn hard.

Zev seems to instantly sense my pain levels rise. "Do you want me to tear him apart for letting you get hurt? Because I will."

I roll my eyes at him. "You two will find literally any reason to fight, won't you?"

He shrugs and doesn't deny it. "It's in our nature."

He twists in his seat and encourages me to do the same so that I can lean my head against him. I close my eyes as he begins a gentle massage around my temples, carefully avoiding the part of my head I hit. The extra leg room of first class clearly has the werewolf feeling better about flying.

"Tell me about your life back on your world," I say. "Rune hinted at the wolf hierarchy but didn't elaborate. What's it like?"

"It's… complicated," he says, his voice soft. "Being part wolf, pack is everything. We are, to some degree, ruled by the instincts of nature. But I am also a man, and so I must abide by the laws of man as well. My father is king and alpha of our pack. But he is also king of other packs, which creates conflict with those alphas. So there is always friction in our kingdom."

"What about you?" I ask.

"I have an older brother, Link. He's by rights next in line to be king, though our race is long-lived so that right will only pass to him if our father is killed in combat."

"I'm sensing a but," I say.

"But he wasn't born an alpha. I was."

"That must be complicated," I say.

"It is. Link and I were close in our youth, but as we grew older, as his future responsibilities came between us, a wall formed that I have never been able to break down."

"So what will happen? Will he ever be king? Will you be alpha?"

I feel Zev shrug. "Those are the questions on everyone's mind. The only way I can become alpha is if I leave the pack to form my own…"

"Or?" I ask as I slowly ease myself up to look at him.

"Or challenge my father and fight him to the death."

I flinch. "That's brutal."

"It is our way. My father killed his father. And his before that. It is a legacy born of blood and teeth."

I reach for his hand and squeeze it. "I'm sorry you have to live under that weight. Sounds like a real bitch of a burden to carry."

"I never gave it much thought. It's just the way it is."

"It's the way it's always been, maybe," I say, my heart hurting for him. "That doesn't mean it has to stay that way." I pause, afraid of the next question but unable to stop myself from asking. "Will you really leave? Once I'm... safe?" It's only now I realize what Zev will be going home to do, and what it will cost him.

Zev stares into my eyes, obviously conflicted. "It's the very last thing I want to do. But I will if I must."

There are no words I can offer that will bring comfort or change our paths, so instead, I squeeze his hand and adjust myself so that I'm leaning with my head against his shoulder.

I fall asleep to the sound of his heartbeat.

When I wake to the sound of the food cart passing by, Rune--who's taken Zev's place in the seat next to me--hands me a cup of steaming tea.

"Zev said your head was still hurting. Next time tell me," he gently admonishes as I sip the concoction. I nod, making a silent promise I'm not sure I'll always keep, and then look around the cabin. It seems Darius has mind-controlled everyone in our section to keep their windows closed so no sun gets in. At least I assume he has, because though I see one guy occasionally glance at his blind with a slightly confused expression, he never reaches to open it, nor does anyone else.

Rain is sleeping in Zev's arms, who looks half asleep himself, though I know from experience he'll be alert in a flash if there's a threat. Darius has his chair reclined and his eyes closed, but I feel his mind whirling, and know he's not resting at all.

It's not a familiar or fun way to travel for any of them. Only Rain, the happiest baby in the world, seems comfortable.

WE HAVE one quick layover and the rest of the flight passes uneventfully, with all of us sleeping in intermittent, restless bursts. When we finally land in Budapest a day has passed and it's nighttime again. Once we're off the plane and heading toward the terminal exit, it dawns on me that we're actually in Budapest. I also become aware that I have no idea what to do now that we're here.

"Does anyone have any thoughts about where we should go next?" I ask the group. "Anyone have my dad's phone number?"

Per usual, my sarcasm is met with frowns and raised eyebrows. I shake my head, which has become my go-to for telling them to move on with the conversation and not try to make sense of my jokes.

"I'd like to inspect my map," Rune says, "though I'd rather do it in privacy."

"We should get a room in the center of town," Darius says. "This land has old magic under the city streets. I'll look around once we have a place secured where Bernie can rest."

The word rest has me taking stock of how tired I am and how dizzy I still feel. Rune and Darius exchange knowing glances and, before I know what's happening, the vampire pulls me into a bathroom and locks us in a stall.

"Third time's the charm?" I ask hopefully, though honestly I feel too disgusting to do anything sexy at the moment.

"You're starting to glow," he says.

"Oh. Right." How had I completely forgotten my glow into the dark problem?

"But you're not strong enough to give blood," he says with a frown.

"Okay… so what's the plan? I assume you have one or you wouldn't have crashed the ladies room with me."

"You need to drink my blood again first. It will heal you and revive you enough to allow me to feed on you."

I swallow nervously. This wasn't what I was expecting. But I remember the instant healing I felt the last time I had a head injury, and I can't deny that would be real handy right about now.

So I nod and he quickly bites into his wrist.

I steel myself against the general unpleasantness of this, then place my mouth against the open wound and suck.

Like before, the viscosity coats my throat and I resist the urge to gag, but once it's in me I feel a zing of power and I can't help but suck harder.

Darius has to gently pull away before I take too much. I sigh, licking my lips, then tilt my head, offering him my neck.

The moment his teeth plunge into my flesh I sag against him, held firmly in his arms, as I cling to him.

This time… it all feels different.

Like a bond that had been tentative between us, like a rope made out of smoke, has hardened into something unbreakable.

When he pulls away, licking the wound to heal it, I can't stop staring at him. At the perfection of his face and the depth of his eyes.

I feel overwhelmed by him and unable to let go.

"What happened between us?" I whisper. "How can I feel you… everywhere?"

He looks just as stunned, his grip on me tightening as if he can't bear to let go. "I didn't expect…" his voice trails off. "Nevermind. We must go. Before the sun comes."

Taking my hand, he guides me out and we catch up with Rune and Zev, who's just changed Rain's diaper.

We step out of the terminal and I start to see and hear things that come with foreign travel--different languages, funny license plates, interesting fashion choices. This is the first time I've ever been outside the U.S. and I wish I could just be a normal tourist. Maybe my estranged and possibly magical father lives in some cool ruins and I can live my Lara Croft fantasies.

Darius flags down a taxi and sits in front while the rest of us cram into the back. There's no room for the carseat, so Darius takes her and straps her to his chest. *She'll be safe,* he assures me mentally.

Once we all have seats, I pay closer attention and realize I'm hearing fluent Hungarian from the front seat and it's Darius doing the speaking. He gives our driver directions and we start weaving through traffic.

It's dark outside but my senses are heightened from feeding on Darius and I take in everything as we head to the hotel. The city is beautiful, with hotels and restaurants lining the central river. Modern buildings line the streets, but the sense of antiquity still has a firm hold on the landscape.

The car pulls up outside a beautiful building with a view of the water. It seems Darius opted for upscale lodging, so hopefully he has a plan for settling the tab.

I let Darius take the lead when we reach the front desk, since I definitely didn't master Hungarian on the flight over. Maybe he'll get us a discount with the whole sexy-as-sin-man-holding-a-cute-baby vibe he's got going. I'd give him whatever he wanted if it were me.

Before he can get more than a few words out to the hotel clerk, the young woman stares at me, her eyes narrowed like she's trying to place me. "You are Bernadette Morgan?" She asks in English.

I nod, surprised at being recognized, and surprised she was able to tear her eyes off of my vampire long enough to notice me at all.

She pulls a manilla envelope from behind the counter and hands it to me. "This was left for you two days ago. I was asked to give it to you when you arrived today."

I exchange glances with the guys, who all look as bewildered as me. Two days ago we didn't know we'd be in Budapest today. And two hours ago we didn't know we'd be at this hotel.

So who could have possibly found us here?

"Who left it?" I ask the clerk, who doesn't find any of this as unnerving as the rest of us do.

She shrugs. "It was left for my manager. I was just told an American woman named Bernadette Morgan with a baby would arrive today and to pass along the envelope."

I thank her for the useless information and move toward the elevator while Darius gets our room keys. As far as I can tell, the only people who know where we are--and possibly where we're going--are those who want us dead.

I'm lost in a trance until I find myself sitting on the edge of a couch in a fancy hotel suite. There's a common room with a couple lazy boys to go with the sofa, plus the TV, mini fridge and wet bar. Double doors lead to bedrooms on either side of the living room.

None of the Sexies speak, they all just stare, waiting for me to do something.

I nervously open the envelope.

Be careful.

Do you smell poison? I ask.

No.

A bomb?

No.

Then the greatest risk is a paper cut. Relax.

I do not, in fact, cut myself on the paper as I pull it out.

It's a thick cream card with calligraphed writing on it that simply says "9 pm Friday."

"What do you think it means?" I ask.

Zev growls. "I think it means someone will be coming for you tomorrow night."

"Is it someone who wants to kill us?" The question doesn't feel all that smart coming out of my mouth, and the looks I receive confirm my assessment.

"Most people with assassination plans don't set up meetings," Rune says, addressing my dumb question far too gently.

"So," the fae continues, "either someone who wants to help us will be here tomorrow night at nine... or someone else plans to kill us between now and then."

CHAPTER FIVE

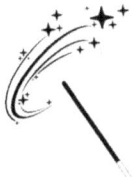

"I just want one semi-plausible reason that anyone--or anything--might know we're here."

Since opening the envelope and getting the incredibly bizarre invitation to my own hotel room for the following evening, neither Rune nor Darius nor Zev has been able to offer any sort of explanation. I don't expect *all* the answers, but I got us on the plane and to Budapest, and now I'd appreciate if one of these magical men could drop some knowledge on a poor little witch from Rowley, MA.

"I'll be back," Darius says, and then is out the door and probably in the street before I can tell him to sit his ass down.

"What's that shit?" I ask Rune, forcing someone else to deal with the anger I feel at Darius bailing.

"He's going to scour the city before he has to spend a day hiding from the sun," Rune says. "I know you want answers, Bernie, and this is the best way to get them."

Rune's right, but it doesn't calm me down. I walk over to Zev, who's putting Rain to bed for the night in the hotel's rollaway crib.

Hang on.

Why's there already a crib in here?

"Let's start at the beginning," I say, trying to keep my voice at a respectable volume while still presenting as much angst as possible. "Why Budapest? My dad is here, someone else knows we're here, my grandfather wanted us to come here when he found out he was going to be murdered. I know you can't solve any of those ridiculous riddles, but maybe someone can tell me why Budapest matters?"

"Oh," Zev says, a trace of confusion on his gorgeous face. "You don't know about Budapest?"

If he was closer, I swear to God I'd bite him.

"Of course I don't know about Budapest! What the hell am I supposed to know?"

Rune walks over and settles me with his calming touch, and not a moment too soon as I realize how tightly my fists were clenched.

"This is the first land," Zev answers, doing that obnoxious thing where he says words that sound important but mean nothing to me. He senses his mistake when I grit my teeth and flare my nostrils.

"When the Fates created humankind, pooled from the three sisters' sweat, it began here," Zev explains.

"Hold up, dude," I say. I can tell he's about to keep talking, like he didn't just undo thousands of years of world religions with one casually tossed out sentence. "Humanity was created from witch sweat?"

Zev frowns. "Well, yes. Obviously."

I purse my lips. "Tell me how that is in any way obvious?"

He doesn't have an answer, because of course none of this is obvious. "There are thousands of religions in my world, and I'm almost 100% certain that none of them have an origin story involving witch sweat."

Zev clears his throat. "Okay. Well, now you know the truth. May I continue?"

I sigh, knowing they will just keep doing this. Throwing out super important, life-changing details like it's nothing. "Be my guest."

Zev nods and begins again like I never interrupted him in the first place. "Generally, of course. The land was different then, but the hills, caves and rivers never lost their importance. And witches have always kept this city as a stronghold, even when vampires pushed them to the brink."

"So," Rune says, assuming the sexy professor role that suits him so well, "for the Last Witch and her mother to be called to Budapest, by whatever power, stands to reason."

"Great," I say, pacing the hotel room impatiently. I'm sure it does stand to reason, as Rune says, but I'd sure as hell love to know what reason that is. And pooled from their sweat? I guess that's as good a primordial ooze as any.

"Either of you have an educated guess about what reason or power brought us here?"

My question is met with thoughtful silence, giving me a reflective beat to appreciate the change I've gone through in a few short weeks. From a pregnant bar owner with dashed dreams and limited prospects, to a single mother keeping company with paranormals who once meant to kill me and have since sworn to protect me, even if it costs them their lives. And also I'm a witch. A glow in the dark one at that.

While I wait for either Zev or Rune to spill the tea about Budapest and why it matters to me and my daughter, I delight briefly in the journey that got me here, commanding these gorgeous, powerful men, and knowing they'll go to hell and back if it means keeping me happy.

"I have a guess," Zev finally responds, his pensive voice rumbling in a low register that always makes me weak-kneed.

"Any witch with an understanding of her heritage knows of this land," the werewolf says as he takes a seat in one of the lazy boys. "We're living through the final stages of an ancient prophecy, one scribed by the Fates themselves after they came here and created life. I'd expect anyone looking for clues would search here. And that includes your father."

Finally, we have the semblance of a theory.

"So you think my dad is here, trying to interpret the prophecy?" I ask, Zev nodding along. "Any thoughts about Gramps' letter and why my dad bailed before I was born?"

"Imagine finding out you'd spawned a being with powers beyond your comprehension," Rune says. "That could certainly drive a man to go looking for answers."

It sounds a little too much like Rune is defending the deadbeat who abandoned me and my mother. My initial reaction is a scowl, but I have to remind myself I'm fresh off of killing my mother because she wanted to kill my baby. Maybe, *maybe*, the man who walked out on her had a half-decent reason. *Maybe.*

"As for your grandfather," Rune continues, "I can't say. I'm fairly certain he didn't write the letter, or wasn't in control of himself when he did."

"What makes you think that?" I ask.

"People can't write when they're dead," the fae states bluntly. It's not quite the insightful answer I'd hoped for.

"I'd say your father planted the letter," Zev says. "I don't know whether he's good or evil, but he's the most likely culprit in my mind."

I stand up and walk toward the window, trying to hide my frustration. I've grown so used to these men teaching and explaining, so to have them confused and searching for answers makes me uncomfortable.

"So what do we do?" I finally ask, hoping to find something to focus on to keep the questions from driving me crazy. "Sit in this hotel room until tomorrow night?"

Zev shrugs. "We'll see what Darius finds tonight, then Rune and I will look around tomorrow. If we don't stumble on some evidence that tells us to do otherwise, yes, we'll wait for our visitor."

"And while we wait," Rune says, walking over and placing his hand on the small of my back. "We'll turn this place into a magical fortress. Whoever means to meet you, whatever their intention might be, won't have an easy time of it."

The words are reassuring, giving me enough peace to notice how exhausted I am. This has been a long, travel day of shitty sleep, and it comes on the heels of a long, sleep-deprived night. Rune notices my heavy eyelids and guides me toward one of the bedrooms.

"Now's the best time for you to rest, Bernie. Zev and I will sleep and guard in shifts while we wait for Darius to return."

I nod, too excited about the prospect of sleep to engage in any more conversation. I give an unenthusiastic wave as I walk into the bedroom, kick my shoes and jeans off, and I'm out the moment my head hits the pillow.

It doesn't take long before vivid dreams consume my mind. I'm walking along the edge of the river, the Sexies trailing behind me, and in every doorway and on every balcony, a shadowy figure stands watching me. It feels like there are hundreds, if not thousands of eyes tracking my every move. I become more anxious with every step and keep looking back to see what my companions are going to do to help me, but they're just falling further behind. I try to slow down, but they can't catch up, and the slower I move, the more people I notice watching.

Finally, I dive into the river. I swim toward the bottom, thinking that the deeper I go, the harder it will be to see me. I hear a splash in the water above and turn to see several dark, faceless figures swimming behind me. I swim faster, going deeper, feeling my air running out but not knowing of any other way to escape.

At the bottom of the river, I'm faced with two different tunnels. I feel my lungs burning up oxygen but I still can't decide. I'm screaming in my brain to go either right or left, but it's like the choice has me paralyzed. *Which way do I go?*

Finally, before my lungs catch fire, I swim through to the right and hover at the entrance of a cave, though it's pitch black inside. I'm terrified to go forward, but more afraid of whoever is swimming behind me, and I cross the threshold into the darkness.

As soon as I swim through, I'm standing in a room. The water is gone, I'm completely dry, and a sense of calm washes over me.

The room is massive, so tall I can't even see the ceiling. Giant shelves stand against every wall, each packed with books. I finally notice the small tables scattered about the room, and all the people who sit at them, casually reading and studying. I'm in some kind of enormous library, and I've got the sense that everyone in here is a student. They're all trying to figure out who the Last Witch is, and I'm suddenly afraid of being seen.

I turn around to see if I can get into the water again, but there's no cave or river to be found. I'm trapped in a room filled with people trying to find me--to find Rain, and sooner or later they will.

As if reading my thoughts, the strangers' eyes start to drift upward, looking away from their texts and discovering me. The mother of the Last Witch.

And then, Darius is there. Right in front of me, staring into my eyes, a smile on his lips. I want to tell him that we're in danger, but I don't want to speak. I step toward him, getting as close as I can to whisper in his ear. Just as our bodies touch, before I can warn him, I feel his teeth sink into my neck.

I feel an immediate release. A release from the fear and the tension.

A release from the dream.

I'm in bed, in the hotel, the fog of sleep lifting. However, one thing from the dream remains.

Darius.

His body hovers over me, his teeth in my vein, my blood flowing through him.

My hands reach up to his sides, and I feel exactly what I hoped I would--no clothes.

I slide my fingers down, gently tracing along his rigid, flexed form, traveling down to the curves of his naked ass and digging my fingers into his flesh.

I'm left wanting as he pulls his teeth out of my neck, but find a new pleasure as his lips meet mine while his hands make quick work of my clothing. After so many failed attempts, I know I'll finally have him.

I reach down and grab his hardness, causing him to moan into my mouth. I'm already on the edge, the passion having built for days, and I just can't wait any longer.

Please, he whispers into my mind, showing he also can't hold off another moment.

I guide him, he pushes, and the most explosive pleasure I've ever experienced fills me. The world melts around us as he goes deeper, forcing my back to arch and my body to shiver. My hands move furiously, trying to touch every inch of him, to bring all of him into me.

I wrap my legs around his back, our hips finding the same rhythm, his pace increasing, my climax building. Darius' short breaths make it clear he's nearing his own precipice, and I contract around him to move him over the edge.

Time freezes. My body convulses uncontrollably and I feel like my skin is on fire. Even with my eyes squeezed shut, I notice the glow of my skin intensifying as wave after wave of pleasure crashes through me.

I float on the swell of that wave for what feels like hours but might have only been minutes, and I'm dizzy and trembling when the hum in my loins finally starts to subside.

I open my eyes only to lose myself in the vampire's dark, penetrative gaze. Never have I felt so intertwined with another soul, so connected to someone outside myself, and I know in my blood that he feels the same.

He leans in and brushes his lips against mine, then trails feather-light kisses down my jawline to my neck, flicking his tongue over his bite mark.

I sigh and fade into his arms, lost to the world until the next morning when the sound of a bird chirping outside our blacked out windows wakes me.

My brain wakes up slowly, processing where I am and what's happened with sluggish reflexes. I'm still naked, so I know at least part of last night wasn't a dream. Darius is still asleep next to me, his naked body exposed after I apparently stole the covers. I don't know if he gets cold when he sleeps, but I gently tuck him in, freezing when I hear my baby cry. In a panic, I dash out the bedroom and, still naked, poke my head out into the common area.

Zev is sitting on the couch, drinking coffee and reading a newspaper, somehow managing to look like a dad on vacation waiting for the rest of the family to wake up. Rain sleeps in the crib next to him.

He eyes my naked figure and gives me a smirk. "Need any help, love?"

A mix of relief and self-awareness pushes me back into my room, where I grab my clothes off the floor and quickly dress. Moderately presentable, I head back out to talk with Zev.

"I imagine that's the best you've slept in weeks," the werewolf says, and I'm not sure if he's talking about the duration of my sleep or the sexy interlude in the middle of it.

"Yeah, I was out pretty hard and fast." *Jesus, Bernie. Word choice.*

Zev lets out a small bark of a laugh, then throws his paper down on the table.

"Darius will sleep for the next two or three hours and then sulk in a closet until the sun goes down, and Rune's off getting some sort of tree bark or frog skin, I can't remember which."

Zev's almost bored description of his magical counterparts makes me laugh. In some ways, he's the most human of the three. He relies on his mind and physical abilities instead of spells and manipulative powers. It gives him a little perspective and sense of humor the other Sexies can't quite muster.

"So," the werewolf continues, "fancy some breakfast? I heard of a great cafe down the street."

Zev stands and extends his arm with an inviting smile that makes my stomach flutter. I smile back. Food sounds amazing, as does a little bit of sun on my soon-to-be-glowing skin.

He straps Rain to him as we head out and I finally get a good look at the city for the first time since we got here. Our hotel is right on the water, and the streets bustle with people on foot, in taxis and on bikes. It's a brisk, sunny morning and I'm immediately drawn to this historical place. I've always been enamored with the famous European cities--Rome, Paris, London and the like. Budapest never made the fantasy list, but clearly it should have. The baroque architecture and beautiful bridges make the city feel like a 360-degree painting, every view pulled off an artist's canvas.

Zev and I settle at a little cafe along the river. It takes exactly one sip of my Hungarian coffee to turn me into a coffee snob who will never go back to the instant garbage I've been drinking up to this point. Why was I never told coffee could be good? I blame not having a father and my mother being a psychopath.

We drink coffee and nibble pastries in silence. Zev seems equally enchanted by our surroundings, though he might be focused on reading whatever smells waft by his nose. Either way, it's as pleasant a morning as I've had in a long time.

When the magic tingle in my skin becomes more of a burn, I know we need to head back to wake Darius. I've got the star in my pocket which helps keep me from lighting up like the marquee outside a strip club, but I still probably shine more brightly than is normal for a human. I've definitely gotten more compliments from random strangers on my beautiful skin since this started.

Zev drops some Euros on the table, which he either stole or just had on hand because he's hip like that, and we walk along the river back toward the hotel.

At first I assume the knot in my stomach has to do with the unchecked magic surging through my body. But as we walk, I realize I'm having a strong bout of *déjà vu*. This path along the river's edge is eerily similar to the route I took in my dream. I pass the same buildings, see the same windows and balconies where cloaked figures watched as I ran along.

I look into the water, and it seems to change color before my eyes. It goes from a dark blue that's nearly opaque, to a more translucent turquoise. The longer I stare, the clearer the water becomes, and now I swear I can see nearly to the bottom. Past the fish and kelp and rocks--to a dark, underwater cavern.

"What do you see, Bernie?" Zev breaks me out of my trance. "You've been locked in on the same spot of water for about a minute."

I don't know how to respond. I see... a memory? A vision from a dream that I can't really define, nor do I think is real?

"I'm not sure. The water... does it look clear to you?"

"Not particularly," he says, making me even more unsure of what I'm seeing. "But," he continues, "I don't have your powers, and this isn't the city of my people. So if you say the water looks clear, I'm inclined to believe you."

WHEN WE GET BACK to the hotel, Darius is awake and hiding in a blacked-out room. My insides turn to jelly the moment our eyes meet, and I feel nearly feverish at the memory of last night and the promise of more nights to come.

But now is not the time for such thoughts.

There is always time for such thoughts, the vampire says, speaking directly to my mind. *And soon there will be time for more than just thoughts.*

I suck in a breath at the promise, but push it aside as I turn my attention to the fae. Rune has the right idea and is busy creating illusions around our suite so whenever our guest or intruders arrive, they'll have some work to do before they can murder us all.

Despite my protests, the three of them gang up on me and force me to nap-- at least for an hour or two--so that I'm well-rested for whatever the night brings.

I insist I can't possibly sleep with so much to do--though we all know there's nothing I can do. Sleep gets the last laugh and I manage to doze for a bit.

I wake feeling refreshed and grateful, and after a shower and a cup of coffee, I'm ready.

Ready to wait for a really long time.

During the remaining daylight hours, I teach the three princes of magical kingdoms poker. Then I proceed to destroy them at it.

They teach me a game called Jokers, and I annihilate them.

Convinced I have a new super power, they all refuse to play more with me, so we each fall into our own rhythms, them taking turns playing with, feeding or changing Rain while I try to read the same page of the same book one thousand two hundred and sixty six times.

After the sun goes down, my heart rate kicks up a notch. Seconds feel like hours and yet each tick of the clock happens too fast, bringing us nearer to what-ever's lurking on the other side of 9 pm.

It's now 8:30 pm and I want to throw up. I wish I could just buzz the front desk and ask the clerk to make a few calls and have the mystery visitor come early.

Darius is equally on edge, rapidly darting between windows every time he hears a noise. If we had more time, I might push him into the bedroom for a repeat of last night and take care of some of this excess energy.

8:40 pm.

The room around us has had a magical remodel. Rune created a labyrinth of walls and mirrors to conceal us, at least momentarily, from anyone that dares enter.

8:47 pm.

Zev morphs into wolf form and sits on the small balcony outside the french doors. He keeps an eye on the street to see who might be coming or going.

8:52 pm.

Rain lays in her crib in the center of the room, as far as possible from any windows or doors, and at the middle of Rune's illusionary maze. I wish I could hide her in a closet or something, away from whatever action might take place, but I've learned from harrowing experiences that she needs to be in my sight always.

8:59 pm.

I stand with the Sexies surrounding Rain, ready as we'll ever be. I face the main door while each of the others faces in a different direction. No reason to believe our guest will come through the front entrance.

At 9:01 there's a knock at the door, which both startles the living shit out of me and makes me feel a little less like we're about to be ambushed. As planned, Darius silently glides to the door, looks through the peephole, and turns the knob.

"Oh, hi," a male voice says from outside. He has a trace of a Hungarian accent but not so much that he's difficult to understand. "I'm looking for Bernadette Mor--"

He can't finish his sentence before Darius grabs him by the sleeve and jerks him into the room. Now that I can see the source of the voice, I honestly feel underwhelmed.

A man in his thirties with shaggy brown hair and ill-fitting clothes stands next to Darius. He might be 5'8" or so, but he looks tiny compared to the strapping vampire. He also looks terrified.

"What's your business?" Darius asks, not even trying to dial back the hostility in his voice.

"I'm here to see Bernadette," the man answers with a tremble. "I left a note, I came alone, I'm not here to cause trouble. Is she here?"

I realize the illusions are still around us and the stranger has no idea that I'm just a few feet away.

Let him go, I say to Darius.

No.

Do it, I insist. *He's not dangerous and you know it. Tell Rune to drop the illusion.*

After a few moments, Darius relaxes his grip and the man's eyes dart over to me, the layout of the room clearly having changed from his point of view.

All the fear I felt earlier has faded, and I can't tell exactly why. It helps that the man isn't at all menacing, but there's something more than that. A connection I never could have felt before, but now registers within my magic spirit.

"Who are you?" I ask, taking a step forward.

"I'm Andor." He smiles as he looks me over, like he's arrived to take me to prom and thinks my dress looks nice. "You're Bernadette?"

I nod and then push past the formalities. "Did my father send you?"

He shakes his head and looks past me, like he's searching for the right response. In the end, he just goes with, "No."

"Then why are you here?"

Andor looks from me to the men standing on either side of me, then up at Darius. He swallows, clearly fighting some nerves of his own, then looks into my eyes.

"I'm, um… I'm your designated lover."

CHAPTER SIX

"My what?" My shock turns to laughter. I can't help it. I'm simply overcome. I have no reservoir left for this conversation. I'm tapped out.

And so I laugh.

The princes are less inclined toward hilarity. They each look ready to rip poor Andor to pieces. He's about 20 seconds away from sharing a fate with my bestie's ex asshole.

Andor turns a bright shade of pink that burns his whole face as he fidgets with sweaty hands. "Err... surely you've been told about this. That is why you have come?"

"Told about a... designated lover?" I purse my lips like I'm thinking, then shake my head. "Yeah, no I'm pretty sure I would have remembered that. What the hell are you talking about?"

"Oh, um, this is very awkward. Not at all how it was supposed to go," the man stutters, desperately avoiding eye contact with me. "Well, you see," he glances at the kitchenette. "Um, could I trouble you for a glass of water?"

Rune steps in his way, turning the kitchen into the illusion of a desert. "Answer the lady," the fae says with a severity to his voice that is always shocking and always effective.

Andor looks as if he wishes the floor would open up and swallow him.

I almost feel pity. In the past, I probably would have. But present-day me is slightly jaded by A: all the people who have tried to kill me, including people I thought I knew; B: all the lies I've been fed like sugar my whole life, sweet until it kills you; and C: all the people who were supposed to be dead who weren't and who weren't supposed to die who did. Sadly, all this has made me more cautious in my empathy.

"Speak!" I say, and though I do not shout, my power fills the room like thunder trapped in a bottle.

The Sexies aren't rattled by my force, but poor Andor looks like he's about to shit himself.

"Right, well, um," he tries to stand a bit taller and he holds out his sweaty palm to me for a handshake. "I'm Andor Maldone, from the *Kő Sorrendje* and I am here to claim you as my own and offer myself to you in service of your magic. *"*

Darius curses under his breath in a rather creative blend of English, French and a bit of Hungarian, which makes our guest's eyes bulge.

You are not going with him, the angry vampire hisses into my mind.

No shit.

To everyone else he says, "The Order of the Stone. I thought your pathetic numbers died out ages ago."

Andor simultaneously puffs his chest in pride and averts his eyes in fear. It's a strange combination of reactions that makes him look like a chihuahua trying to mimic a wolf.

"We did not. We simply allowed the world to think so, in order to protect our ranks and the witches we are pledged to."

I huff in annoyance. "How about someone fill me in on the missing pieces of this conversation, real fast, before I lose my shit."

Darius turns to me, his face shifting from anger to almost amusement. "The order is a society of men employed as the chosen protectors and guides to witches. Through a sexual alliance with those women of power."

My jaw drops as the pieces do in fact come together. "So y'all are basically magic penises."

Zev bursts out laughing. Darius snickers. Rune grins.

Andor loses even more color. "Um, not precisely, no. For the most part, we do not possess magic. Each witch is given a mate--"

"A designated lover," I say, throwing his own words back at him.

"Yes, er, a designated lover, who is meant to protect her and help her control her power."

"Through sex," I add.

"Well, yes, how else?"

"So… powerless magic penises." AJ is going to absolutely die when she hears about this. She'll also be pissed she missed it.

"Thanks for the offer, Andor, but as you can see," I wave to indicate the three increasingly possessive and incredibly sexy men surrounding me, "I'm all stocked up on magic penises. I won't be in need of yours, as lovely as that sounds."

He doesn't need to know I've only actually sampled one of said penises. But there's enough sexual tension between me and all three guys that I feel pretty safe asserting my claim. At least for purposes of dissuading Andor from his hopeless mission.

"Yes, um, well, that's not really how it works."

I cock my head. "How what works?"

"Witches and their mates," he says, as if he's the expert here. "You must mate with a member of the order. That bond will strengthen your power."

I laugh. Again. "First of all, I'm not taking an assigned lover. That's not how *I* work. Second, I do not need to strengthen my power."

"Oh, well, I know it might *feel* like you're strong. It's always a rush when a witch's power comes in, and yours was held back for so long, judging by your age."

Oh hell no he didn't.

Completely oblivious to the quicksand he's walking into, he keeps talking. Poor fool.

"But given how little magic is left in the world, and how weak the witches have become… it is instrumental that you, that is… you will only feel the true reach of your magic--"

"Let me guess, when I sample the magic penis."

He blushes, but he also nods.

"I'm going to let you in on a little secret." I step forward, staring him down as my skin begins to glow again. "Women don't like being told who they're supposed to have sex with. And we definitely don't like being mansplained to about our own bodies and powers."

With my anger comes a surge of magic, though with a different intent and energy than before. I don't feel like I'll hurt anyone, but rather just flex my powers a bit.

As much as I fear my lack of control, I make no attempt to hold back in front of this stranger who's trying to stake a claim in me. I am super tired of secret orders trying to control me. I'm walking into this situation packing… in a manner of speaking.

As the glow in my skin and the magic in my veins reaches boiling point, I don't really know what will happen. I'm as much a spectator as an actor, and I look on as I light the place up.

Literally.

As my hands glow brighter, hundreds of sparkling lights float up from them and hang in the air like fireflies on a warm summer night. It takes me back to when AJ and I would catch them in jars and run around pretending we were magic fairies with the power of light.

If only we'd known then what we know now. Turns out we weren't too far off.

I keep my eyes unfocused as the flying stars of light dance around me, then my fingers move instinctively and begin to shape the light into an ancient symbol that feels familiar and entirely new all at once.

Andor falls to his knees, his eyes wide, his hands pulled up into a prayer supplication. I have no idea what just happened, but I don't want to let him know that.

"Get up, will you?" I say, holding my hands behind my back to hide how badly they're shaking. "I don't want to make a big thing out of all this. Just tell me how you knew I was coming and where my father is. That's all I want from you. Not your magic penis or whatever else you and your creepy order have planned."

When he doesn't rise, Zev steps over to him and jerks him to his feet. The werewolf growls at the man, letting it rumble up from his chest like a predator on the hunt. "How did you know we'd be here?" he asks.

Andor trips over his tongue answering. "We are connected. I had a vision of you in my dreams."

That reminds me of my strange dream and the sense of strong *déjà vu* as we walked through the ancient streets of Budapest, but I don't want to create any shared connection with this stranger, so I hold my tongue. The less he knows about me, the better.

"Do you know my father? His name is…"

"Timót," he says, interrupting me. "Of course I know him. He's the leader of the men in our order. Has been for decades. At least, until he disappeared."

"Disappeared?" The Sexies and I all ask in unison.

"Yes. A few weeks ago. He said you would be coming," Andor gestures to me. "And that you would need a wand more powerful than one we've ever seen. That kind of wand would require a dragon's scale. So he went to retrieve it. And he hasn't been seen since."

MINUTES, hours, days… who knows, maybe months? I'll never know how long I sat in stunned silence after Andor describes my father's disappearance, because I think time stopped working.

Reading Gramps' letter caused my brain to fracture, learning that my father was alive after years of believing otherwise. At the same time, I was almost ready for it. Mom was supposed to be dead, but that wasn't the case. Tilly was bedridden but could still freeze time and give me her powers. Hell, grandpa's letter only came to me because he knew he'd be murdered, so the existence of my father wasn't that big a leap.

Hearing Andor say my father's name, the Hungarian version, shakes my reality in a whole new way. People here *know* him. Until very recently, they were *with* him. I'll be able to ask questions and get answers, and that's a little over-whelming for me.

Sensing that I might be trapped in my thoughts for quite some time, Rune picks up the conversation.

"Are you saying Timothy Trendle was killed by dragons?" the fae asks.

Andor gives a weak shrug. "We don't know. Those caves certainly aren't a safe place to visit, even for someone powerful like him."

"What do you mean, 'powerful'?" Darius cuts in. "He was human, was he not?"

"Yes, he is human," Andor answers, though there's a hesitancy in his voice. "But he is also one of the strongest members of the *Érintett*."

The word means nothing to me, but it prompts Darius to pace toward the window, staring at the floor while his mind probably races through centuries of memories and learning. I don't have that kind of time, so I just request the Cliff Notes version.

"What the hell is an *Érintett*?"

"The Affected," Darius answers from across the room, stealing Andor's chance to be useful.

"Witches are exclusively women," the vampire says, "but certain men, over time and with the proper training, have been said to absorb or inherit their magic."

Comparatively speaking, my dad being a little bit magic doesn't seem like a very big deal.

"So, dad was, what, like a JV witch?"

"Who is JV?" Andor asks, and I instantly regret my ultra-American analogy.

"Nevermind," I say. "What's the deal with the Quartet of Erins? Or whatever you called them."

"There haven't been many," Andor answers. "Those with enough inherited power have brought strength to the *Kö Sorrendje*, defending witches from would-be attackers."

"Not all in your ranks are so friendly," Darius says, as he remains facing away from us. Seems like the vampire still has some past beef with witches that needs to get sorted out.

"Has anyone gone to look for my father?" I ask. "Another Airy Tut, maybe?"

Andor looks at his feet and shakes his head. "No one dares tempt the dragons. Timót was told to stay back, but he refused."

This all hits me a little harder than expected. Assuming any of it is true, which is a sizable leap of faith, I may have come all the way to Budapest to meet my father and realize my powers as a witch, only to be thwarted by dad getting all cavalier and going to fight dragons so he could give his daughter a wand.

"Where are the dragons?" Zev asks. Leave it to the werewolf to get excited about a dance with death.

Andor thinks about his answer for a moment, looking between all of us as he chooses his words.

"Well, since, um... since we won't be consummating our--"

"No, we won't, so just get to the next part." I can't wait to meet whoever *assigned* this man as my lover so I can fireball them through a wall.

"Right, since that won't happen," Andor says, "would you come with me, Bernadette? I'm meant to lead you to the Grand Hall."

The moment Andor singles me out, each of the Sexies inches closer to me. There's no chance I'm going anywhere without them.

Andor takes the point, but makes one last attempt to push back. "I was told by a very powerful witch that only--"

"We will explain to that witch that you were given no choice," Darius says. Andor immediately nods his understanding, possibly due to some mind control, more likely just because Darius could kill him in milliseconds.

"What's at the Grand Hall?" Rune asks.

"Well, it's hard to explain in English... or any language, really," Andor says. "I suppose the best answer is, everything."

I watch the Sexies exchange glances, perhaps doing a little mind-speaking as well. I'm sure they're discussing whether or not this is a trap and all the other logistics of following a stranger into the night.

While they have a silent conference, I stare at Andor. Perhaps he came here with shitty intentions, but I don't think he can take much blame for the shittiness. He seems like a nervous little man caught up in a cause much bigger than himself, and I can't help but feel he probably isn't trying to kill us and may be trustworthy--to an extent. It's not just a judge of character, because that's not a reliable metric in my new magic life. It's an instinct that seems like it's rooted in my powers. Like ancient witch knowledge inherited through Tilly and my mom is guiding my brain.

"Yes, we'll go with you," I say before anyone else can take the lead. I'm not sure where my certainty comes from, other than I'm not leaving this country without some answers, and this seems our only way of getting them.

"Bernie," Rune starts.

"No," I shut him down.

Bernie, Darius tries the mind-speak approach.

"Nope," I shoot back audibly, throwing a glance his way. "You three be on high alert in case there's funny business, but I say we're going with Andor."

The Hungarian man looks at me with a smile, and maybe a sense of hope that I feel inclined to squash, so I add a qualifier: "My designated lover who will never get to do any of the loving."

Andor deflates immediately, but does so with a nod to show he understands. Rune dissolves the remaining illusions and packs Rain into a carrier that he straps to his chest. Zev carries the diaper bag. It's all quite the vision of what modern male parenting should be.

We follow our guide down through the lobby and out into the night. It's a little past 9:30 but the city still buzzes with activity. Bars and restaurants are in full swing with people enjoying the brisk winter evening from covered patios.

After a block or two on the main drag, Andor leads us down a smaller street paved with cobblestone and lined with charming old street lamps. It gives off such a quaint European vibe but also makes me think Jack the Ripper is lurking in the shadows.

The smaller street leads to another busy road, across from which is a large, open square. People mill about in the space, sitting on the edge of the fountain or coming and going from nearby cafes.

"We're headed to the center of that square," Andor explains before leading us across the street. "When I stop walking, everyone please gather close to me."

He doesn't wait for our consent, which is good because I'm not sure Darius would ever acknowledge any sort of obedience to my Hungarian wanna-be lover.

We get to the other side of the street and move into the center of the plaza. Hundreds of people are coming and going from the area, and I'm starting to wonder what exactly Andor has planned.

Meanwhile, my Hungarian man-bride has his eyes glued to the ground, inspecting each slab of cement he steps on. Finally, he seems to approve of a standing area and comes to a stop.

"Gather, if you would," he says. "Stand with shoulders touching, we need to be in a tight little circle."

The Sexies hesitate, as expected, so I take the lead and stand next to Andor.

He smiles when our arms touch, and I'm finding him more harmless and adorable with every passing minute. I'm glad I didn't accidentally kill him with magic back at the hotel.

"Join us please, if you want to go to the Grand Hall." Andor has a little more confidence in his voice now that I'm following his lead and he has some leverage. With a trio of scowls, Zev, Rune and finally Darius move into our five-person cluster. Six if you count Rain, who's still conked out and strapped to the fae's chest.

When Andor's happy with everyone's positioning, he glances around quickly to make sure no one's watching, then pulls a small pouch from his jacket and, in a quick flourish, throws a little dust into the air around us. The powdery substance filters down on our hair and shoulders, but nothing seems to happen. Andor watches each of us closely, seeming to observe something the rest of us aren't. Once he sees whatever it is he needs to see, he stomps on the stone in the middle of our circle three times.

There's a grinding noise, distant at first and then louder as it seems to come up toward the surface below our feet. I look around, wondering if the people nearby can hear the sound, but no one seems to notice or care.

"There we are," Andor says, bringing my attention back to the ground where he stomped. The stone he pounded with his foot is no longer there--it's been replaced by the first step of a narrow staircase leading into the earth below.

"Quickly," Andor says. "The dust casts an illusion to hide our descent, but it only lasts a few moments."

I start to move, but Darius grabs my arm and stops me before I can get to the opening.

"No, not you," he says. "Not first."

Zev growls in agreement and moves into the lead, throwing a look back at Andor right when he reaches the first step. "You go behind me."

Andor nods, his confidence reduced again. He steps in after Zev, then Rune and the baby, and finally I enter with Darius behind me. The grinding sound starts again and we hurry down the first few steps to avoid getting pinned by a closing stone.

Once I'm well below ground level, I look back up to see the night sky disappear. I listen for sounds of the bustling city above, but hear nothing. It's like we've stepped into another world.

I look back down, expecting darkness, but the stairs are lit by torches along the narrow wall.

"So none of the people in the square could see us?" I ask Andor. "Did we just disappear in front of their eyes?"

Andor shakes his head, then starts walking down the stairs behind Zev. "Our shadows lingered and then walked off. To anyone watching, we stopped for a moment and then walked into the darkness. No one expects a secret entrance in a crowded place, which is why this door has remained for centuries."

. . .

THE STAIRS WIND around a central column for quite a while, making me wonder how deep we're going. Through our blood bond, I know that Darius is on edge. Each step makes him a little more agitated, and I reach back to take his hand.

Are you okay? I ask.

I've had bad experiences with witches in hidden buildings, he responds. *I'll be fine.*

Not exactly the answer I wanted, but I don't have time to unpack it as the stairs come to an end in front of a large, stone door. Andor fumbles for a second with the chain around his neck, then pulls it from under his shirt to reveal a long, grey object that looks like a fang or a claw. He sticks it into a hole at the center of the door, and the stone slides back. Andor starts to enter, but Zev grabs his shirt and takes a moment to sniff out danger before letting anyone proceed.

We go in the same order, Darius pulling up the rear as the stone door slides shut.

"This is the Grand Hall," Andor says. "I'll fetch those who can answer questions about... Bernadette? Are you alright?"

His words barely make it to my ears, as too many thoughts and feelings are rushing through my head. As soon as I stepped through the door, my skin started glowing more brightly than ever before.

And, as if the burning in my blood and my glow-in-the-dark skin aren't enough to cause worry, fate scores another point in this game that is now my life, solidly cementing my panic.

"This is the room," I whisper, speaking more to myself than the guys.

The room from my dream.

Vaulted bookshelves climbing walls that seem to go forever.

Tables scattered throughout the space, where people are reading and studying.

And, just like in my dream, all eyes are on me.

CHAPTER SEVEN

The more I look around the room, the stronger the sense I'm reliving that dream. It's not just the similarities of the space, but also the feeling that my legs can't move--that I couldn't get away if I tried.

Everyone is silent, from the men I came in with to the strangers staring at me. The spectators all wear black robes with their hoods drawn, really laying into the eeriness of the moment.

I feel my body moving toward the center of the hall, even though I'd swear my feet aren't doing the walking. It's like I'm being pulled by a magnet, and yet I know it's the magic swirling inside me that's doing the moving.

Before I know what's happening, I've fallen to the ground and Zev is immediately beside me, catching all my weight in his strong arms.

"Your powers are surging, Bernie. Don't try to move."

I want to explain that I'm not trying to move, but speech evades me. From the corner of my eye, I see Andor running through the hall. The hooded faces turn to watch him go, then slowly look back at me. That trust I felt for Andor back in the hotel room is fading fast, as I can't help but think he's led us into a trap.

Darius...

I only need to think the vampire's name and he's at my shoulder, knowing what's needed and ready to take my blood. Still, I feel a hesitancy that's not normally there. He's usually so quick to drink me, but now I feel his face hovering inches away from my neck without making contact.

What's wrong? I ask

"Your skin is burning, Darius."

It's not the vampire who answers my question, but rather Rune. I turn my head back to see Darius' agonized face, smoke rising from his lips as he tries to help. I put my hand against his chest, trying to push him away even as he resists.

I must, he says. *You need me.*

He's not wrong. Whatever pain he's experiencing, I'm confident the burning in my body is worse. Nevertheless, I know his bite won't solve this. I don't know how I know, but it's clear to me.

I put my head down against the floor, trying to concentrate. Maybe I can control this shit, a little mind over matter. Though, it's not really matter, is it? Mind over inexplicable witch powers coursing through my veins trying to kill me from the inside. That's what I'm up against.

Zev and Darius stay close to me, each lending me their strength the best they can as I think of Tilly, how strong my Nanny was the last time I saw her. The calm grace she possessed while controlling an infantry of witches and saving my life. She was so old and frail, but she summoned her powers and made everything okay. *C'mon, Bernie. Just be more like Tilly.*

"*Távolítsuk.*"

The unrecognizable word comes from an unspecified source. My forehead is still against the stone floor, so I don't have any idea who might be around me chanting in Hungarian. While I don't know what's happening, I do know that a tight knot is forming in my chest. It's like a muscle is contracting, but also growing. Maybe I'm having a heart attack? Whatever it is, it doesn't feel great.

The knot grows and the pain magnifies. Just as it reaches an unbearable level, I lift my head off the floor to scream out, but it's not a sound that leaves my mouth. Instead, a ball of light bursts from my throat and into the air above my face. It shocks me into silence, and I'm mesmerized as I look into the shining, floating orb of power.

Because that's what it is. I know beyond a shadow of a doubt that I'm looking at my magic.

The orb of light floats away from me, and as my eyes trail behind it, they settle on the person who must have brought the powers out of me.

A beautiful elderly woman stands before us, her wand extended, pointed at the glowing circle, a look of thoughtful concentration on her face. She has red hair with streaks of silver, light gray eyes and strong cheekbones. If I'd been asked as a child to draw the prettiest old witch, this woman is exactly who I would have envisioned.

Andor stands beside her, a look of relief on his face as his eyes move between me and my floating powers. I glance down at my hands and see that the glow from my body has completely dimmed.

The burning is gone.

But there's an emptiness in its place.

"Hello, Bernadette," the woman says, her eyes still focused on controlling the light.

"You've taken her magic," Zev says, stating the obvious but with a little vinegar in his voice making it clear how he feels about the witch's intervention.

The woman shakes her head. "No one could take her abilities. Not so long as she and the baby are alive." Her wording is very particular and a little frightening. The way she speaks makes me wonder what side she's on. Is she about to kill me to prove her point?

"I've only pulled the magic out of her body," she goes on. "It will return to her the moment I release, and then we'll have to find another way to keep Bernadette from succumbing to her gifts."

Darius, who had been kneeling beside me to this point, rises.

"I'm able to help her. We have a blood bond that--"

"That doesn't work in this Grand Hall," the woman responds, cutting him short. "I imagine you felt quite the discomfort when you tried to feed earlier. This room and the surrounding chambers are guarded by Fate spells as old as time. Perhaps as old as you."

If push came to shove on neutral ground, Darius could probably take this woman down. In this room, however, it's clear who has the upper hand.

"Besides, you shouldn't be here in the first place, Darius."

The old witch knowing my vampire's name throws me for a loop. It's fine if everyone in the witching world knows who I am because of this prophecy bullshit, but I'm not ready for people to be calling my Sexies by name.

When I glance up to see how Darius is reacting to the unexpected recognition, he looks shocked. As I read his face and open myself to his feelings, I get the impression he's not surprised that she knew his name. I sense that he recognizes her as well.

I turn back to the witch, whose focus remains on the powers she's harnessed out of my body. "Bernadette," she says, "I'm going to return your strength to you. When I do, I want you to look to the sky and yell."

I reflexively look up, wondering if I can actually see the sky. Did she mean to say sky, or is she just generally referring to an upward direction--

My scattered thoughts disintegrate as I feel an explosion of magic hit every wall of my skeleton. I'm not sure if I've actually imploded, but I guarantee this is what spontaneous combustion feels like. Clearly, I've been regranted my powers.

As for yelling skyward, it's funny that she even bothered giving me that direction. The jolt of pain hits me so hard I have no choice but to throw my head back and cry to the heavens. When I do, it's like I've fired a flare out of my mouth. It shoots upward, a beacon of light moving through the darkness of this cavernous hall. The blaze continues on until it dwindles to a tiny speck and disappears in the abyss.

I take stock of myself, noting that there's a glow about me, but not an offensive one. Things appear to be in check... for now.

The woman seems happy with how this turned out, walking over and looking me up and down.

"You'll be better for the moment," she says. "But those moments will be fleeting until you learn your powers and find the tools to control them."

Naturally, I have fifty thousand follow-up questions, but the witch has already turned back to the Sexies, who still look like they've seen a ghost.

"Trying to remember the last time you saw me?" She poses the question to the group, indicating the familiarity doesn't stop with Darius.

None of the men answers for long, deafening seconds. At last, Rune slightly bows his head. "Hello, Queen Erzébet."

My head snaps toward the fae. "Wait. How the shit do you know her?"

"Because," the witch named Erzébet says, "these three princes went to school with my daughter, Cara. We met a few times during those years. Then the race wars started. And then Cara was killed."

It takes a moment for my brain to piece together anything Erzébet just said, but the memories finally come trickling back. The sexy princes had schooled together and there was a fourth in their ranks, a woman from the witching realm. Something happened to her and that's when their relationships fractured.

Darius, Zev and Rune are all as stunned as I've ever seen. They're usually at least a little prepared for everything, but standing next to their old friend's mother apparently wasn't something they foresaw.

"And before you ask, Darius," Erzébet goes on, "I don't blame you for my daughter's death. Nevertheless, you can understand if we witches don't welcome vampires with open arms."

At this point I'm reminded that, throughout all of my recent trials and tribulations, we haven't been alone. The Grand Hall still has a few dozen onlookers, and it's being hinted that some of them may hate my vampire, which makes them instant enemies of mine.

"Needless to say," the witch queen says, "a vampire prince inside the final stronghold of the witching realm might put some of our order members on edge. Which reminds me…"

She turns away from Darius to look at Andor, who's been standing about ten feet away since running off and returning with help.

"Andor, for the love of the Fates, why did you bring three hostiles here?"

Andor, who had been in the midst of changing from the street clothes he wore to our hotel into his black robe, freezes. He slowly crosses his arms over his chest and it looks like his goal is to squeeze until he compresses to the size of a bug and can make an unseen getaway.

"I, um, I was not told there would be others with Bernadette," the little man answers. This day just hasn't gone to plan for poor Andor. "I was outnumbered, and they seem very… protective. So… I'm sorry."

Erzébet fires a last disapproving look, then turns back to us. "Members of the Kő work to protect our shrinking numbers, though they have no powers of their own and are often put in situations for which they are outmatched."

"And then they turn us witches into concubines with their magical members?" I ask the question with an extra side of sass, thinking back to why Andor scheduled our 9 pm meeting and getting bothered by it all over again.

The witch queen raises an eyebrow, and it seems we have different opinions about the matter. "It's more the opposite, Bernadette. The status remains with the witch, while a man with allegiance to our cause helps to provide a child."

Provide a child doesn't quite jive with me, and I'm sure Erzébet can tell.

"When you've lived through centuries of vampires and fae trying to infiltrate and decimate your species," she says, taking great care to look at both Darius and Rune as she makes her point, "you begin to take extra precautions with relations."

And with that, she walks off toward a corridor at the other end of the hall.

We all waste zero seconds following, even though we've no clue where she's headed. We came here for answers, and we've finally found someone who might have them.

The Grand Hall is not lacking in grandness, as the walls stretch on forever. It's a never-ending series of bookshelves, and each shelf is packed. As we go, I see men and women walking through the space and giving us quick glances. It's only the men that have the hoods pulled over their heads, while all the women are more exposed. The women are also able to summon books from the shelves, the materials floating directly to them on command. The men, meanwhile, have to jump on floating ladders in order to reach whatever book they need next.

"So, is this just study hall?" I ask. "Witch school? The grown up version of Hogwarts?" A flutter of excitement replaces some of my worry. "What's everyone reading?"

Erzsébet keeps walking, answering over her shoulder without breaking stride.

"Spells," she says. "If a witch has created a spell, good or bad, useful or not, the record is kept here for future generations to learn. Normally you'd find more Kő members in here assisting the witches, but as the prophecy has come closer to fulfillment, their numbers have dwindled, for reasons I don't fully understand."

She reaches the end of the vast room, standing at a small entrance leading to a long, narrow hall. She finally turns back, looking into my eyes and, seemingly, all the way into my witching soul. "Nevertheless, our remaining women and men are studying and preparing for the hardships on the horizon. Most witches start to develop their magic at the age of eleven, twelve at the latest. You're behind."

And she's off again, walking briskly down the hallway as the rest of us trail behind.

At the end of the corridor, we reach another stone door. With a flick of Erzsébet's wand, the door slides open and we follow her through the threshold.

For some reason, I'd been expecting an office. This woman is clearly important, she knows a lot, so surely she's going to sit behind a desk, lean into her leather high-back chair, and tell us things. Now, on the other side of the door, it's clear I still have a very human way of thinking about things.

The small stone doorway has led us into a vast, magical, underground garden. Ferns and ivy and money trees with deep green leaves grow everywhere. Above us, sparkling crystals hang from the ceiling. Brightly colored birds fly from tree to tree, while an enchanting stream runs through the center of this spellbinding landscape.

Rune leans over next to a small fern that looks like it's been bedazzled. Tiny diamonds line the leaves, giving it an impeccable shine. "Amazing," the fae whispers to himself.

"Many witches use Asplenium crystals to tip their wands," Erzsébet says. "It's a small but powerful stone, magnifying light and strengthening spells."

I can't help but feel a child-like excitement when she talks about wands. I really hope she's about to give me one, and I hope it looks badass.

Erzsébet senses my anticipation. "You, however, are not most witches."

My dreams are momentarily dashed. I was about to run over and pluck a diamond off a plant, but I guess I'll hold off.

"Wands help us to control and guide our powers. They aren't a source of strength, but a means of focusing it." She stops to look at me, giving another thorough inspection that makes me feel important but also severely judged.

"You'll get nowhere if your magic overpowers your wand whenever you try to employ it, and that's exactly what will happen if you use the normal ingredients."

She steps away from us, the water coming up to meet her feet as she crosses the stream. When she reaches the center of the garden, Erzsébet waves her wand above her head, and as we look up, I see the most amazing display I've ever witnessed.

My mom conjured images from a fire, and in the moment that was pretty dope. But now I'm staring at a ceiling covered in crystals, colors flooding the translucent spears to create a more vivid, HD image than any screen could ever present. A 3D image comes to life above, and I nearly fall backwards as I tilt my head back trying to take it all in.

Erzsébet first conjures a view of the Grand Hall, looking just as we'd left it.

"Is this right now?" I ask. "Are you able to see anywhere in the world?"

The witch smiles. "Universe, child." With another swipe of her wand, the view morphs to a familiar, worn down room, with a most familiar face wiping a spill off the copper countertop.

I gasp. "AJ."

There's my best friend in the world, larger than life on a screen made of crystals. And of course she ignored my pleas to stay away from my haunted pub. Bless her. She's just tending bar like the world is normal, though she knows better and is probably worried sick about me. God, I wish I could just teleport over there to give her a hug. Can witches do that? I'm going to need to schedule more time with this witch queen to ask questions unrelated to my current quest.

Erzsébet has a distant look on her face as she watches the image she's conjured. "We've spent many an hour watching over Morgan's and Rowley. Watching Lauren devolve from a ray of hope to a breath away from the collapse of all witches was quite harrowing."

Yeah. Imagine what it was like being there.

"If you could see what was happening, why didn't you help?" My question is pointed, but I'm expecting a sensible answer. Erzsébet doesn't disappoint.

"We're not the only ones with powers, dear girl," she says with a trace of regret, like she wishes she could have done more. "Sending an envoy to you would have surely brought attention from others, and it's not like you weren't already in enough peril."

With that, she flicks her wrist again, dissolving the image of AJ and intensifying my heartache. The picture that takes its place, however, forces me to shift gears in a hurry.

We're now looking at the inside of a cave, also covered in crystals, though this one is much larger and without the beautifully tended garden.

"Jesus!"

I can't help but scream when a massive dragon flies through the image. It settles down in a corner of the cave, curling into a ball like an enormous, winged, fire-breathing dog.

"Where is that?" I ask, shock stifling my voice.

"Aggtelek Karst," Erzsébet answers. "Caves in the northern part of Hungary. Many people visit to see the beautiful formations within. If you look a little deeper... you find dragons."

"That's where my father is?"

Erzsébet pauses for a moment in thought. She searches the image in the crystals, like she's looking for him.

"We don't know," she finally says. "If he is, he's masked by a spell. More likely..."

"He's been eaten."

Zev doesn't always display tact when talking about death. This is one of those moments.

The witch nods and sighs, the crystals returning to their normal state as she offers a final flick or her wand and walks back to us. There's an elegance to her movement that reminds me of how my mother moved. I always thought it was the dancer training, but I'm beginning to think women with incredible powers just glide with confident grace.

"It was dangerous for your father to leave, and we told him so," Erzsébet says. "But he's spent more than twenty-five years preparing to help you, and there was no talking him down. Plus..." she starts, then hesitates as her eyes meet mine. It's a look I've received quite a few times in the last couple weeks. The look of a powerful being with powerful secrets, who's wondering if I'm strong enough to hear what they have to say. So far, I've been up to the challenge.

"Go on," I say.

"Your father wasn't wrong to go," she says with a shrug. "It may have cost him his life, but you'll get nowhere without dragon scales."

"What do you mean? Why not?"

"No other wand core can endure your force," Erzsébet answers. "We've seen but a fraction of your power, Bernadette. It will only get stronger until it kills you or you learn to control it. It would take years to master the right spells, so a powerful wand is the only solution. And dragon scales are the only foundation you won't immediately destroy."

Aside from the gentle babbling of the magical stream, there's complete silence. I look to Rune, who's doing nothing to hide his concern. Zev stands next to me, so close that our bodies touch, as is his way of offering comfort. I'm struck by the fact that this progress--meeting a powerful witch and beginning work on my wand--only pushes sand through the hourglass more quickly. It only brings me closer to the moment when my princes will leave. It's almost enough to make me want to stop trying.

I turn to look back at Darius, and his eyes are on the ground, though his thoughts mingle with mine.

I wish I was enough, he says.

You are, my prince. And more.

He looks up at me. I know that neither of us have felt a connection like this before, and I'm sure he's never been as helpless as he is in this moment.

I give him a soft smile, the most comfort I can offer, then turn back to Erzsébet.

"How do I kill a dragon?"

CHAPTER EIGHT

"My kind has a saying." Zev is the first to speak after a lengthy silence. Apparently there's no easy answer to my dragon-slaying question.

"If you want to kill a dragon," the werewolf says, "find an egg that's about to hatch and crush it."

The visual makes me a wee bit nauseous, and I try not to imagine this man I care so much about stomping dragon hatchlings to death.

"That's, um, pretty savage and awful," I say.

"I agree," Zev answers. "But it's the only way to kill the beasts, as far as we werewolves can tell."

"Is there no magic?" I ask Erzsébet. "A spell I can cast or a potion I can use?"

She shakes her head. "Any spell that might kill a dragon is not one we wish to invoke. The creature need not die for you to get a scale."

Oh. I kinda wish she'd led with that. "So we just zip in, grab a scale and leave?"

Again, the witch's head shakes. "The dragons don't readily want to part with their protective plates. If you looked down and saw a mouse removing your toe, things likely wouldn't end well for the mouse."

Solid analogy, Erzsébet. Feels like she may have used that one before.

I'm about to give the queen props for her wordplay when a deep red hue falls over the room, shining down on us from the crystals above. I'm immediately reminded of the shifting colors when I was in the woods with my mother and the Order, and I know this can't be good.

Erzsébet waves her wand toward the ceiling and an image appears of the square above ground where we first came in. There's the normal flow of pedestrians going about their evening, some locals, many tourists. It's the small group standing near the stone that gave way to the staircase who give me pause. They are all clad in black cloaks with black breeches and shirts beneath, and they are studying the humans like they might be dinner. Their skin is pale, almost translucent under the moonlight. And their eyes look just like Darius' when he's about ready to feed.

I suck in my breath. "Vampires."

"Darius…" Erzsébet says, her eyes still on the vision above.

"I've taken an unbreakable oath," the vampire answers before an accusation can be leveled against him. "I'm bound to Bernie, as are Zev and Rune. Any visitor from my realm wants me dead as much as they want the baby."

Erzsébet remains focused on the ceiling, the vision traveling through the cement and earth, looking to see if any assailants have discovered the entryway. By my count, I see ten or eleven vampires, none underground yet.

"Well," the witch says, turning around after she's seen all she needs to in the crystals. "Let's hope this one is stronger than the pact you three made with my daughter."

She leaves us with that parting gut punch and glides out the door and into the hallway. I turn to look at the men, none of whom have started to follow.

"Do we fight?" Rune asks, glancing down at my child's head resting against his chest in a nap.

"If we do," Zev says, starting for the doorway, "best we do it in these halls where the Fate's magic is on our side."

Darius nods in agreement, and then is out the door before I can blink. The three of us rush after.

"We're under siege, and you all have jobs to do."

I hear Erzsébet's voice echoing from the Grand Hall, loud but controlled. She doesn't have to say anything else before the men and women in her order are on the move. As I get to the end of the hallway, I see dozens of bookshelves lifting like garage doors, allowing witches and Kő members to quickly come and go from the main room.

Some witches grab books from shelves before they exit. Others command books with their wands, bringing them under their feet and turning them into antique, literary hoverboards. They fly on books into the vast space, and it's undeniably cool.

I stand in a tight group with the Sexies, and it takes a moment before I notice Andor is also by my side.

"Don't you have a station or whatever?" I ask.

He just looks back and offers a weak smile. "Here," he says. "Protecting you."

As the activity settles and everyone gets where they need to be, a quiet falls over the hall. It's the kind of deafening silence that makes you wish someone would speak.

Maybe they can't get in? I think to Darius.

Perhaps not as fast as they like, but they'll get in.

A loud bang sounds through the room, coming from somewhere above. Moments later, another one follows. Then another.

"They're breaking through the walls," Rune says softly.

"It's just the ten or eleven we saw, right? Or are there more coming?" I ask.

Since we survived the first onslaught of fae, I'm a little worried we're about to be outnumbered ten-to-one by the undead.

"Probably not," Darius says, calming my nerves a little but quite possibly lying to make me feel better. "They'll send more if this mission fails, but none of the kingdoms wish to leave their homelands unprotected. Warriors for all of us are in short supply."

Makes sense, and I guess I'll take the short-term good news over the long-term bad.

Another loud thud sends dust fluttering down from the wall over the main entrance. Seems like the wall thumping vampires are making some headway.

"What will the Fate's magic do to protect us?" I ask, a lump of fear in my throat making me almost inaudible.

"Probably just make the vampire's hands burn while they rip our limbs off."

And with a little parting gallows humor from Zev, the wall above the Grand Hall entrance explodes into the room.

Before the slabs of stone have hit the ground, bursts of light shoot toward the entrance and turn the room into a fireworks display. I notice that Darius has left my side, but before I can freak out about it he's back.

"Rune, cover Bernie," he says. "They're moving around the room trying to find--"

Before he can finish, two fangs are in my face, attached to a terrifying face with bloodshot eyes. I feel hands on my belly, like the creature's searching for my child. The way his fingers dig into my flesh, he might think the baby's still inside of me.

The invasion of my space, the chilling sensation of the fingers on my body, and the general horror rooted in our situation all lend themselves perfectly to some accidental magic. I shove my hands forward and the vampire in front of me both catches on fire and flies through the air in the opposite direction. I look down at my hands, wishing I understood what I did and could do it again.

"Let's get Bernie and Rain out," Rune says. "No need to press our luck and hope for another burst of power that might not come."

I don't try to argue. It's my child the vampires are after, and I've got no control over these crazy hands of mine. No reason to think I'll avoid killing the people I want to keep safe.

"Back through the opening?" Zev asks. "The vampires have given us plenty of room--"

He stops talking just in time to dive out of the way as fire shoots past us. Bodies are running and flying through the room, though most are Kő members thrown violently by vampires. One flailing figure lands with a sickening thud at my feet, the life instantly crushed out of the poor man.

"Wherever we're going, let's do it sooner than later," I say.

"Go back to the garden," Andor says, still a few feet from my side. His face is ashen as he looks down at his fallen comrade. Something tells me this is the first time Andor's witnessed death and I very much empathize.

"There's a tunnel that leads further underground." Andor finally looks up and meets my eyes, his own brimming with tears. Just as he opens his mouth to give more guidance, he's swept off his feet by a blurring figure. He screams, the sound rapidly growing distant as the vampire races Andor toward the exploded entrance.

"Go," Darius says to all of us. "Get to the garden and find the tunnel. I'll guard the entrance."

I'd protest, but I'm learning that's just a waste of time. With Zev and Rune at either side, we break for the hallway. I look back to see if Darius is following, but he's already in a scrape with one of our attackers. He's quickly got the lesser vampire lifted above his head, making me feel good about his odds of coming out on top.

Before we can reach the exit, two vampires flash in front of us, blocking the path.

"Left," Rune says, walking forward with my baby clasped tightly under one arm. I'm not sure what he means or who he was talking to, but before I can think on it, a shifted-Zev pounces on the attacker to the left. At the same time, Rune approaches the other vampire, walking over calmly as though he's going to ask for directions.

Just before the vampire can lunge at him, Rune divides into eight different bodies. I'm sure he doesn't actually do that, but my eyes are very convinced of the existence of seven extra Runes.

Mine aren't the only deceived eyes, as the vampire spins in a circle, swiping at the fae that now surround him. Each strike simply passes through the illusion, the vampire growing more confused and furious by the mystified attack. At last, the real Rune sweeps his leg under the vampire, knocking the teetering adversary off his feet. As the vampire falls, the fae throws a fistful of powder into his face. A horrifying shriek fills the hall as Rune's foe tears at his burning eyes.

By the time I look away from that match, Zev's attacker is already scurrying in the other direction, and it looks like he's holding his own detached arm. When the situation calls for it, my werewolf goes off.

He stays in wolf form and rushes over to me, crouching so I can climb onto his back. Rune has already started down the hall, the two princes working with a coordination that reminds me they've known each other for a really long time. It's like Zev and Darius' sexy striptease, except not sexy and Zev bit off a guy's arm.

I grab hold of the wolf's fur and he sprints toward Rune, catching up to and passing the fae in seconds. When we reach the stone door, it's immediately clear that we've got a new problem.

"How do we open it?" I say, staring at the hole where a magical key would go. Zev's still a wolf, and probably doesn't have much experience picking locks with his paws. I look at Rune, who's already scanning the hallway for another way into the garden. It's comforting to know the witches have strong defenses, but it's a real bitch being on the wrong side of one of their doorways.

This corridor that once felt like an escape route now seems like more of a death trap. Without access to the garden, we're just stuck here, waiting for the vampires to attack.

I look down at my hands, hoping to see charged fingertips ready to pry open a can of magic whoopass. The glow is there, but I don't feel the surge.

Maybe if I aim my hands at the door. Who knows, my magic might just need some clearer intention before it does my bidding. I try pointing my fingers and then lifting my palms, testing different angles that might let out some zesty light.

Nothing. I don't know what my powers are, much less how to control them. I'm the only hope we've got, and I feel absolutely hopeless.

And then the door slides open.

For a brief moment, I credit my pity party. I got so scared and sad that my magic did what I wanted. When I see Erzsébet's face on the other side, I know that's not the case.

"Inside," she says. "Quickly."

Zev rushes us through with Rune and Rain on our heels. The door flies shut right after Rune gets in, crushing the outstretched arm of a vampire as it closes.

"Those pesky monsters are so fast," Erzsébet says, showing she's flustered in the most charming way.

"Bernadette, you already know where you're going," the witch says, announcing something I don't believe to be true. "Rune, you and I will shield the child. I expect they'll make it into the garden, but at that point we'll manage."

"Hang on," I say, climbing down from Zev's back. "I don't know where I'm going."

Erzsébet smiles at me. The calm she keeps while her world gets attacked and her proteges get killed makes no sense, but that's probably why she's been alive forever.

"But you do know," she says with a wink. "Because I showed it to you in your dream."

She offers no other information, just takes my hand and gives me a reassuring squeeze. I glance down at her fingers wrapped around mine, and I really don't want to let go. I'm terrified of witch life without this woman here to guide me, even though we just met. As I'm staring at our hands, I notice she's placed a small piece of paper in my palm.

"For the dragons," she says with a final smile. After that, she rushes toward Rune. "Let's conceal here," she says to the fae. "Hide me until they start searching the walls, then the others will flood in."

I guess Rune doesn't need any more detail than that, as he and Erzsébet instantly disappear into a mesh of ferns and flowers.

The garden is suddenly very still, the trickling of the stream the only source of sound.

Until the vampires start slamming against the wall.

Having seen what they did to the Grand Hall, I know the garden door will be crashing down in no time. That means I've got seconds to figure out how the hell to get out of here. I shove the piece of paper into my pocket and start searching the room for something that will spark my memory.

It's not that I don't remember the dream--it's as vivid now as it was this morning. But it didn't lead me to the garden, just from the river to the main room.

The river?

I walk over to the stream, peering into the waters. Instead of a shallow creek, I'm looking into a deep trench. The water flows gently, but it goes much deeper than I expected. As I stare into the depths, the water stills and clarifies, just as the river did earlier in the day. I see all the way to the bottom of the trench where there are two separate tunnel entrances.

Just like the dream.

I turn to Zev, who's got his hackles up as he faces the door. There are now cracks in the stone; it's not going to stand up to many more blows.

"Can you swim?"

He looks over his wolf shoulder, first at me and then down to the water. In answer to my question, he moves to me as he morphs back into human form, now naked by my side.

"I hate water as a wolf," he says. "I'll tolerate it as a man. Guide me."

I'm about to describe my plan when the wall starts to crumble. Instead of speaking, I just grab Zev's hand and jump into the narrow channel.

We splash through the surface and swim down. Once we're below the banks of the stream, the walls open up and it's like we're in an underground swimming pool. There's plenty of room to maneuver and small silver fish swim around us, creating a shimmer that's obviously meant to light our way. This is without a doubt the world's best pool.

I flip around and start kicking, swimming as fast as I can toward the bottom. In my dream I went into the entrance on the right, so that should take us back to the river entrance next to the city street.

That's not where I want to go, though.

I want to go find dragons.

I also don't want to pop up with a naked werewolf in the heart of Budapest.

Unlike my dream, I'm not afraid of passing into the dark entrance. The only thing pulling me back is that my little girl is in a room full of vampires, and I'm just leaving. I know it's the right choice, and I trust Rune with all of our lives, but that doesn't make it easy.

I feel Zev swimming alongside and just behind me, and with a final push through the water we go into the cave to the left.

Even though we'd been swimming downward, I burst up through the surface of the water as we come out on the other side of the entrance. There's a subtle blue glow coming off the water, otherwise it's completely dark. I don't know where we are and I definitely don't know where we should go.

Zev bursts through the water next to me, inhaling deeply as he does. I hear soft splashing as he looks to the left and the right, trying to get his bearings.

"There's only one direction to go," he says, his wolf vision much sharper than my lame, human sight. He pulls himself up onto solid ground, and the glow from the stream gives me just enough light to watch water cascade down his naked form. His body is perfect, and its perfection is further magnified when wet.

He reaches a hand down and helps pull me up, my momentum carrying me into his body. His arms immediately wrap around me, and it would seem this hug was no accident.

"Where do you think we are?" I ask, keeping myself pressed against him. The warmth feels good with my clothes soaking wet.

"You tell me," he says. "According to Erzsébet, you know exactly where you're going."

As much as I want my powers to manifest fully, I'm not ready to move on from having these princes guide me and carry me and answer all my questions. Now that we're in witch territory and I'm having dreams planted by the witch queen, my responsibilities are on the rise and it scares the shit out of me.

"We're in a cave, trapped between vampires and dragons," I say, doing my best to imitate Erzsébet's calm.

Zev smiles, our faces just inches apart. Despite how often it's happened since these three beautiful men came into my life, I'm still surprised with how quickly fear turns into lust. Of course it's more than that with Zev, our connection running much deeper than our physical beings.

"What do you suppose we should do while we're here?" the werewolf asks with a sly grin.

"Probably find some dragons so I can build a wand before I incinerate," I joke back.

"Sounds like a fine plan," Zev says, stepping out of our embrace but keeping my hands in his. "If nothing else, their fiery breath will warm us up after that swim."

We turn, hand in hand, and start walking into the darkness. I can't see, but I know where I'm going. My clothes are drenched, but the touch of Zev's hand keeps me warm. I miss my girl with all my heart, but I know I'm doing what's right for both of us. Everything is chaos, danger, and uncertainty, and yet, in this moment, I'm right where I want to be.

CHAPTER NINE

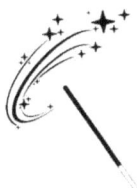

I have no idea how long we've been walking or what time it is. A handful of hours have passed since Andor showed up at our hotel, but I doubt it's light out yet in the real world. I'd ask Zev if he has a guess about the time, but I'm sure he doesn't know or care.

"What did Erzsébet give you back in the garden?" he asks.

This is the first I've thought about the paper, and I immediately panic because it's stuffed in the pocket of my sopping-wet jeans. I reach in to retrieve it--and pull out a miraculously dry piece of parchment.

"Oh my God," I say. "It's not wet."

Zev laughs. "It seems as though the witch knew we'd be going into the water. Would have been a dastardly move to give you an important paper that couldn't handle the trip."

I unfold the note, though there's no reason to do so as it's too dark for me to read. I hold it out for Zev to inspect.

"Looks like an incantation," he says. "Let's put it back in your pocket until we can read it properly. I think we should take our time when you cast your first spell so you don't turn me into a goat."

I laugh, and grip his hand a little tighter. It's unfair for a man to be so handsome and so charming. And on top of that, he's mine, fated to me. It's all a little too much to handle, frankly.

"So... Erzsébet," I say, opening up a discussion we didn't have time for in the Grand Hall. "You all know her?"

"Somewhat," Zev says with a shrug. "We knew her daughter very well, but met the queen only a few times. The last time we saw her was right before Cara and Darius traveled to meet the king of the vampires, Darius' father."

Zev's voice is barely above a whisper by the end of his sentence, and it doesn't take a genius to piece together how Cara died. If Darius was the last of the three

219

princes to be with Cara before the vampires killed her, that explains the dissolving of any friendships.

I'm yanked out of my thoughts--physically and mentally--when Zev stops walking but keeps holding my hand. I look at him, his eyes glued to mine, a curious look on his face.

"We need to stop here," he says.

"Why? It's pitch black and we don't know where we are."

"We're getting close," Zev says. "The air's getting thicker. Dragon's breath."

I trust the werewolf's senses, even if I can't sense these things myself. And how freaking thick is dragon's breath?

"And, a more important reason…"

He trails off as he steps toward me. I can barely see him, but I can absolutely feel him.

"I need to warm you."

Just the words leaving his lips light a fire in my belly. *Mission accomplished, sexy wolf.*

My heart is instantly aflutter, beating against my ribcage with a rhythmic force that feels almost alarming. Zev circles behind me and slips his hands around my waist. I lean into his chest as he bends his neck to whisper into my ear, his lips teasing the tip of my earlobe, sending shivers down my spine.

"No sense being uncomfortable now that we're safe," he says softly.

I snort in a very unladylike way. "Safe?" I say, my voice growing serious. I twist in his arms so that I'm facing him, his hands gripping my hips now, my arms resting on the hardened muscles of his chest. "Just because we're closer to the dragons than the vampires?"

He doesn't answer with his voice, but his gaze says yes. Wherever we were and wherever we're headed, this is the calm of the storm. Zev's green eyes darken as they stay locked with mine, becoming clouded with a need that pierces straight through all of my defenses. He tightens his grip on me, pulling me closer to him. I raise my arms, letting my hands fall to his neck, pressing my breasts into him, wishing we had far fewer clothes between us.

And then I notice the darkness around us brightening slowly, but distinctly, and it takes me a moment to realize I'm the cause. I'm literally lighting the cave up with my glowing skin.

I attempt to step away from Zev, worried I might hurt him, but he refuses to release me, and instead closes whatever microscopic distance remains between us. I suck in my breath, my mind and body at odds with each other. I want to protect Zev from… well, from me. But I also am desperate to be closer to him. A primal need has been growing between us, amplified in ways impossible to ignore after he bit my shoulder during that bath. It feels like that was a lifetime ago, yet the memory is still so fresh.

"Why do you pull away?" he asks, his gaze demanding and intoxicating.

"You saw what I almost did to Darius." Even now, the thought of his lips burning as he tried to feed from me makes me sick to my stomach.

"I can handle your heat," he says gruffly.

I'm trying to think of the perfect comeback for his perfect line, when he silences whatever I would have said with his lips against mine.

His hands spread over my back, working their way down my hips to my ass as his tongue pushes open my lips and his kiss deepens.

I moan into his mouth, momentarily forgetting my fear of blasting him with my witch magic, as I wrap my hand around his neck and pull him closer still.

His heart beats against my chest, our bodies in rhythm to each other as our passions grow.

Before I get swept away by him, I try to grasp any remaining coolheadedness I might still have access to.

This is insane.

I can't do this in a random cave with dragons God knows how close by, while my baby is with Rune and Darius in a fight for their lives, while everything hangs in the balance of me not blowing myself up.

Zev seems to notice my shift in mood, and he lifts his head, breaking contact with my mouth, which is a real disappointment if I'm being honest.

He lifts his thumb and traces it along my forehead. "You've got too many worries, love," he says. "There's no point in dwelling on what's out of our control."

"But--"

He kisses me again, this time pinning me against the cave wall as he does. "But nothing. Rain is safe. I trust Rune with my life--and hers--and yours." He kisses my forehead, where he just ran his thumb over. "Darius is safe. That man is frustratingly hard to kill. He also has something...someone...to live for now." He pauses, his eyes scanning my face for signs that I understand what he's saying.

"Me?" I ask, surprised.

"Of course you. And Rain too. We are all devoted to her. But you, my love," he kisses my cheek this time, and the five-o-clock shadow framing his jaw tickles my skin. "You, we live for." And then his mouth finds mine again, and the passion between us explodes into fireworks in my soul as Zev's fire burns out of him and into me, both of us burning from within.

Any trace of cold leaves my body the second Zev starts to undress me. He works slowly, deliberately, taking his time to peel the wet fabric away from my skin. As he does, I admire the view in front of me, drinking in the sculpted chest and abs I will never tire of seeing.

As he unbuttons my blouse, he somehow snaps open my bra at the same time. My eyes widen in surprise and he chuckles, his hands exploring the shape of my breasts, starting from my ribcage and working up until he's cupping them both.

I reach down and hold the hardness growing between his legs as he rolls his fingers over my nipples, sending shivers of desire and pleasure into the core of my body.

I arch into him, wanting more of his hands on me, needing to feel him everywhere, to quench this desire.

While I don't want his kneading to stop, I also want something more. I move

221

my hands to his hips, dropping to my knees as I do, letting my hair, then my mouth tease the hard length of him.

He growls, the deep thrum of it echoing throughout the cave, and his fingers dig into my hair as I flick my tongue out tentatively.

I feel a whole other kind of power rise up in me with him, the kind that comes from a connection that defies logic or reason. A connection that cuts straight to the soul.

When I take him in my mouth, his pleasure is mine, his ecstatic need is mine... and I feel our destinies knot together into something that can never be broken.

With a jerk, Zev pulls away, and I nearly topple over, as I was precariously balanced on the balls of my feet as I knelt.

He catches me, helping me stand, his eyes a storm. "I'm sorry."

"Did I... did I do something wrong?" Even as I say the words, I regret letting them leave my mouth. I sound too... desperate. Too insecure, and I don't like that.

But Zev grabs my arms and pulls me to him. "Nothing could be further from the truth. But I need to... tell you something."

My stomach clenches in fear of what he's about to say. It seems serious. And so I do my best to prepare for a broken heart.

"Did you," he begins, seeming unsure of his words. "Could you, could you feel a connection forming between us?"

My breath hitches. "Yes." If he's asking me this, he must have felt it too. I can't help but feel hope rise in my chest.

"I've told you that you are my mate."

I nod. I've been wanting to have this conversation since he said that to me, but I've been too scared of what it all might mean--with him and with the others.

"You need to know what will happen if we..." his voice trails off, so I nudge him along.

"What will happen if we...?" But even as I ask the question, I feel the answer within. It is already happening. The bond has already begun to form.

He nods as if reading my mind. "It might already be too late to stop it," he says, looking pained as he speaks. "But if you want to stop it, I will try." He's gritting his teeth now, as if this conversation is really causing him harm.

"Do you not want that with me?" I try to make my voice sound big, strong, confident, but I don't think I succeed even a little.

"Not at all. That's not it. I don't want you to feel forced. For those of my kind, our wolves mate with their Chosen in a primal way. I have no control over it. But I am also a man, and that I do have control over. So I will not force you to be my mate."

My heart feels brittle, and I try not to take everything he's saying as a rejection, but I'm a bit too fragile to pull it off entirely.

"I don't want you to feel trapped in something because of your wolf," I say, feeling suddenly far too exposed half-naked in a cave with a werewolf.

He growls again, and I can feel the rumble in his chest as he pulls me closer.

"Are you daft, woman? I want you. I'm... apparently very badly, asking if you want me. If you want this. If we keep going, our fates will be sealed to one another for life. There will be no breaking it."

I shiver at the promise in those words and I have no fear of sharing fates with him. I have only one fear that needs to be addressed. "What about Darius? And... Rune?" I don't know what's going on with me and Rune, but there's a connection there I cannot deny, even if it hasn't been acted on.

He frowns, and I fear the coming response. If I had to choose between them, what would I do? Picking only one would mean breaking other pieces of my heart. There's no way I come out whole from this.

"Normally," he says, "a wolf doesn't allow other mates to his Chosen."

My stomach clenches in worry of what his next words will be.

"However, a normal Chosen wouldn't be a witch. And I wouldn't share a pledge with your other suitors. You... you are different. For all three of us. And when we bound ourselves to you, we bound ourselves to each other as well, as a byproduct of the sacred oath."

My stomach flips, my mind rushing to piece together the meaning of his words. "Are you saying..."

"I'm saying that Darius and Rune are now part of our pack, love. The three of us have already spoken about this. I'm saying, you don't have to choose just one of us if you don't want to."

And just like that, a great dam is released inside me, and this time I claim his lips, pouring into him everything I have been holding back out of fear.

He accepts my answer, spoken with my body rather than words, and wraps himself around me, trying to move us both closer to each other.

But I need to not have pants on for us to make any progress with this goal, so I begin to slip out of them, with Zev quick to help in pulling them down.

I kick them away as Zev guides my last remaining piece of clothing off my hips, his fingers lightly brushing between my legs, where all the heat and ache is gathering in me.

I bite my lip and try to keep my body relaxed as my underwear drops to the floor and Zev cups my ass and positions his mouth at the perfect spot between my legs.

I'm nearly undone with one flick of his tongue, and I lean against the cave wall, ignoring the stone scraping my skin raw, as Zev treats my body like an all you can eat buffet. I'm writhing in pent up need and nearly at the edge of the cliff about to fly off when he pulls away and raises his body to meet mine.

"You're evil," I breathe, everything in me desperate for the release he promised with his mouth and his fingers.

He slips his arms behind me to support me more, so I don't get torn apart by the wall, and as he nudges my legs apart with his knee, he kisses and nips at my neck and shoulder. "Are you ready?" he asks softly.

I nod. God am I ever.

He bites my shoulder as he thrusts himself into me and I can't help but scream from the delicious blend of pain mixed with the explosive pleasure he offers. My arms are wrapped around him, my nails digging into his back as our bodies unite as one. His thrusts are strong, deep, and powerful, and I hold on to him harder. His hands grip my ass tightly, fingers digging into my flesh, keeping me positioned for the most optimal angle.

I feel the waves crashing and am lost in the forest of his eyes, the feel of his skin against mine, the feel of him inside me. Nothing else exists, and when we both reach the edge of that cliff together, I sink my teeth into his shoulder and bite, and together we fly.

It's NOT until the pulsing of pleasure in my body slows, until we are holding each other on a smooth stretch of stone floor, until the quietness returns, that I feel what is new to feel between us. It is a binding stronger than blood, a soul connection so powerful I know to my core I am changed because of it.

Just as sharing blood back and forth with Darius has made us part of each other in a way that just sex could never do, so too has this experience with Zev been so much more than mere physical pleasure--as mind-blowing as it's been. There is a tether between us that cannot be broken. And I feel a warm sense of belonging that is growing stronger with each of these beautiful men. He is also glowing slightly, his skin casting the same sheen as mine is, though not quite as brightly. My glow, and the pain caused by it, has dimmed since we made love, which has me wondering how this will affect him, being bound to a bomb waiting to explode.

As our heartbeats settle into a new, slower, more relaxed pace together, I finally muster the courage to ask him the question that has been weighing on me, making me feel--unworthy, perhaps. Undeserving, certainly.

These are not emotions I enjoy having exposed to the light, reflected in the most polished mirror of love's pure shine.

And yet to ignore them altogether, to turn a blind eye to my darker thoughts, would be to fester them into something truly terrorizing.

So I expose my heart and I ask. "How is it I can be your mate, when I'm not a werewolf? Won't you be missing something... not being mated to your own kind?"

This question holds so much fear that I am not enough, not enough for Zev, the passionate, deep, unexpectedly brilliant man who is also part wolf. That I am not enough for the mysterious, dark and dashing vampire, with hidden secrets in his past and eyes of a depth I could never escape from. That I am not enough for the beautiful fae who has lost so much and even still gave up more to save me and my daughter. Who has been nothing but kind and pure. Who holds within him so much power, and yet does not use it with ill intention. That I--a silly normal human--am not enough.

And yes, maybe I'm also witch, and maybe I can sometimes shoot lightning out of my mouth, but it doesn't change who I see when I look in the mirror. And it is not a person that could capture the hearts of three incredible beings of magic.

"I may not be a vampire, but that doesn't mean I can't tell what you're thinking, love." Zev's words are soft, kind, as he cups my face in his hands.

We tangle our legs together, our bodies still craving each other too much for either of us to consider moving away.

"What am I thinking?" I ask, wondering if he really can tell.

He shakes his head, then leans in to kiss me. "You are more than you know. And not because you're a witch," he says, kissing me again. "And not because you're part of a prophecy." Each sentence is punctuated with a tender brushing of his lips against mine. "But because of who you are at the core, Bernadette Morgan." He caresses my cheek, his deep forest green eyes penetrating mine. "Darius has been feeding on you. Rune has been in your mind. I have bonded my soul to you. We each have glimpsed parts of your core, your truth. We know what we see when we look at you, and if you can't see that person, you need to take a closer look, because you're missing out."

I can't help the tears that leak from my eyes, and I try to avert my head, to hide my sudden burst of emotion, but Zev holds my face in his hand as he swipes at my tears with his thumb, gently drying my cheek. We both move in at the same time, our lips seeking each other. And this time, as we claim each other's bodies with only the old stone walls as witness, we take our time, exploring every inch, memorizing every curve, tasting and pleasuring and enjoying each other for the few remaining hours of the night.

When morning comes, and the urgency of our quest weighs upon us once more, I stretch and roll over, facing my lover.

His eyes are still closed and I take a moment to study his face. I long to crawl into his arms and never leave, but I know sooner or later, he and the others will have to go home without me. What will happen with our mate bond then? Will we be in pain? Will the loss eat at us? I want to ask, but I also don't want to know. So when he smiles and opens his eyes, I smile back at him, pushing away the dark thoughts for a later time. I can't change what will be, but I can stay present long enough to enjoy what I have now. And right now, I have my werewolf mate in my arms.

"Ready to sweet talk a dragon out of its hide?" he asks.

I grin and kiss him more deeply, speaking into his lips, my breath mingling with his. "Ready as I'll ever be."

CHAPTER TEN

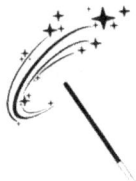

I t's a small piece of paper, insignificant and insanely powerful at the same time. The spell Erzsébet gave to me before we left sits in my palm, a bit of thick parchment with two Hungarian words scrawled across it in a very inky and fancy font: *felfed* and *pálya*. "Reveal" and "path". All I can do is guess how casting this spell works and what it will do. I assume it's going to guide us through the maze of caves to the dragon's lair. And if I'm wrong… well, surprise is on us.

It's also technically my first official spell as a witch. Which is kind of exciting and makes me feel accomplished, like I've finally graduated junior high after years of not making grades.

I stare down at the small slip of waterproof paper, trying my best to stay focused on our mission. And to not think about how my daughter is doing, feeding from a bottle without her mom there to help. Or how Rune and Darius are doing, if they even survived the attack.

They did. I have to believe they did. I feel like I would sense if something happened to them.

Zev walks up behind me--still naked since he refuses to accept any of my clothing, arguing that he's more adept at keeping himself warm and can always shift to wolf form when needed--and pulls me against his chest, his hands gripping my hips. "Soon we'll have the scale and then rejoin the others by this evening. She's okay."

I bend my head back to look up at him and smile. My expression clearly gave away my thoughts. "I know. It's just…"

He kisses my head. "Hard," he says, finishing my sentence. "Of course it is. It's by design. Some moments must be hard, must have weight, must make us fight for them. That is how we know we have found something of true value in our lives. That is how we know what's worth living for."

"What if I can't control my magic for that long?" I ask, expressing my other super stressor.

"Our mate bond is helping siphon some of the extra energy," he says. "It should be enough until we get back to Darius. And maybe between the two of us, you'll have an easier time."

I seal those words with a kiss, then reluctantly pull away.

Zev nods that he's ready, so I take the slip of paper and read aloud the Hungarian spell.

At first, nothing happens. I look at the words and the accent marks, making sure I'm pronouncing it correctly. I can't think of what I did wrong. Two words in and I'm very frustrated by being a witch.

"Try, um…" Zev seems tentative about telling me how to use my powers, as he should. I do appreciate his effort to avoid full mansplaining, or were-mansplaining, as the case may be. "Try saying the words like you mean them. Not like you're reading Hungarian for the first time."

It's annoying, condescending, incredibly accurate advice.

When I try a second time--thinking about the words, our mission, my goals--the sound of my voice ignites a glowing ball of light. It's about the size of a base-ball, pulsing with the ebb and flow of its essence. It bounces twice in the air, then moves forward a bit.

"I think it wants us to follow it," I say, checking if Zev sees what I'm seeing.

He nods and gives my arm a gentle, affirming squeeze. "Let's be off."

The glowing light keeps pace with us. If we speed up, so does it. If we slow down, it does as well, but if we stop for too long, it starts to bounce again until we pick up the pace.

That could get real annoying real fast, but fortunately, we're in a hurry and it seems, based on Zev's sniffing, that we're not too far off.

It brings some small comfort that we don't have to kill the dragon. I'm far too fond of their mythology to harm a real, live one. I can't believe I'm even going to be getting this close to a real freaking dragon! My life is bananas.

We are both quiet as we walk, lost in thoughts as vast as this new world I've found myself in. When I left New York--along with my dreams of a career in music--I thought I knew what every day for the rest of my life would look like, more or less.

Some people may find that comforting, but for me it felt claustrophobic, like the constraints of my narrowing world were suffocating me. Now, I always seem to be one step away from dying, but I'm so much more alive as well.

I smile to myself as I realize how much happier I've been since the three of them walked into my bar, despite all the craziness.

"What's brightened up your somber mood?" Zev asks, breaking the comfortable silence. He slips an arm around my waist as we walk, pulling me closer. "Perhaps memories of earlier?" He nuzzles my neck with his nose and I laugh and shove him away playfully.

"No… but now that I think about it, yes," I say. "I was just thinking that I can't imagine my life without you. Any of you."

My joy in the moment is shadowed by the understanding that the closer I get to mastering my powers, the closer we come to saying goodbye.

Zev senses the shift in my mood and pulls me into an embrace even as our guide ball bounces in place impatiently.

"You'll never be without me. Our mate bond will always connect us, no matter the distance. And I will come back to you. All that I do, I do so that we can be together and so you and Rain can be safe."

His lips find mine, and I am lost in him once again, the taste of his fire in my mouth consuming me.

We are both breathless when the kiss ends, and I grip his hand as we continue our walk together, lost in thoughts of what if.

Lord, what a beautifully messy bed I've made for myself.

After a few twists and turns through narrow passages and enormous, cavernous rooms, our little guide begins to change color, first turning a very pale pink, then slightly darker the further along we follow.

"I think we're getting close," I say, and as if to confirm my suspicion we feel a growing heat fill our lungs. The air is thick with the scent of burnt wood, smoke, and something else. "Please tell me I'm not smelling what I think I'm smelling," I say, covering my nose with part of my shirt and gagging at the stench.

Zev nods, surely having noticed the scent a mile back. "That's the smell of burnt flesh."

Suddenly my excitement about seeing my first dragon is overshadowed by my fear of being a flesh-kabob. The fear for my own safety is compounded with a worry that I'm about to see the charred corpse of my father.

We continue walking much more slowly now, creeping and staying to the walls like we might blend in better that way. I can tell Zev is on the edge of shifting at any moment. I glare at my hands, willing them to produce magic on demand, but I feel nothing to indicate they might obey.

The tunnel we're walking through begins to widen into a larger cavern where sections of the stone wall are charred with ash. This cave is no stranger to fiery dragon breath.

The smells intensify, and my eyes burn from the noxious fumes permeating the air. Let's hope Rune has a potion for whatever damage this is doing to my insides.

Ahead and to our right another narrow pathway widens into a cavern, and the long tail of a dragon peeks out through it, winding around itself.

We both freeze.

I can hardly breathe.

And not just because it stinks in here.

"Let me have a look first," Zev whispers. He doesn't give me a chance to respond, going straight into wolf mode. The grace and ease with which he moves along the uneven floor make it clear he's relieved to be in wolf form for this part.

A sharp and unexpected ache seizes me as I realize this is a part of his life I'll never be able to share. I will always be a witch, never a wolf. He'll never run with his mate through the forest under a full moon; or howl in harmony at the edge of a cliff; or share that bond that must be so special.

I shake my head, pulling myself back to the present circumstances where I'm less than twenty feet from a very real dragon and my mate is about to get close enough to it to become its next appetizer.

I clench my teeth and take deep breaths, praying to whatever gods, goddesses or magic beings are listening that my power will work if we need it. I send out unspoken thoughts to Zev. *Be careful. Come back to me whole.* My heart constricts at the thought of something happening to him.

I don't expect an answer of course, not like with Darius, but I know on some level the words will find him.

Still, I'm stunned when a voice that sounds suspiciously like Zev replies.

I will always come back to you.

Hang on. You can mind-speak?

Zev sounds very pleased with himself when he replies. *Perks of being mates.*

The wolf then disappears into the shadows, his fur spiked out like an animal on defense, his movements cautious, the pads of his paws making no noise.

I don't want to distract him and get him killed, so I hold my three million questions for when we aren't trying to take a piece of dragon.

Our plan, such as it is, involves scouting around the legendary creature, hoping it lost a scale the way a bird might lose a feather. When we find one, use our super stealth skills to take it and leave without being seen, smelled or heard.

That's Plan A, and requires us to be in an action adventure movie where the hero never dies no matter how many times he's shot, stabbed or blown on with dragon fire.

Plan B involves one of us distracting the dragon while the other physically plucks a scale off its hide, which requires us to be actual well-trained NAVY Seals or some shit. I don't even know. Just... like... a real life badass, ya know? This one is not my favorite plan. At all.

Plan C is to die and spend our time in the afterlife discussing what went wrong with Plans A and B.

It feels like ages that Zev is gone, and when he returns and quietly shifts back into a man, my nerves are beyond frayed.

I throw myself into his arms and kiss him fiercely. He responds with abandon, tucking me against his chest as he explores my mouth with his.

Finally, I pull away, breathless and relieved. "You scared me."

He grins, his green eyes twinkling with mischief. "If that's my reception when I scare you, I'll have to do it more often."

I lightly slap his arm, careful to not make any noise. "I'll happily greet you that way for *not* scaring me. Did you find any spare scales lying around? Mission accomplished, time to go home?" I ask, crossing my fingers.

"No," he says with a frown.

"Well, that sucks monkey balls," I say, even though I knew it would never be so easy. "Looks like it's Plan B? Which one of us is gonna be bait?"

"Also no to Plan B," he says, his frown deepening.

"What do you mean? We need to get the scale, one way or another. Or I'm going to blow us all up."

"We don't need bait," he says.

"Okay… do you want to just fill me in on what's going on or are we playing a really annoying game of twenty questions?"

"The dragon is dead," he says finally.

My jaw drops. "Dead? But I thought it's super hard to kill a dragon. You can only kill them while they're still in the egg or whatever."

"It is. You do."

"Then… how? Who?" A horrible thought settles on me and my eyes widen. "What if… what if my father found the dragon first and… and somehow killed it to get the pieces for my wand?"

Zev's eyes soften and he reaches for my hand. "I don't think that happened. Bernie, there's another body in there."

"The smell…" I gently pull myself from Zev and make my way to the dragon.

"Love, wait. It might not be safe."

I don't stop, letting him catch up with me instead. "If everything in there is dead, what do I have to fear?"

I pause at the entrance, stepping carefully around the thick tail and look in, shocked despite myself. The dragon is massive, the size of a house, and fills the cavernous space with its bulk. It's covered in iridescent scales that shimmer and cast rays of blue and green light, despite having no obvious light source.

Near the mythical beast are the remains of a man, leaning against the stone wall and holding something in his hand at his chest. Beyond his human form, he's unrecognizable. I guess this is how I meet my father.

As disturbing as the scorched corpse is, the most startling bit about the whole scene is the fact that the dragon is also charred to death.

Zev leans in, whispering against my ear. "What we both should fear is whatever killed that dragon."

~

RIGHT. That's definitely the thing to be scared of right now. My mind spins, trying to sort out what I need to do before I can get the hell out of this place. "We need a scale. Then we should go."

Zev takes the initiative, wrapping his strong hands around a scale on the right forearm.

I turn away, uncomfortable seeing its poor dead body desecrated like this.

My eye is drawn to the charred human body that is slumped to the left of the dragon. I edge toward it, my curiosity overriding good sense.

"Bernie," Zev says, growling a soft warning deep in his throat.

"I just need to know," I say. It's an almost trancelike state I find myself in as I near the body. I fight against my own gag reflex and lean in to examine what he's clutching in his hand.

Using a bit of my scarf I pry the object out of his fingers and hold it up.

It's a pendant, silver with gold trim and an intricately carved design of an eye with a crystal as the iris.

It feels warm in my palm, even through my scarf, and I wrap it and stick it in my pocket. Just as I do so, I hear the sickening sound of the scale coming free.

Tears burn my eyes and I force myself to look at the dragon's face, into one of its reptilian eyes, which remain open despite its eternal slumber. "Thank you. I know we're not giving you much of a choice, but thank you nonetheless. Your gift is helping save more lives than you'll ever--."

I swallow a scream and fall back when the eye blinks slowly.

"It's not dead," I whisper, dread filling my chest.

"Stay still," Zev hisses. "Don't move."

I've fallen on my ass, so I stay put, trying not to breathe. Or to move. Or to emit any kind of scent.

Puffs of smoke shoot out of its nose like a sneeze, and its body shifts and shuffles just enough to make the stone around us groan and crack as if it's about to cave in.

I can see that Zev did manage to remove the scale. That's a meaningless fact if we die here, but will be awesome news should we somehow manage to survive an encounter with an injured and probably very pissed off dragon.

As the monstrous creature shifts, its long tail unravels a bit, revealing something that breaks my frightened heart.

A massive egg, about six feet tall. Cracked. Hatched.

"I thought you said you crushed the egg," I say to Zev, my eyes never leaving the giant shell. "How the hell does that get crushed?"

"With a very big foot," he responds.

"How big are dragon babies?"

Zev looks at the broken egg, then back at me. "Big enough to do damage when they're a few minutes old."

My eyes well with tears as I look back at the wounded mother. She's nearly dead because she wanted to protect her baby. And now she's here, dying, having lost the thing she valued more than her own life.

I feel like I'm going to vomit.

"I'm so sorry," I say to it, stepping forward timidly as an unbidden tear rolls down my cheek. I've got no reason to believe that this dragon and I can communicate, but I feel an overwhelming need to show my empathy.

"I don't know who--or what--did this to you, but I am truly sorry for your pain and suffering. And for your loss." I swallow tears and continue, as the eye blinks once again at me. "I'm a mother too. Not being near my child hurts so much, I can't imagine the pain of losing her."

It might have more to do with pain than hearing my words, but a tear pools in the corner of the dragon's eye. As it falls, it begins to sizzle from the heat of itself, turning to steam before it can get too far.

My gut sinks when I realize the shared pain is too deep, that this dragon has become something so much more than an ingredient for my wand. She's the most majestic creature I've ever seen, only feet away from me, more concerned with a shattered egg than her injuries.

"We can't take the scale," I say.

"What are you talking about?" Zev asks, definitely annoyed, and I don't blame him. I'm annoyed at myself. But I'm also not wrong.

"She's a mother," I say. "And she's grieving. And dying. I won't treat her like she's anything less."

I stand there, not sure what my decision means for our quest, but already having made it. Zev, meanwhile, isn't giving up on the original plan. "We're taking the scale, Bernie. I'm sorry if it makes me heartless, but I don't give a damn about anything other than saving your life."

My heart swells at his words, but it's not his choice to make.

"I can't explain it, but I know I'm right," I whisper, my throat suddenly very dry. "If I steal this piece of her, if I rob a dying mother of part of her body, my wand will be tainted. It won't work, Zev."

"Then what do we do?" he asks, approaching gently.

"How do you think I ask for permission?"

Zev thinks about my question, looking from me to the dragon. When he turns back to me, his eyes show pure admiration. "Just make her believe in you. The way the rest of us do."

He might as well be reading off a motivational poster in a doctor's office, but the words still strike me. If I can get a tear out of this dragon, I can show her my worth.

I take the scale from Zev and step forward, close enough to the dragon to feel the heat of her breath. Sweat immediately beads on my forehead, but I step even closer.

"You're saving my life," I say, holding the scale in front of the dragon's big, beautiful eye. "And with that, you're saving my child, and countless other souls."

At this point, I've reached the end of my speech. I felt genuine saying those things, but it still feels like I need more. I look at the charred body next to her, the remains of who I can only assume was my father. A man I never met, never knew, and yet somehow brought me to Budapest and sent me on the craziest journey of all time. I return my gaze to the dragon.

"I can't repay you, but I swear on my life I will find and kill whoever, or whatever, did this to you. I will do everything in my power to find your baby and bring it home."

There's no way the dragon understands. There's no way I can make and keep such a promise. And yet, there's something to be said for the power of a sentiment, for the truth of conviction. Another tear trickles and steams off the dragon's cheek--then she lowers her head and closes her eyes.

I shed a tear as well, watching her take what I know will be her last breath.

"She says it's okay," I say to Zev. "I can have her scale."

My gaze stays on the magnificent creature while Zev moves to me and wipes away my tear. "You're brave, powerful, and the most magical being I've ever met."

He gently kisses my head, then whispers in my ear, "Let's get back to your daughter."

Those words spur me into action immediately, and Zev shifts into wolf and pushes into my legs so I'll ride him. It's faster than my running, and I lean into him, wrapping my arms around his wolf torso. I cry some more for the fallen dragon, my tears matting down Zev's soft, white fur.

He doesn't need our guiding magic to find the way back, instead using his nose to retrace our steps. I can't see in the darkness, but I feel the power of these incredible caves. When she's old enough, I'll bring Rain here to meet a dragon.

It feels like it takes mere minutes for us to get back to the watery portal, and Zev shifts back to man as we dive in.

We swim from one underground tunnel to the next, avoiding the garden stream and instead taking the exit that leads to the river running through downtown Budapest. I don't want to walk us straight into the vampire's arms in case they decided to stay the night.

Unfortunately, this means my naked wolf man is going to be a problem.

We push through to the other side and pop out in the middle of the river, right where I swam in my dream. The evening rush is underway, and we're just a couple of tourists swimming in the river.

We get plenty of looks from passersby, wondering where we came from and why we're swimming in the frigid waters. Wait till they see the swimming trunks that Zev definitely isn't wearing.

Hungarians, it turns out, are fun-loving people, as we're met with hoots and hollers after we climb up the ladder of an anchored boat and step onto the sidewalk next to the water. Zev stares at the men and women who whistle and clap for him. He doesn't seem to mind, but I've got too much social conditioning. My face turns bright red as I take my sweater and try to tie it around his waist.

Do I embarrass you, love?

In response, I give his ass a swift, open-hand slap. Dozens of people break into applause. *Not at all,* I say. *But we don't have time for this. Where will we find Darius and Rune?* I close my eyes and think of Darius, imagining our connection, the way our blood sings to each other.

Darius? Are you okay?

I feel his utter relief mentally pour over me. *Thank the Fates you are safe. Across the street from our hotel, there's a narrow alley. Take it until you reach the cemetery behind the church. We will meet you there.*

I break into a jog and Zev quickly follows, waving goodbye as strangers continue to clap.

It feels like perpetual night in Budapest, though I know that's only because I spent the day underground.

Still, it's spooky to step into the sacred and holy ground that is the resting place for so many as the heavy moon casts its silver light over us.

I see Darius first, and nearly trip over my own feet getting to his arms.

Our embrace is passionate and too short, as I pull away to look for Rune. "Where is he? Where's Rain?"

Darius frowns. "They are safe. Given the attack, we felt it best he keep her hidden while I find you two and bring you back, making sure no one follows us."

My heart sinks. I've been away from her for nearly a full day. I know the precaution is justified, but I can't bear to be without her any longer.

Before I can protest, Zev begins to growl as someone walks out of the shadows.

Erzsébet stands in the moonlight. She's dressed in black with her long red and silver hair cascading down her back in waves. She looks more magical than anyone I've ever seen.

"Did you find what was needed?" She asks.

There's something about her tone, her slight surprise at seeing us that gives me pause but I set it aside, rightly blaming it on exhaustion and the stress of the situation.

"Yes, we got a scale," I say, patting my pocket. I remember my other take from the cave and pull it out, unveiling the pendant to the queen. "But the dragon was already dead. Her tail was wrapped around a broken egg shell, so she died trying to save her baby."

Erzsébet cocks an eyebrow. "The dragonling was gone?"

I nod. "There was only the dragon and a dead body. My father."

I study the queen witch's face carefully as she looks at the pendant for a second, then averts her gaze back to me. "How do you know it was your father?"

Huh? Based on everything Erzsébet and Andor have said, this seems pretty obvious. Dad went to get the scale. There was a dead guy next to the dragon. Therefore, dead guy equals dad.

"Did someone else go to the cave?" I ask.

She takes a moment, her eyes never leaving mine. It's not the longest pause, but long enough for me to recognize she knows something. Something she's keeping hidden. Powerful as she is, helpful as she's been, there's something about this woman I don't yet trust.

"I can't say if another accompanied your father," she finally says, "or if they perhaps met him in the cave. But if you say there was a dead dragon, and a dead man next to it, and a missing dragonling…" she trails off, again looking at the pendant before snatching it from my hand and putting it in her own pocket. "It seems as though they had company."

CHAPTER ELEVEN

W ithout another word, the witch turns and starts walking back into the shadows. Since I didn't pick this meeting place, I'm not sure if we're supposed to follow her or not. Which reminds me: "Why are we in a graveyard?"

Darius takes my hand--the feel of his cool touch somehow warming me from the inside-- and we fall in behind Erzsébet with Zev close on our heels.

"And where are they?" I ask Darius, referring to the fae and my baby.

"Nearby," he reassures me, though the fact that they're near the cemetery isn't all that comforting. We're walking along a narrow path, gravestones on either side. I always have a compulsion to read each headstone I pass, like I owe it to the deceased to take a moment and honor the life they lived rather than treating their final resting place like decoration. But this cemetery is massive and we've got places to be--hopefully someplace not teaming with the ghosts of the dead, even though I'm pretty sure Erzsébet brought us here for a reason.

At a certain, unremarkable spot, the witch stops and casually looks around. Despite the fact that it's nighttime and we're surrounded by the dead, I still see a surprising number of people walking about. There are dog walkers and happy couples cruising around as if this were a park like any other. It's a combination of off-putting and charming.

When there's a lull in foot traffic, Erzsébet flicks her wand and the ground in front of a headstone slowly opens up, leaving a hole in the earth about the size of a garbage can lid. With a final glance over her shoulder, Erzsébet steps forward and falls into the ground.

I, for one, have some apprehension about diving into a grave. Darius doesn't share my concern and lets me know it.

She's not leading us into a coffin, my sweet.

I bet you wish she was, I say back, stalling before I'm forced to take the plunge.

Darius flashes a quick smile.

It would be nice to get a decent night's sleep.

The vampire steps forward and drops out of sight, leaving me and Zev to follow. The werewolf takes my hand and gives me a brief, loving kiss, sending sparks of fire through me. I can now always sense our mate bond, but when we are touching it is so much stronger.

"I'm not fond of the under-earth in cemeteries either," he says. "But I've got a feeling your daughter's waiting for you."

He's good at motivating me, this one. With images of Rain in my mind, I repeat the mantra 'I will not die, I will not die, I will not die,' and then take the plunge, my nerves frayed as I step in after Darius and feel gravity give way. What I expect to be a short drop lasts for excruciatingly long seconds as the air leaves my lungs. Just when it starts to feel interminable, my feet finally plant solidly on the ground. I don't stumble, fall, or even land with a jolt. I'm just standing.

As I open my eyes, Zev lands to my side. Darius and Erzsébet are a few feet away, looking back at us. We're all in the middle of a large, underground chamber, light coming from torches stationed along the stone walls.

And there's Rune, standing next to a crib, which looks so incredibly incongruous in the middle of an underground tomb of a cemetery.

I push past Darius and Erzsébet, literally shoving a witch queen who's thousands of years old to the side, so I can go to Rain. I still don't feel safe enough to touch her, and the ache to do so is nearly overwhelming, but I lean over the crib and devour her with my eyes as she sleeps. She looks so peaceful, so content. I hope she always feels this way.

Rune watches, tears brimming in his eyes. His affection for both Rain and myself is palpable, especially when he sees this special mother-daughter connection. I move over to the beautiful fae and bury my face into his chest.

"Thank you," I say while wiping my wet eyes on his shirt. "Thank you for always taking such good care of her."

He wraps his arms around me and speaks softly into my ear. "You two are my reasons for living. It's my pleasure."

When I finally pull away from the sexy fae, I look around to see all four magical, powerful people staring at me.

"Hi," is all I can think to say. "I'm pretty tired and haven't eaten in a day, so does someone else want to do the talking?"

My own mention of food makes my stomach growl. My body goes on autopilot, moving around the room in search of some water. I find a table with a pitcher and glasses on it, and Zev is instantly by my side pouring us water. As I chug a first glass, then a second, then start on a third, Erzsébet does some wand work and mutters *"ünnep,"* which makes a platter of bread, cheese and fruit appear out of thin air. I practically trip on myself running over to it. I need to learn that spell before I learn anything else.

"You should rest," Erzsébet says as I shove half a baguette in my mouth. "Your journey continues as soon as you wake up."

I hadn't thought much about the next step in my wand-making quest, which is silly. I knew there was more to my wand than a piece of dragon, and it would be foolish to assume the other ingredients can just be found at a craft supply store. Unless there's a magical craft supply store hidden between ancient buildings somewhere? Or underground? A black market for magic folk? That seems like it should be a thing. Someone should make that a thing.

I also hadn't noticed, until right now, that I'm hardly glowing, even though Darius hasn't fed on me and Zev hasn't… fed me… in quite a while.

"I don't feel like I'm about to explode," I say to no one in particular. "Is that because I have the dragon scale?"

Erzsébet shakes her head. "This room is keeping your powers under control. We're inside an ancient witch's tomb, built ages ago before the vampires came for us. The spells inside these walls are made to keep the power of a fallen witch in equilibrium, allowing their souls to live on without their bodies."

The room feels more like an unstaged wine cellar than a creepy crypt, but it sounds like they've had a lot of years to renovate.

"Does that mean there's a spirit floating around in here with us?" I ask, thinking of the ghost we left AJ alone with at the pub. Shit. She's gonna be pissed I haven't called her.

"Indeed," Erzsébet says, then just moves right along as if that's not something worth addressing. "As long as you're in here, you should be safe from yourself. It's also a good place to practice spells, like the food summoning I just did."

The prospect of making food appear whenever I want pushes the thought of a long-dead roommate right out of my head. Still, I'm sure I can't just take a long holiday in this magic chamber.

"What happened with the vampires?"

"They'll be back," Darius answers. "We'll be ready, but more *Kő* members will die."

Sounds like we won the battle but still have a long way to go before claiming victory in the war. My thoughts flash back to Andor, ripped away by a blood-thirsty vampire last I saw him. We didn't get off to the greatest start, but I wish he hadn't died.

He lived, Darius says into my mind, responding to my thoughts. *Saved by another Kő.*

I smile with my eyes, happy to hear at least a shred of good news.

Erzsébet bows her head, her beautiful hair draping over her face. "The Grand Hall had been safe for so many centuries. I knew this day would come, but it still feels so unexpected."

It's not lost on me that Rain and I are the only difference between the centuries of peace and the day of devastation. There's a council of paranormals tracking me, combining their efforts and resources to find me and take my baby. And I led them right to the epicenter of witch power.

Erzsébet looks up, reading my thoughts like everyone else always does, because apparently my mind is an open book for anyone to read. "This isn't your fault, Bernadette. I share in the responsibility for bringing you here."

"How so?" I'm still under the impression that my dad lured me here through the words of my soon to be murdered grandfather. What role did the queen witch play in all that?

"There are ways to direct a person to a place without making that intention known," she says. "When I learned you left for Budapest, I set some bits of magic in motion that would lead you to the right hotel at the right time of day. I wasn't going to rest until you were under my watch."

I open my mouth but decide to hold my tongue. It's very suspicious that she makes no mention of my grandfather's letter, the original catalyst for this whole trip. The idea that two parties have been orchestrating my travels makes me uneasy, but I don't feel like opening up about that just yet.

"Let's discuss the matters at hand before you sleep," she says, moving the conversation along.

"Right," I say, tabling my concerns to bring up later with the Sexies. "My wand."

Erzsébet holds her own wand forward and ushers me over with her hand, prompting me to take a closer look.

"The ordinary wand features a wood casing, or sometimes an exterior made of tightly woven feathers," she explains while turning her wand from side to side.

Getting a closer look, I see that hers has thin lines throughout, as if it's made of thread.

"Mine is made of the baleen from a leviathan. That's what gives it the strength to contain the phoenix ashes within."

While the wand sounds very cool and powerful to me, I sense that her words have shocked each of the Sexies.

"Your wand is alive?" Rune asks, a dark concern taking over his light eyes. The fae clearly has some opinions.

Erzsébet nods calmly. She doesn't seem overly surprised by the reaction she's getting.

"In my realm," Rune says, trying to be judicious in his word choice, "some would describe that as dark magic."

"I daresay many witches would agree," Zev adds.

The witch meets their gaze, absorbing the accusatory tones and firing the sentiment right back at them. "To that I would say: when a witch queen, a direct descendant of the Fates, combines her blood, the blood of her fallen daughter, and the ashes of a phoenix in order to cast the spells necessary to save the worlds... one finds the gray area that exists between dark and light magic."

I can't help but enjoy the irony of standing in a tomb and it being deathly quiet.

These princes, once friends before tragedy tore them apart and then I brought them back together, have never been able to mourn their fallen friend. Now they're faced with the girl's mother, made incredibly powerful, seemingly invincible, in the wake of her daughter's death.

That's some heavy shit. I don't know if the Sexies will be able to process it. I don't know when they'll find the time.

"Is that how you, ya know, keep on living?" I ask. It feels a little tactless, but it's the best word combination I can come up with at the moment. Rest is sounding more and more necessary.

Erzsébet nods, and there's a pain in her eyes. "That's the darkest part of all.

No mother wants to outlive her child. Certainly no mother wants to outlive her child for all of eternity."

"Was she, um… was Cara born through the designated lover program you have here?"

There was probably a more tactful way of asking that, but I'm too exhausted to think of it.

The witch cocks her head and studies me. "No, that *program* was created many, many years later when we realized the need for protection and tighter ranks. I was past my childbearing years by then and had already mastered my magic. I did not need such a lover. Cara's father was my husband and greatest love. He died shortly after she did."

As I struggle to find the words sufficient for such tragedy, the queen glances away, walking over to Rain's crib where she stares at my baby in solemn silence.

The sight almost gets me emotional, but instead I yawn, overcome with exhaustion. I need to sleep in a bad way, ideally in the arms of a vampire. Tired as I am, I'd love to give Darius a quick feed and see what happens next. My body and blood have missed him.

I'll prepare the bed, the vampire thinks into my mind, hearing and sharing my needs and disappearing through an opening into what looks like a smaller chamber. I almost follow immediately, but decide to wrap up this conversation.

"Where do I find a leviathan?"

"You can't," Erzsébet says with a shake of her head. "They're long since extinct. Perhaps one or two still swim in the greatest depths of the sea, but we chased them away from the surface more than a thousand years ago."

"Okay," I mutter, my patience wearing a little thin, especially now that my mind has drifted to the bedroom. "So what am I looking for instead?"

"Something natural," Erzsébet says. "The dragon scale gives you great strength, but you need a living element that will transfer power from your hand to the wand's tip."

Annoyed by all the riddles, frustration and impatience builds up in me. I just want to lay my body down and have someone else do all the thinking for a little bit.

"I don't understand," I say with a whimper, my nerves frayed.

"Rest," Zev says, wrapping his hand in mine, letting our mate bond fill me up. "We'll deal with this in the morning."

Rune runs his hand along my back, accomplishing his usual transfer of calm. "I've studied wands, Bernie. I'll find the answer."

I trust the fae with Rain, so of course I trust him with my wand ingredient list. I hug him, kiss Zev, and tiptoe over to the crib to look at my sleeping infant one last time. She flops her tiny arms above her head, a source of pure cuteness in a world that's otherwise a little too ugly for my liking.

After a few moments, I shift my focus to Erzsébet, standing by my side, her striking gaze giving me that conflicted feeling. I trust her, but not implicitly. I need to know more of her secrets. At least I've learned that her immortality comes from a wand full of bird ashes and dead daughter blood. Nothing freaky about that.

"Bernadette," the witch says, her face inching closer to mine until our noses almost touch. "I trust you learned something in the dragon's lair, or else you wouldn't be here with a scale in your pocket."

She might know everything that happened from watching on her big, crystal TV, or she knows nothing and is speaking in relatable platitudes that always ring true. Either way, she's got my attention.

"Your powers found you, but not without your help. Others can only offer so much guidance before your instincts have to take over."

She turns her attention from me to Rain, a warm smile coming to her lips. "Goodnight, my light."

Her face lingers on the baby for another moment, then Erzsébet walks back to the center of the room, stares at me, and flies into the earth above her, like a canister getting sucked into a tube out of the mailroom.

I'm too tired to dwell on anything she said, though I know her words will play over and over in my head as soon as I wake up.

With a wave to the others, I head off in the direction of my vampire. Something about the blood bond makes me need him in a way I can't deny, no matter how tired I am or how connected to Zev I might feel. And though this whole situation of having more than one lover is totally new for me, none of the guys seem to mind, and honestly, it's the lowest concern on the list of strange new things that have happened. I'll probably have to sort out how this will work functionally in the long term, if there is a long term for us. For now, I need them all too much to change anything.

The tomb has different rooms, each barren except for the light furnishings magically conjured or summoned; a table here, a chair there, a few more pitchers of water. We sure don't have the amenities of a hotel, but this charmed room suits us just fine in the given circumstances.

When I round the corner into the room Darius took, he's standing beside an assortment of blankets spread about on the floor. He's already disrobed and is very, *very* ready for me.

My heart lurches at the sight of him. His body sculpted to perfection by a master artist. His eyes dark orbs that pull me into their fathomless depths. I shiver at the prospect of what we are about to do, and heat collects in my center, my body more than ready for him.

I shed my clothes as I move toward him, half-naked by the time we embrace and full-naked by the time we hit the blankets. I guide him inside me, our bodies immediately finding our rhythm, ecstasy overcoming me almost instantaneously. As he sinks his teeth into my neck and he drinks from me, I fully embrace the throes of pleasure, releasing the stress and trials I've faced over the last twenty four hours.

When our passions are spent, I curl up in his arms, my head on his chest, his lips grazing my head.

I have missed you, he says softly into my mind. *I have not known what it means to miss someone in a very long time. And never with this intensity.*

I sigh into his chest, tears pooling in my eyes. *I've missed you too.*

And then my eyes close, and I sleep the sleep of the dead. My mind and body submit fully to unconsciousness, recharging so I can wake up and face another day.

Just before waking, I step into another dream that has the same feeling as my prophetic dream from our first night in Budapest. I'm in a dark tunnel or cave, it's impossible to know because the room is pitch black. I feel my way around, my hands finally sliding over an opening in the rock wall. When I climb through, I'm in the Grand Hall.

It doesn't look the same as it did before; now there's rubble strewn about, and instead of studying from books, the witches are carrying bodies out of the room. My dream is no doubt walking me through the aftermath of the vampire attack.

I feel crippling sorrow as I step through the space, thinking about the lives and history lost to the violence. I hope the Grand Hall can be rebuilt. I hope future witches can learn from it as they have in the past. But I know, even in my dreaming mind, those hopes rest on my ability to keep Rain alive.

Erzsébet stands in the center of the room, tears staining her cheeks while she looks at the spell books on the enormous shelves. She slowly turns in a circle, looking at every wall in the spacious room.

"He can't be trusted, Bernadette."

The witch speaks to me without looking my way, her eyes continuing to search the shelves.

"I knew it wasn't safe to show him, and now the book is gone."

"Who? And what book?" I ask, starting to scan the walls myself as if I might be able to find what she's looking for.

"Bernadette…" I hear a new voice coming from behind me, and turn to see Andor. He approaches cautiously, his eyes darting between me and Erzsébet.

When he reaches my side, he smiles. It's genuine and friendly, making me feel a little bit of peace. He holds out his hand, gesturing for me to take it. He's going to guide me somewhere, show me something. I think I'll go with him.

As I'm about to take his hand, I look up at Erzsébet. She stares at Andor, shaking her head, her face contorting in anger. Why is she so mad? He only wants to help me.

"Come, Bernadette," Andor says, extending his other hand as well. I start to turn to him, but notice Erzsébet has raised her wand.

"Meghal lélek!"

Before either of us can react, a ray of light bursts from the tip, knocking Andor to the floor. He lies motionless, his eyes open, smoke rising from the hole in his chest where the magic blast hit him.

I look back at Erzsébet, her wand now aimed directly at me. Light shoots forth, striking me in the chest, delivering the same fate to me as it did Andor.

And waking me from the dream.

My eyes open, taking in the soft flicker coming from a torch just outside the room. Darius no longer lays with me, and I have no idea what time it is. Mostly, I'm just happy to be alive after my brush with death in that very vivid dream.

I rise quickly and dress, then rush out to check on Rain.

In the main room, Zev and Rune sit near the crib, Rain laying on a blanket between them. She's cooing and squirming about while the magical men just watch her. It's the most heartwarming scene imaginable.

"Good morning," Zev says, the sexiest of smiles on his face.

"How long did I sleep?" I ask, having zero concept of time. It could be ten in the morning or three days later.

"A few hours," Zev answers, shocking the shit out of me. "It's four or five in the morning, still dark out so Darius is patrolling the grounds above."

"Only a few hours? I feel like I was out for days."

Rune rises, walking over to me with a steaming mug of tea. We could be trapped at the bottom of the ocean and this man would still find a way to make me a warm, herbal beverage.

"I've wondered about your sleep since you reclaimed your powers," the fae says. "It might be that your mind and body rest more quickly, as ours do."

I hadn't thought about that, but it makes sense. I've been averaging somewhere between no sleep and a tiny bit of sleep since before we left Rowley. I definitely get tired, but my mind hasn't really failed me yet.

"You're saying my magical brain is better than my old, stupid, human brain?"

Rune dissects my sentence for a moment before smiling, having learned a little bit about how sass works over the last few weeks. "Yes, Bernie. That's exactly what I'm saying."

I sit next to my baby, watching her discover her toes, all while trying to shake the lingering uneasiness from my dream. I want to talk to Zev and Rune about it, and tell them my feelings about the queen witch, but I don't know what to say. So I opt to move the day along instead.

"What did you come up with, Rune?" I ask. "What's the next part of my wand made of?"

"There's an ancient forest a few towns away," he answers. "I can't say if we'll find the element in question there, but I'll be able to better understand the magic of these parts if I visit the elder trees."

"Sounds great," I say. "I'll come with you."

Rune's eyebrows drop to a scowl. Zev growls. Predictable reactions from both.

"I have to be there," I explain. "I have to find the material myself. Zev, you saw how I became connected to the dragon. I can't just give you a shopping list, not for a wand as powerful--and personally connected to me--as this."

Neither speaks, because they know I'm right. I'm silent as well, a little surprised by how confident I am in my words. Especially given that this means I have to leave my baby behind again. Mother of the year, right here, folks. Is this how moms who have to go straight back to work without maternity leave feel? Only... with dragons and werewolves instead of glass ceilings and cubicles?

"What's happening?"

Darius joins us, speaking before any of us had noticed his entrance and causing me to spit tea directly into Rune's face. I apologize, then laugh while I mop it up with my sleeve. He's a very good sport about the whole thing, and I enjoy a few seconds of getting lost in his silver eyes while drying his cheeks.

Meanwhile, Zev explains to Darius that I'll be leaving with Rune, and we all watch the vampire clench his jaw so hard I'm worried he'll bite through his own face. After a few seconds of processing my determined stare, Darius gives a slow, understanding nod.

"I'll have to prepare extra formula," Rune says, pouring a glass of water while he takes a small pouch from his coat. "Zev, you've given Rain a bottle before, correct?"

The fae is going into full worried-mom mode, and I'm a little concerned that I'm being too casual about everything. I've come to trust these men so completely, with such enduring confidence in them, that once I resign myself to the fact that I'm leaving Rain behind, that's the end of my worries. It seems Rune doesn't have the same belief in the others' co-parenting abilities.

He spends another half hour getting everything set up just right, and I keep thinking he's going to end with giving them a post-it note with phone numbers for poison control and the fire department. It's a strong display of neurosis that only Rune could make charming.

I spend those precious minutes giving one last feed and a thousand kisses to my baby, then settle her into her crib. I'd love a shower and a change of clothes, but at least I got to swim in the river last night. And I'm sure Rune will find me some leaf in the woods that will make me smell and feel very clean.

When we're ready to go, I spend a moment in Zev's arms, promising him I'll be safe and return as quickly as I can. Then I embrace Darius, holding him tight and presenting my neck for a final visceral moment. He takes his time to lick my wounds, and I have to pry myself out of his arms when it's time to leave.

With a few supplies loaded on our backs, Rune and I step into the center of the room, ready to get sucked into the human world above, then travel into the unknown, searching for the mysterious.

Before we leave, Darius gives a serious, somewhat ominous look.

"Watch out for vampires," he says.

"And wolves," Zev adds.

I nod, and then, right as I feel my body start to lift, I'm compelled to yell back, "Watch out for the witch."

CHAPTER TWELVE

W ith Darius, he carries me and we sprint at ungodly speeds to wherever we
need to be.

With Zev, he shifts into wolf form, takes me on his back, and he runs with
amazing grace and balance.

With Rune, we get into the back of a truck, and he creates an illusion to
make it look like we're not in the back of that truck.

And honestly, with a life that's changed from no magic to way too much
magic, I'm enjoying the shit out of a casual car ride to the forest.

I look at the passing countryside as we go, enamored with the old architecture that shines through in even the most inconspicuous buildings. New England
has some good history, and I grew up in a family bar that was more than a
hundred years old. Before visiting Europe, I felt like Rowley had some old buildings. This trip makes clear what a baby America really is.

While I take in the sights, Rune's eyes never leave me. Nor does the look of
contentment on his face.

"Yes?" I ask when I finally return his gaze. "Do I have something on my
face?"

"Just your normal magnetic beauty," he responds, dropping a line like they're
going out of style. "It was very difficult being away from you yesterday. I don't
think I fully understood how addicted to your presence I've become."

Words that might sound trite coming from another mouth have my heart all
a flutter when Rune says them. His sincerity is off the charts, and such things said
by a creature so beautiful, it makes me feel like I really am the most important
girl in the world.

"I know... I know I'm not as forward in my affections as Darius and Zev,"
Rune says, not looking away from my eyes as he speaks. "It's... complicated. I
want you. I crave you. I need you. And I haven't felt those things for anyone since

my betrothed died. It feels almost disloyal, and yet I know she would want me to find happiness. I have mourned long enough, but these things take time."

I take his hand and nod, emotion clogging my throat. "You don't have to explain yourself to me. There's no hurry. I'm here." I don't add, *for now*, because that feels too much like a blade in the heart for both of us. The words still sit between us, unspoken but all the more present because of it.

We drive on in silence for a few more minutes while our eyes never leave each other. It's like a makeout sesh for our souls, just staying locked in without our physical forms getting in the way. It's one of the most stimulating, arousing connections I've ever felt, to be honest. Turns out extended eye contact is hot.

It finally gets too hot and I have to break away before my body tries to join in. We both have a lot to process without lust getting in the way, especially him.

When I pull my eyes from the fae's, I look down at my chest, rising and falling with each accelerated breath. And then I remember my dream. Erzsébet killing Andor, then firing a spell at me. The dream is disturbing enough on its own, but knowing that the queen witch has the power to control my dreams makes it even more disconcerting. Is she announcing that she plans to kill me?

"Did you spend much time with Erzsébet yesterday?" I ask Rune. He's now looking at me with some concern, having noticed my shift in demeanor.

"We spent an hour or so concealed in the garden," he says thoughtfully. "Once she'd disposed of our attackers, she brought us directly to the tomb through underground passages, then left until we met up with you last night."

"Did she... did she kill all the vampires?"

Rune nods. "The ones that didn't retreat, yes."

I'm struck and concerned by that kind of power. From what I've seen, vampires are pretty hard to kill when there's just one of them. A dozen seems like way too many.

"She has immense power," Rune says. "The strongest witches are the most feared by vampires, which is part of what led to the wars that have raged all these centuries."

"Vampires attacked the witches because they felt threatened?"

"It depends on who you ask," Rune answers with a wry smile. "Vampires originally served as powerful protectors of all races, invincible defenders against anyone who might wish to harm the Fates or their children. But then the protectors became the provocateurs."

"Why? What changed?"

"They grew dissatisfied with their position, and at the same time realized how much power they possessed." Rune's eyes survey the passing landscape, but he's clearly looking back in time, recalling horrors I'm glad I never witnessed. "The witches developed fiery spells to target the vampires' weaknesses, and the conflict escalated. That's when the fae capitalized on the upheaval, seizing witches' land and trying to take some of their powers for our own."

He talks about events from hundreds of years ago as if they just happened. Things he wasn't even alive for still have a profound impact on this thoughtful man. It seems like quite the load to carry.

"The prophecy was self-fulfilling in that regard," Rune continues. "Witches created everything. Erzsébet herself descends from those with the magical forti-tude to bring planets and people into existence. But it was their own creations that brought us to this point."

We sit in silence as I try to wrap my mind around all this history, and the fact that I'm now such an integral cog in the story. My daughter, a tiny baby who's only just discovering she has toes and fingers, is the final piece in this enormous, cosmic, magical puzzle.

"Do you trust her?" I ask, finally breaking the silence and bringing the conversation back to the witch queen.

Rune takes a long pause before answering. "More than most. Less than some." He turns to me, moving so his forehead rests against mine. If his goal is to make me feel the profundity of the moment, it's working.

"Dark magic leads to some of our greatest sorrows," he says. "You saw it with your mother. However, elements of the same magic that nearly killed your child are what brought Tilly's power to you and allowed you to save us all. So, while I fear the powers that run through Erzsébet and her living wand, I know that dark-ness colors your powers as well. And I trust you with my eternal soul."

I'm glad our bodies are so close, because I don't know if I could deal with the idea of possessing dark magic without Rune's tranquilizing touch.

"Erzsébet trusted the vampires to meet with her daughter," Rune says, pulling his head away from mine as he dips into what must be a painful memory. "Cara wanted to reach common ground, to explain the prophecy as a means of keeping the peace instead of a motivation for war and murder. Erzsébet put faith in her daughter, and faith in goodness."

I know that this story ends with the death of the witch princess, and it seems Rune is struggling to get through to the end of it.

"They opted to go with a simple magic," he says, the slightest quiver in his voice. "They asked for trust. And it worked on Darius... but not his father."

I take Rune's hand again, needing his touch as much as I figure he needs mine. We spend the rest of the drive into the woods in silence.

~

WE PASS through dozens and dozens of tree sentinels lining both sides of the road, and they all look the same. The repetitive scenery makes Rune's decision to stop seem very random to me, though likely he spied some subtle shift in algae on every other tree or some shit. Rune squeezes my hand and indicates it's time to go. I'm about to ask how we're getting off a moving vehicle without injury when the truck pulls over and stops.

Huh. Problem solved, I guess.

Rune and I grab our packs and I groan under the weight of mine, which is sort of pathetic. I had no trouble carrying around a twelve-pound baby, but this fifteen-pound backpack has me feeling overloaded. Nevertheless, we make quick work running into the woods as the driver gets out of his truck and studies the road before him, scratching his head in confusion.

When we're far enough away not to be seen or heard, I stop running and turn to Rune, my breath hitching as I try to slow my inhales and exhales. "What... how did you get him... to stop?" My words come out with exhausted puffs and I slump against a tree, my body drained of all adrenaline.

"I created the illusion of a fallen tree in the road. He will be very confused when it suddenly disappears."

"Poor guy. He's going to be questioning his sanity forever." It makes me wonder how many crazy stories people have told over the years are a result of a run-in with a paranormal and they never knew it.

Rune hands me a little vial of blue liquid. "This will help with the exertion."

"Yes please," I take it, not at all ashamed of my enthusiastic support for any herbal cheats the talented fae is willing to provide. I throw it back like the pro drinker I am, only to gag on the disgusting taste that coats my throat like tar. I start spitting and try hard not to vomit. "What the hell?"

Rune hands me a water jug. "Apologies. It is not the most pleasant tasting, but it is very effective."

"Not the most pleasant?" I ask incredulously, looking up at him even as I know my face is blotching from the gagging. "It's the worst thing I've ever put in my mouth."

I rinse said mouth again, spitting the tainted water out. I repeat this, hoping we have a way to get more water, until the taste has faded enough to function.

"I will carry that putrid taste into my nightmares," I say.

He doesn't seem repentant at all as he patiently waits there, watching me.

"What are you--?" I cut off my own words with a relieved sigh and a smile. "Ah okay. I see now."

Rune grins. "Impressive, yes?"

I nod. All my muscles feel extra pumped, my lungs feel unstoppable and I've suddenly got the energy to run a marathon without a single break. I hitch my pack, straightening it on my back and smile even wider. "I'm stronger!"

"For a time," Rune says. "Do not be careless. You are still working with a human body and can be injured."

I nod. "Where do I trade this one in for a fancier magic edition?" I ask.

Rune scoffs. "Your body is perfect. Do not trade it in. Ever." The heat in his eyes and need in his voice strips me down to my bare emotions, turning me into a puddle at his feet.

But we have work to do and don't have time for sexy sex against a tree distractions, plus I'm giving him time to process his complex emotions. Sexy tree sex can wait.

"Where to?" I ask, trying to break free of his spell long enough to focus.

He shakes his head, like he's clearing it, and coughs, causing my insides to warm knowing I'm just as much a distraction to him as he is to me. "I don't know," he says, making me panic a little. "A decade ago, near here, humans uncovered trees that were millions of years old. They offered a few scientific explanations for the trees' longevity, but I expect there's more to the story."

"So we're just looking for old trees?" I ask. "And if humans already found them, don't we know where they are?"

Rune nods. "We are looking for old trees, but it's not so simple as looking on a map. The earth and power beneath the tree is just as important as the trunk."

"Great. Let's start walking and hope we trip on some magic." Even though Rune's potion makes me feel like I could hike forever, I still can't handle being away from my baby, and from Darius and Zev for so long. I miss my child something awful, and I am determined to get this wand made as quickly as possible so I can hold her and nurse her again. The separation is breaking my heart.

I hitch my bag a final time and Rune and I start walking into the ancient woods of Hungary where who-knows-what awaits.

It's hard to imagine what the fae might be feeling, now that he's in his element, and about to connect even more deeply with nature. He's always moved with impeccable grace, but now there's an added liveliness to his step as his eyes dance around the passing woods.

We hike around for an hour or so, and Rune's potion makes it feel like minutes. We talk of our lives before he walked into my bar, of our interests and dreams and ambitions. Rune tells me about how he learned to play the harp-- from his great grandmother who is a renowned musician amongst his kind.

"You two must be very close," I say, stumbling over a root because I took my eyes off my feet for more than three seconds. It's really clear who's got the spirit of the woods in him and who doesn't.

Spoiler: The woods hate me.

I'm bitten by all the bugs, rocks and twigs jump up from the ground just to trip me, and I can't stop sneezing because apparently the air up here is made entirely from allergy powder.

"We were," he says, his gaze drifting to the past. "My parents were busy running our kingdom, my grandmother was killed in a skirmish before I was born, so my great-grandmother took on the task of entertaining, teaching and guiding a little boy full of mischief and questions."

I smile at the image of Rune as a child and can only imagine the fairytale life he had as a prince raised in a forest palace.

"She taught me secrets of the forest and herbs and of the earth that she learned over many hundreds of years, sacred knowledge passed down only to those intended for Master Alchemy."

I glance over at him, my hand sliding into his, hoping the physical contact helps him as much as it helps me. He smiles and squeezes my hand.

"Was that your destiny?" I ask. "Before all this?"

He nods. "Since I am not the eldest, I was freed of the burden of rulership. My sister has that privilege and took to the training and lifestyle it required with enthusiasm, leaving me to enjoy my passions in peace. Until the wars started, and then there was no peace."

"And then you got sent on a hunt for a fulfillment to a prophecy," I say, sympathetically, as it sinks in even more how much this must have disrupted all of our lives, not just mine.

"And then I got sent to find a new destiny," he says, his gaze lingering on mine, his silver eyes shining like the moon. "One by your side to the end of days."

I gulp, suddenly nervous at the enormity of that promise, but also filled with heat at the safety and joy his words fill me with.

"I, for one, am glad you come packed with all that knowledge. It makes modern medicine look pathetic."

He grins. "I'm happy to be of service."

The forest smells of cold and mulch and all things green and natural. I inhale the pure oxygen as we stop for a brief break.

I shrug out of my pack gratefully and find a place to relieve myself, then take a couple minutes to pump my breasts dry as I pray my milk continues to come in while I'm keeping my distance from Rain.

When I return, Rune pulls thin slices of a dense bread from his pack, handing me a square. "This is an ancient fae recipe. It's packed with nutrients."

I eye the tiny bite of food doubtfully as the fae pops his into his mouth and takes a long swig of our water.

I do the same and am pleased by the taste. It's nutty and sweet, like honey and berries and something else I can't quite place. I chase it with water and lean back against a tree, closing my eyes. I'm not tired per se: the concoction Rune gave me is still in effect, but I am weary on a soul level, and I can feel my powers ramping up again as my skin begins to glow too brightly.

A headache pounds at my skull and a nervous energy zips through me.

"I have an idea to help you on this trip," Rune says, shuffling around in his pack.

I peek my eyes open and see him using a stone mortar and pestle, crushing some herbs in it. He then stands and looks around, studying the trees as if waiting for one of them to tell him something.

Who knows, maybe they will.

Frankly, I'd be disappointed if my magic fae boy couldn't talk to trees.

After a few long moments, he nods and walks over to a nearby cyprus. With deft fingers, he plucks a piece of bark from it and returns to his mortar to grind it down. When it's all a nice fine dust, he glances at me. "I need one more ingredient for this," he says hesitantly, and I know instantly he needs my body fluid of some kind.

I sigh. "Blood, urine, sweat, tears or saliva?" I say, listing off as many readily available options as I can think of.

He raises an eyebrow in surprise. "Blood, if you don't mind."

I hold out my arm. "Have at it."

Rune nods and brings the mortar over, along with a very sharp knife.

First, he pours something over the knife and it glows then dies down to normal metal. Then he makes a swift, clean, cut, releasing a thin line of my glowing blood into the mortar. I flinch at the pain, but it's gone quickly enough.

When he has enough, he rubs a salve on my cut and it heals nearly instantly.

"I always assumed all fae knew how to do what you do. Is that true?"

He shrugs as he mixes my blood with the herbs. "All fae have some connection to the earth that they can use to manipulate their environment. You'll never find a fae who doesn't have a green thumb, unless they've been cursed. Even a drop of fae in your ancestry will guarantee a proper, thriving garden," he says. He

249

stops speaking for a moment and closes his eyes, holding one hand over the mortar, while the other holds it. In that ancient Elven language I've heard a few times now, he mutters some words under his breath. The concoction flares before disappearing into smoke.

I expect him to scrape it out and make a tea from the paste, but instead he surprises me by dipping his fingers into the mortar and pulling out what looks like a small, black pearl.

Before I can ask, he answers my next question. "This should let the forest itself absorb your excess power, to give you control and ease the burden while we are here."

Damn, I'm going to be sharing my magic with ancient trees? That's wild.

"Do I just hold it?" I ask.

He shakes his head. "You ingest it."

Right. Of course.

He drops it in my hand and I feel a thrum of power connecting me to it and it to the forest trees. It's not much bigger than a pill and it's smooth, so it should go down easily enough. I take a swig of the water, then plop it into my mouth and swallow, taking another swig to help ease the journey.

The effects take a few moments, but when it works, I breathe a deep sigh of relief, my body ten times lighter as the stress of carrying that much power disappears.

"Shall we move along?" Rune asks once I've settled into the effects of his magic pill. "I sense we're getting close."

I hoist my pack off the ground and follow him, moving deeper into the woods. Now when I pass each tree, it looks so much more like a living spirit. I can see their wooden bodies exhaling oxygen and absorbing sunlight through their leaves. Trees are goddamn awesome.

When we reach the top of a hill, Rune stops. I come to his side and join him in looking over a strange, stunted cluster of trees. It looks as though all the trunks were chopped down about ten feet from the roots, but there's no cut line from an axe or saw. And I still sense the base of the trees are alive.

"Is this it?" I ask.

Instead of answering my question, Rune comes up behind me, his hands gripping my shoulders to give me a massage.

It seems like an odd time for this tenderness, but I'm not going to fight it. If the fae feels like I need a backrub, then I must need a backrub. To my surprise, he wraps his arms around me and pulls me against his chest as his mouth settles near my ear.

I'm expecting words of comfort, or words of seduction even, but what I'm not expecting is words of warning.

His voice is a harsh whisper full of urgency. "There are wolves behind us, a pack of five. I need you to stay calm, and if I tell you to run, you must promise you will."

I freeze, my body on high alert and in serious adrenaline overdose panic mode. If Rune tells me to run because he thinks we're losing the fight, I don't think I'll be able to leave him.

I feel Runes' hands leave my body as he steps away. With a deep breath, I turn around to face our newest adversary.

The wolves are still about a hundred yards away, crouched and slowly slinking toward us. As strong and cunning as the fae may be, I've got my doubts about these lopsided numbers. I don't think I can fend off even one wolf, and that would leave Rune to fight four on his own. Also…

"What kind of wolves?" I dread the answer, as one option presents a much greater danger than the other. "Like, earth wolves, or… you know."

We've been attacked by the fae and the vampire. Werewolves are the logical next wave.

His eyes stay locked on the approaching beasts as he reaches behind his back and drawers his sword.

"There's only one way to find out."

CHAPTER THIRTEEN

As Rune draws his blade, the wolves attack.

All five rush toward the fae, leaving me safe for the moment but absolutely helpless. I flinch as the first wolf lunges through the air, sharp teeth bared, ready to rip through flesh and bone. At the last second, Rune punches with the hilt of his sword, strong metal connecting with the wolf's jaw and sending the creature crashing to the ground.

At the same moment, another wolf approaches from behind. Rune displays some uncanny awareness, thrusting the blade back into the shoulder of an attacker I was sure he didn't see. The wounded animal limps away, one paw held off the ground.

I have no idea what types of wolves these are. Each is smaller than Zev in wolf form, but he's also an alpha prince and I just assume he's larger. They're certainly not small, and I see no reason why they'd shift into their slower, human forms mid-battle.

The remaining three wolves slow their roll a little, circling Rune cautiously after seeing how quickly he neutralized the first two attacks. They close in tentatively, but still with the same violent intent, their chests rumbling with deep growls.

As fear ramps up in my chest, I feel the familiar burn of my magic reaching its boiling point. Whether or not I'm connected to nature, the energy in my blood is on the rise and needs somewhere to go.

"Rune…" I barely manage to whisper as I lift my glowing hands. I know what's coming, so I'm going to do my best to stay a step ahead of this power surge and maybe, in some way, use it to our advantage.

Whether Rune hears me or senses a magical explosion I'm not sure, but he suddenly does an aerial cartwheel over the wolf behind him, hitting the ground and rolling away. As soon as he's out of my direct line of sight, I stop trying to hold back and expel the energy built up within. The power bursts from my chest and through my arms, forcing an emphatic gesture from my shoulders through my wrists as a brilliant wave of light and fire crashes into the scene before me.

The wolves yelp as the heat burns their fur and the energy knocks them to the ground. Behind them, a row of trees ignites, the smaller branches immediately turning to ash while the trunks burn bright blue.

When my hands have drained of the explosive magic, I look over to see Rune lying in the dirt, seemingly unburned. I rush to him and help him stand.

"Thank you for the warning," he says as we watch four of the five wolves retreat. The fifth, the one Rune stabbed, lays against a rock, its breathing labored and its fur smoldering.

"Those were earthly wolves," he says, returning his sword to its sheath. "I'm glad your spell only took the one. We've come to their home. They've every right to attack."

He walks over to the creature, which makes no effort to escape. Rune kneels next to it, placing a hand over the puncture wound by its shoulder. The wolf whimpers at first, then starts to pant. As Rune reaches into his pocket for one of his many ointments, he suddenly freezes and looks at the burning trees.

"Hurry," he yells to me as he abandons the wolf and runs toward the flames.

I fall in line without hesitating, though I can't imagine what we're going to do with the fire I started. I certainly feel bad about any woodland casualties, but I can't very well suck the heat back into my fingertips.

The fae reaches the edge of the blaze--too close for comfort if you ask me-- and flings a handful of bright yellow powder into the air. As it starts to float down toward the ground, Rune circles his hands with incredible, Darius-like speed, summoning a breeze that carries the dust into the flames. He's like a fire-fighting plane doing a chemical drop, but from the ground and with magic.

I stand next to him, completely at a loss for how I can help. He's working too hard to give me a job, and so far all my powers are good for is lighting shit on fire. I start to feel the dismay settling in; the one time I try to control an outburst and I've torched an ancient forest that was once the home of magical elves and fairies and spirits. This is why humans don't deserve to have nice things.

"Bernie, look at me," Rune says, and I realize that the fires have almost completely extinguished while I was being sad for myself. The fae reaches for my hand and gives me a small vial, this one full of a thick, amber liquid. It looks a lot like tree sap.

"This sap comes from regenerative trees in my kingdom," he explains, confirming my obvious but still correct sap assessment. "One drop at the base of each tree. No more than that, do you understand?"

Instead of answering, I scamper off to one of the burning trees, intent on undoing what I've done. I start at one end of the smoldering grove and Rune starts at the other. There are eleven trees that took the brunt of my force, which doesn't feel like too many, but the haste with which Rune moves makes me think we've got seconds left before the effort becomes futile.

I uncap the vial and tilt it carefully as I stop at the first tree. Heat still emanates off the charred bark, but I don't care about my face getting a little toasted if it means I can make amends. I'm being super careful about letting just one drop fall, and at the same time the viscosity of the sap makes it take for freaking ever to pour.

I'm about to start shaking the vial when a drop finally releases, hitting one of the exposed roots at the base of the old tree. There's a slight sizzle as the sap gets absorbed into the root, and I watch to see what will happen next.

"Keep moving, Bernie," Rune says from across the grove. "They're dying from the inside, you won't be able to see if the remedy works or not."

I pull my eyes off the first tree and rush to the second, keeping the vial tilted so the next sap drop is ready to go. I notice that Rune's already tended to five members of the grove, so it's no wonder he's politely urging me to go faster.

The second drop of sap comes more quickly, and this time I waste no seconds moving on to the next tree. This one is stouter than the others, even though they're all short from whatever event cut off their top halves. I aim the sap droplet above the largest root I can see, my feet already poised to carry me off to the next tree as soon as the sticky liquid hits its mark.

But when the tree lets out a blood-curdling scream, my feet fail me.

I fall backward at the sound, my heart jumping out of my throat because the noise so shocks me. I manage to keep the vial in my hand, but the sap misses the root and settles into the dirt and ash a few feet from the tree.

Rune has a look of horror on his face, though he still manages to get to the last of the burning pillars before rushing over to me. As he arrives, another shrill screech pierces my ears and ripples goosebumps across my flesh.

"What is that?" I ask, even though I know the answer. Rune's pearl has me connected with the natural world in a way I could never have imagined. And while the surrounding trees helped steady my powers before the wolf attack, now I'm hearing the pained wails of death from one of their family members, because I can't control what flows through my veins.

"We've hopefully saved the others," Rune says in an attempt to comfort me. "For this one, I fear it's too late."

There's a tear in the fae's eye as he stands, walking from my side to the smoldering trunk. As upset as I am, Rune obviously feels this on a deeper level. Nature is a part of him in a way I will never fully understand. But it feels akin to the loss of a close family member, and that breaks my heart.

He comes to the trunk and, in defiance of his own nerve endings, places his hand against the scalding tree. Rune grimaces in pain but leaves his palm on the bark, absorbing the hurt or communing with the earth or something that he clearly believes is worth doing despite the intense pain.

As he stands there, I notice a shift in the tree to his right. There's a slight ripple within the bark, quick but noticeable. From the flattened top of the trunk, a body starts to emerge.

Rune stays focused on his searing palm and the dying tree, so I'm alone in watching an indescribable figure grow out of an ancient stump. It looks like a pile of kindling in motion, but as more of the form comes into view, it starts to take a human shape.

I look back to Rune to see if he's noticed yet. His head is turned to the side where another figure is climbing out of a different trunk. Now, with the exception of the tree I couldn't save, every blackened stump has a body crawling out of it.

Rune backs up to join me. He keeps his eyes on the creatures moving toward us, but he doesn't unsheathe his sword.

"These are dryads," he says to me in a low voice.

"They live in the trees?" I ask, a lump in my throat as I face down nearly a dozen homeowners who might now be homeless.

"They live *with* the trees," he says. "It's a kinship humans could never understand. A deeper connection than most beings ever experience."

Each dryad stands nearly ten feet tall, and they slowly form a semi-circle around us. They have legs, arms and faces, sharing many qualities of a human body, but they're also like walking trees, with leaves and branches giving them shape. With each step, roots flow from their feet into the ground, keeping them constantly connected with the earth.

"I guess they're pretty mad at me?" I try to sound lighthearted because I'm 100% scared shitless. It's a different kind of fear than when wolves or vampires attack; this is the feeling of getting caught doing something wrong and awaiting judgment.

Rune doesn't answer, only takes my hand as the tallest of the tree people steps forward.

"You've slain one of my own," the dryad says, its voice like a loud gust of wind. The sound is horrifying and beautiful at the same time.

"I'm so sorry. I didn't... mean to," I say, stumbling on my tongue as I try not to cry. "I tried to save it. Him. Her." A squeeze of my hand from Rune indicates it's time for me to pass the microphone.

"Are you the queen?" Rune asks the dryad that approached. It, or rather she, gives a subtle nod, the leaves around her head rustling as she does.

"We were attacked by wolves, who we fended off without harm." Rune points to the injured wolf, still panting over by a rock, it's wound now mostly healed.

"You've entered the home of Cupressus without invitation," the tree says. "You've used dark magic to kill one of our family. Of the two, which shall pay the price?"

"Who two? Us two? What's the price?"

Rune squeezes my hand again, imploring me to shut the hell up. He's very right to do so.

"Neither," the fae answers, stepping toward the dryad queen in a way that could be perceived as either defiant or reverent. I guess we'll find out the queen's take soon enough. "My name is Rune, prince of the fae realm, long friend to the dryads and all growing life."

All the tree people lean forward to look more closely when he says his name. I'm really hoping his ancestry gives him some celebrity status in the forestry world.

"I've come on a quest, along with Bernadette, mother of the Last Witch."

Now all the wooden, leafy faces turn to look at me. For some reason I'm surprised to see recognition from trees, but I guess word of this ancient prophecy has made the rounds.

"Where is the child?" the dryad queen asks. It seems she wants proof of the claim, which is totally fair, but I'm guessing Rune didn't pack Rain's birth certificate or immunization card when he was loading up our bags.

"With our companions, princes from the other realms and the witch queen, Erzsébet," Rune answers, craftily name dropping. "We're bonded to save the baby witch and her mother, to keep any kingdom from acting on the prophecy."

"And why is that?" the dryad asks, stepping forward and towering over the fae. "Do you not wish to save your kind? Or are you spellbound to this witch?"

"Only by our own spell," Rune answers, standing his ground. "There's a magic within Bernadette, and surely within her child, that can't simply be sacrificed to a single race. I have seen this and it is why I willingly risk my life to protect her even against my own kind."

The queen of the tree folk turns and moves toward me. I don't have quite the same gumption as Rune, stumbling back a few steps as she approaches. Her face is exquisite but intimidating, with skin that looks like smoothed bark, eyes like shining knots, hair a woven mess of twigs and leaves.

"What is so special about your magic that you can kill?" she asks. "Wherefore do you get the right to strike down a tree soiled by the Fates themselves?"

Goddammit. I killed a tree that's as old as the planet. Thanks for making me feel even worse, tree lady.

"I... I don't have that right."

I don't know what else to say. I also know my riffing hasn't been great thus far, so I just turn back to Rune, hoping he can help.

He takes his cue right away, stepping back to my side. "She bears a burden none of us could understand. Magic only recently came to her, days after she learned of her daughter and the prophecy. Our quest, that which fated this moment, is to help Bernadette control her powers so that she may protect her child and save this world, as well as the other realms."

The dryad keeps her gaze on me as she takes in Rune's words, seeming to consider it all for an extended beat before speaking again.

"Nevertheless, her magic is dark. What answer do you have to that, to ensure the safety of my kingdom?"

Rune looks into my eyes, his face warming as his expression softens with love and admiration.

"She has the powers of her mother within her, which, as you can sense, brings a shadow to her light. But there is only good in her heart, and only kindness in her soul. I've spent nearly every waking second in her company since coming to this world, brought by a prophecy that should have pitted us against one another. And yet there is no way not to fall in love with this woman's entire being. The care with which she treats all those in her presence. The love she provides for her daughter, even in the direst of moments. She brings constant light to a world in which there's a constant effort to extinguish her glow."

I've entirely forgotten why we're here and the point of Rune's monologue. His words are striking so deep in my core that I just want to kiss him and then live in his arms forever.

"Whatever darkness exists in Bernadette has no measure against her light," he says, turning back to the dryad. "This I promise you, and it's why you must be compelled to forgive."

The queen's eyes haven't left my face the entire time Rune speaks. Her expression hasn't changed either, but that might be because her face is mostly wood. I can sense the slightest shift in her perception of me, thanks to Rune giving the most inspired introduction in history, but I have no idea if it will be enough.

The dryad leans even closer, bending down so that the leaves atop her head nearly touch me.

"I sense the magic you describe, fae," she says. "But I must feel it for myself."

At those words, she starts to lift one of her gnarled arms, the tips of her branchy fingers directed at my chest.

"My queen, I implore you--"

As soon as Rune starts to speak, I raise my hand to silence him. I can't quite explain why, since his words have very much kept me alive to this point. Still, something in my witch's intuition says it's time for the dryad to commune directly with me.

"Bernie, you mustn't," Rune pleads. "You don't know what you're about to experience."

"I know that," I respond truthfully. "But neither do you."

He shakes his head, but now it's the fae's turn for words to fail him. He might understand what's about to happen, but he doesn't know what I will feel. And my gut says that the queen of the dryads, who has every right to consider me a murderer, will find the goodness she's hoping to see, through whatever method she uses to see it.

I raise my chin and take a deep breath, standing ready for the queen to do her bidding. Her arm inches closer to my chest, hovering above my heart, the pointed branches of her hand pushing past my clothes to touch my bare skin. And then I feel the worst pain I've ever experienced in my life.

Pushing out a baby hurts like hell, but I prepared myself for that and could understand the agony. As the queen spears me with her arm, puncturing my flesh and sticking her wooden fingers directly into my heart, I'm lost entirely to the excruciation.

Somehow, my body understands that this horrifying experience is not meant to kill me. My arms remain at my sides instead of flailing and trying to end it. My head tilts back but doesn't thrash. My feet stay planted and don't try to get away.

Through it all, the hurt doesn't dull a bit. I feel like pain receptors are supposed to go numb after they cross a certain threshold, but I'm getting no such treatment. I only feel it more intensely, like my heart is pumping anguished blood into my veins.

And then there is another layer of a new kind of pain as her magic plunges into my very soul. Waves of emotions overwhelm me, spiraling me into the darkest corners of my heart. Flashes of moments from my past flicker in my mind: lies I told, hurt I caused, all the ways I inflicted pain on others or myself over my lifetime. I feel sure I'm going to die, that I am being judged and found wanting and I am now seeing the worst parts of my life flash before me until finally I will come to the afterlife and discover where it is we all end up, if anywhere.

I feel myself tumbling into the darkness of eternity only to be pulled back to my body when the queen speaks.

"Hmmm," the queen murmurs, leaning her face even closer to mine. "I know you," she goes on. "Yes... I know this blood."

It's definitely what a serial killer would say while eating a still-living victim, but it has a different meaning coming from this ancient, powerful tree-being. If she recognizes the blood that flows through me, that has to mean something, right? Hopefully a good something.

As fast as it started, the pain retreats when the dryad pulls her branch hand out of my chest. I look down in time to see the gaping wound close and slowly heal, leaving just a small leaf-shaped scar where the tree stabbed into me.

The queen steps back and Rune jumps to my side, offering support as my legs start to wobble a little. I keep my eyes locked with the dryad's, waiting to see what she'll say or do next. Having offered my heart for her inspection, I feel pretty confident she'll let me live.

Instead of addressing me, she and the other dryads turn away in unison, reforming their half-circle around the dead tree. For a long time, everything is completely still, the only sounds are leaves shifting in the slight breeze. Rune and I stay silent as well, paying our respects for the life lost. I glance to the side and see the fallen wolf is back on its feet, gingerly walking to rejoin its pack.

I return my eyes to the stump that died today, that I killed with errant, dark magic, even if it was an accident. A tear falls down my cheek, and I vow to hold onto this pain so I'll remember the cost of power gone astray.

Once the dryads conclude their silent ceremony, all but the queen return to the trees from which they emerged. Meanwhile, her highness returns to me and bows her head.

When she stands erect again, I see a new growth coming from her center. A thin branch stretches toward me, like a sapling sprouting in front of my eyes. It's just a foot long, a mix of green and brown, with smooth bark.

The dryad queen wraps the thin twigs of her fingers around the new branch, and with a swift pull, rips it from her body. It's a little startling, like watching someone reset a dislocated shoulder, and I try not to cringe too visibly.

She looks at the branch for a second, inspecting it carefully, and then hands it to me.

"You are forgiven," the dryad says, then turns and walks back to her tree.

I watch until she's gone, retreated back inside the stump, before finally looking down at the gift she gave me. It's not much to take in, but it feels special, important, even alive.

"Do you know why she gave me this?" I ask Rune.

The fae smiles at me, then looks back at the row of ancient trees.

"If I had to guess," he says with a smile, "I'd say that's your wand."

CHAPTER FOURTEEN

The death of the dryad weighs heavily on me as we hike back to the main road. Even though I now carry the casing for my wand, it feels like a gift and a condemnation in one. I am blessed and cursed by this magic in equal measure it would seem.

We are quiet on our hike, as Rune takes my hand, allowing his warm, calming energy to flow through me.

It works, though I still feel an inexplicable ache in my heart, in the place where the dryad queen pierced through my soul, and I wonder if that will ever go away. Part of me hopes it doesn't, as I don't want to ever forget the price of my power.

With my free hand, I rub at the scar that remains, tracing the lines of the leaf design.

Of all the things I've seen and experienced since the three princes walked into my bar, this has been the most surreal.

When we reach the end of the forest that connects to the main road, Rune casts his charms to once again hide us in the back of a pickup, and I fall asleep with my head in his lap as we head to Budapest.

I don't wake until we arrive in the city. It's midday, the sun high in the sky, casting warm rays of light that take the bite out of the winter cold.

By the time we reach the cemetery and make our way into the tomb, I am desperate to see my baby.

My gaze lands on her small form the moment my eyes adjust to the dimly lit underground space. She's on a blanket on the floor with Darius, who's singing her a song in a language I've never heard. His voice is soft and soothing, and I melt a little at the sight.

Not wanting to interrupt, though I know the vampire knows we're here, I stand and wait, watching with a small smile on my face.

When the song ends, he looks up, his dark eyes shining, his smile when he sees me luminous, and I rush over to him and Rain, throwing myself into his arms. Rain coos and seems to smile when she sees me, but it could just be gas.

Either way, I'll take it.

Success? he whispers into my mind. I tilt my head to look into his eyes and nod.

Darius kisses me, taking his time to explore the texture of my lips, his tongue flicking into my mouth, warming the center of my body instantly, then he moves to nuzzle my neck. "You are glowing, my love," he says.

I nod. "Rune helped me control my powers while in the forest, but I've been bursting since we left."

"Allow me to remedy that," he says.

I moan into him at the promise of such delights, but get distracted by the baby next to us.

He winks. "I was about to put her down for a nap."

"Where is Zev?" Rune asks as he putters around the room tidying things that aren't dirty.

"Out getting food. We ran out this morning and haven't seen Erzsébet since you left."

Rune raises an eyebrow at that. "If you both are okay here, I will go find her and let her know we have been successful in our quest. We need to make your wand as soon as possible."

"Be safe," I say, reluctant to let any of these men out of sight with so much uncertainty in our lives right now.

He crosses the room and kisses my cheek, then kisses Rain's head. "I will be very safe," he says. "Stay here until I get back."

He leaves, getting sucked up into the world in a way that feels like a sci-fi movie. Beam me up, Scottie.

Shaking my head, I return my attention to Darius as he gently lays Rain in the crib and covers her with a blanket. She falls asleep instantly, with the innocence of a well-protected child. I wish, not for the first time, that I could document her strange start to life with a baby book. It would certainly be the most unique one any child has had, I'm sure of that.

Darius is ready and waiting to take my blood as I move back to him. Wordlessly he pulls me close, slipping his arms around my waist, pressing his strong, muscular body against mine. I tilt my head and with gentle fingers he brushes the hair off my neck and leans forward, his breath warm against my skin.

When his teeth plunge into my vein, I'm once again set on fire with the mixture of pleasure and pain it brings. I close my eyes and grip his body, my fingers digging into his back as I press closer against him.

He drinks in my blood, the glow in my skin fading back to normal. By the time he finishes, both of us are desperate for each other.

We could go to the back room, he says into my mind.

Before I can respond, Zev returns, carrying two grocery bags. The werewolf instantly zones in on us, his nostrils flaring and body immediately reacting to the sexual charge in the room.

"I would ask how you are, but I think I already know," the werewolf says, his green eyes devouring me in one look, his voice husky and filled with his own need.

He sets the groceries on the table and slowly walks over to us. Darius still has his arms around me, and Zev positions himself behind me, so that I'm sandwiched between the two men.

My heart rate ramps up as the electricity between the three of us nearly overwhelms me.

Zev places his hands above Darius's, wrapping his arms around me just below my breasts, brushing against them as he does.

He brings his lips to my ear and whispers. "I am so glad you are back safely. To be apart from my mate for so long is... unpleasant."

As it always does, the word mate makes me swoony and I lean into him, allowing the two men to tighten their hold on me. I have no idea what this might lead to, but I enjoy the feeling of them both against me. And they clearly do as well, if the hardness in their pants is any indication.

Darius kisses me as Zev nuzzles my neck, exploring the sensitive skin with teeth and lips and tongue. His hands push up, caressing my breasts, his fingers brushing against my hard nipples through my clothes.

I'm lost in the sensations of both of them. They are in my skin, my blood, my heart and soul. They are so much a part of me, I don't know where I end and they begin.

After some time, which could be minutes or hours, as time has lost all meaning, Zev turns me to face him. "It's my turn," he says gruffly, as he claims my lips with a barely contained and nearly bruising passion. Darius pulls my ass against him and begins to slide his hands down the front of my pants.

He teases me at first, while Zev nibbles my lip and cups my face as he unleashes his desires into me. Darius lets his hands explore without giving me what I really need.

When the vampire's fingers finally slide into me, I moan into Zev's mouth, nearly exploding then and there, but he doesn't give me the satisfaction quite yet, instead he pulls out until he's barely touching me, then rubs at the most sensitive spot before plunging back in.

Zev has moved his hands to my breasts, and as he kisses me, he slides his hands under my shirt and bra, cupping my breasts, his thumbs rubbing over my nipples--now without any clothing interfering.

I'm delirious with the pleasure, stunned that I get to enjoy them both.

I'm about to fly off the edge of the cliff, overwhelmed by the feeling of having both men play my body like an instrument, one they are very skilled at finding the right notes on.

As the climax inside me builds, Zev moves his mouth to my shoulder, the same one that already has a small mark where he bit me before. He bears down with his teeth, claiming that spot again, as Darius increases his rhythm between my legs, and I close my eyes and let it all roll over me. My mind explodes in fireworks as the waves crash into me and my body is rocked to the core. My legs are jelly but both men keep me on my feet as they coax my climax out longer and longer, as more and more waves hit me, until I spill into their arms, a limp noodle so blissed out I can hardly think.

Without words, because none of us have any, Zev lifts me into his arms and takes me to the makeshift bed Darius made. He lays me down and spoons me while Darius stays to watch Rain--through some unspoken agreement between the two.

I pull the werewolf's arms more tightly around me, enjoying the feel of him pressed against me, and fall into a dreamless nap where I am safe and warm.

I wake sometime later to the sound of arguing and a baby crying. Zev is no longer by my side, and I'm so groggy I can't tell how long I've been out.

When I walk into the main room I see Erzsébet there with the three Sexies. Rune is comforting Rain, who needs a diaper change by the smell wafting from her, Zev has food laid out and is eating a sandwich, and Darius is yelling at the witch queen.

"It's not safe. She's not going. Final word."

Erzsébet narrows her eyes at the vampire, then turns to Zev, who shrugs casually, less heated than Darius. "Her safety is most important," he says between bites. "I agree with the vampire."

Rune finishes changing the diaper and cradles her. "I agree," he says. "Going back to the Grand Hall poses too many risks we can't account for. Bernie's enemies already know she's been there, so the council surely has it surveilled."

Erzsébet frowns. "Your commitment to this woman is impressive, but it is misguided. The longer she is without a wand, the less safe she is."

Tired of being talked about, I walk forward. "What's going on?" I ask. I move instinctually to hold my baby, then stop, putting my hands behind my back. The episode from the forest has me more afraid of my powers than ever.

"You must return to the Grand Hall to complete your wand," Erzsébet says.

"Can't you just take the materials and do it then bring it back?" I ask, though as soon as I say the words I know that's not going to be enough. Like acquiring the pieces, I have to take part in the crafting. It's an instinctive knowledge that hits me, and Erzsébet notices when it does and nods.

"You understand, then," she says.

I sigh. "Yeah. I do."

I look at Darius, the angriest of the three. "It won't work if I'm not there."

"Then make it here," he says through gritted teeth.

Erzsébet shakes her head. "We must go to the crystal cave within the Grand Hall for her to choose her tip, then we must forge it over the ancient fires. Only then will it be strong enough to contain her magic."

"It's going to be okay," I say, trying to assure myself as much as I am the Sexies. "At least one of you should stay here to protect Rain. Maybe two of you, just in case. She's the real target."

Erzsébet nods. "That is wise. Which one of you would like to accompany Bernadette?"

All three step forward.

"It is still full daylight," Erzsébet says. "So perhaps the vampire should not travel during this time."

"I'm the best able to fight off my own kind should it come to that," Darius says, "and I have a mental bond with Bernie that can help protect her. I suggest we should wait until dark. Bernie needs to eat before she goes at any rate."

Zev growls. "I am her mate. It should be I who accompanies her."

"And I know the most about wand making," Rune says.

I look at all three of them, torn about who to bring. I need them all, but I'm determined at least two of them should stay with my baby.

"I wish I could pick all of you, but I think Darius is right. So far only vampires have found us, and he's our best defense against them. Plus he can communicate with you two telepathically if needed".

Erzsébet nods. "Very well. Eat and rest. I will retrieve you at sunset. Be ready."

She leaves quickly, without any other niceties, and Zev hands me a sandwich I didn't see him make. "Eat. You haven't been eating enough."

I haven't been doing a lot of things enough. Showering and brushing my teeth come to mind. But sweet Jesus I am starving.

So I sit and eat and think about all the things going on right now. "I don't suppose you bought a phone charger at the store today did you?" I ask Zev.

He shakes his head.

"Damn. I need to call AJ. I'm worried about her, and Morgan's. Need to make sure it hasn't burned down. Again."

"It didn't burn down last time," Rune says. "It was just singed a bit."

I chuckle at that. "Right. Either way, she's probably just as worried as I am."

"I'm sure she knows you're dealing with a lot and will be in touch when you can," Rune says.

I laugh. "You don't know AJ."

Sandwich finished, I grab a water bottle and guzzle it, then head to the makeshift area we are using as a bathroom. Makeshift area is my fancy way of saying "bucket in the corner." It's not elegant and I try not to think too much about it. At least it magically empties itself.

I handle my business and find some clean clothes waiting for me, courtesy of Zev. Grateful--especially for clean underwear--I change into some trendy jeans with ripped knees, a long-sleeved top with giant lips on the chest, and a very comfortable gray cardigan.

Feeling as refreshed as I'm going to get, I join the guys and wait for Erzsébet to return.

While we wait, I ask Darius about the song he was singing to Rain.

"It is an ancient song we used to sing on the longest night of the year, when my people had the most freedom to wander. It is a song of hope and cheer. My mother used to sing it to me, once upon a time."

We continue talking about our lives before we met, their lives, of course, being much longer and more dramatically filled with interesting things than mine.

I tell them about my time at Juilliard and how my love of piano developed. I tell them about the man who fathered Rain, who broke my heart. About my friends there who didn't stay in touch once I got pregnant and left. About the crazy shit AJ and I got up to as children.

When Erzsébet returns, Darius and I are ready to go. I say goodbye to my baby, who's freshly fed and swaddled, then I kiss Zev and Rune before heading into the night with a vampire and queen witch and glowing skin that paints a bullseye on my back.

The Grand Hall looks as it did in my last dream. Crumbled and broken, though the dead bodies have been removed, thank goodness. Andor finds us as soon as we arrive, his face a mask of worry and anger.

"Where have you been?"

I look around. "Me?" I ask, confused by the aggressive tone in his voice.

"I've been worried sick since the attack." He takes my hand in his, his eyes wide and sincere. "I know you do not want to be my lover. But I hope at least we can be friends. I have spent my life waiting for you, waiting to protect you and help empower you."

"Um… thanks," I say, unsure how to respond to his intense claim on me. It doesn't feel good, but it's their way and I can't judge them for it. I just can't play along either.

Erzsébet purses her lips. "Step aside, Andor. We are here to make Bernadette's wand."

His eyes widen in shock. "You got all the ingredients? Already?"

Feeling a bit cocky with my success, I nod. "It wasn't that hard." It totally was, but he doesn't need to know that. For some reason I feel inclined to make it very clear how much I do not need him.

I wonder if he can trade for a different witch to bond with. Maybe file for designated lover divorce.

Erzsébet clears her throat and leads us through the tragically demolished hall and through a corridor that takes us to the crystal cave, according to her very curt guided tour.

Andor follows, of course, but at least I have Darius by my side. He doesn't seem to like the guy very much, which I don't hold against him. He's already sharing me with his two best friends. A random guy isn't going to be able to get a foothold in our group.

When we enter the cave, a hush falls over our small group as the magnificent beauty of it all settles into us.

Lining the walls and ceiling are crystals of all shapes, sizes, and colors, glistening and glittering with an internal light that illuminates the entire cave. In the center is a large fire pit with a glowing blue flame burning within. A giant black cauldron hangs over the blaze, suspended by nothing but magic.

Witch fire.

Erzsébet stands next to the fire. "Bernadette, take out your dragon scale and wand casing and come here."

Darius follows me, pushing Andor aside when he tries to scoot in, and stands at my back like a bouncer while I follow the witch's instructions.

A WEREWOLF, A VAMPIRE, AND A FAE GO TO BUDAPEST

"I understand you were gifted a piece of the dryad queen, yes?" Rune must have filled her in when he fetched her earlier. "That's very special indeed. She's been alive for millions of years, and I don't know of another wand made from her being."

Shit. No pressure.

"Place the branch and the dragon scale into the cauldron," Erzsébet says.

I do as instructed, and a light flares up then dies down. Heat engulfs me and I resist the urge to wipe away the sweat dripping down my face. Erzsébet moves closer to me and produces a sharp blade, then slices a chunk of my hair off.

"Hey, that's going to grow back all uneven."

She ignores me, handing me the clump of hair. "Put this in."

I do.

Another flare of light.

Another burst of heat.

"Finally, you must bleed into the cauldron while reciting this spell." She clears her throat before continuing.

"A test és a vér, a csont és az iszap annyira isteni tartja a varázslatomat."

That's a lot of Hungarian to learn in one sitting, and I ask her to repeat the words twice before I attempt them myself. I take her knife and slice into my arm, holding it over the cauldron. Then I do my best attempt at speaking the spell.

For a moment nothing happens, and I worry I've messed up, but then the contents of the pot begin to sizzle and purple smoke pours out. As the sizzling gets louder, I hold my breath, waiting.

I'm so on edge that when the entire cauldron explodes into pieces, sending shards of cast iron everywhere, I scream in alarm.

Darius is lightning fast, pulling me away and shielding me with his body, though he needn't have bothered as Erzsébet had already cast some kind of containment spell to keep everyone safe.

When the pieces fall to the ground and the fires return to normal, I pull away from my vampire and look around the room at what remains. "Does this mean I've ruined my wand?" I ask, heartbroken. That would be just my luck. There's no way the dryad queen will give me another body part, and that's assuming I can get another dragon scale without getting burned to death.

Tears burn my eyes and Darius takes my hand, speaking directly into my mind.

We will find another way.

I shake my head, swiping a tear. *There is no other way.*

When I look to Erzsébet, I'm surprised to see a calm smile on her face. If my wand is destroyed, she's taking it very well, which makes me think not all is lost. She raises her own wand and speaks a word that sends all the pieces into place. With the floor cleared, I now see what sits at the center of the fire.

A beautiful wand engulfed in blue flames, the base slightly thicker than the top, the green and brown coloring of the wood now slightly darker. My jaw drops. It seems to glow and beckons me to it.

"Go on," Erzsébet says. "Only you can wield it."

I take a tentative step forward, afraid to stick my hand into the flames but

265

also compelled to do so. I bend down to pick it up, the heat constant but never burning me. Immediately I feel magic connect to the wand as golden light glows around us both.

The wood is carved in an intricate design that looks elven to me, and I smile, pleased at the beauty of it.

Be of pure soul.

The voice in my mind isn't Darius's and with a start I realize that it was the dryad queen's voice, as the mark on my chest begins to ache.

I smile, turning to Darius and Erzsébet. And Andor, I suppose, who's standing behind Darius looking sad.

"It's incredible!" I say. "Now what?"

Erzsébet smiles a truly happy smile and it brings out the beauty in her stately features. "Now, you must allow a crystal to choose you. The wand itself contains the magic, but the crystal tip allows you to control it."

I look around the cave. "How do I know which one is choosing me?" I ask.

Erzsébet gives a slight shake of her head. "You have to find one that speaks to you. I won't be able to hear it, so the decision rests squarely on your shoulders."

I turn back to the walls of shimmering stones, now panicking that I don't speak crystal well enough to make the right choice.

I try to follow the witch's instructions, listening to each gem I pass, but none of them are in a chatty mood. I make another round, trying to start the conversation, but get nothing in return. It goes on forever. I throw out Hungarian words, speak in funny voices, try to communicate telepathically, and it's all for naught.

Hours later, I slump to the ground in exhaustion. "I'm not vibing with any of them," I say dejectedly.

Erzsébet scans the room, then walks over to a ruby and plucks it from the wall like she's picking berries from a bush. "Try this. Rubies are especially useful for protection."

I like the sound of that.

"Put it on the tip of your wand and say *kötvény*."

I do as she says, and as soon as I speak the word, the stone embeds itself into my wand forming a beautifully smooth tip.

"I love it," I say, studying every detail.

"Now try a spell," Erzsébet says.

"Um. I don't know any off the top of my head."

She frowns. "We must remedy that. Now's as good a time as any for you to learn the food spell you seemed excited about. Say *étel*."

I swish my wand and repeat the word.

Instantly the ruby explodes in my face. Fortunately, Erzsébet has her wand at the ready and deflects the careening shards so they don't blind me. The base of the wand, thank heavens, is still good as new.

"That was clearly not the correct crystal," she says, moving on to pick another. "Try a diamond. They are very powerful."

She hands me the largest, most perfect looking diamond I've ever seen and I gasp. This is worth a fortune. Holy shit.

Unable to process the fact that I'm holding more wealth in my hand than probably exists in my entire hometown, I place it on the top and speak the spell to bond them.

The resulting wand is so stunning I'm rendered speechless. I nervously prepare to try a spell, praying it works.

It too explodes in my face.

I just destroyed two priceless gems, but I don't have the energy to dwell on that because I'm starting to doubt my powers will ever be controlled.

Undeterred, Erzsébet picks another gemstone. And another. And another. Each with the same result as the last.

After several more hours of painfully awful attempts to make the tip of my wand, nothing works. We are surrounded by bits and pieces of the stones and I'm no closer to having a functioning wand than I was when we arrived.

I rub my eyes and yawn, and Darius comes to me, putting an arm around my shoulder. Andor's face turns dark at the contact, but quickly smooths out to neutral when he catches me looking at him.

Erzsébet paces the cave. "I'm sorry, child. It's clear an element of your wand is at odds with the others. I'd venture it's the tip, but we've tried every type of stone."

For someone who was already feeling pretty sad, her words take me to a whole new plain of sorrow. "You're saying there's something wrong with the scale? Or the branch?"

She shakes her head, eyes still scanning the room in search of answers. "That would never be my guess, but I've also never seen a quality wand reject this many gems. I'll need time with my spellbook in order to..."

Erzsébet freezes as a green hue fills the room. It doesn't come from the crystals lining the walls, but rather the walls themselves.

"Someone's in the garden," the witch says.

"What?" Andor says with disbelief. "That's impossible, my queen. Apart from yourself and Bernadette, no one knows of the underwater passage."

"Timót knows," Erzsébet answers, eyes boring down on Andor. "Weren't you with him as he prepared to leave for the caves?"

Andor appears stunned by the queen's statement, pushed back on his heels. He shakes his head. "No, I only helped him prepare. I had nothing to do with his travels."

Erzsébet turns to me, reading my face for information before asking her question. "Have you shown or told anyone of the entrance?"

"Not unless someone's reading my mind," I answer honestly. "And that happens way more than I'd like, so I can't make any promises."

Darius is already standing at the exit to the crystal cave, waiting for the rest of us to follow. "No sense in letting intruders make the first move," he says. "Lead us to the garden."

Erzsébet follows the vampire's command, moving quickly to the exit and into the corridor. I head after them with Andor close on my heels. I hear him muttering under his breath, but can't make out the Hungarian. I'm sure I wouldn't understand even if he was slowly speaking directly at me.

We reach the garden door and the witch queen puts her hand against the stone before reaching for her key. "I feel magic... but nothing dark."

She lifts her wand and aims it at the door while her other hand retrieves the key. "Darius, stand in front of Bernadette. I'll blind the cave when the door opens."

I move behind the vampire, putting my hands on his sides and peering around his right arm. He reaches back and rests a hand firmly on my side, offering what little comfort he can provide in this nerve-wracking moment.

With a quick flourish, Erzsébet opens the stone door and yells, "*fényes vak!*"

I'm impressed and jealous as I watch the brightest burst of light leap from the tip of her wand. Whatever crystal she's got has no problem doing shit without imploding. The light envelopes the garden cave, as every plant inside disappears in the hot, white glow.

"Jesus Christ, bub, turn that shit down!"

It takes all of a half second for me to recognize the voice. Against my better instincts, I rush into the room, blinded by the light as I do so.

"AJ?!"

"B?!" my best friend's voice cries back. "Where the hell are you? I feel like I'm back in high school getting the shine down from the cops."

With me in the room, Erzsébet has no choice but to retract the blaring light and let everyone be seen. It takes a moment for our eyes to adjust, but I finally see AJ standing at the edge of the stream with Zev by her side. He's dripping wet from the swim, but it looks like my water nymph gal just shook the droplets off.

We sprint to each other and hug like sisters who have been separated for years instead of days. I look over her shoulder at Zev, who's doing an excellent job at containing his jealousy after not getting the first hug.

"What the hell are you doing here?" I ask when we finally pull apart.

"Well, some bitch who's name rhymes with Mernie won't answer her damn phone, so I had to buy a goddamn plane ticket to... where are we, Hungary? Turkey? I confuse the two every damn time..."

"But A," I cut in, trying to get her bouncing brain to settle in one place. "Why did you come? Did something happen?"

She takes a deep breath, suddenly serious now that she has to explain herself. "I've been talking with that ghost, the one you stuck in the bar with me. Thanks for that, by the way. Nothing like doing bar prep while a freaking ghost sings old pirate songs--"

"A!"

"Right, sorry. Anyway, he's been around a long time, knows a lot about Morgan's, your family, the witches, everything."

AJ takes a beat to look at the other faces in the room, then back at me, a sadness taking over her eyes. "The ghost thinks your grandpa is full of shit."

"What? What do you mean?"

"The letter, coming to Budapest, all of it," she says. "He says it's a trap."

CHAPTER FIFTEEN

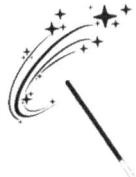

Too many of AJ's words clash in my brain, keeping the sentences from leading to any sort of comprehension. As I wait for the pieces to fall into place, Erzsébet walks over and steps between me and my friend.

"Very pushy," AJ says in response to Erzsébet's arrival. "You must be the witch wolfy was talking about."

"I'm sure I am," the queen responds in a soft tone that belies the look on her face. "May I ask how you got here?"

"I'm Bernie's best friend, and I'm also a water nymph so don't try any shit."

Erzsébet looks a little confused, and rightly so because AJ's answer doesn't make a lot of sense. Zev walks over to join our little pow wow, taking my hand in his while putting his other hand on AJ's shoulder.

"I brought us through the channel, remembering the way after Bernie showed me," he says, then gestures to AJ. "She arrived this morning and I caught her scent after you all left the tomb. Our seance back in Massachusetts brought forth a spirit who apparently continues to offer valuable information."

"Sidebar," AJ says to me with a smile, "the ghost is totally hot." I'm not sure if she's joking or not, since I'm pretty sure the ghost is invisible.

"What did the ghost say?" I ask. My brain's finally caught up enough that I know gramps has been pulled back into this and I need some clarification.

"His name is Leo Ransom," she says, "and he said the letter arrived *after* all the shit went down." AJ has an excited look on her face as she dives into her mysterious story. "No one brought it, it just arrived, like floated down into the basement and went inside that keepsake box."

"What?" I fire back skeptically. "How can a letter just fly itself into a box?"

AJ raises an eyebrow, not all that impressed with my dubious tone. "I don't know, Bernie, maybe it has something to do with ALL THE MAGIC."

She punctuates the yelling with a cute little smile, which is a classic AJ move. It drives me nuts but it's also pretty endearing.

"So what does that mean?" I ask. "What does it mean about my grandpa?"

AJ shrugs. "Beats me. It did seem a little weird that he left a letter saying he knew he was going to die, but then he hid it away for half a year, and then was just like, 'go to Budapest, bitch'."

Spelled out like that, it does feel a little insane that our first response was to follow the letter blindly, hopping on a plane to head straight to Budapest. That said, I've since met a dragon, been heart-stabbed by a tree, and had the best sex of my life. If this is a trap, it's very slow to spring.

"Who did the letter advise you to meet?" Erzsébet asks me, a quizzical look on her face.

"My father, I told you that--"

"But what was the name given, child? What name did the letter use?"

I have to think for a second, but I'm sure I remember correctly after reading that letter at least fifty times before accidently burning it to ash. "Timothy Trendle."

Erzsébet continues staring at me, though her mind has clearly gone to a far off place. Her brain seems to be sorting through puzzle pieces, just as mine had a few moments before. The difference, of course, is that I was trying to make sense of a single sentence, and I'm sure Erzsébet is sifting through the entire history of magic.

"Interesting," she says, slowly turning away and pacing between the deep green ferns. "Unless done in secret and with a magic envoy, your father and grandfather never met. Lauren and Timót kept their relationship secret, as they were advised to do, and then he returned to Hungary before you were born."

I never gave it much thought growing up, but neither Tilly nor Ed ever really spoke of my father. Mom did all the storytelling, and even that was sparse. He was an all-but-forgotten figure.

"But what does that prove?" I ask, not yet seeing the point. "I've never met him either, but I can still find out his name and come looking for him."

She stops her pacing and nods, then looks back at me. "If you were to introduce me, how would you do it?"

"Huh?"

"Tell AJ my name."

For the love of all that's holy, why do magical beings love speaking in so many goddamn riddles?

"Fine," I say, knowing that the only way to get through is to play along. "This is... Erzsébet. It sounds much better when she says it. You happy?"

I look back at the queen, who is, indeed, looking rather happy.

"And why don't you translate my name into English? Why not call me Elizabeth?"

I'm not entirely sure where this is headed, but my interest has definitely turned a corner.

"Because that's not the name you told me," I answer. "You're not American, feels like it would be weird to change it."

"I agree," Erzsébet says. "And yet that's what your grandfather appears to have done with his letter. He took the name Timót Tarijan, which your father was given at birth and used all his life, and offered you a translation. Why?"

She's clearly five steps ahead of me and I harbor no illusions of catching up, so I'm just going to see if I can get the answer. "I don't know, why?"

Her smile fades and her eyes narrow. "I don't know, either. I consider it very fortunate that you came here. I ensured your safe passage to the Grand Hall once you arrived in Budapest, but I knew nothing of this letter. Someone else motivated your voyage, and it's of the utmost importance we find out who... and more importantly, why."

Super. All that wordplay and we've got more questions than we started with, plus my fated Budapest trip now feels like a bad decision.

Darius flashes over to my side, taking the hand not held by Zev. It's not a possessive or jealous move, just his attempt to comfort. When AJ sees that I've got a Sexy on either side, each holding a hand, she crosses her arms and flashes a knowing smile. My cheeks immediately turn fire-engine red.

"Who do you suspect?" Darius asks Erzsébet. "Surely you have suspicions."

"Suspicions, yes, but I don't know where to cast them," she answers. "Until we find Timót or the one responsible for his death, I have no information worth acting on."

"So you don't think that was my father in the cave?" I ask. Since seeing that charred corpse, I've had a nagging doubt about who it was. For whatever reason, I feel like the experience would have been more visceral if it was actually him. Does Erzsébet share in my disbelief?

"I can't say, Bernadette," she says in an apologetic tone. "But with a dead dragon, a stolen dragonling, and this..."

She reaches into her pocket and pulls out the pendant that I took off the body, the one she quickly snatched away from me. I forgot about that feisty maneuver and now I'm back to not fully trusting the witch and wanting that necklace back.

"These pendants go to the *Érintett*--those who, like your father, are able to glean some magic from the witches in their stead," Erzsébet says while looking at the pendant.

"So the body *could* have been my father's?" I ask impatiently, cutting off the witch's thought even though I know there's more to it. I'm also just giving AJ a few seconds to catch up because she looks unbelievably confused.

Erzsébet shakes her head. "It's still possible, but the *Érintett* pendants are made of white gold. This piece could never endure dragon fire, much less the heat needed to kill a dragon."

I look at the pendant in her hand. Aside from a smudge here or there, it's still in pristine condition. Meanwhile, the body next to the dragon was all but turned to ash. In retrospect, the whole thing seemed pretty damn staged. Sort of like someone wanted me to take that pendant and leap to the conclusion my dad was dead.

"Enough," Erzsébet says, hastily pocketing the white gold charm and looking at everyone in the room. "We have much to do and, I suspect, little time to do it.

And we've added another non-witch member to our ranks, which makes things more difficult."

It's not a jab, per se, but the look on AJ's face shows she's definitely taking offense to the witch's words.

"Bernadette, you'll need to work on your wand in solitude," Erzsébet continues. "I'll give you a book on power binding and cursed elements. Read it carefully."

I'm not going to argue, but I definitely don't love that I've been given homework while the entire magic world is trying to find and kill me. Especially when I bet the queen of the witches could probably give a pretty quick synopsis of my reading assignment.

"Andor," she says, turning to look back at the little man who's still standing by the door. Once again I'd forgotten he was with us, and with how much he wants to be noticed by me, I'm sure he's aware that I keep losing sight of him. "Any luck locating that other spellbook? The one that's gone missing?"

Erzsébet really slows down and emphasizes each of her words, laying on the subtext pretty thick. I'm not sure what they're talking about, but they've obviously had this conversation before.

In response, Andor gets a bit fidgety. He might be thinking about his answer, or just nervous about giving it.

"No, my queen, nothing yet," he says quietly. "I've asked nearly every witch who would have had access, and no one recalls seeing it around. With how few in our ranks have the power to possess and read those spells, I'm at a loss for who could have taken it."

Erzsébet keeps her eyes on Andor while he makes no attempt to meet her gaze.

"What's gone missing?" I ask. I don't really care if this is a private conversation between the two of them. My daughter is in the most danger and I come in a close second, so I feel like I've got a right to know anything and everything at this point.

After another few seconds of beating down Andor with her glare, Erzsébet turns back to me. "An old book, one known to contain dark spells. It went missing two days after your father left."

Another interesting tidbit that seems ultra-important and yet just leads us to one more dead end. What the hell was my father up to and where did he go? And who sent the letter to get me here?

Just as Erzsébet opens her mouth to give further instructions, AJ raises her hand. It's a strange, schoolgirl gesture, and she's got an impatient, angry look on her face while she waits to be acknowledged.

"Do you have something you need to say?" Erzsébet asks, a thin veil of politeness covering her testy words.

"Yes, I do, thank you... *Elizabeth.*" AJ would never hesitate to mouth off to a stranger, and it seems being in a magical garden in the presence of the mightiest witch has changed absolutely nothing. "Just to clarify... B, did you see a freaking dragon?"

We all stare at AJ silently for a moment. I'm the first to burst out laughing, followed immediately by Zev and Darius. I'm guessing they've missed having AJ around almost as much as I have. Hopefully someday we'll have a little extra time to get her caught up on everything that's happened.

Erzsébet simply turns and walks to the exit, calling over her shoulder as she goes. "Bernadette, the spellbook will be waiting in the tomb. Andor, guide them back." She pauses after giving him the instruction, like she's waiting to see his reaction. It seems like she doesn't trust him, yet she's still giving him responsibilities. It's hard to keep up with the witch's mind games.

"Take extra caution," Erzsébet says to all of us. "I expect we'll be visited by vampires again before too long."

AJ's eyes go wide. "*Again?*"

I take her hand and we all follow to the door.

"Yeah, again,' I say. "I also talked to a tree. Lots to catch you up on, but not until I figure out how to make my stupid wand work."

We reach the exit and Andor takes the lead. He still looks a bit rattled, and I'm starting to wonder exactly what's affecting his mood. The missing book sounds like it might have Andor more preoccupied than the hunks who are always by my side, keeping him from the prize he thought he'd won.

"Who's the small guy?" AJ asks as we walk down the corridor and start to head through the Grand Hall. There's no way Andor didn't hear her, but he doesn't bother looking back. I don't answer, instead just shush AJ with a finger to my lips and give her an *I'll tell you later* look.

THE WALK to the tomb is thankfully uneventful, even a little entertaining as AJ, who's never seen the outside of Massachusetts, gawks at old buildings and signs in Hungarian. She seems genuinely perplexed that people don't speak English in this foreign country. God love her.

I actually have to clamp my hand over her mouth when we arrive at the graveside portal into the tomb because she won't shut up about her fear of getting buried alive. When she watches Zev disappear through the hole in the ground, Darius has to stop her from running away and physically holds her over the opening until she's sucked into the tomb. When I follow and land next to her in the spacious room, she immediately slugs me in the arm.

Thankfully, before we end up in an all-out brawl, Rune walks over with my sweet little girl, and AJ rushes over to hold her.

And when Rune casually--seemingly without noticing--glances his fingers against her hand as he hands her Rain, I wink at him. His calming power takes instant effect on my shaken best friend.

"Oh my God, look how big you are!" AJ says, even though Rain has at most gained a third of a pound since they last saw each other. "Did you miss your auntie? Fart, barf, or do nothing if the answer is yes." She doesn't cast her gaze away from the child as she tilts her head in acknowledgement of Rune. "Oh, hi elf."

Rune gives a playful wave, then looks to me as AJ wanders the tomb without paying much attention to her surroundings, totally distracted by the baby. It's very sweet to see them together again, and it gives me a moment to collect my thoughts and discuss things with the guys.

"Wand still doesn't work," I say to Rune, answering the question I'm sure he would have asked. "Either the dryad gave me shitty wood, the dragon let me take a shitty scale, or I need to track down a crystal tip that the world's most powerful witch has never heard of."

Rune nods solemnly, then heads over to a small table and grabs a book I don't remember seeing before we left. "This arrived moments before you did," the fae says, reminding me that Erzsébet said she'd send a book about wands.

"Oh good." I accept it from his outstretched hand, enjoying the brief but calming sensation as our fingers touch. "Any chance you already read it and have all the answers?"

My question is mostly in jest, but also loaded with hope that Rune will have some sort of guidance to offer. Now that I'm away from Erzsébet and Andor, in this empty space with a chance to sit with my thoughts, I realize how close I am to my breaking point. The dragon scared me, the dryad queen scarred me, but neither of those things rocked me the way this failure has. Killing the ancient tree, exploding crystal after crystal, feeling lost in a language I can't speak but need to cast spells--it's all too much.

I feel the impossible weight of what I'm carrying slam into me like a physical force, knocking me to my knees, breaking the floodgates of my heart wide open.

I'm torn apart by every decision I don't know how to make. Every problem I don't know how to solve.

A sob forces itself out of me, clearing the way for the storm of emotions that has been building to pour out.

Tears flood my eyes, blinding me as I bury my face in my hands, my shoulders shaking as I unleash the torrent of pain I wanted so badly to ignore and bury.

But pain never stays buried long. It grows from neglect into something fierce and wild that demands attention. Ignoring your pain only feeds it.

The time of reckoning has come as I give an honest accounting of the unfair burden I've been given.

And I feel so alone. Without my grandparents, who were always there for me. Tilly who always knew the right thing to say at the right time. Ed who worked harder than anyone I ever met and would give you the shirt off his back if you needed it.

I feel...

So.

Utterly.

Alone.

And then... I feel them. Three sets of hands reaching to comfort me. To soothe me.

Three strong, solid bodies forming a tight circle around me.

Zev to my right, Darius sitting before me, and Rune behind me, his peaceful calm flowing over me, though it's not enough this time to ease the hurt that's consuming my raw and beaten heart.

"I don't know what to do," I say between sobs. "I don't have any control. No wand works for me, and there's no time for me to figure this out."

"We'll make time," Darius says softly, his cool fingers brushing my hair out of my eyes as he speaks. "We are here to fight this battle as long as it takes."

I sniff and wipe at my eyes. "Yeah, well, a lot of your old friends are going to come fight too," I say. "And I don't think they'll be all that eager to let me learn more magic."

Zev puts his head on my shoulder, offering companionship instead of words. It's a sweet gesture, but I know it's because he has nothing to say. There's no solution.

"I murdered a magical being that had been alive for millions of years," I say, the tears returning with force. "*Millions* of years, and then I showed up. You're all in danger because of me, and I'm only making things worse. Everyone who comes near me gets hurt. I should just give Rain to one of you to hide, paint a target on my back, then sit and wait for the council to come for me."

"Or maybe I'll just break your neck so you can't say dumb shit anymore."

AJ's returned to listen to the conversation while still rocking the baby, and though her words sting, I had missed the bite of them, of her. The hard truths that the Sexies don't always have the heart to share with me.

Darius takes my hands in his, ignoring AJ as he leans forward so our faces are inches apart. I hesitate a moment before looking up, unsure if I'm ready to look anyone in the eyes without breaking down again.

When I finally do, I see tears in his dark eyes. Darius has shown his heart and passion over the last few weeks, but I don't think I've seen him this emotional. I grip his hands tighter, trying to give us both a little extra strength.

As he maintains eye contact, I feel our connection pulsing in my veins. It doesn't so much comfort or calm me, but instead reinforces what has been growing between us through our shared blood exchange, that we feel each other's pain; he's not just trying to make me feel better, but also show that we're going through these trials together.

"When Cara died," he begins, his voice so soft it's barely audible, "my world came to an end. It wasn't just losing a dear friend, but losing the faith I had in a greater cause. I stopped believing in goodness, and stopped believing in myself. Nothing gave me hope, not my friends, not my family, least of all my life. After all, I was an immortal beast and the heir to a throne occupied by the monster who killed someone I cared deeply for."

Though I'm not looking at Zev or Rune, I know they're hanging on every word, just as I am. Perhaps even more so, as the vampire is describing what ultimately ended their friendship.

"I gave into my bloodlust and took thousands of lives," Darius says, anger starting to color his voice. "Without a reason to care, I had no reason not to kill. I spent centuries embodying my worst self, and I would have gone on that way... if not for your grandmother." I squeeze his hands tighter at the mention of Tilly, and Darius gets a little brightness back in his dark eyes.

"She fought with such bravery in the face of endless rage. Love compelled her to risk her own life, to help others, to bring light into the darkness. Whether or not she knew then, it was all to create you."

For the first time since he started speaking, Darius looks away from me. His mouth hangs open, waiting for the words to come, but struggling to get them out. I feel his internal strife inside me and I will him to power through.

"I intended to kill Matilda Morgan the night we met."

His words hit me like a shotgun blast to the chest. A generation before I arrived, my blood-bonded soulmate wanted, and maybe tried, to kill my beloved grandmother.

"Perhaps I would have," he continues as I refocus on his words, ignoring the burning in my soul for the moment, "but not for looking into her eyes and understanding that she wasn't afraid to die." Darius meets my gaze once again. "She feared more for my wayward soul than she did her own life. I hadn't felt that since my days with Cara, and Zev and Rune. I hadn't felt cared for, and that made all the difference."

I'm compelled to reach up and wipe his eye, to touch his face, to show that I don't fault him for what happened, but rather appreciate him even more for what didn't happen. He pulls my hand away from his cheek, kissing my fingers gently, and then continues.

"Since you came into my life, every day between this one and the moment I met your grandmother has been a validation. Your light is the antidote to my darkness. I would relive every moment of anguish from my past for a moment in your eyes, seeing the love you have for the goodness in others."

Darius stands gracefully, going from seated to upright in a way that only someone with crazy strong thighs could manage. He holds his hand in front of me to help me stand as well.

"You've already changed lives, Bernie," he says, a look of pure reverence on his face. "Before you were even born, you managed to change hearts. The three of us have found our way because of you, and, by the same token, you shall find your wand."

I take his hand and stand, immediately clutching his face and bringing him toward me, kissing him passionately because I might die if I don't.

But then I pause, struck by something.

I look into his black eyes, my own eyes as wide as saucers, forced open by a major epiphany.

"You didn't find your way because of me," I whisper.

Darius says nothing, too confused to respond. Everyone is silent, waiting for me to explain myself.

"You found your way… because of this."

I reach into my pocket slowly, my hand trembling as I do, and grasp the star that's been with me throughout all these adventures, subtly helping me control my magic. Is it really this simple?

I take a second to wet my lips and remember the word I repeated countless times back in the crystal cave. I close my eyes and press the tip of my wand against the star. It's far too big to serve as the tip, but I feel in my heart this is the right choice.

"*Kötvény,*" I say, speaking the word with confidence for the first time.

There's no explosion. Nothing backfires. No one in the room yelps in pain.

Rather, I feel the star fracture in my hand. It's quick and painless, like I've broken a cracker. When I open my eyes to check out my handiwork, a small chunk of the star has broken off, and is now fused to the end of the dragon scale wrapped in dryad skin. The star is cut to perfection, revealing a luminescent shine, like it truly did just get plucked from the sky and placed on my wand.

I exhale a breath I'd been holding, relief coursing through me. So far so good. But I'm not in the clear quite yet.

"You've done it," AJ says, stepping forward before I stop her with a raised hand.

"I made it this far before," I say. "This next part is the real test. If I kill us all, I'm super sorry."

I take another breath, then envision the food I've had in my mind since everything went to shit earlier this evening.

"*Étel.*"

A sparkle of light swirls out from the tip of my wand, dancing a few feet in front of me before disappearing. Now, in its place, sits a plate with two enormous, glorious lobster rolls.

I look around, still in shock, checking to make sure nothing blew up without us realizing it. But everything looks in order. And my spell actually worked.

Tears burn my eyes, but this time for an entirely different reason. My throat clogs with emotion when I speak. "I did it," I whisper, staring at my wand in surprise.

I had no doubt, Darius says to my mind.

Zev skips the words and instead pulls me into a passionate kiss, ending it with a quick nip of my lip.

Rune just smiles, and I see the pride and joy in his eyes.

AJ, well AJ responds in typical AJ fashion.

"Oh, I know you brought enough to share with the class," she says, a huge smile on her face.

I pick up one of the buttery rolls and sink my teeth in. Holy hell. It's just as good as the ones Nanny and I used to get on our summer trips to the beach.

"I'll trade you the other roll for my baby." I can feel the wand steadying my magic, containing the pressure, and I know for the first time since this all started that I'm in control. I may only know one spell, but it's a start. And I miss holding my baby more than anything.

AJ's quick to take me up on the offer, practically throwing Rain into my arms as she rushes for the food. I hug my baby girl tightly, feeling like I'm not about to accidentally kill her for the first time since these powers took up residence in my body.

"You're safe with mama now, sweetie pie," I say as her cute little eyes slowly open. "I'll protect you from the bad guys."

I'm nuzzling her nose with mine when there's a popping sound and a very annoyed voice interrupts our celebration.

"Where is he?"

Erzsébet's voice shatters the mood and scares the shit out of me. She stands below the entrance to the tomb, though none of us saw her come in.

"Did Andor not remain with you?" she asks, deep lines of concern running across her forehead as she looks around the tomb.

"No," I say. "Darius was the last to come through the ground, I assumed he went back to find you."

The witch shakes her head. We've been through a lot in the last couple days, but this is definitely the most upset I've seen Erzsébet.

"Where should he be?" I ask. I'm really not sure if everyone sleeps back in the Grand Hall, if there's a curfew, how any of it works. Also, Andor's powerless compared to, like, everyone. What's the problem?

"He should be helping me locate an important book full of dark magic," she answers. "Instead, I think he's helping someone else steal it."

CHAPTER SIXTEEN

I swallow the last of my lobster roll awkwardly, licking my lips of crumbs while
I think of a response. "Um... what?"

Way to wow them with your articulateness, Bernie.

Erzsébet sighs, and with a wave of her wand and a spoken word, creates a
luxuriously overstuffed loveseat made of indigo velvet that she sinks into. "I've
had my suspicions about him for some time now. I've been subtly testing him
over the last few days, seeing what choices--"

"Wait, hold up," AJ says, stepping forward, hand on hip, sass on face--typical
AJ. "You're just gonna Mary Poppins some shit for yourself but my bestie is
getting it on werewolf style with her men on the floor? She's the mother of the
Last damn Witch, and these guys are all princes. You're really going to keep them
in a shitty, unfurnished grave?"

I press my lips together to keep from laughing out loud. Leave it to AJ to
ignore the big problem and focus on what really matters. Comfort. Nothing
lightens the mood like AJ. Also, how the hell does she know I've crossed the
threshold in my relationship with the guys? Well, two of them, at any rate. Does
her nymphness give her sex spy powers? My cheeks burn with embarrassment at
that thought.

Erzsébet narrows her eyes at AJ, staring at my friend for several long
moments.

"You dare speak to a queen that way?" she says in an icy tone.

AJ just shrugs, taking a big bite of lobster roll and speaking through a mouthful. "I don't discriminate," she says. "I talk to everyone like this."

I worry for a moment that Erzsébet is about to turn this uppity lass into a
frog or something, but then the super serious queen of the witches laughs. She
laughs. To say I'm stunned would be an understatement. I don't think I've seen
her laugh--or even really smile much--since we've been here.

"Fair enough," Erzsébet says. She waves her wand again, speaking several words under her breath, and the air sparkles with electricity before the space transforms itself.

I gasp, but I think it's more of a collective gasp. Everyone in the room who isn't Erzsébet is stunned.

Where once were the remnants of an ancient tomb dotted with a few chairs, a table and a makeshift crib for my child, is now a room fit for royalty.

The loveseat Erzsébet reclines on now has a matching couch and two chairs, with a complementary ottoman with a full-service tea tray. Side tables have appeared in a rich mahogany wood.

The ground is covered in overlapping rugs featuring Hungarian designs in bright colors. And the walls each have a few accent art pieces that are bold, full of emotions, and exquisitely rendered.

One in particular looks like a sunrise and sunset overlaid with each other... with a single leaf of undetermined color in the center. It evokes every emotion, every season, every fleeting and infinitely important passage of time that has affected humanity. I blink.

And then I see it.

The gleaming white grand piano in the corner. Rune, knowing me too well, takes Rain as I nearly trip over my own feet to get to it, walking as if in a trance. I sit at the stool and reverently open the fallboard exposing the black and white pattern that has been a staple in my life since I can remember. I run my fingers lightly over the keys, like a lover memorizing their partner's skin. "How did you know?"

Erzsébet walks over and puts her hands on my shoulders. "I've watched you, child. Many a moment from your life has played out on the crystal viewer in the garden."

She sits down next to me on the bench. "Play something," she says. "I've seen, but never heard you play."

I don't have to be asked twice. Without any self-consciousness, I strum my fingers over the ivories, setting their songs free.

The melody fills the cavern, bouncing off the walls and echoing in the underground space. I pour myself into the tips of my finger, transferring my soul to the piano itself, trusting it will translate my core being into music.

I am not disappointed.

I'm so transfixed by the depth and beauty of the song that the world around me disappears, just as it always has. When I play, it is just me and the music.

When I finish, I'm surprised to note my skin is glowing. I frown and reach for my wand. When my hand grips it, my skin returns to color.

Erzsébet's eyes are shining, and if I didn't know better, I'd almost say she's about to cry.

"That was more than I could have ever imagined," she says, turning away from me to inconspicuously wipe her eyes.

"Why did I start glowing when I played?" I ask. "I thought my wand would fix that."

Erzsébet sniffs, then turns back to me, her face once again composed. "When you play, you channel your deepest magic. You can't help it. It's a part of you." Before I can ask another question, like how to stop it from happening if I'm playing in public, with humans, she continues speaking. "It is why I put the piano here, to help you learn control of your powers. You have used your music as a kind of wand--a channel--your whole life, even before your magic was returned to you. Some of it has always been inside you. You cannot strip a witch of all her magic entirely without killing her."

She frowns, her eyes unfocused as she appears lost in a memory from the past, and I wonder if she's thinking of her dead daughter. My heart constricts and my gaze lands on my own child. A chill pierces through me, throbbing at the scar over my heart, as I imagine what it would feel like to lose her. And I know with everything in me that I must become as strong and as powerful as possible.

My child might die if I don't.

Erzsébet clears her throat and refocuses on me, her light grey eyes now sharp and clear. "You need to master your powers, Bernadette," she says. "Which means mastering yourself. Your discipline with music will be of benefit. If not for that, I fear you would not get far enough in your training quickly enough to be of much use in the coming days and weeks."

The way she says 'coming days and weeks' makes goosebumps form on the back of my neck. I mean, I already know the three kingdoms are after me and my kid... but I get the distinct impression she means something else entirely.

Erzsébet presses her lips together and begins pacing. Rain coos at the fae who's holding her as he rocks her gently, AJ by his side like a sexy sentinel. Darius is standing still as a statue, watching us both with unreadable eyes, and Zev has taken over the couch and looks like a restless wolf as his eyes follow Erzsébet's movement.

Everyone's waiting for the witch to say more.

"Besides those coming from the other realms," she says, "I fear we have dissenters here in our homeland to contend with."

Awesome.

"Are you saying there are witches coming for my baby as well?" As I ask the question, I start to feel a little rage building up. "Even though she's the one who can save them all?"

"If you recall, I mentioned diminishing numbers within the Kő when you first arrived at the Grand Hall. For several years, the men who show the greatest talents for magic, those most likely to become *Érintett*, have been disappearing without word. I have long held my suspicions, but never had proof. Given recent events, I believe..."

"My father's behind it," I say, giving voice to a small suspicion that's been slowly growing in the depths of my mind.

She looks up in surprise. "What do you know?"

This will be hard to explain, because I don't really *know* anything. I just have questions and doubts. "Pieces haven't added up," I say. "That letter to my grand-father that AJ's ghost crush says was a lie. Men with magic going missing. The burned corpse with my father's medallion in perfect condition. I... knew something was off in the dragon's lair but now... now I'm sure. Plus... it makes sense, given human nature. It seems inevitable that men who serve the ambitions of more powerful witches would look for a way to gain the upper hand eventually."

Erzsébet nods. "Your instincts are strong, Bernadette, as I've always suspected they would be. Your mother was powerful in her own right, if misguided, and your grandmother was one of the strongest witches I've ever known. Even your father had more power than most men. In hindsight, that seems to be part of the problem."

"What did he do?" I ask. I've only been able to piece together the basic shape of what's happening. Erzsébet clearly knows more details.

"I can't speak to specific crimes, but power and status have always been on your father's mind. He petitioned fervently to be the Kő chosen for your mother. To be the one to sire the mother of the Last Witch. He knew it would give him prestige and authority within our order, and he worked hard to earn it. It was a privilege many wanted, but none so much as Timót."

I cringe. It's so gross to imagine all these men arguing over who gets to sleep with--and impregnate--my mother.

Erzsébet continues. "He also championed Andor to be your chosen, which seemed strange but nothing of too great concern. It has made me more aware of Andor's movements these last few months. I suspect it was him that placed your grandfather's letter."

"Why? Why him and not my father?"

"Timót would not have wanted to bring any extra attention," Erzsébet says with a shrug. Then, with a slight sneer, she adds, "plus, translating your father's name into English seems like the type of stupid thing Andor would do. All while thinking he was being very clever."

The witch's distaste for my former Chosen lingers on her face a moment longer, then her look is once again reflective.

"I should have paid Andor more mind when plans changed. When your grandmother refused to send you here when it was time, and instead, you went to New York and chose your own path."

Her words stir in me a memory of when I first told Nanny about my acceptance into Juilliard. She still had the occasional lucid moments back then. I don't really think she knew what Juilliard was, but she still seemed so happy about the news. "Good," she'd said, taking my hands in hers. "Carve your own path. No one owns you, Bernadette Morgan." Her tone had been fierce, her eyes focused, and I remember being surprised she'd used my full name. She never did that except when I was in trouble, or when she wanted me to really remember her words. At the time I chalked it up to her deteriorating mind.

Now it seems she had a very real point to make, and it was about this order and their plans for my uterus.

Gross.

"Nanny always wanted you to go," AJ says, surprising us all.

I turn to her. "What?"

She shrugs. "Nanny. Even after she started going nuts, she still talked about how Bernie was going to leave to do big things with her big dreams."

There are tears in AJ's eyes as she walks over to me and sits on the bench to my right, her fingers plunking discordant keys as she talks. "I'm not as selfless as her. I wanted you with me. Life in Rowley was miserable without you. But I know you didn't belong, and so did she. You were always meant for bigger things."

Erzsébet cuts in, ruining whatever moment AJ and I were about to have. "I don't know what Timót is planning. But if he does have a grand scheme, he's been working on it for decades. And now it would appear he has a book of dark magic, a dragon, and perhaps a small following of angry, power-hungry men."

"What an ass-wipe," AJ says. "But what can he do? He's got shit on our Bern here, right?"

Erzsébet shrugs. "Hard to say until we know the extent of his plans."

I stand and walk to the couch to sit next to Zev, who pulls me against him. "I'm losing track of how many enemies we have," I say. "And now the order that's supposed to protect us is also against us?"

Erzsébet's eyes narrow, her face fierce. "Your father is not the order, as much as he might like to imagine himself being. And we witches have far more power than them. We will not let you fall into their hands. But you need to train. Starting now."

She waves her wand and chants some words under her breath, and against three of the walls shelves appear, filled with books and ancient scrolls. It's more than I could read in several lifetimes, let alone memorize in a few days.

I instantly feel way too overwhelmed. I pull away from Zev to stand and study the books, taking one out and flipping through the pages. Frowning, I put it back and do the same with another and another. "These are all in Hungarian," I say, feeling frustration tighten my gut. "How am I supposed to learn enough to be of any help when I can't even speak the language?"

I'm expecting some kind of pep talk or even scolding from Erzsébet, but it's Darius who speaks first. "In a way, you do know the language," he says, walking over to me.

I set the book down as he approaches and takes my hand in his. "Our blood exchange binds us, almost as one."

I nod. That's definitely true, but I have no idea how it solves our problem.

"I am fluent in Hungarian," he says, then turns to Erzsébet. "If I'm not mistaken, there's a spell that might allow us to share more than just our emotional and physical connection. It would allow us to share our knowledge. Experiences. Memories," he adds softly.

My pulse quickens at the many layered implications in his offer. "So I would become fluent in Hungarian as well?" I ask.

He nods. "Eventually. I can't simply transfer the information, but as you study, the words and knowledge would flow into you like music, quickly and organically."

Erzsébet purses her lips. "A spell does exist, Darius. I'm glad to see you remember your studies. Unfortunately, it would likely mean her dreams would become consumed by you and eventually drive her mad."

Well that's not a great side effect. Darius might not remember all the details from his studies.

"That's not true," Zev says, standing and walking to us. "Bernie is my wolf's... and my... mate. That bond strengthens her mind."

I glance at Rune, who is standing with Rain, watching us with such kind, loving eyes. And I feel a twinge of sadness that he and I haven't had as much time together as I'd like. Especially in this moment, when his brand of magic feels so necessary.

He seems to be on the same page as he stares into my eyes and nods thoughtfully. "There's an ancient tonic fae drink before they pass to the other side. It enables the mind to stay strong even as the pain of death encroaches. If Bernie were to drink it before the spell was cast..." Rune trails off, mercifully doing all the complicated fae math in his head instead of saying it out loud. "I think Zev is right," he surmises. "She would not fall into Darius's mind the way another might. She would be well protected."

"This is not a spell I ever invoke on a young witch," Erzsébet says. "But clearly Bernadette has chosen a much different path than most witches." Erzsébet pauses, considering. "That might be for the best. I'm willing to try it if Bernadette is," she says, looking at me. "But it must be your choice. This could be very dangerous."

I look to Darius, then Zev, then Rune. Each of them nod, giving me the only confirmation I need. "Let's do it. There's no way I'm going to learn all this without the help."

AJ pops up from the piano, closing the fallboard so hard I flinch. "Hold up. You're about to download hundreds or thousands of years of memories and knowledge into my bestie. That seems like a thing we should chat a bit more about first, don't you think?" She turns to me, her eyes full of worry. "Will you even still be you? What if he turns you into his mini-me?"

Darius scowls. "My mini-what?"

I chuckle and just shake my head. "I think I'll be okay, AJ. I don't know why I feel so certain, but I do. And I need this if we're going to save Rain."

AJ looks over at her godchild, her face softening instantly, then her gaze snaps back to Erzsébet. "Fine, but is there any way of backing real Bernie up? Just in case?"

Erzsébet looks confused and I can't help but laugh. "A, they can't upload me into the cloud. You have to trust me. I'll be fine."

THREE HOURS LATER, I'm about to eat my words and hope I don't vomit them back up.

Rune has made his potion. Zev and I had a quickie in the other room to solidify our mate bond. His idea, not mine, but I didn't hate it. I don't think it was at all necessary for the spell, but I'm not complaining. Meanwhile, Erzsébet left and returned with a bunch of crystals that she laid out on the ground to form a pentagram.

"You and Darius will stand in the center and exchange blood as I recite the spell," Erzsébet says.

I nod. "Got it."

Rune hands me the potion. It's steaming and smells like feet. He looks at me apologetically. "I'm sorry I can't make it taste better."

I shrug, figuring I've had worse.

I shoot it fast and as it burns down my throat I fight against vomiting up everything I've ever eaten and some internal organs as well.

I gag and struggle to breathe. I definitely have not had worse.

But I feel the power thrumming through me as I take Darius's hand and step into the center.

His dark eyes are luminous as he stares at me. "Are you sure about this? What is done cannot be undone."

"I'm sure," I whisper, knowing this is going to bond us in a way that is frankly terrifying. There won't be any part of each other we can hide from the other after this.

With sweaty hands I grip his, my body shaking as Erzsébet begins to speak in Hungarian. This is a long, complicated spell, and it reinforces what I'm about to do. There's no way I could learn something like that right now. Not when I struggle with basic nouns.

"We must drink at the same time," he says, cutting open his own neck with a small knife, letting the blood pool.

Darius leans in and I feel the familiar tingle of anticipation as his teeth brush along my pulsing vein, sinking into my flesh.

I lean into him, letting my tongue flick at the blood trickling bright red against his pale skin. And then I move my mouth over the wound, sucking more deeply as he takes in my blood.

Before I close my eyes, I notice golden light swirling around us, creating a cocoon. And once I close them, I feel the magic pulsing like a drum beat inside me as his hands tighten on my back. Erzsébet's words fade, though I know she still speaks, but now all I hear is Darius.

He sings into every pore of my body, every molecule of my existence.

I ride the wave of these feelings, and can sense myself falling into him.

Then darkness rises, and a panic grips me as I realize I'm

falling

falling

falling

falling.

I can't stop.

I'm losing myself to him and the panic threatens to overwhelm me entirely.

Before I reach the bottom, I hear a growl and feel the claim of my wolf mate on my heart, pulling me back into myself.

And I feel the calming magic of Rune protecting my mind. Protecting me.

I let the wolf and the fae hold me as the vampire takes me in and gives me all he is, and I see into the mind and heart of a being with darkness and light at war within himself. With memories too buried to unearth. With crushing heartache and aching beauty. And I hold all three of them to me, filling them each with my light, my love, my soul.

It might have been a moment or an eternity, but when I come back to myself, to my body, to the pentagram and the reality around me, everything is as it was.

The furniture is still there. AJ sits watching, biting her nails, which she hasn't done since grade school. My child sleeps peacefully in Rune's arms. Everything is as it was.

Except it's not.

I'm not.

And one look at Darius proves he is not either.

He pulls me against his chest, his grip desperate, his eyes gleaming. "Bernie. God, Bernie. I love you."

After some time I pull away and smile. "I love you too. Now let's get to work."

~

I SPEND the next several days pouring over books and blowing a lot of shit up with my wand. Darius and I are closer than we have ever been, as my mind shifts to contain more and more. My knowledge expands in a way I could never have imagined, and I relish the power I feel at how quickly I'm learning and memorizing a language I only first heard a few days ago.

While I focus on training, the Sexies take turns serving as lookout above the tomb. They seem more nervous with each passing hour, waiting for the inevitable attack. I try to stay optimistic, thinking that every day without a vampire assault might mean we're closer to being in the clear. No one else shares that point of view.

My progress is impressive, but Erzsébet is never satisfied. She's chosen to stay in the cave with us, keeping me on task every waking second of the day. When I'm not eating or sleeping, I'm working.

She pushes me hard, and on more than one occasion Darius or Zev or Rune has stepped in to protect me, but I usher them away each time, knowing I have to be pushed, even if it feels like it's going to kill me, even when I feel like my head will explode. If I don't go the extra mile, I won't be ready, and I know time is running out.

It's the sixth day of my training, just after sunset, that time officially runs out.

We are in another training session--really just one long ongoing session that I sometimes get a break from to eat or nap--and I'm trying to use magic to grow a seed into a tree.

"It is easy to destroy," Erzsébet says. "It is so much harder to create."

I've finally made progress as something green and alive pushes through the dirt, when Erzsébet freezes, her face alarmed.

"They are here," she says, her eyes wide.

The three Sexies all stand at full attention, and I feel waves of worry hit me.

AJ looks around confused. "Who's here?"

Darius looks at me with worry on his face as Erzsébet answers. "Everyone."

286

CHAPTER SEVENTEEN

No sooner have the words left Erzsébet's mouth than Darius flashes out of the tomb. Rune and Zev instinctually step to my sides, prepared to fend off whatever might harm me. AJ steps closer, wanting to be part of the circle of protection. I clutch my wand, ready to fling a few spells at whoever tries to mess with us. I may not have memorized--or even opened--all the books Erzsébet brought me, but I got the guys and AJ to help me find the most useful spells for combat, healing and protection.

"We need to get to the Grand Hall," Erzsébet says, though she shows no signs of moving.

"It's not safe for us to travel."

I know he's fast, but it still surprises me to hear Darius' voice back in the tomb.

"How do you know?" I ask as I turn to look at him. "What did you see in the five seconds you were gone?"

"I know where to look," he answers briskly. "Vampires have the city surrounded."

I want to believe he's exaggerating, but that's not really the vampire's style. If he says that Budapest is surrounded, it kinda means we're in deep shit. Plus, after our bond, I can feel everything. And right now, I feel his worry.

"Wolves?" Zev asks.

Darius looks between Zev and Rune. "I imagine the wolves and fae are walking the streets, looking for signs and smells."

Rune turns to look at Erzsébet, my child still cradled in his arms. "Where are we safer, here or the hall?"

The witch queen looks at me as she answers. It's clear that the only real "we" that matters when it comes to safety is Rain and me.

"There's more magic at our disposal in the Grand Hall, but we can expect more visitors there as well." She looks around the room, assessing our current home base. "While we're harder to find here, we're trapped."

"See, Bernie?" AJ says, making some obvious point that's not yet obvious to me. "This is why I said I didn't want to go into the tomb. Bad shit happens."

"Can't you just, you know, magic us over there?" I ask Erzsébet.

"I can move books and chairs and loaves of bread," she says, waving her wand around and making those very things disappear, as though to prove her point. "But a living being can't be pulled apart and reassembled that way. Many have tried, just as many have died."

I guess that'll just count as part of my lesson for the day, and it's one I'm certainly glad I learned before murdering myself trying to save time on travel.

I glance back at the Sexies, who are having a hushed discussion. Their group asides usually involve these three taking on enormous personal risk in an attempt to keep me safe. Darius is trying way too hard to shield his thoughts and emotions from me, so I waste no time butting in.

"What?" I shout across the space, bringing the secret conversation to a halt. "What's this little pow-wow about?"

Zev checks in with the other two before walking over to me, losing the game of *who gets to argue with Bernie.* They chose well, as his sexy voice can usually make me cave.

"I'm going to walk through town and then north along the river," he says, telling me the plan instead of asking. "That'll give me a sense of who's been sent and where they're looking."

"While he walks," Darius jumps in, keeping the thread going before I have a chance to tell my mate he's not going anywhere. I'm automatically opposed to any division within the group, to the point I'm hardly listening to the words as Darius continues. "I'll travel the back streets between here and the entrance to the Grand Hall, finding the most clandestine route. Zev and I can aid each other if needed, and he might also distract a few watching eyes away from the streets as I walk."

"No," I say the moment Darius finishes his sentence. "If we break into smaller--hey!"

But my mate has already been sucked into the world, out of our tomb before I can even finish my thought. I'm shocked by him leaving, and I can't quite tell if it's because I feel legitimately betrayed or because I'm so used to them doing as I ask.

Darius follows right behind him, our mixed blood stinging in my veins as I watch him go. Rune comes to me, bringing me into his arms, remaining as my one true pillar of support. And then he outs himself as an accomplice.

"The last word we shared on the matter was to not let you have a say in it," he says with a sheepish smile.

"Why the hell not?" I spit back at him. "We're stronger together, you know I'm right. Separating is the stupid choice in like every horror movie ever--when the group breaks up, they're picked off one by one."

"And yet the dragon scale and the dryad arm came when you set out with just one of us by your side," Rune answers smugly. He's not acting smug, but the swiftness with which he pokes a hole in my argument feels very self-satisfied.

"This is different," I murmur back, not really sure if that's true.

"It is, and it isn't," the fae says. "We are stronger together. I'm stronger when you're by my side, undoubtedly. But I gain strength from doing something that could help you, even if we're separated. The same is true for Zev and Darius right now. They know their success will help you and Rain, and that compels them forward. It strengthens them."

His argument feels too much like a set up for when the three of them leave me to face their families...and that hurt is too close to the surface to touch on right now. Instead, I focus on the present, and Rune is right. They are focused and driven. They are furious but contained. Calm. They will do anything to keep us safe. And they will make anyone who hurts me pay.

Damn right we will, Darius mentally says. This is the first time our mental connection has reached this far, and I get some small solace from that.

I smile at Rune. The fae always knows how to make a case that plays to my logical side and touches my heart. I lean into him more, wrapping my arms around his back and enjoying the comfort. Who knows how many more minutes or seconds of this peace I'll have before we're all running for our lives. Or saying goodbye for who knows how long.

"You've managed to attract three smart, sweet men, Bernadette." Erzsébet now faces me, finished with the business of sending books and furniture back from where they came. "And they're right, this is our best hope for getting to the hall without being noticed. Inside, we can regroup and decide where to go."

"Do the tunnels lead anywhere other than the river and the dragon caves?" I ask.

"Oh yes," Erzsébet says. "If we know where we need to be, the channels beneath the hall can take us almost anywhere. We can head to the vampire realm and send a bolt of fire right up the king's asshole, if we please."

It's the very last thing I expected the queen to say, and I assume I misheard until AJ chimes in. "Yeah, boss bitch. Bern, this queen is wicked better than your mom."

Erzsébet fights back a smile and I'm sure she enjoyed the compliment. Then the serious expression returns to her face. "Enough of this, you need to learn a spell in the next few moments so you can cast it without killing anyone."

I hope her plan is for me to somehow grow a shitty radish, because I feel like that's about where my skills max out.

"What's the spell? What does it do?" I'm terrified of the answer, and get even more freaked out as Erzsébet raises her wand and points it at her own chin.

"*Arc a mások.*"

My gaze is on the tip of her wand as she mutters the spell, but my focus immediately shifts to her face as it turns into a swirling ball of flesh and light. I'm horrified and fascinated watching her face glow and melt and move. After just a few seconds, it finally settles back into place, and the sight is even more disturbing than what just transpired.

She's Zev.

"Holy shit," AJ and I say in unison. I turn to Rune, my eyes the size of apples, to see if he witnessed the crazy face theft I just saw. I'm immediately annoyed at how unimpressed he looks.

"What?" he says, gauging my reaction. "Did you think she was going to do something else?"

I spin back to the witch, in no mood to lose a magical IQ test. "Does that spell make us all look like Zev? Are there different, non-Zev-face spells?"

"Bernadette, have you ever thought that you ask too many questions and could stand to have more patience waiting for answers?"

This is the wrong time to be scolding me, especially while wearing the face of my wolf mate, but when AJ laughs I know I've already lost this fight.

"Yessah mum, she's definitely been told she has that problem." AJ always sounds extra Massholey when it's at my expense.

"Please continue," I say in my most patient voice, eager for everyone to get their goddamn heads back in the game and off of my case.

"The words always stay the same," Erzsébet explains. "What changes is your intent and the image in your mind."

It's so strange to hear these words coming from Zev's mouth yet carried by the witch's voice. I try to shrug off the weirdness of it all and focus on what I need to do to learn the spell.

"Is there a way I can practice?" I ask, thinking of all the tiny plants I murdered earlier in the day.

"*Visszatérési,*" Erzsébet says with the wand pointed back at her face, thankfully returning to her normal self. "You must first practice on yourself, but I'm confident you'll master this one quickly."

"*Arc a mások* and *Visszatérési,*" I say, repeating the spell and counter-spell. I'm mostly interested in my ability to get my own face back so I don't get stuck looking like some rando for the rest of my life. "Alright, here I go. Does it hurt?"

"Hm," Erzsébet says thoughtfully. "It's been so long since I experienced pain the way a new witch does. Probably. I imagine it does hurt."

Fun.

I point my wand toward my chin, absolutely terrified of myself but trying to maintain confidence and a clear vision.

"*Arc a mások,*" I mutter breathily, struggling to push the words out because I'm so afraid of what they'll do.

First I feel warmth from the wand in my hand, which is always a byproduct of a spell. The heat quickly hits my chin and begins to spread over the rest of my face. Just as I start to think it's not that painful, the sensation changes from burning to gripping, like someone with a giant hand has palmed my face and is squeezing with all their might. It definitely hurts and it's ridiculous that Erzsébet had to think about it.

It only lasts another second or two and then stops abruptly. I feel entirely normal, and start to wonder if anything changed at all, but the look on AJ's face confirms that something's different.

"Welp," she says, fighting back the urge to either laugh or vomit. "You didn't nail it."

"No, she did not," Rune confirms, looking somewhat sickened.

"What? What's wrong, what do I look like?"

Erzsébet approaches, an eyebrow raised as she thinks of how to fix my problem. "Who did you envision when you incanted?"

"A guy," I answer plainly. "Just a generic guy. I sort of imagined a man I walked past when we first got here, but I was going for a very general look."

Now Erzsébet cracks a smile. "That explains it," she says before conjuring a reflection in front of me. The face that stares back is only a partial face. The nose is missing and my mouth is an empty, toothless hole. The eyes are also missing pupils and I've only got bangs, no hair on the rest of my head. I'm like an unfinished mannequin.

"Jesus! I'm gonna have nightmares about me," I say right before Erzsébet dissolves the reflection.

"You can't do this with a general picture in your mind," the witch explains. "It needs to be a face you know, perhaps not intimately, but well enough that you can picture the details."

That makes sense. Could have used the full lesson before I disfigured myself, but maybe she knew this was the best way to learn.

"*Visszatérési,*" I say with the wand to my chin, feeling a less intense but still noticeable pressure as my face returns to being my face. "Okay, let me try again." I lift the wand, steeling myself for the abuse I'm about to endure, but then pause. "I guess it still needs to be someone who won't draw attention, right? I shouldn't, like, turn us all into Darius."

Erzsébet nods. "We want to blend in with the crowd as best we can. A powerful being might still sniff us out, but this gives us a fighting chance of making it to the hall unnoticed."

With that, she says the incantation with her wand pointed to her own mug, and I watch as her bright, churning face slowly morphs into the mask of a younger woman, someone I don't recognize at all. The new face smiles, then Erzsébet's voice speaks. "This is a barista at my favorite cafe downtown."

The image of a powerful, centuries-old witch stepping out for a cappuccino makes me really happy for some reason. Maybe someday she'll stop by Morgan's and we'll whip her up one of Rune's fancy drinks.

I refocus on the matter at hand, pointing my wand at my face and thinking of who I should impersonate. Who won't draw eyes? Or, perhaps more importantly, who do I want to be if eyes are drawn?

"*Arc a mások,*" I say for a second time, now much more prepared for the sensation about to overtake me. It definitely still hurts, but much less so since I know what's coming. If I keep at this for a few thousand years, I too will probably forget that it's painful.

When the spell completes and the shifting stops, I look around the room, waiting for reactions.

"Fascinating choice," Rune says thoughtfully.

AJ walks over to inspect my handiwork. "Yeah, you look like a guy this time. Less of an abomination. Oh wait, you look like--"

"Andor," Erzsébet cuts in. She seems thoughtful, weighing the pros and cons

291

of my decision. "This could go either way, Bernadette. Depending on who we see, that face could either hasten our problems or buy us precious minutes."

I'm mostly glad the spell worked and I have a believable face, but also thinking those same thoughts. "He can't be too well known by vampires and the other attackers. But if there are defected members of the Kő anywhere, this might be the face I need."

Erzsébet doesn't answer, but I see approval in her eyes as she looks at both Rune and AJ, who's still holding a sleeping Rain. "Now it's time to shift the others."

AJ shakes her head and raises a hand. "I'm good, I'm just a girl from Mass walking the streets of Budapest, no one knows--"

"They know, AJ," Erzsébet says in her disappointed mother voice. "You've been with Bernadette through all of her recent trials, and the connection between you two is more than skin deep. You'll have a magnetic pull for our adversaries if you walk out looking like yourself."

For perhaps the first time in her life, AJ doesn't argue. Maybe, like me, she's wondering what the witch means by our connection being more than skin deep. Is there another crazy secret being kept and we're actually sisters? I can't dismiss anything, but I suspect it's more likely there's a power within our friendship. A bond so strong it has its own kind of magic.

AJ turns to me, a look of love in her eyes that fades quickly as she gazes into the face of a Hungarian man she's never met. "Okay, who are you going to turn me into?"

I smile as I lift my wand. "You'll see," I say. "Also, this hurts like balls the first time."

"What--"

"*Arc a mások,*" I say, cutting her off before she can do anything. Her face ignites with brightness and then rearranges itself, finally coming to rest as a familiar face that no Hungarian will recognize. "Can you do the mirror thing for her?" I ask the disguised witch queen.

She quickly does so and I watch AJ, who no longer looks like AJ, stare back at herself with a big smile.

"Oh hell yeah."

She looks at the reflection, seeing Michael, my ex-boyfriend who was secretly gay and, more secretly, a shifter.

"This is awesome," AJ says at her reflection. "I'm a freaking unicorn."

"Let's move along," Erzsébet says. "We'll want to leave the moment Zev and Darius return."

I walk over to Rune, forming a clear image of Joe, the regular at Morgan's who was another casualty of all this witch business. It's an emotional choice, but a face that will blend here and will be easy for me and AJ to spot in case we all get separated. Rune doesn't care to look in a mirror, trusting that his face has changed and otherwise not worrying about it.

We decide Erzsébet will take Rain, since she'll be the best prepared to cast a protective spell and also has the face of a young woman who would make sense to be carrying a child. I hug my baby tightly, fighting off the fear of what might happen to her if plans go south tonight. I don't kiss her the way I normally would because it feels strange with a face that's not mine, but I mutter a thousand I love yous as I strap her into the harness.

After a few more minutes of standing in awkward silence, both me and AJ compulsively touching our strange, male faces, Zev and Darius return. Erzsébet steps forward immediately to show them Rain and explain the spells we cast. It's good she does, otherwise I might have rushed over to kiss one of them and that would have gone horribly wrong.

"The main streets are teeming with fae," Zev says after it's been sorted out who he's talking to. He averts his eyes every time he looks my way, which is understandable. I wouldn't like it if my lover suddenly looked like someone I was inclined to kill. "The disguises will help, but we need to try and keep our distance from those standing watch."

"I walked two routes," Darius says, looking at me but clearly not liking what he sees. "I suggest we start traveling together at first, but break into smaller clusters if need be."

We agree to move together following Darius' lead, and Erzsébet and I each cast spells to transform the beautiful faces of the werewolf and the vampire. I turn Darius into my high school music teacher, who's face I'll never forget since I spent a billion hours in his classroom. Erzsébet morphs Zev into an older man who she says used to sit in the square above the Grand Hall and feed the pigeons.

Wands in hand, faces obscured, and a route selected, it's time for us to move from the safety of the tomb into the uncertainty of the city streets. One by one we get sucked up and spat back out above ground. The sun has set and the darkness makes me fully realize how frightful this next step is. A vampire could swoop in unseen and kill any of us before we knew what was happening. I'm practically paralyzed with fear as we start to walk out of the cemetery.

Rune, his gorgeous face turned into the less handsome but still appealing mug of Joe, walks by my side and puts a hand on my shoulder. The new face has done nothing to take away from his calming powers.

"Push that fear away, Bernie," he says, his soothing voice unchanged. "We all feel it in these moments, but it can only hold you back."

"Maybe I need to be scared in order to stay alert," I say back, my argumentative instincts taking over.

"True awareness comes from confidence," he responds. "Not from fear. You're an incredibly powerful witch, surrounded by those who love you and want to protect you. Put your belief in that, not in your fears."

It's a good pep talk, as I've come to expect from Rune. As we step through the cemetery entrance and head into the crowded streets, buzzing with nightlife, I grip my wand a little more tightly under my sleeve. Let's do this.

The first few blocks are the scariest, and my eyes dart from face to face, trying to figure out who's a harmless Hungarian or hapless tourist, and who's a paranormal fighter here to kill my child. Everyone looks exactly the same.

We naturally split into two pods, me walking with Erzsébet, my baby, and Rune while Zev, Darius and AJ stroll together about ten feet behind us. This makes us a little less conspicuous, I hope, and also lets us move more quickly through the crowds.

About halfway to the Grand Hall I start feeling less threatened. The disguises are working and the streets are too busy for us to stand out. I'm not sure how we'll get into the Grand Hall once we get to the square, but so far this travel plan has worked.

And then we round a corner, and I come face to face with the one person I didn't expect, and certainly didn't want to see.

Me.

But not me.

Andor.

We're feet apart, staring into each other's eyes. I know exactly who he is, but he's got no idea what's going on. He'd been walking with his head down, wearing a cloak, clearly trying to get somewhere unnoticed. But now unnoticed isn't an option.

Before I know what I'm doing, my wand is raised and a flash of light shoots from the tip, hitting him in the chest and knocking him down. We're close enough to each other that passersby likely didn't see the wand, but they definitely see the man fall to the ground.

I've got no strategy beyond staring at the person I magically tasered, but Erzsébet is instantly kneeling by him and chanting some sort of quiet spell. After she does so, Andor stands next to her, still as a statue, eyes glazed over.

"He'll be in a trance until we're at the Grand Hall," she says to me in a hushed whisper. "But the magic blast from your wand almost certainly…"

Her eyes finish her thought instead of her words, as she looks over my shoulder. The rest of us follow her gaze and see a group of men walking in our direction. They're dressed like Darius was the first night he walked into my bar, and their menacing looks and skin tone give them away pretty fast. Regular people won't immediately know who or what they are, but these vampires definitely don't blend in.

They're half a block away from us and moving at a brisk pace. I turn back to Erzsébet, hoping she's got an awesome plan that will diffuse the situation quickly.

She looks back at me, a frantic energy in her eyes.

"Run."

CHAPTER EIGHTEEN

"Run? From vampires?" My voice is incredulous, but I, like everyone else, am already following the command, my legs pumping hard as I try to escape a flock… or is it herd?…of vampires trying to eat me.

Which begs the question, what do you call a group of vampires?

Setting that thought puzzle aside, I pull my wand out of my sleeve, aim at our pursuers and mutter *tűz*, the Hungarian word for fire, grateful that my connection to Darius allowed me to learn so much so fast, even if it still doesn't feel like nearly enough. Behind me, several vampires burst into flames. My stomach turns on itself at the sounds of their screams, and I don't feel any sense of victory.

Erzsébet flicks her own wand and whispers a spell, casting a kind of net around us that glows white against the night sky.

"This should mask your location, for a time at any rate," Erzsébet says, holding my child out to me. "Take her. I will throw them off your trail. Use the river to get to the garden."

Oh shit.

With fumbling hands I strap Rain onto my chest and tuck her blanket around her just as something hits me from behind, knocking the wind out of my lungs and sending my legs lunging out from under me.

Panic clutches my chest, making it hard to breathe for a moment until I realize what's happening.

Shock is replaced by relief when Darius catches me into his arms. "I've got you," he whispers. It's weird AF coming from the face of my high school band teacher, but comforting all the same. *We're going to the river,* I think to Zev, making sure he knows where to go in case he can't see us to follow. I don't bother sending a thought to Darius, as our minds are already linked.

I twine my hands around his neck and hold on tight as he carries me at super speed, zig-zagging and changing direction now that we're cloaked.

Before she's out of sight, I watch Erzsébet charge in the opposite direction, letting herself be seen long enough to catch the eye of a vampire. And either she or Rune casts an illusion that makes it look like we're with her.

My eyes search for the others, frantic to make sure everyone is safe. Zev has shifted to wolf form, dropping his magical disguise entirely, and he's giving AJ a ride so she can keep up. I don't see Rune or Andor, which panics me for a moment, but Darius calmly assures me mentally that the fae is fine. He can take care of himself--and the traitorous order member.

Erzsébet seems to glide on wind, making excellent time as she lures the enemies away, and I make a mental note to get that spell from her when this is over.

The net of power around us is still visible as we make haste, but it seems less vibrant. Like it's fading.

Hurry, I whisper into Darius's mind. *What will they do if they catch us?*

They won't catch you, Darius says, answering my question by not answering it.

Hopefully Erzsébet's spell will last long enough to get us where we need to be so we won't have to find out.

I want to help more, to whip out my wand and blast them with more fire, but that would negate the effects of Erzsébet's cloaking spell--giving away our location, and we can't win in a faceoff with them, not out here. Maybe not even with the magic of the Grand Hall, but at least we'll have a slight advantage there.

As we get more space between us and the attackers, I wonder if I can guide us to the right spot in the Danube River. I can visualize the area where Zev and I emerged after visiting the dragon cave, but I'm shit with directions and not sure I can guide us there easily. Suddenly I know the answer, and I know it's my connection to Darius providing the knowledge. I have a map in my head of Hungary, and I can zoom in to see different areas in more detail. I also instinctively know where we are in relation to the map.

This is a wicked cool gift.

Zev, I'm going to need AJ as soon as we get to the water.

This wolf mate telepathy could not be more useful. I look over my shoulder as Zev increases his pace and Darius slows enough to let him catch up to us.

We are going so fast, weaving through alleys as Darius follows the map towards the river that runs through the center of the city. The river that should give us a back door to the Grand Hall, since getting to the courtyard portal would 1: take us longer since it's on the other side of the river and 2: for sure be surrounded by fae or wolves or the undead, or if we're super lucky, all three.

The river has the advantage of spanning the length of Budapest--a much larger target to try and defend. The vampires can't have every inch of the banks guarded, even if they know about it being a portal, which hopefully they don't.

Let's hope I'm right.

I choose a part of the river that's close but also most likely to be free of any witnesses--or vampires.

Darius never tires as he carries me and Rain through streets, then woods, until we reach the water's edge. He sets me down gently and snow crunches under my feet. A tree heavy with icicles and gleaming a brilliant white in the darkness gives a winter wonderland vibe to the moment. The ebb and flow of the tide creates a gentle soundtrack to our adventures, but I know the water is going to be freezing.

Which won't be a problem for Darius, but the rest of us might die from it.

Zev and AJ catch up, and I see the cloaking web around us cracking and fading and know we only have a few more minutes before we will be visible to the enemy again, though it seems Erzsébet has done a good job of sending them on a wild goose chase. I just hope she's okay. But first thing's first.

"AJ, I need you to use your water nymph powers to, I don't know, put us in a bubble once we dive into this river," I say, wasting no time as she climbs off my wolf mate's back.

"No prob, B, but that looks colder than a witch's titty. Why are we diving into a river anyways?"

"It will take us where we need to go," I say. "Where's Rune?" I'm not leaving without the fae. And Andor, I guess.

An illusion flickers before me and Rune and Andor appear. Andor continues to act under the spell Erzsébet cast, his eyes glazed over. He offers no resistance.

I sigh in relief at seeing the fae, though I need a moment to process him having Joe's face. "Everyone ready? We dive in on three." I hold Rain close to me and say a silent prayer to whatever gods or goddesses are in charge of keeping people from freezing to death. Then I count. "One. Two. Three."

I expect the cold, but I am not prepared for how *cold* the cold is. Zev wraps himself around Rain and me, letting his werewolf heat warm us both as AJ does her thing. She puts her arms around Zev and me, so we're all swimming downward in a big, clumsy hug. As far as speed is concerned, it doesn't feel like the ideal formation.

However, a moment later, the water is sloughed off of us, and though the temperature hasn't increased, we are dry and drifting down into the depths of the Danube, swimming but not. It's a strange kind of flying swimming as we are cushioned by air bubbles. Turns out AJ knows her shit.

I lead us deeper and deeper until I see the small cave that leads us out of the river.

Though we could talk if we wanted, we are all silent, and the muted sounds and heaviness of being underwater surround us.

We have to go into the dark entrance one by one, and I'm sure the others feel as claustrophobic as I do squeezing into the pitch-black tunnel. When I feel the break in the passage, where we could go to the Grand Hall or the dragon caves, I stay to the right.

Seconds after I move through the opening, I'm swimming up toward the water's surface inside the Grand Hall garden. I climb onto dry land, amazed that I'm not hypothermic, or even wet.

I do a quick headcount once the others have joined me, starting with my baby, who's stirring a bit but otherwise seems okay. Her early childhood is either going to make her the coolest person ever or scar her for life. Probably both.

It dawns on me that we all have our normal faces back. AJ's a girl again, and the vampire, fae and werewolf are once again their sexy selves. I'm guessing the threshold of the Grand Hall undoes enchantments. If I had a magical underground stronghold built to protect an endangered species, I wouldn't want anyone sneaking in disguised.

Darius is at my side in a moment, our beings tethered together like magnets. Zev, who stayed in wolf form, shifts back to human, and AJs eyes bug at his sexy nakedness. I ignore her and instead look for Rune, who appears last with a bleary-eyed Andor in tow, looking like he's starting to regain his wits.

Good, because I have questions.

Darius, always in my head, instantly restrains Andor, and Rune, who doesn't need to be in my head to know what I'm thinking, uses his fae plant magic to will some vines to grow from the garden and tie Andor to a tree.

"Thanks, boys," I say, as I hand Rain to the fae and walk over to Andor.

His milky brown eyes widen in alarm as I approach. "Bernadette, it is not what you imagine."

I cock my head. "Really? What do you know about my imagination?" I ask.

"I have done nothing with bad intentions. I am only trying to help you."

"You're lying," I hiss, rage boiling in my veins like lava.

"I only wanted to help your father protect you. Together, we could be very powerful," he says, his expression pathetically hopeful.

I hold out my wand and let lightning dance on the end of it. "I'm already powerful," I tell him, my voice much colder than the white-hot anger in my gut. "Tell me what you and my father are planning. Is he still alive?"

Andor pinches his lips closed, as if that might help him avoid saying anything incriminating.

I look deep into his eyes and feel a new kind of power welling up in me. Once it reaches my throat I throw it at the man before me, wrapped in the force of my words. "Tell me!"

Something cracks in him, I see it in the flicker of his eyes as his soul is dimmed, and then, he begins to begrudgingly speak.

"Your father is the strongest of us all. He promised to make me your Chosen and that together we would create the Last Witch and rule." His face contorts and he bites his tongue to keep from saying more.

Darius steps up to me, a frown on his face. "You are compelling him," he says softly.

"But... that's not one of my powers."

"It is the vampire's powers," Erzsébet says, now standing at the edge of the stream, completely dry and the picture of elderly stealth. "And now, it appears, it is one of yours. No witch has ever survived a vampire mating ritual of this nature for so long with her sanity intact, so we really don't know what to expect from you."

"Am I... am I becoming a vampire?" I don't know how to feel about that.

298

Not bad exactly, but at the same time I have a child to raise, and I'd like to be able to do that in the sun.

Erzsébet shakes her head. "No, you are becoming something more. What that is will be determined by time."

So many questions, but Andor struggling against the vines reminds me we are in the middle of something more important than the subtleties of my magic as it relates to my mate bonds.

I do glance at Zev though, wondering what surprises my connection to him might have in store.

The wolf nods. *Our dance has only begun,* he says to my mind, and I shiver at the promise there.

Erzsébet walks over to Andor, stopping a few feet in front of him. "You have betrayed our order, you have betrayed my sisters. What is Timót planning with the book of dark spells?"

His eyes fill with tears, but I have no sympathy left. "I do not know. I swear it. He said we needed them to protect Bernadette and the baby. That even though I was not the father, I could still serve Bernadette and be her prince, if only I brought him the book."

Zev growls and I can tell he's ready to rip Andor's guts open. Darius is still, expressionless, and looks ten times scarier than if he was all ragey. And Rune is holding my child, but if he wasn't…

"What did my father want with a dragonling?" I ask, trying to use that compulsion trick again, but I don't feel the power in the same way anymore. "It was him who took it, yes?"

Andor looks away, unable to make eye contact with me. "He did not tell me about the dragonling."

Erzsébet laughs, but it is not one that reaches her eyes or sounds in any way joyful. "You are a tool, Andor, and Timót has been using you. You are useless."

She waves a wand over his head and speaks the word *alvás.* Andor instantly falls asleep.

"We must head to the Grand Hall where the base of our power is stronger, and gather the other witches to raise our defenses. I bought us some time, but it won't take them long to find us. Come."

We follow her, but I glance back at Andor limply hanging from the tree, the vines still wrapped around his torso and legs. "Are we just going to leave him there?" I ask.

"He would probably prefer that to what I will do if I see him again," Darius hisses, his face hardening in anger.

Zev grunts in agreement, and I don't argue further. I'm pretty pissed at him as well. And at the choices made that put him in this position. It might have started as a plan for protecting their kind, but this whole order needs a serious facelift to bring it into the modern era of women getting to make their own decisions about their bodies.

I reach Rune and take Rain from him as she begins to fuss. "She needs a feeding," I say. He nods but looks worried.

"This isn't a great time for that," he says.

I shrug. "Tell that to the crying baby."

I tuck her into my chest and let her suckle for the first time in a long time as we keep walking. I'm relieved that my supply is still strong enough to feed her, but mostly pleased at how skilled I've become at nursing on the go. Here's hoping I'm getting some awesome upper arm definition from it. That doesn't feel like too much to ask given how heavy she starts to feel after a while of doing this.

When we enter the Grand Hall, at first I think it's empty. It's dark and seemingly vacant, but my skin crawls at the sense of someone...or something present. I instinctively slip Rain back into her harness, freeing up both my hands, wand in one. "They're here!" I whisper, fear clutching my throat.

But my warning comes too late.

Dozens of vampires step out of the shadows, surrounding us. Then an equal number of fae step out, and finally the wolves slink toward the center of the room.

It's a real party.

Pandemonium breaks out as Erzsébet begins fighting them with blasts of magic. I follow suit, using my wand to cast fireballs as I search for a path to freedom and safety.

Rain begins to cry and I try to cover her face as I continue fighting hostile creatures from all the realms. Zev is back in wolf form, attacking everything in sight. Rune is creating illusion after illusion to keep them away from me and Rain, creating a small break in the onslaught.

Holding my child tight to my chest, I run for it, flinging fire around me until I'm surrounded by a wall of flames I didn't even know I could make.

This buys me enough time to get out of the main room, and just as I turn a corner into a darkened tunnel I've never been in before, a hand grabs my arm.

I scream and pull away, raising my wand. But the person on the other end of the hand steps out of the shadows, mutters a spell and blows purple dust into my face.

I cough and choke, and when I try to speak my vocal cords don't work.

I've lost my voice.

I can't cast spells.

I try to scream but nothing comes out. I try to pull away, clutching my child, fear crawling into me like a thousand spiders.

"Be still," the man says. "I have not come to harm you. I'm trying to help you."

I narrow my eyes and point to my throat, hoping I'm making very clear how I feel about his *help*, and his iron grip on my arm which is definitely going to leave a bruise.

"Your voice will come back in a few minutes. I didn't want to draw attention and this was the fastest way."

His words make a kind of sense, but I'm not in the mood to listen.

"Bernadette, I know you don't know me, but I promise I only want the best for you." He pauses as if considering what to say next, and I try once again to yank away from him, nearly dislocating my shoulder in the process. Damn he's strong. Too strong.

But as I look more closely at him, my chest tightens. The cheeks. The shape of the eyes. I gasp, though no sound comes out, and he nods, smiling.

"You see the resemblance, do you not?"

Without the power of speech, I simply nod.

I'm finally meeting my father.

CHAPTER NINETEEN

I'm powerless to scream, cry, or question.

I can't do any of the things I thought I might do if I ever met my father. All I can do is stare.

And feel afraid.

For the second time in as many months, I'm meeting a parent I long thought was dead, and everything about the encounter feels treacherous. There are vampires and wolves and fae all battling to find and sacrifice my child, almost definitely with the intention of killing me in the process, and yet I'm just as frightened staring back into the face of my dear old dad.

His hazel eyes look gentle. They don't have the same anxiety that Andor couldn't help but display. Despite the alarm bells clanging in my head, Timót looks calm and collected. He's clean shaven, his curly black hair peeking out from under his hood. He doesn't look as evil as I want him to.

"You fear me," he says, hitting the nail on the head. "And you should. You should fear everyone, dear daughter. That's what comes with being so important to so many."

Fighting continues in the room behind us, as all of the attackers and my sweet princes clash mere feet away. I want to reach into their minds, to ask them for help, but I can't distract them. Not when so few are up against so many.

One thought from me could get them killed.

Timót follows my gaze, watching as bodies fly through the room. "It didn't have to come to this," he says softly, then looks down at Rain. "I'm sorry your ancestors put you in this position, little one."

He looks fondly at the child, not with the love of a grandparent, but the admiration of someone who knows Rain's importance. It's a bit chilling since he should care about the baby regardless of this cursed prophecy. I'd tell him as much if I could speak.

"Wait here," he says as he moves back toward the main room. The last thing I want to do is follow his command, but I'm in a tough spot. The passageway behind me is pitch black and I've got no idea where the hell it might take me. Meanwhile, I'm not going to rush back into harm's way with my baby strapped to my chest. That feels like the quickest way to get everyone killed.

Timót pauses in the entryway to the main room, taking a small pouch from his pocket and emptying a fine powder into his hand. He gives one last look back at me, then throws the dust into the air in front of him. It forms a cloud as it settles between him and the hall, and then he strides right through it.

Walking boldly into a room full of vampires seems like a very stupid move, but the effect of the powder immediately explains his boldness. As the particles settle on his hair, skin and clothes, Timót becomes invisible.

It's a nifty trick, and I can't help but wonder if he brought enough to share. I remind myself that he's not on my side, that he's betrayed the witches, stolen from Erzsébet, put all of us in harm's way. Not to mention he tried to auction me off to his lackey. At the same time, the enemy of my enemy is my friend. He's got to be better than the vampires currently attacking all the people I love most in the world.

I'm worried sick about AJ, caught in the middle of this with no real magic to protect herself unless she's underwater. I'm nervous for Erzsébet, who's powerful as shit but also old as dirt, and probably getting really tired of fighting vampires all the time.

I'm worried for Rune.

For Zev.

For Darius.

The second I imagine my vampire lover, it's as though I inhabit his body. I don't see what he sees, but I feel his movements, I sense the danger around him. It's too much to bear, and I shake my head to regain my own thoughts. Now, noting my own sensations again, the constriction of my throat feels better.

"*Tüz útmutató,*" I whisper, proving that my voice is back and summoning a small ball of flame that rests at the end of my wand. I turn back to the dark corridor and send the fire out in front of me, illuminating the narrow space which seemingly goes on forever. I don't see any doorways or connecting halls, so my choices are stay put, walk into battle, or head for the darkness. Something tells me I'll be choosing darkness.

"B!"

I spin around, breaking my concentration and losing my fireball, but happy nonetheless as I see AJ standing at the end of the tunnel in front of me. She's got a gash above her cheek and burn marks on her arms and clothes, but she's alive.

She runs over and hugs me and Rain, and I squeeze her back while keeping my eyes over her shoulder, hoping no vampires are about to follow her into this room.

"Is everyone okay?" I ask, thrilled to pieces that I can speak again.

She nods, then shrugs. "Erzsébet's riding on Zev and shooting fire all over the freaking place. It actually looks pretty badass. I was with Rune and he's been casting illusions left and right so no one could see us, except for one wolf," she points to the gash on her cheek. "Rune saw you come in here and he told me to follow. " She pauses. "I'm not sure where Darius is."

My heart knots up at her words, and I reopen my mind without hesitation, hoping I can connect with him enough to at least know where he is. I feel him in battle, moving with unimaginable speed through cold air, and I breathe out my worst fears. He's alive.

And no longer in the Grand Hall.

He's too far away for my comfort, but I hope he's at least safe. Being apart is almost physically painful, which doesn't bode well for our future.

"My father's here," I say to AJ, my mind leaving Darius and coming back to join my body. AJ spins in a circle, looking every which way.

"Where? In this tunnel?" She pushes her sleeves up and starts to walk past me. "I'll bust his goddamn lip."

I grab her arm to keep her from going further into the darkness. "He pulled me into this room, then turned himself invisible and went out into the main hall."

"Uh-huh, sticking with the absentee father act," she says. "So what, are you waiting for him? Are we killing him? What's happening?"

I look back down the dark passage, feeling more and more like that's our only option. If AJ could stumble over and find me, it's only a matter of time before a vampire or werewolf does the same.

"I think we need to go this way," I say as I take AJ's hand. "We just have to trust everyone will be alright, but I want to get Rain as far away from the vampires and my father as I can."

I can tell AJ's nervous but on board. I conjure my little torch again and we start to slowly head down the hallway. It feels like the floor slopes down, taking us deeper into the heart of the earth. Even with my fire lighting the way, it still feels oppressively dark in this confined space.

We've moved a few hundred paces or so when I hear more than just our footsteps. The sound is soft at first but grows louder as it nears, and I wheel around, wand raised and ready to bring fire and pain to whoever's in pursuit.

I've got a harming spell on my lips as the figure nears, but right before I speak it the words catch in my throat. Thank God they do, otherwise I might have killed my sweet fae prince.

Rune looks frightened and winded, and I rush into his arms. The normal calm is missing from his touch, which is alarming as anything else, but understandable given what he's been through.

When I pull out of his embrace, I nearly scream. Timót stands next to Rune, having just shed his invisibility charm.

I step back and start to raise my wand, but Rune reaches down and stops me.

"No," he says in a hoarse whisper.

"Rune, you know he's not on--"

The fae cuts me off by raising a finger to his lips. "He's guiding us out. Please."

I've never heard desperation like this in Rune's voice. I look to my father, anger coursing through me for so many different reasons, but still feeling like I might need his help in order to survive. I glance at AJ, who looks just as lost as I feel, but the fact that she's not screaming at my dad to get bent must count for something.

I take one last look back up the corridor, wishing with all my might that I would see Zev and Erzsébet's charging down the hall, coming to our rescue. All I see is darkness.

I grip my wand tightly, ready to use it in the most violent ways, and then step aside to let Timót lead the way.

"You're sure about this?" I ask Rune as my father steps past. The fae gives a quick nod, then gently touches my arm. I'm worried he saw something out there that has him so disturbed, because his normal powers just don't seem to be there. What could have happened? I shudder at the thought and turn to follow Timót, taking AJ's hand in mine so I can keep her close.

The path widens as it goes deeper. We walk on and on, and it's starting to feel like we're miles below ground.

Finally, the hallway leads into a large, open space. It's a perfectly circular room with a soft orange hue. I let my guiding fire go out and can still see from the natural brightness in the space.

In the middle of the room is an enormous star, with hundreds of points extending from its sapphire center. The blue glows and pulses, flooding light into each of the points that seem to direct to small doorways along the rounded walls.

Erzsébet mentioned that the tunnels beneath the Grand Hall could take a person anywhere. Seeing this star, I know instantly that this is the room of portals.

I look at Rune, whose eyes are dancing between the doorways that might take us to any number of places. Timót is counting the points on the star, seemingly trying to pinpoint a certain direction. AJ has her eyes on me, probably hoping I've got some idea about what's going to happen next.

Sorry, girl. I'm wicked lost.

"Here," Timót says, walking to the center of the star, then turning and moving along one of the points until he reaches the wall. "This will get us to safety."

"And where is safety?" I ask. I followed blindly enough to this point, but I need more answers before I walk behind this traitor through another dark doorway.

"A different realm," he answers. "Where we can't be followed. And where I can tell you everything you need to know."

My eyes move to Rune. He's never led me astray in the past, and I'm trusting him to help me stay alive now. He meets my gaze, grits his teeth, and nods. It's clear he's not 100% comfortable with the choice, but I understand there are no perfect answers at this point.

I walk to the center of the room and then pace the point of the star, just as my father did. AJ follows me, with Rune bringing up the rear. The sapphire glows beneath all of our feet, but most brightly under mine. This room knows my powers. Hopefully it won't let my steps be misguided.

"Ajtó tól halál."

The spell Timót mutters sounds incredibly dark, both in the way he says it and the words he uses. I'm not familiar with the specific incantation, but I definitely recognize the Hungarian word for *death*.

"What realm are we--"

Timót grabs my hands.

I feel a strong shove in my back.

And before I can ask, we're all falling in a portal.

Darkness ripples around me, and I have the same sensation of dropping that I did when traveling into the tomb. This one lasts much longer and feels much more tumultuous. I clutch Rain close to my chest as she cries at the top of her lungs, finally rattled from her blissful sleep. Beyond Rain I can also hear AJ's screams, which tear at my heart, but at least let me know she's still alive. I keep one hand tightly clasped on Rain while the other holds my wand. If I'm going to survive--if anyone is going to survive--I must keep these two things safe.

And then stillness.

I'm on my knees, planted on the ground. My fingers reach down and touch smooth stone below me. I open my eyes and see a gray, rocky landscape. The sky above is an ominous shade of ash, like a volcano erupted not too long ago. The rocks around us are the color of charcoal, and I can't see a single living plant in any direction.

If I were to draw a picture of a safe place, this would not be it.

This whole place is the color of death.

Timót stands before me, a curious look on his face. He reaches a hand down to help me up, then shakes his head when he sees me raise my wand.

"As I said, you're right to fear me. And I know you don't trust me, and likely never will." So many of his words sound like they were pulled from the exact playbook my mother used the first night we met. It's the worst kind of eerie.

"But," he goes on, "I swear on all the stars that I'm trying to keep you alive. You and Rain. Fight me as you might, I'll still make you the princess of the new *Érintett*."

With a baby strapped to me and him having the high ground, I decide now is not the moment to start a duel with my father. I reach for his hand and let him pull me to my feet. I'm sure he's expecting questions, but I'm not ready to give him the satisfaction of speaking more, so I turn to find Rune.

And that's when my last shred of hope floats away.

Where there should have been my trustworthy fae, another now stands.

Andor.

I knew something felt wrong, and I should have listened to those feelings. The calming touch, the sound of his voice, none of it was right. I listened to my eyes when I should have trusted my instincts.

"I needed a familiar face to help move you along," Timót says. "And I wanted to bring your future prince along for the journey."

My stomach churns as I look at Andor--pathetic, meek, and hopeful. He's been lied to his whole life about how relationships work, and it's made him a pretty disgusting person.

"There's a useful spell that allows you to change the face of--

"Yeah, I know the spell," I say, loathing every word I have to speak to this so-called father. Whatever he says about wanting to protect me, and however much he believes it, I'm going with my instincts now. He's a piece of shit.

"Impressive," he says in response to my magic knowledge. "You're learning quickly. I'm excited for the day when you'll rule, use your powers for good, and finally understand the purity of my intentions."

"You know Bernie can destroy you, right?" AJ asks. I appreciate the support, but she's talking smack I'm not sure I can back up. If this guy can pull one over on the queen witch, he's got some tricks up his sleeves.

As if on cue, he pulls a slender wand from the arm of his robe and aims it at AJ. Since hearing that the witch line was limited to just females, I've wondered exactly what powers the *Érintett* possessed. For some reason, I figured wands were a bridge too far for the men; looking at the slender staff in Timót's hand, jet black and shimmering, it's clear I was wrong.

"I most certainly do know that. I, in turn, could also destroy her, so I'm hoping we can reach a truce until our plan unfolds."

"What plan?" I hiss. "Are you just hoping to siphon power off a baby witch like the rest of them?"

Timót looks at me but leaves his wand pointed at my friend. Andor slowly inches toward me and the hairs on my neck perk right up. "We don't want the child sacrificed, Bernadette," my father answers. "That's a foolish interpretation of the prophecy, meant to mislead the other races. No, we want to keep the mother and child together."

That would sound like good news coming from a man who exuded less evil. The way he pairs me and Rain, I can't help but picture the two of us chained together while a bunch of powerless warlocks feed off our magic.

"But there are many steps in the plan before anything comes to pass," Timót says, now returning his focus to AJ. "And the first step is to remove unnecessary obstacles. *Lélel nak a szikla!*"

I turn, a scream ripping from my throat as AJ falls in a heap on the ground. Before I can think about what I just witnessed, I'm raising my arm, wand aimed at Timót, ready to unleash every bit of anger and power I have onto his worthless soul.

But my arm doesn't move.

My hand is frozen by my side.

My wand drops from my fingers, clattering on the stones below.

A few feet away, Andor stands with his own wand, a band of light stretched between it and my right elbow.

"Excellent work, young prince," my father says. "Your secret practice has done you well."

Andor beams at the compliment, though he keeps an apprehensive look. He's wronged me and he knows I don't like it.

I look back to AJ, slumped on the ground like a puppet whose master has gone to bed. I squeeze my eyes shut, willing it not to be so but feeling the deepest despair engulf my heart.

"Why!!!" I scream, feeling power surge through me in a way I haven't felt since my wand first touched my palm. "Did you kill her?"

Timót looks at the body, then down at his wand. "I don't know, honestly. I've never tried that spell before. I don't believe she's dead, but we have to leave her all the same."

The fire raging in my soul burns even hotter, and whereas I used to fear these moments, I'm now inviting the powers to flood through me and strike this man down.

"I'll explain in due time, Bernadette," my father says, his wand now trained on me as though he expects some type of reaction. "There's a movement in the magic world, led by myself and others who have long been forgotten. What you see now as betrayal is the exact opposite. I'm leading men who want to expose the wrongs of the vampires, of the fae, of the wolves. And yes, of the witches. They're not so innocent as Erzsébet would have you believe."

Darius, I speak into my mind, trying the only thing I can think of.

No response.

Zev, my prince, I say, hoping the mate bond travels between realms.

Silence.

Tears rush from my eyes, falling onto the head of my poor child. I wanted to save her from danger and I've made things infinitely worse.

"Bernadette--"

Hearing my name on Andor's lips is the final straw. That he feels any power over me is something I'll die before I accept, and a combination of magical compulsion and angry free will turn my face toward him.

The last thing I see are the whites of his eyes as I scream scorching light. Flames flood out of me, knocking him to the ground and searing his flesh. I watch as he writhes for a few moments and then stops moving completely, his body already blackened, almost as grotesque as the corpse from the dragon cave.

I look back to Timót, who keeps a steely gaze on me, though he's lost a bit of his luster.

With a clear mind and the utmost control, I summon my wand into my hand, aiming it at my father. Killing my mother hurt my heart a little. Seeing my dad die won't be nearly as sad.

"Before you do anything rash," he says, his wand still targeting me, "you should know that we're not alone."

"That's fine," I spit back. "I'm happy to kill everyone else you brought here."

He cracks a pitying smile and shakes his head. "I know you feel that way, but these others... they're not so easy to kill. *Lobogás!*"

He points his wand straight up as he yells the incantation, sending a bolt of deep red light into the sky. Seconds after his action, before I can think to react, we're surrounded.

I blink.

Then blink again.

They approach in the sky, coming from all directions.

We're surrounded by dragons.

Dozens of them. They all have that iridescent glow coming off their scales, but they present different shades of blue, orange, green and purple. Giant wings create flurries of wind with each flap as the creatures hover in a circle above us.

None of them is as big as the mother dragon we found dead, so I assume these are all younger dragons. *He's been stealing baby dragons from their mothers.*

Young as they may be, they are still huge, easily big enough and probably powerful enough to roast me and my baby like marshmallows.

My wand feels impotent in my hand, and I feel real terror well up in me.

Timót walks over to me slowly, wand still drawn to show he's not taking any chances.

"You'd be wise to calm down if you want to live." He holds my gaze for a long moment, trying to convey some sort of message, trying to make me see something.

"*Bizalom,*" he whispers. It's the Hungarian word for trust, and him saying it makes me want to scream.

He approaches me cautiously, but with too much confidence for my liking. "Together, we can rise to greatness. We can conquer all other nations and rule, taking for ourselves the eternal youth of the vampires, the strength of the were-wolves and the magic of the fae. We will be undefeatable."

I frown. "Does what I want matter in any of these worlds domination plans?"

"I assumed you would want no part of this," he says smugly. "Which is why I've brokered a deal with someone near and dear to you. I get eternal life and the baby… and he gets you."

My heart skips a beat, as my gut twists on itself at the implication of his words.

I feel him before I see him.

I turn slowly, desperate to be wrong, certain I'm not.

I squeeze my eyes shut, pushing away the tears, before I open them and face the man who has betrayed me. Who has made a deal with the devil to save me… by paying far too high a cost. A cost I will never be able to forgive.

And the truth of that crushes my soul.

I open my eyes, schooling my face into neutral at the beautiful man before me. "Hello Darius."

KEEP READING FOR MORE!

KARPOV GAUSTAD

A
WEREWOLF
A VAMPIRE
AND A FAE
GO HOME

CHAPTER ONE

 *hy?*

WHAT ARE YOU DOING?

Please, talk to me.

Darius stares back at me through narrow eyes. His expression is cold; his face unreadable.

Every effort I make to connect with him, to hear his thoughts and reveal mine, is met with stone-cold silence. I feel his emotions coloring my own, dancing around the edges of my heart, but that's all. Just a steady sense of anger-- nothing more, nothing less.

After so many hours of living with souls intertwined, this distance between us feels immeasurable. I can't understand what's changed. My eyes bore into his, trying to find a window into our bond, but I'm shut out.

There's a throbbing pain in my veins. I started to notice it in the passage in the Grand Hall, but ignored it because there was too much going on. Now it's all I can think about, and being near Darius is only making it worse.

Every fiber of my being wants to break down, to scream and cry and fire bolts of lightning into the air, but I push back. It's not that I don't want to show myself to Darius, because I'm sure he can already feel my emotional assault; I don't want to give the satisfaction to Timót. AJ's lying still on the ground, Darius has betrayed my baby, and I'm surrounded by a thunder of dragons, but I will not let my father assume he's taken an ounce of my power.

I keep my eyes on Darius as he walks toward Timót, the vampire's gaze never leaving mine. I'm still baffled by this mental wall he's erected between us. We did a magical blood ritual that was supposed to meld our brains together, and suddenly it's like he's opted out of the contract. And it's not like he's been drifting away--our minds were one and the same less than an hour ago.

Darius arrives next to my father, and the sight of the two of them side by side makes me clutch my wand so hard I'm worried it will break. Good thing we went with the dragon scale model.

"You didn't have any trouble using the pendant?" my evil father asks my potentially evil blood-bound lover.

Darius nods slowly, his dark, unreadable eyes still on me. His gaze is unsettling, unbreaking and completely lacking expression. If he knows how badly he's wronged me, why won't he look away? If he has some sort of explanation, why doesn't he offer it?

He holds up the *Érintett* medallion that I found in the dragon cave, the one Erzsébet had taken. "I didn't know such a small piece could serve as a portal between realms."

"I spent many years charming that pendant," my father says with a sense of pride, taking the medallion back and putting it around his neck. "I failed repeatedly until an ancient sorcerer gave me the enchanted blood of a Sylph, and now I have the ability to travel at will."

I'm appalled by the coordination between Darius and Timót, and confused by the importance of this pendant I found on a charred corpse in a cave. "Why leave it behind then?"

Timót smiles, a pompous look on his deceitful face. "Oh, I didn't leave it behind. As it happens, I was there when you came for your scale. After killing the dragon I created the illusion of my death, lying in wait to bring you and your baby here. I can't tell you how disappointing it was that you didn't bring your child. Irresponsible, really."

Thank God I can transfer power into this wand without destroying it, because the rage inside me right now is off the charts. "Thank you so much for the parenting tips. You've always been so good at it."

I'm not going to crack. He's not going to kill me or my baby--not yet, anyway--so I'll keep my cool and hope it ruffles his feathers. He doesn't look like he's enjoying my barbs, but I haven't quite gotten under his skin yet.

"Fortunately," he says, looking at Darius, "the delayed timeline worked in my favor. Now we have an escort to the temple."

Darius doesn't return the look, his gaze still penetrating my own. My ears fill with deafening silence as I try to pry open his thoughts and find out what's happening.

"You'll be happy to know," Timót says to me, "that my dragons and I are going to destroy the sacrificial chambers meant to bleed the Last Witch. Without that element of the prophecy, the vampires will assume their fate is as good as sealed."

"And then what?" I ask, while keeping my eyes on Darius, as the question readily applies to either traitor.

"Then I'll keep the child while slowly convincing you of the promising life that could be yours. It's hard for you to understand now--"

"Yeah, you've mentioned that," I say, cutting him off. "That's the type of argument someone without a convincing argument says over and over. You're a trash ball and everyone knows it, so let's stop pretending someday I'll understand otherwise and we'll be one big happy family of psychopaths."

My dad flares his nostrils as he takes a deep breath, making a face similar to one I've seen all too many times in the mirror. When he exhales, he's no less angry. "If you weren't such a foolish young girl, maybe you could be made to see the grander themes at play, as your vampire friend managed to do."

"Yeah, well…" The staring match between myself and Darius continues, and it's harder than ever to keep my cool. "He might be garbage, too."

For the first time since he arrived, I feel a blip inside me, a small bubble in our emotional union. Nothing registers on the vampire's face, but I can sense a tiny wound from my words.

Why? I say again, practically screaming inside my head while trying to keep my face still, hoping that little word will slip through the small crack that's appeared in the wall between us.

Nothing. Trying to connect with him only makes the throbbing in my veins worse.

This tiny sliver of an opening is gone, sealed up tight once again.

I raise my wand, not aiming at Timót, but Darius. I don't know what spell I plan on shouting, I only know I'm at the end of my rope and I either need to find out why he's done this or make him hurt. Since I'm not sure he can feel the pain coursing through me, I might need to see it on his face.

"I'd be careful, Bernadette," Timót says in a disgustingly condescending tone. "I believe Darius is the only vampire who doesn't want you to die. Any harm you cause him won't help you or your child in any way."

My current despair makes it hard to care about what might happen and when. Whatever his intentions, Darius betrayed me. Perhaps he couldn't bear the thought of us being apart, but this wasn't his decision to make, and it wasn't the right choice. I mean, does he think we'll ride off into the sunset together after my daughter's ripped away and my father adds immortality to his list of powers?

"When do we leave?" Darius asks.

"As soon as you subdue Bernadette," Timót says, his eyes on my wand. "As a show of good faith. I need to know you're on my side before you deliver me to the king."

Darius' eyes pull away from mine for the briefest moment, glancing at my father and then returning to me. In the fraction of a second while he looks away, I feel him return to me. I feel his pain, sense his sorrow and his rage. But the sensation disappears as quickly as it comes, leaving me empty again.

"Of course," Darius says, his tone sending an ice-cold dagger into my heart. "So you're aware, the king won't trust to turn you until he sees the baby on the altar. Even then…"

My wand trembles in my hand. To hear these words from Darius' lips shreds any sense of control I have left.

You're a monster.

Hatred pushes out the pain and betrayal, leaving nothing but rage toward this man I once loved with all of my soul, who I allowed to become myself, to inhabit my very being. The anger is maddening, and it's finally pushed me too far.

"Sebhely tüz!"

I scream the first fire spell that comes to mind, one meant to maim but not necessarily to kill. A thin line of light darts out of my wand, sparks flying from the tip. As fast as the blast leaves my wand, Darius is somewhere else. It would appear vampires move faster than the speed of light, and we hadn't covered paranormal speed in my witching lessons before the attack. Poor planning, I guess.

Before I can plot my next move--having barely thought out my initial attack--I feel a burning rope wrap around my body. Timót has seized the opportunity to wrangle me, as a bright cord extends from his wand and tightly binds my arms to my sides. I look down to see my hands trapped at my thighs, my wand uselessly pointed at the stone beneath my feet.

Looks like my first instinct to keep my shit together and not lose my cool was the right call. Now I'm helpless and hopeless, with a screaming baby pinned even more tightly to my chest.

There's no longer any chance of keeping my emotions at bay, and tears roll down my cheeks and dampen Rain's little hairs. Through my blurry eyes I see Darius and Timót moving in my direction. They stand next to each other, two men who I thought were on opposite sides of this war and in opposite spectrums of my affection. Things haven't made sense for a long time now, but this is the most incomprehensible development.

"You're powerful," Timót says. "There's no question of that. But you're not prepared to fight the forces at odds with you."

"Let's go," Darius says, his black pupils looking more hollow than fierce. I don't think I even recognize this man anymore.

"Not until everyone is ready," Timót says, his eyes narrowed as he glares at the vampire. They've clearly agreed on the basics of a plan, but implicit trust is definitely lacking in this partnership.

"I don't want any foul play from the young witch. And, let me remind you," Timót says as he points his wand toward the sky, "that you're quite outnumbered."

The tip of his wand brightens, but instead of sending out a flare of light, it emits a deep, pulsing hum. The sound reverberates in my ears for a few moments, and then my eyes dart from side to side as various figures appear around us. Some wear cloaks like Timót, others are dressed in unfamiliar styles, and some don't look human at all. It's an eclectic assortment of men, now forming a circle around us and making a bad situation feel infinitely worse.

"There was no shortage in disenfranchised people and creatures wanting to join a greater cause," my father says as the strangers draw closer. "These men understand the real damage the witch's prophecy has brought. Someday you will both see what they see."

As Timót's army appears, Darius' stare never wavers from mine, though a quick blink shows me his hesitation. Whether he's trying to decide an action or swallowing his pride, I can't tell.

That momentary lapse gives me a glimmer of hope. Perhaps this is all part of a ploy--lead Timót on long enough to make him complacent, then rip him apart. After all, Darius wouldn't break a sweat killing this *Érintett* leader, I don't care how powerful he is or what army he's brought. There's no way any of these men can match the strength and cunning of the vampire prince.

The more I think about it, the more convinced I am that this is the moment my love will return to me. Timót will feel protected by his men, and that's when Darius will strike and rip his wand away. Then I'll be free to use my magic and we'll send the dragons and the *Érintett* followers running for the hills.

My hope strengthens with each second. Darius is conflicted, but not about what to do, just how to do it. Is it really this simple? All of Timót's careful planning laid to waste by trusting the wrong vampire?

He starts to walk toward me at a slow, steady gait. He'd move faster if he meant to disarm or hurt me. The pace will allow him to pick his moment, kill the lot and carry me to safety.

Any second now, he'll move at an imperceptible speed and plunge a dagger into my father's chest. Or snap his neck. Or cut his throat.

Any second now.

Any...

Second.

Darius reaches my side, his eyes devoid of feeling as they stay locked with mine. I sense the same steady stream of anger inside him, but I can't understand where it's directed. For all I know, all the hostility could be aimed at me.

He reaches up and wraps his fingers around my wand, his cool touch passing through the piece and into my hand.

Then the sensation--and my wand--are ripped away.

He walks back to Timót and unceremoniously hands over the beautiful, rare, exquisite wand I worked so hard to make. Timót grins and slides the stick into the sleeve of his cloak.

"Thank you," he says to Darius.

The vampire nods and steps away, his gaze still on me. If his plan was to kill my father and save my child, he's just made it infinitely more difficult. As for me ever forgiving him, he's made it all but impossible.

"Now we may go. Come, my *sárkányok*," Timót says, and with a wave of his arm the dragons descend to the ground around us. All of the soldiers that were just revealed begin climbing on the beasts' backs, making it clear we're traveling as a pack. The strangers throw sideways glances at me and Rain, but I can't be bothered to pull my focus away from Darius and my father. I glance between the two, not knowing who to hate more. In their own ways, both gave me life, and now it feels like they're both trying to take that away.

Timót points his wand at me and mutters *úszó*, sending me and Rain floating a few feet above the ground. "You'll ride on Agoston, Bernadette. She's the oldest of the thunder."

I feel a warm, scaly body slither beneath me as I'm lowered onto the creature's back. Agoston is bright orange with purple markings along the edges of her wings. I wonder if she was also stolen from her mother in the deep caves.

The warm tether that had just been wrapped around my torso now snakes around my legs as well, strapping me to the dragon's back. As I study my mythical transportation, my gaze drifts back to AJ's body. I have no idea if she's alive or dead, but I can't bear to leave her either way.

"Please," I say. "Can't we save her? Or at least bring her so I can say goodbye?"

Timót, now mounted on a dark blue dragon, looks at my fallen friend, his expression skeptical. Before he can answer, Darius speaks.

"If she's not already dead, the vampires would kill her quickly. Chances of survival are better if she stays here."

We're in a different world, in the middle of nowhere, with no idea what kind of help AJ might need, and he thinks it's best to just leave her? If there had been a tiny flicker of hope left that my Darius still existed, it just got snuffed out.

He climbs onto the back of a large, green beast. With his head turned away from me, I feel his soul flash through mine. When he pauses his climb, I know he feels it as well.

Forgive me, he whispers into my mind.

Hearing his voice again almost breaks me, but my anger is a living fire raging in my soul, and it consumes my grief, using the fodder of my crushed heart as fuel for growth. He's taken us past the point of no return, and no words can fix that.

Never, I whisper back.

CHAPTER TWO

My dragon keeps to the center of the pack as we fly above the rocky, colorless landscape. I realize that the overcast skies aren't part of any weather pattern, but rather the constant of the vampire realm; the sun never touches this place. There's a huge mountain range to our left with just the slightest glow along its highest ridge. I'm guessing it's daytime on the other side, but the rays never make it this far.

Because of that, I don't see any forests or fields. No bees buzzing around flowers or birds nesting in trees. There's the occasional stream of rust-colored water running through the scarred face of the hardened ground, but otherwise the view is completely desolate.

And even that water looks less... watery... somehow. Like if you tried to drink it, it would definitely stick in your throat.

It matches my mood perfectly.

I've stopped trying to feel any union with Darius. The effort is exhausting and being stonewalled only deepens the wound in my heart. My focus now rests solely on Rain, who cried herself to sleep in the first few minutes of flight. I hum different lullabies to her, hoping to keep her resting peacefully. My poor girl has endured so much already in her short life, and it feels like the worst is still to come.

No one speaks as we fly, but I get my fair share of looks from Timót's gang. There are dwarves, giants, goblins, shifters--it's a pretty diverse spread on the backs of these dragons. The only consistency is the testosterone count; every one of them is male. They all leer at me and my baby, thinking whatever awful thoughts run through the brains of the type of men who would join this type of cause. *Hey, come with me, we're going to gain power by kidnapping my daughter and stealing her kid.* Shocking that he couldn't get any women on board.

Darius rides behind me, my sense of him ebbing and flowing as we travel.

He's still distant, perhaps even more so since I stopped trying to connect with him. It's for the best, I suppose. His aloofness makes it easier to pretend he never existed.

Zev, please, I whimper in my thoughts. *Come to me.*

I wait for an answer, even though I know it's hopeless. I feel a howl inside my heart, but that's just my lonely soul crying out for its mate.

After twenty minutes or so in the air, the thunder of dragons begins to descend. We settle on another patch of gray stone, this one just as bleak and dead as every other part of these lands. On the horizon, I see the outlines of tall, angular buildings. I wonder what they look like close up, but I'm sure that question will be answered soon enough.

Timót slides off the back of his dragon and turns to face his legion, all of whom sit at various levels of attention. "Welcome to Vaemor."

The men smile, nod, some even laugh. They're excited. This is fun for them. Gross.

"I'll venture into the temple with Darius, the mother, and the child," he says, referring to me as *the mother*, like any good father would. What a brutal parenting hand I was dealt.

"You'll hear and see activity as the Ancients head to the pantheon and prepare the altar," he continues. "The moment you see my flare, flood the city with dragons."

The Ancients, huh? Vampires sound pompous as hell. Then again, how else do you describe old dudes who have been kicking around since the dawn of all things?

This loose outline of a plan doesn't make me feel particularly safe. Call me crazy, but attacking vampires with dragons right before my baby gets sacrificed sounds like an awesome way to get everyone killed. Especially my baby.

My father points his wand at me and does the little levitating trick, flying Rain and me off the dragon and onto the ground. I give the other dragons a quick glance, thinking about how sad they must be, and wondering how broken they are by this man. Like horses ridden by Confederate soldiers, unwittingly aiding an evil cause.

My insides slosh around like jello on a slick platter as dear ol' dad jerks me around, and I do my best to protect Rain, who starts to scream again as my feet hit the ground. She hasn't eaten in hours and, well, everything sucks. No real surprise she's fussy. It's a solidly relatable mood right about now.

"Can I feed my child?" I ask, keeping my tone cold and my voice quiet in an attempt to stave off the hysteria that's nearly overtaking me.

Timót's face shows a trace of empathy, either completely staged or bubbling up from some hidden part of his heart that's still human. "Of course."

The cord of light loosens around us and then slithers back into his wand. My arms are stiff from being clasped against my sides for so long, but I shake it off and unstrap Rain as fast as I can to get her feeding. Wrecked as I may be, I can still give her some contentment.

As she takes the nipple and starts to drink, I'm self-conscious about the feeding process for the first time since she was born. All of these strangers stare at me, making no effort to look away or not appear to be total creeps. So far I'm really loving the company my dad keeps.

"As soon as she finishes, let's begin the walk," Timót says to Darius. I haven't given the vampire so much as a sideways look since getting off the dragon, though I can feel his eyes boring into me like icy daggers. As long as I live, which might not be much longer, I'll never understand what happened to him. Or has he always been this much of an ass, conning me into trusting him while working backroom deals?

No. There's no way. After all, he's gaining nothing from this he didn't have to begin with. I was already pledged to him eternally, our souls fused together as one. If this has been his plan all along, he's just walking away with no baby, a fallen kingdom, and a scorned lover who wants him dead.

There has to be more to it.

Why?

I try sneaking the question in again, hoping to catch him off guard. I feel a twinge of pain from him, but nothing else. No meaningful response.

I hope Rain will feed forever so we don't have to march her into the vampire stronghold, but she pops off the breast and delivers a satisfied burp, all but announcing to my captors that she's ready to roll.

"Very good," Timót says. "Let us away to meet King Vladimir."

Darius walks briskly past me, wasting no time leading us toward the ancient temple of the vampires. This is exactly what his oath was meant to protect me and Rain from, meaning he either had his fingers crossed when he made the pledge, or magic is bullshit.

While I toil with a dismantled world and the blurred lines between fact and fiction, my father seems to be feeling more invincible by the moment. He walks in a brisk stride, strutting like he's walking into his own kingdom, not an enemy stronghold. I know he wants the strength of immortality, but I still can't fit together all the pieces of his puzzle. He's after power, but what's his strategy for getting it? What does the Last Witch mean to his efforts? What's his plan for me and my powers, especially since all I really want to do is melt him down and then pour his molten shit corpse into an ocean?

And when--Jesus Christ Almighty WHEN--did he rope in Darius? The vampire has been at my side nearly every second since we arrived in Budapest, and when he was away our souls were still connected. They've clearly had enough communication to work out a pretty involved scheme, so were they writing letters? Was it all done while I was away with Zev? Or Rune? Did it happen because I was away with another prince and Darius got jealous?

I fight the urge to search the vampire's mind for answers, because I know he'll just shut me out and hurt me more. I can only hope I get some clarity before I detonate like an atomic bomb and kill everyone. I'm not quite there yet, but I've got enough confidence in my powers to at least give it a shot when the moment arrives.

As we start down a slight incline that leads to the city, I can finally study the fascinating metropolis a bit more. The structures are very gothic, with tall points and turrets capping all the roofs. The hardest thing to reconcile is the lack of roads. One building merges into the next, with no room for vehicles or foot traffic. It strikes me as odd until I notice the vampires flashing about above the different premises. They leap and bound, grabbing hold of the erected pinnacles and then entering through horizontal doorways. I open my mind a little and it makes more sense; why travel on roads when cars would slow you down?

It doesn't take long for a few vampires to notice our arrival. One by one, figures clad in dark velvet and pristine silks begin zipping over to us, standing along the perimeter of the city while they assess the visitors. I see one vampire whisper to another, and the second is gone in a flash. If I have to guess, he's recognized Darius and is off to fetch someone with authority.

More and more vampires join the crowd until there are at least fifty, with many more watching from a distance. I wonder if every envoy receives this big a greeting party. Now that I think about it, Vaemor probably doesn't get many visitors; it's all dead, devoid of sunlight, and full of vampires. Not a lot of travelers passing through these parts, for business or pleasure, I imagine.

Excruciatingly long seconds pass in silence, with Darius and Timót in a winner-take-all staring contest with the locals. Finally, I see a figure in dark robes exit one of the taller buildings. A few deferential men walk behind him, I'm guessing they're guards or servants. He walks with another, younger man, dressed in more modern attire, gold trim lining his black coat. The closer he gets, the more handsome and stylish he appears, almost as though he could be--

"Brother."

He addresses Darius before I can finish connecting the dots. Darius doesn't say anything back, only offering a swift nod before moving his gaze to the older vampire, who can only be the king.

"You've been away for some time, my son," Vladimir says, his wrinkled face and pitchy voice the epitome of villainous. "It seemed you had strayed far from the prophecy."

"Well," Darius says, clearing his throat in that way people do when they're fighting the urge to say what they really think. "It seems there's no such thing as a tidy ending to a prophecy as old as time."

Darius' father smiles, making sure to show his long, yellowed fangs as he does. I can't imagine how many lives those daggers have taken, and I try to push the thought out of my head before I start doing any nauseating calculations.

The vampire king turns his attention to me, the hideous smile still resting on his face. "Here you are, in the... flesh." He takes his time with the last word and lets his eyes drift over my neck and down to my child. It puts me a big step closer to pulling the pin on atomic bomb Bernie.

I sense an urgency in my legs to step forward, to move closer to the monster as he looks back up from my baby and into my eyes. It's a familiar feeling, and I know immediately he's trying to compel me. I stare back at him, willing my legs to stay right where they are. I push back with my mind, fighting to compel him instead. After a few grueling seconds, the pull in my legs fades away, as does the vampire's smile.

"Hm," he says as he studies me. "I suppose I should have expected as much from a witch who is so desirable. Very good, girl. This means the blood of your child will be that much stronger."

Leaving me with that charming sentiment, the king turns to Timót and stares expectantly.

My father quickly picks up his cue. "My name is Timót. I sired the mother of the Last Witch and brokered the deal that brought her safely here. I've been promised eternal life in exchange for the child."

Vladimir quickly looks from Timót to Darius, cocking an eyebrow. "Brokered a deal, Darius? A very bold move for someone so eager to toy with treason."

As mad as I already am, I feel my blood boil a little more, and I know it's Darius that I feel. I may never understand what's driving his decision-making in all this, but it has nothing to do with loyalty to his father.

Before Darius can speak, his brother steps in on his behalf. "I think we can trust that the challenges presented have been substantial, father." The brother looks between me and Darius, trying to glean a little insight from our expressions. There's probably too much going on for him to get a clear picture.

I'm certainly clueless about half of what's happening, particularly if it involves my traitorous vampire lover.

"This is why Darius was sent and not you, Emerus," King Vladimir says with a grunt. "You try too hard to see the good. And you may have rubbed off on your brother."

Vladimir returns his attention to my father, sizing him up and weighing the bargaining chip. "Any reason not to simply kill you and take the child on my own terms?"

"Because..." It's Darius speaking up on Timót's behalf, which takes everyone by surprise. "I've made a pledge and it deserves to be acknowledged. If the vampires are saved by the blood of the child, why defy the wishes of the man who helped fulfill the prophecy in our favor?"

Darius standing up to his king father on Timót's behalf instead of fighting to save Rain causes me more pain than I thought I could feel. I was sure my senses had been bludgeoned into numbness, but apparently I still have the capacity to break further.

Vladimir sneers at Darius, then shrugs. "Very well. No use wasting time arguing with your flawed reasoning, son. Best to bring the child to the temple with haste. Emerus, fetch the Ancients. We will begin immediately. We've no time to waste."

Vladimir turns and heads back toward the city walls. Emerus lingers a second longer, looking into the eyes of his brother, then he disappears in a blur. By this time, I can see hundreds upon hundreds of the city's residents watching from the tops of their buildings. Word has spread and they're all stepping out to bear witness.

The nearest vampires follow their king, throwing the occasional look over their shoulder to see the Last Witch. The sacrifice that will give them the power they've desired for hundreds of thousands of years.

Timót comes to my side and takes me by the arm, leading me after the pack. Before I can lash out at him for the unwanted touch, he mutters under his breath. "I'm only standing close to protect you. While the vampires don't care what happens to the Last Witch's mother, I do."

I can't fight or argue with him, because even if he doesn't give two shits about my life, he's definitely not wrong about the vampires. To them, I'm just a body waiting to be drained. I can see it in their anxious, bloodshot eyes.

"You might not want to trust me," my father goes on, "but you've heard the plan and know of my fleet. I'm your only hope for survival."

I will say this: my father is the biggest piece of shit and worst father since Cronus. He's also pretty smart and seems to have his bases covered in this impossible quest.

As we head toward the entrance of a small building, more and more vampires circle around us. It doesn't take long for me to feel a modicum of comfort having Timót by my side, which I find disgustingly ironic. The vampires don't bother to keep their distance, and I can feel some of them breathing against my neck and shoulders. I keep my arms wrapped tightly around Rain, who's thankfully fallen back to sleep.

We walk through the rounded doorway of the stone building. The entrance leads to a stairway that descends into the rocky ground, and I'm suddenly worried that Timót's plan has a giant flaw--how are we going to get a squadron of dragons underground?

The vampires lead us down the steps and into the darkness. Before we get too deep, the stairs turn into a level hallway. Looking past the people in front of me, I can see a sliver light trickling in from an opening at the end of the passage. The light gets steadier as we get closer, and at the end of the hall we step into a giant, open room. The ceiling above rounds into a dome, with an open mouth at the top, which allows me to breathe a small sigh of relief. Dragon door: check.

Then I see what stands in the middle of the space, and my breath catches again.

A large, stone slab sits in the center of a raised platform. The stone is at a slight incline, with grooves running down toward the vertical sides. Those deep creases lead to more lines, spider-webbing into a vast network that surrounds the altar.

A series of channels.

Below the altar.

For my baby's blood to drip.

Do not *let this happen,* I plead to Darius.

It's too late.

The words send a shock of horror through my body. It's not just the sentiment, but the voice that's doing the speaking.

Welcome to my kingdom. Vladimir's voice pierces my mind, cutting it open to speak as he faces me from across the room while sitting in a large, obsidian throne.

I try my best to wall off my mind, praying I'll never have to hear his thoughts again and hoping to God he's not going to keep listening to mine.

The vampires that walked into the temple with us have climbed into seats above in rafters that circle about the room. We're on a stage, everyone here to watch something abjectly grotesque.

Through an entrance at the other end of the temple, Emerus leads in a trio of men, their faces obscured by hoods. They move over to three stone benches that are stationed around the altar. I can't see their eyes, but I know each of them is staring at me. Staring at my baby.

My body jolts when two hands tightly grip my arms. I struggle briefly to break free but it's no use. I'm no match against vampire super strength, and I feel even weaker when my boiling blood shows that the one gripping me is Darius. A touch I used to long for now pushes me closer to my deepest despair. As he holds me, I feel the straps of the baby harness loosen and fall away from Rain. Vladimir coaxes the air with his fingers, controlling her little body as she lifts from the harness and floats toward the altar. A muffled sob escapes my lips as I watch her move away from me, my heart bursting from the gut-wrenching fear that I've touched my darling girl for the last time.

I glance down at my hands to see a familiar glow building within. I'm not sure I'll be able to fend off the evil surrounding me for long, but I'm damn willing to light this place on fire and see what happens.

The moment I entertain the thought of putting my magic to use, a pair of fangs diving into my neck sucks all the air from that idea. Darius drinks away my magic, my blood, and my hope.

No, I think, perhaps not even audibly as I feel myself drain.

Wait, he says in response.

I don't know what it means, but I'm surprised to finally get any connection from him in return. Wait for what? For my child to die? That's exactly what I'm not willing to wait on.

"Do you plan to save any for the rest of us, Darius?" Vladimir's joke is met with a chorus of laughter from the gallery above. My eyes open as Darius releases me, and I see that Rain now lies flat on the stone altar, the Ancients standing about and inspecting her.

"Just keeping her powers from overwhelming and killing you, father," Darius snaps back. There's no love lost between these two, and I'm not sure why he didn't just let me burn the piece of shit to a crisp.

The Ancients move back to their benches, having completed whatever inspection needed to happen. Rain is now awake but completely still, as she looks around but makes no noise. She's still under the control of Vladimir and I know she's terrified.

Everyone's attention shifts as my sleaze of a father steps forward. "I have fulfilled my end of the agreement," he says. "Now I expect the same."

The room falls silent as Vladimir stands and approaches Timót, the vampire king taller than I realized as he towers over my father--not a small man himself.

A kind of ancient power radiates out of him, and I bristle at the nearness of it even though he's still several feet away from me.

I try to study everything and everyone, to learn what I can that might be of use in rescuing my baby.

It's so hard to tear my eyes off her, but I know my focus should be elsewhere if I have any hope of getting us out of here.

The king leans in to speak to Timót, his voice cold and bloodthirsty. "Not everyone survives a Turning," he hisses.

To my father's credit, he doesn't flinch. He's still an ass of the highest order, but it's good to see someone standing up to Darius's super awful dad.

Looks like I'm not the only one with daddy issues.

"I'm prepared to accept any consequences of this decision," Timót says with an air of confidence that doesn't sound fake. He really believes he's going to win.

That might be the scariest part of all of this. His unwavering confidence in the face of the king of vampires.

"Very well," the ancient vampire says. "I will honor my son's word--foolish though it may be--and give you our gift that very few receive. Let us hope you are worthy."

My father just smiles, so freaking smug in his worthiness.

My heart thuds in my chest as I watch my child, praying for a way to save her before it's too late. Hating Darius for taking the only means I had of protecting us. How could he condemn us to this fate? None of this makes sense.

Vladmir's teeth extend into predatory sharpness and pierce Timót's jugular. My father's face is stoic as the vampire feeds on him, but after a few moments it's clear the blood loss is having an excruciating effect.

The color drains from his face at an alarming rate. His body is shaking, and he looks ready to collapse at any moment.

Is Vladimir going to kill my father? Like, for good?

I want him to. I want my dad to pay for what he's done with his life. At the same time, it can't happen yet. Not until he's done his part to save me and Rain from a city full of vampires.

The king lets my father fall to the ground like a sack of potatoes. I flinch, but I don't feel any sympathy for my mom's sperm donor.

I might have. Once upon a time. When I was a little girl with fantastical and silly dreams about who and what my father was. An astronaut stuck in space? A prince in exile who couldn't risk our safety by coming to us? A spy who lived a secret life?

But adulthood disabused me of those silly notions.

What I do feel is an urgent need to do something, anything, to save my daughter while the vampires are distracted by this charming ceremony.

Throwing caution to the wind, I'm about to rush the altar and take my chances, magic or no, when a crushing grip squeezes my forearm painfully.

Wait.

Again, only one word. No context. No explanation. No nothing.

This is utter bullshit.

I let out a string of expletives into his mind that would make a sailor blush as I try to yank out of his grip to no avail.

So help me god if anything happens to my child I will stake your cold, dead heart, then behead you, then burn your body and scatter your ashes to the four corners of the earth and beyond.

I feel only sadness from him, but then it's cut abruptly like a faucet being turned off.

My father moans, distracting me from my focus on Darius and back to the scene before us.

Vladmir is leaning over Timót, holding a bleeding wrist to his mouth. My father is drinking the vampire king's blood.

The two of them exchanging blood can't be enough to turn him. Darius and I have done that so many times, I'd for sure be a vampire by now if that were all there was to it.

There is more to it, the king whispers into my mind as he locks eyes with me. I clearly failed to keep that damn wall up.

He smiles in a way that's totally creepy, and then very viciously snaps my father's neck, killing him instantly.

And with that final, brutal act, the man who had been nothing more to me than a childhood curiosity turned nightmare, slumps to the ground.

I suck in my breath as Vladimir stands, his thin lips twisted into a gloating smile as he turns his attention to Rain.

CHAPTER THREE

I stand frozen in place, stunned by what has just happened. Even if Darius does loosen his grip, I won't be able to move.

"And now, the ceremony," Vladimir says.

The three eldest vampires begin to chant, softly and quietly, and the rest of the temple falls silent. Aside from the king and the Ancients, every vampire crosses their arms in an X over their chest and stares down at the ground. The uniformity of it is impressive, like they've been running daily prophecy fulfillment drills for hundreds of years. Shit, maybe they have.

Just as Vladimir takes in a deep breath, ready to launch into something terrible, Darius interrupts. "Father, do we not first wish to bless the mother and child, as the prophecy reading would dictate. Lest we waylay our plans entirely through improper planning."

Vladimir holds up a hand, pausing the chanting. "You are quite right, son. It seems thousands of years of waiting have me acting rashly. We would be remiss in taking any shortcuts on this most auspicious occasion. Priests, bring forth the unholy waters for anointing."

Unholy waters? Oh hell no, are these dead assholes trying to give me and my kid a reverse baptism? My Catholicism has long since lapsed, but even I don't want to mess up my afterlife chances, especially with how frequently my child and I seem to flirt with death.

Two priests in long gray robes step forward holding small pewter bowls filled with--apparently--unholy water. I don't even want to know what makes water unholy. I also have questions about what makes these guys priests.

As one moves toward Rain and the other toward me, they chant together in a strange, ominous language. When each priest arrives at his mark, they draw water from the bowls and use the pads of their thumbs to paint a half circle with a dot in the center on our foreheads.

I don't expect to feel anything but annoyed, but a zing pulses in my spine, then fades, and I shudder.

What did they do to me? And more importantly, what did they do to Rain?

Darius keeps his grip on my arms, and I start to pull against him, ready to die if it means I go out trying to save my baby girl. No matter how hard I strain, he keeps me still. I doubt he's even putting in much effort.

"The mother and child are now duly blessed," Vladimir says as the priests walk back into the shadows. "We may begin."

The chanting resumes, now accompanied by a low hum from all the vampires who continue looking at the ground with their arms crossed.

I stop fighting against Darius when it's clear I'm just wasting my strength, and I turn my attention to Timót. No one else is paying any attention to my father, as he's pretty dead looking. Maybe it takes a long time for the transition to happen, or maybe all Vladimir did was kill him for good. In any case, the vampires pay Timót no mind, so when his body twitches, I'm the only one who sees it.

My eyes dart around the room, trying to gauge where we are in the process. Vladimir still stands away from Rain, and all the vampires have intensified their humming. The vigor of the ceremony is really ramping up, as is my heartbeat.

When my eyes shift back to Timót I fight the urge to gasp as he blinks. His eyes slowly focus on me... and then he smiles.

Daddy is back, and now in addition to magic, dragons, and an army, he's also got access to all the cool vampire tricks.

He looks toward the opening in the ceiling. He has a vampire on either side of him, but they have their arms crossed and their eyes closed. To the vampires, this ceremony is about the survival of their kind, so commitment levels are very high. That makes it easy for my father to sneak the tip of his wand out of his sleeve and point it to the sky. I try to blank out my mind in case the king might be looking into my thoughts.

Fortunately, Vladimir is entirely focused on Rain, now walking toward her with a shimmering dagger in his right hand.

"From the beginning," the vampire king announces to the room, "we have been shunned by our creators, and feared by the other creations. Our powers were seen as a plight on the world, not a gift. Our demands for respect were met with calls for our heads. No more."

He continues his slow walk toward my baby, his stare frighteningly entranced by her presence. I sneak another glance at Timót and see that his lips are subtly moving while a tiny speck of light drifts from his wand toward the open ceiling.

"The Fates gave us life in death, they created the prophecy for all to see, and now we will make our realm absolute."

At the edge of the altar, Vladimir raises the dagger over his head. The humming from the room grows louder, and a scream that has been brewing in my knotted stomach is about to leave my mouth when Timót shatters the silence.

"Excuse me," he says, getting to his feet and brushing off his knees like someone who just tripped and is apologizing for creating some commotion. A collective gasp ripples through the temple, and the rage on the king's face can be felt by everyone.

"You dare interrupt?!" Vladimir spits.

"Sorry, just woke," my father says, feigning ignorance. "Has the ceremony started?"

The king's lip curls and his disgusting fangs extend, making it clear what he wants to do to Timót. "I should have killed you the moment you arrived."

"Perhaps," dad says with a shrug. "A bit late for that now."

"There are still ways, you fool. Bring him to me!"

The vampires at either side of my father reach for Timót, but with equal deftness he steps back, grabs them by the arms and throws them to the ground. In the same instant, Darius has released me and is on top of the fallen attackers, keeping them away from Timót.

The king glares at his son, surprised and appalled by his actions. "What are you doing?"

"He's only taking precautions," Timót says, his wand aimed at the king. "As he knows what comes next."

Right on cue, an ear-piercing roar echoes through the room. All faces turn upward in time to see dozens of nose-diving dragons fly through the opening in the dome, swarming the temple.

My eyes immediately shoot back to Rain, completely exposed in the center of the chamber. Vladimir stands next to her. I see terror in his eyes as more beasts flood in through the open ceiling. As the vampire king moves out of the center of the room, I sprint to the altar, practically throwing my body over Rain in case a burst of fire is about to hit. As soon as she's wrapped in my arms, someone lifts me and starts to carry us away. I expect to see Darius, or perhaps Timót. Instead I'm shocked to see Emerus rushing me off to the sidelines. He tucks us into a small recession in the stone wall, out of the reach of the dragons and hopefully unseen by the vampires.

"The child cannot die like this."

Adding the qualifier "like this" takes away from the kindness of the gesture, but I'll take what I can get. Emerus flashes away from me, presumably to save himself.

I look above to see that Timót has mounted his dragon, but the creature stays on the ground, marching over to the three Ancients who are pinned in the corner. A few vampires run to their defense, only to be lit on fire by the scorching dragon breath. There's a strange moment where the elderly vampires seem to accept their fate and bow their heads. I wonder briefly if Timót might spare them, but that thought dies more quickly than the Ancients as a stream of fire erupts from the dragon's mouth and consumes them.

While the undead relics flail, Timót turns his attention back to the altar where Rain had been. The look on his face is one of unbridled power. His plan has worked and his life is eternal. He believes he's the most powerful man to ever grace the universe... and there's a chance he's right.

He steadies his wand and aims it at the altar--an ancient piece of stone built for the sole purpose of staging my baby's death. In this moment, I'm one-hundred-percent team psycho dad.. I want him to wreck that goddamn thing. Don't leave anything behind but dust. And then take that dust and make it more dust until it's microscopic. Then scatter that to all the worlds so this monstrosity can never be rebuilt.

"*Elpusztítani teljes,*" he yells, and a ripple of red light bursts forward and into the stone. There's the briefest pause before the altar explodes into tiny particles, floating into the surrounding space and coating everything nearby in tiny flecks of debris.

Good goddamn riddance.

Timót gives one last look at the spot where the altar used to be, admiring his destruction, before turning back to find his next target--King Vladimir.

The vampire leader has been carefully dodging flames and alluding fighters, but making no move to escape the fray. His fangs are out, looking longer than ever, ready to kill anything that comes near.

"I'm sorry things haven't gone quite to plan, Vladimir." My father approaches the king, his dragon ready to do its worst. I wonder if someone as powerful as Vladimir might be able to survive a blast of dragon fire. The way his eyes keep jumping between Timót and the giant creature's nostrils makes me think he's not feeling too confident.

"What shall you do?" Vladimir asks. "Run off with the child? Hide away until the vampires find you? Don't think for a second that we won't."

"But whatever for?" Timót says with a laugh. "You've no altar. No Ancients to perform your rituals. Your poor interpretation of the prophecy has no chance for fulfillment."

The king snarls, taking a step closer to my father and the dragon. Maybe I was wrong about him being afraid. Maybe nothing can kill this old monster.

"Altars can be rebuilt," he hisses. "Songs from old lore can be rediscovered."

Timót nods, a pompous smile on his face.

"That's all true. Perhaps things will go exactly as you say. But you certainly won't be around to see it."

His face turns from cocky to crazed as he wrenches back on the reins around the dragon's head and a massive swath of fire circles around the king. I watch as Vladimir stands in the fire, his body not moving. He's either invincible or welcoming death, and I won't know until the flames subside.

But that might never happen.

The dragon continues to scorch the king, moving closer as the hot blue fire wraps around the vampire. Now I can hear Vladimir's screams, though his body is unmoving. The dragon leans closer still, now practically on top of its target. Timót keeps his grip on the reins, not letting up at all.

With their faces inches apart, the dragon fire finally stops. I hold my breath as I wait to see what's become of the king, but I'm never given the chance. In one swift, gruesome motion, Timót's giant creature takes the vampire king into its mouth, its colossal teeth shredding charred flesh and crunching through old bones.

No more wondering about the vampire king.

I duck back into my hiding place as Timót looks around the room. I'm not sure how much more killing he wants to do before he starts searching for me.

The vampires have largely fled from the room. The fiery attack has forced them away, and only a few fighters remain. I glance around, looking for Darius, and while I can't see him, I feel him more strongly. I feel less anger, and a sense of calm. The timing feels odd, what with dragons everywhere breathing out fire and ending the previously endless lives of vampires.

Where are you?

I don't know why I ask, because I hate him. Still, something about the change has me wondering enough to ask. I'm not sure I'll get a response, so when I hear the words, and the voice that puts them in my brain, tears of hope and joy burst out of me.

He's with us, love. We're coming for you.

CHAPTER FOUR

Z *ev.*
Oh my God, Zev.

I hug Rain closer to my chest, my tears spilling onto her little head, my heart pounding through my ribs.

They're here. And Darius is with them? Confusion and anger war within me, even as an actual literal war is waging all around me.

I slink as far into the wall's recession as I can to keep my baby and myself safe. My magic is still weak from the feeding Darius did, giving me yet another reason to forgive him never. He fed to disarm me. His intention was to weaken me. As my baby lay on the sacrificial altar, he sought to make me powerless.

Wait for us. Stay safe.

Zev's voice breaks me from a spiral into despair. Having my wolf mate so close gives me hope I didn't have a few minutes ago. I can feel his presence in my mind, in my heart, and it renews my strength and helps heal a little of the pain caused by Darius.

Or at least it helps me avoid falling into pieces at the very worst possible time.

My confused and broken heart does not get to dictate my child's survival right now.

Pushing my emotional wounds to the side, I refocus on the only thing that matters: getting Rain out of here safely.

I strap her to my chest to free my arms. I need my wand, which is still tucked up the sleeve of my undead dad.

This is… tricky. He didn't want me or Rain to get killed by vampires, but only because he wants to force us to come with his weird tribe. If I go after him to get my wand, I'll probably just end up magically roped to a dragon again.

New plan. I skip the wand and get the hell out of dodge. Whatever problems arise can be figured out by future me, who will hopefully not be in the middle of getting blown up and attacked.

Though given my recent track record, that's not a guarantee. After sitting with it for a few seconds, the thought of being without my wand seems a bit calamitous.

I frantically review my options again--hoping something new pops out that makes this an easier decision--as I wait to see what Zev and the others are planning. Taking in the scene around me only makes things worse.

Above are fire breathing dragons.

Within are bloodthirsty vampires.

Without... is a desolate, dry land no human can survive.

Somehow I have to get back to my own world.

If there's a portal here, there must be one back.

Unless Zev has a better plan.

I'm really hoping Zev has a better plan.

Zev? I ask, the desperation and fear I feel bleeding into even my mental voice.

We've got a plan, love. Stay where you are. I'm coming for you.

He's coming for us. I kiss Rain's head and slink further into the shadows. It feels too passive, and part of me wants to dive into the fray and kick some ass. But without any control over my magic, I'd be the one getting my ass kicked.

Even with the wand, it'd be a tough round that wouldn't leave me unscathed. If it were just me, that'd be one thing, but... I look down at my child and my entire soul fills with a raw need to protect this small being. This little person I love more than life. More than myself. More than anything in this universe or beyond.

The feeling of that love fills me so completely that it warms me from within.

It takes me a moment to realize it's not just love that's filling me.

Rain is glowing, her skin a shimmering pearl in the darkness.

And so is mine.

My magic is ramping back up at an alarming rate.

Shit.

Back to Plan A. I need to get my wand back.

Zev, I'm turning into a night light. I need to move.

He lets out a protective growl. *I'm almost there.*

I look down at my hands and shake my head. *We don't have time.*

It's not just the lightning storm exploding under my skin, but the fact that I'm a glowing target for anyone who wants to find me or Rain. And our enemy list is pretty long.

I have to move. If Zev can track me this far, a hundred more yards shouldn't present a problem. I need to find my father and get these powers under control.

No more accidentally burning down ancient groves or singeing people I love.

I worked too hard to get my wand to come back to this again.

I dart out of the nook I've been sheltering in and scan the area, looking for my father and trying to avoid being seen, which seems mostly impossible at this point. I'm the only glowing witch in the joint.

It takes my eyes a moment to adjust, with smoke billowing, fires burning, dragons screeching, people on both sides screaming, yelling, dying.

But it's clear which side is holding stronger. Which side is sustaining fewer casualties. Which side will walk away the victor.

My father's side. And there he is, riding above it all on his stolen dragon, his wand out, his eyes surveying the carnage.

"The Eternal Night of the Ancients is over!" My father screams, to cheers from his army, even as they continue to slaughter the remaining vampires. By the body count, many have fled or been killed. Only a few remain, scrambling away from the flames, trying to take one last life before they die for real.

"It is a new era!" he says to another round of hoots and hollers.

I see my wand, the tip just visible at the edge of his sleeve, though I have no way of reaching him while he's on a dragon. I need him to notice me and come.

A thought occurs to me, though it seems too easy. But what if?

I focus my attention on my father, trying to catch his eye. If the king could get into my mind, and so can Darius, maybe Timót can as well? Can I get his attention? I don't love the idea of bringing him into my head, but if it helps me lure him somewhere discreet where I can retrieve my wand, then it's worth it.

Father. Can you hear my thoughts? Father? I'm in danger. I need my wand or I'll lose control and destroy us all. Help!

It doesn't take much in the way of acting to inflect my plea with sufficient desperation and need. I have both in spades at the moment. But it still makes me cringe to ask for his help.

Though technically I'm just insisting he return what he stole from me.

His head jerks and I can see that he heard me, or at least sensed my presence.

When his eyes land on mine, I know he got my message.

Help.

I say it again, to hit that note a little harder. When he directs his dragon down toward me, I turn and run back into the tunnels so none of the remaining vampires or *Érintett* will see us.

I have to trust that Timót will follow me and he'll try to keep us safe.

Fortunately, I'm like a walking LED bulb. My father had to have noticed and will assume something's wrong.

I squat in the corner of an empty hall with Rain, hiding in a carved out nook and waiting for Zev and Timót to find us. Time seems to pass in slow motion, and I resist the urge to crawl out and go looking for one or both of them.

They can each find me. I will wait.

Bullshit. My skin is getting hot enough to melt my baby, I'm not waiting for anyone.

Just as I start back toward the main room, Timót arrives on foot and alone, the halls too narrow for his dragon to pass through.

As I'd hoped.

I hold out my hands, giving him a good look at my skin, at the electricity zapping through my fingers. "I'm not safe. To her or you or anyone here. I need my wand back."

He cocks his head and smiles. "Look at you. So much raw power and you don't even know what to do with it. This is why we are the perfect team." His eyes glow with a maniacal light that does nothing to win me over. "I can help guide that power. I've had to work harder than most to cultivate my magic, and I can teach you how to tap into it, how to use it to create a better world."

"A better world? For who?" I bite my tongue before I say more. I still need my wand, and getting him pissed off at me isn't the way to make that happen.

He pulls the wand out of his pocket, and my whole body responds, lurching forward almost involuntarily, desperate to hold it, to channel my magic into and through it.

"This is a crutch they gave you to weaken you. You should let your power out!"

This isn't the direction I was expecting the conversation to go and my stomach sinks when I realize what he wants from me.

He doesn't know that getting it could kill him as well.

Maybe he thinks he's invincible now, and he largely is. But as he's just seen, vampires have vulnerabilities. The fire released from my magic could take him out lickity split.

As my hands snap, crackle and pop, I hold them out and toward him, pushing the intention of my powers toward my father. Magic shoots out of my hands, uncontrolled, and flies everywhere, in all directions. Nothing in this hall is flammable but a rug hanging on one of the walls, and it catches fire instantly, nearly singeing my father who has to step to the side to avoid getting burned.

Instead of being scared, he claps.

"Don't you see, Bernadette? We can tap into this and become the most powerful sorcerers the world has ever seen."

"We?" I ask.

He nods. "Of course. Ever since I felt my first surge of power, I've studied the witch's ability to transfer and share magic. You don't have to bear this burden alone. If you only allow me to help, together we could do great things."

My stomach clenches at his words. He wants to steal my magic.

"Sorry, I've already had my powers stolen once this lifetime. That's quite enough."

He frowns. "I would not be stealing your magic. Only helping to give it focus. You would still be the most powerful witch in the world."

"I need my wand," I say, skipping the argument. "Please."

I hold out my hand as another random lightning burst shoots out and hits his right shoe, burning the leather with a hiss.

I'm close. Zev's voice is a reassurance I can't let show on my face.

I just need to keep Timót focused on me.

"You don't need it. You just think you do," he says, frustrating me beyond comprehension. Thanks for the mansplain about my own powers, dad. Just give me my damn wand. I work hard not to let him hear my thoughts, though, since I'm still playing the nice game.

As I open my mouth to plead some more, my wand suddenly travels from Timót's hand to mine. My look of surprise is matched by my father's, and the flurry of activity in my blood tells me a certain vampire I know has joined the conversation.

Darius moves in a blur and stands beside me, his mind still shuttered, but this time I feel regret and pain and sadness. I can't let myself soften or think about him. Not yet. Not while everything is still so volatile.

Instead, I channel all my hurt, all my rage, all my fear and pain into my wand and point it at my dad. "Call off your men, father. Release your dragons and surrender. I have every right to kill you here and now, and unless you beg forgiveness and then try to right some of your wrongs, I will."

My father laughs, which is not at all the reaction I was hoping for. "Dear girl. You're still not seeing straight. In that case, I'll take what's mine by rights and go. You'll change your mind eventually."

He whistles and the stone walls around us begin to shake, the rocks cracking as dust falls around us.

I try to take cover, but it's impossible to find anywhere that's safe. It feels like the entire structure is collapsing.

As the ceiling begins to crumble and stone falls in large chunks around us, a dragon pushes through the rubble and my father grabs hold and mounts.

I scream and begin shooting him with my wand, aiming all that pent up magic his way, but he calmly flicks his wand and creates a protective shield that deflects my blast.

As I continue my attack, his dragon blows fire between Darius and myself, sending us diving in opposite directions. I hit the ground, understanding his intention--he's slowly separating us with uncrossable lines of fire.

Darius' mind breaks open, his fear for my safety palpable. *Bernie!*

His panic spurs me to move, and I leap away from a wall just as it falls. Enormous columns are crashing to the ground and light from the sky above has started peeking into the dark halls. This ancient chamber isn't going to last much longer.

I feel Zev in my mind, and Rune's calming presence nearby. I know they're all here, but the fire separates us. I can barely hear anything over the sound of walls crumbling and dragons screeching. It's hard to see or breathe with smoke burning my eyes and choking me. I cover Rain loosely with my shirt and try to block the worst of it.

With all my senses a jumbled mess, I'm taken off guard when my father rushes me with his dragon, zapping the straps to my child carrier and swooping by to grab her from my arms.

The girth of the dragon knocks me back, and I stumble to the ground as my baby is wrenched away from me. Giant gusts of wind send dirt and ash into my face as the dragon pumps its mighty wings, lifting higher, taking my daughter further from my arms.

"No!"

I react without thinking, jumping to my feet and pointing my wand at the ground.

"Dob val vel tűz!"

A blast of light shoots into the stone beneath my feet, propelling me like a rocket toward the flying beast above. When it comes to saving Rain, I will not hesitate to turn myself into a missile.

The jolt of magic launches me at a horrifying speed, giving Timót no time to get away. When it's within reach, I hold my wand between my teeth and grab the harness around the dragon as tightly as I can, then start pulling myself up toward Rain, tucked tightly under my father's arm. I'm reminded of how horrified I was when my car seat back home would jiggle slightly, and now she's unsecured on a dragon a hundred feet in the air.

Timót's focus is forward, not having expected me to fly at him. I didn't really expect it either, but here I am, inches away from taking my child back.

As my hand finds her leg, Timót notices the stowaway on his dragon.

"How in the name of--"

Everything happens so quickly. I let go of the harness while pulling Rain free from my father's grip. As we start to fall back, I unleash everything I have into my father, blasting him directly in the chest. I don't use an incantation or try to summon a particular spell, I just shoot pure energy into this man and pray that it hurts.

Then I scream.

And we fall.

I look up into the sky, no idea how far the ground is below me, no idea when I'll feel the crushing impact as my body connects with stone.

I wrap my body around my daughter, fearing what will happen next.

In trying to save her, I have killed us.

And then my body hits... but it's not the rocky floor I expected.

Strong arms wrap around me, pulling me close as our momentum changes from straight down to a new, lateral, safe trajectory.

I squeeze my eyes closed, clutching Rain, tears leaking onto my cheeks.

All anger is gone, for the moment at least, as the familiar voice settles into my mind once more.

I'm sorry.

Darius... my thought trails off as I feel the motion stop and we come to rest on the solid earth. I look down at Rain, her eyes open and yet she's somehow not crying. Either she's scared stiff or she's getting too used to almost dying.

I look up from her and into the face that I'd come to love, then come to hate, and now can't understand.

Darius stares back at me, his dark eyes flooded with sorrow, remorse, and relief. Looking into those striking eyes, it's clear he thought he might lose me.

We hold eye contact a moment longer, then Darius drops to a knee.

And weeps.

CHAPTER FIVE

I stare at Darius knelt before me, head bowed, body trembling as he sobs. The sight stirs up a mix of empathy and apathy within me. My feelings are too conflicted for my own good, but one thing I am super sure of is that I'm tremendously relieved Rain is okay and I'm still alive.

I look to the sky and sigh with relief as I watch the dragons fly away. They started their departure as soon as Timót grabbed Rain, and now the massive fleet is headed off without the baby they did all this for.

Even at this distance, I can see the limp body of my father riding side saddle on his dragon. I'm under no illusions that I've killed him, but ecstatic that I at least knocked him out. I wonder how far they'll get before realizing their leader is unconscious.

With or without my baby, their victory isn't contested. In one vicious and bloodthirsty stroke, the *Érintett* crushed their fiercest opponent. The Ancients are nothing more than ash, and their king rots in the belly of a dragon.

I shake with rage as I think about how close he came to getting Rain as well.

After how close she came to dying on that altar.

And it's all because Darius betrayed me.

He slowly looks up from the ground, his face soaked with tears. My eyes bore into his, and though a big part of me just wants to kiss and hold him, I take a small perverse pleasure in the pain I see in his eyes.

My rage takes a momentary respite when I see Zev through the flames, his eyes frantically searching for me. When his gaze locks on mine, it's magnetic. He leaps through the fire in a move that forces my heart to skip a beat, and then is by my side, our mate bond like a pulse I can feel in every inch of myself.

He grabs me brusquely and wastes no time kissing me. It's a brief, passionate kiss, then he pulls away to look at my baby. He kisses Rain's head and whispers to her. "You're the bravest little girl in the world."

His words make my lips twitch into an almost-smile sprung from a grateful mom heart. How I've missed my wolf in all this chaos.

I nearly jump out of my shoes when Rune lands by Zev's side, having leapt over the fires to be near me. He's clearly seen his share of battle in recent minutes, his elvish clothing stained with soot and blood.

My vision blurs at the sight of my beautiful fae, and he immediately cups my face, sending waves of calm through both me and Rain, who pauses her sniffling to look at the man who's taken such good care of her.

I'm reluctant to give her to anyone, to ever release her from my own arms, but I must. "Will you check her? Make sure she's okay? See if anything's wrong, aside from her desperate need for a bath and bed."

Zev grunts. "We could all do with a rinse."

Rune nods and gently lifts the child from my arms, and responds to my unspoken concern. "I'll look her over, but be assured, she has a strong constitution. She's a powerful witch in her own right."

I hope that's true. I need it to be true.

Our little tribe is complete again... except for AJ. I try to hold off thinking about my friend, because I know if I give into the grief I'll never stop. I can't go there yet, not when there's so much to say. To do. Too many questions to ask.

But I'm shaking, and the adrenaline that got me through this is fading fast.

Darius, somewhat reconnected to me but still so distant, lifts me into his arms and starts walking me through the rubble.

"Put me down."

He ignores me, and Zev chuckles. I glare at the wolf. "You want to be on my shit list too?"

He shrugs. "You should hear him out, Bernie. He deserves that at least."

We climb out of the wreckage, Rune carrying Rain, who looks content in his arms, Darius carrying me--a definitely not content expression on my face--and Zev scanning the area for any remaining vampires looking for one last fight.

I have half a mind to scream at Darius now, but I'm exhausted and he's saving me the trouble of climbing out of this mess, so I keep my mouth shut and just think angry thoughts. I'll have my time to lay into him, once we get to wherever he's taking me.

We finally reach the outer walls of the chamber, only half of which still stand. A doorway leads us into a small sitting room, probably an old waiting area. It's dusty and I can still smell the burning coming from the main hall, but this place at least has a few benches where we can sit. The moment Darius puts me down, I step away from him and channel all my anger and rage. Pulling out my wand, I aim it at him, the tip pulsing silver like the fallen star it is, waiting to deliver a high-octane spell.

"You betrayed us," I say. A part of me knows he must have had a reason, but I'm too angry to want that reason, too angry to willingly forgive him.

Darius doesn't defend himself. He sits on a bench, staring back at me.

I see the pain in his eyes and feel it in my soul, and it breaks me just a little.

With a sigh, I sit next to him.

Rune and Zev have moved off to the corner to tend to my poor child and stand guard. Darius and I are left alone to talk.

I lower my wand, not from lack of anger, but my arms feel too heavy. My body hurts now that all the fighting is done. I glance to Rain, who is taking a potion from Rune. Good. She must have felt the shock of everything too.

Darius examines me with his dark gaze, then uses his teeth to slit his wrist open. "Drink. It will heal you and help repair our bond. You will see everything I did."

"What do you mean, 'repair'?" I spit back. "What happened to it?"

"I broke it," he says plainly. "And then I did my best to compel you out of my mind once we arrived in Vaemor. I needed you to feel betrayed. Now drink so you can understand."

Mission accomplished on the betrayal, I think loudly. He doesn't flinch, just keeps his wrist outstretched for me.

The red viscous liquid pools on his pale flesh, and I finally cave. I need to know. I can't keep letting this hurt in my heart fester.

I make sure he knows I'm still angry as I take his wrist to my mouth.

The moment his blood touches my lips, the last of the walls between us crumble and I fall into his memories.

Darius is with Erzsébet. It's during the battle in the Grand Hall. They're speaking privately, in a corner enclave. I see everything as though I'm perched on Darius' shoulder, almost seeing from his point of view but still aware of him.

"She can't know," the witch says. "Any insight she takes from your mind will only make things harder."

Darius' lips tighten. "This will hurt her."

Erzsébet glares back. "So will being dead or watching her daughter die. It is the only way." She hands him a small vial, amber liquid steaming within.

He hesitates, then takes it from her and pours it into his mouth.

A long moment passes before anything happens, but then he drops to his hands and knees and cries out in such despair it nearly breaks my heart. Through our bond I can feel the intense agony he's in as the potion rips through his body, shredding his mind and soul. Blood seeps from his eyes, nose and ears, and his skin glows red like it's about to catch on fire. The longer I watch, the duller the feeling becomes for me. I know he's suffering this concoction as a way to weaken our bond.

Seeing his pain, I can't help but let out a sob. A hand reaches for me, and I realize his present self is now with me in the vision.

Keep watching, he says to my mind.

Though my heart feels like it's being ripped out of my chest, I do as he asks.

Eventually, the vampire recovers enough to stand, but his eyes are alight with the horror of what he's undergoing and his voice is laced with pain as he speaks. "I'll find Timót now and ensure they escape safely. But I'll have to leave you all to fight this battle without me. I won't leave Bernie alone a second longer than I must."

The witch queen nods. "I wouldn't have it any other way. We'll survive, and

341

I'll watch your every move through the crystals. We'll come to you as soon as the moment is right. Just keep the mother and child safe."

Darius holds a fist to his heart. "On my life. I will not let what happened to Cara happen to Bernie and Rain."

Erzsébet's face flinches briefly at the mention of her dead daughter, and my heart newly aches for her after nearly losing my own child twice in a matter of minutes.

With that, Darius flashes away from the queen. My mind starts to return to the present moment, but Darius' pulls me back into his memory.

There's more you must see.

The image blurs, and now we're in the cemetery above the tomb where we spent so many nights. It's dark and quiet outside, probably early in the morning, just before dawn. Darius and Erzsébet walk slowly between the tombstones.

"Is there no other way?" Darius asks, though it's clear he's resigned to his task.

"We have two active threats we can't contain," she says. "Vampires, fae and wolves will continue coming after us, and Timót has amassed power beyond what I ever could have imagined."

"How do you know?" Darius asks.

A worried look comes over Erzsébet's face. "Dragons."

Darius stops walking. The queen stops as well, turning to face him.

"There had been stories and signs for years, but no explanation. Dragonlings gone missing and mothers found dead. At first we assumed it was just the unbalance in the magical kingdoms, but then Bernadette spoke of the broken egg in the cave where Timót had gone."

"You think he's trying to build some kind of dragon army?"

"I think he's already built it, Darius." Erzsébet's words have great weight, and the vampire clearly feels it.

"He means to kill the vampires," Darius says, and I can almost see the images of his home and family dancing through his mind.

Erzsébet nods. "He wants a throne for himself, and he'll destroy anyone who might hold him back. Vampires pose the most immediate threat."

"Then why should I lead him right where he wants to go?"

"So that he'll take the bait," the queen says. "We must move this fight to a new realm, if not we'll just watch more people die. Also, I believe you can lure Timót with an offer few others can make."

Darius raises an eyebrow, unsure of what bargaining chip Erzsébet refers to.

"You're the vampire king's son," she says. "If Timót will promise Bernadette to you, you can offer him the eternal life only your father can grant. A man like Timót could not refuse such a proposal. But..."

She stops, the creases in her brow becoming deeper as a look of concern takes hold.

"But...?"

"But Bernadette can't know. Should everything go exactly to plan, it will still be incredibly dangerous. She wouldn't agree to take such risk with her child, even if it is the only path forward. You'll have to force her to go along. And she'll have to think you've broken your pledge."

Before I can fully process the exchange, I'm thrust back into Darius' memory from the fight in the Grand Hall. He's now face to face with my father, standing in the shadows only feet from the doorway that led us to the room of portals. Darius holds a frightened looking Andor by the arm.

"I've kept him safe, now do what you must and get everyone out of here before the vampires find you," Darius says.

Timót points his wand at Andor's face, mutters his spell and I watch the man shift into Rune. Seeing everything that preceded that treacherous moment is really hard to stomach.

"You've made a wise choice, Darius," Timót says as the spell takes hold of his protegé. He then hands Darius the infamous pendant, which I now understand to be a mobile portal forged with dark magic.

Darius nods, and I'm back to sensing our slackened bond, which reminds me of the potion that caused him so much pain.

"I'll see you, Bernadette, and the child on the other side."

With those parting words we pull out of the memory, both left with our blood boiling as we consider the events that brought us here. I can feel that Darius hates my father with a passion that is fierce and protective, and his love for me and Rain is all-encompassing. He would do anything for us. Even this.

Even the thing that he feared would ruin our relationship.

As long as it kept us safe.

I'm silent for a moment as I stare into the face of a man I love, but still feel so hurt and confused by. "So you led my father to massacre your people?"

He looks at the floor, searching for a good answer. "The fight was bound to bring me here. Once I pledged myself to you, I pitted myself against my family, my ancestors, and my laws. I'm not proud of what happened here today, but Timót would have come with or without my help. This way, I could make every effort to protect you."

His explanation makes sense, but the feeling I had when he took Rain... When he took my wand... When he took my magic...

It could have gone so badly.

It almost did.

I know. He says silently. *I know I hurt you. But please know I never betrayed you. Or us. I did what I did to save you. I knew we couldn't fight Timót and the vampires at the same time. Frightful as this plan was, King Vladimir will never again send assassins to find your child. Still, I'm eternally sorry.*

"I understand," I say, speaking out loud. I leave it at that, too drained by the day and these revelations to unpack any more of my emotions.

Darius acknowledges those feelings and stands to leave me in peace. I want to reach out to him, longing to feel the love between us that was once so strong, but then another memory rocks me to my core and my anger surges again.. "What about AJ? We left her for dead."

He turns to me. "I would never leave your best friend for dead," he says softly.

"But… I saw you. I asked you. We just left…"

"Vampires have a pretty strong sense of when something is alive or dead," he says. "Her heart was strong and I knew Erzsébet was watching."

Erzsébet is with her now.

Zev's voice chimes into my mind, making my heart go a flutter for two reasons. First, his voice just does that to me, and second, my AJ is okay.

I drop to the ground and cry my freaking eyes out, letting every bit of needless mourning pour out of me. I've been fighting for my life, pushing away any thought of AJ being dead but knowing that a huge piece of my heart might be gone. Now I know she's alive and I'm just letting it all flow.

As I flood the small room with my tears, Zev's strong hands grip my sides and lift me from the ground. I'd love to keep crying, but I also have been longing for a deeper embrace with my wolf.

I bury my face in his chest and relish in his hug. The safety. The warmth. The comfort of it. Even as I do, I feel Darius on the other side of the room, his emotions and thoughts nudging against mine, and I know I will have to fully absolve him eventually. I won't be able to live with my own mind if I don't. And he did everything for us. As close as it brought us to death, we're still here.

"WILL AJ and Erzsébet come to us?" I ask as I reluctantly pull out of the hug with Zev. As much as I long for his touch, I'm giddy at the thought of being reunited with my dearest friend who's been through so much because of me.

"We'll have to see," Rune says, finally stepping forward to join the conversation and holding a baby that somehow looks clean and content. Where the shit did he find a fresh diaper? "Before we can safely--"

Rune abruptly stops talking, his eyes on Darius. I look to the vampire as well, who stands near the door, a serious look on his face as though he's lost in thought. A few seconds of silence pass, then he looks at me.

"I need everyone to stand behind me but stay close."

"Why? What's happening? Where are we going?"

Darius puts his hand on the large, marble door handle, listening through the stone for sounds I definitely can't hear.

"They're waiting," he says. "It does us no good to stay hidden away."

"What's our plan?" Zev asks.

The four of us exchange looks, and the haunting realization that we're still in the vampire kingdom washes over us. We're surrounded by angry survivors without a plan of action, and companions of a prince who just brought death and destruction to his own doorstep.

"I don't want to force you to fight," I say to Darius. Pledged to me or not, I can't ask this man to kill more of his brethren.

"I don't know if we'd win a fight at this point, without the dragons flying overhead," Darius says.

"Can we get them on our side?" I pose my question to Darius, but I'm happy for anyone in the room to answer. "Help them see our cause?"

The moment the words leave my mouth, I realize how important they are. The Sexies see it on my face. "That's it," I whisper.

The three princes look at each other, not yet as sure of my epiphany as I am.

"You all believe the prophecy is bogus, right?" I say to a chorus of nods. "Then that's what we have to do. We can't fight everyone. We have to make them understand that--"

"That the Last Witch is more important alive than dead," Rune says, finishing my thought with a little artistic license. "She can save us all, or fall into the *Érintett's* hands and save none of us."

This is the only path forward. Timót's army is too big, his dragons are too fierce, his magic is too powerful. If we want to stand a chance, we need a united realm.

I can feel in my lovers that they know I'm right.

Without another word, Darius opens the door and we all walk out. I grip my wand, terrified of what might come for us. Rune keeps Rain held tight against his chest, putting her safety above his own, as always. Zev stays right beside Darius, prepared to fight and die for his old friend.

As we move into the open air, climbing on top of the fallen debris from the earlier battle, there's no immediate threat. No vampires jump out at us. I don't hear any sounds from them as we step out, and I'm not sure what Darius was listening to earlier.

When we move a little higher, climbing up the fallen columns, the scene becomes more apparent.

I thought most of the vampires died in the attack.

I clearly underestimated their numbers.

Hundreds of them stand on top of buildings and fallen structures, staring down at us as we emerge.

No one looks to attack. No one even moves.

Except for one vampire, who slowly walks toward us, coming out of the rubble that was once a sacred chamber.

It's Emerus.

And he's carrying King Vladimir's crown.

CHAPTER SIX

I t's not so much that we're out-numbered. I mean we are, greatly so, with vampires on every rooftop and some certainly lurking unseen in the shadows.

That's not what scares me. We've been outnumbered before, and if there's one thing I trust my powers to do, it's light shit on fire. The vampire's greatest weakness is my greatest strength. The numbers don't scare me.

It's the volatility.

It's the fragility of this shaken realm, and the realization that just hit me like a ton of bricks.

We need them.

Every last one of them.

Timót's army flies on the backs of enormous, unbreakable flame throwers. He has countless men following his lead, and I'm confident he has even more fighters waiting back at a camp somewhere. Now he has the strength and durability of a vampire. He's all but invincible.

I've spent the last few weeks wondering if I'd be on the run for the rest of my life, trying to raise my child in hidden chambers while a council of paranormals chased us down. In an instant, that's all changed. I don't want to run from these vampires, and I don't want to kill them--even if that's what they want to do to me.

I want to convince them to join us.

Emerus leaps off a crumbling wall, landing gracefully in front of his brother. He and Darius stand just a few feet apart, staring at each other in silence. Given the stakes of this showdown, I have to keep reminding myself that these are two brothers who just lost their father.

Darius has his own issues to sort out with the king's death, but it's nothing he won't recover from. With Emerus, I don't know anything about their relationship. I don't know if he saw his maker as a despicable, murderous monster, or the head of state who helped promote the best interests of his kind. I guess we'll find out soon enough.

"I know why you came, brother," Emerus says, keeping his voice diplomatic while his balled fists show he's ready to throw diplomacy out the window if need be.

"I don't believe you do," Darius responds. He's calm and collected. A face-off with his brother could be violent and scary, but now that he's done fake-betraying me it's clear he feels a sense of relief.

"No? I understand how pledges, bonds, and oaths work." Emerus gets a little more oomph in his voice after each word, the anger starting to peek through. "I can smell your blood bond a mile away. I read your thoughts even as you tried to keep them from her, and if our father's mind wasn't so poisoned with anger over you leaving, he would have seen through you as well."

Darius looks at his feet, flashing back to those moments when he was still shunning me, moments I now know nearly crushed him. I'll have scars from those heartbreaking hours, but I'm positive the vampire's wounds will take even longer to heal.

"Then I'm lucky," Darius says. "We're all lucky. If the king saw through me and killed Bernie, we'd all be dead. That *Érintett* army would have murdered every last one of us, but the goal was to keep the mother and child alive."

"He killed hundreds! And had we sacrificed the child--"

"It would have done nothing!" Darius spits as he yells back, as impassioned as I've ever seen him get regarding the prophecy. He climbs past his brother, standing atop a chamber wall so he can address all the vampires, most of whom are probably just waiting for Emerus to give them the cue to attack this traitor.

"Don't you see? There's no sense in the prophecy, written by the Fates themselves, if the final act is to kill the last of their kind." Darius lets his words hang while the angry crowd considers what he's said. "The battle for magic and power has led us here, with three races at each other's throats and one nearly killed off, and the baby's blood would do nothing to change that."

Darius looks over the faces of the men and women he's addressing; some seem thoughtful, others still too scorned to listen. I don't know if he's expecting a response from the masses, but Emerus leaps up to the same platform to make the conversation more intimate again.

"A simple explanation from a man with simple, compromised intentions," Emerus says.

And thus the stalemate continues, the two brothers arguing two different truths. Unfortunately, the one on my side is viewed as the treasonous son and has an uphill battle if he wants to get anyone on his side.

"I suppose," Emerus says, finally breaking the silence, "that you plan to assume the throne. Perhaps your standing as the eldest heir made the decision to lead all these foreigners into our kingdom easier."

"I meant only to save the child and her mother," Darius says back, his voice barely above a whisper. "I didn't kill our father."

"His blood certainly colors your hands more than it does mine."

Again Darius' eyes scan the waiting vampires, like he's weighing their loyalty to the throne against their loathing of him.

"I'll put it in the hands of the citizenry, Emerus."

Everyone in earshot freezes, listening intently to see if Darius actually means what he said. I'm as on edge as anyone else; putting his future in the hands of those who hate him most seems like a foolhardy move. I'd speak up and tell everyone Darius has been huffing glue and doesn't know what he's talking about, but I've admittedly been a few steps behind the clever vampire for a number of days.

Emerus looks more skeptical than surprised, trying to determine his brother's angle.

"There are no Ancients to oversee a vote," he says.

"I'm aware," Darius responds.

"Nor any priests to sanctify the outcome."

"As I said, this is a decision for those who remain. Unprecedented times call for unprecedented measures." With great trepidation, Darius raises a hand and places it on his brother's shoulder. "You know I'm torn, and you know exactly why. I believe there's a life for our people beyond this prophecy. I'm willing to stake my life and my throne on it. But I won't force anyone to bend to my will."

It's as good a speech as I've heard in a long time, but I'm pretty biased. I don't imagine vamp bro will be as quick to let vamp boy slide as I normally am.

To my happy surprise, Emerus reaches a hand up and clasps his brother's. The two share a moment, perhaps trading thoughts back and forth, perhaps just embracing the mutual respect they have for one another. I don't get anything concrete through my shared thoughts with Darius, only a strong sense of adoration.

"We must duel," Emerus says, his words throwing ice water on the tender moment.

"I know," Darius says back, his response nearly knocking the wind out of me.

What? Why? I fling my questions into Darius' mind without a care for whatever other thoughts he's dealing with. We've all nearly died too many times already to be waltzing into an extra, avoidable fight.

Emerus stares at me with a penetrating gaze. It's immediately clear he was privy to my thought exchange with Darius. "If I may be so bold... please stay out of this."

With that, he turns to face the throngs of vampires, all anxiously awaiting word from someone who will claim to be their leader.

"You need a trustworthy king. Darius and I will fight for that title. To the Pit!"

The crowd breaks into a strange, guttural chant as the brothers turn and walk back toward the center of the city.

SINCE DAY IS night and death is life for vampires, it makes sense that up is also down. The Pit stands at the highest point in Vaemor, with long columns rising from the buildings below to support the open-air arena. There's no raked seating like in a normal stadium--everyone just forms a circle, crowding around and elbowing through to get a better view of the spectacle.

I don't want to watch. I think, all things considered, this is a stupid plan. If Darius dies, the vampires will try to make quick work of me and my child. If he lives, there's no reason to assume that will turn him into a respected leader. It feels like a lose-lose.

Zev and Rune stand as close to me as possible, each holding an arm and standing their ground to make sure we don't get trampled by the restless vampires behind us. We walked close behind Darius and Emerus on the way over so now we have front-row seats, but that means we've got hundreds of vampires pushing at our backs.

I never liked mosh pits.

I keep my wand at the ready, trying to think of the spells I've learned and which would be best for stopping angry throngs of vampires coming from all directions. So far I'm drawing a blank.

Darius and Emerus have shed their cloaks and tunics. Their matching chiseled frames are a sight for sore eyes, but my mind and body are a little too weary to care about sexy visuals. I have to figure out how this is going to end, because I don't think Darius is looking that far ahead.

All this work tricking me and Timót to keep us alive, and now he might throw it all away because he's so goddamn alpha.

The look in his eyes is one I haven't seen before. As he stands opposite his brother, both with their hands clasped in a prayer position, there's a devoutness in his aura. He might not put stock in the prophecy, but he still believes in some of the vampire ways and traditions.

Like fighting one's brother to the death to pick a new king.

I'd admire his steadfastness if it wasn't so stupid.

There has to be another way, I say into his mind.

Perhaps, he says back. *If you know what it is, please let me know.*

I'm in no mood for sarcasm, but I can't fault him the attitude. There isn't an easy answer to any of our problems, and asking the guy on the verge of battle to come up with an alternate plan isn't really fair.

A female vampire stands on the opposite side of the Pit from us, carrying a blood-red pillow that supports the crown. It looks made of pure gold with rubies embedded like blood drops around the base and pointed spikes framing it.

I turn to Zev, hoping to get a little peace of mind. "Is Darius the better fighter?"

Zev's green eyes bounce between the royal vampire brothers, sizing them up before he answers.

"I think they're fairly equal."

Not exactly what I wanted to hear.

"It comes down to motivation," Zev continues. "Darius fights for you and your child, Emerus for his kingdom. It should be an impressive match."

Impressive match? I'm sorry, are we at a sporting event, or does the existence of all things hang in the balance of who wins or loses this fight? These paranormal princes seem to take cataclysmic events in stride and it's making me feel insane.

Fortunately, sweet Rune has a better hold on how emotions work. His touch pours calming energy into my veins, quieting the disturbed sensation I get from Darius' blood.

"I think Darius has something his brother lacks," the fae whispers to me. "Breaking his bond with you over the last day was a fate worse than death for him. I don't think he's ready to lose you again."

I take a little bit of comfort in that, though my confidence still wanes a bit.

"How…" I try to think of a delicate way to word my question, but there isn't one. "How do they kill each other?"

Rune takes a breath, and he's either trying to remember how it works or searching for an answer that won't make me cringe. Again, no such answer exists.

"By either ripping off the other's head or taking out the other's heart."

Perfect.

Any sense of calm I had disappears right away as my mind starts reeling for another option beyond the fight. I'm not sure how long I have before the duel begins, but hopefully--

Too late.

Without any warning, Darius and Emerus leap at each other, colliding in mid-air with their arms outstretched and their teeth bared. Each prince grips the other's arms, digging fingers into strong flesh as they fall back to the stone floor below.

Emerus is the first to strike, throwing an elbow into Darius' sternum that knocks him back a few steps. As he stumbles, Emerus follows up with a swift kick to the thigh, dropping his brother to the ground. When Emerus makes to kick again, Darius swiftly recovers and catches his brother's leg, twisting and violently forcing Emerus to jump and spin as the only way to keep the bone from breaking.

I'm watching every MMA fan's wet dream and hating every second of it.

Darius pounces on his brother, but Emerus catches him with his feet and throws him back with his strong thighs. The two both stand slowly, squaring off for another round. This time Darius goes on the offensive, feigning a punch and then catching his brother with a roundhouse kick to the shoulder. The blow throws Emerus off balance but doesn't bring him to the ground.

"Your legs seem weak, brother," Emerus says with a slight smile. "Not as forceful as when you were young."

Darius smiles back, and it's just so unbelievable to me that they're poking fun when one of them is about to die.

"I've been on the run for weeks," Darius says. "Fear not, I'll get my second wind."

Just as he finishes the word "wind," Darius propels himself like a torpedo, feet first and somehow spinning through the air. It's a move I've probably seen in a video game. You know, where physics don't matter.

His feet connect with Emerus' stomach, and while the younger brother tries to grab hold of the weaponized legs, there's too much torque. He falls back and Darius lands on top of him, pinning his arms to the ground with his knees.

Emerus grimaces under the weight while trying to kick free, but Darius holds strong.

As Darius lifts his hands to his brother's throat, I try to get inside his mind. I don't have anything to say, but I want to listen in. I need to know what could possibly be going through a person's head in a moment like this.

It's a confusing jumble inside Darius' mind, and I think I hear fragments of thoughts from Emerus as well. I'm sure the connection is strong between these siblings.

Ask for mercy, I hear Darius say. I can't make out a response, but it's clear from looking at him that Emerus doesn't plan to concede.

Darius digs his fingers into the skin around Emerus' neck, and the possibility of a gruesome murder becomes very apparent.

Please.

Darius asks again, but Emerus only kicks harder. Blood now drips from the younger brother's throat and the elder's grip tightens.

I honestly don't know if Darius has the heart to kill his brother, and the hesitation suggests he wouldn't do it, but I'm not willing to find out. I've found a better way. At least I think I have.

"Stand guard," I say to Zev and Rune, handing Rain to the fae. "I'm not sure how the vampires are going to react to this."

"React to what--"

"*Éget!*"

Before Zev can ask his question, my wand is up and shooting fire at Darius. Flames lick all around his naked back as he dives to the ground, trying to smother the blaze.

As soon as he's off his battered brother, I take aim and say "*menö,*" extinguishing the fire. Darius lies still as steam rises around him. He and Emerus sprawl out on the ground, both looking worse for wear.

What are you doing? Darius says in my mind, clearly still in agony from the burn.

Trying another way, I answer.

I walk forward, coming to a stop between the brothers, turning in a circle to look at all of the vampires. None of them makes a move toward me, but it feels like that could change in an instant. Zev and Rune quickly follow, standing at my sides in case some shit goes down.

"This won't save you," I say to the crowd. "Losing one of your leaders isn't how you gain a king. If Emerus got his goddamn head ripped off, would that make you swear allegiance to Darius?"

I was hoping for a more responsive crowd, maybe someone to throw out an Amen, but all I get is stone-faced silence. I guess I'll keep going.

"Darius' blood runs in my veins. Our minds and bodies are bound, and I feel the reverence he has for this kingdom. But I've watched you tear each other apart, giving in to your bloodlust even as Vaemor crumbles and war wages on without an end in sight. You're so blinded by a tradition of violence that you've lost sight of the real enemy. It's not Darius. It's certainly not Emerus."

Emerus has slowly pushed himself up to one knee. He still looks pretty roughed up, but he's on the road to recovery. Darius is also sitting upright now and only a little bit of smoke billows off his burnt back. I'll have to remember to apologize for that later, and maybe send Rune to find some aloe. I take a breath and look back to the crowd, hoping to deliver a strong finale.

"Your enemy has never been the witches, it has never been the fae, it has never been the wolves. Until a few weeks ago, your only adversary was the prophecy. But now you have a real problem. Now there's a deranged man with a fleet of dragons and a massive army. He destroyed your city, killed your king, and he'll be back to take more of your lives if you don't do something about it."

No one speaks, so it's time to make the final pitch, and then my idea has run its course.

"We're going to stop him. If it's going to work, we need your help. All of your help. Darius, and Emerus. If that means lighting you all on fire so you stop fighting each other, then that's what I'll do."

I raise my wand, now aimed at Emerus.

"So what's it gonna be?"

CHAPTER SEVEN

The tension is thick in the Pit as Emerus weighs his options, and I fake full confidence in my ability to follow through on my big speech.

I mean, I'll definitely unleash my wand powers on anyone who tries to kill me, Rain, or any of the guys. Whether we would survive the after-effects of that is less certain.

Still. I wait. Wand held high.

And if there's a trace of nerves making my hand shake, well… I try to ignore it and hope everyone else will too.

"You're playing with fire," Emerus says, his eyes narrowing at me.

My lips twitch and I can't help but channel a little AJ 'tude with this guy as I hold out a hand and let fire dance on my palm. "Haven't you heard? I *am* the fire."

Tread carefully, Darius says in my mind. *My brother is not one to trifle with.*

I'm not trifling, I say. *I'm trying to salvage our plan. A little help would be great.*

While I'd love to reach out to Zev and Rune to aid me, I know they aren't the most welcome in the vampire kingdom. It's up to me and Darius.

Not that I'm exactly welcomed with open arms, but they certainly have done their damnedest to get me here. They also just watched me light the traitorous brother on fire, so I'm not sure anyone's gunning for me yet.

"One of us will have to become king," Emerus says. "If we don't complete our duel…"

He's awfully cocky for a vamp who was about to face real deadness, I tell Darius. His lips twitch as he tries to suppress a laugh.

Emerus narrows his eyes, and though I feel a push in my mind--like he's trying to get inside my thoughts--I resist. The sexy brother glowers at me and I keep my face schooled in total innocence. Let him fester. I owe him nothing.

Darius stands and walks away from the center of the Pit, heading toward the woman carrying the crown. Everyone nearby shoots odious glares as he snatches the royal headwear, but no one tries to stop him.

"I have a simple solution," Darius says as he turns back to his brother, but Emerus cuts him off before he can get to the point.

"You can't just take the crown and expect our people to follow you after betraying our king." His voice catches, and once again I wonder at his relationship with his father. Were they close? Is he as evil as daddy vampire was? I don't get that vibe, but I can't get a read on this guy and Darius has never gushed about family. Though I try to dig deeper into my mind connection with Darius, to see if I can pull the answer up the way I learned to speak Hungarian, the effort is in vain.

I squint, a sudden throbbing headache puncturing my concentration.

Darius quickly glances my way, a grimace on his face, and I can tell he's feeling what I am. Knowing he must stay focused on the pressing issue, he shakes it off and he returns his attention to his brother.

"Our *king*," Darius says with a solid dose of disdain, "betrayed many when he waged war against everyone who wasn't a vampire. When he sent assassins after Bernie and Rain. When he let an unproven interpretation of an ancient prophecy destroy our kingdom. One of us will have to undo his many centuries of damage."

Darius maintains eye contact with his brother for a long time, and I resist the urge to try and listen in. It's clear there's a battle of the alphas going on internally and I don't want to get in the way.

Sometimes doing nothing, saying nothing, is the right course of action, albeit the much harder one to follow. I'm itching to make them talk, but I bite my tongue.

For a moment, the sheer insanity of all of this once again smacks me in the psyche. I should be tending bar and telling the regulars to go home to their wives, not playing chicken with the two royal princes of the vampire kingdom, but here we are.

The rest of the vampires might as well be mannequins, so still and quiet and oddly patient. Previous interactions had me thinking of this race as angsty and always on the go, but that might have something to do with them chasing and trying to abduct me. Now that we're all standing around and dealing with the future of their kingdom, I don't think any of them have so much as inhaled since this showdown between brothers began.

When the silence continues, I reject my commitment to staying out of it. Typical Bernie.

"Your numbers were decimated, and that is a tragedy" I say. "But your king was killed by an army of dragons and a guy who seems pretty eager to destroy you. We may not be natural allies, but we share a common enemy. Like it or not, you know we are stronger together. I'm not all that thrilled to be allying with kingdoms that have been trying to kill me and my baby, but sometimes you gotta make exceptions. So, are you going to be smart about this, or are you going to fight over your dad's hat while everyone dies?"

Darius walks over to Emerus, and I suck in my breath as we wait to see what he will do.

"I am the first to admit I have mixed loyalties," Darius says. "I am bound, by honor, by blood oath..." he glances at me, "and by choice, to Bernadette and her child. She has my heart, what is left of it."

His words soothe an ache that has been growing in my soul since his first perceived betrayal. Really since the moment he drank that potion and our entangled spirits were torn from one another.

"What are you saying, brother?" Emerus asks.

I'm encouraged by his use of the word brother instead of, say, traitor. Perhaps we're making progress.

Rather than answer, Darius steps forward, and I sense what he's about to do before he does it. Still, the act itself is emotionally moving. It feels heavy with meaning and future consequence.

Darius places the crown on his brother's head and then takes a knee, bowing. "I hereby relinquish my rightful place as the next king and bequeath this duty to my brother, Emerus of Vaemor."

The sound of murmuring vampires is not something easily described. Their voices carry on a different wave. Not quite words, not quite music, something in between but entirely new. Still, it's clear to all of us that what Darius has done is unprecedented.

Emerus, for his part, hasn't breathed since the crown was placed on his head.

Like he forgot to exhale.

I, however, still seem to need human amounts of oxygen, and so I suck in a breath and exhale as if I've just emerged from the depths of the ocean.

I'm pretty sure Rune and Zev use real air to breathe as well, but they're more inconspicuous than myself, which unfortunately results in me making an alarmingly human sound in an arena full of immortals.

All eyes turn to me, and despite being fundamentally opposed to blushing, I feel the blood rush to my cheeks.

"All hail King Emerus?" I say, my voice lacking in conviction as I try to navigate dicy vampire politics.

Color me shocked when a throng--I'm going with throng because they didn't cover vampire group names at Julliard--of vampires echo my words.

"All hail King Emerus."

Figuring it's best to err on the side of kissing ass right now, I bend the knee, mimicking Darius and hoping women don't have a whole different code of conduct.

Kneel! I say to Zev, who is stubbornly glaring at Emerus and refusing to budge.

Even my gentle fae is standing tall, his chin jutted out in uncharacteristic defiance.

Seems the other princes might be ready to form alliances but haven't reached the point of allegiances. Fair enough. When Emerus finally nods his head, tension eases from my shoulders. Darius stands, and I hear the two brothers exchange some thoughts I can't understand. Even though I can't translate, I have a strong sense they're speaking amicably.

In a show of good faith, I lower my wand.

Emerus raises his hand to draw everyone's attention to him, as if all eyes weren't already glued to the new king. Still, a little showmanship is probably a good quality in a leader. "Your proposal will be given due consideration," he says to me. "I will honor the codes of knighthood and guarantee your safety in our kingdom. Then I will give you my answer."

Consideration? That's all we get?

Hey, didn't you just make him king?? I ask Darius. *Wouldn't helping us out be the brotherly thing to do in response?*

I did make him king, yes, Darius responds. *And now he's going to decide what he feels is best for his kingdom.*

He says this like it's law, but it seems a little ridiculous.

Hot as my temper may be, I keep my freaking mouth shut as Darius stands and gestures for me to come forward. "Emerus, I'd like to officially introduce you to Bernadette Morgan. She's... very special."

Emerus nods his head in acknowledgment, so I follow his lead and hope I'm not embarrassing myself but also like, so what? It's really confusing being a woman in a normal world. It's extra extra confusing being a woman--a witch-- and constantly bouncing between different cultures and worlds.

I follow Darius' and Emerus' lead as the two walk down from the Pit and head across a wind-swept patio of stone, orange dirt and cacti-like plants.

I can feel Zev's annoyance at this subservient treatment, but I admonish him to keep silent. A lot is riding on this partnership, and giving the new king 'tude won't do anything to help our cause.

We are ushered into a room that looks extravagant for one person but a bit cramped for four.

I don't need my mental/emotional connection to Darius to know that this was his room.

I try to take in every detail, gleaning as much as I can from my lover's life before we met. Frankly, there's not a lot to take away from it.

It's an austere space, with a large bed, a dresser, a desk and a fireplace with one chair set beside it. A door on the north wall leads to what I hope is some semblance of a modern bathroom, because my bladder has been stretched to capacity and I have to pee like I've never had to pee before.

A woman's postpartum bladder does not pause for war, it seems. This is another thing they didn't include in the What To Expect books. Honestly, they need a whole subseries on what to do when you have a baby and crazy paranormal shit happens.

I can't even pay attention as Emerus and Darius say their farewells. I'm legit trying not to pee myself.

When my kinda brother-in-law leaves, I instantly turn to Darius. "Tell me there is a bathroom?"

He points to the door I've been pinning all my hopes on and I don't even pretend decorum as I beeline it to relief.

What awaits me is less than encouraging.

There's a hole in the floor. That's it.

I eye it skeptically, but the urgency in my bladder propels me forward.

The pit is deep, and I can't smell or see what awaits anyone who might fall into it.

Though this does nothing to give me comfort, I stand over the hole and drop my pants, squatting and trying to aim as best I can.

What I wouldn't give for a shewee right now.

Last summer, AJ couldn't stop talking about a thing that could let us girls pee standing up like boys. At the time it seemed ridiculous and I told her so. Now, I'm eating my words as I try not to fall into the neverending pee pit. I'm also fighting back tears thinking of AJ. I need to get to her and Erzsébet ASAP to make sure everyone's okay.

I finish my business and try to shut my emotions down, knowing sadness won't get me any closer to finding my friend. Cleaning myself is a challenge best not discussed in polite company. When I return to the guys, I desperately wish for a proper bathroom, and I tell them so.

"This isn't...civil."

But honestly, we are all too exhausted to care.

The bed isn't big, but it's big enough. We arrange ourselves as best we can, with Darius on an edge, then me, Rain, Zev and Rune. It doesn't take long for us all to fall asleep.

I expected nightmares, but when I wake sometime later, it's a relief to realize I had a dreamless sleep after all the horror of the previous day.

I'm especially grateful to see a platter of food readied for those of us with human-esque stomachs. I feed and care for Rain then help myself to dried fruit and dried meat.

I'm surprised to wake before the guys, but am glad I've had a few moments to myself with my child before they rise.

I can feel the tension rolling off Darius as soon as he moves from the bed.

"My brother will make a decision shortly," he says.

I don't ask him how he knows. I assume it's either a vampire thing or a brother thing. Either way, time to get ready for what's to come.

Darius looks sallow and pale and when Rune takes Rain, I pull the vampire into the makeshift bathroom. "Feed on me."

He shakes his head, refusing. "I've betrayed you."

"Oh my lord, you are a pain in the ass. You need blood; I have blood. I'll get over the betrayal, but only if you stay... undead. And not like dead dead."

Frustrated by his unnecessary restraint, I pull him toward me and push his mouth towards my neck. It doesn't take much more than that to get him to feed.

I wish I could avoid the pleasure I feel in this act. I'm still processing the deceit, even though I understand the motivation. Nevertheless, I can't deny the relief present in the act of giving my life essence to him.

Zev and Rune have finished the refreshments by the time Darius finishes feeding, and I strap Rain to my chest as we make our way through winding halls to Darius' brother.

We find him sitting on a throne, with attendants on either side. He's wearing his father's crown and totally looks like he's practiced sitting on the throne before. I narrow my eyes at Emerus, suddenly suspicious of his motives as a wave of unease rides over me.

I want to flee.

To take my men and run.

And this urge makes me extra nervous.

Be careful, I say. *Something doesn't feel right.*

Darius doesn't reply. Instead, he focuses on his brother. "What have you decided?" he asks without preamble.

Emerus takes a long pause before speaking, making me doubt he's going to give a simple thumbs up to my request. He gestures to a couple plush pillows on the floor in front of his throne. "Please. Sit."

The hair on my neck stands on end at his words and I suck in my breath and hold my wand tightly in my hand, ready for whatever he's about to say. Darius sits without hesitation, so I steel my nerves and follow his lead.

"I have decided to offer an alliance to your cause and any who might join it, to stop Timót and his army. After that is done, I make no promises of peace."

"Understood," Darius says. He seems relieved by his brother's words, but I still feel like there's more to come. Emerus holds up a finger, proving me right when I had really hoped to be wrong.

"I have one condition to this agreement. It's not particularly pleasant, but it aligns with our laws… and it's non-negotiable."

Shit. This isn't good. I want to tell Darius to run. I want to blast Emerus with my wand before he has a chance to speak. Making him king was not the right call. Amiable as he may have been before, Vladimir's crown has made him shitty. I just know it.

"I will give the support of the vampires," Emerus says with a look of unearned triumph in his eyes, "if you, dear brother, agree to accept your due punishment."

Darius stiffens at my side and I shudder at whatever he is trying to avoid thinking. Whatever it is, it absolutely terrifies a vampire who almost never gets scared.

My heart feels on the precipice of breaking at the newly crowned king's next words. "I sentence you to the Tomb of Time for three passages of the moon. You will suffer one day for your sins, one day for mine, and one day for our fallen father, for whose death you will accept the blame."

Darius looks more like death than any vampire I've ever seen. His light skin is even lighter, his dark eyes sullen, his mouth slightly agape. Yet still he nods, accepting this fate I still don't understand.

What is the Tomb of Time? I ask, trying to hide the panic I feel. *What does this mean?*

Darius doesn't look at me or answer, toiling with too much panic of his own. Instead, I get a response from Emerus.

A chamber, deep in the bowels of our kingdom. Time passes at its own speed there. One day lasts for a thousand years.

His words hit me right in the knees, and if I wasn't already seated I would surely fall.

My sweet lover, who only just came back to me, will be locked away for three millenia.

CHAPTER EIGHT

M y world spins and I feel dizzy, but I can't tell if it's me or Darius.
Most likely it's both of us.

I don't understand anything beyond the unfathomable number I just heard. *Three thousand years?* I'd be worked up if he'd said a week. This is unconscionable. I'd think it was a joke but the fear I feel in Darius makes it seem very real.

"No way. Hard pass."

Emerus frowns and Darius hisses in my mind. *Do not be foolish. We haven't been given a choice.*

What are you saying? We'll all be dead!

Darius gives me a sideways look, and it seems like I've missed something. He hesitates a moment before I push him. *What don't I get about three thousand years in a tomb?*

He speaks to me slowly, like he's finding the silver lining in some really bad news. *Only three days will pass before I see you again. It will be but a short while for you, but I will live through three thousand years of solitude. It was a punishment designed specifically for the immortal.*

That clears things up, sort of. It makes me happy in one respect, because three days isn't so bad--for me. But to leave Darius here knowing what he's about to endure... I don't think I can do it. *No. Nope. Nada. Niet. Nine. I'm pretty sure those are all legit languages and all mean the same thing. No.*

Darius ignores me and addresses his brother. "May the sentence begin after my friends have left for the fae kingdom?"

I grab Darius' hand and squeeze it hard, digging my nails into his palms. "No. I do not agree to this at all, and I am not leaving without you."

"I'm not sure who you think is seeking your agreement," Emerus says with all the condescension of a king who earned his crown by lucking into the right bloodline. Kings suck.

"Listen, buddy," I start speaking well before I know what I'm going to say, but I'm sure I'll figure something out. "You're on that throne because I didn't let Darius kill you. You're alive because Timót doesn't want me dead."

"And you're alive because I helped you and your baby hide from the dragons," he answers, sneaking in a little fact that weakens my argument a hair. "We both have a debt to each other, which is why I'm willing to join forces with sworn enemies."

He looks at Zev and Rune for this last line, clearly less than pumped about having princes from the other kingdoms as guests. The fae and the werewolf stare back, less than thrilled about visiting the vampire city.

Emerus stands and walks over to me. At first, it feels like another power move and I grip my wand more tightly. Then he raises his hand in a classic "I come in peace" sort of way, and I try to quell my anger and my nerves. He stops a few feet from me, a thoughtful look on his face, trying to choose his words wisely.

"Outside these walls, the vampires are afraid, directionless, and angry. I intend to convince them this is a cause worth joining, but you cannot forget that a day ago, their previous king had your child on our sacred altar. Victory was declared, and then many of us died."

He turns his attention to Darius, and I sense a bit of remorse in my blood. The two brothers feel an equal sadness that it's come to this.

"I trust my brother," Emerus goes on. "I may be hurt by his priorities, but I understand them. And, as you both might be surprised to hear, I share many of Darius' feelings about our dead father."

Thank God. The jury's been out on Emerus this whole time, but the fact that he's not totally blind to his dad being horrible will make this united front thing a little easier.

"It pains me to bestow this punishment, but it must be done," King Emerus continues. "Darius knows as well as anyone that our people won't commit to me or a new way unless there's penance for the betrayal."

Darius doesn't have to speak or nod or anything for me to know he agrees. I still want to fight it, but it's clear I'm not going to have any authority on the matter.

"One day," I counter, putting my last bit of hope on a haggle. "One thousand years of tomb torture seems like plenty, right?"

The understanding look fades from Emerus' face, and he's instantly back to being a king with a boner for himself. "No. The sentence begins in one hour."

He heads back to his throne and a couple of vampire guards, who up until now had been creepily hidden in the shadows, move to escort us out. Darius turns to leave without any resistance, and I'm forced to follow.

We walk in silence back to Darius' cramped quarters, the guards on our heels to make sure we don't try anything funny. Once inside the small room, we stand for another few moments of quiet. Zev is the first to speak, and the softness in his voice shows he's plenty worried for his friend.

"We'll be waiting for you," he says. "In four days, we'll all be laughing about this. Or three thousand years and one day, for you."

Darius smiles, if only to acknowledge the werewolf's attempt at cutting the tension.

"You won't wait here," the vampire says. "You'll need to move on to the other kingdoms, to warn and persuade the others. It's possible Timót has already staged another attack."

"We also need to get to AJ and Erzsébet," Rune says. I feel a brutal mix of terror and excitement as I think about finding my friend, and worrying about whether or not she's okay. Rune takes my hand, helping me to manage the emotional overload.

For three days, I'll be torn apart, wondering what's happening to Darius. For infinitely more time than that, he'll suffer in ways my human brain can't begin to comprehend.

But that's just the way it has to be.

When it's done, we'll all be alive, and that's the most I can hope for on any given day. Maybe we can find him a good undead therapist to help him process three thousand years of torture that only he experiences.

"Let's go," I say to Zev and Rune, though I keep my eyes on Darius. The last twenty-four hours have lasted a lifetime. I thought it might take longer for me to process and move past the deception that brought us here, but I don't need any more time. Darius acts almost exclusively out of love for me, and I'm surprised I couldn't see that the whole time.

Whatever claim to pain I might still have pales in comparison to what he's about to go through, and now all I feel is fear and sorrow for this man I love.

"We'll give you two a moment," Zev says. I let the werewolf take Rain from me, and my baby steps outside with two of her three paranormal dads. If we ever make it back to our world, she's gonna have the best Bring Your Parent To School days.

When the door shuts behind us, Darius and I are immediately in each other's arms, kissing fiercely. God, I've missed him. And goddammit, I will miss him.

"How will you find us?" I ask, when we finally come up for air.

"I will always find you," he answers. "On any world, in any realm, I will find you."

The magical fusion of our souls might be weaker than it once was, but the bond of our love is as strong as ever. I trust him, and I know I'll see him soon. My heart will break for him every second we're apart, but then it will mend. And I hope he will mend from this as well.

I give him one last kiss, trying to inhale his spirit, to keep him inside me as we separate. I'll need his strength as we start this next leg of our journey.

And he'll need my strength even more.

Rune, Zev and I stand in quiet thought outside Darius' door. There's really not much to say. Again, Zev is the one to break the somber mood and push us forward.

"We've only got three days until Darius shows up and starts bragging about how much longer he's lived than the rest of us. Better get a move on."

It's a good enough line to make Rune smile, and I give the slightest grin. I'm not at all in a laughing mood, but I appreciate Zev's efforts.

"Let's go find AJ," I say, wiping my cheeks that had become damp without my knowing. "How do we get there, where is she, what's next?"

"This part of our realm hides behind the Kilarean Mountains," Rune says. "That's what keeps sunlight away, but it also means the land is narrow between the mountains and the sea. We'll start heading south, and trust your powers and intuition to guide us to Erzsébet and AJ."

I want to ask what intuition he's talking about, because I have yet to see an improvement in my sense of direction. I decide to leave my pride intact and save the self deprecation for when I actually get lost

"Lead the way," I say to my two Sexies.

With a quick look at the vampire guards who wait to escort Darius to the Tomb, we head down the hall and out into the open.

Vampires watch us go, and I'm banking on Emerus having told them they're not allowed to kill us. Trust is a crazy thing, as it can get you killed as easily as it can save you. If I didn't trust Emerus' word, I might start a fight and die. If I trust him and he's a liar, I'll get killed when I'm not looking. I clutch Rain a little tighter, offering my thumb as a pacifier while we walk.

Nearing the edge of the vampire city, it looks like the trust was earned. Hundreds watch us leave, none of them make a move to harm us. That's one fear I can let go of; time to move on to the next.

Coming into this kingdom I was roped to a dragon, surrounded by evil strangers and emotionally destroyed on pretty much every level. On my way out, I can look around with a little less trepidation. I'll need to be alert and paying attention to whatever signs and landmarks might jar my memory and point me in the right direction.

Trouble is, this part of whatever world we're in has nothing but rocks and dust. It's like walking across the salt flats in the middle of the U.S., but somehow less appealing.

I look behind us at the city, trying to remember the direction from which we entered. Seems like the best bet is to walk straight into the nothingness and then reassess in a few hours.

We walk for a couple minutes before I feel eyes on me. Judgemental, questioning eyes.

"What?!" I snap at both Rune and Zev as I spin around to face them. "I feel your stares and I'm not vibing. What's up?"

Zev tries to hide a smile while Rune cocks an eyebrow, falling into their typical reactions to my sass.

"Is your plan really to retrace your steps through the barren stone land?" Rune asks.

"Even though you came in on a dragon, hundreds of feet above?" Zev tacks on.

"Right now, yeah, that's my plan," I say, equally annoyed with the attitude and my dumb ideas.

"You're a witch, love," Zev points out, like a sexy asshole. "You've got spells and powers... and you've got access to your memories that you've never had before."

Huh? Access to my memories? I cannot wait to know more about myself than everyone else seems to, because this shit is getting old.

"Step out of your mind," Rune says, sounding a little too much like a guru who's full of crap. "You get lost in your thoughts and can't see what's there."

This mumbo jumbo is going to drive me insane, but before I can tell them as much, Zev asks a final question.

"Where did you leave AJ?"

At the same time as the words *I don't know* flash through my head, so does an image of my dear friend, collapsed on the ground. I see her in my mind's eye, reliving the memory as it happened while I was there. Then, something shifts. I'm not looking through my eyes in the moment, but later as the dragon lifted into the air. I go higher and higher, AJ getting further away but still remaining in view.

It's the craziest thing. It's like I'm rewatching my flight to the vampire kingdom but from a different point of view. The DVD of my memory has special features and it's blowing my mind.

The vision dances through my head a few times, and I slowly piece together a direction and a general area. She's a few miles away, not nearly as far as I thought. When I pull myself out of my thoughts, both Rune and Zev are smiling.

"Did you learn anything?" Zev asks with a smirk.

I nod, still not fully believing what I saw. "How?"

"Magic opens the mind," Rune says, sounding like a stoner but still making a good point. "You aren't beholden to the linear thoughts of a human anymore. You have an extra eye."

Hell yeah I do.

I take one last peek into my past to get my bearings, then start to walk with a determined pace. "She's this way," I say with blooming confidence.

About ten steps in, the boys ruin my swagger.

"What? Why aren't you moving?"

"You've got a magical mind, love," Zev says as he steps towards me. "But you're not very fast."

He gives me a quick kiss and a bite of the lip, then transforms into a wolf. I swallow a small amount of pride and climb onto his back. "That way," I say, pointing to the horizon.

Rune breaks into a sprint, and we all charge off, guided by my new, badass witch vision.

The land passes quickly beneath Zev's paws and Rune's feet. I'm sure Zev could outpace the fae if he wanted, but Rune runs plenty fast when compared to a non-magical sprinter, and I can tell we're getting closer to the mark.

Even though the landscape still looks the same, I sense we're nearing the portal and the spot where AJ fell. I squint, trying to make out anything I see in the distance. Hundreds of feet away, the faint outline of a shape catches my eye. It could be a rock, it could be nothing, but we're going that way.

A few of Zev's strides closer and I know we're in the right place. My skin crawls just nearing the spot I had to deal with so many blows--AJ, Darius, Timót... Andor. I haven't processed that one enough. Deceitful and criminal as the little man was, I took a life. As soon as my brain makes space for it, I'm sure that will haunt me.

The shape I saw in the distance has now become a human form, and my heart skips far too many beats as I try to figure out who it is. A few feet closer I spot the flowing gown, the long red hair, and the general poise of a powerful witch.

Erzsébet.

Standing.

Over AJ.

It's been a day, maybe more, maybe less, and my best friend, my non-amorous life partner, my sister from another mister, still lies right where we left her.

The wound from Darius' betrayal opens back up a tiny bit.

My desire to shoot Timót out of a cannon and into the sun returns with a vengeance.

When we're probably twenty feet away, with Zev still running at a good clip, I find myself standing and leaping off his back, using our momentum to propel me forward. In my mind, I look incredible, flying toward the ground in slow motion. In reality, there's a good chance I'm about to break my ankles.

Maybe it's the sight of Erzsébet that has my brain remembering tricks from my training, or maybe it's the lesson I just got on how to access my mind--I point my wand at the ground I'm sailing toward and say "*párna.*" When my feet touch the stone they sink in gently, and I stick the landing like a professional, magical gymnast.

It probably saved me half a second, but I look freaking awesome.

"What's wrong?" I ask Erzsébet, saving our pleasantries for later when I know what's up with my fallen friend.

The witch queen looks at me, then at my feet as she admires my abilities, then back to my face with concern.

"She's alive, insomuch as she has a pulse," she says. "But I must know the spell in order to summon an antidote, if any exists."

For a split second, I revert back to the idiot brain I was trained to use by other idiots and family members who lied to me about my powers (no hard feelings, Tilly, I love you forever). Then I remember that I've got magic memories and I step inside my own mind, seeking out that moment that shot a harpoon through my heart, but now with the intention of undoing what was done.

"*Lélel nak a szikla,*" I say with more certainty than I've ever said anything. From the outside looking in, I can see it all unfold clear as day. I can hear the spell as though my father were standing next to me, whispering it into my ear.

It sends a chill down my spine.

Erzsébet wears a dubious look. "Are you sure?"

I nod, now trusting my memories implicitly since I can watch them like a detective analyzing a surveillance video.

Erzsébet kneels by AJ again, studying her and listening for either breath or a heartbeat. "Bernadette," she says softly. "I need you to come put a hand on AJ's shoulder. Hold her steady while I cast a spell."

I'm eager to do anything and everything to help, but am consumed with guilt after leaving her alone. If I can't save her now, it's my fault. I'm a shit friend. I had no choice, AJ would have told me to go if she'd been able, but that doesn't change how I feel.

I follow the queen's instructions and kneel beside AJ's body, stiff as a board but still warm.

"I make no promises," Erzsébet says. "I've one trick to try, then this is in the hands of the Fates."

I place my hand on AJ's shoulder while looking into her frozen face. Even if she's alive, her face doesn't make it seem that way. It's almost too much to bear.

I squeeze her arm, sending as much of my life force into her through my fingertips as I can manage. I don't know exactly what Erzsébet expects of me, but I'm doing my best.

"*Élettel teli,*" the queen says, a faint flicker of light coming from the end of her wand. There's no fanfare, nothing that makes me or Zev or Rune jump back in surprise. Only a slow breeze that circles around and wafts into AJ's slightly open mouth.

The lack of excitement makes me fear the worst. If the spell had worked, AJ would have shot up instantly, wondering where she was, looking for a vampire to fight.

I'm starting to crumble. I don't know if I can do any of the things I need to do with this hanging over me.

I lean over her, tears starting to trickle down my nose. She's still completely rigid, her hands balled into tight fists. I stare into her eyes, wondering if I'm about to say goodbye.

And then she blinks.

Her chest starts to rise and fall and her eyes wander around, trying to figure out where she is.

Finally, her gaze settles on me.

"You bitch."

CHAPTER NINE

I completely dissolve. I throw myself on top of AJ and start to cry like a baby, nearly crushing my actual baby between us.

For the first time in our long and storied friendship, AJ's crying as hard as I am.

"I watched you leave," she sobs. "I was paralyzed, and I watched that asshat tie you up and then you all flew off on dragons. Jesus Christ, B, I've never been so sad."

I help AJ up so we're both sitting. She takes a break from crying and talking to lean over and kiss Rain. I notice she's got a pendant clutched tightly in her hand, something I don't remember ever seeing before.

"Not many can withstand being turned to stone," Erzsébet says.

"Is that what happened to me?" AJ asks.

"More or less. Your body stops moving, even your cells and blood. Seems you have an impressive constitution."

AJ stares down at her pendant, then back up at me. I've got questions, but they can wait.

We resume crying for a few more moments, then AJ looks around to take stock of our present company.

"Witch lady, wolfy, elf man... where's the bloodsucker?"

When I open my mouth to answer, the lump in my throat gets too big for words to come out. I try to feel for our connection, to see if I can sense where he is or what he's going through, but there's nothing. Not a trace of Darius. He's in the Tomb.

I should have answered AJ's question more quickly, because now she's in a panic.

"No. He can't be dead. He--"

"He's not," I say. "He's alive, but... it's complicated. Like really complicated, there's a whole time and physics thing going on that I don't understand. I'll explain it while we travel."

AJ looks at me with hope in her eyes but fear on her otherwise grimacing face.

"Are we going... home?"

I shake my head.

"Back to Budapest?"

I shake my head again.

"Land of the water nymphs?"

A final head shake breaks her spirits. "Goddammit, just tell me then."

I stand, then help her to her feet. AJ's always been the picture of exuberance, so when her knees give out and she hits the ground again, I'm more than slightly concerned.

"What's wrong? Are you hurt?"

She looks more confused than agonized. "Just so. Damn. Thirsty."

Before I can ask, Rune is kneeling by her side with a leather bladder. She practically breaks his thumbs as she takes it and drinks it all down in a couple gulps.

"Better?" Rune asks, turning the bladder upside down and shaking it to prove she finished every drop.

AJ licks her lips and then shakes her head. "No. I'm still wicked thirsty. Water nymph needs water."

She's being tongue in cheek about the whole thing, but I get the feeling she's right. Rune's nod makes me even more sure.

"You need to do more than hydrate," he says. "I wonder if it's the water in your body that's kept you alive all these hours, and now it's nearly run out."

I look to Erzsébet to see if Rune's theory gets approved by the ancient witch. She nods as well. Seems like everyone agrees, which is awesome, but maybe we should do something about it?

"Where do we go for water?" I ask. "This clearly isn't the spot, so where do we go and how do we get there?"

Erzsébet adjusts her robes. "We can't find the help she needs in Vaemor. The vampire kingdom is toxic, as you might have noticed. We need to get to Aevelairith. The fae waters are renowned for their healing properties."

"She speaks the truth," Rune says with more than a little pride in his voice. "There is nothing more healing than water, and no water more healing than that of the fae. They say the ancient trees gained their spirits because of the waters that feed their roots. All of nature is more alive that is fed from these waters."

"Well, great, that's where we were going anyway, so maybe let's stop talking about it and get there," I say.

My own statement brings me to a very obvious question.

How the hell do we get to Aevelairith?

There has to be a portal here, because this is where I landed after Timót pulled me through the door underneath the Grand Hall. Looking around, I see nothing but barren grounds that stretch on indefinitely.

"You won't see the portal door, Bernadette."

Erzsébet's been doing a little mind reading these last few seconds, but her smile says she's got an answer that won't make me angry.

"The doorways between realms were opened shortly after the creation of all things, but the wars made them more of a danger than a useful means of conveyance. Aside from the singular room in our Budapest fortress, all the access portals have been hidden."

Cool. But also not.

"So how do we find our way out?"

Erzsébet turns her attention toward the ground, looking like an old woman who dropped a hairpin. "You just have to know where to look."

After staring at the ground for a minute or two, she pops up. "Here it is!"

We all move over, Zev and Rune each propping up AJ, to see what the powerful witch has found.

It's a rock.

Like, a pebble.

So… maybe she's lost it?

"*Felfed portál,*" she says with her wand pointed at the tiny stone. In an instant, an undulating doorway sprouts up from the ground, standing in front of us like a vertical sheet of water.

"Shit," AJ says, vocalizing what I was certainly thinking.

"How the hell did you know it was that rock?" I ask, probably sounding more annoyed than I really am. Except, for real, how?

"I just… remembered. Come along, just a few seconds before it disappears."

And with that, she steps through the magical passageway and vanishes into another realm.

She remembered.

Of course. And if I ever end up back here, I'll remember as well. Though if I ever end up back here, I might just lay down and hope to die. This place sucks.

Zev and Rune edge through the portal, still supporting AJ and moving quickly and safely.

I step in after them, a million things running through my head. I'm blissed the hell out to be back with AJ. I'm stoked to be in the company of another, more powerful witch. I need to feed and change my baby, and she's probably due for some tummy time.

I miss Darius beyond words. I miss his touch, I miss our connection, and I can't handle thinking about what he's experiencing.

And I'm glad we're on the move. Time to find some fae water and then go save the effing universe.

ROUND TWO OF falling through the witches' portal doesn't mess me up nearly as much as the first time.

For starters, I'm not pushed through by a creepy little shit disguised as Rune. This magical journey between realms also doesn't involve my father, and though my heart aches constantly for the pain Darius is enduring, I'm at least not worried that my friends and lovers are being slaughtered by vampires. All of those things make this teleportative outing much less stressful.

When we pass through the crazy rock door in Vaemor, we end up right where I started, underground in Budapest. I have a brief longing to run up and feel sunshine, maybe eat a bagel, do some quick human things, but I know there's no time. Erzsébet shows us right to another point on the portal room star, this one directing to a doorway that will drop us somewhere in Aevelairith.

That's what *really* separates this trip from the first portal voyage.

Landing in a remote corner of the vampire kingdom, where the sun is permanently blocked by imposing mountains and a gray haze--that's pretty upsetting to the senses.

Conversely, when you pop out in a cave behind a waterfall, then walk through the cascading stream and your eyes fall on a green, luscious valley, with even more waterfalls in the surrounding hills and all manner of plant and animal life frolicking about, it's pretty awesome.

They keep telling me these kingdoms are part of the same world or realm, but I don't see how that could be. The vampires live on Mars or Venus, some arid rock with nothing that can sustain biological life. The fae live in the freaking Garden of Eden. Traveling from the Sahara to the Amazon wouldn't produce this stark a contrast.

"Portals aren't what I expected," AJ says as we stand on the face of a cliff that's overgrown with beautiful ferns and flowers. The clearest, most brilliant water I've ever seen splashes down behind us, pools at our feet and then falls again into the watering hole below. We're up high enough to see for miles.

Erzsébet flashes a skeptical grin. "What were you expecting?"

AJ shrugs, but the effort appears to exhaust her and she leans against Rune for support in her weakened state, clutching the pendant at her chest. "I don't know. Something crazy like a unicorn piss portal or something."

I burst out laughing. "Unicorn piss? That's absurd! And gross." I shudder imagining having to walk through Michael's pee stream in order to fast travel.

"Maybe," she says. "But it would be interesting."

"Interesting isn't always better, A."

She rolls her eyes at me. "Interesting is always better."

Everyone else seems to have tuned out of our convo, and for good reason. I'm certainly done with these unsanitary visualizations. I clutch Rain against my chest as I refocus on the breathtaking beauty around us. I just wish Darius were here to enjoy it with us. Albeit at night, where he won't get fried by the sun, which honestly feels glorious on my skin. I can't remember the last time I was out during the daylight hours. My poor child probably has a massive Vitamin D deficiency.

"Do you know where we are?" Erzsébet asks Rune, who's surveying the grounds with a twinkle in his eye.

"It's the Valley of Hilinea," the fae answers. "I visited here with my grandmother in my youth, to see the dance of the willows."

Erzsébet nods, and it's clear she wasn't asking for directions but rather checking to make sure Rune knew his history. With how powerful and spry the queen is, I sometimes forget that she's crazy old and sometimes just wants to talk about old stuff.

"Hilinea was a powerful, kind woman. I met her when I was a child, she would come give lessons to young witches learning to make potions. A pity that this valley took on her name after it was forcibly annexed from the witching realm. I don't imagine she would have approved."

It's a passive-aggressive dig, but years of persecution have earned her the right. Rune has nothing to say in defense, just a solemn nod of acknowledgement.

Everyone stands in silence for a moment longer, then the quiet breaks as AJ cannonballs into the water below, nearly giving me a heart attack.

"AJ!" I scream, worried when she doesn't resurface immediately. Rune takes my hand, steadying my frayed nerves. "Wait. Watch."

So I do. I wait. I watch. I hope to heavens I'm not waiting and watching my best friend drown after being basically turned to stone.

I study the surface of the water looking for any signs of life, and if not for the calming effects of Rune, I'm sure I would be losing my mind right now.

I'm expecting her little head to bob up at any moment sucking in a huge breath, but then I remember she can breathe underwater and I feel like a huge idiot. Still, she's so weak that I'm not totally convinced all is well.

When something shoots out of the water and into the air like a playful dolphin, I nearly fall off the cliff. Rune catches me as I stare in awe.

AJ is flipping through the air laughing and hooting, and I don't blame her for one single second.

Her long blond hair dances in the wind, but now has streaks of teal blue through it. Her skin is iridescent and shimmers under the sun, and her legs... well, her legs are now fused into a beautiful teal fish tail that matches her eyes and the new streaks in her hair.

Also, she seems to have lost her clothes underwater, as she is totally naked now, save her jewelry and her newly acquired scales.

"AJ is... a mermaid?" I ask in awe.

"We always knew she was a water nymph," Rune says with a smile. "If the blood line is strong enough, they can take on a form similar to mermaids, though it's very rare. Their scales are different, and their gills are slightly larger."

"Right, so like the difference between a crocodile and an alligator."

Rune shrugs. "I suppose."

I grin. "AJ's gonna be thrilled to hear this is super rare. But why is it happening now and not all the other times she went into water?"

He looks at AJ thoughtfully. "A combination of things. It's the magical waters of these lands unlocking her deepest truth, and likely healing a fracture within that was keeping her separate from her magic. It's also that she knows who she is now," he says with a grin. "At any rate, she has the right idea."

Without warning, Rune plunges into the water below, joining AJ. He swims to the surface, shedding his wet shirt and climbing up on the water's edge. We've all got a million worries on our minds, but Rune is taking a break to feel at home. Water drips off his slender frame as he tilts his head back, eyes closed, feeling the warm sun on his face.

Zev quickly follows suit, swan diving into the water below and then joining the fae on the shore. AJ continues to dance with the water. I can't describe it in any other way. What she's doing right now is so much more than swimming, and I feel a twinge of envy at how connected she is with this element. It suits her.

I've got Rain strapped to my chest, and I'm not really one for high-diving, so I look to Erzsébet to see what she's got planned for her descent. My look is met with a sly smile.

"Hand me Rain and swim with your men and your friend," she says. "If I were an eon or two younger, that's what I would do."

It's a sweet offer, and a salient point. Who knows how many chances I'll have to dive from fae waterfalls into fae pools and then snuggle up with my werewolf mate? Plus I definitely want a closer look at AJ's tail.

I hand Rain and her harness to Erzsébet, panic for a second, then take the plunge. The fall is exhilarating and my heart is pounding hard in my chest when I hit the frigid water, but my body adapts quickly and it becomes a pure source of refreshment and magical regeneration.

AJ splashes up to me, using her tail to send a spray of sparkling water raining over me like a waterfall. "B! Look! I have a tail!"

I laugh as I tread water, weighed down by too many clothes. "I noticed. What's it like?"

She giggles and does a backflip, then resurfaces and sprays water from her mouth like a fountain. I just try not to think of the fish poop that's definitely in that mouthful. "It feels freaking amazing!" she says. "Like I was born to this. I never want to leave."

That innocent sentiment sends my heart lurching. In all our talks of me leaving Rowley, it never occured to me she might be the one to leave. Why would she want to go back to a town with such bad memories, where she's not treated great, when she could spend her life lazing in the sun and swimming like a fish?

Given the choice, I know which I would pick, and if it comes to that, I'll be happy for her.

Sensing my mood as always, she sprays me with water again, this time more forcefully. "Stop moping. I'm not leaving you, not even for a water paradise."

I smile and the words give me temporary comfort, but I hadn't realized until now that she could have a much more enjoyable life in this world. Is it possible to relocate? To become a permanent citizen of Aevelairith? Are there, like, immigration laws or paperwork to fill out? It's something to look into. I want my friend to live her best possible life, even if that isn't with me.

I swim to the shore with the guys and undress down to my underwear and bra. This gets me a few appreciative glances which I smile at before diving back in. I can understand why AJ never wants to leave. It's like swimming in the original waters of creation. I feel a bubbling of joy within me that radiates through my skin as it glows in the water. Everything feels possible, and suddenly the task of convincing a couple more rival kingdoms to align doesn't seem nearly as daunting.

Let's just hope no one from our worlds gets their hands on this magical treasure. It would be bottled up and sold on Amazon within a month.

I swim back over to AJ, who let's me more closely examine her skin and scales. "You're beautiful," I say in awe.

She smiles even wider. "This is the best thing to ever happen to me in my whole life, and it's all because of you," she says, growing suddenly serious, her eyes glossy with emotion. "Thank you, Bernie. You're my best friend in the world, and you've brought so much magic into my life, I can't even begin to tell you how you've changed me."

"I almost got you killed," I say, the words sticking in my throat painfully.

She rolls her eyes. "Please. First, I'm totally better. Better than better. I'm the best I've ever been. And your dipshit dad was responsible for that, not you. By that token, I almost got you killed when my ex showed up with a shotgun."

Solid point. In all the craziness, I'd nearly forgotten about that. Crazy how a guy almost killing you then dying by vampire-werewolf attack in your living room can seem so inconsequential in the right--or wrong--context.

"How about we chalk up our near death experiences to the asshole men in our lives and enjoy the awesomeness of this world. Cuz I am here for this."

I smile and nod my head. "Fair enough. Race you to the shore?"

What an idiot I am.

As kids I always beat her in pretty much every foot race.

But that wasn't in the water, and she wasn't sporting a mermaid tail.

She's laughing at me as she does a magnificent spiral in the air and lands near the shore in a blink.

I take a bit longer and am laughing along with her when I arrive.

She continues playing in the water, and I wave to Rain and Erzsébet, but realize they're no longer there.

A quick look around finds them having located an easier trail down, and now lounging under a weeping willow on a patch of thick green grass that looks like luxurious carpet. Erzsébet is giving Rain a bath in the magic waters, and my daughter's skin is glowing like mine as she babbles. I mouth a thank you to the witch and crawl out of the water to lay on the grass between Zev and Rune as they look up at the clouds.

Zev puts his arm around me and pulls me into his chest. His heat dries my undergarments quickly and the sun feels amazing on my skin. I close my eyes and soak in the rays, the calm, the bliss of this moment.

The water laps at our feet, pushed by the currents from the waterfall, and continues to work its magic on all of us.

I peek through eyelashes to see that Rain is now napping on the grass, Erzsébet keeping a close eye on her. AJ is lounging on a boulder pushing out of the water, like the Little Mermaid. Rune looks like he's napping, and Zev has his gaze locked on me.

"You're beautiful," he whispers, his lips now inches from mine.

"It's my waterfall look. Carefully cultivated," I joke, tugging on the wet, wavy mess that is my hair now.

"It's a good look," he says with a grin. "The only flaw I can find in it is that you are wearing too much clothing."

I laugh. "Some would say I'm not wearing enough, given we're not alone."

"Who says being alone is a requirement for anything?" he asks, a darkly seductive look on his face.

"You're naughty. And I'm not having sex in front of everyone." Honestly, Rain is too young to know what's going on. I'm sure plenty of new parents have sex with their sleeping infant in a crib nearby. And AJ--Eh. Not really into exhibitionism, but we've seen worse from each other. Rune? Actually, the idea gives me a little tingle. But there is no way in hell or hades I'm getting frisky with the queen of witches eyeing us. Nope. Hard and fast and solid nope.

Zev sighs dramatically, then pulls me up with him in one smooth move and dives into the water with me.

With my skin freshly warmed by werewolf heat and the sun, the water is shockingly cold once again, but I relish it and duck my head to submerge myself completely. Zev joins me, and the water is so crystal clear we can see each other in detail.

He makes funny faces and reaches for me, and I try not to laugh and inhale the wrong oxygen source for my body.

My best friend may be easily able to switch between water and air with ease, but I'm still solidly in the air camp.

When he presses his lips to mine, the air from his lungs enters me, and I inhale him and kiss him, our bodies slipping against each other in an extremely pleasant way.

I wrap my legs around his waist and let the hardness of him press into me as he moans in my mouth.

He clearly has a larger storage of oxygen than me, but eventually we both run out of air and have to resurface.

I'm laughing and spitting water, so it takes me a moment to catch that the energy around us has changed.

I look to the shore and see Rune standing with his hands up. AJ is on shore, human legs returned, completely naked, also raising her hands.

And surrounding the shore are dozens of fae holding longbows, all of which are pulled tight and aimed straight at us.

Frantic, I look around to find Erzsébet and Rain, but they are nowhere to be seen. I say a silent prayer of hope that she left before being noticed and is taking care of my baby. Because whatever is going down right now isn't good, and I don't want my child anywhere near it. If Rain got away with the queen of the witches, I know she'll be safe.

The leader of the armed fae, a tall man with long black hair streaked with silver, steps forward. "Quite a lot of foreigners to be swimming in a sacred fae pool. Keep your wands where we can see them. Reach for a weapon or shift and you'll be dead."

I eye my wand on the shore and curse myself for not keeping it with me.

Zev and I approach cautiously, trying our best to stay out of view.

"Come out of the water, you two."

Not out of view enough, it would seem. We step onto dry land and move over to join Rune.

My usually calm companion glares at the man in charge with a hatred I have never seen on his face, even when confronting our most dangerous enemies.

"Hello cousin," Rune says. "I expected a warmer welcome than this."

His cousin smirks. "You weren't expecting a welcome at all, or else you wouldn't be sneaking in through the south end of the valley. Too bad for you we still run patrols to keep vampires and wolves out. Tell me, Rune, when did you become such traitorous trash?"

He grabs Rune by the neck and pushes him forward. The other fae take the rest of us by the arms and start marching us away from the water.

Before I can be corralled, I sprint over to grab my wand, but just as my fingers touch it a large boot comes down on my hand. I yelp in pain and feel a strong grip on the back of my head, pulling me up by my hair.

"No, no, no," Rune's cousin says. "You've caused enough trouble as it is. You can have your stick back when you're released from prison… should such a day ever arrive."

CHAPTER TEN

W*here's Rain?* I ask Zev mentally as we are pushed into a thick forest, the threat of being shot by an arrow ever-present.

They got away before they were seen. Don't worry, Erzsébet will protect Rain and find us later. His voice is husky in my mind, and there's a simmering rage he's barely repressing under his words. I glance at him and see his muscles bulging as he resists the urge to wolf out.

How do you know? I ask.

Because she's the queen of the witches, caring for the Last Witch, he says curtly. *What else would she do?*

It's the answer I hoped for, but I still breathe a deep sigh of relief at hearing it. As much as it terrifies me to have Rain out of my sight, there's no one I'd rather she be with, and I'm extremely happy they snuck off unseen.

I'm pulled out of my thoughts when I feel a guard's hand grab my arm and yank me forward. "Keep the pace," he says, his hard gray eyes boring into me. "So you're the witch everyone's been talking about? What's so special about you?" he hisses as he drags me along, his grip creating an instant bruise around my arm.

"Give me back my wand and find out for yourself," I spit back.

He squeezes even tighter, causing me to flinch. I really got the wrong impression about the fae; basing them all off Rune's pleasant demeanor was a big mistake.

The guard's eyes shift from me when we hear a low growl coming from my side. Zev easily rips out of the grasp of the surprised fae holding onto him and pushes my guard away from me, grabbing him by the throat in the process. "I will cut off any body part of yours that touches her again. Do you understand?"

Everyone stops walking to turn and look at us.

And AJ uses this moment to speak up. "Hey, I'm naked here in case you hadn't noticed!"

She. Looks. Pissed.

I have never seen my bestie this angry, and I've seen her plenty riled up. I notice a few of the fae soldiers leering at her, and that makes my blood boil.

"You'll have to make do," Rune's dick bag cousin says as he turns away. "Keep moving, we don't have time for distractions. And you," he says to Zev. "Another move and I'll put an arrow through your heart, then turn you into a wolf-skin rug."

They push us along, no intention of heeding AJ's request. I'd love at least a shirt to cover a little skin, but poor AJ's naked as the day she was born.

"Ouch!" The fae holding onto AJ yelps and jumps back from her. We all stop and stare.

I widen my eyes at her hair, which is now floating above her head in the shape of spikes. That bitch used her water powers to make frozen daggers with her wet hair, and her captor now has a gash across his face that's seeping blood.

On the one hand, go girl. On the other, Rune's cousin hasn't been stingy with the threats. I'm not sure how far we can push before someone gets hurt.

AJ's eyes blaze, and the pendant she's clutching almost glows. "Give me and Bernie some clothes, or you won't like how this ends."

Rune's cousin sneers for a moment, then nods at two of his men. Looks like we walked up to the line but didn't cross it.

The guards take off their vests and hand them to us. AJ and I slip them on, and I feel a little more confident now that I'm a bit more clothed. The vest acts as a very sleeveless dress.

My guard does not touch me the rest of the hike, and he flinches every time Zev glances at him.

In fact, none of the guards get heavy-handed with us again, and I wonder if they realize we could for sure take them in a fight. Or if they have another reason for getting us to the royal family unscathed. I mean, Rune is their prince. That must account for something, right?

It's unfortunate we're surrounded by fae assholes, otherwise I'd really enjoy the scenery. As we get closer to the outer walls of Aevelairith, I notice more houses built within the trunks and branches of trees. We cross beautiful streams every hundred feet or so, walking over carefully carved wooden bridges.

We finally come to a giant drawbridge nestled between two mountain ridges. A handful of guards stand in front of the massive gate, while others lean out of turrets above, their bows drawn.

Rune's shitty cousin yells up to a guard stationed atop the barricade. "Lower the gate and send a runner to the palace. Tell the king and queen their son's come home."

The sound of gears turning echoes off the mountains as the drawbridge lowers. I sort of expect to see paved streets and something representing a city on the other side, but all I see are trees. As we start to move through the threshold and I can look higher, I see the city I wanted is mostly there, just several stories higher.

Bridges, branches, vines and ropes connect a massive overhead metropolis, held in place by every kind of tree you can imagine. Redwoods act as huge pillars for the bigger structures; birch trees grow in tight clusters to form barriers; incredible oaks reach in every direction, creating walkways on different levels. It's what a child might imagine a squirrel motel would look like, but full of grown adults and way more extravagant.

We're ushered along by our unfriendly captors. As we pass other fae, they seem intrigued and confused by us. Some of them recognize Rune and gasp. All in all, they strike me as more fae-like than the patrolling squad that found us.

Crap cousin reaches a massive sequoia trunk with a small opening and gestures for us to enter. The gesture isn't a suggestion, because our accompanying guards shove us ahead and don't give us a choice.

Inside the tree, a spiral staircase is carved along the inner edge of the trunk. I can't explain how big this sequoia is, except to say I immediately forget it's a tree once we're in the trunk.

The stairs go up for quite a few flights, occasionally passing openings to branches that lead off to another tree. I start to wonder how long it took to build this place, then stop myself before a migraine sets in.

Finally we're shown an exit, though the doorway out of the tree doesn't really take us outside. Instead we find ourselves in a spacious chamber with a roof that looks to be made of enormous leaves. The walls are made from a variety of woods that seem fused together, creating a natural, rustic look.

At the end of the hall are three chairs, or humble thrones. The king sits in the center seat, his long white hair matched by a long, silky beard. Aside from being completely gray, he doesn't look that old.

The queen sits beside him, with curly hair I want to describe as blond, but it's just so damn light I can't tell. Maybe she's gone gray too, but it looks sort of like Rune got his coloring from her.

And on the other side of the king sits who I'm guessing is the princess, Rune's older sister. She somehow popped out of her mother with auburn hair, so I'm guessing that's how Rune's pop's was colored many moons ago.

Each of the three wears the same concerned expression, and they've all got their eyes on Rune.

We're led into the center of the room while more guards pour in and stand around the perimeter. You'd think the envoy accompanying the prince of this realm, all of whom just got caught skinny dipping and are still underdressed, would draw less hostile attention.

The king looks at each of us, then finally speaks. "Where are you coming from?"

"Found them at the Mystelian Falls," the cousin answers. "Marched them straight here."

The looks of concern on the royals' faces take on a shade of confusion.

"Did you not give them a chance to dress?" the queen asks.

"Well, your majesty, the intrusion--"

"As you can see by my borrowed vest that barely covers my ass and has to be pulled shut so you can't see my hoo-ha, no they did not."

Sometimes I wonder what movie AJ saw as a child that made her think speaking her mind at all times, no matter the company, was the best choice. The king and queen seem a bit taken aback, but then turn back to the leader of the guards.

"Why would you treat your cousin this way, Eliar?" Now the king looks upset, but not at us.

"My lord, he's betrayed you in more ways--"

"So you march him naked through the woods? If he's to be tried and put to death, so be it, but he is still your prince until that verdict comes, and I daresay I'm not going to give it."

The cousin, Eliar, chomps down on his lip so he won't dig this hole any further. The king rises and walks toward Rune, who kneels before his father.

"Stand, child," the king says, and as he does so the queen walks down to join them. "I don't need your forgiveness when I don't yet know what's happened. Above all, I'm overcome with gratitude to see you alive."

"Thank the gods," his mother said. "We've missed you, Rune."

On the heels of meeting Darius' father, and then thinking about my recent parental interactions, it feels like Rune hit the mom-and-dad jackpot. The sister also stands, looking happy to see her brother but staying a few feet back. While Rune embraces his parents, his sister does a quick survey of the rest of us. I'd probably do the same if I were in her shoes. She and I hold brief eye contact, but her stare lingers on Zev the longest.

Rune makes quick work of explaining what's happened. Since the king and queen--who I gather from the conversation are named Rivelis and Scocha, respectively--are good listeners with concern for their family, he's able to make salient points and gets them nodding pretty earnestly while describing the flawed view of the prophecy.

When he gets to the part about an alliance, the air gets sucked out of the room. Rune's sister, Revia, steps forward to join the conversation, her mood seeming very tense.

"What word do you have that they might hold their end of the bargain?" she asks. "And why would we ever trust that?"

I see the body language of the guards shift while the conversation turns to teaming up with the vampires. Centuries of battle and fending them off has made for some pretty bad blood, so to speak.

"We have word from their new king, and we have a sworn oath with the king's brother, Darius," Rune says.

Rivelis cocks an eye at Darius' name. "Your old friend? That vampire prince, you have an oath with him?"

Rune nods, and I really can't tell how his dad is reacting to this information. He slowly strokes his beard while digging through his memory.

"We liked him before this all started, I remember. Before he took on his father's disposition."

"Which has gone since he met Bernadette," Rune says, gesturing to me, "and her daughter."

Rivelis shows a warm smile as he walks over to me, but stops short.

"I can't believe I didn't ask... where is the Last Witch?"

Great question, sir. Where is the witch who has my baby? I'm about to ask that very question, when Rune comes in with an answer.

"The child remains in the Earthly realm with Erzsébet," he says. "Bernadette was pulled from that world without her baby, and as trying as that's been, it's kept the child safe."

It's a calculated lie, but I'm not quite sure why he's telling it. The king and queen seem to be entirely on his side. Now we're locked into not asking about--or looking for--my baby and our very powerful companion.

Far be it from me to question Rune's assessment of the situation, especially in his own kingdom. As I move through these thoughts, my eyes again meet with Rune's sister's, and I can't quite get a read on what she's thinking. She looks away after a beat, and the king's voice draws everyone's attention.

"I, for one, am moved by your story and compelled to act," Rivelis says. "But not until I've spoken with the queen and spent some time in the Elder Roots. The issue of an alliance with the vampires comes with great delicacy."

"Unless we establish ourselves as the leading race with full authority," Revia says, "I see no case for such a coalition. It's a setup for betrayal."

"I agree... or rather, I would have,' Rivelis says, putting a hand on his daughter's shoulder, "but the death of King Vladimir and this argument against the prophecy turns my mind. After all, who among us doesn't want to see the end of this endless war?"

The king gestures to the whole room, bringing the dozens of guards into the conversation. A few give small nods, most stay stoically still. Revia doesn't look convinced, but she holds her tongue.

"How about you, Prince Zev?" Rivelis asks the werewolf with a small smile, while Zev looks a bit shocked that he's being addressed directly. "Wouldn't you like the slaughtering to end?"

"More than anything, Your Highness."

"Then let me mull our options while you all rest. Rune, show our guests to the western madrone lofts. The Celebration of the Sun begins tomorrow, and you'll have an excellent view of the festivities."

"We'll have clothes brought to the rooms," Scocha says with a smile. I goddamn love this fae family.

Rune gives a quick bow, then turns to us and gestures toward the door. The large group of guards that walked us in here no longer has the job of escorting us around, and the sneer on Eliar's face shows that he doesn't love it.

I, on the other hand, am thrilled to feel like an honored guest and not a prisoner. I might get some rest and enjoy myself for a day. Except that my baby's off in the woods somewhere, hiding out. And my lover is still at the very beginning of his three-day torture sentence. Perhaps my mind isn't going to let me just enjoy these comforts.

On the way out, Rune stops in front of his cousin and holds out his hand expectantly. A moment later, and with a look of pure resentment, Eliar hands my wand to the fae prince, who in turn passes it to me. I give Eliar the absolute sassiest smile on my way out.

Rune leads us down a couple of tree flights after we leave the royal chamber, then we start across a long bridge made of ivy vines that runs between treetops. We're high enough up that I can see a lake in the distance, and a nearby hilltop that's covered in grapevines and fruit trees. I can't turn my head without being charmed to death by Aevelairith.

We finally reach our rooms, which are quaint little yurts at the end of individual walkways atop a massive madrone. I'm reminded of the fancy tropical resorts, where you have your own room at the end of a dock over the water. Instead of being over the water, these rooms stand over an entire forest.

We each have our own space, and in mine I find a plush four poster bed draped with colorful silks, a sitting area with a loveseat and two chairs made of wood so supple and carved so beautifully that when I sit on one I don't even miss the cushions. There's an armoire with a decorative depiction of a large tree with roots that run down to the floor, a bathroom complete with a tub, a fancy looking toilet and a shiny mirror to show just how shitty I looked when I met the king and queen of the fae. Throughout the space are open windows, letting in the fresh evening air carrying a hint of lavender. Hanging in my wardrobe is a beautiful yellow and green gown in just my size. I'm not all that big on dresses, but this one just falls over my body in the most comfortable way.

"Eff me, this thing fits like a dream!"

AJ's voice is a little piercing, but I appreciate that she's having the same dress-wearing experience as I am.

There's a knock at my door and I turn to see Zev and Rune waiting at the entrance. They are both dressed in the simple yet elegant style of the fae, with fitted vests edged with gold and silver leaves. Zev comes to me first, taking me in his arms and admiring my new threads. After a tender kiss, I pull from my mate's arms and walk over to hug Rune.

"Of all the magic I've seen, this place might be the most magical," I say. "And your parents are, like, parents."

Rune smiles, then looks to Zev. "The werewolves have seen a different side of them from time to time, but our familial connection is strong."

He pauses, throwing a quick glance at the door before looking into my eyes. "I felt compelled to lie about Rain because I don't trust everyone's intentions just yet. My cousin is a fine example of the more hostile members of our kingdom, who perhaps aren't ready for this war to end, and certainly aren't ready to believe the prophecy has a different interpretation."

I nod and hug him again, showing my understanding and siphoning off his calming energy. I'm glad he lied about my baby's whereabouts and I'm feeling more confident now that she's safe with Erzsébet. Food, shelter and warmth won't be an issue as long as she's with Granny Witch.

I look out the window, taking in the alluring view and breathing in the sweet, clean air.

"What's the Celebration of the Sun?" I ask.

Rune moves over to my side, equally enamored by the sight of his homeland. "It's a month-long celebration at the end of our Spring. The days grow longer until we reach a day without darkness. Starting tomorrow, the royal family hosts a feast each day as the fae bring the Spring bounty to share with one another.

During these years fraught with battle, this month has been a lone bright spot in Aevelairith."

Zev joins us at the window and puts his arm around Rune's shoulder instead of mine. It's a bit of a surprise, but my heart flutters at the show of affection between the two.

"I fear the wolves may have ruined a celebration or two, my friend."

Rune responds to the touch by leaning his head down, resting it sweetly against Zev's. "And we did the same or worse to you."

It's all I can do not to turn into a blubbering baby. I imagine if a civil war had broken out in Mass and somehow AJ and I ended up on opposite sides. It seems like an impossibility that we'd turn against each other, but I'm not so naive to assume everything would be peachy.

"Did you guys try to stay friends when it all started?" This level of intimacy between the two has me feeling bolder than normal about diving into these old wounds. They turn to face me, keeping their arms around each other's shoulders.

"For years," Zev answers. "At the beginning, we considered the four of us the great hope for a united future."

"Cara's death broke our connection with Darius," Rune says. "After that, we didn't see or speak with him until arriving at your bar. Zev and I lost touch a few years later."

I'm about to ask more, yearning to learn every detail about these men I love, but Rune's eyes shoot up to the entryway and his mood changes. I spin to follow his gaze and find his sister standing in the doorway.

She walks in, eyes darting between each of us, and closes the door behind her.

"I didn't get a chance to say hello, Revia," Zev says with a slight smirk. I'm sure these two have some sort of history, and the princess's response makes me think it's not all great.

"I don't fold as easily as my father," she snaps, then brushes past Zev to face her brother.

"You've brought a wolf into our most sacred rooms, and the Last Witch is here in Aevelairith." She punctuates this statement with a look at me, and it's clear that I had some sort of tell when Rune told his little fib in the royal chamber.

"I know you've told lies, and I need to know how many," she goes on, her gaze back on Rune. "Give me the truth, or I'll have all of your friends killed."

CHAPTER ELEVEN

Rune and Revia are locked in a tense staredown, while Zev and I stay watchful, showing no reaction to the threat against our lives. That doesn't mean inside I'm not bristling like an angry porcupine. Our peaceful stay in the fae realm has taken a quick and unexpected turn.

"I'm a little surprised by your hostility, Revia," Rune says.

"You shouldn't be. Perhaps your time off in another world, forming bonds with sworn enemies has made you forget the needs of our people and the crimes of others." She doesn't need to look at Zev on that last line for us to know who she's talking about.

"Lest we forget our own crimes," Rune says. "And perhaps you're right, time away has changed my mind on some things, but only because I had a chance to realize our reading of an ancient prophecy is flawed at best."

"On what grounds? Everything else has come true, Rune. The three kingdoms are locked in eternal war. We are losing the strength of our magic. Our numbers have dwindled as our mothers cannot bear children. You've fallen in love with a witch and suddenly decided the prophecy has no merit. Tell me I'm wrong."

Rune hesitates and looks at me. I know that I love him, but something about his sister accusing him of *falling* in love with me puts a whole new spin on our relationship.

"Yet everything you mention stems from the death of the witches. As their power has been extinguished, so has our own. The prophecy felt valid because we made it so. And might I ask, what magic do you think will be unlocked by killing an innocent child?" Rune now has a little more edge on his voice than before. "What other fae rituals fall in line with killing an infant? How far outside your moral code are you willing to step for a contested interpretation?"

Revia again turns to me, but the anger in her eyes has turned to concern. I don't think she likes the idea of taking an innocent life. Rune's framing might have her rethinking things.

She takes a moment and then changes the topic when she speaks. "Where is the child? I know she's alive and I don't believe she's on Earth."

I can tell Rune's thinking of how best to play this. Sell the lie or see if the truth will set us free? I'm not surprised when he opts for the latter.

"Yes, she is here. She's with the queen witch, hidden somewhere on the edges of the valley. You won't find her unless Bernadette wants her to be found, however."

Revia considers this thoughtfully. She came in with a full head of steam, but the sincerity of her brother seems to have her on a different track.

"It was wise to keep that from our parents, I think. Knowing the Last Witch was within the realm might cloud their vision."

"It seemed like the safest version of our story," Rune says.

The siblings share a pensive moment, and I see the similarities in them. Rune might be on the calmer side, but I think that comes with being the younger child without the same pressure of leading.

"I'm sorry for the threat," Revia says. "These have been difficult times, and battles haven't stopped while you were away. Until today, I was expecting the vampires would stage an attack during Celebration, as they often do." She raises an eyebrow and looks to Zev. "Now I only have to worry about the wolves it would seem."

"If they come, I'll fight by your side, princess," my wolf says in response. Revia smiles, then heads for the door.

"Such strange times. It's nice to see you, brother. And welcome to Aevelairith, Bernadette."

She takes the tension in the room with her when she leaves, and I sink onto the bed, exhausted by... everything.

I miss my daughter, but I know she's safer wherever she is.

I worry about Darius, and I have to constantly shift my thoughts away from imagining what unthinkable loneliness and despair he's enduring.

The guys are standing side by side, staring out the window as the sun sets completely and the moon rises full in the sky, letting in moonbeams that cast shimmering rays of silver light across my room.

"I feel the pull of the full moon," Zev says, speaking gruffly. "I must shift."

Rune frowns. "There will be patrols everywhere. You won't be safe in wolf form."

Zev looks meaningfully at the fae. "I will be safe. I know how to evade your kind, brother. And being back in my homeworld on a full moon, I have no choice."

Rune nods and Zev comes over to me and pulls me from the bed into his arms. His kiss is bruising and passionate and I can feel his wolf at the surface, ready to come out and play. How I wish I could go running through the woods with him. I feel the call of it in my blood as his mate, but have no outlet for that impulse.

When he pulls away, his nails already growing and his body shifting, I feel the absence, and I watch in awe as his fancy fae clothes are shredded in his shift from man to wolf.

I'll be keeping an eye on you. We can't trust everyone here. Call if you need me.

His parting words give me a small comfort, knowing he'll be out there if anything happens.

I'm just hoping nothing happens. One night of no one trying to kill me would be super fab.

Zev leaps through an open window in a fluid motion born of instinct and disappears into the woods. I still feel our connection, our mate bond singing through my blood, which eases my anxiety.

I turn to Rune, whose eyes are trained on the horizon beyond our rooms, when AJ bursts in. "Yo. Did Zev just wolf out in the middle of enemy territory?"

"He's fine," I say with more conviction than I feel.

Oh come now, love. Have more faith in me than that.

I cringe that Zev felt my uncertainty.

It's not you I doubt.

AJ yawns and glances down at her pendant. Her lips purse like she's about to say something about it until she notices me watching.

She yawns again, this time with way more exaggeration. "I'm wiped. Heading to bed." She grins at Rune and me. "Don't do anything I wouldn't do."

I snort. "That leaves a lot on the table."

"Exactly. Have fun," she says in a sing-songy voice as she leaves, closing the door behind her.

I glance at Rune, who is now watching me with such intensity I blush. Then I feel stupid for blushing, given this guy helped me birth my child and has already seen me at my most vulnerable.

"You must be tired," Rune says, though he makes no move to leave.

"Not as much as I thought," I say as my heartbeat escalates until I can hear the whoosh of my own blood.

Rune steps closer to me and takes my hand in his. "I apologize for how my cousin treated you. I should have done more."

He glances away, the mood that was building between us fizzling like dying soap bubbles. "It wasn't your fault," I say. "And your parents laid into him publicly. Almost made it all worth it."

"I'm relieved they were welcoming. I was worried," he says.

"I know. But it must be nice to be home?" My voice lands on a hopeful note and he smiles and brushes a stray hair from my face with his free hand.

"It is. But as I'm sure you know, homecoming is always a mixed bag."

"I feel that," I say. "I'm surprised your parents weren't more committed to killing my baby," I say, then flinch at how badly those words came out of my mouth. But Rune doesn't seem bothered.

"In truth, I am as well. Something must have happened while I was gone to soften their stance on this, but I can't imagine what. We still don't have a final answer, so we'll have to see how this ends. They will speak with other fae leaders, including my sister, who may not be in favor of allying with enemies who killed so many of our brothers and sisters."

We both walk out onto the balcony and sit on the bench facing the vista. A sky full of stars set like diamonds against velvet, the moon hanging heavy overhead, casting the world around us in an ethereal glow. Rune slips an arm over my shoulder and I lean into him as we continue our conversation.

"It feels like the fae will make or break this alliance," I say, speaking the truth we both know all too well. It would be hard for the wolves to say no when both the vampires and fae were in agreement against all odds. Without the fae, the wolves have much less reason to trust the vampires alone.

"Zev will secure the wolves," Rune says, and I hear the message he's not saying out loud. There is a way Zev can secure allyship with his kingdom... if he's king.

I lean forward and rub my temples, as the beginning of a headache sneaks up on me. "What exactly is happening in this world that you each thought the prophecy and my baby could fix?" I ask as Rune rubs my sore back with his strong, skilled hands.

"The magic is fading. Procreation has all but stopped. Vampires can no longer turn others except the king himself. Our races will die out if we do not reverse it."

"Right, you mentioned that. But what does that look like specifically? How do you know it's because magic is dying and not because, I don't know, people are taking the wrong meds?"

He pauses his ministrations on my back as he thinks. I would have asked a less riveting question if I knew it meant he'd stop massaging me with those exquisite hands.

I twist to face him and he takes both my hands in his. "I want to show you something, if you don't mind?"

I nod, expecting us to slip into his memories like before. But instead, he stands, pulling me up with him. Rather than jump out the window like Zev, we leave via the door and down through winding trails and thick trees that glow a luminescent green in the night.

In fact, between the full moon and how much of the foliage around us has that graceful glow, I don't need a light to see just fine.

We hike together in companionable silence, holding hands, and I take in as much of the intoxicating fae evening as I can. The air is thick with the scent of lavender and something else... something sweet. It's a balmy evening, and part of me thinks the weather here is always some version of perfect. I can feel the bite of chill in the air that still speaks of warmer days to come.

"It's incredible to me, how all the plant life glows," I say, and he pauses to turn to me with an intrigued look.

"You can see it?"

"Uh, yeah. It's hard to miss. How do you think I'm able to see in the dark?" I ask.

He looks past me, lost in thought for a moment. "What you're seeing is the life flow of the plant kingdom. Their spirits. All my life, I've only known fae to see their true nature." He shrugs, his expression still a bit vacant and turns to continue walking.

I don't know what to make of his words. "Maybe when the queen of trees stabbed me, I got some kind of new plant super power?" I ask.

He tilts his head, pondering it. "Perhaps."

He doesn't sound convinced, but whatever it is, I enjoy the walk through what feels like pure magic.

It seems very sudden when we stop at an impossibly tall gate to a massive garden. Towering stone walls stand before us covered in vines dotted with glowing silver orbs.

"How did I not see this until now?" I ask, looking behind me. I should have been able to see it for the last ten minutes of our walk.

"It is part of the magic of this place. You'll understand in a moment."

He places his palm into a hand shaped mold on the door. Something clicks and Rune pulls his hand back, wiping blood off his palm as he does.

Slowly the door grunts and grinds open, sounding as if it hasn't budged in eons.

When we step into the garden, I become more convinced no one has been here in a super long time.

It's an incredible and wildly overgrown paradise of lush trees, crystal growths glimmering iridescent, blue, red, wild flowers letting off the fragrant scent I could smell even back in my room. In the center of it all, a massive tree that towers over the rest, branches spread thick and long, roots clearly going deep and wide through the earth.

Everything in the garden is alive and glows with that magic I shouldn't be able to see... everything except the mighty tree.

I suck in my breath and step forward, holding my hand out. I place my palm on the tree and squeeze back tears at the emptiness I feel from it. "What happened to her?" I ask, feeling very strongly this was not just an ordinary tree. Though it is nearly fossilized, I can still sense what once was within.

"She is the Tree of Life. The epicenter of magical harmony in our world. As you can see, she is dying. Perhaps she is already dead and the magic she left behind just takes longer to disappear entirely. Either way, without her, all of this world will slowly perish."

"And everyone thought sacrificing Rain would wake her back up?"

Rune doesn't glance away from my harsh tone, instead he holds my gaze and nods.

"She doesn't want blood," I say, feeling into something I don't quite understand. "Not the way you think."

This gets the fae's attention, and he is immediately by my side, almost as fast as Darius. "Can you hear her? My grandmother said the tree spoke to the royals, once upon a time. Do you know how to bring her to life?"

There's so much hope in his voice, I feel I'll crush him when I tell him the truth. "I don't. All I know is she doesn't want what you think she wants."

I let my hands fall away, knowing I'll get nothing more from her and it will just be frustrating to try.

Whatever part of my power is letting me see plant souls and talk to trees is still very much a training wheel gift. I don't really know what the hell I'm doing.

Rune cups my face in his hand and I glance up at him. "Do not feel bad for not having answers to questions that three long-lived races have been asking for centuries."

"Well, when you put it like that…" It doesn't mean I'm not going to feel bad that I can't do more. That I've inadvertently brought so much chaos and death to this world, a world I didn't even know about two months ago. That said, I'll shed any sense of guilt for a moment and just enjoy being in this magic garden with this magic man.

The wind ripples around us, caressing our skin and Rune's silver eyes become pools I get lost in as he gazes so lovingly at me. "Oh Bernie…"

I lose my patience and grab the back of his head, pulling his lips to mine as I stand on the balls of my feet to reach his mouth.

The passion that infects us with this kiss is nothing like we have experienced before with each other.

It can't be compared to anything I've experienced ever. It's like lightning striking my soul, cracking me open and filling me with the most extraordinary burst of energy. I'm blinded by the light that burns through us as our bodies press together, and the world around us disappears.

An urgency grips us and we run our hands over each other as if we might never feel the touch of a lover again.

The moonlight guides us, and Rune's skin glows just like the plants and flowers. His eyes alight with silver, his skin dusted with diamonds.

We undress each other slowly, forestalling our own desperate need to touch, to bind our bodies to each other. When we both stand naked under the moon, the plants and flowers around us seem to light up even brighter, casting a glow over our bare flesh and somehow amplifying our desire.

Rune lays me on the lush carpet-like expanse of grass under the Tree of Life and holds himself up over me as his lips and hands continue to explore my body, memorizing the taste and feel of my skin. His long hair tickles at my breasts as he moves down… down… down…

And I lose myself in his touch. In the feel of him. In the ecstasy of emotion that overtakes me at his closeness, his energy that merges and blends with mine as our bodies come together.

When he enters me, my magic curls around him like he's part of me, and we are held together by the tethers of my power as we move as one.

When we reach the edge of our pleasure, we topple over together and into delirious flight. I have one hand around him, fingernails digging into his muscular back, and one hand clutching the earth, my magic shooting out of me as the waves of climax continue to rock me.

Rune collapses next to me, keeping us close as we both catch our breath, and I spare a glance for the tree, hoping my surge of power didn't kill anything in the garden. Instead, it looks as though it did the exact opposite. For a fleeting second, the Tree of Life has a subtle, almost imperceptible glow.

As the light from my magic quickly fades from the grass, I'm startled by the sound of a deep sigh.

I turn to Rune, eyes wide. "Did you hear that?"

He blinks at me, clearly still lost in the pleasure of our coupling. "Hear what?"

I shrug and tuck myself into his arms, laying my head on his chest. "Nothing. I must have imagined it."

We don't intend to fall asleep under the tree and stay there all night, but that's exactly what we do.

And in the morning, as the sun rises, casting the garden in a golden light, I awake to the sound of a wolf's howl.

CHAPTER TWELVE

*L*ove, hurry back to the rooms. The king and queen have requested counsel.

I communicate to Rune what Zev said, and we both dress quickly and stand to leave. Before we get to the gate, I turn back to look at the Tree of Life one last time, as if she called my name. There's the hint of a whisper on the wind, but then it's gone and I'm not sure if I really heard it to begin with.

I turn away from the magical garden and head to our rooms with Rune. Zev is there waiting for us, shifted back to human form but apparently he hasn't bothered to find clothes.

"You know, given how often one of us appears buck naked in front of Rune's parents, they're going to think we're running some kind of nudist colony," I say, before mentally adding, *though I certainly am not complaining about the view.*

He gives me a little growl, then draws in a long breath through his nose. I know what he's smelling, and it's made even clearer as he looks between me and Rune. My emotions creep toward nervousness but then dance back. I don't know if I'll ever be able to explain the understanding that exists between my trio of lovers, and how I can continue to love each of them more without loving any of them less. I'm half-convinced I've got a bunch of separate hearts in my chest, each devoted to another person. And then a final, bigger heart for my baby, who's hopefully off having a magical time in a cave or something.

AJ joins us, looking exquisite in a flowery skirt--literally made of flowers--and a fluffy sweater. Whoever runs the fae fashion department is nailing it and deserves a raise.

"We going to see the king and queen? And then maybe somewhere for lunch?"

Rune smiles, enjoying the strange bit of our world AJ is bringing to his. "To the royal chamber, yes. Then we'll eat, either to celebrate good news or decide what to do next."

Zev finally succumbs to the social pressure of wearing clothing, and the four of us head off, the rope bridges and branch walkways as charming this morning as they were last night. For this walk, however, my tiredness is replaced with anxiety. Last night felt hopeful, but things can change. Minds can change. They almost always do. And it certainly can't be an easy decision to align with enemies who have been killing your people for so long.

When we walk into the sprawling, wooden hall, Rivelis and Scocha immediately stand from their thrones. Revia stays seated, which seems as good an indicator as any of what's to come.

"How was your sleep?" the queen asks, looking mostly at me but I assume addressing the group.

"Freaking bliss," AJ answers first.

"Yeah, it was wonderful," I say. "Your kingdom is just... indescribable."

"Thank you," Rivelis says. "We agree, and we have battled with all our might to protect our home. Which is why..."

This guy gets straight to the point, which is very refreshing after meeting so many powerful people who like to speak in riddles.

"The timing seems right for a change in approach," the king continues. "I have every apprehension about an alliance, and I know very little about this new enemy. But I trust my son. And I believe in a new interpretation of the prophecy, since every past step has only pushed us closer to the brink. We've been caught in a self-defeating cycle and I'm ready to break free. Rune, Bernadette--you have the commitment of the fae."

AJ hoots, fist in the air and everything.

I suppress a smile as relief washes over me. Though it felt like a win last night, nothing is ever guaranteed.

Revia finally stands and comes forward with a forced smile. "I trust, brother, that you'll have treaties ready for ratification in the coming days. Abnormal as this situation may be, there must be some normalcy of process."

Rune nods, but his words belie his body language. "There's no time for a political approach, Revia. Timót's army did to the vampires in a matter of minutes what our kind could not do in centuries of war. We either go on the offensive immediately or die waiting."

"Buzzkill," AJ mutters under her breath. The tone has taken a considerably negative turn.

The king looks upward, twirling his fingers in his long beard. "What, then, is the first step? I'll agree to an alliance, but I won't welcome the other races into our kingdom first."

"That's fair and wise," Rune says. "I trust the commitment of the vampires, and of our brother in pledge, Darius. We'll return by portal to Vaemor as soon as we've gathered our things."

The king and queen's faces drop a little. So does AJ's, as she was dead set on eating some delicious fae food and probably has a little PTSD from her waterless experience in the vampire realm.

"Will you not stay for the first night of the festival?" Queen Scocha asks. "I think it will be important to have the entire family present for the opening feast. A show of solidarity before we announce such a striking change of course."

"If I may," Revia cuts in, "I think they should move on as quickly as possible, if what Rune says is true about this stranger and his army of dragons."

"Revia's right," Rune says, but I butt into the conversation with a point he may have forgotten.

"Actually, there's one reason we might want to stay. Aside from another night in a bed and a delicious meal, we still have to wait on Darius. He's got at least another night in the Tomb and the vampires won't move while he's still serving."

All the royals look at me, unaware of this news.

"They've put your friend in the Tomb of Time?" the king asks.

"As punishment for betraying the vampire cause," Zev offers, speaking for the first time and causing a lot of heads to whip his way in surprise. I can sense he's being tactical--using his position as an outsider to speak about another non-fae-- and trying to show the unity of the three princes. "He went willingly."

There's a moment of silence, this news seeming to weigh heavily on the king and queen. I kinda wish Rune had offered it up last night, might have saved us all the hours of waiting.

"Well," Rivelis says at last, "then it is settled. You will stay and enjoy the first night of celebration before returning to Vaemor in the morning."

Rune smiles in agreement as Queen Scocha tries to hide her excitement. I'm just as happy; even though we have dragons to kill and werewolves to win over, I'll let all of that wait one more night. I need more time with Rune in his king-dom, seeing his true self surrounded by impeccable beauty.

The king looks like he's about to say something else when Revia quickly bows and exits through a doorway in the back of the chamber. It seems a little abrupt, but I don't know anything about how anything works in this royal family--or any royal family for that matter, though I have read an impressive number of articles about the British royal family and the Queen. Still, I doubt this family has rules about which shoes the women in the family must wear.

"I'm sure she's off to oversee preparations," Scocha says, then looks at me. "The first night of the Celebration spares no expense."

The king and queen bow to us and we do the same in return--even Zev, after refusing to lower his head an inch in the vampire kingdom. Either he's got a better relationship with the fae or he's softening to this whole alliance thing.

As we leave, I sneak a quick, hushed conversation with Rune. "Is it safe to try and find Rain?" I assume it is, but I'd rather not bring up Rune's lie in front of anyone else.

He thinks for a moment, then takes my hand as he shakes his head. The mixture of his calming energy and my sadness leaves me feeling pretty neutral.

"The situation is volatile enough without exploring my dishonesty. We'll find them on the way to the portal tomorrow."

And I'll track the witch queen and check in with them tonight, Zev says in my mind, offering a true bit of comfort. If I can get word that they're safe, I'll rest much easier.

Before going back to our rooms, Rune takes us down to a river outside the main gate. It looks like it's full of beaver dams, but a closer look shows each little mound of sticks is actually a different food vendor. It's like taco trucks, but waterside huts that actually float along the water. Rune plays the royalty card and we get samples of everything, from fresh fish to fruit to baked goods. Most of the food I've never seen before but would happily eat until I die. It's the best lunch I've had in ages, if not ever. The only problem is listening to AJ yell "MMMMMMM" after every single bite.

At one point she asks if eating a fish taco is considered cannibalism now that she has fins. No one validates the question with a response, and she has no problem shrugging off the moral conundrum as she decimates the fish, inhaling it like a starving person.

Once our tummies are full, we walk along the river until we reach a small cave that a section of the river channels into. Rune steps into the water then ducks into the entrance. We all follow, our hands reaching out to keep us steady as light gives way to darkness. A few steps into the cave, a sparkling blue light illuminates every wall, turning it into a magical, glowing cavern. The river widens into a swimming hole with narrow rock platforms along the edge of the water for people to stand or sit.

AJ is immediately out of her clothes and swimming, this time keeping a bra on but losing the pants so her fins can wiggle free.

"There are caves like this all along the river," Rune says as he strips down. "Enough that you can almost always find one with privacy."

He dives in, swimming deep into the water below. Zev comes over and puts his arm around me, whispering into my ear and making my skin turn into a field of goosebumps.

"Some real privacy would be nice," he says. "A night away from you makes me need you so much more."

I turn toward him and capture his lips with mine, also taking the opportunity to reach down and give a quick tease with my hand. "I've been needing you, too. Will you have to shift again tonight?"

He moans at my touch and growls at his reality, making it clear he'll be off in wolf form after the banquet instead of wrapped in my arms.

"Another night, then," he says. "When we get to my kingdom, expect to be properly ravaged."

I feel his rigid member for a moment longer, until we both might cave, then dive into the water. Seconds later I hear him splash in after me.

As I swim away, I feel another set of hands trace along the sides of my ribcage, and the pleasing touch makes clear it's Rune. I spin toward him, smiling underwater at his beautiful face, warmed by the smile he gives me in return. I'll miss Zev tonight, but I'm already stirring with the anticipation of another night with my fae prince.

I give Rune a kiss and then head for the surface to catch my breath. When I break through the water, I see AJ sitting on one of the rock ledges, her tail dangling into the river below. She's got a sweet but almost melancholic look on her face and I see that she's staring at her little pendant again. I throw a glance back at the Sexies swimming behind me, and they take the hint that I'm heading off for some girl time.

I swim over and climb out to sit by her side. She tries to tuck the pendant away, but she's too much of a fish and doesn't have pockets.

"No more sneakiness, A. Where did you get that and why are you obsessing over it like Gollum?"

"You know how I feel about Gollum, B," AJ says with sincere admonishment. Always the contrarian, AJ decided when we were younger that Gollum was the true hero of The Lord of the Rings since he never let the ring fall into the wrong hands. It's complicated, but she's got a whole theory and I guarantee she was talking about it most nights while running Morgan's.

"Right, sorry. Also, don't change the subject."

"You're going to make fun of me," AJ says, staring at the pendant with a blush in her cheeks.

"When have I ever made fun of you?" I say back.

She thinks for a second, then laughs. "Fair point. I guess, if I were you I'd make fun of me." She takes a deep breath, sucking in some vulnerability, then proceeds. "It's, um, from the ghost. In the bar, the one you summoned or whatever. He didn't give it to me because he's a freaking invisible ghost, but he told me where to find it, down in your cellar."

"So... it's Tilly's? Or Ed's?" It's okay if AJ keeps something that belonged to my grandparents, but I want to know if this ghost is giving away stuff that isn't his to give.

"No, no, the ghost--his name is Leo, by the way, so hot--he brought it through from his... from the other side. He can touch and carry things there, but it's a lot harder in the living world. He's explained it all but it's pretty complicated."

"I bet. So what's the deal?"

AJ looks longingly at the pendant. "He says he can live inside here so... Jesus, it sounds cheesy AF when I say it out loud--so we can always be together."

It would sound cheesy, but I know it means something to AJ and there's nothing sappy about it. A couple weeks with this invisible dead man in my bar has really changed something in her.

"Hell, AJ, you finally find a guy who isn't trash and he's already dead."

"I know, right?" The tragedy of the situation isn't lost on her. "Still, I can hear him through this, and he can hear me." AJ stops, emotions catching in her throat and forcing a pause before she can continue. "He whispered to me the whole time you were gone, when I was paralyzed in the vampire place. I swear to God, B, I'd have died from insanity if he wasn't there."

Her story rips me apart and I bring her in for a hug so we can both do a little crying. I can't wait to get back to the bar and try to figure out a way to bring this Leo guy back from the dead. If it means giving AJ the man she deserves, I'll break into some dark magic.

After a moment of reflection, we're both ready to dive back into the sparkling water. The four of us swim around, enjoying a type of calm we haven't had in so long. I can't give into it fully, though. Whenever I get close I think first of Rain, then of Darius. There's no way to be completely happy without them near me.

The swimming eventually winds down, and only AJ is left splashing and frolicking with her impressive tail. We all get out, dry off, dress and head back into the kingdom. Rune says the festival starts in the late afternoon and carries on through the evening, so everyone has time to rest up before a night of revelry.

I'm balancing my sadness at missing Rain and worrying about Darius with my excitement at having a night of fun and celebration.

Even after a good night's sleep, I still hit the mattress like a sack of potatoes and power nap as soon as we get back. My dreams are practically the same as the reality I'm living, only with my baby by my side. I splash with her in the water and lay her down on a blanket in the middle of a grassy field. She's absolutely coming to Aevelairith for the Celebration of the Sun each year.

I'm left feeling a bit empty when I wake up, having such vivid dreams of my child and then finding her gone again. I remind myself that it's okay, she's with the most powerful woman in the universe, and it's nice to have a few nights off. Rain's probably happy to be away from me for a little while, since all I do is traipse her from one dangerous place to the next.

More clothes have been delivered when I wake up. The same must be true for AJ, because her yelling "DAMN!" is actually what wakes me up. I've got a short dress with a swirling pattern of purple and green, a scoop neck and three quarter length sleeves with a tasteful frill around the edges.

AJ bursts in and we both squeal with delight to see our dresses are matching, with hers in pink and blue. Zev and Rune come in to see what the fuss is about, and they both look dashing in similar worn leather pants and silk shirts. If they were going to a cocktail party on Earth it might be too much; for the Celebration of the Sun in the fae world, it's just right.

A selfish part of me longs for Darius to be in our company, but I know tensions would shoot through the roof if there was a vampire in the land. There's a lot of animosity the fae will have to overcome for the races to join forces, so it's best to take these changes in small doses.

Darius is no small dose.

Rune leads us from our rooms to a stone walkway on the ground floor, heading toward a part of the kingdom we haven't seen yet. The path is lined with tall flowers that sway in a non-existent wind, moving on their own to absorb the final rays of dusk's sunlight.

I notice other fae walking along parallel paths, heading toward the same open meadow. When we reach the gathering, it's like a classy carnival. There are food carts and games and musicians and jugglers; a man rides by on what looks like a short giraffe; colorful birds flutter around us, ready to pick the ground clean of food.

It's a fun, casual version of magic and I love it.

As we move through the crowd, we see a long, oval table, with the king, queen and princess sitting behind it. Other people sit around the table eating as well, and it seems like the purpose is to mingle the royal family with the rest of their people. Rivelis and Scocha smile and chat with anyone who comes near, while Revia has her usual, distant look.

"Let me speak with the king and queen, then we'll walk the grounds more," Rune says, giving my arm a gentle touch before heading off.

"Let's go eat everything," AJ says. She's always had an appetite, but I think maybe this new mermaid thing has her burning calories faster. She ate like a line-backer at lunch and now she's ready for more.

"Yes, please," Zev says, looking extra hungry with a night of wolf-prowling on his mind.

"You two go ahead, I'll wait for Rune and then catch up."

I get a kiss from my mate and a wink from AJ and then they're off, leaving me to take in the scene. I'm enamored with all of it--the way the fae look and conduct themselves, the world they live in, the food they eat, the plants they grow. I would do a lot to save this kingdom, these people. Rune's family. Almost anything. Anything except sacrificing my child. That's a few steps too far. In the thought exercise where your child gets stuck in the gears needed to lift a bridge and if you don't lift it, a boat full of people will die, what do you do? Save your child and sacrifice the boat full of people? Or kill your child to save them? I'll always pick my kid. Star Trek's original Spock might have judged me for that choice. But end-of-life Spock would have understood. The needs of the many do not always outweigh the needs of the one or the few.

"Lost your clan?"

It's not exactly the voice I wanted to hear, and I turn to see Eliar standing behind me.

"I'm fine, thank you."

"Forgive me if we got off on the wrong foot," he says, extending his hand. "You can appreciate that unwelcome visitors have long been a source of anguish, and, well…"

He leaves it at that, not needing to say more. I put my hand in his and allow him to give a courteous peck just above the knuckles. It seems harmless enough, but then he pulls me into him and presses against me. There are people all around, but he sways like we're dancing and doesn't cause enough of a scene to catch anyone's eye.

"You need to let go of me," I say through gritted teeth, offering the only warning he's going to get.

"I've heard you humans love fae," Eliar says with a lecherous smile. "I happen to love foreign women, so this should work out fine."

I've got my wand strapped to my thigh so it's hidden under my dress, and I'm trying to think of a way to discreetly grab it and turn this piece of shit into a beetle. But before I can make a move, Rune sticks a hand between us, grabs Eliar by the chest, lifts him off his feet and slams him onto his back. While the unwanted advance didn't get anyone's attention, this encounter surely does.

"You're not worthy of the air she breathes, much less the touch of her body," Rune says, a fire in his eyes like I've never seen before.

Eliar's eyes are still wide and he returns the fiery stare. "Careful, Rune. There's still a lot of doubt as to which side you're on."

More fae have stopped to watch the scuffle. I think Rune senses that as he hoists Eliar back to his feet and gives him a firm, faux-friendly pat on the shoulder.

"The same could probably be said about you, cousin. Go enjoy the festival, and perhaps go light on the drink."

Eliar gives me one last look before briskly walking off. Rune watches him go, then turns to me.

"Are you alright?" he asks, the fire in his gaze turned to love and concern.

"Yeah, nothing happened. He's just an idiot."

Rune nods, looking me over as though there might be an emotional injury I missed.

"War brings out the worst in us. I'm glad we may have a chance to end it."

He takes my hand and leads me off to see more wonders of the festival. We find AJ and Zev a few minutes later, both greedily eating some kind of kabob. I sample half a dozen fruit wines, we play a strange game where you throw beans into a Venus flytrap, and AJ and Zev split another sandwich.

As the moon grows brighter, Zev bids us all adieu, sneaking off to become a wolf before the need becomes too great. We share a long kiss behind a food stand, each getting a little handsier than is suitable for public, and then he sprints into the darkness, beginning his shift just before he's out of sight.

I walk back to AJ and Rune, and I'm almost lost in the joy of the moment. I feel like everyone is, even just for this brief flash of time, safe. There's nothing else I ought to be doing. It's okay that I'm here and I'm allowed to enjoy myself. It's a very relieving feeling.

And then there's a scream.

Bloodcurdling, coming from the direction of the main table.

Rune sprints toward the sound without hesitation, and AJ and I are a step or two behind.

All of the guests have frozen, looking toward the same spot, and I'm terrified and confused by the sight when it finally comes into view.

The king and queen still sit at their table, but their heads have dropped to their plates. Scocha's wine glass has toppled over, and the contents mix with the red blood trickling from her nose. Rivelis is in the same position, blood pooling below his ear.

Revia stands over them, staring back at us.

Just as I start to wonder what happened, what she's done, she raises her finger and points at Rune.

"Traitor!"

CHAPTER THIRTEEN

There's silence throughout the kingdom.

All eyes are on Rune, waiting for him to speak. He looks between his lifeless parents and his sister, his hands balled into fists. He's trying to maintain some calm, but I can see he's starting to tremble.

"Revia..."

"Don't deny what you have done!" the princess screams. "You chose a witch over the fae. You side with the vampires now. Tell everyone, Rune. Tell them of your choices."

Guards have started to form a circle around us. I hear footsteps a few feet behind me and there's not a doubt in my mind it's Eliar.

This is all very coordinated. Rune's done nothing wrong and had the blessing of the king and queen, but they're not alive to say so.

Revia killed her own parents to foil our plans.

What's she willing to do to her brother?

I'm not about to find out, and I can only hope Rune's on the same page. I spin around, grabbing my wand from my Tomb Raider-style thigh holster and blasting Eliar in the chest all in one fluid motion. The moment the light leaves my wand, Rune puts up an illusion that covers everything and everyone in thick white mist.

I instantly feel like it's harder to breathe, even though it's not real and can't possibly be impeding my airways. The mind is a crazy powerful thing, but it's also easily fooled it would seem.

AJ grabs my right arm, leaving my hand free to keep my wand at the ready, and Rune reaches for my left hand, guiding us out of his illusion as I hear guards scramble to find us.

I have no idea where we're going and can't see a damn thing, but that should mean they can't see us either. Unless playing this game with fae is like a child thinking that closing their own eyes will render them invisible to others.

I trust Rune knows what he's doing. He wouldn't create an illusion that didn't work.

Nevertheless, I've got fire spells on the tip of my tongue.

There's commotion everywhere, and I feel bodies brushing by us while I continue to follow Rune's lead. I have to assume none of the people I bump into are guards, because I really don't want to hurt an innocent fae. While I can't see, it seems like we're moving against the flow of traffic. Hopefully that means anyone looking for us is going in the opposite direction as well.

Rune winds us through the mist until we reach a solid stone wall. I only know because I walk right into it before Rune can stop me.

He pulls on something--I can't see what--and a secret passage opens. The three of us slip into a dark opening, the door closes on us and the mist disappears.

In the silence, with only the tip of my wand giving us light, I throw myself into Rune's arms, tears I've been holding back leaking down my cheeks. The sadness hits me like a tidal wave, and I think I'm channeling Rune's feelings as well as my own, though he's remaining much more stoic than me.

He squeezes me tightly, nods brusquely and then pulls away. Through his touch, I can feel the turmoil he's in. The pain and sense of betrayal. And I know I can't do anything to help him right now.

"We must hurry. I'm not the only one who knows of these passages," he says.

AJ looks back from where we came, her eyes shooting daggers at our newest enemies, but in rare style, she doesn't say anything. She can sense this isn't the time for the standard AJ sass.

The passage leads to a narrow stairwell that takes us down underneath the kingdom grounds. As we skulk through the passageway, trying our best to be fast but stealth, I reach out to Zev with my mind. *Where are you?*

But he doesn't reply.

I pray with all my soul that they didn't go wolf hunting while this double-cross was happening.

I know Revia was against the alliance, but I never could have fathomed something like this. This is Shakespearian-level villainy. Maybe Rune, when things are calmed down and he feels like talking about it, will have some insights into how everything went so horribly wrong.

For now, we just need to get out of this kingdom.

Rune silently guides us through the dusty, cramped, spider web covered stone halls and down a second long stairway, then out an inconspicuous wooden door, where we find ourselves standing on an underground dock, a wooden boat bobbing in the waters, tugging at the rope that moors it.

"The river is the fastest way past the kingdom walls and it flows toward Wiceraweil. That's where we need to get to right now."

"I can be of some use there," a voice growls, stepping out of the shadows. Zev walks over to us and pulls me into a fierce hug. "I'm sorry I couldn't answer you," he says, kissing my forehead and stepping back to address us all. "I came running when I heard commotion, and I was with Erzsébet before."

I open my mouth to speak but he beats me to it. "Rain is happy, healthy, and safe. And I think having a baby to care for has done Erzsébet a lot of good."

I snap my mouth shut, relief pouring into me at his words.

Unfortunately, I sense a big but, and he's right on time to deliver it.

"But there is some bad news too. I'll explain when we're on the river."

As we are boarding the boat, we hear shouting coming from the passage we just left.

I hold up my wand to do something about it when AJ shakes her head, then closes her eyes. She reaches a hand over the side of the boat so her fingers graze the water's surface. For a moment nothing happens. Then everything happens.

Water pours from the river and begins to circle around itself, forming a huge ball. Once it's positioned in front of the door we just walked through, it freezes into a giant boulder.

"Let them try to get through that," she mutters, a gleam of pride showing in her eyes. I stare at the massive ball of ice, my mouth hanging open. She's really taking to her powers, and I'm impressed.

Once we're all in, AJ gives the water a nudge and we make fast time down the river. The mountain is still giving us shelter for a time, but eventually, we'll pop out into the open world. Hopefully, they'll have lost our trail by then.

As Rune navigates the boat and AJ manipulates the water, I fill Zev in on what happened. I do it mentally so Rune doesn't have to rehash his parent's murder.

This is devastating, Zev says when I've finished. *For Rune and for all of us. We would have had an easier time convincing the wolves to join us had we already aligned the other two kingdoms.*

"I know," I whisper out loud, squeezing his hand.

AJ continues magically propelling us downstream, towards the werewolf kingdom. After a moment of silence, I remember Zev had some news to deliver.

"So where were you? Why didn't you bring back my baby? And what did Erzsébet tell you that's so terrible? And also, why didn't you bring back my baby?" I need my damn baby.

"The witch queen intercepted a message sent by crow with the *Érintett* plans. She didn't know who it was intended for, but the use of hidden ink made her believe it came from Timót." Zev's nostrils flare before he continues. "He's poised to attack Wiceraweil during the Blood Moon. In three nights. It's a mating time for dragons, meaning they'll be particularly… aggressive."

"But didn't we just have a full moon?" I ask. "That was the whole reason you had to shift."

"In our world the full moon lasts longer. A full seven-day cycle every month, with each day carrying a different significance."

"That's not enough time," I say, my pitch and volume rising with my agitation. "We lost the fae, who might even be working against us at this point. The vampires are only on our side because half of them are dead and the rest are scared. And the wolves…" I look away from Zev, reluctant to finish my sentence.

"I know, love," he says. "That's why we must hurry. The werewolves, vampires and two powerful witches will have to be enough. And I'll do whatever it takes to get the wolves on our side. Especially knowing that's where the dragons are headed."

Ugh. Why is shit so hard all the damn time?

I sound like a whiny toddler, even to myself, but I'm really over all this. I just want my baby, and my bar, and maybe a piano. That's it. That's the perfect life.

But then I glance at Rune, his aristocratic profile, his kind eyes, and I think of all he's given up to help me. And I look to Zev, whose gaze searches the distance, towards his homeland, but whose heart, I can feel, is diving deep into the past. And I think of Darius, enduring unimaginable torture to hold together this fragile alliance.

And I know.

I can't give them up for an easier life. I won't.

Sometimes it's the hardest paths, the steepest hills, that provide the greatest reward.

Life isn't meant to be easy. It's meant to shape us into someone capable of handling the hard times.

My poor baby is gonna be the toughest kid in town.

I shake my head, tearing myself away from my thoughts, and take in the scenery around me as we float down the underground river. We've come to the base of a slope and Rune now pulls on a massive rope, guiding our boat up a watery incline. AJ sits at the back of the vessel, magically prompting the water to help push us along. After a minute or so, we emerge through a small cave leading from under the fae kingdom and into the main river channel. Rune sits down, his first moment of stillness since we ran.

I inch closer to the fae and take his arm in mine, leaning my head against his shoulder.

I open my mouth but really don't have anything to say. No words can help in a situation like this.

He shakes his head slowly, a single tear trickling down his cheek. "My sister and I have always had our differences, but I never imagined..." He pauses, his voice catching. "I never imagined she'd be capable of this."

For a hot second I wondered if someone else did the murdering and Revia just assumed it was us, but Rune's instincts confirm my own.

That bitch.

Zev joins us, holding Rune from the other side. The two press their foreheads together, and I squeeze the tears out of my eyes seeing the affection between them. I hate that it took war, death, and a cruel prophecy to bring these three men back to one another, but I can't argue against the end result. They are closer than brothers. Closer than lovers in many ways. It's a bond that goes back lifetimes and shatters barriers. They have loved and lost and suffered together.

For her part, AJ has been unusually quiet. She's sitting on the edge of the boat in mermaid form, letting her tail dangle in the water as she uses her fin to guide us. But her real focus is on her pendant. Leo.

After all these years, it looks like we've both finally found our type: not human.

We pass the rest of the journey in silence, Zev and I offering what comfort we can to Rune, who continues his long stare into the distance. He has many human lifetimes of memories to reflect on right now, and a boat ride to another kingdom won't be nearly enough time to process all that, but at least it's a start.

~

I GET a sense we're almost there when the sun starts to rise and I notice a change in topography. The type of tree is different, and mountains loom in the distance. Not the snowy peaked ones that cut down the middle of this world, but the green, lush mountains surrounded by the shimmering blue waters that look just as magical here as they do in the fae land.

I can also feel that we're getting closer by how Zev's energy shifts. I'm always connected to my mate, but the closer we are physically, the stronger that connection is. He's nervous about being home, and I don't blame him one bit.

If this whole adventure has taught me anything it's that homecomings are fraught with drama. Holy hell.

We hear wolves howling in the distance, and I'm startled when Zev begins to join in. Though he doesn't shift, what comes from his throat is more beast than man.

"They know we're here," Zev says, when the howling dies down.

"No shit, Sherlock," AJ says, twisting to face him. "You just announced our presence."

Zev rolls his eyes at my salty friend. "I responded because they knew already and were going to attack. Now we will have an escort instead."

AJ snorts. "Escorts. Guards. Sounds like the same thing to me."

I can't disagree with her, so I just shrug. "What now?"

Zev lifts his chin to indicate a bridge in the distance. "Dock there. They will meet us and escort us to the king and queen."

I stifle a yawn as AJ begins to guide our bow to its destination.

When we disembark, a dozen wolves surround us, teeth bared, snarling. Zev instantly shifts and nips at a few of them, putting them in their place. They all submit, whining and creeping back, offering their necks. It's clear Zev is asserting his dominance as an alpha and prince, but God it's such a pissing contest it's hard to take too seriously.

The only wolf that doesn't shrink back much is a large gray one in the front. The gray wolf shifts and Zev does the same. The two men have similarities: their body shape and hair color mainly, but where Zev is much taller and exudes alpha energy, the other man is definitely a beta who wishes he was an alpha. It sours his looks, and his whole vibe. I instantly know A; this is Zev's brother and B; this guy gives me the sceevies.

Zev reaches for my hand, and I join him, clutching his arm and trying not to act like I'm scared of being surrounded by wolves. "Alden, this is Bernadette, the mother of the Last Witch, and my mate."

The wolves scrape the ground in agitation and Alden raises an eyebrow. "Mate? That's...unexpected."

AJ clears her throat, clearly annoyed at being ignored.

"And her friend, AJ," Zev says with an amused grin.

AJ gets Alden's attention, that's for sure. Little does he know he's in competition with a ghost.

"Bernie, this is my brother Alden."

I hold out a hand to shake his, but he ignores it and I drop mine, my cheeks burning in embarrassment but also anger that he's being a dick.

So far, the only family members of my guys who have been pleasant are dead.

"Mother's waiting," Alden says turning on his heels.

We've only taken a few steps away from the water and towards the hill leading up the mountain when the wolves freak the hell out.

That's when I hear it. The voice a gentle breeze against my mind.

"Darius!" I scream his name, tears blurring my vision as I search for him.

He's by my side in a flash, and Zev has to puff out his chest to get the other wolves to settle themselves as Darius pulls me into a hard embrace.

As our flesh touches, our souls connect once again, and the piece of me that's been emptied out is refilled with painfully sharp reminders of his torment. When we finally push our bodies apart, I study his face. He looks... different. His eyes are darker, his face narrower. I run my fingers through a streak of silver hair that wasn't there before. "I thought you had another day," I ask softly.

He shakes his head. *My brother freed me after the second night. As a show of good faith.*

There's an agony in his voice that shakes me to the core. Even serving two-thirds of his sentence, he just sat alone in the darkness for two thousand years. I pull him closer to me, trying to transfer my lifeforce to him.

Zev's brother sneers. "I thought she was *your* mate? Not some bloodsucker's whore."

That was exactly the wrong thing to say right now.

Zev, Darius, and even Rune, who's been mostly checked out, come together as one to offer an incredibly menacing and threatening display that sends Alden stumbling back and mumbling something incomprehensible.

I'm not sure that won't come back to bite us in the ass later, but either way I'm grateful we're all together again.

Except my damn baby. I need Rain so much it hurts. That witch better not let a hair on my precious girl get touched or I'll never forgive myself.

As much as I know she shouldn't be here, it's still so hard to be away from her. I guess this is what it's like as a working mom. Though my work is decidedly a bit unique.

"Let's press on before the sun brings full daybreak," Zev says with a wink to Darius. Alden growls at the show of affection to the vampire then begrudgingly leads us all forward.

I try very hard to keep my mind from mentally slamming Darius with word vomit, but I can't help but ask at least one question. *Are you okay?*

He glances over at me. He still hasn't let go of my hand. *I will be.*

His dark eyes pierce into me, and I promise him that as soon as we have a minute, he needs to feed on me. I can tell he hasn't had blood since last I saw him and it's not having a great effect on his general health.

We enter the werewolf kingdom through a mountain tunnel that looks like it's for trains... but that's because I have a dumb human brain. As soon as we pass through the threshold, the tunnel walls give way to a massive, underground city, with stone streets passing between clay buildings. It's the secret village every kid dreams of constructing in a mound of dirt, just a billion times more extravagant. Lighting columns along the street look like they filter sunlight from the mountain down to underground luminaires, though right now everything is lit with fire pits and candles. It's rustic and futuristic all at once.

Our handlers, or whatever the wolves escorting us are called, lead us along the roads to an unbelievable palace at the center of the city. Marble cylinders stand in front of the entryway, with gold patterns decorating the entire structure. I keep worrying that an earthquake will bring the mountain crumbling down and destroy all this beauty, but then I remind myself that this city has clearly been here a long time and won't be going anywhere anytime soon.

We are escorted down a hallway and through enormous double doors made of oak and elaborately carved. I know that we'll meet the king and queen of the werewolves on the other side of this door, and they just so happen to be the parents of my werewolf mate. My nerves start to spike as we walk in and turn towards the thrones.

Except there's only his mother, not his father. That takes some of the pressure off, but it also feels odd. The queen sits on her throne with a sad expression on her aged yet timeless face. Her eyes are the same green as Zev's, but her hair is lighter, grayed by time.

Zev lowers himself to a knee, though he keeps his eyes on his mother with a confused expression in his eyes.

"Rise my son. We need not stand on ceremony. Not when times such as these are upon us," the queen says.

Zev stands and approaches his mother, taking her hand. "Where is Father?"

The queen shakes her head. "Your father is sick. We hoped you'd come back in time, and I wish I could greet you in higher spirits."

"A new war is coming," Zev says. "We need the wolves. How ill is he, and for how long?"

She frowns. "He's gone to Mount Arys. He's said his farewells."

She turns away from Zev, looking now at the empty chair beside her.

"We cannot help you. Not when we are about to lose our king."

CHAPTER FOURTEEN

Things just keep going from bad to worse with family affairs. I reach for Zev's hand instinctively, as worry and tension radiate off of him.

His mother raises an eyebrow in surprise. She sniffs the air, making me super self-conscious about BO, then frowns. "You've mated. With a *witch*."

She doesn't even bother trying to hide her condescension.

Zev pulls me closer to him. "Yes. Mother, this is Bernadette, my mate."

The queen ignores me as her gaze lands on first Rune then Darius. "And you've brought our enemies with you as well, I see."

This time her tone is harder to read, but she's for sure not happy about any of this. Then again, her husband is dying. She's probably not happy about anything.

"He is unfit to lead," Alden says bluntly, turning his mother's attention to himself. "He consorts with the enemy, and not only is his mate a witch, she's already mated to a vampire and fae."

The queen's eyes are sharp when she turns them on Zev. "Is this true?"

Zev squeezes my hand, assuring me the queen's judgment means nothing. "Bernie is a powerful witch, more powerful than any we have ever known. Through hardship and oath, she has formed a bond with all three of us. But we chose to bind ourselves to her. And whether she's a wolf or not, my wolf chose her. You know that is unbreakable, in life or death." He growls at the end, his alpha energy consuming the room.

His mother waves him off. "None of this matters while our king faces the end of his life."

"What happened to him?" Zev asks.

His brother answers. "Magic is dying. He took a tusk during a hunt, and now he cannot heal or shift back. The wound is festering, killing him slowly. You were meant to bring back the prophesied child who would save us, not mate with the mother and destroy your kind in the process."

He throws each word like a dagger at Zev, who remains stoic in face of the verbal wounds.

I'm done with this bullshit, and I do not remain so stoic. "Listen, shithead. That's my daughter you're talking about. Killing my baby won't fix your magical drought, and you all need to really start thinking more creatively if you don't want to go the way of the DoDo birds. The Last Witch will not die in your kingdom. And if you help us, she might not even be the *Last* Witch."

Alden, who I can tell really loves being called out by a non-wolf female, nearly shifts in front of us and looks ready to tear out my throat. Zev steps forward, his eyes glowing as he growls at his brother. "Do not lay a hand on her."

"Stop this, both of you," the queen says, standing. "Someone will show you to your rooms. Do as you please tonight, tomorrow we will talk about this... situation," she says, her eyes flinching at Zev's penetrating look. Then she turns and storms out.

Alden hisses at me, then turns to follow her, and one of the other guards steps forward awkwardly. "I guess follow me?"

We follow the guard through the palace. It seems like Zev is being treated as a stranger in his home land and I can't tell if that's custom or my fault. If I had to guess, I'd say I'm the problem. Or really, our whole entourage is.

I'm intrigued by every bit of architecture in the city. Floating down the river, I didn't know what to expect. Do werewolves live in caves? Penthouses? Tree forts? My mind put in plenty of hours trying to envision what this land might look like, but it was always filtered through my limited human perceptions. At some point I'll have to learn not to listen to that part of my brain.

Turns out, it's sort of a mix of all of it. Our suite features exquisite natural materials, with stone walls polished until they gleam a deep smokey gray with flecks of sparkling quartz, floors covered in hand woven carpets of earthy colors, overstuffed furniture for lounging before the fire, and bedrooms for all of us. The guys choose to stay in the rooms closest to me, while AJ takes the furthest one away.

"I need some alone time," she says softly, one hand on her pendant.

I purse my lips, worried about my bestie, but then nod. "Sure. Get some rest. It's been a long day."

She snorts at that and closes her door behind her firmly. A few moments later I hear her talking to her ghost.

I take a quick pass through my room, charmed by the decor but feeling like I can't really enjoy it.

My closet comes stocked with a few fancy garments, and though I don't much feel like dressing up, I'm grateful to be able to get out of the dirty clothes I've been wearing. I change into a periwinkle dress, kicking my tattered fae clothing into the back corner of the closet.

I head to the common area, looking prettier than I feel. Zev won't stop pacing the room, even when a meal of venison and roasted vegetables are delivered.

"You should eat something," I plead.

Rune usually helps in these situations, but he shuffled off to his room for some well-earned wallowing.

And Darius has been withdrawn since he returned from his torture, which I definitely don't blame him for. I can't even imagine what he's processing.

My poor guys have lost so much.

Zev ignores my pleas to eat, and I set the plate down, unable to muster up much of an appetite for myself either.

Zev's wolf is close to the surface, making the man edgy and anxious.

I cross the room to take his hand, my worry for him creasing my brow. "If you want to go spend some time with your mother, we'll keep ourselves busy."

He stops pacing to face me, his forest green eyes full of unexpressed emotion. My beautiful werewolf has only been back in his kingdom for a few hours and already seems different. He's more distant, more serious than usual. But through our bond I can feel the truth. He's scared. He's scared of his father dying, or not dying but staying incapacitated. He's scared of what's coming and what will happen to his people.

I feel all this through our bond as I offer what comfort I can.

"There's nothing to be done," he says gruffly as he pulls me into his muscular arms, sliding his hands around my hips. "If a wolf knows they're dying, they leave for Mount Arys to go in peace. My father, and all his subjects, are simply waiting for death."

The words sound hollow coming from his lips.

"Are you going to go see him?" I study his face to try and read him, but his heart speaks to me more powerfully. Grief rises in him like a wave, coming from the depths of his past, an old pain that has never healed.

He nods, his eyes glossy with emotion. "It's not customary to visit the still living at Mount Arys, but... the news of this has shaken me. I had no idea how bad things had gotten..." he drifts off, and I see in his eyes he's trying to make sense of this. He had a plan. To convince his father to join us, or challenge him to a duel. But how can you duel a dying man?

After a moment he shakes his head to refocus. "If he was as he used to be, things would be different. Now, I don't know what to do."

"I'm sorry," I say softly. "I feel like getting people on our side shouldn't be this hard."

"Nothing is as it should be in the world right now," he says, his jaw tensing as he speaks. "The magical imbalance destroying us will eventually be felt in all realms. Even yours."

I think of my little Irish pub on the outskirts of Rowley and wonder what that would mean for my small town. Up to this point, every person I know is blissfully unaware of magic, the feuding realms, and certainly the fact that I'm a witch. They think I'm on vacation--not in a werewolf palace.

It's something we've talked about before, but the reality has never felt so immediate as it does now. Sure, we've been attacked, and I've nearly died more times than I can count since meeting the three Sexies. But being here, in the different kingdoms of my men, I realize more than ever what the stakes are for all of them. And though I'll always put the well being of my baby above everything else--even if that means being away from her for days--I finally understand the desperation all of the kingdoms are dealing with.

They want to save their people from extinction.

And if they'll let me, I'm going to try to help.

Before I can dwell on these big-picture issues, we need to defeat Timót and his army. Aside from a squadron of dragons, I don't know exactly how many fight in his ranks. After the showdown in Vaemor, I feel very confident we need more than just the vampires on our side. The fae blew it, and now things are off to a rocky start with the wolves.

Kings and queens have been picking really shitty times to die.

Zev looks at the floor, battling his emotions. I lift his chin so our eyes meet, then pull him closer and seek out his lips.

The kiss starts tenderly. A kiss of shared pain, shared love, shared sorrow and shared joy.

But as we lose ourselves in each other, the kiss changes to something passionate and deep. It holds within it all the swirling complexity of emotions we are both feeling. I feel our bond more profoundly when we are intimate, and the power of it swells up in me, merging with my own magic, creating a euphoria that's almost addictive.

A soft hiss from behind me interrupts our kiss, and I turn in Zev's arms to see Darius walking over. The vampire studies me with his obsidian eyes, consuming me with just a look.

"I need you," Darius says, his gaze locking on mine. He flashes to my side with his vampire swiftness, and I find myself pinned between him and Zev in the most delicious possible way. Two sets of hands has my skin begging for the dress to be removed.

I lean against Zev's chest as Darius presses into me, and the feel of them both ignites a deep, burning need in me that only my lovers can satiate.

Darius leans in, his teeth sharpening as he studies the vein in my neck. I sigh as he begins to drink from me. Though I no longer need him to feed from me for survival, the act remains incredibly intimate and powerful. And I know he needs not just my blood, but me, my essence, to heal the cracks that his centuries of confinement created.

Zev's body responds to the moment and I feel his hardness pressing against my back just as Rune steps out of the bedroom for the first time since we got here. He stares for a moment, then walks over to us. Darius pulls away from my neck and takes a step to the side, making room for the sexy fae who can't pull his eyes from the three of us.

My sweet, heart-heavy fae had only just opened himself to love again, and now I'm worried about how his horrible loss might affect him. I pull his face to mine, our noses and foreheads touching.

His silver eyes still hold the pain of loss and betrayal, but there's also a gleam of desire as well. It gives me hope that all three of them seem to take comfort in not just being with me, but being with each other as well.

As Rune's lips land on mine, Darius and Zev stroke my body into a heightened sense of arousal, and I feel all three of them in my soul, mixing with my magic, with my breath, with my very essence. I close my eyes, letting their hands, mouths and bodies blur into one orgasmic experience.

Zev's teeth are on my neck, scraping at the now healed flesh where Darius just fed. Rune continues to explore my mouth, nipping at my lower lip as he cups my face with his hands, and Darius is using one hand to tease at the hot, pulsing need between my legs, pressing through my gown, while his thumb rubs against my hardened nipples through the silk and satin.

Nothing has ever felt more right than having all three of my lovers with me like this, and I'm desperate to tear off all our clothes and find out what more we can do together, but just as I'm about to send buttons flying through the room, there's a knock at our door following the creaking sound of it opening.

Flushed and slightly embarrassed, I pull away from my men and adjust my dress as a servant comes in. She looks middle-aged, with some graying streaks in her dark hair, though for a werewolf that likely means she's very, very, very old, given how slowly I've heard they age.

"The queen has sent this for you, Your Highness," she says in a subservient voice, not looking directly at Zev but bowing in his general direction. Zev frowns, and the sexual tension we were all floating in just moments ago dissipates quickly with the reminder of why we're here.

He accepts the parchment from her and nods. "Thank you, Ally."

Ally bows again, glances my way quickly, then shirks back when we make eye contact. With mumbled apologies she quickly exits the room, leaving us alone once again.

I straighten my spine, trying to stay strong for whatever the night brings. But I know the guys can feel the nervous wave of energy threatening to consume me.

Rune takes my hand, and for the first time since his parent's death, his calming magic flows into me, soothing my unsettled mind.

"Thank you," I say with a smile. "You might want to give Zev some of that."

Zev just huffs in response and continues reading.

Darius approaches me from behind, dropping his lips to my neck seductively. *I would rather continue what we started than deal with anymore wolves.*

I turn to face the vampire, smirking at him. *Would that we could,* I say back to his mind. *But we should follow Zev's lead.*

Putting action to my words, I take Zev's hand and squeeze it. "What does it say?"

Zev looks up from the letter, his face a few shades paler. "It's from my mother. She…"

He walks over and drops the letter in the fireplace, watching it burn. "She's worried my brother will try to kill my father and become king. She wants me to stop him."

THE FOUR OF us make all haste in heading to Mount Arys, not knowing what we'll find when we get there.

We are silent as we hike through the woods, Darius keeping to the shadows to avoid the late afternoon sun. Zev suggested he stay back, but the vampire made it clear he's had enough alone time and would rather risk catching on fire than spend another moment with just his thoughts.

It's a tense hike for me. This isn't how any girl dreams of meeting her lover's dad, and I'm a little worried my presence might be the thing that actually kills him. Not only am I a poor bartender from New England who's 100% not a werewolf, I'm also bonded to a vampire and a fae--the two races this king has been at war with for centuries. I'm like the least ideal mate for the future werewolf king.

I shut out the uncomfortable thoughts by looking at my mate, trying to give him strength through my loving gaze. He doesn't look back, but I know he feels me.

I have a lot of questions about Alden. Is he really thinking of killing his father, or is the queen just trying to stir shit up? He seems like a dirtbag, but that could just be the magical imbalance destroying his realm that's affecting his mood.

Probably a combination of both.

As we reach the opening to a cave deep in the woods, Zev sprints off without a word. I'm confused for a second, then I hear the mournful howls of a dying wolf that had already caught his ears.

Darius has rejoined me and Rune beneath the shade of the trees, and we approach the entrance with a bit more caution. This is not a mountain we will be welcome inside.

When we reach the mouth to the cave, we hear the growling. It's not the sound of one wolf growling through pain, but three animals showing aggression. I pull out my wand, Darius pulls out his teeth, and Rune draws his sword as we follow. We find two wolves attacking each other; a large gray wolf lying on the ground covered in blood, one wound clearly fresher than the rest.

Rune runs over to the king and tries to work his healing magic on him. I aim my wand as Zev and his brother go at it, but I can't get a clean shot with the two constantly biting at each other's necks. Finally, when there's a bit of separation, I send a jolting shot into the gray wolf's chest that knocks him back. He's not seriously injured, but the way he whines you'd think I'd just shot off his balls.

When Darius steps forward, his elongated teeth on full display, brother dearest seems to realize he's way outmatched and runs away, dodging us as he leaves the cave and heads home with his tail between his legs.

Zev shifts to human form and runs to his father, bending over his near-lifeless body as the king slowly shifts back from beast to man.

I wait for a Hallmark kind of death, where father and son say their last goodbyes and make amends. Where Zev's dad gives his blessing for his son to lead and bring peace to their people.

None of that happens.

The king never opens his eyes again.

With his last exhale, all is silent.

Zev looks far more angry than sad. He's lost his father, but his need to protect this new family carries more weight. He stands and turns toward the exit, murder in his eyes as he thinks of what his brother's just done.

"Zev..." I say, not knowing what he plans but thinking a little reflection might be useful before he acts. He doesn't seem to share my assessment.

"He'll try to rally the wolves," Zev says. "He may already be trying to kill our mother. If we..."

He stops talking, cocking his head to the side so he can listen. I can't hear a thing, but Zev's got wolf ears that put mine to shame.

Then I hear it. It starts softly before becoming unmistakable.

The sound of large, beating wings.

We run out of the cave and look up through the trees, my heart dropping in my chest at the site.

The evening sky is filled with dragons, circling around the wolves' mountain stronghold.

"I thought we had more time," I breathe, terror gripping me.

"We don't," Darius says.

The new war has begun.

CHAPTER FIFTEEN

Dragons descend from every direction, sheets of fire coating the hillsides and mountaintops. There's not a lot of excess foliage to burn, but the heat of the dragons' flames is so intense it doesn't need much fuel.

And we're running straight towards it.

Zev runs ahead as a wolf while I ride on the speedy Darius' back, sprinting with incredible speed and grace while avoiding even a flicker of sunlight. I'm not sure what the plan is, other than to face an impossibly strong army head-on. I race through different spells in my mind, but each feels like throwing an ice cube at a house fire. I'm not ready for this.

Scores of dragons flutter above the mountain, each with a handful of fighters on its back. They breathe fire mercilessly, and I'm starting to think Timót's plan is to melt the entire werewolf kingdom. Which will be a real drag, because we're heading inside.

The dragons have their focus on the mountain, so passing under them isn't too difficult, though the flames feel way too close.

I'm drenched with sweat in seconds, which is how long it takes us to get inside the tunnel to the main city. There's a brief sense of relief at not being out in the open anymore, but that's quickly erased by the panic coming from being trapped inside a mountain.

Zev disappears into the city streets, maybe looking for his mother, maybe still planning to find and kill his brother. I'm not going to bother trying to have a mental conversation with him at this juncture.

Darius and Rune stay right by my side, neither with a plan beyond sacrificing themselves to save me.

We move further into the center of the city and away from the main entrances. I'm starting to wonder if this is the first time anyone has ever attacked the wolves and they have no plan to counter, but Darius steps into my mind and shoots that thought down, reminding me that all the races in this realm have been at war for hundreds of years.

"Where do we go?" I ask, not particular about who gives me an answer.

"Into the city center, then we wait for Zev to find us," Rune says. "No reason to come up with a plan other than whatever he thinks is best."

I appreciate the deference to the wolf prince, but since Zev isn't standing with us right now and I can see dragon fire sneaking through the entrances, I'd love to hear some additional ideas.

At that moment, every structure in the city bursts to life. Wolves leap and scramble through doorways and windows, climbing up narrow paths along the inside face of the mountain. None of them heads for the main tunnels, but instead climbs to smaller coves along the gigantic mountain walls.

Clearly, they have a plan.

Distracted as I am by the sight of the wolves in action, I turn immediately when Zev comes to my side and shifts back into human form. He's followed by AJ, which almost makes my heart burst. The world is chaos and death feels eminent, but my wolf still went to find my friend and make sure she was safe. There's no time for me to hug and kiss and thank him, so I just welcome as much of his spirit into me as I can while his body's close.

"We have tactical positions to assume," he says, "but a thinned army of wolves is no match for dragons. I can't imagine we'll fare better than the vampires."

"Can we run?" I ask, with AJ nodding at the idea. There's not enough water for her to play with here, so she'd clearly rather be on the move.

"There are passages beneath the mountain that fan out to the headlands, but they're too narrow to fit a large group. Besides, most wolves would bark at the idea of leav--"

Zev's sentence is cut short when an arrow whips through the air behind us and strikes him in the shoulder, the impact taking him off his feet and slamming him against a nearby wall. Darius flashes over to help Zev as I turn to see where the attack came from.

Revia.

She and another twenty fae stand just inside the entrance on the opposite side of the mountain.

We've got dragons to our left, fae warriors to our right, and nowhere to go.

Rune has his sword drawn, standing his ground. Zev has morphed back into a wolf, the fur on his left front leg damp with blood, but the arrow is out in Darius' hand.

"We will kill you before you can kill us," Revia yells at her brother, another arrow drawn in her bow.

"How did our parents raise only one of us to be so dense?" Rune yells back, then swings his sword with incredible precision to deflect the arrow shot in response to his words. "We're trying to help all the races! We're trying to undo what's been done. Your actions only ensure more will die."

"You're blind, brother." Revia loads another arrow as the fae behind her begin fending off a few wolf attackers. She's got enough of an infantry to keep her safe while still having another ten guards stay focused on us. Meanwhile, the goddamn mountain around us is on fire.

"You've been led astray by the very subject of the prophecy," she says, slowly advancing towards us. "I've met this Timót you seem to fear so much. In fact, I sent him word right after your escape. He wants to save the fae from the vampires, then have the wolves bow to us as they were meant to. With him as our ally, the Last Witch--alive or dead--will bring magic back to our woods." She takes a break from her speech to fire another arrow, which again Rune strikes away. "If your pledges hadn't made you so disloyal, you'd understand."

Rune's teeth grind. "Interesting talk of loyalty from someone who just killed her own parents, the rulers of the kingdom she claims to love so fiercely."

His words strike a chord, as Revia's face scrunches in reaction, but she shakes it off and dives back into her self-deluded narrative. "Leadership comes with a price," she says.

She plucks another arrow, but an enormous rumble makes everyone freeze. The entire city shakes and all of the buildings sway. From the mountain walls above the far entrance, hundreds of wolves run back inside, many with their fur singed and smoking. There's a momentary lull...

And then the mountain wall explodes.

Dirt flies in every direction as a cacophonous mixture of crashing debris and howling wolves fills the air. Before I know what's happening, Darius has lifted both me and Zev and rushed us around the corner of a building for shelter.

When he sets me down, I peer out and look for Rune. The air is thick with dust, but I see his profile standing right where he was, still facing off against his sister. I get the feeling they'll both try to ignore the dragons in favor of settling this very personal score.

As visibility returns, I can see daylight coming through the massive hole leading into the outside world. Zev now stands in human form over my shoulder, his rage almost bubbling over as he takes in the damage. Seems like the dragons weren't trying to melt the whole mountain, only soften it enough to break through.

"These mountain walls have withstood every attack since my great grandfather claimed this land," Zev says in a shaky voice. "Those dragons will pay."

Darius puts a hand on his friend's non-wounded shoulder. "Let's start with the man who controls the dragons. It's his head we want."

I expect to see a burst of fire or a massive reptilian head slink through the opening, and hold my breath while waiting for what's to come. A quick glance at the fae soldiers shows they're waiting as well, though they all look pretty calm.

The army we hoped to align with has allegiance with our enemy.

God I hate Rune's sister.

When there's finally movement along the exploded wall, I ready my wand to cast some sort of shield, though I don't know if any spell can protect us from dragon breath.

Instead of a dragon, however, I see men. Timót's soldiers.

They come in by the dozens, using the walkways the wolves took to come down to the ground floor. When we flew into Vaemor, Timót had maybe fifty men; now there are hundreds. It's a larger sampling of the different races I saw before, with orcs walking alongside humans alongside shifters and dwarves. They march in, firing arrows or shooting spells at any wolf that dares approach.

I'd almost rather face off against the dragons than this army of creeps.

Even though it's a long way to the opening in the mountain wall, I still recognize my father when he steps into rubble, backlit by the sun and looking as powerful as he thinks he is.

I want nothing more than to take him down a peg.

Behind him, his enormous dragon flaps its wings, hovering outside the entrance. It'll be a tight squeeze, but I'm not about to bet that thing can't make its way inside the city. Looks like I might get to face off against these shitty soldiers *and* a dragon.

Timót barks orders at his troops, but he's too far away for me to hear. If I had to guess, I'd say he's telling them not to kill me or the baby. Even though Rain isn't here, just the idea of her is making our attackers approach with caution. We'll see how much we can use that to our benefit.

I'm shocked when Rune appears beside me, as I can still see him standing in the open street facing his sister. My brain knows he's created an illusion, but my eyes don't trust my brain at all. The fae sees Zev's wound and sets to healing it while the army continues descending into the city. We're not well hidden, but we're not in a direct sight line. As the *Érintett* fighters get closer, I can hear some of their calls--"bring out the witch and the city lives," and "deliver the Last Witch or face the dragons."

We're huddled against a wall, trapped in a mountain. Hiding won't save us.

I'm about to stand, to offer myself up, when Darius grabs my arm to keep me still.

Don't you dare, he says.

It's the only way. Timót won't kill me.

You don't know that.

Our conversation is interrupted by a loud crash that answers my question about the size of the opening in the wall--Timót, on the back of his massive dragon, has landed on the city floor not too far from Rune's illusory self. He's covered in a shimmering cloak from head to toe, one that looks like iridescent chainmail. There's a matching helmet that leaves a small slit for his eyes and mouth.

Dragon armor, Darius says in my mind. *To protect him from the sun.*

Oh shit. I completely forget that my disgusting dad was also a vampire. And apparently one who scaled a dragon so he could still enjoy the daytime. What a prick.

Revia fires an arrow, not at Timót since apparently they're great friends, but at what she believes is her brother. It passes through his pretend body and dissipates the illusion.

"Where are they?" Timót asks.

"Near," the fae princess answers. "Though they don't have the child."

"What?" My father sounds angry. He's kept his cool through horrifying situations, and that was before he became immortal, so his rage is extra unsettling.

"They escaped Aevelairith by boat, the witch queen has the baby--"

"You didn't make that clear in your missive," Timót seethes.

"What does it matter?" Revia fires back. "The child can be tracked later and returned to the fae to fulfill the prophecy. First we can capture or kill the others."

My wand is shaking with magical anxiety. This feels like an opportunity to bring down at least one enemy, but there are too many and I don't know where to start. I'm also a little curious to see where this argument is headed.

Peering around the fallen column of a building, I can see my father on top of his dragon, his wand at his side. He stares at Revia, calculating his next move.

"You don't quite understand my intention," Timót says. "The child has a greater, more important purpose within the *Érintett* kingdom."

"Your agreement was to help the fae," Revia says. "You swore an oath."

"I did. A living oath."

Oh shit. What a tricky bastard.

"And then I died."

Before Revia can make sense of what's just been said, Timót rears back on the reins at his dragon's neck and the beast sends a flurry of fire toward the fae army. Some are far enough away to run or dive to the side, evading the worst of the fire. Standing front and center, only yards away from the dragon's mouth, Revia becomes charcoal before she can move an inch.

That takes care of one of our problems, and yet I don't feel one iota safer.

The surviving fae lower their weapons, looking as sheepish as they should. Fooled by this sinister man into thinking he believed in their cause. Now they have the blood of the royals on their hands.

"Bring in the rest of the dragons," Timót bellows. "Search the grounds for the witch's mother and keep her alive if you can. If we don't find her within the hour… burn the mountain to the ground."

I feel Zev's growl in my bones before I can hear it, and know he's about to go die a fiery death if I don't do something. I ignore Darius' pleas and Rune's effort to grab my arm, and step out from the crumbled wall that was concealing us.

"Dad, why can't you be less evil?"

I don't have a plan, but that's never stopped me from talking shit in the past. I only hope AJ doesn't join in, because last time it almost killed her. My princes rise to stand behind me, though none makes a move to draw me back or come between me and my father. They know better at this point.

Timót smiles at me, and he looks genuinely happy to see me. How broken his brain must be, that he wants me to stay alive and be part of the vile kingdom he's trying to create.

"My girl, I've been worried. You knocked me out for days with your spell in Vaemor, and I wondered if the vampires had killed you while I was incapacitated. I'm so glad you're alright."

As he speaks, dragon after dragon crawls through the devastated mountain wall. Big as this underground city felt when we first arrived, the introduction of multiple dragons makes it feel much smaller.

A bright yellow dragon crawls toward us, a number of ogre-ish men on its back. There's anger in the monster's giant eyes, and I feel in my bones it has more to do with those riding it than the people it's approaching.

"Wherever have you left your child, Bernadette?" my father asks. "And how can you bring yourself to let the Last Witch out of your sight?"

"I don't know, dad, maybe it's because everyone's always trying to kill me and it's harder to point a wand with a baby on my tit."

Speaking with this wretched man really brings out the bartender in me. It's like talking with a belligerent drunk who's after my phone number, only worse in every conceivable way.

"I understand your feelings, but you must see the error in your choices." Timót gestures to the ravaged city around us, a shell of its former beautiful self. Wolf bodies are scattered around the grounds, while the living animals sit with their tails tucked, fearful of what will happen next. He's not wrong--destruction follows wherever I go.

"You can't have her, dad," I snap back, not ready to take the blame for the atrocities he's causing. "You can keep fighting and killing and destroying, and maybe one day you'll get your way, but then you can live alone in a shitty world surrounded only by the people who were shitty enough to be your followers."

I was just barfing out insults because I'm pissed, but this last line seems to have hit its mark. I can see the anger in Timót's eyes as he throws quick looks at the men in his command. They're a strange collection of angry and ornery, the type of guys who want to get in fights to distract from their other shortcomings. My dad's smarter than them, clearly, and wants to be better. But this is what his cause attracts. I see now that he wants to gain respect through his powers, and so far he's only respected by people he loathes.

The yellow dragon draws even closer. Should its riders pull the reins, me and my companions will meet a fiery death within seconds.

"You make this very difficult, Bernadette," Timót says, trying to keep his cool even as angry spittle flies out of his mouth. He starts to raise his wand, taking aim at me. I fight my fear, still believing he won't try to kill me, and trusting I have the speed and power to deflect a spell. I'm not really that scared, more curious to see what he'll try to do.

But I don't get a chance to find out.

A burst of light comes from the highest point inside the mountain walls, and rocks and dirt come falling down as we all shield our faces. From a new opening in the underground castle, a glowing figure twirls down toward the city floor. No one makes a move; we're all too mesmerized by this dramatic entrance.

When she lands, I feel the most powerful sense of relief.

Accompanied by absolute terror.

Erzsébet.

And Rain.

She holds my baby in a neat little bundle, looking like the coolest grandma since Tilly. She smiles at me with her eyes before turning her focus to Timót.

"What a nice surprise," my awful dad says. "You've brought just what I needed."

"Oh, I'm dreadfully sorry, Timót," the witch responds. "The baby's not for you."

In the fanfare of Erzsébet's entrance, I missed the rest of the dragons crawling into the city. There are probably still more outside the mountain, but we're now completely surrounded, with twenty or more of the enormous creatures along the perimeter, all facing the witch queen and my child.

I really admire this woman, but her arrival was disastrously timed.

There's hot breath warming my shoulder, and I look briefly at the yellow dragon. It's the only one not focused on Erzsébet or Timót. Instead, its eyes are on me. That shouldn't come as a relief, but for some reason it does. I'm reminded of my moment with the dying mother in the cave, and finding peace in the creature's eyes. This dragon has the same look, even though peace should be the last thing on my mind.

"It's not too late to form an alliance, Erzsébet," Timót says. "When will you see that your plans for protecting the witches will never work?"

The queen stares back at him, a mix of pity and disgust on her face. "Blinded by power, young Timót. Just like so many who came before you. I'm sorry I couldn't offer better guidance. You've always been a clever man, and there was a better path for you to take."

Timót looks bored by the lecture and tries to move things along. "Give me the baby and save some lives. Perhaps even your own, depending on how I feel."

"Your threats don't carry much weight with an old woman like myself," Erzsébet says, slowly moving in my direction. "Bernadette, come to your baby. She's missed her mother."

I feel panic radiate off the Sexies behind me as I step further out into the open. I keep my wand aimed at Timót, knowing an attack from him is the only thing I can fend off. I just have to trust the dragons aren't about to light us up. As I move, there's a gutteral noise that comes from the closest dragon. I don't speak it's language, but I'd swear it's calling to me.

Timót's angry glare bounces between Erzsébet and me, but he makes no move to act. The queen's right about his intelligence, and he knows he's currently outmatched magic-wise, plus he doesn't want to hurt the baby. What he'll do after the exchange remains to be seen.

It's so hard not to drop my wand and bring Rain in for a giant hug, but I manage as I take her into my left arm. The touch of my child almost brings me to my knees, but I stay strong for her. I keep my focus so I can keep her alive.

"Back away, dear," Erzsébet says to me, her eyes again locked on Timót. "I have to endure a quick duel with your father."

I do as she says, though I'm not excited about what this all means. One on one, I've got my money on the queen. One on one with the backing of a dragon army--I think we're all screwed.

"You've always thought your powers were enough," Timót says, keeping his wand trained on the queen as she strides gracefully over fallen stones toward the center of the city. "Your hubris has been the downfall of your kind, and now it will bring about your end."

Erzsébet reaches a platform and steps upon it, bringing herself closer to eye level with Timót, who's been turning on his dragon so he can keep the witch in his sights.

"I view it as a new beginning," the queen says.

I'd say my heart is racing, but I actually think it's stopped. I'm so racked with terror that my insides are paralyzed.

Timót stares a moment longer, then lifts his wand, aiming it not at Erzsébet but instead toward the hole in the mountain ceiling above. The witch queen holds her own wand in front of her, gripping it with two hands, waiting on her enemy's next move.

"*Támadás!*" Timót yells. Nothing happens with his wand, but I think the posture was just that--posturing. The action comes from all around us.

In unison, every dragon rears its head back, then sends fire at the target. The heat is excruciating, even though I'm far from where the flames are headed. It burns my eyes, but I can't look away from Erzsébet. She's too smart, too strong, too powerful.

She's too important.

There's no way she can survive this onslaught of fire, but there's also no way she can die. I need her too much.

Rain needs her too much.

At first, the blaze encircles but doesn't touch her. There's a blue forcefield around the queen that keeps her from melting. Her eyes are closed and she looks relatively peaceful, though I'm sure her mind is super strained as she fights for control.

Slowly and with great purpose, she starts to lift her wand. My spirits perk up just a smidge, expecting she'll do something absolutely wild, like send all the flames back into the dragons' mouths and explode all of our enemies. She must have something cool like that up her sleeve.

Then she does something I don't understand--she turns her wand so the tip faces back toward her. She keeps both hands on the hilt, with the diamond point directed at her stomach.

Why?

In a sudden burst, the force field disappears, the flames engulf her--

And she plunges her wand into her gut.

She instantly disappears in the flames, a huge fire column in her place, reaching all the way up to the opening at the top of the mountain.

She's dead.

She's gone.

Or is she?

High above where she stood, in the middle of the skyward flame, two giant wings fan out.

A mighty red bird hovers in the fire. Or perhaps it's part of the fire. The cry of a phoenix rings out through the underground city. While the dragons continue leveling their fiery breath at what was once the queen of the witches, the powerful wings repel the blaze back to the source. The dragons seem confused and flustered, and they keep scorching the center of the city where Erzsébet stood.

It's mayhem.

And it's given us our chance.

I spin to Rune, who knows my thoughts immediately, wiping his hands frantically to create an illusion.

Zev, I say in my mind, *get us the hell out of here.*

The words have barely left my thoughts when I feel teeth on my back.

But they're not vampire teeth. And they're not werewolf teeth.

Bigger.

Hotter.

Dragon teeth.

Aside from the burn, it doesn't really hurt. There's pressure from the grip, but it's not crushing my bones. I hold onto Rain with all my might, not bothering to aim my wand because I've got to make sure my baby doesn't fall.

I'm lifted into the air, swung around and gently thrown--right onto the back of the yellow dragon. For the briefest second, I'm face to face with a mean-looking orc, who's just as surprised to see me as I am to see him.

Just as he opens his mouth to scream, the dragon's teeth chomp down on him. This bite isn't nearly so gentle. The creature thrashes his body from side to side, and I listen to bones breaking while watching blood fly. The forceful shaking knocks the other men off the dragon's back, then the beast flings the now lifeless body to the ground.

"Grab on!" I yell to my friends.

The sense of peace I got from this dragon holds firm, and I know it's on our side. I don't know why, but I'm not about to doubt it. With four friends needing to join us and the dragon having four legs, I figure this is the perfect vehicle to get us out of here--until Darius speeds off in the other direction.

I open my mind to scream, but he speaks first. *I must travel in the tunnels and the shadows to avoid the sun. I will find you at Aevelairith, my love.*

Everyone else leaps to hold onto a leg just as the expansive wings start to flap. I look up to see if the rest of the army has turned on us, but most of the dragons are still breathing fire on the inflammable phoenix. The cylinder of fire still stretches between the floor and the roof high above.

While Timót's dragon continues its fire barrage, my father has turned his attention in our direction, confused by both the illusion and the yellow dragon that's broken ranks. He doesn't really see what's happening, so this is our chance.

"*Unar,*" I say under my breath, though the intensity of my voice makes the spell as powerful as if I'd screamed it. A second later, Timót's wand flies out of his hand, clattering to the ground behind him.

One less threat. Now I just hope this young dragon is up to the task of outmaneuvering all its friends.

Another few beats of its wings and we're in the air, picking up momentum faster than I would have expected. I'm also surprised when our living transport heads upward and toward the center of the underground city as opposed to the larger opening in the side of the mountain.

We're going straight for the column of fire.

As we close in on the blaze, I see the head of the phoenix turn in our direction. It's like slow motion as we move closer and I stare at the bird, wondering if it's Erzsébet I'm seeing.

When we're only a few feet from the cylinder of fire, the bird dives back toward the ground, bringing the flames down with it and washing the city floor in a blue fire. Now it's chaos below us--and freedom above.

I squeeze Rain tightly against my chest while holding the reins with my other hand. This ascent better not last much longer or gravity will get the best of me.

The other dragons have left the ground to get away from the fire spread at their feet, but they don't seem to care about us. The men on their backs don't know what to do without Timót shouting orders, and he's trying to gather his wand without getting burned.

As we near the top of the mountain, I look back to the flames below us. To the last spot I saw Erzsébet standing. Now it's just scorched ground and ash.

Our dragon bursts through the opening in the mountaintop, continuing to fly higher. I keep my hold on the reins, finding a strength I didn't know I possessed to keep me and Rain alive. There are dragons flying around the outside of the mountain, as I thought there would be, but they're all lower than us. Before any makes a move, we're soaring well above them.

The dragon levels out, finally giving my arm a break, and continues flying through the clouds, never slowing down as it rushes us away from the danger.

I look down and breathe a sigh of relief. AJ, Zev and Rune are all safely holding on to the dragon's slender legs. I close my eyes and sense Darius moving beneath the earth, escaping the melay.

My family is safe.

Except for one.

CHAPTER SIXTEEN

The dragon flies through the clouds for a few more minutes, then ducks its mighty head and takes us back toward the ground. It keeps swerving and changing course, which is absolutely nauseating, but probably meant to keep any trackers off its path.

Frankly, I don't understand how this creature knows to be so helpful.

Is... is Erzsébet the dragon?

She's not, of course, because I saw her turn into fire as we escaped. That doesn't stop me from wanting to believe that she sent a part of herself into the dragon's mind so she could stay with us but in a different form.

I need to believe something like that. It makes it easier to understand what she did.

Tears blur my vision, and I don't have a hand to wipe them away. I just stare into space, wondering where--and if--this dragon will set us down.

The crunching of branches answers my question in short order as the magnificent yellow flyer breaks through a dense canopy of trees and lands with a jarring thud on the ground below. The choice was probably made to stay hidden from overhead, which is great; the scrapes and scratches endured by the people holding onto the dragon's legs are less appreciated.

She lowers her head, turning her long neck into a slide for me to climb down. I do so as gracefully as possible, and when my feet touch the ground, I finally have the chance to kiss and cuddle my sweet baby girl.

I feel like she's bigger, smarter, more alert since the last time I saw her. I missed so much in the last couple days and I'm about to mourn the lost time, when a calming touch from Rune reminds me that our distance probably kept Rain alive. Whether or not that's true, I'll just have to believe it so I don't hate myself too much.

"Where are we?" AJ asks, tending to a decent-sized cut on her forearm. "I need water before I go insane and try to fight this dragon."

I turn back to the majestic, gorgeous beast, sitting calmly with its head still on the ground. It seems so gentle now after causing such terror when it was part of an army helmed by shitbirds.

My companions stand a few yards away, not quite as trusting of the creature as I am. I don't blame them; it certainly seemed like I was the only one the dragon planned to save.

I pass Rain to Rune and kneel in front of the gentle monster's face, the hot breath coming from her nostrils making my eyes water.

We stare into each other's eyes for a minute in silence. I'm not sure what to say to my new yellow friend. Not how I knew to speak to the mother…

Wait.

I set my wand down in front of the dragon, her huge, glassy eyes following my motions as I do. The grass below my feet rustles as she takes sharp inhalations, sniffing at the dark stick I've laid before it.

I jump back a step when her forked tongue darts out, licking the wand once, then again, then wrapping around the wood casing. I worry for a second that I've just fed a dragon my most precious possession, but the tongue stays extended, snaking along the wand like a blind person studying brail. It's a strange, miraculous thing to watch.

I look back into the dragon's eyes and see tears starting to form.

She senses her mother.

"I promised your mother I'd save you," I say to the mythical beast, pretty confident my words won't fully register but sharing the sentiment all the same. "But now you've both saved me."

I look over at my partners in crime. Zev has a look of understanding, and I think Rune has pieced it together by now. AJ looks super baffled.

"I met this dragon's mom, right after Timót stole the baby away. She gave me the scale for my wand."

Things don't seem any clearer to AJ. "Did she like, sell it to you? Put it in an envelope and leave it at your door? Use eBay?"

"She *let* me take it," I say with a roll of my eyes. "She chose to let me go instead of burning me to death. That help?"

AJ shrugs, and it's as much of a yes as I can hope to get. I look back at the dragon and smile. "Thank you."

She releases my wand for me to retrieve, then I stand and join the others. "Let's get to some water and then go to… somewhere."

We take just a couple steps toward the edge of the grove before hearing the dragon rise to her feet, smashing a couple saplings with her tail as she does so. A few more steps and she starts to follow us.

Looks like we've got a new team member.

"Is this dragon like our pet now?" AJ asks. "God we're cool. Buncha magic bitches with a pet dragon."

Jokes aside, I do feel a little awesome. We escaped death, earned a dragon, and I've got my baby back. After I conjure a nifty harness for her out of thin air, I feel even better.

Naturally, that bit of happiness is fleeting. The sacrifice it took to get us free was perhaps the greatest I've ever witnessed. Erzsébet didn't have to die. She could have cast some spell, created some shadow, turned the air to ice--I don't know, done something to live and fight another day.

And while she gave her life willingly to help our cause, the wolves weren't so lucky. We brought terror to their once beautiful kingdom and it cost them everything.

I sense that Zev's thinking the same thing.

Not too far from the edge of the forest, we come to a small stream. AJ's already splashing in the shallow water before I know it's there. The dragon and Rune both kneel at the bank of the stream to drink, making quite the adorable pair. Like a boy and his dog.

I step over to Zev, who's staring at the water, lost in thought.

"Do you think any of them got away?"

He nods solemnly. "Wolves will fight until their last breath, but they won't die senselessly. I'm sure the ones that could, ran as the dragons came in."

That could be good news. "Where would they go?" I ask.

"I'm going to find out," he answers briskly as he leans down to take a drink of water.

I'm not sure what he means, and I'm mostly positive I won't like the answer.

"How do you plan on finding out?"

He steps up from the stream and gives me a deep, passionate kiss before pulling away and gazing at me with those enchanting green eyes.

"By finding them. I'll meet you in Aevelairith."

His words are still dancing along my eardrum and he's already shifted and started to sprint away as a wolf. He's lost in the trees before I can even think *get your self-sabotaging wolf ass back here!*

I know it's too late. He's gone and I could never convince him to stay anyway. I swallow my pride and sadness and get myself a drink from the stream. I have no idea how thirsty I am until the water hits my lips and I suck it down until my stomach feels full.

"So," I say as I fall back into the grass. "Back to the 'where the hell are we' question."

Rune plucks a few blades of grass, and I start to think he's going to throw them into the air like a golfer checking the wind, but then he does something even more strange and eats them.

"We gotta get Ru-Ru a sandwich, stat," AJ says, her short-term memory dismissing everything we've been through and getting right back to name calling. Fortunately Rune is too focused on his meal to hear the dig.

"Still to the south and east of Aevelairith, but only a short distance," he says with unflappable confidence. What the hell did he taste on that grass? "The stream will take us toward the main river."

In a different life, I'd yell for everyone to stop what they were doing so Rune could explain how a mouthful of plant and dirt worked as GPS, but now I just hop up, walk over to him for a quick, grassy-mouthed kiss, and start heading upstream.

No time like the present to stop trying to make sense of all this.

I only get a few steps forward before I stop, Darius' voice penetrating my mind.

I'm in the woods, safe from the sunlight. Turn to the left and you'll see me.

I spin almost too quickly, nearly tumbling backward into the stream. Through the trees, I can make out a figure.

"Wait here!" I yell to AJ and Rune as I sprint to my vampire. Rain was sleeping until this, but now her eyes are open as she tries to figure out why she's bouncing so much.

I reach Darius and take his face in my hands, kissing him all over his cheeks and lips.

"How did you get here?" I ask.

"Through the tunnels at first, then by staying beneath the canopy. I can travel when clouds pass or beneath the shade of a tree. It's not ideal, but it will do. More importantly, I've spoken with King Emerus, to tell him of these events."

I had forgotten about coordinating with the vampires. Now that the attacking has started, I wonder if it's already too late.

"He says the vampires will deploy immediately to aid our cause."

"That's great," I say, though I'm still wondering how it will all work out. "How are they getting here?"

Darius nods skeptically, picking up my tone. "They'll climb through the mountains as soon as the western sun sets. It's no short journey, but they'll move as fast as they can."

Okay cool. So we need to stay alive until at least nightfall. And we've got no time to lose. I kiss Darius again, then run back to my waiting travel companions.

They return to moving upstream as soon as I'm close, AJ riding on a wave she's created with her feet, looking like the happiest little girl in the world. The dragon, who I've started calling Sunflower, mostly walks alongside us and then occasionally bursts into the sky for a quick bit of flight.

Worry hits me every now and again that Timót and his army will descend on us without warning, but the calm of the others keeps me in check. Sunflower didn't take a straight route toward the fae kingdom, and I don't think my father will waste time searching every inch of the realm. Apparently he has eyes and ears all around, so he'll likely wait until he gets word.

Which is why the sooner we get to Aevelairith, the sooner we need to prepare for war.

My fear leads me down a path of reflection, as memories of the earliest days with the Sexies pop into my mind. I'd never known terror like I felt being trapped in my bar with those three strangers, and now I'll never know a life without them. We're either together, or I die.

I think about arriving in Budapest and meeting the queen of the witches, how her riddles frustrated and flustered me, but her patience and care made me into a powerful witch. Within my magic, I'll always carry a part of Erzsébet. And so will Rain.

I think about my parents, both deadset on ruining my life for different bad reasons. Mom because magic had cost her so much, and dad because he's always felt slighted by those better than him. What a terrible pair of parents. Maybe if they'd stayed together they'd have balanced each other out. Or killed each other earlier and saved me all this trouble.

In the distance, I see the mountainous walls that surround the valleys of Aevelairith. If there was a kingdom I had to fight in, and perhaps die in, this would be it. I feel the power of the earth moving below my feet. The old magic of the Fates is sowed into the soil here. In the strangest way, this land feels like home.

Our small stream merges with the river and we begin the final leg of what might be our final journey. I don't expect to go on another quest before we have to put our lives on the line to save the Last Witch, my pure and innocent baby, from those who would treat her as a magical prize to be coveted and captured.

When we reach the gate leading into the kingdom, no guard stands watch. It's eerie after our first visit, even if we did arrive as naked prisoners.

Rune quickly scales the wall and sets the gears in motion to open the stone barrier.

Inside, it's like a ghost town. A night ago there was merriment at every stop, and now it's like the people have gone into hiding. They probably have, but I'm not sure what Revia told them to hide from.

"I assume the fae are gathered at the Cliff of Liliolyn," Rune says. "To send my parents' ashes off to be with their ancestors."

He starts marching through the kingdom with a purposeful stride. Sunflower takes to the sky overhead while AJ and I follow our leader.

We walk to the outer edge of the city and then turn off on a path leading up a golden hillside. As we walk, the distant sound of humming and chanting can be heard. It gets louder as we approach the top of the hill, and then all of the fae are suddenly before us.

They stand overlooking a cliff, with two caskets resting at the edge of the precipice. It's a solemn, focused ceremony, so they don't notice our approach.

They do, however, hear the sound of beating dragon wings as Sunflower crests the hilltop.

There are cries and screams at first, but the crowd settles when they see Rune, standing with his hand raised. I have no idea if anyone here still trusts him, but the fact that he's calmly standing in front of a dragon means people will at least hear him out.

"Revia is dead," Rune announces.

"You killed her too!" a voice shouts from the crowd.

"I killed no one," the fae prince answers calmly. "Your king and queen were killed by the same blindness that's been murdering the fae for generations. The mindless adherence to a prophecy that no longer holds true. My mother and father finally saw the error of our ways, and for that, Revia killed them."

Lots of murmurs. Lots of head shaking. It wouldn't surprise me if this turned into an angry mob situation, so I keep my wand at the ready.

"We have a new enemy now," Rune says. "He and his army ride on the back of dragons. He'll be in Aevelairith by nightfall, perhaps sooner. We have no choice but to defend our kingdom until our blood runs dry."

"Our greatest fighters have fled," a woman yells out. "Gone in search of you."

Rune nods. "I know. They were tricked and killed by the man of which I speak. That's why…"

I'm pretty sure Rune was going to mention the fact that a bunch of vampires might show up, but the arrival of Zev in wolf form cuts him off. He shifts to human as people scream and gasp but make no move to attack. Perhaps his nudity and impressive manhood keeps everyone distracted.

Alden died in the attack, Zev whispers to me. *Mother perished as well. The remaining wolves will regroup and come to fight alongside their new king.*

I take Zev's hand and squeeze it tightly. The loss might sting, but right now he's focused on a greater good. I love him for that, even as my heart breaks for him. He's lost his whole family in under a day, and now must go to war. That shit is not easy to process.

The werewolf stands between me and Rune, also taking the fae's hand in a show of solidarity. Rune smiles and then returns to addressing the crowd.

"We may be joined by vampires tonight," he says to more gasps from the crowd. He looks at Zev, who nods. "And wolves. Those we fought for so long, Fates willing, shall come and take up arms beside us. To protect Aevelairith. And to protect the Last Witch."

The people are silent, with the soundtrack for this heavy moment just the steady beating of Sunflower's wings. They see Rain strapped to me, the prophetic baby alive and well. I try to smile at anyone willing to make eye contact. To show we're not the enemy.

Finally, a tall, elderly fae steps forward.

"What would you have us do, my liege?"

Rune smiles, relieved that he won't have to do anymore arguing or convincing. For now.

"First, we send my parents to join the ancestors. We mourn our loss and give them our blessings."

The fae nod, support for their new leader growing.

"And then," Rune continues, "we prepare to fight as though our entire world depends on it, for it truly does."

CHAPTER SEVENTEEN

I pace the war room--which is really just a cool way of describing the room with all the maps and little toy soldiers--as I think through a convoluted and twisty plan that has more holes in it than swiss cheese--or my brain after childbirth.

Darius arrived shortly after the fae said a final goodbye to Rivelis and Scocha. I found him lurking in the shadows just at the bottom of the hill. With our group at full strength, Rune led us into this small but impressive space, within the trunk of a mighty oak tree.

I keep pouring over the maps laid out on the large stone table the five of us are sitting around. Well six, if you count my baby. There are little fae, wolf and vampire wooden figurines spread over the different kingdoms. I wonder who carved these? We don't have any dragons, so AJ helpfully made a few tiny paper airplanes to represent them. Though she keeps stealing them from the table to launch at Zev's stoic face.

He ignores her, but when his thoughts bleed into mine I have to hold back an inappropriate laugh.

I offered to find a piece of shit to stand in for daddy dearest, but that idea got rejected.

Vaemor, the vampire kingdom, is located in the Northeast region of the world. The fae kingdom of Aevelairith sits opposite them in the Northwest region, and Wiceraweil is directly below the fae in the Southwest region. There's a massive mountain range running down the center, cutting the vampires off from the rest. It's part of what allows them to bespell their territory in magical sunblock.

I keep looking at the map, trying to think of a place we might run to, a way we can escape and join forces with the other races, then get the high ground. No matter how I slice it, no such place exists. For one, it's kind of hard to get a higher ground than dragons.

Timót will come through the air, with an army that dwarfs ours. Fighting in Aevelairith is our best bet. And the odds really aren't that good.

"I'm working on an idea," I tell the guys. "But I don't think you'll like it."

They already have their eyes narrowed, trying to read my thoughts and feelings, ready to dissuade me of any suggestions that sound risky. Unfortunately for them, the window for avoiding risk got shattered back in Rowley.

"We need a plan that's better than 'fight and win'," I say. "We don't know when or how many of the wolves and vampires will show up. We're assuming my father will arrive soon, but 'soon' is our best guess. We have one dragon. He's got dozens. We've got a decimated fae army that doesn't know who to trust. Our plan can't rely on brute strength. We have to be smarter than that." I look down at Rain, blissfully unaware of this chaotic world that's so obsessively aware of her. "We need to lure him in."

The guys look disgusted. I turn to AJ for backup, but she's frowning. "I don't like it," she says, but before I can chew her out for not taking my side, she holds up a hand and takes Rain from me, giving the baby's head kisses. "But I think you're right. We have to try."

The Sexies are none too happy, but appeasing them really isn't the goal.

I take Rain back and hold her close to my chest, marveling at what a calm, sweet little thing she is despite everything.

I mean, I'd take a bout of colic or cradle cap over someone constantly trying to kill my poor kid, but I'm insanely grateful she is such a perfect little peanut.

I kiss her nose, then get back to it. "We don't know how long we have. Rune, I assume the fae have a system of defense in place given all your warring?"

He nods. "We do, but not against dragons. Fighting off an aerial attack will be a very different thing than targeting vampires or wolves."

"You have archers?" Zev asks.

"Yes. The best left with Revia, but we still have some."

"Let's use 'em," I say, studying a different map that shows the outer walls of the fae kingdom. "We don't know which direction he'll come from, do we? If they flew straight from Wiceraweil, they'd already be here."

"We don't, but we can control the ease with which they fly into our kingdom," Rune says.

I smile, sensing the direction he's going. "So we can make giant illusions?"

Rune nods. "With enough fae working in concert, we can make the kingdom disappear... for a brief while."

"Then how will the vamps and wolves find us?" AJ asks, pointing out the big flaw in my plan.

"That's a problem," I admit, looking around the table, hoping someone smarter than me has an idea I haven't thought of.

When no one immediately speaks up, I give it my best shot. "Can the illusion just work from the bird's eye view? So anything approaching on foot doesn't have to deal with it?""

Rune scratches his chin. "Yes, as long as everyone casting the charm takes the same approach. Though it won't be as strong of an illusion."

I shrug. "I think we have to risk it. We need all the help we can get."

Rune nods. "We shall make it so."

I look back at the map but I'm not really seeing it. My mind is on the inevitable showdown between me and my father, and no drawing or figurines will help with that. The others sense where my head is at, but none of them has an easy solution.

"I need to lead my father into the tunnels below the city," I say, voicing this realization before I've had much time to process it. "Fending off the dragons is important, but we need to get to Timót. Cut off the head, kill the beast."

"And if his dragons cave in the tunnels, crushing you and your child?" Darius asks, his dark eyes piercing me.

"Timót's only here for Rain," I say. "Yeah, he wants to kill everyone who might stand in his way, but none of it matters to him without the Last Witch. He won't let his own army hurt the baby."

"Then we'll come with you to the tunnels," Zev says, determined to shield me from harm as much as possible.

I shake my head. "He's an immortal with a dragon armor suit and a lifetime of witch training. If there's an obstacle he doesn't mind killing, he'll kill it. Besides, you three will have your hands full. You have to defeat his army... with or without help."

"And how do you expect to destroy a being too powerful for any of us?" Darius asks in his righteous way.

I shrug. It's not like I fancy myself an equal match against my father, or consider myself stronger than anyone in this room. Experience-wise, I'm the least equipped for this fight. The one advantage I have is that he'll hesitate before killing me, and take every step not to hurt my baby. I think back on my lessons with Erzsébet, and while nothing sticks out as the perfect solution, I trust the magic will find me.

"Annnnnnnd, does anyone have any use for the water nymph?" AJ jokes, but she probably is feeling a little left out. She likes to drive the action, though she recognizes we're not fighting in her best arena.

"I need you to just stay alive," I say. "If something happens to me, but we somehow save Rain, I need you here for her." The pressure of the moment keeps me from crying, but it doesn't stop AJ. She hides her face and gives me a thumbs up.

We sit in silence, processing the strategy I've just thrown together on the fly. I'm not sure when I took charge of the mission, and I'm alarmed that my scheme has me facing our most powerful rival all on my own. That's the way it has to be, though. And that's why it fell on me to propose the master plan. No one else is willing to put me in harm's way.

"So... what does everyone think?" I don't really want feedback but I need to break the silence.

"How will you draw Timót into the tunnels?" Rune asks. "He'll see the same illusion as the rest, provided it works."

I've got a half-baked thought for this, and I'm hoping everyone can help me cook it all the way through. "Can we, if I'm able to do the crazy thing I'm thinking of doing, create the illusion right after my father and I land on the ground? Before the rest of the dragons arrive?"

"Theoretically," Rune says in a voice that still needs some convincing.

"Let's say, hypothetically, I take to the sky on our dragon. We know she's fast enough to outrun the pack, and we know Timót won't send one of his goons after me instead of giving chase himself. As soon as he and I cross a certain threshold, can the fae throw up the illusion and confuse the shit out of everyone else?"

Zev and Darius both turn to Rune, clearly employing a pressure campaign to make him say it's impossible. The more I talk about using myself as bait, the angrier the thoughts of my lovers become.

Rune's too devoted to logic to cave. "Yes, we can. We'll confuse the shit right out of them."

Nothing diffuses the tension like Rune doing a little human talk.

Both Darius and Zev try to plead with my mind, begging for another solution, but I reject every effort. My gut hasn't led me astray yet, and I don't see another path forward.

"No more time to waste," I say. "I love you all very, very much."

It might undercut the power of my previous speech, but I need to get gushy for just a quick second. I'm scared to death of what's about to happen, so I'm taking this chance to tell them how I feel. In case another chance doesn't come around.

Darius kisses me deeply before disappearing into the shadows.

Zev takes his turn next, nuzzling my neck after his kiss, nipping at the bite mark he used to claim me.

And then Rune takes me into his arms. His eyes are a mix of sadness and strength. So much has happened to him in the last day, it seems unfair that he could still endure more pain. I make a silent promise that he won't experience another loss.

God I hope I can keep my word.

Rune kisses me tenderly, holding my face as he does, and then he brushes away a tear I didn't know I had before running off to prepare the fae.

I sniff, then take AJs hand and lead us to the garden Rune shared with me just a couple nights before. There are small streams and so much beautiful plant life, it seems like this is where AJ should be. Sunflower sits just outside the garden walls, looking like an adorable, enormous, scaled puppy.

AJ and I stroll over to the Tree of Life, neither of us able to speak. This is the hardest goodbye to say because AJ doesn't have a task to busy herself with. She just gets to watch me walk away and then hope for the best.

I hug my best friend and kiss her cheek. "Stay safe. Don't do anything stupid."

Now we're both crying, but the bitch uses her magic to make her tears change shapes and dance around, to a delighted cry from Rain. "You've impressed your god daughter," I say with a wet laugh.

There are more hugs and tears and kisses. And then it's time.

"I'm proud of you, B," she says, just as I turn to leave. "A real queen."

I pause and smile at her through wet lashes. But I don't turn around to look at her again.

I can't.

Destiny is calling.

And for that, I need a dragon.

Sunflower is waiting for me when I step out of the garden. When she sees me and Rain, she stands, unfurls her wings and lowers her head so that I can mount her more easily.

And then we are off. I've got the baby tightly strapped to my chest, knowing we might be in for a bumpy ride. As we soar into the clouds, my heart lurches and my pulse speeds up from sheer nerves. I really hope this plan works.

I direct the dragon in a sweeping circle around the kingdom, so we can cautiously scout to see what direction my father's army will be coming from. It shouldn't be hard to spot an entire thunder of dragons coming at us; the hard part will be making sure they don't spot us first.

The wind rushes through my hair, and with nothing but clouds around me I feel at once free and terrified. The moments of solitude help me settle my mind, and I pat the dragon as we soar through the sky. "I lost my mom too," I tell her, though my voice hardly carries with the wind. "Maybe we can be each other's family now," I say, though lord help me I have no idea what I'd do with a dragon at Morgan's Pub.

It makes me wonder: what *is* going to happen to us all once this is over, should we survive to the end? It's a question that plagues me, even though there's so much danger that stands between myself and an answer. I wish I could spare a few moments to think about the long term, or to spend time with Darius alone to help him process his torment. Or with Zev and Rune who should be busy grieving right now.

It's all been put on hold for a senseless war, and I hate it. I want this over with. I want it done. I want my father out of my life forever. Out of all of our lives. It would be real nice if this were a normal dad problem that could be solved with a block button rather than a whole war.

Then my thoughts wander back to the task at hand, and the possible outcomes of today. Each more gruesome than the last.

As my thoughts turn dangerously dark, the dragon beneath me stops short, nearly toppling me from her back.

I see in the distance the glint of dragon scale against the fading sun just as my dragon whips around and begins flying slowly towards the underground entry to the tunnels.

I wait, twisted in the seat with my wand at the ready.

I don't take action until I can see my father's eyes.

Until I know he can see his coveted prize.

I kiss my sweet girl on the head, trying to show that I love her despite what's about to happen.

And then I blast a firebolt at him from my wand, and we race off through the sky, the wind piercing as my father gives chase.

The other dragons follow, but my father stays well in the lead. So far, so good, even though it all feels mostly bad.

"Hurry," I whisper to the dragon as I lean forward, trying to make my body more aerodynamic. Being a lumpy human meat suit holding a baby does little to decrease air resistance.

We are nearing the planned disembarkment site, and my nerves are frayed. I clutch the bundle to my chest with one hand, and raise my wand with the other as my dragon lands and I slide off in a fluid motion that's movie quality, if I do say so myself.

I make the mistake of looking behind me to see if my father has caught up. The lightning bolt that explodes the ground at my feet indicates he has indeed.

Bastard.

I climb down through the tunnel door and speed along the dark passage, knowing my dad will follow. I try to keep my strides smooth, not wanting to bounce Rain too much and make her scream.

The deeper in we go, the narrower the tunnel, which works to our advantage. I stop when I reach a cavern with a few different exits. I plan on walking out of here the victor, but I'd at least like to keep the option to run away available.

I face the opening nervously, my wand drawn, my back straight. I try not to shake.

My father arrives on foot and alone, just as I'd hoped. He stands taller than life with his dragon skin armor. Just seeing him in such an atrocity makes my stomach lurch.

The earth around us shakes as he approaches, and he looks up and smiles. "It sounds like my dragons have started the attack. You have the power to end this and save many lives."

I want to brag, to showboat all the ways we are keeping his dragons confused, but that would be stupid and ego-driven. I keep my face stoic and say a silent prayer everything is going okay up there. I have to trust the Sexies to handle the battle above while I fight my own down here.

"Give me the child," he says, holding out his hands like I'm just going to do what he says, no biggie. "I won't harm her. She will grow up to be the witch queen, ruling every realm, with me the Grand Emperor of all."

"Forgive me if your penchant for murder doesn't instill the utmost trust for my daughter's safety." And then, because I don't want to make the mistake of every villain in every B movie and spend too much time talking, I unleash my wand into my father, fully determined to strike first.

He draws just as quickly, a counterspell causing my fire to fizzle without doing any harm.

"You mistake raw magic and luck for power, Bernadette," he says, slowly stepping closer. "I'm sure the witch queen tried to get you to understand your magic, but she didn't teach you the control it takes to be powerful."

A spark flies from the tip of his wand and slices my shoulder before I can react. The pain is hard to bear, but I'm even more concerned that a strap on the harness has been cut. Once he gets Rain away from me, I've lost my child... and my leverage.

"I know these things because I was in your shoes, hoping to learn how to harness these powers, yet being taught nothing. Erzsébet spent centuries blaming the other races for the downfall of the witches, when it was their own hubris and pretension that led us to where we are now."

Another spark flies from his wand, but this time I'm ready to deflect. A bubble of light forms around my wand and saves my right arm from the same injury as my left. However, in the moments I waste celebrating my success, Timót fires another shot that tears into my hip, breaking another strap and cutting deep into my flesh. I drop to a knee, fighting through the searing pain so I can keep an eye on my father as he steps even closer.

When another tremor pulls my father's attention to the cavern walls above us, I try to sneak in another shot. As soon as I mutter *tűz*, he moves his wand in a small circle and sends the fire back toward me. I fall to the ground, covering Rain to keep her from burning while I feel the heat run across my back.

I'm outmatched. Timót's envisioned this fight for decades, and my list of spells is maybe three pages long. My heart was in the right place bringing this final battle to my doorstep, but I'm out of my depth.

I hear his footsteps getting closer. I don't fear for my life, not yet. I only fear for my baby. For the life he'll force her to live. I've brought her to this moment, hoping things would go my way in the end. I wanted so badly to offer the protection no one offered me. I think back to my mother, devastated by her powers, betrayed by her magic, trying to take her own life to save the others around her. I fight back tears, hating even the inkling of sympathy I might feel for that woman.

My father stands right behind me, leaning down to put a hand on my shoulder.

"Despite what you may think, I don't want to hurt you. I want you to raise your child in the *Érintett* Kingdom, to discover at last the powers you possess, and to pass those gifts on to your daughter. I fight to give you what's best, Bernadette."

I slowly rise from the ground, first to my knees, keeping an arm wrapped around Rain so she won't fall from her carrier. I slowly get to my feet and turn to face Timót, not making any move to back away from him.

"I guess that's the difference between us," I say as I raise my wand, just inches from his face.

He keeps his eyes locked on mine and brings his wand up to eye level, the two tips glowing as the competing powers push and pull against each other.

"What's that?" he asks, the light from our wands flickering in his eyes hiding behind the dragonskin mask.

"You'll kill everyone to try and keep us alive. I'll kill us to make sure you can't hurt anyone else."

My wand has been aimed at his eyes, and he's ready to defend himself. What he's not prepared for is me turning the wand toward my chest.

Toward me.

Toward Rain.

His eyes go wide, confused and afraid of whatever I might do. He doesn't even react as I grab him by the shoulder and pull him into a tight embrace, summoning all the strength of a mother who's had enough.

"Goodbye," I whisper into my dad's ear. Then I scream "*dominálnak lélek!*"

And the world goes white.

CHAPTER EIGHTEEN

I t's quiet.
I don't hear, see, smell or feel anything.

My mind is like a blank slate, the only thought running through is the awareness that I have no thoughts.

The space around me is incredibly bright, but it doesn't hurt my eyes or force me to squint. Ever so slowly, the white glare begins to fade, replaced by a soft yellow. Walls start to come into view as a room takes shape around me. I notice that I'm in a chair, comfortably seated, my wand in my hand.

My baby strapped to my chest.

"We don't control our magic."

Erzsébet sits in front of me, just a few feet away and not at all dead. She carries on with a casual lesson, her voice calm and soothing.

"Instead, we become it. This is why powers take time, and spells don't get thought up overnight." She stops talking for a moment to look at Rain and make a silly face, eliciting a cute little giggle.

"When you first arrived in Budapest, it wasn't simply that you couldn't control your powers, Bernie. That's too simple a solution. That's what some... less thoughtful witches--and others--might have you believe."

I know she's talking about my father. But I also know this conversation is taking place during our trainings, back before I took the portal to Vaemor, before I knew anything of my father's plans.

"You have to think of controlling magic the same way you think of taking a breath. Or looking into the sky. Or enjoying a friendship. You simply do those things, because your body and your heart and your mind are part of your greater being. So too is your magic."

More thoughts crystalize in my mind as she speaks. I've just traveled through all of the kingdoms, running and fighting and hurting and loving. I've just been in the darkness, hugging my baby tight, trying to protect her.

To save her from Timót.

"The more you let magic bind with you, the more it becomes who you are and what you can do. The more you become it. The longer you grow with your powers, the greater your abilities. Eventually, the spells and knowledge live in your body as part of your genetic makeup, more than just an education. The power comes to your aid when you need it, not simply because you can recite an incantation. Your wand, special and useful as it may be, becomes less important."

I'm in the tomb in Budapest. This is a lesson from Erzsébet.

But I'm in the tunnel with Timót, our bodies closed around Rain as magic explodes around us.

That's where I really am. My mind, however, is walking through a memory.

"If I teach you nothing else, dear girl, let this lesson get through to you," the queen says, leaning in close. "Magic binds to nothing so tightly as love. It is more than a feeling. It is at the core of who you are, and it is a very tangible thing in the magical world. Love has kept you alive, has brought three very powerful men to your side. In your time of greatest need, it is where you will find your greatest power."

The white light slowly returns, and the smiling witch before me is washed away by the brightness. The senses I once lacked start to return, bit by bit. Smells, tastes, sounds. Pain. Tremendous, glorious pain. Tremendous because it's so strong I want to pass out; glorious because, looking into the lifeless eyes of Timót, his head on the cavern floor next to mine, I know he can't feel it.

As I slowly regain consciousness, I'm riding a wave of numbness and traveling at superspeed. Darius has me in his arms, sprinting me through the tunnel.

I lean my head against his chest. I can't use my arms or hands. Everything hurts as the adrenaline fades and the pain hits hard and fast.

I moan in his arms and he holds me closer, his voice a calm presence in my mind. *You'll be okay. It's all okay. You're going to be fine.*

I don't know if I believe him. I hardly trust I'm alive right now, much less that I will continue living for the next few minutes.

As we run, Darius makes me drink some of his blood. It drips into my mouth and then runs down my cheek. I don't have the power to swallow.

His cheeks are stained with tears as he carries me out of the tunnels and to the secret garden. I can hardly see, but the smell of the plants and the feel of cool night air comes as a welcome relief.

The sound of battle is loud around us. I don't know if Darius has been weaving between warring factions or if the fight is further away. I've lost the ability to focus on anything, and I trust him to avoid the worst of it.

In the distance, I hear a howl. Zev, perhaps? Then I hear another, and another, and more howling voices until it sounds like a whole pack.

"Wolves?" I say, my voice barely above a whisper.

Darius reaches an empty patch of grass and sets me down gently. He sees my flesh wounds, but I think he knows that's not where the real damage is.

"Yes," he answers. "They arrived just before the flash of lightning shot up from the ground. I came to you as fast as I could."

I try to ask Darius what's happening, but he just shushes me and tells me it'll all be fine.

Except I can tell he's lying.

He knows I'm dying.

And so do I. I summoned a spell to challenge every soul in that family embrace. I unleashed powers great enough to bring down the living dead.

I thought that maybe magic bound by love could somehow live on.

Hopefully in Rain. I'm not sure I'll be around long enough to find out.

My head rolls to the side and I see the Tree of Life, standing tall above me. I wish I could have lain beneath it in earlier times, before the witches died, when magic flowed freely.

I hear footsteps as AJ cries out and runs over to kneel beside us. She reaches down and starts to carefully unstrap Rain.

"What happened? What do you need me to do, B?" She asks through her tears.

"Is she alive?" I ask with what little breath I have left as my friend cradles my baby. Even as I ask, I'm afraid I don't want the answer.

AJ stifles a sob as she lifts Rain. "I... don't know."

"Can you lay her on my chest?" I ask. "Put her little head under my chin." As AJ sets my baby down, I flash back to her birth, the first time I held her in my arms.

For every first, there is a last. And I have reached mine.

"What happened," AJ whispers. Thankfully, Darius answers on my behalf.

"The ground beneath our feet lit up, then I raced into the tunnels. I found Bernie and Rain beside Timót. Both their wands were shattered."

I hear a howl coming closer to us, and then Zev is here, shifting from wolf to man. "Bernie," he falls to his knees at my side, his expression matching Darius.

Rune arrives seconds later, probably having guessed I caused the flash. He looks angry and sad and all the things I can't deal with because my life is fading really fast and I'm about to feel the touch of my daughter for the last time and I can't bear it.

Tears slide down my face as my arms lay uselessly at my side, my fingers dusted with dirt.

"You all need to help the wolves" I manage to croak. No sense in watching me die while Aevelairith burns.

"The vampires arrived," Zev says. "Seconds after the sun settled behind the hills."

Thank God. Emerus held true to his word. That gives me a bit of hope not just for this fight, but for the future of the kingdoms when this battle is done.

He did keep his word, Darius says, picking up on my thoughts. *He was the first over the mountains, leading his men like a true king.*

I wish I could thank him, I say back.

You cannot, Darius says sternly. *He died in the dragons' fire. And you will not go to the other side to meet him.*

Poor Darius. So many years of immortality, and now so much death. Cara, father, brother... and now, me.

Rune looks to the sky and I follow his gaze. In the air I see dozens of massive dragons. It's a sight that would bring terror, except they're flying in the opposite direction.

"The dragons are leaving," the fae says. "It appears they've left without the *Érintett.*"

"Timót's wand," Darius says softly. "You broke the spell and set them free."

That brings a blip of happiness into my heart. Those beautiful beasts deserve much better. I also find some peace in knowing my beloveds might not die today. But the feeling is fleeting as I look back at the Tree of Life, in dire need of magic only my kind can provide. While the different interpretations of the prophecy might have been off base, the truth remains that this world's magic is in short supply.

I have no wand. I have no strength. I need a miracle.

You are the miracle, a voice in my mind whispers. A voice who is decidedly not either of my mates.

Who are you? I ask, wondering if this is the voice of death come to take me to meet AJ's beau.

You know who I am, she says. *Look upon me.*

My eyes are on the trunk of the massive tree, but I let them drift up toward the foliage. While nothing stands out as drastically different, I notice for the first time a face, made of branches and leaves. It might have always been there, but I can only see it now because it's talking to me.

Am I dead?

You could be, she says. *Do you want to be?*

No.

Then live on.

The skin above my heart burns anew, even though I thought my body was done feeling pain. This is a different sort of agony, though. And it strikes me at a particular point--right where the Dryad queen punctured me. My heart rate increases, and I feel blood trickling from my wounds and dropping onto the earth below me.

Ah yes, I know your blood, the tree says. *It is of the Fate who planted me, and who breathed life into the fae.*

My blood?

The leaves of the tree shake, like it's nodding. *You have the blood of a creator. One of the givers of life.*

My family's blood? My family traces back to one of the Fates?

That's right, sweet girl.

This is a new voice, and it's one I recognize in an instant.

Tilly...

There's a new face in the tree, one that somehow, while still made of twigs and leaves, looks just like my beautiful nanny.

Our magic flourished in this garden and in these woods, nanny says. *I think the Tree of Life is happy to see you here.*

It's then I notice that the talking tree, with faces made of branches, has started to regain its glow. My eyes drift back down, and I see my magic surging through my hands and into the ground.

You found the love we'd all been searching for, Bernie, Tilly says. *It's bound to you, and your magic to it.*

I didn't want to hurt Rain, I say in my mind while tears stream down my face. *I didn't want either of us to die, Nanny. I'm not like my mother.*

Of course you're not. That's exactly why you're going to be alright.

Even in the tree, Tilly has the sweetest smile.

You won't be seeing me anytime soon. Wake up, she says.

Wake up, the Tree of Life repeats.

Wake up.

Bernie, wake up. Bernie!

Love!

The voices no longer belong to the faces in the tree, but rather to Darius and Zev. I can feel arms clutching me as I jolt up. I've got my arms wrapped around Rain, and as I feel my breath come back, I can hear my baby's heartbeat. She's alive.

I look at Rune, whose face is drenched with tears, his eyes locked on the Tree of Life.

The beautiful, vibrant, *living* Tree of Life.

White and golden light runs through the trunk, spilling out of the branches, bringing the tree back to life. I look down at my hands, at my body, and see the magic still pulses through me and into the soil beneath my fingertips.

Glancing back at the tree, I can just barely make out the outline of the face. A gust of wind rustles the leaves, but I know it's a smile.

Rune looks in awe as he speaks. "You brought her back to life, Bernie."

Without looking away from the tree, I reach out and take Rune's hand, swapping some of my Fate-forged magic for his eternal calm. "*We* brought her back to life," I say as I look at Rain, her sweet face lighting up my heart brighter than any sparkling tree.

Darius stands, looking off into the distance.

"I hear cheers," Zev says, filling the rest of us in on the sounds only a wolf can hear.

"Yes," Darius says. "I can sense it in the vampire soldiers. The *Érintett* have surrendered."

I squeeze and kiss my child, then take a moment to look at each of my Sexy companions and my dearest friend.

The war is over.

We get to start the rest of our lives.

CHAPTER NINETEEN
5 MONTHS LATER

"So, a werewolf, a vampire and a fae walk into a bar..." Frank says, as he sloshes his Guinness before taking another sip. Frank's a beefy type, with a thick body and a thick dark beard that covers his aging skin. He was a truck driver for 40 years and is now a professional barfly at my pub.

"Does that joke even have an ending?" Phil asks from a barstool a few seats down. Between them is a pint of beer. Every night they buy one in memory of Joe--who died in a way they'll never know the full truth of--and leave it in his regular spot, regardless of how busy Morgan's gets.

Frank shrugs. "That's what I'm trying to find out. I figure if I start the joke enough times, someone will finish it and then we'll finally know how it ends."

I feel the sting of a hand towel slapping my ass and turn to glare at AJ. "Bitch!"

She just sticks out her tongue, then looks to Frank.

"A werewolf, a vampire, and a fae walk into a bar..." she says. "And then everyone falls in love."

Frank frowns and then takes a long pull of his beer. "I don't get it."

I laugh. "It's got a lot of layers, Frank. Give it some time."

"Hey Bernie, when you gonna play for us again?" Phil asks as he raises his glass to his lips.

"Soon!" I glance at my beautiful piano and sigh. There hasn't been enough time for my music, though I have been working on a related project whenever I get a spare moment.

The bell above our door dings and Alice, Frank's wife, comes in, sees her husband, and beelines to the bar, avoiding Joe's seat to take the stool on the other side of Frank. "Bernie, where's that beautiful baby of yours? I have a gift for her."

Alice pulls a lovely knitted blanket from her purse and hands it to me. It's pink with tiny blue unicorns designed into it.

I hold it to my chest and smile. "Thank you, this is beautiful. She's with her dads right now, but I'll have her here with me tomorrow."

AJ snorts. "*Dads*. Spoiled little witch," she says under her breath.

Alice raises an eyebrow, and leans in like we're going to have a private conversation--but everyone can still hear us. "Are you really going to keep seeing all three of those men? And let all of them raise your child?"

This has been an ongoing conversation for the last five months, because of course it is. This is Rowley and I walk around with three dudes on my arm. Whatever. Let the people talk.

"Yes, I'm really dating them all, and yes, they are all taking the role as father for Rain." They've certainly earned it.

Alice gives me a skeptical, judgy look, but then follows it up with the perfect question. "Does that mean the dark-haired one won't be dancing for us anymore?" she asks.

AJ howls with laughter and I really wish Darius was here to answer for himself. "Oh, he'll still dance. I'm not the jealous type. I'm happy to share my eye candy with the world."

I squint at the time and sigh. "Okay, last call folks. I've got a meeting to get to."

Frank looks like I've just informed him he has a terminal illness. "But Bernie, it's too early to call it a night. Christ, it's still light out!" He legit looks like he might cry.

Alice nudges her husband. "How about we take the party home? We've got beer in the fridge and we can rewatch one of the Pats' Super Bowl wins."

The idea of beer and football on his own couch cheers Frank up, so much so that he leaves half a pint unfinished as he chases his wife out the bar, both of them giggling like school children. God bless small town New England folk.

Phil, the last one left, leaves cash on the bar and nods his head. "See you tomorrow. Good luck with that... meeting." He eyes me like he knows more than he's letting on, but I know for a fact he's clueless.

Hell, even I'm living in suspended disbelief. I wake up every morning wondering if this is actually my life.

Once I've locked the front door and turned the sign to closed, I meet AJ at the door leading down to the basement. We're totally in a hurry, but I still hesitate. I need a moment to look around Morgan's, to soak up some nostalgia before I take this next step.

"Don't stress," AJ says. "You're not saying goodbye, you're just... leaving for a minute."

"Sure," I say with a little eye roll. "Let's go with that. Got my makeup?"

AJ nods and then follows me downstairs to the basement. At first glance, this place looks like it always has. Dusty and stacked with extra supplies for the bar. The only notable difference is a big book shelf with a locked glass door. It's full of books of spells that I wanted to keep close at hand as I continue my magical studies.

The most important difference, however, hides within the inner-workings of my old piano. It's been down here since the Sexies went all Extreme Home

Makeover back when they first arrived. Over the last few months, I've been engaged in some heavy magical lifting. First I had to enchant each key on the keyboard. Then I had to create spells that were summoned with musical chords instead of recited words. Lastly, I had to bend space and time to cater to the songs played on my childhood piano. Here in my basement, under my family bar that secretly housed generations of witches, I've created a portal to multiple realms.

It's been the craziest undertaking of my magical career, and apparently the entire magical world is floored by my efforts. Perhaps the wildest part is that I did it all without my wand. I've found that since I died and came back, my power lives within me and doesn't need a conduit to do my bidding. My magic is always available to me, and more and more I'm learning control of it.

AJ sits on the bench next to me and I start to play. It's a newer piece, written with elements of Hungarian music and then little influences from each of the kingdoms of the other world. As I play, the bench below us starts to glow, and a ring of light forms a circle around me and AJ.

When I whisper the word "*Sulvara,*" we're whisked away to another world.

We step out of the blinding light inside a cluster of trees behind the back entrance to a sprawling, stone estate. This portal leads straight to the heart of Sulvara Castle, the newly established kingdom of the witches… and all other magical creatures. The name itself was pulled from the Hungarian words for magic and unity.

This portal was the easiest and first I created. The hardest part has been negotiating with the werewolves, vampires and fae regarding portal use and placement. Magic returning to the realm has helped a lot with easing tensions, but it'll take more than a few months and a commitment to peace for trust to be rebuilt.

That's what I'm working hard on, and today will bring us a step closer.

I hope.

Before my eyes even clear from the blinding light, my best friend is dragging me toward an open door with witches standing guard at either side.

"No time to lose, B. Do you know how much work you need to look good tonight?" she asks.

"Gee thanks, A."

She nudges me through the door, and we both smile politely as the witches gesture for us to go in. We keep moving at a good clip until we reach the kitchen. It's packed with castle staff who are putting the final touches together for the feast planned after the ceremony.

I smile at the head chef, a young witch with a knack for the culinary. "Tressa, everything looks and smells outrageous. Can I sample anything"

She beams at the praise and reaches for a small puff pastry, but AJ pushes me forward before I can take it.

"Not now, we need to move."

Sad and hungry, I let my dearest, meanest friend direct me up a spiral staircase and then down another long hall. At the end of it is a double-door leading into my suite.

443

My eyes light up as I open the door and see Rain sitting on the ground--all by herself!--playing with a dragon plushie someone at the pub gave her.

She looks every bit a princess dressed in sheer peach tulle with tiny embroidered flowers. I coo at her and crawl to face her. "How's the best little girl in all the worlds?" I ask as she reaches her chubby hands to cup my cheeks and giggles.

I kiss her and sit up, smiling at Rune, Darius and Zev--the dad sitters today. "How was daddy day care?" I ask, noting that my powerful men all look a little tired, but still entirely enamored with baby Rain.

"She's a genius," Rune declares proudly.

"She's strong," Zev says combatively.

"She's clever," Darius says with a wink, and I can't help but laugh at the three of them.

"She's a little of each of you," I reassure them. "Now, you all need to kiss me and scat so I can get dressed." I look down at my jeans and T-shirt ensemble. "I don't think this is gonna cut it."

They stand to go, with Rune leaning in to take Rain, but I stop him. "Let her stay. I miss her, and besides, she might as well learn early the great pains women take to look beautiful. Maybe she'll be the generation that puts an end to this nonsense."

AJ rolls her eyes. "There is nothing nonsense about wanting to present the most beautiful artistry in your appearance."

"Agree to disagree," I say dejectedly. "Let's get this over with."

Each of the handsome kings kisses me on the way out and AJ begins her work. It takes all of five minutes before Rain is fussing and we have to take a break for me to get her set up in a swing.

Two hours later--two very long two hours later--AJ and her minions have determined I am ready.

They pull over the full-length mirror and I gasp as I study myself.

My sleeveless A-line gown is made of layers of cream silk chiffon with flowers embroidered along the hem... just like Rain's. My dark hair is woven into braids with tiny gemstones dotting them, and my makeup is dramatic and expertly applied.

I smile. "Let's do this."

I turn to leave, but AJ stops me and pulls out a tray with two shot glasses from Morgan's filled with Powers Irish Whiskey. This was always her go-to when she was stealing liquor, and now the name has made it my preferred pour as well.

She raises one. "May the best of our past, be the worst of our future." She reflexively places a hand over the pendant resting at her heart as she speaks.

We clink glasses and drink, then hug. I pick up Rain, who instantly wants to catch all the gemstones in my hair, and we walk to our future.

This castle was repaired from the remains of the school the Sexies all attended in their youth. It was abandoned during the war, as was the original kingdom of the witches. In the last few months, this and the other lands have been undergoing repairs, with all races working together to lend their skills to the tasks.

It hasn't always been easy, and there has been some in-fighting--but we are turning a corner. Today will mark a new path for all our people.

The guys are waiting for us when we arrive in a large sitting room at the opposite end of the castle. They are all dressed in the formal royal style of their kingdoms, and all three are wearing their crowns.

I can hear music coming from the courtyard out front, and people cheering.

My palms are suddenly sweaty, and Rune takes my hand, letting his calm slip through me.

I smile appreciatively and straighten my back while handing my child to AJ.

French doors lead out to a balcony. Sheer curtains hang in front of the glass so I can't quite see the crowd gathered below. Just a couple more seconds of pretending this isn't a big deal before it becomes obvious it's the biggest deal ever.

A vampire and a werewolf stand at each side of the French doors, and they pull them open when AJ gives them the go ahead. The kings walk out first, taking their seats on the lower level of the two-tiered balcony. I walk out behind them, AJ at my side, the Last Witch cradled in her arms.

Except she's not going to be the Last Witch. We made sure of that. And that's why this massive courtyard is flooded with people from all the races who have come to bear witness to this momentous occasion.

I step toward a large, elegant throne, made from the elder woods of Aevelairith, brandished in the fires of Vaemor, and carved with bones of the felled warriors in Wiceraweil. My three kings watch me take my seat, looks of absolute pride and adoration on all of their faces. When the crowd sees us all seated, the vision of unity sends them into a frenzy of applause.

As the noise finally subsides, Rune rises and speaks.

"Today we unite our kingdoms in a way never before seen in our world," the fae says, capturing the attention of the audience easily with his eloquence and charisma. "As kings of our respective kingdoms, we each here today lay our crowns at the feet of the True Queen, Bernadette Morgan, who returned magic to our lands, who brought us together after centuries of war, and who now leads us forward to a bright, peaceful future."

Cries of joy fill the air and my cheeks burn that all of this is for me.

But not me. Not really. None of this could have been done by one person alone. I had a lot of help from those who are here with me, and just as much from some who have gone.

Zev covers my shoulders in the royal mantle of his people, a deep purple fur-trimmed cloak.

Darius hands me the golden scepter from his kingdom, with an obsidian crystal at its head.

And Rune places the crown on my head--a special piece crafted by the Dryad queen, using bark from the Tree of Life and the scale of my dear dragon. It's a living crown, to symbolize the life I am bringing back to this world.

The gravity of the moment feels almost overwhelming as Rune gently sets the crown atop my head. The touch sends shivers through me, as the piece is practically weightless and yet carries the weight of the world all at once.

When the cheering dies down, I hold up my scepter to address the crowd.

"While I may hold this seat, it is not my accomplishments alone that brought us to this day. No amount of magic can match the power created by you, all of you, finding unity when it mattered most. By forming alliances even when you had cause to fear, resent, or hate. By trusting me to bring about a new vision for this world."

I take a moment to look at my trio of kings. Once friends, then enemies, and now truly family. I glance back at AJ, who has always been more family than friend. My eyes finally fall on Rain, who isn't friend or family. She is my heart.

I can't stop the tears from running down my cheeks as I give the final part of my speech.

"Our kingdoms are not bound by treaty or pledge. No one swears an oath or follows the words of an ancient prophecy. We share something much greater. Much truer. It is love that has brought us together, and love that welcomed magic back into the land. As long as that is true, we cannot fail." I choke up a little on my last line, but it doesn't matter because the people have already lost it. They scream and cheer and hug and smile. All they've ever known is war and hate, and this move toward peace and the common good has everyone beside themselves with joy.

I look down at my men, and they are absolutely beaming.

When I look at my daughter in AJ's arms, I see her smiling. Then she laughs and holds up two glowing silver hands. She claps and fireworks spark all around us.

It startles the shit out of me. For a second I worry the way any mother would if fire came out of their kid. Then I remember who--and what--my kid is.

This is just the beginning of what my magical ball of love will be able to do.

What a crazy baby book she's going to have.

THE END

Want more romance, fantasy and adventure? Check out I Am the Wild. When Eve Oliver loses everything: her twin, her job, her apartment, she accepts a job at a mysterious law firm. But the Night brothers aren't what they seem… and neither is Eve.

Also, if you want to read… and VOTE… on a book as we write it, join us here:
Patreon.com/karpovkinrade
Find us online at KarpovKinrade.com
On Facebook /KarpovKinrade
On Twitter @KarpovKinrade
On TikTok @KarpovKinrade
And subscribe to our newsletter at ReadKK.com for special deals and up-to-date notice of new launches.

SILLY BONUS CONTENT

When we discussed making this trilogy into an omnibus, we knew we wanted to add a little extra something to the end to make it fun. But what? We didn't know. So we started a Google Docs chat about it, and here's what we ended up with. You're welcome. I think. Or we're sorry. I'm not sure which one is most appropriate. Either way, here's the raw draft of what we wrote to entertain you.

LUX: Hey Evan, should we write a whole new story for the omnibus? Or like another sex scene or something to give this omnibus something fun? Or maybe... MAYBE we could just write a few of the scenes we really wanted in the books but couldn't fit. Like for example, I STILL WANT my unicorn pee (is this how you spell pee? It looks wrong to me) portal scene. I REALLY WANT UNICORN PEE PORTALS TO BE A THING.

EVAN: I think it would be a great idea to include something new. There are so many great directions we can take these characters, so much world building left to be done, all the endless options for Rain and what becomes of her. I guess my only caveat is that we don't write anything about a portal made of unicorn pee because I think that might single-handedly ruin the series. Other than that I'm game for anything! Let's do it!

LUX: Why are you always trying to ruin everything? :(I think you're just not imagining it well enough. Let me set the scene.

***

The cold, icy wind cuts through the trees like blades, whipping the leaves in every direction. Zev has an arm around my shoulder, his werewolf heat keeping me warm. Or warmer, at least. I'm still freezing my ass off. Rune is plucking leaves off the dead tree to our left. That fae can always find something to keep

447

him occupied. Darius looks the most annoyed, pacing back and forth. If he had a watch, he'd be checking it.

"Where is he, Bernie?" Darius asks.

"He should be here soon." Rain is back at the bar with AJ, who has been teaching the toddler her alphabet by using liquor bottles. My daughter has had an unusual life to date, that's for sure.

I shiver again, and Zev scoots closer, pulling me against his broad chest, when Michael finally arrives as if from mist.

He doesn't look happy to see me. I don't blame him. This is a… strange request.

"Is this really the only way?" Michael asks, skipping the hellos entirely.

I nod. "I wish it weren't. But." I shrug.

"And this is really the only thing Rain wants for her birthday?" he asks, shuffling back and forth nervously.

I nod again. "I wouldn't ask if it weren't important."

Rain's birthday party is this weekend, and she wants what every girl wants. A unicorn. But there's only one place to get a real baby unicorn to come to her party, and this is the only way to get there.

Michael sighs again. "Fine." He unzips his jeans and I avert my eyes as he whips out his johnson. This is so awkward.

I can hear the stream of his urine and when it stops, I hear him zip back up. "You can look now," he says dejectedly.

I don't know what I'm expecting. The only way to create a portal to unicorn world is with unicorn pee. And since Michael is a unicorn shifter, his counts. It sounds gross, I know, but parents do what they must to make their kids happy.

The portal does not look or smell like piss, thank the gods. Instead, it is a beautiful rainbow arch that glows golden in the center.

Michael waves his hand. "Go on then. They should have a unicorn waiting for you. But you have to return it within a week or there's an extra rental fee."

Who knew you could rent unicorns for parties… with the right connections of course.
***

448

LUX: See? That wasn't so bad. Oh, we should have Rain write a college entrance letter as a teen graduating high school, but she writes about something related to her life with three dads and going back and forth between an Irish pub and a fantasy realm full of vampires, fae and werewolves where she's a princess. Here's a question idea: Discuss an accomplishment, event, or realization that sparked a period of personal growth and a new understanding of yourself or others.

EVAN: The way I pictured it, Michael would have to take unicorn form to make the unicorn pee that would be a portal to the unicron realm. This, unfortunately, is much worse. Thanks for not putting this scene in the actual books!

Okay, here's Rain's college entrance letter.

Describe a time in your life when you faced adversity, but were able to persevere with help from an unexpected source.

Being a teenager is hard. I can't say whether or not it's harder than being an adult since I haven't tried both, but no one can deny these adolescent years are tough for everybody. All things considered, I've had a charmed life: a mother who loves me beyond words, an auntie who's like my best friend, and three amazing men that I call my dads.

Even so, I'm no stranger to hardship. I was kidnapped twice before I turned two months old, and was nearly stolen by a man riding a dragon not much later. Scary as those moments must have been (I can't remember, of course), it all pales in comparison to my mother shooting a magical charge into my infant chest that killed my grandfather, almost killed my mother, and somehow miraculously didn't kill me.

What's funny is that those moments, even though I've heard the stories hundreds of times, don't come to mind immediately when I think about the struggles I've faced. Instead, my mind flashes to my first dance in high school, and how I was so nervous that I sweat actual crystals. They glowed coming out of my pores and you could hear them hit the ground. Or I think of eighth grade, when I got into an argument with my soccer coach, lost control of my temper and lit his shorts on fire. I got kicked off the team and grounded for the rest of the semester. I might have deserved it, but it was still a really dark time for me.

Recent, teenage hardships are the ones that hit me hardest. And, if I had to pick one trial to write about, it would be the time an army of gnomes found my home through the basement portal I left open after going to a fae music festival. Mom trusted me to stay out late, and I let her down. Her only rule was that I close the portal before going to bed, and I blew it. I didn't really think of what the consequences would be, which made it all the more terrifying when I found myself being dragged along the floor in a magical burlap sack that made all of my powers useless.

The gnomes planned on taking me and holding me for a ransom, knowing my queen mother had no trouble paying off a bribe if she felt like the stakes were high enough. I'm sure it all would have worked out, so I wasn't even worried about dying—I was worried about getting grounded forever. Like, for EVER.

After so many years of using magic to fix my problems, I didn't know what to do in the predicament. I was helpless. The magical bag stifled all sounds of my pleas, and it didn't make a noise as I bounced down the stairs from my bedroom to the basement.

Just when I thought all was lost, help showed up in the strangest form. My cat, Matilda, named after my great grandmother, arrived on the scene. I could see her through the sheer fabric as she pattered over and then, calmly and casually, just started batting the gnomes with her paws. The little kidnappers didn't see it coming, having not prepared for house-cat stealth, and they were flying off walls and bouncing under couches before they had any clue what was happening. Matilda stayed after them until they either escaped through the portal or she ate them. Then she clawed through the bag and set me free.

I think about this story for two reasons. Yeah, my cat was a very unlikely, unpredictable hero. I live my life surrounded by the most powerful beings in any universe, and my little gray kitty is who actually saved the day. If that's not an unexpected source of strength, I don't know what is.

More importantly, I learned about respect that day. Respect on all levels. Respecting my mother's wishes that I close the "goddamn portal that goes to all the goddamn magical realms" as she describes it. Sometimes we think our parents' rules are nothing more than that: rules. In reality, they're safeguards. They're put in place out of love and worry. That's something everyone should respect.

I learned about respecting things both big and small. I'm not going to lie, I've made some gnome jokes in my day. Not to their faces, but definitely within ear shot. I felt big and powerful and confident, and instead of using my position to lift others up, I pushed them down. Being dragged across my own floor by thirty or forty testy little gnomes made me regret being so dismissive and unkind. The best version of myself is one who always shows people and creatures respect, no matter what the size difference is.

Lastly, I gained a newfound respect for the natural order of things. Since I straddle this line between normal and magical worlds, I get lost in the hierarchy of who fights best or casts the strongest spells. Those things matter, but we can't forget the innate power of all forms of life. Sometimes, the greatest magic in the world is a wicked fast swat from a tabby.

These are lessons I carry with me, and I try to live them every day. This is why I think I would be an asset at your university. Not only am I a hard worker and a good student, but my life lessons have turned me into a person who brings a deep respect for all things wherever I go.

Respectfully Submitted,
  Rain Morgan

EVAN: Spoiler: Rain gets accepted but isn't awarded scholarship money.

You know what would be a fun scene the book didn't quite have time for? A passive aggressive note from Bernie to the Sexies about cleaning up after themselves. I mean, yeah, they're charming princes who dote on Bernie 24/7, but they're still men so you just *know* there's the occasional cabinet left open, empty ice tray put back in the freezer, laundry left on the floor. At some point, the lady of the house/kingdom has to get fed up, right?

LUX: I'm pretty sure her parents are rich enough to pay for college up front. Though we never really talked about how or why they were so rich, I guess I'm kind of imagining they all have a lot of treasure in their respective kingdoms and now Bernie is a queen so that seems like it would produce wealth. I could also totally see Darius talking Rune into selling some potions online or something. And the bar is kicking ass now.

Also this is a great prompt except you've made me very annoyed with the Sexies now that I'm thinking about what slobs they are. So you'll have to live with that knowledge that you've tarnished them in my eyes.

Recipients: Dariusthevampire@yahoo.com,   RunetheFae@hotmail.com, zevthewolf@wolfking.com

From: Bernie the annoyed

Re: guys really? I love you but omfg clean up your shit for the love of all that's holy!!

First of all, did you three coordinate your email addresses? Because that's weird. And not stealth at all. And Zev really? You started your own website?

Second, we need to talk about messes.
    Darius. You're up first. I know you hired someone to come clean the apartment and bar, but you can't expect them to also clean up the blood you leave behind. You need to be less messy when you eat. Honestly why are vampires like goddamn toddlers about food? It's weird. Stop leaving blood stains everywhere. It's gross and bad for business. And you owe me a new kitchen rug.

Rune, my love, I know you are a genius with the herbs. But this morning I found Rain eating something from one of your jars and it was... still alive? Please keep this shit under lock and key and make sure Rain is okay. She's been puking up rainbows. It's not been fun for any of us.

And Zev. I... think you might need a hair cut? Maybe in wolf form? You've been shedding everywhere and I can't get it off the couches. Like... is your wolf hair made of glue? I'm so confused. Either way, can you please handle this?

And moving forward I think we need to have our weekly house meetings via email since they keep ending up... with all of us naked. And while that's obviously more fun than discussing whose week it is to make dinner, it's also not very productive.

Love you all. Call me when you're done cleaning. I'll be at AJs until then.

Bernie

***

Keep reading if you want to see ridiculous outlines, notes and ideas we had before writing some of these books. It's... a little scary. You've been warned.

SILLY EARLY NOTES AND OUTLINES

You've been warned… here are some notes, outlines and thoughts we exchanged back and forth in the making of this series. It gets… uncomfortable in places. Don't say we didn't warn you. (Also, this is riddled with typos. RIDDLED. Like they are EVERYWHERE. Don't report them. Don't make a scene. This is our raw process. Behind the curtain of the magician, as it were. If you get weird about it, it will make us sad. If you can't handle stupid ideas and typos up the wazoo, don't read this part. It's okay, you wouldn't actually be missing much.

RANDOM BITS FROM OTHER DOCUMENTS:

From document "The Fucking Prophecy":

3 Witches - Each creates one race, using a part of their self as the primordial soup

• One uses her blood to create vampires

• One uses her hair? To create werewolves bones

• One turns her favorite succulent into all the Fae I DON'T KNOW breath

Because each race comes from the actual being of the Fates, the survival of witches is intrinsically part of the survival of each race.

When the final witch dies, so will all the other magical beings, unless that final witch is

• Entombed or saved or sacrificed or loved

These (or better words) can be the confusing part of the prophecy, leading each race to have a different plan for the child, and then at the end it's Bernie's love that clearly fixes things.

Witches fled the magical world to go to Earth after the power of their creations grew too strong and forgot about where they came from. After centuries of worshipping the Fates, they began to rewrite the history to change their relationships with the witches who were so important, and the alternate interpretations of the prophecy started getting traction.

Once on Earth, witches were still hunted by magical assassins, who would steal their powers maybe to bring back to their realms? This could potentially tie in with Tilly stealing Bernie's powers.

Predicting when the last witch would be born - WHO KNOWS

Evan's bullshit outline for Book 3

Chapter 1 - Get into the pact between Darius and Timót -- Darius promising safe passage into the vampire realm if Bernie will be spared. Bernie HATES this idea because it seems to mean Rain will die. Darius tries to convince her that he had no choice, this will buy them time to think of a new plan, if he hadn't made the agreement he would have lost them both. Bernie's still pretty upset. Maybe we find out later that this allowed Darius to get some insight into Tim's plan and pass that along to Liz. Also when did they make the plan?
They arrive at the vampire castle and meet Darius' dad - Carn..scraggle. He sucks, but in a different sort of sucky way than Tim. He's like, we're the undead, we drink blood, the witches made us, I have no sympathy.

Chapter 2 - Tim and Carnscraggle make a deal - Vampires get the baby, Érintett get eternal protection from the vampires. The ritual will happen, the baby will be murdered, and then Tim and Bernie will have free passage away from the vampire realm to join the rest of his forces.

We learn a little more about his forces. They're people who feel forgotten and underrepresented, magical beings from all realms. Tim has convinced them the witches left them behind and that he'll help, but he won't. He's a liar. He sucks. By the end of this book, people will not have any doubt as to whether or not he sucks.

Chapter 3 - DRAGONS! Tim's army of dragons shows up, and he kills Carnscraggle! Oh no! Carnscraggle's dead! Now the vampires need a new king.

Tim tries to take Bernie with him during the destruction, but she does witch shit and he flies off on a dragon, vowing that he'll return for her and that she needs to remember that vampires, no matter what they say, are not on her side. He steals

Rain? Maybe that's too much. But then we wouldn't have to deal with carrying a goddamn baby around everywhere and she's already drinking from a bottle so I give two shits about logistics. But still he probably doesn't.

Chapter 4 - They're semi-safe in the vampire realm, as Darius won't let anyone near Bernie and the vampires are preoccupied trying to figure out who will be the new ruler. It should be Darius, but no one wants Darius because he's a traitor. The only person defending Darius, in private, is Darius' brother, Hamp..bringle. Hampbringle has quietly been supporting Darius throughout all of this, but hasn't offered support publicly because he needed to keep some sort of standing.

Zev and Darius and Elizabeth and AJ arrive! Liz brought AJ back to life, they all came through the portal because Darius left clues or something. It seems like there's gonna be a showdown between Darius and the vampires but then Liz makes everyone see the truth and says the vampires need to unite with them to fight the Érintett, that's the real threat to everything. Especially since Tim has the baby! Unless he doesn't. Liz says she trusts the vampires to help. And this coming from the mother of the princess they killed matters, or at least it matters enough for Hampbringle to take a stand.

Now they just have to get the rest of the realms on board.

Chapter 5 - Realm travel. They leave vampire land and travel to a new realm. The fae realm? Sure, the fae realm. It's pretty.

Chapter 6 - They're in faeland and have to fend off an attack, a bunch of fae who think they're intruders. We get to see how this beautiful place has been under siege for centuries and everyone is always on high alert. Rune requests consult with the king. He's going to have to make a plea for help and also not to be killed. They also have to convince the fae not to steal the baby, which is either with them or not, depending on whether or not Tim steals it.

AJ is in bad shape. The spell from Tim almost killed her and Liz brought her back, but she's a water nymph and vampire land had no water and she needs to get some magic water or something soon. Liz says she may need to travel to… Water World. Rune and Bernie get dooooooooooooown.

Chapter 7 - Rune makes a compelling argument. The whole chapter is a trial. It's boring and no one reads past this chapter. Or, something better happens. Maybe there's some undercover Érintett action. A magical being living in the fae realm does something and someone dies/almost dies. Rune and his sister, Quit...skinip, argue. She's all about show of force, but Rune says that's not the way. They both work to convince the fae leader, Meh, of their case. Quitskinip gets poisoned. ?

Chapter 8 - They leave without having convinced the fae to join their cause. They don't die, but it's otherwise a failed effort. The fae simply aren't ready to team up with wolves and vampires. Plus they just lost Quitskinip and that leaves Rune next in line and he's viewed as a traitor. Realm travel. Werewolf time?

Chapter 9 - Werewolf time! They know exactly what's going to happen because Zev has to kill his dad. Zev is received with mixed reactions. Some are impressed that he mated with the mother of the Last Witch, thinking that brings power to their kind. Others hate him because he won't let them kill the baby. After Zev challenges his father, Berz...agoggle, there's a big banquet dinner. It's weird how formal the murder challenge process is. Bernie's freaking out because it's like 50/50% Zev will die.

Chapter 10 - The night before the fight, everybody has sex.

The next day, Zev kills Berzagoggle. The werewolves unite behind him, but some of them defect to join the Érintett. Or something. It's scary. Now what? Where do they go? They've got ⅔ of the realms on their side, but still don't know what they're up against or where to take the fight.

Liz and AJ come back from Water World. AJ is fine, and they've learned from the sea creatures some important information. It's so important. It's very telling. It will help a lot when they hear this information from AJ.

Chapter 11 - Flanked by Darius and Zev, Bernie speaks to the wolves and the vampires, who have been fighting each other and now have to fight side by side against an army of unknown size and unknown number of dragons. Bernie gives a great speech and unity abounds. Now she's got an army behind her, and that incredibly useful bit of information from AJ about where to go or what to do or just fucking ANYTHING, and they all head out to fight the bad guys.

Chapter 12 - They start traveling somewhere cool. When they get there, it's crazy. AJ's information is helpful.

Chapter 13 - DRAGONS! A dragon attack really fucks things up. Lots of vampires die and wolves run away. It looks like all is lost and it sucks because no one can kill a dragon and they don't want to because it's Tim's fault not theirs but still they have to do something about these goddamn fire breathing dragons. But then Bernie finds the baby dragon! Whose mom's scale is in her wand and she changes the mind of a dragon that's about to kill her. The dragon leads the other dragons away, ending the onslaught, then comes back to Bernie and is owned by her now.

Maybe Liz does the thing with her wand here and it seems like she dies to save the others.

Chapter 14 - With diminished numbers, they forge ahead, getting closer to the crazy place where the crazy stuff will happen. They capture Bernie! Oh no!

Chapter 15 - Bernie gets brought in front of the Érintett army and they all, predictably, suck. Tim unveils his plan for winning the battle. It's a very scary plan.

Chapter 16 - People come to the rescue! And the fae are there! They've had a change of heart and they stop half of Tim's army with fae bullshit!

Chapter 17 - Lots of people die! What's going to happen? What will happen with Rain? People are having doubts! Vampires want to eat the baby!

Bernie does something! With her wand! It changes everything and everyone learns that the prophecy was about love and family! Except not shitty biological fathers! Hooray!

Chapter 18 - Bernie lives forever with three husbands in a new realm called Olyp...vulk. She's the queen of Olypvulk. Tim's dead.

Lux's Book 2 outline with Evan's ideas in <u>underline</u>

1 - Bernie and the Sexies investigate what the letter could mean, how Ed could have had that info, and what it means for their future. They decide the only way to get any of the answers is to go find Timothy Trendle in Budapest.
   -We also get some info from the Sexies about the history of witches in Budapest, establishing that it was the original home for earthbound witches.
   -cliffhanger?

2 - AJ and Bernie have a sweet scene where Bernie puts her in charge of the bar. Michael maybe stops by to assure he'll help look after AJ and Morgan's. Then he creates a portal with his unicorn <u>thoughts and feelings that are not in any way related to urine rainbow made of</u> not piss piss and they walk to Budapest. Fortu-nately, none of this happens. While the Sexies and Bernie focus on what they'll do when they get to Budapest, AJ says she'll book travel because she's got a connection and understands human travel better than the Sexies. They don't trust her, she says trust me, then they end up flying Delta
   -Bernie's never left the US so she's terrified. Plus they're walking through a portal.
   -On the otherside they're met by someone we don't expect - I say Rain's father, but it could also be a member of the order or Darius' brother or they're in the middle of an open market and they hear a voice and can't tell where it's coming from and it turns out it's a cat or a bird or something

3 - The group is taken to meet the Order of druids who have served the witches since the beginning of time. This is where Bernie's dad is and they... meet him? Probably. End of the chapter or early on?
   -Meanwhile, Bernie's powers are flaring and going nuts as they walk through

these sacred magical grounds. She's starting to think she can't make it unless they get this under control ASAP. And then... they do.

4 - Timothy tells everyone that they need to find the right materials in order to make a wand capable of managing Bernie's powers. Unfortunately none of them will be easy to find - they have to steal vocal cords from a Phoenix and grind up leviathan teeth (AJ COMES BACK TO HELP THEM SWIM TO THE DEPTHS) and sperm please not sperm. The chapter ends with AJ getting swallowed by a leviathan.

5 - AJ kills the leviathan from the inside and they all stay the night in a lighthouse. A pirate ship comes to visit. Fae pirates. Elves of the sea. AJ is on the elf ship? Give me one good reason why this is a bad idea. Shut up, Ash.

6 - Bernie's wand is almost complete, but before they can finish that task they need to find a more permanent solution for the star that she keeps in her pocket, because she keeps losing it and lighting shit on fire then almost dying. They turn it into a necklace. OR they grind it up and she snorts stardust every couple of hours. Or earings. Or Docter Zev surgically implants it in her fucking shoulder. They realize that the star can be the fourth and binding ingredient in the wand. They probably realize this in a later chapter.

7 - Her dad dies. Bummer. But she meets the guy who she'll have sex with in book 3. Also she has sex with someone.

8. Some vampires show up and tell Darius he's going to be exiled or murdered. Or they try to murder him and our group wins. Now they really need to get a move on and also there are still 12 chapters left in the book.

9. The dad has been missing, isn't confirmed dead, and the only place the
    20 - Captured before they can escape Transylvania and taken to the vampire realm. It's scary and perhaps hopeless, but at least she's with her strong and cunning Sexies

NOTES:
    The wand needs 3 ingredients, so they quest for them, encountering trials along the way.
    1. Leviathan teeth

2. Phoenix feather or something

3. Dragons' scale

Maybe they have to break into a museum for something for the wand?
    I like this, they break into a museum to steal something unexpected--like there's a gem embedded into an old piece of pottery or something, or an elixir

written on the back of a painting. The witches/druids hid the their important stuff in the human world were hunting vampires wouldn't think to look

Maybe star is used as crystal tip, or cyrstal is third ingredient. They go on quests for these things.

There could be some training, with guys and maybe with druids or dad, on meditation and mastery of powers? And maybe exercising these powers throughout the quests.

Find cool places in Budapest and Transylvania, buildings, monuments that they can be in.

Also, 4th guy could be whiny loser but actually bad guy behind the scenes? Mayben order members are being killed off? Dad is missing or dead? Mystery of who's killing them. Lose guy might be an obvious suspect so he could be a red herring and we have a different bad guy. Maybe it's daddy. Or it's a sea fae, or the sea fae is a love interest?
I'm starting to think the dad should be dead and he died shortly before she arrived. Feels like a strong cliffhanger and that can open the door for them trying to figure out who's killing off the druids. Also, who the fuck is killing off the druids? Maybe there's a faction of witches trying to burn it all down, kinda like Lauren was? Or a magical race we haven't been introduced to yet?

Pirate love interest?
But D says we might not want to have a fourth serious love interest since the title has the three in them. I'm not sure I agree.
**
Final note, we obviously did not have a pirate love interest, much to my sadness. But someday. Someday I will write a sexy pirate. Bye for now!

ABOUT KARPOV KINRADE

Karpov Kinrade is the pen name for the husband and wife writing duo of USA TODAY bestselling, award-winning authors Lux Karpov-Kinrade and Dmytry Karpov-Kinrade.

Together, they live in Ukiah, California and write fantasy and science fiction novels and screenplays, make music and direct movies.

Look for more from Karpov Kinrade in *The Night Firm, Vampire Girl, The Last Witch, Dungeon Queen, The Witch's Heart, Of Dreams and Dragons, Nightfall Academy* and *Paranormal Spy Academy*. If you're looking for their suspense and romance titles, you'll now find those under Alex Lux.

They live with their three teens who share a genius for all things creative, and seven cats who think they rule the world (spoiler, they do.)

Want their books and music before anyone else and also enjoy weekly interactive flash fiction? Join them on Patreon at Patreon.com/karpovkinrade

Find them online at KarpovKinrade.com

On Facebook /KarpovKinrade

On Twitter @KarpovKinrade

And subscribe to their newsletter at ReadKK.com for special deals and up-to-date notice of new launches.

~ ~ ~ ~ ~

If you enjoyed this book, consider supporting the author by leaving a review wherever you purchased this book. Thank you.

ALSO BY KARPOV KINRADE

A reverse harem paranormal romance with humor and good liquor. (with Evan Gaustad)

The Last Witch

A Werewolf, A Vampire, and A Fae Walk Into A Bar (The Last Witch, 1)

A Werewolf, A Vampire, and A Fae Go To Budapest (The Last Witch, 2)

A Werewolf, A Vampire, and a Fae Go Home (The Last Witch, 3)

A reverse harem Greek Mythology adventure with a badass heroine and some serious kickass action. (with Liv Chatham)

Dungeon Queen

Warrior Queen

A standalone reverse harem paranormal romance with mystery, suspense and plenty of twists. (with Heather Hildenbrand)

The Witch's Heart

The Night Firm

A reverse harem fantasy romance with mystery, suspense and depth.

I Am the Wild

I Am the Storm

I Am the Night

A standalone dark paranormal romance with mystery

Wanted

In the Vampire Girl Universe

A fantasy romance with mystery and intrigue.

Vampire Girl

Vampire Girl 2: Midnight Star

Vampire Girl 3: Silver Flame

Vampire Girl 4: Moonlight Prince

Vampire Girl 5: First Hunter

Vampire Girl 6: Unseen Lord

Vampire Girl 7: Fallen Star

Vampire Girl: Copper Snare

Vampire Girl: Crimson Cocktail

Vampire Girl: Christmas Cognac

Of Dreams and Dragons

Standalone fantasy romance novellas

The Winter Witch (with Heather Hildenbrand)

The Spring Witch (with Heather Hildenbrand)

Forever Bound

Get the soundtrack for I AM THE WILD, OF DREAMS AND DRAGONS and MOONSTONE ACADEMY wherever music can be found.

Nightfall Academy

Court of Nightfall

Weeper of Blood

House of Ravens

Night of Nyx

Song of Kai

Daughter of Strife

Paranormal Spy Academy (complete academy sci fi thriller romance)

Forbidden Mind

Forbidden Fire

Forbidden Life

Our ALEX LUX BOOKS!

The Seduced Saga (paranormal romance with suspense)

Seduced by Innocence

Seduced by Pain

Seduced by Power

Seduced by Lies

Seduced by Darkness

The Call Me Cat Trilogy (romantic suspense)

Call Me Cat

Leave Me Love

Tell Me True

(Standalone romcon with crossover characters)

Hitched

Whipped

Kiss Me in Paris (A standalone romance)

Our Children's Fantasy collection under Kimberly Kinrade

The Three Lost Kids series

Lexie World

Bella World

Maddie World

The Three Lost Kids and Cupid's Capture

The Three Lost Kids and the Death of the Sugar Fairy

The Three Lost Kids and the Christmas Curse

ABOUT EVAN GAUSTAD

Evan grew up in Northern California before moving to Los Angeles in 2001. He worked as an actor and a writer in LA until 2015, and now splits his time between writing and running the drama department at the School of Performing Arts and Cultural Education in Ukiah, CA.

Follow him on Amazon.

ALSO BY EVAN GAUSTAD

A series about that time the world didn't end even though it was supposed to.
by Evan Gaustad and Clint Gage
It's Not the End of the World (Sisyphus Series, Book 1)
Countdown Phoenix (Sisyphus Series, Book 2)

A reverse harem paranormal romance with humor and good liquor. (with Karpov Kinrade)
The Last Witch
A Werewolf, A Vampire, and A Fae Walk Into A Bar (The Last Witch, 1)
A Werewolf, A Vampire, and A Fae Go To Budapest (The Last Witch, 2)
A Werewolf, A Vampire, and a Fae Go Home (The Last Witch, 3)

www.ingramcontent.com/pod-product-compliance
Lightning Source LLC
Chambersburg PA
CBHW060758030726
47503CB00002B/300